The Sandman Diaries
Best Kept Secrets

David Alan Ovegian

Bloomington, IN Milton Keynes, UK

authorHOUSE™

AuthorHouse™
1663 Liberty Drive, Suite 200
Bloomington, IN 47403
www.authorhouse.com
Phone: 1-800-839-8640

AuthorHouse™ UK Ltd.
500 Avebury Boulevard
Central Milton Keynes, MK9 2BE
www.authorhouse.co.uk
Phone: 08001974150

This book is a work of fiction. People, places, events, and situations are the product of the author's imagination. Any resemblance to actual persons, living or dead, or historical events, is purely coincidental.

First published by AuthorHouse 11/11/2008

ISBN: 978-1-4259-3519-1 (sc)

Printed in the United States of America
Bloomington, Indiana

This book is printed on acid-free paper.

Reader discretion is strongly advised...

This book is rated "R" by the author for violence, strong language and graphic detail and was written for the adult reader.

Warning: The author will not be held responsible for anyone who may seek to use the methods described in this book to cause harm to anyone.

Do not attempt to use any of the methods described in this material for any reason what so ever.

The methods of assassination described in this book, if used, will cause death to another human being and therefore are not to be used or attempted by anyone.

This book is about death and should be read with that understanding in mind.

This book is not to be read by anyone under the age of eighteen.

The names of companies, products and businesses, used in the book are registered trademarks and were used with the utmost respect for the excellence of their individual product and quality of service to the general public.

This book is dedicated to my sister: Kerri Lynn Perna.

Thank you for your love, friendship and for not giving up on me when everyone else has.

"And when the Lamb broke the fourth seal, I heard the fourth living being say, "Come!" I looked up and saw a horse whose color was pale green like a corpse. And Death was the name of its rider, who was followed around by the grave."

Revelation, Chapter 6, Verses 7 & 8
Bible

We who have seen war, will never stop seeing it.

In the silence of the night, we will always hear their screams and see their faces.

Author Unknown

Acknowledgements

To my brother and friend Raymond 'Doc' Decker. Without your help and support this book would have never made it to print. Thank you my dear friend for loving me with such a true heart. You will always be my brother and friend throughout life and into death, until the very end.

This book is the sequel to A Sniper's Sin ISBN #1-4033-7652-2.

See through the eyes of the author as he once again takes you through chapter after chapter of Mafia and CIA assassinations, giving you an up close and personal look into the mysterious Cloak & Dagger world of organized crime and the Central Intelligence Agency Black Operations Division.

Introduction

I had been home from Vietnam for almost two months now. Lying on my bed with my dog Pookie at my side, I felt the cold gun barrel of Colonel Boris Kalashnikov's Russian-made handgun press against my forehead. Opening my eyes, I felt my heart surge with fear as I looked up and into the Russian Colonel's cold blue eyes. "I have come a long way to kill you David. No one escapes me and lives to talk about it," Boris whispered with hate filled eyes. Reaching slowly under my pillow, I gripped my P-38 German automatic, sweat running down my forehead and into my eyes. Seeing that I was in trouble, my faithful dog Pookie barked, and with that bark a brand new adventure has begun…

Chapter One
The Call

Sitting straight up, I tried to focus my thoughts. My body trembled, as my heart raced to the point of making me dizzy.

I looked down and saw my faithful dog, Pookie. She was a black Terrier my sister Ruth had given to me as a puppy. When I went into the Army and to Vietnam, she began what the veterinarian called a grieving process that almost killed her. She refused to eat and all day long would wait for me at the front door; at night she would lie on my bed. My mother said it had taken a lot of love from me for my dog to experience that much pain. Pookie was my best friend and remained true even to this day.

"David, are you alright?" my mother asked as she opened the bedroom door to check on me.

"Yeah, mom, I'm fine. It was just a bad dream, that's all," I replied in a shaken voice.

"You're not alright, son, you need help. Let me call the VA Hospital. Maybe talking to someone there will help you," my mother advised with a worried look on her face.

"I'm alright, mom, really, I am. Pookie woke me up when she saw I was having a bad dream. Didn't you, girl?" I explained to my mother as I picked up Pookie and gave her a big hug.

Shaking her head in a way that only a mother does, she left the room and closed the bedroom door behind her. Setting my dog back down on the bed next to me, I let my upper body flop back down in a prone position.

"Oh, man, this is crazy," I whispered softly as I lay still, staring up at the ceiling of my room.

Reaching up with my right hand, I rubbed my finger against the scar on my chin and then touched the scar on my right collarbone where I was burned at the POW camp.

"Colonel Kalashnikov," I whispered, "I'm going to get you for this." My mind began to drift back to the Iron Hand pilots that were betrayed by our government and taken to Russia.

The ringing of the telephone in the kitchen was followed by my mother's voice. "David, it's for you," she yelled.

Getting out of my bed, I walked to the kitchen and picked up the telephone. Putting the receiver to my ear, I said, "Hello."

"David?" the voice on the other end asked.

"Yes," I responded.

"Are you tired of the mundane life yet?" the voice asked.

"Who is this?" I questioned.

1

"Let's just say that I'm the friend you haven't met yet. Your country still needs you, David. Are you interested?" the voice asked with no emotion in its tone. "You have ten seconds to decide, David."

After letting about eight seconds tick by, I answered, "Yes."

"Go to the Pine Knob Ski Lodge. Once you're there, go into the main lodge and sit down by the fireplace. You have fifteen minutes to get there. If you make it on time, your life will never be the same again. If you don't make it in exactly fifteen minutes, you'll spend the rest of your life wondering what could have been. I'll be gone in sixteen minutes," the voice explained as he hung up the phone.

"Shit," I whispered in a low voice. "Who in the hell was that?"

Looking at my watch, I moved quickly back to my bedroom, put on my boots, and grabbed my blue goose-down jacket. Pausing for a moment, I remembered my Seal team instructor telling me to always expect the unexpected.

Opening the top drawer of my dresser, I reached in under my T-shirts and pulled out the gray T-shirt I had wrapped in plastic. Unwrapping the plastic, I opened the folded T-shirt and pulled out the .9mm, P-38 Walter Gray Ghost pistol I had brought back with me from Vietnam. A gift – a war trophy given to me by Captain Bell, just before I left Vietnam to return home.

The smell of gun oil was sweet to my senses; I checked the clip to make sure the pistol was fully loaded. Sliding back the action, I chambered a round into the firing position and put the safety on. Opening up my jacket, I tucked the pistol into the hidden pocket. Moving quickly, I went out to the driveway and climbed into my black 1970 Chevelle Super Sport and started the engine.

It took less than five minutes for me to travel the short distance down Sasabaw Road to the Pine Knob Ski Lodge, which was located just a few miles down the road from my parent's home in Clarkston, Michigan. Parking my car next to the front entrance, I walked into the main lodge and stepped to the right side of the door, placing the wall to my back. Looking around, I saw about twenty people sitting at the bar and in the lounge chairs scattered around the large room.

It was getting warm outside and the snow was slowly starting to melt. I didn't recognize any of the faces inside, so I walked over to the large fireplace and sat down. Unzipping my jacket, I reached inside my shirt pocket, pulled out the tiny glass vial of liquid Methadrine, and placed a drop under my tongue. Within seconds I felt the surge of blood flowing through every vein in my body. Taking a deep breath into my nose, I let it out slowly and smiled.

2

"You realize that stuff will kill you, don't you?" the lady said as she walked up to me with a mixed drink in her right hand and an open bottle of cold Pepsi in her left.

She was in her late twenties, stood about five-feet, seven-inches tall and had short jet-black hair. She wore a pink ski suit with black ski boots and a pink scarf draped around her neck

"No, thank you," I replied as she reached out to hand me the bottle of Pepsi. "I never drink anything that someone else has opened."

"Right answer," she said as she sat down next to me. "Mind if I join you?"

"Sorry, ma'am, but I am expecting someone. Maybe some other time," I replied softly.

"You made pretty good time, David. My name is Kathy, I've been looking forward to meeting you," she said as she introduced herself and held out her hand for me to shake. "You, Butch, Nick, and Danny are a legend with our department at the Agency," she explained with a smile. Shaking her hand, I slowly began to scan the room with my eyes trying to detect anything or anyone that looked out of place. "I'm by myself, David," she said softly, as she took a sip of her drink.

"The person that I talked with on the phone was a man. I doubt that you're alone," I explained sarcastically with a grin.

"Well, I am," she replied as she set down her drink and stood up. "Why don't you walk me to my van and I'll explain why I'm here." Walking out to the parking lot, we went to her 1971 Ford van with dark tinted windows and got inside.

"David, by now I am sure you have figured out that I am with the Central Intelligence Agency, Black Operations Division. We keep track of certain people with extraordinary talents that return home from Vietnam, especially the ones that worked for us while they were in country. We approached Danny, or Chopper as you so proudly call him, right away. We knew that he would be looking for a way to get back into the game as quickly as possible and we were right," she explained in a calm voice, as her blue eyes searched my face for a reaction to her talking about Chopper.

"Is Chopper still alive?" I asked keeping my eyes focused on the people walking around in the snow covered parking lot.

"Oh, yes, David, your friend Chopper is very much alive and, believe it or not, back in Vietnam working for us now," she explained, still watching my face.

"Damn, I miss him, Kathy," I answered as a smile crept across my face.

"I'll bet you do, David. Danny told us the same thing about you, that is why I'm here," Kathy explained.

3

"You're here in Clarkston, Michigan talking to me because Chopper said he misses me. Why don't I believe that?" I questioned cautiously, still looking out through the windshield of the van.

"Partly, but most of all, I am here because of a Russian Colonel named Boris Kalashnikov," she answered quickly, still looking at my face.

Turning my head slowly, our eyes met for the first time since we got into the van. I didn't speak, but I could feel my heart race with the full surge of Methadrine and anger.

"Do you know where the colonel is?" I asked.

"Right at this very moment, no, I don't. But we know where he lives in the Motherland of his country and our intel in Russia tells us that you, David, are the topic of many of his conversations with his leaders and the KGB," she explained calmly, showing no expression or emotion on her face.

"Really, that's interesting. I was just thinking about him this morning," I answered, as I turned my head to look back out at the parking area of the ski lodge.

"It's just a matter of time, David, before the KGB sends someone to kill you. You saw too much in that POW camp and you can put the Colonel there, which makes diplomatic relations between the United States and Russia very tense right now. The Russians are not supposed to be involved in Vietnam. We knew they were, but could never prove it until you became a POW and escaped. Now the shit is in the air at a level at which our President has never had to deal with before," she explained calmly.

"What do you want from me, Kathy; why are you here?" I asked.

"We want you to come back into the Black Operations Division, David—back with the Company. Not as an agent, but as an operative to do what we call 'wet work' for us. You'll do things that agents can't legally do. You had a Class Twelve security clearance in Vietnam, David, which means that we can get you a Q-clearance rather quickly," she explained.

"What's a Q-clearance?" I asked.

"It's the Government's highest, Top Secret clearance. You'll have access to things – locations, equipment, information – that the President himself doesn't have access to. But you're going to have to take some tests and go through some special training before you'll be cleared to do 'wet work'," she explained, as she turned her head once again to look at me.

Taking a deep breath into my lungs, I let it out slowly through my nose. My mind raced with the thoughts of seeing Danny again and getting back into the 'Cloak & Dagger' game of Black Op's. Looking back at the CIA agent that I only knew as Kathy, our eyes met once again.

"Do you have any eight-track tapes of James Brown?" I questioned.

"Sure I do, why?" she asked.

4

"Turn on some James Brown, pretty lady, its time to rock and roll!" I explained smiling.

"Fantastic, David. Chopper said that you would want to put on some Motown music and dance," she explained with a grin. "Welcome back, David," Kathy said as she extended her right hand for me to shake.

"Hoo yah," I whispered out loud as I took her hand into mine and shook it.

"Meet me at the Pontiac Airport on M-59 at 9 p.m. sharp tonight. Don't bring anything with you; just the clothes that you're wearing at the time and whatever is in your pockets, nothing else. We will supply you with everything you'll need—razor, soap, clothing, money, everything. And by the way, leave the gun you're carrying on your left side at home," Kathy explained, as she smiled and turned the key in the ignition to start the van.

"I'm impressed," I replied with a nod of my head.

"You haven't seen anything yet, kiddo. See ya at 9 p.m. and don't be late," she explained.

* * * * * * *

"Smells like rain," I commented as I looked up at the darkening sky.

"That's funny," Kathy replied, as we walked up to the silver Learjet parked on the tarmac of the Pontiac Airport.

"What's funny?" I asked.

"There are no clouds in the sky. It's only dark because the sun has set. Why on earth would you think that it was going to rain?" she asked, as we climbed on board and fastened our seat belts.

"Like I said, it smells like rain," I replied as I took a mental picture of the inside of the plane.

The plane was a lot smaller than I had imagined it would be. It had wood grain paneling, thick carpet, black leather seats, and a section that held computer components. Two telephones and what I would later find out was a scrambler box attached to the phones and computer to scramble any and all communications coming to and going from the plane. This kept unwanted ears from hearing the classified information of the CIA Black Op's Division. Both the pilot and co-pilot looked to be in their forties, medium built; both wearing dark Ray Ban Aviator sun glasses. Neither smiled, nor said a word.

"So Kathy, where are we headed?" I asked.

"Well, because you're my new recruit, I have to take you to the Farm. Because you've already received some very extensive training from the Agency, you won't be there long. But we have a few more things you need to learn before we send you back out into our little world of dark secrets," she explained, as the plane now began to taxi out onto the runway for take off.

"Sounds like fun," I replied, as I looked out through the small side window of the plane and grinned.

"Something funny?" Kathy asked as she twisted her head slightly to look over my left shoulder at my face. "David, listen," she continued, "from this point forward, I'm responsible for you and everything that happens with you and to you. Do you understand that? I chose to accept this assignment because you intrigue me. I've followed your every step since John recruited you in Vietnam. I'm a Patriot, David, and I will gladly die to protect this country. So please, if you have something on your mind, share it with me. We have to learn to trust each other, right?" she asked.

Nodding toward the window, I never turned to look at her, I simply said, "Rain," and then smiled.

"How did you know?" she asked in a confused tone as she looked out through the window and the plane shot forward on its take-off from the small airport.

Turning my head, I looked Kathy in the eyes. "To survive in the jungle, you must become the jungle," I explained. The plane slowly lifted up into the air, while the rain began to come down a little harder. "So where is this Farm of yours? Does it have lots of animals and stuff on it?" I asked jokingly.

"Well, the Farm is located on nine thousand acres of land and is fenced in. You won't be there long because your thoughts and mind are already tuned in to our way of thinking. We are now going to teach you to look for things that most normal people never see, to see beyond sight. When we're done with you, we will walk you into a restaurant full of people and within seconds you'll be able to memorize everything and everyone in the room. You will be taught everything you will need to know to become a spy and enter into the real world of espionage," she explained with a serious look on her face.

"Really?" I replied.

"Yes, David, really. There is more to what we do than shooting someone from a mile away with the Nighthawk sniper's rifle; which, by the way, was one hell of a shot your team made in Cambodia for us," she added with a grin on her face.

"Boy, I am impressed," I responded, as I turned to look back out through the side window of the plane.

"You should be. Most people only dream about this stuff or watch the bullshit they see on TV and wonder what it would be like. You're actually going to be doing it, David," Kathy explained in a serious voice.

"No, Kathy, that's not what I meant. What I meant was that I was impressed at how you said all of that and never answered my original question. So much for trust, huh," I pointed out, as I raised my eyebrows and twisted my head slightly to the right.

Smiling, Kathy leaned back and rested comfortably in her seat. "We are going to Camp Perry. The Farm is located near there, David. The training center is on nine thousand heavily wooded acres surrounded by a barbed wire topped fence. It's near Williamsburg, Virginia. Once we land, I'll have you sign some papers and then we will begin," she explained calmly, as she closed her eyes.

"Sign some papers; for what reason?" I asked.

"Once you step through the front gate of the Farm, David, if you don't make it and get a green light from the instructors, you'll be taken to a small building. Once you enter that building, you won't come out alive. I, on the other hand, believe this will be a cakewalk for you. Your addicted, kiddo, you love this stuff, the rush of adrenaline and fear. You were made for this shit. That's why I asked for you personally when I found out that the Agency was going to try to recruit you again," she explained calmly.

"Why would you ask for me? That part doesn't fit, Kathy. Why me?" I asked as I let my body relax in my seat.

"Hey, that's the question that's easy to answer," she replied. "I wanted to meet the legend."

"What are you talking about, Kathy? Now you've really got me confused," I explained.

Keeping her eyes closed, Kathy placed her right hand over her mouth and yawned. Turning her head slightly to the right, she squirmed in her seat to make herself more comfortable. "A dozen trained recruiters from the Company each wanted to be the one to recruit you, David, but I got you. I threatened to resign if they didn't give me the assignment. I wanted to meet him, David. He's in there and I want to see him up close and personal. Believe me, kid, no matter how hard you try you won't be able to keep him in. Sooner or later he will come out to play, then I'll get to see him," she explained in a tired and lazy voice.

"See who, Kathy?" I asked once again in a soft voice.

"The Sandman, David. Now get some rest, it's going to be a long ride," she explained.

Taking a deep breath of air into my lungs, I let it out slowly. "Better be careful, Kathy," I thought as I closed my eyes to rest, "you might not like what you see."

* * * * * * *

7

The Farm was a very secure area near Williamsburg, Virginia. I spent two months there and left the same way I came in — through the front gate with Kathy on June 18, 1971. The exact location of the Farm and the classified training I received there will not be revealed; not even for the writing of this book. Kathy and I walked out together. It was 1 p.m. and she was smiling.

* * * * * * * *

Leaving the Farm near Camp Perry, we went to the headquarters of the Central Intelligence Agency in Langley, Virginia. Moving through the heavily secured building, Kathy took me to a very large and plush office. It was there I met the Director of the CIA.

"Hello, David, do you know who I am?" he asked with a smile, as he shook my hand.

"Yes, sir, I do," I responded.

"Have a seat, young man, and make yourself comfortable," he explained as he opened his top desk drawer and pulled out the leather covered identification holder. Closing the desk drawer, he again looked at me and then at Kathy. Smiling, he looked back at me. "Before I give you this, David, I need to ask you a very serious question. In fact, I need to ask you two of them. Ready?" he asked.

"Yes, sir," I responded.

"If you were given an order by the Agency, or in fact by Special Agent Eckland, and you were told that for matters of National Security we needed you to assassinate the President of the United States, would you do it, David?" he asked, never taking his eyes off of mine.

Even though I knew that I wouldn't do it and that this was a trick question, I responded, "Yes, sir, I would." My eyes never left the director's, not for a second.

"You wouldn't question, why, David?" he asked.

"No, sir, I would follow my orders and trust in you to make the right call," I explained calmly.

"And what if we were wrong, then what, David?" he asked again never taking his eyes off mine.

"Oh well, sir, life goes on, doesn't it," I replied.

"Are you willing to die for your country, David? Just as all of us here are willing to do at any given moment?" he asked in a slightly colder tone of voice, as he leaned forward resting his arms on his large oak desk.

"No, sir, I am not. Only a fool dies for his country, sir," I replied calmly, noticing a look of surprise on the director's face as I said it.

"What?" he snapped back loudly, as he looked over at Kathy and then back at me. "You're not willing to die for your country, David?"

Leaning forward slightly, I kept my eyes focused dead center on the Director's eyes. "No, sir, I am not and you should not be willing to die for your country either. I was given some very wise advice from Master Chief Jeff Mareno, United States Navy Seals. He said, and I quote: "Only a fool dies for his country, David. You make that other sorry bastard die for his. Do you understand me, Sergeant?' I replied loud and clear, yes, Master Chief! As for you and the CIA, sir, don't expect anything less from me now. If you want somebody dead, then I will put him or her to sleep, and I'll be the one that comes home alive. If I don't make it out alive, then I screwed up, and that makes me the stupid one. If you want me in with you, sir, then look me in the eyes and shake my hand, but don't ever betray me no matter what happens and I'll always be loyal to the very end, sir," I explained, never once breaking eye contact with the director.

Standing up, the middle-aged man with the touch of gray in his hair extended his right hand out to me. "Welcome aboard, David," he greeted, as he reached over with his left hand and handed me the leather ID holder.

"Hoo yah, sir," I responded as I shook his hand and took the leather wallet. Opening the wallet, I smiled, "Q-clearance, huh," I whispered with a huge grin on my face.

"That's right, kiddo, Top Secret clearance, which means you're in all the way now," Kathy explained, as she reached over and shook my hand with a big smile on her face.

"From this point forward, David, you will receive all of your missions from Special Agent Eckland. If anyone else tries to contact you other than me personally, kill them because you're being set up. Then call the emergency number and we will send a cleaner to clean up whatever mess there is and dispose of any bodies, understood?"

"Understood, sir," I said with a smile.

"Agent Eckland will take you to our shop so you can pick up the weapon of your choice and anything else that you may need. If, while you're out in the field and out of pocket and should need anything and I mean anything at all, contact Special Agent Eckland and we will get it to you immediately, understood?" he asked.

"Yes, sir, I understand," I said as I nodded my head slightly.

"Well then, good luck, son, and stay safe," the director commented as he sat back down in his leather chair.

Leaving the office, we took the elevator to the basement where I picked out several weapons, both of which were handguns. A .22 magnum automatic with screw-on silencer and a .9mm Berretta with an extended barrel, which was threaded on the end, also for a screw-on silencer. Placing the handguns, silencers, holsters, and ammunition for both in a leather-covered metallic lined security case, Kathy and I went down the hall to the Special Op's room where my photographs were taken.

"Sir, we will be giving you a total of six different passports, driver's licenses, social security cards, and birth certificates. This will give you a total of six different identifications that will pass anywhere in the world. Step over here, please and speak into this microphone," she explained.

"What do you want me to say?" I asked.

"As soon as I push this green button and you see the little green light come on right here on my panel," she explained, as she pointed to the unlit green light, "tell me where you're from, where you went to school, and what your nickname was in Vietnam. Ready?"

Nodding my head yes, she pushed the red button and the green light lit up on the black panel board. "I am from Clarkston, Michigan, I graduated from Clarkston High School, and my big brother Chopper nicknamed me Sandman while I was in Vietnam," I said calmly into the microphone on the table.

Taking off her headphones, she pushed the red button and turned off the machine. "Thank you, sir, your voice identification code number is *'Delta-Seven Alpha-Six Sandman.'* Whenever you contact us, or any of our field operatives anywhere in the world, remember to use your voice identification code. If you don't, we will hang up. There will be a few seconds delay when you call in. It takes a few seconds for our computer to identify the voice on the phone and match it to you. Now then, if you're in trouble and need to let us know, or if you have been captured by enemy agents of another country, your emergency code word is *'Necromancer',*" she explained, as she typed the word into the computer next to the black panel in front of her. Do you have any preference for names on your fake identifications, sir?" she asked looking over at me calmly.

"No, ma'am, whatever names you choose will be fine with me," I answered.

"All right then, sir, welcome to the Agency. Agent Eckland will take you out from here. Your passports and ID's will be ready in 48-hours and will be delivered to you at your safe house," she explained.

"My safe house?" I asked in a confused tone of voice as I looked over at Kathy.

"Don't look over at Special Agent Eckland, sir, this is my office and I am in charge here," the older lady with no name explained as she walked over and opened the large safe in the corner of the room. Reaching into the safe, she pulled out a manila envelope that had my name written on it. Handing the envelope to me, she continued, "Enclosed in this envelope is the deed to your safe house, which is fully furnished, I might add, the car in the garage of the home is also yours. The title to which is also in the envelope along with keys to the car and home. You have three different credit cards in your name that are also in the envelope. Use the credit cards to pay for everything as long as you're at home and using your real name. If you're going out on a mission and you're leaving the country, Agent Eckland will issue you two credit cards that will be in the name of one of your fake passports. Use it and do not be concerned with how much you spend. The Agency pays for everything, understood, sir?" she asked.

"Yes, ma'am, kind of like 007, huh?" I answered with a small grin on my face.

"Your Q-clearance gives you a license to kill, sir – any time, anywhere in the world. Enemy agents of this country would love to get their hands on any one of our agents, such as you, David. So I'd keep the smart-ass fucking comments to myself if I were you," she scolded sternly. "When you step out of this building it all becomes very real and people's lives will depend on you getting whatever the job you're called to do, done. I take my job very seriously, sir, that's why I wear this," she explained as she pulled the thin diamond cut neck chain out from under her sweater. Dangling the tiny glass cylinder that was attached to the neck chain, in front of me to see, I knew right away that the small glass capsule inside of it and visible to see was Cyanide. "I know too much about all of our agents in the field, David. At the first sign of trouble, I bite into this capsule and I take all of my secrets with me. That's how serious I am, sir, and that's how serious your job is. Have I made myself understood, sir?" she asked calmly.

"Completely, ma'am. May I ask what your first name is?" I asked politely.

"Need to know basis, sir, and you don't need to know. Ma'am will do just fine," she said as she turned to walk away. "Good luck, David," she said as she walked into the next room, closing the door behind her.

"Come on slick, I'll buy you supper and then we'll get a couple of rooms and get some sleep," Kathy explained as I followed her out of the Black Op's office and down the hall to the elevator.

Looking at my watch, I had not noticed that the day had gone by so quickly. I felt stupid for the '007' comment I had made, but I kept it to myself. I was sure that Kathy already knew how I felt, but she never once said a thing.

* * * * * * *

The flight back to Pontiac, Michigan was quiet. I spent the time memorizing phone numbers and code names. The Agency had purchased a house for me in Waterford, Michigan, which was next to where I had grown up in the town of Clarkston. The homes on Waterford Hills were real nice and above average compared to the middle-class home that I had grown up in.

Dropping me off at the Pontiac Airport, Kathy told me that she would be in touch and said goodbye. Getting into my black 1970 Chevelle Super Sport, I drove to my new house in the Waterford Hills Estates.

It was a beautiful four-bedroom home with a plush green lawn, a few trees, fenced in backyard, and a three-car garage. Getting out of my car, I walked up to the front door and used my key to let myself in. I couldn't believe my eyes. The front room had a brick fireplace, leather furniture, oak end tables, and a beautiful mirror above the sofa. The refrigerator and cabinets in the kitchen were completely stocked with food. Pulling the note off of the cold can of Pepsi, I read it and smiled. It read, "Didn't think we would forget the most important part, did you?"

Opening the ice-cold can of soda, I walked around the house and looked everything over. The den was downstairs, with my security phones and scrambler box system, on my desk. The large full-size grandfather clock chimed at the top of the hour. The basement had a full-size bar that was fully stocked, a full-size Brunswick pool table, a large leather reclining chair, and a television set. Going back up to the master bedroom I was amazed. The closet and dresser drawers were full of suits, clothing, shoes, blue jeans, T-shirts, underwear, socks, ties, and on the dresser was a jewelry box made out of polished wood. Opening the jewelry box, I saw cuff links, two diamond cut, gold men's neck chains, and three gold watches.

"This is going to be sweet," I said out loud, as I jumped up onto the queen-size bed. "Boy, have I got it made," I whispered to myself as I yawned and closed my eyes for just a moment. What I didn't realize at the time was that it would be very exciting, but very costly in the end.

Chapter Two
The House

It was late July 1971, as I sat in the sun porch of my grandparents' home. Looking out through the window, I watched my grandmother's dog, Laddy, as he barked at the red squirrel that was taunting him from the top of our apple tree.

My grandparents had bought this beautiful red brick home with the insurance money the United States Army had given them when my Uncle Tommy was killed in World War II. The home faced Telegraph Road and was located in Pontiac, Michigan. It had red-and-white striped aluminum awnings over each window, and large oak trees in the front yard. The backyard was full of fruit trees – sweet cherries, sour cherries, pear, apple, and plum. As I watched Laddy bark at the squirrel, I couldn't help but smile. "Some things never change," I thought to myself silently.

When the phone rang, it was my grandmother who answered it. She was a full-blooded Armenian woman in her early sixties, a survivor of the Armenian Massacre of 1915. The Turks were brutal, savage people. They invaded the peaceful Christian country of Armenia and massacred three million men, women, and children in an attempt to wipe out our race. My great grandparents, Vector and Sophie Negoshian, were able to flee the country and relocate in the United States. Coming through Ellis Island, New York they made the decision to settle down in Pontiac, Michigan. I had never met my great grandparents, but my grandmother, Helen and my grandfather, John, both loved me as if I was their own son. For this I have always been grateful. Their two sons, Tommy and Sammy, were both killed within six months of each other. Tommy was a radio gunner on a B-17 bomber. He was shot down during his last bombing mission over Germany. He, and two of his crew members, survived the crash only to be killed later as they tried to reach the French underground. Tommy's younger brother, Sammy, was killed six months later as he and a friend were hit by a drunk driver, while riding on the new scooter bike my mother and uncle had bought for him. I was born in 1950, and had an uncanny resemblance to my Uncle Tommy, in both looks and things I did as a child growing up.

"Hello?" my grandmother said softly as she spoke into the telephone. "Augh, you filthy man," she said in a disgusted tone of voice as she hung up the phone.

"Mamo, what's wrong?" I asked as I stood up and walked into the dining room toward my grandmother. Mamo is the Armenian word for grandmother; Babo is the Armenian word for grandfather.

"Some filthy man saying some bad things again," she explained, as she threw her right hand in the air and started walking toward the kitchen.

"Again?" I questioned. "How many times has this happened?"

"Three, four days now," my grandma answered in broken English.

It was then the phone rang again. As I answered the phone, I quickly walked into the small bedroom and closed the door. "Hello," I said calmly.

"Who in the hell do you, motherfuckers, think you are?" the man shouted through the receiver of the phone. Before I could answer, he continued, "I'll sell my drugs any fucking place I feel like selling them and to anyone who wants to buy them. Do you hear me?" he shouted.

"Oh yeah, I hear you," I replied calmly.

"Interfere with us again, you old motherfucker, and I'll kill your whole worthless family. I don't give a rat's ass if you're Mafia or not – I'll kill the lot of you. I'm here and no one tells me how to run my fucking business. You got that, old man?" the voice shouted out again.

"You sure that you've got the right phone number?" I asked calmly, even though my temper was beginning to rise.

"Don't play stupid with me, you coward piece of shit. 332-6770, that's your home number, John," the voice said.

"Yeah, that's our number, but I'm not John. My name is Dave; I'm John's grandson. I'll make sure he gets your message," I explained calmly. "Just do me a favor and don't call here any more."

"I knew it, you coward punk. Big time mob family my ass! Tell the Don, or Godfather, or whatever you fucking people call yourselves, that he's old and I'm young. I'm also backed up with big connections out of Miami. Fuck with me one more time, and life, as you know it is over. I'll kill your whole family – your cat, your dog, everyone and every living thing, understood, motherfucker?" the voice threatened.

"Loud and clear, sir. As I said before, I'll make sure your message is delivered. All I ask is that you do not call here again," I explained calmly as he hung the phone up in my ear.

Stepping out of the small bedroom, I hung up the phone. I couldn't believe what I had just heard. My grandfather was the kindest man I had ever known. He wasn't in the Mafia, let alone a mob boss. This is insane I thought to myself, as I picked the phone back up and dialed the number to the Agency.

"Hello?" the female voice said softly.

"Hello, voice identification code *Delta-Seven, Alpha-Six, Sandman*," I said. There was no reply, just silence. In less than thirty seconds, the response came.

"Hello, David, are you on a secure line?"

"No, ma'am, I need a back trace on phone number 332-6770, area code 313, Pontiac, Michigan. The call came through two minutes ago," I explained.

"Hold please," a short pause. "Sir, the last call made to area code 313-332-6770, Pontiac, Michigan came from phone number 672-4832, which is a home located in Waterford, Michigan, 4281 Cass Lake Drive. Owner's name, Henry Fleming. Is there anything else, sir?" she asked politely.

"No, ma'am, that will do it, thank you," I replied as I hung up the phone. "So you want to threaten my family, huh," I said to myself, as I took the small vial of liquid Methadrine out of my pocket and placed a drop under my tongue. "Let's see how tough you really are!"

* * * * * * *

It had now been three weeks since I started my surveillance of the house on 4281 Cass Lake Drive and its three occupants. There were two men and one woman living in the modest three-bedroom home. Both men appeared to be in their early thirties. One had blonde hair, stood about five-feet, ten-inches tall, and was well built. The other had longer black hair and stood about six-feet, three-inches tall. He looked to be about two hundred and forty pounds in weight and wore a well-trimmed goatee. He looked a little older than the other two and seemed to be the boss of the three people living in the home. All of his actions pointed a finger at him as being the loud mouth that had threatened my family and me. The female stood five-feet, four-inches tall, and had a slender built frame with long brown hair that touched the waist of her blue jeans. She appeared to be in her late twenties.

What I was waiting for was the one mistake that all three would make that would expose their vulnerability. Three weeks of waiting patiently had paid off. Running a check on their Florida license plates, confirmed they were, indeed, from Miami, Florida. Having the Agency down load all of the NCIC information that law enforcement had on them, also confirmed that they left Miami because the Federal Drug Enforcement Agency was closing in on them fast for sales of controlled substance. Our Agency, the CIA, told me that the two men were dealing in some major drug trafficking at the international level. Killing these three would be no loss to the world.

It was Tuesday evening and just as they had done for the past two weeks, all three of them put on their bowling shirts, grabbed their bowling bags, and climbed into the new dark blue Cadillac. Their destination was the Thunderbird Lanes Bowling Alley on Elisabeth Lake Road in Pontiac. Following the dark blue Cadillac to the bowling alley, I went inside and ordered a Pepsi from the bartender.

Another hour passed as I sat and watched the Midnight Doubles Bowling League begin. I wanted to make sure that all three of these people were occupied. The last thing I wanted was to have one of them walk in on me as I was preparing my trap. I knew I couldn't simply shoot them. That would open up a homicide investigation, and a police check of the phone records from their house would show that they had called my grandparents' home on a number of occasions. No, I could not allow that. I needed this hit to look like an accident something that the police would consider an open and shut case. You should never let law enforcement into your business. Once you do, you'll never again get their nose out of your business.

Driving back to the home on Case Lake Drive, I felt the summer air blow on my face. I was driving my 1969 white Chevy Corvette, with black leather interior, with the T-tops off. Looking down to check my speedometer, the white Corvette was cruising at a steady fifty-five.

Pulling into the driveway, I turned off the ignition and got out of the car. Wearing a pair of slip-on black dress shoes, black dress slacks, and a blue pullover golf shirt; I adjusted my dark Ray Ban Aviator sunglasses, reached into the passenger seat, and pulled out my black leather doctor's bag.

This was a beautiful neighborhood. The sun was starting to set, yet it was still light out. The neighbors across the street were sitting on their front porch watching their children play out on the lawn. Walking toward the backyard, I opened the gate on the chain-linked fence and stepped through, closing the gate behind me. I walked up to the backdoor, and looked around to make sure no one was watching me. Setting down my doctor's bag, I opened it up and pulled out the small hydraulic car jack and the two pieces of two-by-four I had folded and placed in the bag. I had fastened them together with a small metal hinge that I had purchased at Sears.

Opening the two-by-four to its full length, I placed the butt end of the jack against the opposite side of the wooden doorframe, just underneath the doorknob. Quickly working the jack lever, I felt the tension increase on the doorframe. Within a few seconds, I could see the bolt of the deadbolt locking system as the wooden doorframe gave way to the pressure that was being applied to it. As the wooden doorframe bowed, I pushed the bottom of the door with the toe of my right shoe. A smile spread across my face as I watched the door open freely and swing into the house.

Releasing the pressure from the jack, I quickly folded the two-by-four back up and placed it, along with the small hydraulic car jack, back into the leather bag. Picking up the leather bag, I quickly stepped into the house and closed the backdoor, resetting the locks. Smiling, I shook my head, stepped up the three small steps, and entered the kitchen.

I set my bag on the top of the kitchen table, and snugged my leather driving gloves a little tighter on both of my hands. Reaching behind me

16

and under my shirt, I pulled out the silenced .22 magnum automatic that I had tucked between the small of my back and the waist of my belt. Moving quickly, I searched the entire house even though my research told me that it was empty. Remembering my Seal team instructor, Master Chief Jeff Mareno, "Always expect the unexpected, David. Never forget what I am telling you. One day it may very well save your life," he used to always say this to me over and over again. The house was clear.

Tucking my pistol back in between my belt and the small of my back, I walked over and opened up the refrigerator. Looking inside, I whispered out loud, "Coke, my God, who in their right mind wants to drink that crap?" Seeing that there was no Pepsi available, I went to work. Pulling a kitchen chair out from the side of the kitchen table, I placed it under the ceiling light, and then went down the stairs and into the basement. Finding the main fuse box, I opened the front cover of the box and removed the main breakers. In doing so, I completely cut off all electricity to the entire house. Setting the main breakers on top of the metal fuse box, I went back upstairs and into the kitchen.

Standing on top of the kitchen chair, I carefully removed the light cover and placed it on the kitchen table. Reaching back up to the light, I removed one of the now exposed light bulbs and stepped down off of the chair. Placing the bulb on the table, I opened my doctor's bag and pulled out my glasscutter, a syringe, a small tube of glass sealer, and a small plastic bottle of gasoline. I sat down in the chair, picked up the light bulb and the small glass-cutting tool, and very carefully cut a small pin-size hole through the glass bulb at the base of the metal screw on end. I then loaded the syringe with gasoline and carefully injected the fluid into the light bulb, being very careful not to damage or break the delicate light filament inside. Reloading the syringe, I injected a second load of gasoline into the light bulb. Setting the syringe down, I picked up the tiny tube of glass sealer, opened the tip and placed several drops of the fast drying sealer over the hole to reseal the light bulb.

I waited ten minutes to let the sealer completely dry, picked up the bulb, and very carefully stood back up on the chair. The trick now was to screw the light bulb back into the kitchen light without splashing any of the gasoline onto the delicate light filament. If the filament were to break, I would have to start the process all over again using another light bulb. Patience is truly a virtue. It took me almost twenty minutes to screw the light bulb back into its socket. As my luck would have it, the spot that had the glass sealer on it was facing up and away from the liquid that now filled the bottom section of the bulb.

Replacing the light cover, I then went back downstairs to the main breaker fuse box. Opening the front door of the box, I picked up the main breakers. "Well, David, if we get a power surge through the line when you stick these back in, that light's gonna blow," I said out loud to myself. Sticking the main breakers back into the sockets, I smiled. "Oh yeah, hoo yah," I whispered out loud. There was no power surge; the gas-filled bulb didn't blow. Closing the fuse box door, I went to the furnace, opened the small metal door at the bottom, and blew out the gas pilot light. Closing the small metal door, I could hear and smell the hiss of raw natural gas as it slowly began to fill the basement area.

Going back upstairs, I reached into the left corner of my doctor's bag and pulled out the small glass vial of sulfuric acid. Removing the metal grills from the four top-surface burners of the gas-operated stove, I blew out all four of the tiny flames called pilot lights. I then opened the vial of sulfuric acid and placed a drop of acid on the gas line, next to where the pilot light had been burning. The acid immediately started to bubble up as it ate its way through the gas line. Replacing all four of the grills to their original positions, I then opened the oven door and blew out the pilot light flame in the oven. "Real stupid, David," I whispered to myself out loud. I should have blown the oven flame out as soon as I blew out the top burner lights. "No harm done," I thought to myself, as I put the sulfuric acid back inside the black leather bag. Double-checking to make sure that I did not leave anything out of place, I left the house. Looking at my watch, it was 8:05 p.m.

* * * * * * *

Looking at my watch it was 12:32 a.m., early Wednesday morning. In my Corvette, I sat at the end of Cass Lake Drive waiting for my prey to return home from the bowling alley.

"Right on schedule," I whispered softly to myself as the dark blue Cadillac drove past me. Placing a drop of Methadrine under my tongue, I felt my heart rate begin to pick up with the thought of what was about to happen.

Even though I was parked at the end of the street and seven houses away from the 4281 Cass Lake Drive home, I raised my night-vision binoculars and watched as both men and their female companion got out of the car. The taller, older man went straight to the front door and began to unlock it, as the other two opened the trunk of the car and pulled out the three bowling bags. I sat quietly and watched as the first man opened the front door, then pulled his head back quickly and stepped back, motioning for the other younger man to put out his cigarette.

Even at this distance, I could almost read his lips. I knew that he was telling his two friends that he smelled gas in the house and that a pilot light must have gone out on the kitchen stove. Now they would do what everyone does when they smell gas in their home. Open both the front and back doors, and turn on the light in the kitchen to check the stove. As I had planned, that was exactly what they did.

Once they turn on the kitchen light, the filament in the kitchen light bulb will ignite the gasoline causing it to explode into flames. That flame will ignite the natural gas that was now permeating the entire house. When that happens, the gas filled house will explode killing everyone inside.

First, the older man with the goatee went in, followed by his other two companions. Excitement filled my entire body as my heart began to race even faster.

"Come on, tough guy, turn on the kitchen light," I said to myself out loud, as I continued to watch through my binoculars. What happened next caught me completely by surprise. I saw a quick flash of light, and within a mega-second the entire home blew up with such a violent explosion that the entire roof of the house broke away from its support beams. The roof flew up into the air about six-feet and then came crashing back down into the center of the home that was now completely engulfed with flames. The explosion was so massive that it blew the windows out of the homes beside, behind, and in front of it.

"Oh, my God," I said in a shocked tone of voice. "I hope all that flying glass doesn't hurt any innocent people, especially the children in those surrounding homes."

Starting my car, I left the area and went back home. I was tired but the thought of innocent kids being hurt bothered me so much that I drove back to Cass Lake Drive. This time, I took my 1970 black Chevelle Super Sport.

The whole area was blocked off with Police and Fire Fighting vehicles. Parking my car on the side of the road, I walked up to one of the Sheriff Deputies and asked him if he needed any help. This would be the quickest way to get information on how many people were hurt.

"Hey, Deputy, do you need any help?" I asked.

"No, sir, we've got it under control. Thanks for asking, though," the Deputy replied.

"What happened, Deputy, anyone get hurt?" I asked.

"Well, sir, from what little I know, a house blew up. Probably a gas leak from the size of the explosion and damage that was caused. The good thing is that even though there are a lot of broken windows in the homes around the blast area, no one was hurt. We still don't know if anyone was in the house that exploded. I guess that it will be a few hours before the Fire Department will get it all cooled down enough for our people to search the debris," the deputy explained.

"Well, at least no one got hurt, that's the important thing. See ya later, Deputy," I replied as I walked back to my car and drove back home.

"David, you stupid idiot," I said out loud to myself. "You went in too early. I should have gone in at ten that would have still left plenty of time for the house to fill up with gas. 8 p.m. was two hours too long; don't ever make that mistake again. Damn, I could have gotten innocent people killed and that's not acceptable."

When I arrived home, I put my black leather bag away, took a shower, and went to bed. Tomorrow would prove to be an interesting day, I thought to myself as I fell asleep.

*   *   *   *   *   *   *

"Hey, Babo," I said as I kissed my grandfather on his cheek. "Want to watch the evening news?" I asked.

Nodding his head, yes; I turned on the television set in the front room of my grandparents' home, and sat down in the reclining chair next to the front room windows. It was 6:00 p.m. and Channel Seven Action News with Bill Bonds and Doris Bisco was just starting.

"We have an update on that terrible explosion that claimed three lives early this morning in Waterford Township. Doris, are you there?" News Anchor Bill Bonds asked as the camera went live to Doris Bisco at the scene of the explosion.

"Yes, Bill, I'm here and with me is Waterford Township Fire Marshal, Joe Evens. Mr. Evens can you tell us what happened here last night?" Ms. Bisco asked as she placed her hand-held microphone in front of the Fire Marshal's mouth.

"Yes, I can, Doris. We received a code three fire alarm at approximately twelve twenty-one this morning. Arriving at the scene, we found the home of 4281 Cass Lake Drive burning completely out of control. Knowing that there was nothing we could really do, we began to put out the fire and water down the homes on both sides of the burning residence to keep them from catching on fire also," the Fire Marshal explained.

"Was anyone hurt, sir, any casualties?" Ms. Bisco asked.

"Yes, I'm afraid so. We removed three bodies from the debris of the home. We will have to wait for the medical examiner in order to identify the remains. They were burned beyond recognition," Joe explained.

"By the looks of the homes surrounding this one, it's a miracle that no one else was hurt, wouldn't you say, sir?"

"We are very lucky that everyone else was in bed. The window curtains stopped most of the flying glass; yes, ma'am."

"Any idea what caused such a massive explosion like this, Joe?"

"Yes, ma'am," the Fire Marshal responded. "We found a worn out gas line on the kitchen stove. It's a sad thing, Doris, but it does happen from time to time."

"Well, there you have it, Bill. A home explodes, killing three people, a sad, sad thing. This is Doris Bisco, Channel Seven Action News reporting live and signing off."

Turning my head to look at my grandfather, I found him staring at me. Looking down he slowly shook his head, got up, and walked out of the room.

I could feel my heart break. I loved my grandfather so very much and now I felt as though I had let him down. Getting up, I went into the sun porch where I found him sitting on the couch.

"Are you mad at me, Babo?' I asked.

"David, you do this?" he asked in broken English.

"Yes, sir," I answered.

"Why, David, why you do this?" he asked, turning slightly to the side to look directly into my eyes.

"Babo, the man calls here and says dirty things to grandma over the phone. He threatens to kill you and Mamo. What do you think I am going to do? No one threatens my family, Babo. No one," I answered.

"Oh, David," my grandfather answered sadly. "I no want this for you. You can have anything you want, David. Go to college, be a doctor, a judge, a president, but not this, honey."

"Babo, Vietnam changed me. I did things there I never thought I could ever do," I explained, as I looked down at my feet. "I know it sounds crazy, but I miss the action. I miss my friends, I miss that feeling I used to get Grandpa," I explained.

"What feeling? What feeling you miss, David?" he asked in a curious voice.

"I don't know how to explain it, Babo. It's like a combination of fear and excitement both at the same time. I know it sounds crazy, but I miss it," I explained.

Taking a deep breath, he let it out slowly and looked out through the sun porch window into the backyard.

A few minutes of silence passed, and then I asked the question that had been bothering me for almost a month now.

"Grandpa, can I ask you a question?"

"Of course you can," he replied. "What is it?"

"The man that called here, said you wouldn't let him sell drugs in this area. He said you were a Don, the Godfather of the Mafia. Is that true, Babo, is there something that you and I need to talk about?" I asked.

Turning his head to face me, our eyes met once again. Nothing was said for along time; then we took a long walk together.

George Bernard Shaw was right, "The best kept secrets are the secrets that keep themselves" . . .

Chapter Three
The Set Up

"Hello, David," the voice whispered into my right ear as I felt the cold metal of the Russian made .10mm automatic pistol press against my forehead.

Startled, I quickly opened my eyes. Feeling my heart race with fear, I slowly moved my right hand under my pillow toward my Colt .45 caliber, Gold Cup automatic pistol.

"I come long way to this country you call America just so I can see you once more before I kill you," the Russian Colonel whispered calmly.

Feeling the sweat from my forehead drip down into my eyes, I slowly placed my hand around the pistol grip of my gun. "I'm going to kill you, Kalshnikov," I replied in a cold tone of voice.

"I think maybe no, David, this time you will not escape from me," the Russian Colonel said calmly, as he cocked the hammer back on his gun and applied more pressure to the trigger.

"Hoo yah, motherfucker," I shouted as I spun around quickly, pulling my gun out from under my pillow.

The ring of my doorbell brought me back to full consciousness. Pointing my gun in all directions, I sat on my bed covered with sweat, my body trembling.

"Shit!" I shouted as the doorbell rang once again. Still shaken, I got up and walked into the front room and opened the door.

"Hello, David," Kathy said with a smile. Looking down and seeing the gun in my hand and the upset look on my face, Kathy's smile quickly vanished. "What's wrong?" she asked.

"Bad dream," I responded as I opened the screen door. "Come on in. Make yourself at home," I explained. "I'll be right back." Going down the hall to my bathroom, I washed up and came back out to see Special Agent Eckland.

"Here, I think you can use this right about now," Kathy explained as she handed me a cold bottle of Pepsi.

"Thanks, I can sure use this," I explained as I took the bottle, sat down on my sofa, and took a drink.

"Don't thank me, kiddo, I took it out of your refrigerator," she explained with a grin as she took a sip from her bottle of Pepsi. "Are you okay, David?"

"Yeah, I'm alright. Just a ghost from the past came to see me. So, what brings you here?" I asked in hopes of changing the subject.

"A mobster named Joe Colombo out of New York," she explained as she opened her briefcase, and began to pull out some 8×10 color photographs and documents concerning Colombo. "We alone?" she asked as a second thought, looking up at me.

"Just me and my ghosts," I answered with a smile, as I took the picture out of Kathy's hand and looked at it.

"We have a small problem with this one, David," Kathy explained.

"For every problem, there's a solution," I replied as I continued to study the face of Joe Columbo.

"We have word that Mr. Colombo is talking to the FBI about some things that could connect us to a situation that needs to remain quiet. We need him dead in less than five days, David. Put this guy to sleep by June 28th and make it look like someone else did it for some other reason, understood?"

"We have any contacts in New York?"

"Yes, they'll meet you at the airport. You can use our Learjet. It's waiting for you at the Pontiac Airport," she explained as she got up and headed for the front door. "Good Luck, David, and hurry."

Looking up, all I saw was my screen door closing behind my new boss. Five days to hit this guy and I have to cover up everything so the heat goes in another direction. This should be interesting, I thought to myself as I began to put my gear together and head to the airport. Looking at my watch, it was 7:04 a.m., June 24, 1971.

* * * * * * *

Landing in New York, I was quickly greeted by an older man that looked to be in his late forties. He stood five-feet, ten-inches tall, weighed about 210-pounds, had dark skin, black hair, and brown eyes. What caught my attention was that his accent was not from New York.

"Hello, sir," the older man said as he extended his right hand for me to shake.

"Hello," I replied as I shook his hand and noticed his very powerful grip.

"Can you tell me, sir, is there a phone booth that I could use? I need to make a call," I asked calmly with a straight face.

"No, I'm afraid not. Ducks don't swim, they paddle," he responded with a grin.

"Sorry, my friend, you can never be too careful," I explained.

"Not in our business, you can't. Come on and let's get you out of here. I'll take you to a place that's safe so you can freshen up a bit and then I'll take you to one of the best steak houses in the city," he explained as he patted me gently on my left shoulder.

The airport was huge and the ride to Manhattan was just as I had remembered it from when my grandfather had brought me here to see Uncle Pauly. The Agency had a penthouse on the top of one of New York's high-rise buildings. The view was spectacular. All in all, it was everything that I had come to expect from the Agency.

After cleaning up, the older man extended his hand out to me once again. "My name is Gary," he explained as we shook hands once again.

"Call me Dave, nice to meet you, Gary," I replied.

"Would you like a drink, Dave?" Gary asked. "The bar is fully stocked and I was told to have plenty of cold Pepsi on hand for you," Gary explained with a grin, as he walked into the next room to refill his drink.

Sitting on the bar stool, I again looked around the penthouse. "They sure know how to treat a guy don't they?" I commented as Gary poured me a glass of Pepsi from behind the bar.

"Oh, it's not always like this, kid. I've been in situations that had me sleeping in back alleys, while people were trying to hunt me down to kill me. Sometimes it takes time before our people can get you a safe exit out of a hostile country. Enjoy this while it lasts," he explained, as he raised his glass of Scotch and ice in a toasting gesture.

Raising my glass, I tapped it gently against his and whispered, "Hoo yah."

"Are you from around here, Gary?" I asked.

"Nice day, isn't it," he answered with a grin.

"Okay," I said as I took a sip of my soda and remembered my training from the Farm. "Sorry, Gary, I'm still kind of new at this."

Raising his glass in a toasting gesture, Gary acknowledged without saying a word.

"I don't understand this, Gary. Why would the Agency send me to whack this Colombo fella when they could have hired some street punk to do it for fifty bucks? And why would our people be doing business with a guy like this anyway?" I asked.

"Don't expect to be told the truth about why you're hitting a guy, David, at least not this early in the game. I seriously doubt that we're involved with some low-level mobster like Colombo anyway. My guess is that the 'Big Boys' at the top are doing a favor for someone in organized crime. You know, we scratch their back and down the road they scratch ours," Gary explained calmly, as he took a sip from his drink.

"Yeah, but why me?" I asked with a confused look on my face.

"That's simple. They're testing you kid. Hell, your team became a legend with our Agency. We used to take up money pools to see who would come closest to guessing how quickly you guys would strike and get out safely, while accomplishing your mission successfully."

"You're kidding, tell me you're kidding, Gary," I answered.

"Nope, it's the truth kid. The Deputy Director of the Agency would never put himself in harms way by going to Vietnam. But he did for 'Team One'; he did for you, Butch, Nick, and Danny. It's called respect, kid, and you guys earned it the hard way," Gary explained. "But the one thing you have to remember is, that was Vietnam, David. Now you're back in the free world and you're in cement city. New York, kid, the Big Apple, and this is a mob boss you're after. They threw you into the shark tank and there's some serious money on you blowing this hit. It's a different playground now, buddy."

"You guys bet that I would blow this hit? You guys still bet on people?" I questioned.

"Not on everyone, David, just on you and Danny," Gary answered as he poured himself another drink.

"Damn, nobody bet on me, huh?" I asked as I reached up and rubbed the scar on my chin, feeling disappointed.

"Only our boss, Agent Eckland, and Marge, the older lady that put together your identifications, house, and stuff," Gary explained.

"So that's her name, Marge, huh. So much for need to know basis," I said with a grin.

"So, why are you here if you bet against me?" I asked.

"Hell, kid, I wouldn't miss this for the world," Gary answered.

"They bet a lot of money on me, Gary?'

Raising his eyebrows, Gary nodded 'Yes' without saying a word.

"Well then, I need three pieces of ID All in the same name and some Secret Service identification credentials with my picture on it, but in the name that's on the bogus ID's. Oh, by the way, Gary, I need it by tomorrow morning, 8 a.m. Think you can handle that?" I asked.

"Secret Service credentials, for what, David?" Gary asked.

"Need to know, Gary, and you bet against me. You don't need to know. Come on old-timer, you can buy me dinner," I explained as I got up and headed for the door.

* * * * * * *

June 25, 1971: Looking at my watch, it was 7:30 a.m. as the man that I only knew as Gary walked in through the front door of our penthouse.

"Here you go, hot shot," Gary said as he handed me the sealed manila envelope. "Marge said to tell you that there are two credit cards and five thousand dollars in cash in there," Gary added.

"Did she ask what I needed this for?" I questioned.

"Nope, not a word. She just handed me the envelope, explained that she added two credit cards and the cash to your request. Then she crossed her arms in front of her, grinned, and asked me if I wanted to raise the bet," Gary explained sarcastically.

"Hey, Gary, this information package that Kathy gave me says that this Columbo fella is having one of his 'Unity Day' rallies on the 28th. Are there any black guys around here that don't like Colombo, any that you know of?" I asked.

"Boy, I'm not from this area, Dave. I really wouldn't know. You could call it in and see what's on file with our people back in Langley," he suggested.

"Good idea," I replied as I reached over, picked up the telephone, and dialed our Black Op's number.

"Hello," the lady's voice answered softly.

"Voice identification code number - *Delta 7, Alpha 6, Sandman*," I said calmly into the mouthpiece. There was no reply, just silence on the other end of the line. Twenty seconds later the response came.

"Hello, David, what can I do for you?" she asked.

"Do you have any information on anyone that might be upset with the name 'Joe Colombo', or anyone that might have a bone to pick with the 'Unity Day' rally people in New York?" I asked.

"Hold please." Six minutes later, "David, I have a list of people that is longer than my arm," she replied. "Colombo and Unity Day are not well liked by these people."

"Can you break it down to maybe two or three people that hate him for personal reasons, or anyone that is an ex-federal employee, or someone that was trying to become a federal employee but failed?" I asked.

"That might make it a bit easier, sir. Let me see what our computer has to say," she responded. Listening carefully, I could hear the young lady on the other end of the line tapping on the computer keys.

"Well, this is interesting. I have four names for you. One white and three blacks, all male," she explained.

Picking up my notepad and ink pen, I looked up at Gary and smiled. "Alright, ma'am, I'm ready. Please give me their full names, addresses, phone numbers, make of their vehicle, license plate number, driver's license number, and social security number," I asked.

Writing down all of the information, I thanked our friend for the help and hung up.

"I'm going to need a car, Gary. Do you have one I can use?" I asked.

"In New York, my friend, we call a cab," Gary answered with a smile.

"Keys to your car, Gary," I asked as I held out my hand.

"You'll get lost, David. This is a big city," Gary answered.

"If I can find my way through the swamps and jungles of Vietnam, New York will be a piece of cake," I responded. "Keys, Gary."

"I'll drive you, kid," he answered, as he stood up and pulled the keys out of his pocket.

"Not this time, Gary, I go solo on this one," I explained as I pulled the keys out of Gary's hand and headed for the door. "See ya, later," I said with a chuckle, as I pushed the door closed behind me. "Well, this should be interesting, David," I whispered out loud to myself, as I got into the elevator and began to descend to the lobby. "Real interesting."

* * * * * * *

I spent the rest of the day tracking down the first two names on my list. The white male named Brian Jenks was a burned out mob-wanna-be. The first black man was Kevin Reese, who I found out had been killed in a shooting at the local party store a week earlier. Renting a room at a downtown hotel, I found myself quickly falling asleep with my mind wondering if I really could pull this off all by myself.

* * * * * * *

June 26, 1971. As I left the hotel, I couldn't help but be upset with myself for sleeping in so late. It was almost 10 a.m. and I was getting a late start.

It took me three hours to find Benny Lombowsky, who was a very serious alcoholic and the only black man I had ever met with a Polish last name. Looking at my watch, I realized that I was quickly running out of time.

It was almost 6:30 p.m. when I finally found Jerome A. Johnson sitting alone at a bar, minding his own business. Going across the street to a small restaurant, I called the bar and asked the bartender to page a Mr. Jerome Johnson for me.

"Hello," came the response in a cautious voice.

"Mr. Johnson, Jerome A. Johnson?" I asked.

"Yes, I'm Jerome Johnson. Who is this?" he asked.

"Well, Mr. Johnson, my name is Jim Nelson, United States Secret Service. If you have a few minutes to spare I would like to talk to you about a matter of National Security," I explained calmly.

"Secret Service, National Security, you're kidding, right?" he asked with a chuckle.

"No, sir, I am not kidding. In fact, I am so serious that this could very well get you that job you wanted with the Federal Bureau of Prisons along with a — well lets just say, a very large bonus check, tax exempt, of course," I explained calmly. "If you're interested, sir, I am parked across the street in the dark blue Chevy two-door Impala Super Sport. You have one minute to decide. If you're not in the passenger's seat of my vehicle, sitting next to me in one minute, I'll be gone and you'll spend the rest of your life wondering, what if?" I explained, as I hung up the phone and returned to my vehicle outside.

Jerome A. Johnson was sitting next to me in less than thirty seconds. At this point, I knew that the rest would be a simple matter of brainwashing him and convincing him that he was completely bulletproof. Jerome Johnson was a very simple minded man; this would be a piece of cake.

* * * * * * *

June 27, 1971: Sending Gary out to get the credentials and weapon that I would need for Jerome, I spent the entire day and night fueling his anger toward Joe Colombo and convincing him that he was completely safe with us, and that he would be highly rewarded for the service that he was about to perform for his country.

* * * * * * *

June 28, 1971: Keeping Gary limited to only meeting Jerome one time, which was when he delivered Jerome's phony newspaper photographer credentials, camera, and handgun, I sat Jerome down one more time to go over the plan.

* * * * * * *

Standing in the crowd of people next to Jerome, I watched as mobster Joe Colombo, once again, lead the march of one of his Unity Day Rallies in New York City with his armed bodyguards at his side.

Convinced that the crowd was full of Secret Service agents who would cover his path of retreat, Jerome stood poised and ready to make his move.

Jerome, wearing his phony newspaper photographer credentials, emerged from the crowd of people, pulled his gun, and shot Joe Colombo three times in the head. Joe Colombo's bodyguards quickly pulled their weapons and opened fire, killing Jerome A. Johnson at the scene. Turning around, I slowly made my way out and away from the crowd, and returned to our penthouse.

Shot three times in the head by the amateur gunman, Joe Colombo lied in a coma for seven years before he finally died. The word on the street was that the hit came from the Gambino crime family, even though it was well known that Joe Colombo had tipped off Gambino that there was a plot to kill him, which saved Gambino's life.

* * * * * * *

June 29, 1971: A dozen red roses with babies breath flowers were delivered to Special Agent Kathy Eckland and my contact lady friend in Langley Virginia, who I only knew as Marge. A note was attached to their flowers, which simply read: "You win, Sandman."

Chapter Four
Diplomatic Immunity

The Pontiac Airport was small in size and located on the north side of Highway M-59. It had a bar and dining area that allowed you to see out through the windows in all directions. To my right, I could see the steady flow of traffic on the four-lane highway. Looking to my left, a smile crossed my face as I took a sip of my Pepsi and watched Special Agent Eckland walk in through the double glass doors facing the runway. Watching Kathy, I couldn't help but think about what a pretty young lady she was. Walking toward me with her metal briefcase in hand, she smiled as she looked up and saw me staring at her.

"Hello, David," she said as she set her security case on the table and sat down.

"Hello, boss," I replied with a grin.

"Thank you for the roses. They were beautiful," she explained. "I'm told that it took Marge a full ten minutes before she actually closed her mouth, when they delivered the flowers to her. I guess no one has ever taken the time to send her roses before," Kathy explained with a smile. "She is also trying to figure out how you found out what her name was in such a short time."

"Really," I said, looking down at my drink with a smile.

"How did you know about the bet? Did Gary tell you?" she asked.

"Yes, he did. He also told me that he had bet against me, so I kept him out of the loop. He was a little sucked up about it but I'm sure he'll get over it," I explained. "Have you eaten yet? They have a great prime rib dinner here."

"Sounds good to me, I'm starving. I haven't eaten anything since seven this morning," she explained as she looked at her watch. "My gosh, it's after six already."

Placing our order, Kathy took a sip of her rum and coke and opened the security case she had brought with her. Taking out several photographs, she slid them across the table for me to look at.

"Her name is Mia Ty Linn. She is a diplomat with full diplomatic immunity from the Chinese Embassy in New York. She is bilingual and has a Ph.D. in Medicine from Harvard University. Mia is single, 42-years of age, five-feet, two-inches in height, and weighs 114-pounds. She is also highly trained in the Chinese Martial Arts and is deadly if provoked," Kathy explained.

"So, what's so important that you asked me to meet with you on such short notice?" I asked, setting the pictures face down on the table and taking a sip of my soda.

"Our people have intercepted some telephone communications coming out of her Embassy. We believe that she is meeting with a Russian double agent this weekend and that the meeting is to take place in New Orleans. We need to know who the double agent is and, if at all possible, we need to know what they're talking about," Kathy explained.

"Do you know where the meeting is going to take place in New Orleans?" I questioned.

"A place called Smiling Jacks on the corner of Bourbon and Toulouse. We know that something big is taking place, David, because of the location of the meet," Kathy explained with a serious look on her face.

"I'm not following you, Kathy. What do you mean?"

"Smiling Jacks is a strip club, David. Why would a diplomat meet with a double agent at a strip club in New Orleans unless it's because they don't want their faces seen by anyone that might know them?" Kathy explained.

"Makes sense, a double agent from Russia, huh. I wonder if he knows Colonel Kalashnikov?"

"This spy is also part of the KGB in Russia, David. The odds are that he at least knows of him, if nothing else," Kathy explained.

Finishing our meal, we walked out onto the tarmac where the Agency's Learjet was waiting for Kathy.

"Try to be in place by tomorrow, David. We have more intel coming in. I'll contact you at this phone number," Kathy explained as she handed me the address and phone number, which she had handwritten on a piece of paper. "Go to this address and ask for Mama Chu Lu. She works for us from time to time. She's not with the Company, but she is trusted by us and feared by most of the people in New Orleans," Kathy explained with a grin.

"Feared, what is she, mob connected?" I asked.

"Not even close. Most mobsters are afraid of her also. She's very deep into the world of Black Arts, you know, Voodoo. You two should hit if off great," Kathy explained as she climbed up the steps and entered the plane. "I'll call you in twenty-four hours at that number with an update on the status of your mission. Stay safe, David, and good luck," Kathy added as she disappeared into the plane.

Turning around, I began to walk to the parking lot where my 1970 Chevelle Super Sport was waiting for me. "Mama Chu Lu, Voodoo, Black Arts, what the fuck is this all about?" I asked myself out loud, as I set the metal security case down on the seat next to me and started the engine.

"Well, New Orleans, here I come," I whispered to myself as I pulled out of the parking lot and headed home to get ready for my flight.

* * * * * * *

New Orleans, the magical town of myth, mystery, and mythology; its history is legendary. Catching a cab at the airport, I had the cab driver take me to the end of the street that had Mama Chu Lu's address on it.

"Mama Chu Lu live that way," the cab driver explained as he pointed his finger down the dirt road.

"You're not going to drive me to her house?" I asked.

"No, mon, Mama Chu Lu bad Mojo. She put the gris-gris on them she no like. No go I farther than this," he explained in a frightened voice.

Paying the cab driver, I grabbed my bags and began walking down the dirt road in the direction of Mama Chu Lu's home. There were no houses on either side of the street, just swamp and an eerie stillness to the air. Only the occasional sound of a snake slithering across the lily pads and a gator moving slowly across the still swamp water could be heard. The air was hot and humid, and sweat began to run down my back and forehead. There in the distance, I saw the cabin sitting alone at the end of the dirt road surrounded by swampland.

"You've got to be kidding me," I whispered out loud as I reached up under my windbreaker and pulled my Colt 45 automatic from its shoulder holster. Walking up to the one-room log cabin, I cocked the hammer back on my pistol and knocked on the old wooden front door. The cabin had to be at least a hundred and fifty years old. It was covered with moss and had old rags hanging in the windows as curtains.

"What it be you looking to see, you?" the voice behind me asked in a whisper.

Startled, I turned quickly, pointing my Colt in the direction of the voice. Standing fifteen feet away from me was an old Cajun black woman who appeared to be in her late sixties. Her hair was all white, her skin wrinkled, and her eyes were a dark shade of green. She wore a dark blue dress that was worn thin and an old pair of sandals.

"You it be, I know you from my dreams. You scare me, not, you," she explained calmly.

Lowering my gun, I quickly placed it back in the holster. "I'm sorry, ma'am. I didn't hear you come up behind me. You startled me, I'm sorry for my actions. I meant no disrespect. I'm looking for Mama Chu Lu," I explained.

"That I be," she said softly as she walked up to me and placed her right hand on my left cheek. As she looked into my eyes, I could feel my heart start to pound in my chest. "Calm down, David," I said to myself in my mind. "She's only an old woman, nothing more."

"More I am, you see," she explained as she took her hand off of my face.

Saying nothing, I couldn't believe it. Did this old lady just read my mind? My thoughts quickly went back to the time I had met Chopper's mother. She had looked into my eyes and told me things about myself that no one else knew. She explained that the eyes were the windows to a person's soul.

"Wait here, you, I gather my things," she explained as she walked into the old cabin and closed the door behind her.

Caught off guard by an old woman, I felt stupid as I stood outside in the hot spring air. Twenty minutes had passed when Mama Chu Lu came back out of the cabin carrying an old burlap sack. Hearing the sound of a car coming down the dirt road toward us, she looked at me and handed me the sack to carry.

"Now go you, with me," she explained as the car pulled up in front of us. Getting into the old 1954 Plymouth, we turned around and drove away from the old cabin.

The driver was a black man in his mid-thirties. He didn't say anything. His eyes looked dead, which matched the way he was dressed and smelled. He looked as though he was in a trance of some sort. But I kept my mouth shut and my hand wrapped firmly around the butt of my Colt .45 just in case something went wrong. "What in the hell was Kathy thinking?" I thought to myself.

We drove about thirty minutes and arrived in the city limits just down from Bourbon Street. Mama Chu Lu's apartment home was located above one of the many restaurant-bars that New Orleans is famous for.

Now I understood what Kathy meant, when she said that she would call me within twenty-four hours of my arrival at Mama Chu Lu's home. The cabin out in the swamp certainly didn't have any electricity let alone a telephone. This apartment home was, much to the contrary, more modern and up-to-date with today's living standards.

Walking up the stairway to Mama Chu Lu's front door, I watched as she reached for the door key that was attached to the piece of rope she used as a belt around her tiny waist. Opening the door, I walked into the front room behind Mama Chu Lu, carrying my bag and the burlap sack that she had handed me back at the old cabin.

"Come, bring bag this way, you," she explained, as I followed her down the hall and into the bathroom. Taking the sack from my hand, the old lady opened it and dumped its contents into the bathtub. Raising my eyebrows, I whispered, "Oh, my God," as I stood watching in amazement.

Two cottonmouth snakes, eight frogs, a bunch of weeds, two dead bats, some tree moss, and a variety of other crawling things began to slither around and hiss in the tub.

Saying one word, that I did not understand, Mama Chu Lu raised her right hand and waved it over the bathtub. Immediately, all of the swamp animals became quiet. Looking up at me, Mama Chu Lu smiled for the first time since I had met her. "Mama scare them, yes?" she asked.

"Yes, ma'am, I believe that you're right about that. Can I use your phone?" I asked calmly.

"Kitchen, phone you find there. You no scare me, you. I see, I see, no scared me," she explained as she smiled and waved the finger of her right hand from side to side at me.

"Mama Chu Lu, I no come here to scare you. I'm a friend of Kathy, I'm your friend, Mama Chu Lu, I'm one of the good guys," I explained calmly.

"No, you say, you he, you come, grave follow you, I see. Mama Chu Lu see you. Dreams, I see you, yes. You he," she said as the smile disappeared from her face.

"I'm he? I don't understand, Mama Chu Lu. I'm who?" I asked, with a confused look on my face.

"Death," Mama Chu Lu explained in a serious tone. "Grave follow you. Holy book say you come, now I see, yes, I see," she said in a whisper of a voice.

Turning around, I picked up my bag and walked into the kitchen. I dialed the telephone, and waited.

"Hello," the man's voice greeted.

"Voice identification – *Delta 7, Alpha 6 – Sandman*," I replied.

Almost twenty seconds passed before the voice spoke again. "Hello, David. How may I help you?'

"Patch me through to Agent Eckland," I responded.

"Hold, please."

"David, is that you?" Kathy asked.

"What is this, some kind of a sick fucking joke, Kathy?" I asked in a bitter tone.

"Hey, when we called Mama Chu Lu, she said that she already knew what we wanted and who we wanted to send to meet her. She insisted on meeting you. She said that she has seen you in her dreams and that she wasn't afraid of you. Don't you just lover her?" Kathy asked excitedly.

"She has a bathtub full of cottonmouth snakes, bats, frogs, and God only knows what else is in there, Kathy. Find me a room to stay at, or I'm out of here," I insisted.

"You don't want to stay there?" Kathy asked with a chuckle in her voice.

Hanging the phone up in Kathy's ear, I picked up my bag and headed for the door. "Bye, Mama Chu Lu. I'm leaving now," I shouted out as I opened the door to leave.

"Go, you, where?" she asked.

"Ah gees, Mama, would you stop doing that," I insisted in a startled voice, as I walked out of the door and right into Mama Chu Lu who was standing on the other side of the door in the hallway.

"You no scare Mama Chu Lu," she whispered.

"Mama Chu Lu scare me," I replied as I tried to calm myself down.

Smiling, Mama Chu Lu laughed out loud. "If you need Mama Chu Lu, you come, yes?" she asked.

"Yes, Mama, if I need you, I come," I answered, as I shook the old woman's hand and walked down the wooden stairway and out onto Bourbon Street.

Looking around, I followed the smell of barbecued chicken to a nearby restaurant. Ordering a meal of barbecued chicken, dirty rice, and a cold Pepsi, I tried to gather my thoughts. I needed someplace to stay that was close by, yet far enough away so if I ran into trouble I would be able to escape quickly. Asking some of the locals that were drinking at the bar, I decided to take their advice. Walking three blocks off of Canal Street, I went to the Saint Charles Hotel, which was located on Saint Charles Street. Renting a room there, I paid in cash, went upstairs, and sat on the edge of the bed. Watching the cable car pass by my window, I couldn't help but wonder what I had gotten myself into. I reached into my shirt pocket, took out my tiny vial of liquid Methadrine, opened it, and placed a drop under my tongue.

Looking at the phone located on the nightstand next to the bed, I knew I needed to call in and give Kathy my location. "Boy, she is going to be pissed that I hung up on her," I thought to myself. As I reached for the telephone, it rang before I had a chance to pick it up.

"Hello?" I asked.

"David, if you ever hang up on me again, I'll have your ass. Do you understand me?" Kathy explained in a stern, scolding voice.

Hanging the phone up in Kathy's ear, I smiled, and waited for her to call back.

The phone rang again, but this time when I picked it up I said, "Hello, Wong's Chinese Laundry, you get dirty, we clean you up," my attempt at a Chinese accent wasn't too bad.

"Wong's Laundry?" Kathy questioned. "David, you son of a bitch, this isn't funny!"

"Neither was your witch doctor, Mama Chu Lu," I responded coldly.

After a slight pause, I knew that Agent Eckland had started to realize that she had made a mistake by sending me to see Mama Chu Lu and that I was indeed very upset about it.

"Yeah, well, I guess you're right, David, I'm sorry. But I really did think that you would find her interesting," she added, with a touch of humor in her voice.

"She plays with snakes and dead bats, Kathy. I hate snakes, remember?"

"Yes, I do, I really am sorry, David, it won't happen again," Kathy explained calmly.

"Then I accept your apology," I replied. "Hey, wait a minute. How did you know I was here at this hotel?"

"Mama Chu Lu told me when I called her."

"Oh really, Mama Chu Lu doesn't know I'm here Kathy. I never told her where I was going," I answered sarcastically. "What'd she do, follow me?"

"No, she didn't follow you, David. She just knows these things; that's why we use her. Besides, she really likes you. She said that you're the one that the Holy book talks about. She said that you're the one that collects the dead. I thought that was kind of spooky though, when I heard her say it," Kathy explained in a soft tone of voice. "Hold on a second, David, something is coming across my computer."

Looking out through the window of my room, I waited quietly for Kathy to say something. "We just got confirmation that Mia Ty Linn will be meeting with her contact tonight at the Artist Café Strip Club, on Iberville Street, at 11:00 p.m. Do you have a camera with you, David?" Kathy asked.

With a light tone of laughter, I answered, "No, I seem to have forgotten that. I could go down to K-Mart and purchase one if you would like me to," I said sarcastically.

"Hang on, David, something else is happening. Stay where you are, don't leave the room until I call you back," Kathy explained as she hung the phone up in my ear.

Pulling the telephone receiver away from my ear, I looked at it for a few seconds and then hung it back up onto my phone. Reaching into my bag, I pulled out my .22 magnum automatic pistol and slowly screwed on the silencer. "Always expect the unexpected, David," I whispered to myself. "Remember your Seal team training and don't get careless."

It had been almost twelve minutes since I had talked to Kathy. I couldn't help but wonder what was going on at the Agency and why would a Chinese diplomat be meeting with a Russian double agent? Sliding a fully-loaded clip of .22 magnum rounds into the butt of my automatic, I pulled the slide action back on my weapon and loaded a round into the chamber. Checking to make sure that the safety was on, I tucked the pistol into my waist between my belt and my lower back.

Hearing the phone ring once again, I picked up the receiver and placed it to my ear. "Talk," I said calmly.

"David?" Kathy asked.

"What's up, boss, everything alright?" I asked.

"Wait for the exchange to take place and then try to recover whatever it is that he gives Mia Linn," Kathy explained.

"Exchange?" I questioned.

"We have new information that tells us that Mia Linn is picking up something from the Russian, David," Kathy explained, and then paused for a few seconds.

"Kathy, what's wrong?" I asked, when I sensed the tension in her voice.

"David, we just received some sensitive information that the Russian double agent is selling information to the Chinese in exchange for technology about some secret project the Chinese are involved in. We believe that it has something to do with a nuclear trigger device. We're just not sure. Wait for the exchange to go down and once Ms. Linn leaves, do whatever it takes to recover what the Russian gives her. Even if you have to kill her. Remember that she has diplomatic immunity, David, but it doesn't matter," Kathy explained.

"Understood, boss," I replied in a soft tone of voice.

"Be careful, David. These people are very dangerous and very, very lethal. Call in as soon as you retrieve it," Kathy explained. "Remember, David, this isn't Vietnam, it's a whole new ball game now."

"I understand," I replied as I hung up the telephone and pulled the tiny glass vial of liquid Methadrine out of my shirt pocket. Placing a drop of the liquid under my tongue, I felt my body surge with new-found energy. "Russians and Chinese, huh?" I whispered out loud to myself. "This isn't Vietnam my ass, Kathy. This is just like Vietnam, the only difference is we're playing in my backyard now and this time I'm making the rules!"

* * * * * * *

The Artist Café was just one of many nude strip joints in this area of Iberville Street. Most of the female dancers ranged from the age of 18 to 30. Some white, some black, some straight, and some junkies strung out on one or more illegal narcotics that were readily available for purchase from the big Cajun bouncer that sat quietly in the corner of the dimly lit room.

Taking a sip of my Pepsi, I looked down at my watch; it was 11:01 p.m. Looking back up, I turned my head slightly to the side as I watched the pretty female Chinese diplomat walk in through the front door. She looked a lot younger than her forty-two years of age. What surprised me was that she was dressed in a blue halter-top, blue jeans, and wore a pair of flat leather slip-on shoes. Her dark sunglasses matched her jet-black hair, which was cut in a stylish short fashion. It was the fact that she wasn't wearing any socks that caught my attention.

Kathy had warned me that this five-foot, two-inch, 114-pound female was highly trained in Chinese Martial Arts. Now I believed it more than ever. While being trained at the CIA's Farm, one of my instructors had taught me well as he trained me in the art of detection. Ms. Mia Ty Linn wanted to be able to get out of her shoes quickly if need be, and when she did she would put her feet into action in what I believed to be true Kung Fu fashion. The Eastern Art of Kung Fu prefers the bare foot snake/crane technique, which makes it easier for the person or student to manipulate the desired maneuver and strike with lightening speed. I had no doubt, after watching Ms. Linn walk to the back table of the club with such a fluid, deliberate, calculated movement, that she was indeed a master of this ancient art. Sitting down at the table, Mia placed her black leather handbag on the table in front of her and ordered a drink.

It was 11:10 p.m. when the older gray haired man came walking into the club and up to the bar to order a drink. Everything about him fit the middle-class American male profile of a horny older man who was looking for some cheap thrills. Everything except his Russian made watch and the bulge, in what looked to be an ankle holster, protruding from his pant cuff just above his right ankle.

Reaching into my pocket, I pulled out my tiny glass vial of liquid Methadrine and placed a drop under my tongue. Placing the vial back into my pocket, I took a sip of my Pepsi and grinned. The effect of the liquid was instantaneous as my body began to tingle with the full surge of blood rushing through every vein in my body. The combination of excitement, along with the full pump of the speed coursing its way through my veins had me at full alert.

"My God, how I miss this feeling," I thought to myself as I watched the older man make his way to Ms. Linn's table and sit down, placing his hat on the table next to him.

While several of the strippers began their routine and danced slowly to the music being played for them, I realized just how comfortable Ms. Linn and the older Russian felt doing business at this bar. They were not paying any attention to their surroundings or to anyone that might be watching them. I knew from my training that whatever it was they were going to do, it wouldn't take long. They would make the exchange quickly without drawing any attention to themselves and then separate, each going their own way. As predicted, Mia Linn and the Russian engaged in some idle chit-chat and watched the strippers.

"Something's not right with all of this," I said to myself as I continued to watch Mia Linn and the Russian talk softly to each other.

It was impossible to hear anything they were saying. I was too far away and the dance music was way too loud. Hearing a table full of men start to hoot and holler as one of the strippers pulled off her bra, I looked over at her for just a second. It was then I caught it. The Russian, he's a man but his fingernails are way too long! "Damn," I whispered softly as I took a drink from my glass and gazed back over at the Russian and the female Chinese diplomat. The special training I received at the Farm in detection had just paid off. I watched the Russian slowly reach over with his right hand and peal off the fingernail from the small finger of his left hand and place it on the table top next to his napkin. "Gotcha, you vodka drinking piece of shit," I whispered to myself.

A few minutes passed as they smiled and laughed, and then Mia Linn picked up the piece of fingernail and quickly placed it between the bottom gum and the lower lip of her mouth. Standing up, she headed for the door, leaving her small purse behind. "The payoff money must be in the purse," I thought to myself as I stood up and headed for the door right behind her.

Reaching into my right pant leg pocket, I placed my hand firmly onto the grip of my stungun. Walking through the first inner door and into the small ten-foot section of hallway that led to the outer exit door, I said, "Excuse me, miss, I think you dropped this."

Now, no more than two-feet behind the Chinese diplomat, Mia Linn, turned her head slightly to look at my left hand as she pushed the release bar of the outer door to open it. I knew that this pretty, small lady was lethal and dangerous in a number of Chinese Martial Arts. Looking down at my empty left hand, she said, "Excuse me?" The look on her face told me she knew she had just been had. Her pretty eyes widened as she tried to counter my move with a sweeping left hand, but it was too late.

The two metal prongs of my stungun were already pushing into the back of her neck. Pressing the button on the gun, I sent 150,000-volts of electricity surging through her body. She dropped like a rock, straight downward and onto the black and white squares of the tile floor. Bending over, I hit her with another three-second jolt of electricity, just to be safe. She was too dangerous to take any chances with.

Kneeling down, I quickly pulled her bottom lip out and away from her mouth with my left hand and reached between her lower lip and gum with the first finger of my right hand. Starting at the back of her jaw, I moved my finger forward until I felt the piece of fingernail. Securing it between my thumb and finger, I quickly stuck it into my top shirt pocket and stood up, putting the hand-held stungun back into my pants pocket. Reaching for the door to leave, I was startled when the door opened by itself.

Looking at me, then down at Mia Linn and back up at me again, the overweight black man asked, "She drunk?"

Nodding my head up and down, I said, "Sure looks like it. She's lucky I'm in a hurry. If I had the time, I'd take her out to my car and fuck her brains out," I explained as I stepped over her body and walked past the older man and out through the door.

The temperature was hot and there was no breeze as I quickly moved to my car, climbed in, and started it up. Looking up, I smiled as I watched the older black gentleman carry the Chinese diplomat's limp body out to his old delivery truck.

"Boy is he going to be in for the surprise of his life when she wakes up and catches him pulling off her clothes. But then again, he might actually get lucky. The stungun will only knock her out for about ten minutes. He looks to be about forty-years old. He might actually have enough time to get some before Mia Linn wakes up and kills him," I thought to myself as I headed straight for the airport.

Once at the airport, I called Kathy on our secure line. "Hey, pretty lady, what's up?" I asked.

"Did they meet?" Kathy asked in an anxious voice.

"Yup," was all I said. I knew that Kathy and everyone in the office were sitting on pins and needles waiting to find out what happened.

"Yup? Yup? Are you fucking crazy, David? Where are you?" Kathy asked in an angry voice.

I really enjoyed getting Kathy upset with me. After her little prank with Mama Chu Lu and her bathtub full of snakes, frogs, and dead bats; I wanted some payback.

"Airport," I replied.

Hearing Kathy take a deep breath of air into her lungs and let it out slowly, I knew that she was ready to blow.

"David?" she said softly.

"Yes, dear," I answered tenderly.

"You're a dead man!" she explained calmly.

"Really? That's the same thing Major Dinh and Colonel Ky said," I explained with a chuckle.

"Do you have something for me?" Kathy asked calmly.

I thought about a sexual type of reply, but then changed my mind quickly. I didn't want to push my luck too far.

"A piece of fingernail," I explained calmly.

"Microchip?" Kathy asked in an excited voice.

"Either that or a dried booger," I said jokingly.

"Don't go back to your hotel room, David," she explained.

"Didn't plan on it, kiddo. What do you want me to do with this thing, Kathy?" I asked in a more serious tone.

"Bring it straight to us," Kathy explained. "Do you need anything cleaned up out there?" she asked.

"No, they're both still alive, but Mia Linn got a pretty good look at my face before I turned her lights out," I explained as I looked around to make sure that no one was listening or watching me. "I've got to go, Kathy, they just made the boarding call for my flight. I'm on Delta Airlines, Flight 704. Pick me up at the airport on your end, will you?" I asked.

"We'll be waiting for you, David. Good job," Kathy replied as she hung up the phone.

* * * * * * *

Debriefing took less than two hours, once I got back to C.I.A. Headquarters in Langley. It took our lab technicians less than thirty minutes to remove the tiny Russian microchip from between the fingernail and clear nail sealer that held it in place. All I was told was the Russian technology of the microchip was superb. Decrypting the coded microchip would take some time, but I knew our people would get it done quickly.

Kathy took me to dinner. We were becoming closer to each other as friends and that made me feel good inside.

"So, tell me, David, did Mia Linn meet the Sandman?" Kathy asked as she looked deep into my eyes, waiting for a response.

Thinking about the North Viet Cong girl that I had caught taking our pictures in Bien Hoa and the water-hose torture treatment I had used to get her to talk, I smiled. "No," was all I said.

"Am I ever going to get to meet the Sandman, David?" she asked, with a child like look on her face.

"Let's hope not, pretty lady," I answered with a smile, as I took a drink of my Pepsi and looked into Kathy's pretty blue eyes. "Let's hope not..."

Chapter Five
Oath of Silence

The memories of Vietnam continued to haunt me as I tossed and turned throughout the night. Unable to sleep and covered in sweat, I got out of my bed and went into the bathroom to take a shower.

"This is crazy," I thought to myself as I left the bathroom and went into the kitchen. Opening the refrigerator door, I smiled. Inside was a large pizza with everything, a bucket of fried chicken – extra crispy, two jars of dill pickles, a jar of green olives, four bottles of A-1 steak sauce, and four cases of ice-cold Pepsi, in long neck bottles.

Grabbing a bottle of Pepsi, the pizza, and a full bottle of A-1 steak sauce, I sat down at the kitchen table. Opening my Pepsi, I took a drink, opened the bottle of A-1 steak sauce, and began pouring it all over the top of my two-day old pizza. "Now this is how real men eat," I said to myself as I picked up a slice of the pizza and took a bite of it. Hearing the doorbell ring, I looked up at the clock on my kitchen wall. It was 4:37 a.m. "I wonder who this is?' I said out loud as I walked over to the front door and opened it.

"Wake you up?" Andy and Don asked as I grinned and looked at my piece of half-eaten pizza that was still in my left hand.

"Yeah," I answered as I waved my grandfather's two bodyguards into the house.

Andy Hiffner was German-Indian, and stood five-feet, ten-inches tall. He was medium-built, black hair, brown eyes, and strong as a country ox. Don Meloche was six-feet tall, had brown hair, brown eyes, and slender build. Both men had been with my grandfather for as long as I could remember. At a glance, you would never suspect that these two men were cold-blooded killers working for the Mafia. They were two of the nicest guys you would ever want to meet – just don't piss'em off. If you did and you weren't part of our family, it would be the last time you did.

"Hungry?" I asked as we all sat down at my kitchen table.

"Got any cold beer?" Don asked.

"Yeah, but you'll have to go get it. It's in the refrigerator in the garage," I explained. "Or jump downstairs and grab some from behind the bar. That cooler is a lot colder," I explained as I took a long drink of my Pepsi and emptied the bottle. Without saying a word, Andy got up and grabbed another bottle of Pepsi out of the refrigerator and handed it to me.

"Thank you, Andy, but please don't wait on me, I'm not the Godfather," I explained calmly.

"No," he answered. "But you will be one day," he replied with a grin, as he picked up a piece of pizza and began to eat it. "Got any pickles?" he asked.

Pointing my thumb at the refrigerator, I kept eating as Andy got up and grabbed a jar of dills.

"My God," Don said out loud as he sat down across from us. "How can you two eat that shit this early in the morning?"

"Like this," Andy said as he pulled out a large dill pickle, took a bite of it, then a bite of his pizza and began to chew.

"That's why I love you, Andy, you're just like me," I said with a smile. "You've got balls!"

"You're both fuckin' nuts," Don explained as he handed Andy a cold Budweiser beer.

"So what brings you guys out here this early in the morning?" I asked.

"Your grandfather told us that your standing beside him in the family business and that you made your 'bones' by blowing up that house with those drug dealing pieces of shit in it a few months ago."

"Yeah, so?" I asked.

"You broke the old man's heart, David. Your grandpa didn't want you to ever know about that part of his life," Andy explained.

"Yes, but he also knows that Vietnam changed you and after your talk with him, you're in at the top," Don explained with a smile.

"There is a big meeting going down at the Desert Inn Casino in Las Vegas this weekend. The whole commission is meeting. The heads of all five families will be there. We're suppose to make sure you're there," Don explained.

"This weekend? Tomorrow is Friday," I replied.

"That's right," Andy said. "Pack your best suit and take a shower. We're out of here as soon as you finish eating!"

* * * * * * *

I guess that it shouldn't have surprised me when we got to the Pontiac Airport and drove up to one of the large metal and brick hangers that housed both of my grandfather's Learjet's and limousine. One Learjet was white in color, the other jet matched the limousine; both were a beautiful shade of silver.

"I'll bet you've never been in one of these before," Don questioned, with a smile on his face.

Thinking about the CIA Learjet I had been in several times and now had full access to, I replied, "Nope."

"You're going to love this," he explained as we drove right into the hanger and parked next to the limo.

"Anything else I should know?" I asked, as we all got out of the dark blue Blazer and pulled out our suitcases.

"Well," Andy said with a strange look on his face. "Your Uncle Paul in New York and your Uncle Sammy in Chicago?"

"Yeah, what about them?" I asked as I began to get a bit frustrated.

"They're the heads of the crime families out there," Don explained as he jumped in and interrupted Andy.

Shaking my head, I said, "Why doesn't that surprise me?"

Climbing on board of my grandfather's silver Learjet, we took off heading for Nevada. All during the flight, both Don and Andy brought me up to speed on who was who in the pecking order of the five families and what to expect once we got to Vegas. It was hard for me to accept the fact that these men, who used to come over to my grandparent's home on Saturday nights to play Pinnacle with their wives, were gangsters. As a little boy growing up, both Sam Giancana and Paul Castellano would smile at me and then give me a brand new crisp ten dollar bill. At the age of nine years old, that was a lot of candy money for a kid in 1959. Now I was going to Las Vegas to meet with the men that I grew up calling uncles. To think that these men came up under Al Capone and now to find out my grandfather was the one, who actually was Capone's mentor, was just unbelievable. "Why should this surprise me?" I thought to myself. "Always expect the unexpected, David. Remember what Master Chief Jeffrey Mareno used to always tell you. Remember your training, David, you're back in the jungle." I was now very deeply involved with the CIA as a black operations agent, and within the next twenty-four hours would be initiated into the mysterious world of the Mafia and neither side would know that I'm also working for the opposite side. "Holy shit, David," I whispered to myself quietly. "You're walking the razor's edge, bubba. You better not slip, because both sides are deadly and they play for keeps!"

* * * * * * *

Landing at the Nevada International Airport, I called Kathy to check in and let her know where I could be reached, just in case something should happen and I would be needed.

Stepping off our plane, two stretch limousines pulled up to greet us.

"The car in back is full of Gambino's hit men. The one pulling up close to us has Tony Rosario in it. He's the man that runs the Desert Inn Casino for your Uncle Sam," Andy explained in a whisper, as Mr. Rosario got out of the shiny black limo to greet us.

"Why hit men?" I questioned cautiously, never taking my eyes off of Mr. Rosario, who was walking toward us with a smile on his face and his right hand extended out toward me to shake.

"Protection for you. They'll bodyguard you around the clock while you're here," Andy whispered, as he smiled and reached out to shake Mr. Rosario's hand.

"Andy, Don, welcome," Tony said as he shook both of their hands.

"Mr. Rosario, I would like to introduce you to John's grandson. Tony this is David, David this is Mr. Rosario, your Uncle Sam's partner," Don explained.

"Sir, it's a pleasure to meet you," I said as I shook Tony's hand.

"David, it's an honor to finally get to meet the Don's grandson, and please, please, call me Tony," he explained. "You're Uncle Sam is waiting for you. Boy, do we have a weekend planned for you. Welcome my friend, welcome to Las Vegas!" Tony said as he waved his right hand out toward the area the Las Vegas Strip was in.

The drive from the airport to the Vegas Strip was short. I was in awe as we reached the actual strip with all of its bright neon lights. It was dark out and this place was lit up like a well-lit Christmas display. Driving past the red, white, and blue colored "Welcome to Fabulous Las Vegas Nevada," sign with the red neon star shining brightly between and above the word "Welcome," I smiled. "Oh, hell yeah, now I could get used to this," I said out loud, as I placed a drop of Methadrine under my tongue and smiled.

"Welcome to 'Sin City,' David," Tony said with a smile.

"Tony, if it's anything like Saigon, this is gonna be fun!" I replied.

Walking into the main lobby of the Desert Inn was an experience far beyond what I had expected. It was packed full of people. The slot machines were clicking away as people pressed coin after coin into them hoping to score a win. The gambling tables were running full tilt and a middle-aged lady yelled far off to our right as she hit 'twenty-one' on the Black Jack table to win.

Standing at the front desk waiting for us was a young well-built fella with blonde hair, blue eyes, who wore a two thousand dollar suit. Next to him were three of the most beautiful women that I had ever seen.

"David, I would like you to meet Sonny," Tony explained as Sonny and I shook hands, both smiling at each other. "Sonny is our floor host! Anything that you want, David, and I mean anything at all, you see Sonny and he'll get if for you. Sonny, this is the Don's grandson, David."

"It's an honor to meet you, sir. This is Heidi, Ginger, and Tammy. If there is anything that you should need, they'll be more than happy to take care of it for you," Sonny explained with one eyebrow raised and a very large grin on his face. "Anything whatsoever, at any time, day or night," Sonny added.

"Thank you, Sonny, please call me Dave, my grandfather is the one that you call 'sir'," I explained.

"No, David, I'm sorry," Sonny said in a lower tone of voice. "Your grandfather is my Godfather; that is what I call him," Sonny corrected.

"Point taken," I replied. "Speaking of which, is he here yet?"

"Everyone is here, sir, they're all upstairs in Sam's suite waiting on you," Sonny explained. "Shall I take you up to see him, Dave?"

"No, that's okay," Tony said quickly. "I'll take him up. I have to attend this meeting also."

Walking over to the elevator, we went up to the penthouse suite and stepped in.

A smile crossed my face when I saw my grandfather sitting with Sam, Paul, and four other men that I did not recognize. Walking over to my grandfather, I bent down and kissed him on the cheek. Turning to both Uncle Sam and Uncle Paul, who were both now standing and smiling, I gave both men a hug; a kiss on the cheek, as a show of deep respect; and a handshake. It was then I noticed seven other men, who were standing at the bar with drinks in their hands.

"How was your trip?" Sam asked.

"Good, Uncle Sam. How have you been?" I asked.

"Ah, I'm getting old," he said with a smile. "I want you to know that we are all very proud of you with what you did in Vietnam and all."

"Thank you," was all I said.

"Your grandfather tells us that you want to join our family. Is this true?" Sam asked.

"Yes, sir," I answered.

"You understand that what we do is very dangerous?" Paul asked, as he placed his right hand on my left shoulder and patted gently.

"Yes," I answered.

"Your grandfather tells us you made your 'bones' already. So we have all gathered together today for a very special and very secret initiation ceremony. What happens in this room must never be spoken of ever again, understand?" Sam asked.

"Yes, sir," I answered.

"Let me introduce you to the men who stand witness that are here with us today," Paul explained, as he began to introduce me to each of the men and their underbosses.

Everyone then gathered around as Uncle Paul opened up a black silk cloth that was sitting on the coffee table in front of us. Picking up the beautiful Italian made silver dagger, Sam reached over, took my right hand

and cut my palm. He then put a piece of rice paper, that had a picture of the Virgin Mary on it, in the palms of my two hands, which were now open, cupped slightly, and side-by-side. Lighting the piece of paper, Uncle Paul told me to repeat after him. It was here, at this moment in time, that I took the "Blood Oath of Silence" as the paper burned in my hands. Cutting the palm of each man's hand, we shook hands, sealing the blood oath and making me a member of the real and very dangerous Mafia.

We spent the next hour laughing, drinking, and talking. Most of which was about the good old days and what the family went through to build Las Vegas. It was then I learned of how my grandfather, Sam Giancana, Carlos Marcello and Paul Castellano had built the Copa Cabana Club in Cuba; only to lose it a few years later when Castro took over the country.

Now, at almost midnight, everyone gathered around to hear Tony Provenzano as he brought a complaint to the commission.

"Talk to us, Tony. What's going on?" Sam asked with a concerned look on his face.

"With all due respect, I am asking this commission for permission to 'hit' Jimmy," Tony Pro asked.

"Why?" Uncle Paul asked as he raised both hands upward in a questioning gesture as he looked around the room at all of the men that were gathered with us.

"First, we have all of the trouble that he brings to us when he and that little Bobby Kennedy punk but heads during the Senate hearings. Does he do it quietly? No! He does it on national television for God's sake. We tell him, Jimmy, back off, you're drawing too much attention to the families. Does he listen? No! Does he care? No! Just two weeks ago, I call Jimmy and tell him that I need thirty-four million dollars of the Teamster's pension fund money so I can build my Casino. Do you know what he tells me?" Tony Pro asks as he looks around the room at each of the heads of the five families and their underbosses, with his hands held out to them. "He says, 'No problem Tony. Give me back sixty-eight million in three years.' Can you believe it?" Tony asks, slapping the back of his right hand into the palm of his left hand. "I made this arrogant bastard the most powerful Teamster President ever and he spits in my face," Tony shouts out loud. "I told Jimmy when we were in prison together, I said, 'Jimmy, I'll make you a very powerful man, but if you ever cross me, they won't find so much as your fingernail!'"

"Be patient, Tony," my grandfather says softly.

"But, Godfather, Jimmy spits in my face. He disrespects me and in doing so, he disrespects Lafamilya," Tony says calmly. Letting out a sigh, my grandfather looks down at his wedding ring and gently rubs it.

"If you get permission, Tony, how would it be done?" Uncle Paul asked.

"Tony Jack will put it all together through the enforcer family out of Detroit. I'll send four of my shooters from the Teamsters Union out of Jersey. We'll use one of my cars that can't be traced and when it's over, Tony Jack will have the car crushed and my people will fly home," Tony Pro explained.

"Jimmy is no fool, Tony," Sam said calmly as he sat back down next to my grandfather. "He knows that you're upset with him. How will you get him alone and without his bodyguards?"

"I have his stepson in my pocket. I'll use him to talk Jimmy into meeting with me to make the peace. Jimmy trusts Chucky. He'll come," Tony Pro explained calmly, as he sat down in one of the plush black leather recliner chairs and accepted a drink from one of his men.

"What do you think, Paul?" Sam asked.

"In Michigan?" Paul commented. "Oh mama, the local cops will have a field day with the publicity on a hit this big."

"I have them covered," Tony Pro explained. "Tony Jack and his brother have two FBI agents on their payroll. As soon as it becomes public, they'll step in and take over the investigation."

"Won't work," Paul's underboss explained.

"Why?" Paul asked.

"The Fed's don't have any authority in a local shooting," Gotti explained.

"Who said that they were going to find his body?" Tony Pro asked. "I am known by all of you as a man of my word. I told him that if he ever crossed me that they wouldn't find so much as his fingernail. I meant what I said, gentlemen. With your permission, Teamster President Jimmy Hoffa disappears," Tony Pro explained.

The vote was taken. It was agreed that Hoffa was a threat to the families. He was bringing way too much attention to the families. My grandfather, Sam Giancana, and Paul Castellano voted 'No'. The rest of the men in the room voted 'Yes'. Hoffa was a dead man, but a second decision was also made. The 'hit' would have to wait. There was too much family business going on at the moment. It was too risky to do it now and have the news media and police bringing up the war between Bobby Kennedy and Jimmy Hoffa. My grandfather was the best kept secret in the world of organized crime. Nobody was willing to draw any attention to him, especially if the hit went down in Michigan, which is exactly where it was agreed to take place.

"I must go now," my grandfather explained as he stood up. "My wife worries when I am gone for too long," he explained.

"I'll go with you, Grandpa," I said with a smile.

"No, no, David, you stay and have a good time. Donald, Andy, stay with him and enjoy yourselves," my grandfather explained, as he placed his hands on the sides of my face and kissed me on the forehead. "Where did you disappear to all last week?" he asked kindly. "I was worried about you."

"I went to see a friend in New Orleans, Grandpa," I explained.

"Ahh, I see. Have a good time. I'll see you later," he answered as everyone lined up and began to, one by one, say goodbye. My grandfather was getting old. His health was failing, but these very powerful and wealthy men all loved him. As they each said goodbye to him, it showed.

As the meeting broke up and everyone went out to the Casino, I looked over at Tony. "What time does this place close, Tony?" I asked as I looked at my watch.

"Never! This place hasn't closed for over thirty five years," he said with a smile. "Welcome to the Devil's Playground." Picking up the telephone in the penthouse suite, Tony called Sonny and told him to meet us in the main lobby. Once there, Tony told Sonny, "David has an unlimited expense account. He doesn't sign for anything. Mr. Giancana said to give him fifty-thousand in chips to start with and put him in the penthouse suite next to mine," he explained. "David, welcome to the family," Tony said with a smile, as he gave me a hug. "Sonny will get you squared away. I really need to make my rounds. I'll see you later, okay?"

"Count on it, Tony, and thank you," I answered, as I placed a drop of Methadrine under my tongue and looked over at Andy and Don who were standing at my sides. "Well, fellas, show me around, its party time," I explained with a huge smile on my face.

"David, here is fifty-thousand in chips and another twenty-thousand in cash. Heidi and the girls have your weekend all planned out for you. Your Uncle Sam wants you to have a good time. Trust me, my friend, this is one weekend that you're never going to forget!" Sonny explained, as Heidi walked up to me and smiled.

"Ready?" Heidi asked.

"Pretty lady, I was born ready," I answered as Ginger and Tammy grabbed both Don and Andy by the arm.

Walking back up to our suite, followed by our bodyguards and a dozen of the hottest strippers in the world, I found it tough to see past the Brazilian bikini waxes and the six breasts that were bouncing off my face. I did, however, notice a growing pile of thongs on the floor of my room.

I had given both Don and Andy ten thousand dollars each, then handed each of the six Gambino bodyguards two grand each and told them all to relax and have fun. I fully expected all of these men, including the bodyguards, to party right along with me, and boy did they!

The stereo was pounding as three completely naked nympho supermodels began doing things to each other that would make the best Saigon whore blush. First they started rolling around, alternately slapping and slurping on each other; then they decided to 'dance' for us, with occasional breaks to go downtown on each other again.

"It can't get any better than this!" I said smiling, but boy was I wrong. Friday night flights are stripper shuttles; girls fly in in droves to make more cash in two Vegas nights than they can in a month at their local House O'Babes. By Pepsi number four, the decision was made. We'll gamble later; it's stripper time!

Jumping into our limo, we follow a tip and went to the Pussycat Lounge. The Pussycat is an all-nude club, so there's no booze and no hot chicks. Don yells, "Hey Dave, screw this place." So we leave and head for the old reliable Crazy Horse. On the way there, one of the bodyguards spots a billboard that reads, 'Sapphire – the world's largest gentlemen's club!' Hey, it's on a billboard, so it must be true, right?

One foot in the door and we know we've made the right choice. This place puts the tit in Titanic; two huge rooms with 30-foot ceilings, four bars, and more poles than a light bulb screwing seminar. After a few hours here, we find our laps are chafing from all of the lap dances and we are starting to get hungry. Another decision is made and we head to the Palace Station for a late night breakfast. After eating, we all head back to the Desert Inn. While the morning sun is burning my eyes and early bird gamblers walk past us into the Desert Inn Casino, a silver limousine pulls up and out steps Frank Sanatra.

"Hey, David, I didn't know that you were in town. Is your grandfather here?" Frank asks.

"He knows, Frank," Andy whispered as he leaned in close to Frank's ear to speak. "The Commission swore David in last night.

"I see," Frank said with a smile.

"Your Godfather left to return to Michigan around 1 p.m. Frank. He'll be sorry that he missed you," I explained.

"How is his health, David; is he alright?" Frank asked.

"So-so Frank, he's getting old," I explained sadly. My grandfather had come into the United States in 1915 as a young man, coming through Ellis Island after the Armenian massacre. The country of Turkey had invaded the country of Armenia in 1915 and tried to wipe out our race by massacring over three million of our men, women, and children. We were the only Christian faith people in all of that land. My grandfather, who was in his early twenties at the time, worked as a spy to fight against the blood thirsty Turks. He was a handsome young Armenian man who wore his long handlebar mustache with pride. Because of the invasion of our country, all of his paperwork was lost. We never really knew how old he was. During his last six birthday parties, I would ask him, "How old are you, Grandpa?' and he would always answer "Eighty-six", and then smile. He spoke very little English and was one of the greatest men that I had ever known, but now, at close to a hundred years old, his health was beginning to fail.

"Listen, Mohammed Ali and Smoking Joe Frazer are fighting tonight at Caesar's Palace. I'll have seats waiting for you next to mine. Don, Andy, bring your lady friends and come with him. The fight starts at 9 p.m., David, pre-fights start at 6 p.m., so get there early," Frank explained as he patted me on the back and smiled.

"Thanks, Frank. We'll be there," I said with a smile. They called Frank 'Ole Blue Eyes' and he had a voice that was so smooth that my grandfather would always say, "Frankie sings and the butter melts in the kitchen."

Going back up to our suite, we left the girls behind so we could all take a shower, clean up, and try to get a few hours of rest. Sitting on the huge leather 'play-pen' sofa, I placed two drops of Methadrine under my tongue and handed the tiny glass vial to Andy who was sitting next to me.

"This stuff going to kill me?" Andy asked as he placed a drop under his tongue and took a sip of his long neck bottle of Budweiser beer.

"Hell," I said with a laugh, "Last night should have killed you!"

Laughing, we both looked around the room. Don and all six of the Gambino bodyguards were passed out and snoring away. They were fast asleep from a fast run of booze, whores, strippers, and just plain too much fun!

"Wanna go racing?" Andy asked with a grin. Andy knew that I loved to drive fast; so I knew he was up to something and whatever it was, it was gonna be fun.

"Lead the way brother," I answered as I took a drink of my cold Pepsi and tossed the empty bottle onto the pile of bikini underwear the strippers had left behind.

"What about them?" Andy asked as he nodded at Don and the bodyguards, who were all fast asleep in my bedroom and on the floor.

"Ahh, let them sleep. We'll stop by and pick them up later," I explained as Andy and I got up and left the suite.

* * * * * * *

Forget the Bloody Marys or Aspirin for a hangover. The best cure in Vegas is to head to 'Derek Daly Academy'. After spending an hour in the classroom, Andy and I climbed behind the wheel of two 145-mph formula cars at the Las Vegas Motor Speedway and let it all hang out!

From there we went to Hard Rock's swim-up blackjack tables. Stripping down to our underwear, we tossed our clothes onto a pool side chair, which freaked-out a group of daiquiri-sipping soft rockers, and dived into the 'no-diving' pool with our hands full of cash, then dog paddled over to the tables. Our total winnings, next to chicks splitting 10's and hitting 17's; negative $1,400.

But some girls know how to double down. The 'Chicken Ranch' is only forty-minutes off the strip and offers a free limo if you're staying at a major hotel. Now, I'm not saying that Andy and I went, and I'm not saying you should go either if you're reading this book, but the 'Ranch' charges about $400 a load, including a shower, wet naps, and condoms, or so I've heard, anyway...

Going back to our suite at the Desert Inn, Andy and I walk in to find three empty whiskey bottles, music blasting, and a room full of beautiful, hot, sexy, dancing women. Don and my six bodyguards had their hands full and were partying hard once again.

Walking up to me, Don shakes his first finger up and down at me as if to scold me. "David, you got some 'splaining to do," he shouts in his best Dezi Arnez – Lucy Ball imitation. "Where you been?' Don asked.

"Oh, feeding the chickens, I guess you could say," I replied as Andy and I looked at each other and began to laugh.

Before I knew it, the stereo is turned up, our clothes are on the floor; and four hours before the 'Ali – Frazer' fight is to begin, I'm getting another lesson in what makes Las Vegas the Valhalla of debauchery!

* * * * * * *

I walked into the 'Main Event' at Caesar's Palace with Tony Rasario, Don, and Andy; we left the girls and bodyguards at the suite. Walking up to the open front row of seats, we were greeted by Frank Sanatra and quickly introduced to his closest friends, Sammy Davis Jr., Peter Lawford, and Dean Martin. It was 8:45 p.m. and the 'Main Event' was about to begin. Tony had explained to me that the real "Hollywood Stars and Big Players", never make their appearance or walk in until just before the "Main Fight Event" starts. Sitting down next to Frank, I looked around in awe. The Palace was full of high rollers and big time celebrities.

Leaning close to my ear, Frank explained, "This fight is going to be a war, but Ali is going to beat Smoking Joe in this one."

Shaking my head from side-to-side, I looked at Frank. "I'm impressed, this is awesome," I said as I placed a drop of Methadrine under my tongue and sat back to listen as the ring announcer began to speak.

As promised, the fight was a war and Mohammed Ali won by wearing Smoking Joe Frazer out with his 'rope-a-dope' fighting style.

From the fight, we went to Frank's private table for dinner. Manicotti, Lasagna, Fettuccini Alfredo, and Spaghetti with real Italian meatballs covered the large table. The drinks were flowing as I listened to Frank, Sammy, Peter, Dean, and Tony laugh and talk. It became very obvious to me that behind all of the glitter and stardom, these big time celebrities were just everyday guys out having a little fun.

After spending another two hours with Frank and his friends, we excused ourselves and headed back out to the casino to win back some of our money. We spent the rest of the night at the Sapphire, Club Paradise, Rios, and the Sands. Did we win any of our money back? No! Did we have a good time? Unbelievable!

Now of course, this story is 'fiction' and none of this every really happened, but if it would have been a true story and you were going to Las Vegas for a bachelor party or with a couple of your friends to have some 'Gangster Style' fun, I would recommend: Las Vegas Bachelor Party, 800-834-2712. They'll get you on the V.I.P. list of every club in town, book limos and hotels, and even arrange in-room entertainment. Book a limo from the airport with Mammoth Limousines, 866-804-5699, and watch the hotties come a running. Club Paradise, 702-734-7990, L.V. Motor Speedway, 702-644-4444, Rios, 888-746-7784, are all great. But for a top rate, high-class operation call: George Maloof, owner of the Palms Casino, 866-942-7777, and then call Sapphire: The Worlds Largest Gentlemen's Club, 702-796-6000.

As for the 'Chicken Ranch', well heck, we never went there, remember, and neither should you. I'm a lot of things, but I'm not a book-writing pimp! But at $400 a pop, I have no doubt you'll figure it out...

* * * * * * *

Saying goodbye to Tony, Sonny, and the girls, we left the Desert Inn Casino and boarded my grandfather's plane. Once in the air, I sat back in my seat and looked at both Don and Andy. "My God, it's Sunday night already," I said as the glittering lights of the Las Vegas strip slowly began to fade away in the darkness of the Nevada night. "Where did the past 72 hours go to?"

"Time sure does fly by in Vegas. Thanks, David, that's the best time I've ever had in 'Sin City'," Don explained with a huge grin.

"How much money did you spend?' Andy asked with a smile.

Reaching into my right pant leg pocket, I pulled out a thousand dollar poker chip that read 'Desert Inn' on one side of it and $1000 on the other side. "Sixty-nine thousand," I said softly, with a sigh and a grin on my face.

Clapping his hands together, Don broke out in a laugh. "Who would ever believe it!" he said with a chuckle. "Boy, those Gambino boys sure do love you. They'll be 'die hard' loyal to you now, David. No one ever treats them the way you just did, not even their own people. You gave those boys a lot of respect. I'll bet you they've never gotten that much pussy before in their entire lives. Hell, David, you're still young. Someday you can tell your friends about this weekend," Don added laughingly.

"Shit," Andy said softly. "Before its all over, you'll be able to write a damn book about everything that you're going to see and do."

" A book?" I said in a low voice. "Hmm, now that's an idea. If I do I think that, I'll have to write it as 'fiction,' huh?" I asked in a questioning tone of voice with a grin on my face, as I sat back and stared out the window into the darkness. "I'd have to invoke my Fifth Amendment rights against self-incrimination. Ah, hell, nobody would waste their time reading a book about this kind of stuff," I said softly as I closed my eyes and yawned. "Whatever happens in Vegas stays in Vegas. Nobody would believe it anyway." My mind turned a shade of gray as my body began to come down hard from three days use of liquid Methadrine. Then darkness called upon me once again, as the memories of Vietnam snuck back out to remind me of my past sins...

Chapter Six
Chicago's Finest

Lying on the thick plush green carpet of grass, I reached up and gently rubbed the palm of my right hand across my water soaked face. Opening my eyes, I stared up through the branches of the large old oak tree that I was laying underneath. It had been raining now for almost three hours and I was soaking wet from the Michigan rainstorm. Hearing my phone ring again, I spread my arms out to my sides and lay still. "God, this feels so good," I said softly as I held my mouth open to catch some of the rainwater on my tongue.

I had been home from Las Vegas for almost ten days and nothing was going on. Watching the rainstorm from the window of the sliding glass doors in my basement, I simply said "Fuck it," smiled, stripped down to my underwear and walked out into my backyard and lay down.

"There you are," I heard Andy say as he walked from my house, out to where I was laying.

Keeping my eyes closed, I didn't say a thing as I focused my thoughts on Andy's footsteps as he walked up and stood next to me.

"I was starting to worry about you, brother, but I see you're alright," Andy said calmly, as he stood next to me in the rain.

Opening my eyes, I smiled and broke out laughing. Standing next to me, wearing only his underwear and holding his Colt .45 automatic in his right hand, Andy smiled.

"Mind if I join you?" he asked as he sat down next to me. "You okay, boy?" he asked in a concerned voice.

The sound of lightning echoed off in the distance. "Yeah, I'm okay," I replied.

"Damn, I thought you and I were better than that," Andy said sadly, as he lay down on the grass next to me.

"You're gonna get wet," I said sarcastically, hoping to change the subject.

"Hell, son, I'm eighty-percent Indian remember? I don't know where the twenty-percent German came from," Andy said calmly. "I love the rain. It's the only time I ever really feel clean. Now, answer my question. You all right?" he asked once again.

"I miss my friends, Andy. I miss Vietnam and being with them. I can't sleep. Every time I close my eyes, the faces of the people I killed come back to haunt me. I can't get 'em out of my head, Andy. Even the ones I didn't kill, the dead Americans that I saw come back to haunt me," I explained sadly. "I think I'm loosing it, Andy. I think I'm losing my mind," I explained as I reached up with both of my hands and rubbed my face.

"Yeah, I know the feeling. I was in Korea," Andy explained.

Rolling onto my right side, I looked at Andy. "What? I didn't know you were in the Korean War?"

"101st Airborne, Special Forces," Andy explained as he sat up and looked at me. "I thought that damn war was never gonna end," Andy explained. We would sit in our fox holes, covered with snow, freezing to death. A few times I would get up at night and go out hunting them. Talk about stupid, would ya? Yes it was, but it was my Indian nature to stalk 'em, plus it kept me semi-warm," Andy explained with a grin.

"Man, Andy, I didn't know you were in that war," I said, once again.

"You're not the only one that has nightmares, David. Those Koreans were bloodthirsty bastards. We should have dropped the big bomb on the whole damn country, both North and South," Andy explained with a look in his eyes that I had never seen before until now.

"Come on, big brother. Let's go inside and I'll make you some of my famous 'Sneak-Greek-and-Arabian' chili," I explained with a big smile on my face. Andy was more than a bodyguard to me now. He was a combat war veteran and that made him my brother.

"Yeah, we should go in," Andy said as we walked toward my house, dripping wet, in our underwear. "I hear that it's suppose to rain sometime today. I damn sure wouldn't want to get caught out in the rain. Hell, we might get wet!" he explained with a serous look on his face, never once showing any sign of a smile.

As promised, I made a big pan of my famous chili with extra beans, lots of freshly ground round steak; which is what I use rather than hamburger, large chunks of onion, and a full jar of hot yellow chili peppers that I cut up into small pieces. Throwing some Polish Kielbasa onto my grill, Andy and I sat down to eat. He liked his food spicy and hot just like I did, and that's exactly the way he got it—Hot! Armed with long necked bottles of ice-cold Pepsi and Budweiser beer, we ate and shared some of our 'Best kept secrets' and war stories with each other.

Several hours had passed and we now found ourselves sitting on the floor of my den in front of the fireplace, watching the yellow and blue flames as they danced on the pine logs burning within. Quietly we sat, saying nothing, as our memories took us back into the dark hidden corners of our mind. There, hidden in the darkness were the faces of our own personal ghosts, silently waiting to come out and play...

* * * * * * *

It was the ringing of my telephone that woke me up. The logs in the fireplace had burned down and Andy was fast asleep off to my right.

Covered with sweat, I shook my head, trying to clear my thoughts and get the smell of the jungles of Vietnam out of my nose. Standing up, I walked over to my bar and picked up the telephone that continued to ring.

"Hello," I said softly into the receiver.

"Are you available?' the voice asked on the other end of the line. This was a code that the family used when a 'Contract Hit' was needed. I never really knew who it was that called, and the person who would deliver the 'Information Package' was never the same person.

"Yes," I replied as I heard the telephone go dead on the other end.

Making my way upstairs, I headed for the front door of my house. Within one minute someone would either knock on the door or ring the doorbell. At that time I would receive a manila envelope. Inside of the envelope, which I call the information package, I would find 8×10 photographs of the person that was to be killed. Along with the photographs, would be detailed personal information. Medical details, favorite foods, work place, and schedules, the time that he would wake-up and got to bed. It was so detailed that I would even know what time the person would get up at night to take a leak! Hearing the doorbell ring, I opened the door. Standing in front of me was a pizza delivery boy with a large pizza box in his hand that said "Pizza Hut" on the top of it.

"Here you go, sir. Enjoy your meal," the young redheaded teenager said with a smile as he handed me the pizza box, turned, and walked away.

"Thank you," I replied as I closed the door and locked it. Walking into the kitchen, I set down the box, opened it and smiled when I saw the large pizza with extra cheese, pepperoni, mushrooms, green peppers, and onions. Lifting the pizza up and out of the box, I placed it on the kitchen counter and picked up the manila envelope that was hidden between the cardboard bottom of the pizza and the box itself. Unwrapping the saran wrap that the envelope was sealed in, I opened the envelope and dumped its contents out and onto my kitchen table.

"What ya got there, brother?" Andy asked as he yawned out loud and ran his fingers through his long black hair.

"A hit," I answered with a smile on my face as I grabbed a piece of pizza and sat down to look at the photograph of the target. Handing me a cold Pepsi, Andy opened up a bottle of Budweiser, took a long drink of the cold beer and sat down across from me at the table.

"Anybody we know?" Andy asked as he picked up a piece of pizza and took a big bite out of the end of it.

"Not me. I've never seen this guy before," I answered as I handed Andy one of the 8×10 photographs. "How about you, you know him?"

Looking at the photograph for only a second, Andy said, "Nope," and then tossed the photograph back onto the table next to the pizza. "What'd he do?"

"Says here that he was suppose to deliver a briefcase to one of the family boys in Chicago and decided to keep it for himself," I explained as I read more of the information. "Damn, Andy, this guy's a police detective with the Chicago Police Department. Says here that the family has been paying him twenty thousand dollars a month for information and protection and this idiot rips off a hundred thousand in cash. What a moron!" I explained as I set down the papers and began to eat. "Why would he do something so stupid?" I asked.

"Money in the hands of someone that's never really had any before makes people greedy. Figures he's a cop and that the family won't mess with him because of it. How long has he been with the police force and on the family's payroll?" Andy asked.

"Says here that he's forty-three years old and that he's been a cop for fifteen-years and with the family for ten-years," I explained as I glanced down at the paperwork to read it.

"Do they want him hurt of dead?' Andy asked non-chalantly.

"Dead," I explained as I picked up another piece of pizza and began to eat it.

"How much they paying for the hit?" Andy asked.

"Twenty-five thousand," I answered as I picked up the tightly wrapped pile of brand new one hundred dollar bills and grinned.

Looking at the stack of cash, Andy raised his eyebrows and smiled. "Want some company?" he asked.

"Sure, why not," I answered. "This shouldn't take more than a day or two.

* * * * * * *

The flight to Chicago from Michigan, across Lake Michigan took about twenty minutes. We could have had a car and anything else we wanted or might need for this hit waiting for us at the airport; however, whoever put this contract out, ran it through the enforcer family in Detroit. They must have been worried that someone in Chicago may have owed this cop a favor. If true, and they knew about the hit, that knowledge would get the books cleaned and the favor cleared if they were to tell this cop he was about to get iced. Besides that, if your gonna whack somebody, you don't want anyone to know you're the one who is doing it. If somebody knows you committed a murder and they get in trouble with the law later, they could make a deal with the police and prosecutor and get a 'free walk' by testifying against you.

Renting a new Ford Thunderbird from Avis car rentals, Andy climbed behind the wheel and started it up. We had already committed the address, phone number, and face of our target to memory. The man, who was now known to us as Big Jim Brown, was a dead man. He just didn't know it yet.

Big Jim lived in the Lincoln Park area of Chicago in a middle-class apartment. He stood six-feet, four-inches tall, had shortcut brown hair, brown eyes, and weighed two hundred and sixty-five pounds. Most of which was muscle. He was forty-three years old, divorced with no children, a cop for fifteen-years, and bought and paid for by the Chicago crime family for the past ten-years. His apartment building only had six apartments in its two-story structure. One apartment was empty and being painted by the owner of the building, the other four apartments had elderly retired people living in them. Next door to his building was an Italian restaurant and across the street was an Irish pub-style bar. Big Jim worked the four-to-midnight shift and was a supervisor for the Chicago Police Drug Enforcement Department. He was well known for busting prostitutes and letting them go in exchange for free sex. His drink of choice was Jack Daniel's Old No. 7 Sour Mash whiskey. He was also well known for beating up street level drug dealers and stealing both their money and dope. This would make the hit easier to get away with. If done right, nobody would ever suspect the local crime boss or his family of having anything to do with his death. Whoever put out the contract made it very clear they wanted the 'heat' to go in another direction and not toward the family. Big Jim's apartment faced the main street, which also would prove to be very helpful.

Parking our car down the street from Big Jim's apartment building in a small parking lot, Andy and I got out, locked the doors, and began to walk down the crowded sidewalk.

"I'm impressed! Look at this place, Andy," I said as I looked down at my watch. "It's 7:30 p.m. and this place is packed."

"Most of these bars will have a packed house by nine o'clock. This is one of Lincoln Park's most popular areas. All of the younger eighteen to forty-year-old partying crowd hangout down here," Andy explained.

Stopping in front of Big Jim's apartment building, I glanced at the three cement steps that lead up to the main entrance and then up to his apartment window. The building was brown brick, and the front door was solid oak with a double light above the entrance. There was no light on in Big Jim's apartment.

Smiling at Andy, I asked, "Hungry?" as I looked around at all of the pretty young women who were making their way to they're favorite nightclubs.

Walking into the old family style mom and pop restaurant, my senses went on full alert and my mouth began to water. The smell of real home cooked Italian food and fresh baked Italian bread was unbelievable. The place was packed full of customers. Lucky for us we only had to stand and wait for about five-minutes before a couple sitting at a booth in front of the main window got up to leave. After the table had been cleaned, we were led over to the booth, seated, and handed a menu.

"We have about three and half hours to kill, brother, so take your time," I explained. After placing our order, I got up and went to the pay phone next to the door. Placing a quarter in the phone, I called Big Jim's apartment. I wanted to make sure he was gone and not sleeping off a drunk. I let the phone ring thirty times and then hung-up. I then called the police precinct he worked at and asked the desk sergeant if I could speak to Big Jim. I was quickly told that Jim was out on assignment and to call back later between 11 and 11:45 p.m.

Hanging up, I went back to my table and took a sip of my Pepsi. "He's at work," I said softly as the waitress brought us our meals.

Waiting for the waitress to leave, Andy asked, "What time are you going into the apartment?"

"Eleven thirty," I replied as we both began to eat. We spent the next hour and half eating and talking. The one good thing about a real old-style Italian restaurant is that they're in no hurry to make you leave. Italians love to talk, laugh, and have a good time when they gather around the table to eat. We were no exception to the old time tradition.

We left the restaurant at 9:45 p.m. and went to the bar across the street. The Irish Pub was packed and the party crowd was rocking!

Sitting at a small table by the window that faced the street, I looked at my watch. "It's eleven-thirty, brother, I'm going in. Stay in here and watch my back in case anything should happen to go wrong," I explained.

"I got ya," was all that Andy said as I got up and left the crowded bar.

Walking across the street and up the stairs, I pulled on my thin leather driving gloves and reached into my jacket pocket for the door key that was sent to me along with the information package. I had placed the entire package, photographs, and all in my fireplace and burned everything to a crisp just before we had left; keeping only the key that was suppose to work both the front door and door to Big Jim's apartment.

Sliding the key into the lock of the front door, I turned it. 'Click' was the sound that I heard as I turned the doorknob and walked into the building. Moving quickly up the stairs, I went to room Number 4, put the key into the lock and turned it. I heard the 'click' but the door wouldn't open. Being in a hurry I didn't notice the deadbolt lock face on the door. Big Jim had added an extra security lock to his apartment door. Reaching under my jacket, I pulled out my lock pick set and quickly began to work the deadbolt lock. I could hear a television set in the room across the hall. The hallway was clean with fresh paint on the walls and ceiling. The hallway lights were all bright, which told me whoever owned this building really did care for his elderly tenants. "Work the lock, David, work the lock," I said to myself as I worked the pick. The sound of the second 'click' brought a smile to my face as I opened the door to Big Jim's apartment and quickly stepped inside. Closing the door behind me, I locked both of the locks and put the lock pick set back into my inside jacket pocket.

I knew now why they called Chicago the 'Windy City'. It was, in fact, windy and cold. I was glad that I had brought this lightweight jacket. It concealed my handgun and helped me to keep the few extra tools I would need to do this job hidden. Pulling out my silenced .22 magnum pistol, I stood silently and listened. Just because no one had answered the phone didn't mean that no one was in the apartment, "Always expect the unexpected" was what Master Chief Jeffrey Mareno used to tell me. In this line of business you better damn sure live by that rule, because anything could go wrong at any given moment. I didn't even put on any aftershave. I didn't want Big Jim to smell it when he came home. I had already made one very stupid mistake. I had eaten at an Italian restaurant and my clothing and breath would smell like it. I was really lucky because Big Jim had eaten and left his leftovers on the kitchen table. It was Italian food with lots of garlic. He must have been running late for work, because other than that his apartment was spotless.

Shining my small, penlight flashlight around, I walked through the tiny two-bedroom apartment. Walking into Jim's bedroom, I noticed a wide-back wicker chair that sat in the far corner of the room. Walking over to it, I sat down and looked at my watch. "Seven minutes after midnight," I said to myself as I put the penlight flashlight back into my pocket. Crossing my legs, I placed my pistol on my lap.

"Shouldn't be long now," I thought. "He is always home by 12:30," I reminded myself as I placed a drop of Methadrine under my tongue and waited in the darkness of the room.

* * * * * * *

Sitting quietly in the large bedroom, I glanced over at the clock that sat on top of the nightstand next to Big Jim's bed. A yellowish glow illuminated the far side of the room. It came from the combination of streetlights and bright neon signs that reached in through the bedroom window that faced the main street of Lincoln Park. Looking at the clock, my heart raced from the combination of fear, excitement, and Methadrine as I heard a key unlocking the front door.

Cocking the hammer back on my .22 magnum automatic, I raised the pistol up and off of my lap and pointed it at the bedroom door. It was 12:37 a.m. as Detective Jim Brown entered his apartment, locked the door behind him, and walked into his kitchen. He was following the exact pattern that was described in the information package. If he stayed true to his normal routine, he would now open the refrigerator, grab a beer, and head to the bathroom to take a leak. Staying true to form, that was exactly what he did. Hearing the toilet flush, my heart raced as Jim walked into his bedroom, flicked on the light switch next to the door and walked to his bedroom closet; which was on the opposite side of the room from where I was still sitting.

Now I knew why they called him Big Jim. This guy was huge!

Setting his bottle of beer on top of his nightstand, Jim pulled off his jacket and hung it up in his closet as he continued to chew on the day old breadstick that he held in his mouth. Taking off his shoulder holster, Jim hung it up on the corner of the closet door. The heavy automatic pistol that was holstered in it made a thumping sound as it bounced up against the wooden door. Keeping a steady aim at Jim's head, I sat and watched as the big man bent forward, raised his left pant leg up to his knee and pulled off the ankle holster that carried his smaller .380 automatic handgun that was hidden there. Standing up, Jim placed his throwaway, back-up piece on top of the shelf that was closest to him in his closet.

Turning around he took two steps forward and reached for his beer with his right hand as he took the last part of his breadstick with his left hand and gently pushed it all the way into his mouth. It was then that Jim looked up and saw me sitting quietly at the opposite side of the room with my gun pointed at him.

"Oops," I said softly as Jim's eyes got wide. Turning his head, he looked at his shoulder holster that was now slightly behind him and off to his right. "Don't be stupid, Jim. You've already made one dumb mistake. Why make another one?" I explained.

Looking back over at me, Big Jim took a deep breath of air into his lungs and let it out slowly. "Damn," he whispered as he looked down at the floor. "Anyway we can work this out?" he asked.

"Maybe. Have a seat on the bed, Jim, and keep your hands on your knees where I can see them," I explained. "Relax, Jim, it's not as bad as you think."

Sitting down on the side of his bed, I could see some of the tension on Jim's face ease up. Putting his hands, palms down, on top of his knees, he slowly rubbed them back and forth on his legs. "You mean you're not here to kill me?" Jim asked curiously.

"Not unless you do something stupid, Jim. If I was going to kill you, you would be dead already," I explained.

"Oh man, I though I was dead," Jim explained with a sigh.

Standing up, I walked over and stood on the opposite side of the bed. "All I want to know, Jim, is why? Mr. Giancana pays you twenty grand a month. You should be rich by now, Jim. Why would you rip off a lousy hundred thousand?" I asked out of curiosity.

"Awe hell, I don't know. I opened that briefcase and saw all of that cash and said, fuck it—what's a hundred grand to these boys? They make millions. To be honest with you, I figured that Donny the Chin would take the blame and that they would go after him," Jim explained.

"Donny's family, bubba. Family never rips off family. Not ever, it's bad business," I explained. "Do you have any of the money left, Jim, or did you spend it all already?" I asked.

"Naw, man, its right here," Jim explained. "I never touched a penny of it, honest. It's still in the same briefcase they gave it to me in."

"Well that's good, big man. It's your ticket out of this mess. Where's it at?" I asked.

"Right here, man," Jim said anxiously as he jumped up off of the bed and moved toward the closet.

"Freeze," I shouted quickly. "Back away from that gun, Jim, or I swear I'll blow you away!"

"Woe, woe," Jim said quickly as he put his hands behind his head. "I'm sorry, man, I'm sorry. I wasn't thinking. I just wanted to give you back the money, that's all," Jim explained.

"Drop down to your knees, big man," I said calmly as I moved to the foot of the bed and closer to Jim.

"Awe, come on, man," Jim said sadly as he lowered himself down onto both of his knees. "Please, don't kill me, please."

"Chill out Jim, I'm not going to kill you. I thought you were going for your gun, that's all. Lets just get through this without any bloodshed, brother. When we're done, I'll buy you a drink. Now then, where did you say the money is?" I asked once again. My heart was racing. I thought Big Jim was going to grab for his gun. I don't know who was more scared at this moment, Big Jim or me.

"It's in my safe, buddy. Inside of the closet and to the right," Jim explained.

"Alright, here's how we're going to do this, Jim. Keep your right hand behind your head and crawl into the closet. Unlock the safe and pull the door of it open with your left hand. Jim, listen to me. I didn't come here to kill you. If you try to grab a gun, I'll have no choice but to defend myself. Don't make me shoot you. Once I see the money is still all here, I'm going to call Mr. Giancana and explain to him that this was all a misunderstanding. Then I'll hand you the phone and all you'll have to do is show some respect and say you're sorry and that it won't ever happen again," I explained. "Do you understand?"

I knew that Jim was right handed so by making him use his left hand only, keeping his right hand in plain sight, I had the advantage. Jim was scared and that made him dangerous. I was even more scared than him and pumped up on speed. I also had to pee, and that made me even more dangerous than him.

"Yeah, I understand. Slow and easy, right?" Jim explained.

"That's it, brother. Slow and easy," I replied as Jim crawled into the closet, turned to his right and pushed a bunch of clothes out of the way.

Moving up behind Jim, I kept my gun pointed at his head. Reaching up, I pulled the thin chain that turned on the closet light. Watching Jim turn the dial on the big safe, I could hear the tumblers click. Reaching down with his left hand, he turned the handle on the front of the safe and pulled.

"Holy shit," I whispered. I couldn't believe what I was seeing. The briefcase sat inside the safe and off to the right. There were two metal security drawers at the top of the safe. The rest of the safe was packed to the brim with cold hard cash and bags of white powder, which I was sure, were drugs.

"That's what I was trying to tell you. I didn't need the money. I don't know why I took it," Jim explained as he slid the briefcase out of the safe and began to back out of the closet on his knees. Backing up all of the way to his bed, Jim then reached over with his right hand, grabbed the side of his bed and pushed. This gave him the help he needed to get up and off of his knees so he could sit back down on the side of his bed. Using both hands, Jim opened the black leather briefcase and set it down next to him on the bed.

"Want me to count it for you?" Jim asked.

"No, Jim, it looks like it's all there. You're home free now. Its a good thing you didn't spend any of it," I said with a grin on my face.

Taking a deep breath of air into his lungs, Jim let it out slowly and began to relax. "All's forgiven?" he asked softly.

"I told ya, big man, I didn't come here to kill you. But take some advice, will you?" I asked.

"What's that?" Jim asked with a half smile on his face.

"Don't do it again, Jim. This time it's a mistake and all is forgiven. The next time they'll kill ya. Understand?" I explained with a smile.

"Yeah, man, thanks," Jim said with a look of relief on his face.

"Don't thank me, Jim. Now that I see all the money in your safe, you're the one that's going to buy drinks and supper," I explained.

"You got it," Jim replied with a chuckle in his voice.

"Grab that phone, Jim, so we can call the old man, will you? Do they have any good places to eat around here that's open this late?" I asked.

Turning to his left, Jim reached for the telephone that sat on the night stand next to his bed, "Sure do, there's a..."

The two shots from my .22 magnum cut Jim's sentence short as they both struck Big Jim in the back of his head. This was a mob hit gun and not the longer slender .22 magnum that I used for the CIA. These hollow-point bullets entered the back of Jim's head at point blank range and exploded inside, turning Jim's brain into mush. Falling gently to his side, Jim lay still. Two small spots of blood were all I could see as I walked over and raised Jim's eyelid. His eye was a smoky fog color—he was dead.

Moving quickly, I stepped into the closet and grabbed one of the two gold Samsonite suitcases that were sitting off to the left on the floor. Opening the suitcase, I began to fill it with the money that was in the safe. Once all of the cash was in the suitcase, I pulled open the first metal drawer at the top of the safe.

"Oh, yeah," I said out load. "Jim, you're my kind of guy."

The drawer had two diamond faced Rolex watches in it and a black velvet case. Opening the velvet case, I whistled softly. It was full of large sparkling diamonds. Putting both watches and the velvet case into the suitcase, I smiled and pulled open the other metal drawer.

The smile quickly left my face as I reached in and picked up the large stack of Polaroid pictures. Thumbing through the pictures, I became angry as my mind took me back to Vietnam and the little six-year-old girl who had been raped by the Viet Cong soldiers and left to die in the jungle. These were photographs of children—both boys and girls. All were nude and posing in sexual positions. All looked scared and looked to be between the ages of eight to twelve.

"And to think that I gave you a quick death, you sick bastard," I said out loud.

Putting half of the photographs back into the metal drawer, I kept the other half and grabbed a bag of the white powder with the Chinese dragon on it. Setting the suitcase and briefcase next to the bedroom door, I tore the plastic sealed bag open and poured it out onto Big Jim's head. I then threw the photographs of the naked children on the bed next to his body.

Turning the bedroom light on and off six quick times, I waited a second and did it again to signal Andy I was coming out. Turning off all of the lights in the apartment, I picked up the briefcase and suitcase and left, leaving the apartment door closed but unlocked.

Leaving the apartment building, I stepped down the three cement steps and onto the sidewalk just as Andy pulled up and pushed the passenger side door open for me. Tossing both the suitcase and briefcase into the backseat, I got in and closed the passenger side door.

"Running away from home, little boy?" Andy asked with a grin.

"Let's go," was all that I said.

Seeing that something was wrong, Andy stopped joking and became deadly serious. "What's going on, David, what's wrong?" he asked as we pulled away and drove down the road.

"I found photographs in his safe, Andy. Photos of scared, naked children. That sick bastard was a child molester. Motherfucker!" I shouted as anger built up inside of me.

Not saying a word, Andy kept driving. Andy loved kids just as much as I did.

"Children are a gift from God. You don't touch kids, not ever," I said in a softer voice as I looked out through the side window of the car. And to think that I killed that sick pervert quick. I should have gutted him!" I said softly as I tried to calm myself down. "Try to find me a pay phone, Andy, I need to make some phone calls."

Reaching over with his right hand, Andy grabbed me by my left arm and gently squeezed. Without saying a word, Andy said everything with a simple touch of his hand.

Finding a phone booth at a Clark gas station, I got out of the car, stepped into the phone booth and made two calls. One was to the Chicago Tribune, the biggest newspaper in Chicago. The other call was to the Federal Bureau of Investigation. The message was the same:

"A dirty cop has just been shot to death. He was a drug dealer and a child molester. The evidence is all in the bedroom of his apartment located at 4710 Lincoln Park Avenue. The door of apartment Number 4 is unlocked. The body is inside. You better get there fast before the Chicago Police Department gets there and covers it up. As for me, I'm the father of one of those children."

Our next stop was to the bus station, where I placed the briefcase with a hundred thousand dollars in it into a storage locker. Addressing an envelope to my Uncle Sam at his home address, I placed the locker key into the envelope, sealed it, put a stamp on it, and dropped it in the blue metal U.S. Postal Service mail box at the bus station. Climbing back into the Ford Thunderbird, I told Andy what I had said to the Chicago Tribune and the FBI. "Think they'll go to the apartment and take a look?" I asked.

"Oh, hell yeah. By tomorrow it will be all over the twelve o'clock news. The Chicago cops will run for cover. They'll close this case fast and put it in a dead file. Nobody likes a dirty cop, brother, especially one who molests and rapes children. Not even the FBI," Andy explained. "What's in the suitcase?" Andy asked as we drove to the airport to catch a flight back to Michigan.

"Cash," I said with a straight face.

"Cash? You needed a suitcase to put some cash in?" Andy asked with a curious look on his face. "I thought you just sent the hundred grand back to your Uncle Sam? Which by the way was stupid. You should have kept it, David. Nobody blows away the target and then returns the stolen money."

If you saw how much is in that suitcase, Andy, you would know that a hundred grand is pocket change," I explained with a smile.

"Really?" Andy asked with both eyebrows raised.

"Really," I replied calmly.

"How much?" Andy asked once again.

"At least a million, maybe a bit more," I answered as I turned my head and looked at Andy with a big smile on my face.

"What are you going to do with it?" Andy asked.

"Well, half of it's yours, so you can do whatever you want with your half. As for me, I'm going to give my half to Mrs. McBride, Chopper's mom," I explained as I nodded my head in agreement with my thoughts.

"You talking about that young black guy, your partner from Vietnam. His mom?" Andy questioned.

"Yup," I answered as we pulled into the Avis rental service at the airport to return the car. "He's my brother, Andy. I really do miss him. I hope that one day you'll get to meet him," I explained as we got out of the car. "You would really like Chopper," I said proudly.

"His mother's that cool, huh?" Andy asked as I pulled the suitcase out of the backseat and closed the car door.

"I went to see her after I got home from Vietnam. She treated me like I was one of her own kids. She even slapped me on the side of my face and told me to, 'mind my elders'," I explained as the memory of Mrs. McBride brought a smile to my face. "She lives in a small house out next to a swamp in New Orleans. She's had a hard life, brother. This money will let her live out the rest of her life in ease and in a brand new house just like Chopper promised her," I explained.

"I'll tell you what," Andy said. "If she's family to you, then she's family to me too. Give her my half too, then," Andy explained calmly. "Boy, oh boy, I know some damn good spots to have a good time at in N'awlins," Andy said in his best New Orleans slang.

"It's not N'awlins, Andy, its New Orleans," I explained as we walked into the airport terminal.

"Hey," Andy said sternly as he gently slapped me across the side of my face. "Mind your elders boy. It's N'awlins," he said as he smiled and put his right arm around me and gave me a brotherly hug. "You're just like your grandfather, David. You respect and honor your friends and family. I love you, kid, don't you ever forget that cuz I won't say it again," Andy said as we walked up to the counter and booked a flight back to Detroit Metropolitan Airport.

* * * * * * *

As was expected, the death of Detective Jim Brown turned into the top news story the next day. "A drug dealing, child molesting, dirty cop was shot to death in his apartment late last night. Police and FBI officials suspect that the killer was an outraged father of one of the thirty-eight missing children whose nude pictures were found next to the dead body of the Chicago Police Detective."

Selling the diamonds and both Rolex watches to one of Sam Giancana's friends who just happened to be a Jewish New York diamond dealer. We ended up with a grand total of two million, three hundred and twenty-seven thousand dollars. Making a deal with the bank manager of the Chase Manhattan Bank in New York, who just happen to be a member of the Gambino crime family. We sent one million dollars to Dannys mother, Mrs. McBride. We then sent a million dollars to my brother Nick's mom and dad. Nick was my other brother and partner, who died in my arms in Cambodia while we were searching for a missing Marine pilot named Captain David B. Williams. We gave the bank manager one hundred thousand for laundering the money through his bank and sending the checks. That left Andy and I with two hundred and twenty-seven thousand dollars to play with.

"Maybe I'll just have to introduce Andy to Mama Chu Lu. Yeah, that's what I'll do," I thought to myself. "After all, it's not New Orleans. It's N'awlins. Right?".

Chapter Seven
LaFamilya

Wearing a pair of cut-off blue jeans, my Army airborne leather jump boots with the zippers on the sides, and my Navy Seal team ball cap; I turned off my lawn mower and wiped the sweat from my forehead. Taking off my ball cap I began to fan myself with it in an effort to cool myself down. "Damn, it's hot," I said out loud, as I looked at my freshly mowed backyard and smiled. Putting the lawn mower back in the garage I went straight to my basement, walked over to the large oak bar, and sat down on one of my bar stools.

"What can I get for you, sailor?" Don asked jokingly as he reached into the refrigerator, pulled out an ice cold, long neck bottle of Pepsi and slid it down the solid oak top of my bar to me.

Taking a long drink of the cold soda, I let out a sigh of relief. "Boy, that's good," I said as I looked at my watch. "Next time I'm going to hire one of the neighbor kids to cut my lawn. It's too damn hot out there," I explained as I looked over at Andy, who was flipping some hamburger patties over on the grill that was behind my bar. "Boy, those smell good, Andy," I explained with a hungry look on my face.

"It's my special blend of hamburger," Andy explained. "Half dog meat and half horse meat," he explained with a straight face. "I call 'em 'Indian burgers'."

"Sounds like something I ate in Saigon once. You ever work in Saigon?" I asked jokingly, as I looked over at Don and winked.

It was almost noon and it was a hot and beautiful Thursday. Both Andy and Don had come over early this morning. It had been almost three weeks since Andy and I had gone to Chicago after Big Jim. We were planning a trip to New Orleans, but just hadn't gotten around to going yet.

Hearing my front door bell ring, I looked at Andy. "You guys expecting anyone?" I questioned as I got up and went upstairs to answer the door.

Opening the door, I looked out across my front lawn and saw a sky blue Ford van parked on the side of the street next to my lawn. Looking down, I saw the little girl with long brown pigtails in her hair, wearing a Girl Scout Brownie uniform with badges and scout patches on it.

"Hello, sir, my name is Tara and I'm nine years old." Stopping to think for a moment, she continued as I smiled at her. "I'm... um... I'm with Brownie Troop 121," she said with a smile. It was then that I noticed the older lady standing off to the side of my front porch, keeping a close eye on the young child, and smiling. "Would you like to buy a box of Girl

Scout cookies?" she asked shyly, almost looking afraid of what my answer might be.

"I thought you said you were a Brownie. How can you sell Girl Scout cookies if you're not a Girl Scout?" I asked as I looked over at her Scout mother and winked.

"Well, um.... I'm helping my big sister. She's a Girl Scout and if I can sell enough boxes of cookies, then I can be a Girl Scout too," she explained with a half smile on her face.

"Who is it, brother?" Andy asked as he walked over and stood next to me at the door.

"Girl Scout," I said with a smile.

"She's not a Girl Scout," Andy corrected as he looked at the cute little girl. "She's a Brownie. See, that's a Brownie uniform that she's wearing."

Hearing what Andy said must have made the little girl feel bad. She dropped her head slightly and frowned.

"Only because she hasn't sold enough boxes of cookies," I explained as I elbowed Andy in his ribs.

"Oh," Andy replied as he rubbed his left side.

"Hey, do you have any of those chocolate mint cookies?" I asked quickly.

Looking up the little girl didn't say anything. She simply nodded her head up and down saying, "Yes".

"Really, oh man, I love those mint cookies," I explained.

"Do you have any peanut butter cookies?" Andy asked.

"Yes, sir," she said softly.

"Peanut butter cookies?" I asked, looking at Andy as if he were nuts.

"Yeah, peanut butter cookies. I like those," he said snapping back at me.

Andy must have read my mind, because he had jumped right into what I was about to do.

"Peanut butter, yuck," I muttered with a sour look on my face.

"Mister, peanut butter cookies are good, too. Huh, Mrs. Carlson?" the little girl said as she looked over at her Scout mother.

"Yes, honey, peanut butter cookies are very good," she explained as she walked over and stood next to Tara, smiling.

"Well, Tara, how many boxes of cookies do you have in your Scout van and how much does each box cost?" I asked with a straight face.

"Hey guys, what are you doing? The hamburgers are done," Don explained as he walked up behind us and looked over Andy's shoulder.

"Girl Scout," Andy whispered.

"That's not a Girl Scout, she's a Brownie," Don explained calmly.

Looking at Don, both Andy and I then looked at each other and smiled.

"I'm almost a Girl Scout," the little girl said sternly, as she put both of her hands on her hips and stood up for herself.

Looking back at the little girl, I asked once again, "How many do you have and how much are they?"

"How many boxes do we have, Mrs. Carlson?" Tara asked as she look up at her Scout mother.

"We have five different flavors of cookies and they're a dollar a box," she explained kindly.

"How many boxes total do you have in your van, ma'am?" I asked.

"Well, sir, your house is our first stop in this neighborhood. I have a total of 500 boxes in my van, why?" she asked curiously.

Looking down at Tara, I reached into my pocket and found it was empty.

"We'll take 500 boxes," I explained as Tara's eyes got wide and her mouth fell open.

"Really, mister? Really? Honest?" Tara blurted out in an excited voice.

"Sweetie, if you ever saw these two guys eat then you would understand," I explained. "Andy, Don, unload the van while I go and get this young Girl Scout her money," I explained.

Going into my bedroom, I grabbed five hundred dollars of Big Jim Brown's money, went back outside, and paid Tara.

Watching Don and Andy as they unloaded the last six cases of cookies from the van and took them into the house, I looked down at Tara. "I'll bet that you're a Girl Scout now, huh?" I asked with a smile on my face.

Little Tara was so excited that she could barely talk. Her smile was ear to ear. "I am now, mister. I'm a Girl Scout now, huh, Mrs. Carlson?" she asked with one hundred percent confidence in her voice.

"You sure are, Tara, congratulations, honey," her Scout mother said with a smile, as they turned and walked back toward their van.

Looking over her right shoulder and back at me, Mrs. Carlson smiled and mouthed the words, "Thank you". Smiling back at her, I nodded, "You're welcome".

Walking back into my front room, I looked at all of the cases of Girl Scout cookies that were now spread out across my front room floor. I didn't know who was more excited, little Tara or Don and Andy, who were tearing open the boxes of cookies and stuffing cookie after cookie into their mouths.

"You're gonna get sick eating like that on an empty stomach," I explained as I grabbed a box of chocolate mint cookies and headed to the bathroom to take a shower. "Save me a couple of hamburgers, fellas. I'm gonna take a quick shower," I explained. There was no reply, just a couple of grunts, and the steady sound of crunch, crunch, crunch as I closed the bathroom door behind me. It was then the phone rang.

A few seconds later Andy opened the bathroom door, "David?"

"Yeah," I replied as the cool shower water ran from the showerhead over my body.

"That was your grandpa. There's a meeting in New York tomorrow and he wants you to be there at his side," Andy explained.

"Alright, you guys, go and pack your suitcases and then come back here," I explained.

"Okay. Hey, want a cookie?" Andy asked.

"Now, what kind of a moron would try to eat cookies while he's taking a shower?" I questioned.

"Good point," Andy said calmly. "We'll be back in a few hours."

"Okay. Hey, take a couple of cases of those cookies with you. We'll drop the rest of em off at the Oakland County Children's Home when we get back," I explained. "The kids there will love it!"

"Alright, see you in a little while," Andy said as he closed the bathroom door and walked away.

Reaching up to the top of my sliding shower glass door, I carefully reached into my box of chocolate mint Girl Scout cookies, pulled out two cookies, and popped them into my mouth. "God, I love these things," I said out loud as the shower water ran through my hair and down onto my face and body.

* * * * * * *

It was almost noon when we arrived in New York. It was a sun shinny Friday afternoon as the limousine dropped Andy, Don, my grandfather, and I off at the St. Regis Hotel in Manhattan.

On the plane, my grandfather had explained to me that this meeting was put together quickly, because some of the families wanted to expand the business of selling drugs beyond the elite rich group and into the middle-class working man's world of America. My grandfather was against narcotics of any kind being sold to anyone.

"Narcotics are a disease, David. But it's also a big moneymaking business. One day children in the school system will be affected by these drugs," he said sadly. "Your Uncle Paul will stand with me on this vote, but even Sam will vote against me. Ah," he said as he raised his right hand in a gesturing manner. "The times are changing. The old ways are fading away fast," he explained sadly.

Stepping directly into the elevator, we stopped at the seventh floor and got off. The elevator we had gotten into was standing open with two people guarding it, now I knew why. Stepping out into the hallway and onto the dark blue carpet, I looked down both sides of the long hallway. It was lined with men who were all standing around smoking cigars and cigarettes. Most of these men had drinks in their hands and all of them smiled when they saw my elderly grandfather step out of the elevator into the hallway. The men all greeted my grandfather by calling him Godfather and asking how he was feeling as we walked to Room 707 and stepped inside. Once inside, these men who had secured the entire seventh floor would stand a careful watch, making sure no one other than family members would be allowed to step foot into the hallway. No one would interrupt this meeting until it was over with and all of the heads of the families and the men that accompanied them were gone.

Looking around I saw that this hotel room had been modified. The walls on both sides of the suite had been removed. What were once three suites, Rooms 706, 707, and 708, were in fact now all Room 707. The huge suite had gold carpet, solid oak wood tables, and crystal chandeliers hanging from the wood beamed ceiling. This was impressive. The long bar was on the far left of the room. Leather furniture was everywhere and the conference room was to the far right. Once everyone had shook hands and greeted each other, we all talked for a few minutes sharing some light chitchat, and then went into the conference room and sat down at the long oak wood table that was waiting for us inside. Sitting down next to my grandfather, I reached over, picked up the solid crystal water pitcher, and poured a glass of water for my grandfather.

It was Mr. Joseph Tortelli of the Miami, Florida crime family that spoke first. It was just like my grandfather had said. The request to expand the narcotics business was made. Uncle Paul, Sam, and some of the other men sitting at the table asked a lot of questions. Who would supply the drugs? Who would guarantee protection? How would the profit of these sales by split? Looking at my grandfather, I could tell that he did not want to be here. Deep in my heart, I knew his heart wasn't in this kind of activity any more. He was old now and all he ever talked about was mama, my grandmother, Helen.

As the questions and answers went back and forth, some of the older men sitting at the table began whispering into the ears of their underbosses who sat next to them. Raising his right hand slightly, my grandfather took over the conversation and drew every eye in the room to himself.

"You men all know me and you have all come to me at one time or another asking for guidance, for advise. Have I ever misguided you? Have

I ever said no or turned any of you away?" he asked softly as he looked around the room and into the eyes of each man sitting at the table.

"No, Godfather. Of course not, Godfather. Never, Godfather," the men all responded simultaneously with respect.

"I realize that the objective is millions of dollars—lots of money. Fast and easy, but at what price?" he asked. "This expansion that you ask for will one day affect innocent women and children. This is a poison you sell, a poison some men crave for. When men crave for narcotics, they become very dangerous. They will do anything whatsoever to get it. They will rape, commit robbery, and will even murder other innocent people to get what they want. With this, many policemen will come; and when they do, who do you think they will look at, the man selling it on the street? No, they will look at all of us, the families that supply these drugs," my grandfather explained calmly.

"Oh, please," Paul's underboss, said sarcastically. "What are you saying? Are you saying that you don't think we can handle this?" he asked quickly and almost defiantly.

Every eye in the room went to Paul's underboss, John, then quickly to my grandfather and then even more quickly to my Uncle Paul, who was directly responsible for his underboss's actions.

John Gotti was well known for his outbursts when he wasn't getting his way. He came up fast in the New York family. He was a leg breaker who had his eyes set on one day taking over the Gambino crime family when Uncle Paul retired. He was now testing the waters to show everyone in the room he had the nuts to speak out against the Godfather who was now getting old.

Paul Castellano quickly broke in and took over the conversation in an attempt to clean up the insult that had just taken place against my grandfather. I kept my eyes fixed on Gotti who now sat back in his leather chair with a cocky grin on his face as he listened to his bodyguard, who was now whispering in his ear. Uncle Paul was in a bad position. He had to try to correct the insult, because my grandfather was his mentor and the one who made him the head of the New York family. In doing so, Paul had to try to save face with his own men who were watching his every move. My heart raced with the full surge of anger and rage.

"Who in the fuck does this piece of shit think he is?" I said to myself as I tried to remain emotionless on the outside, trying not to draw attention to what I knew I was about to do.

"Sometimes emotions can become our worst enemy and we say things that we don't really mean. I have known you all of my life, Godfather. You took me out of the Bronx in New York and taught me how to be a man. You made me the man I am today. You are my mentor, my Godfather; and above all else, John, you are my friend. I love you and look up to you. You are a man of great wisdom. My vote on this matter is no," Paul explained. "We do not need this kind of trouble in our family," he added as an after thought, as he sat back in his chair and smiled at my grandfather who's first name was also John.

The only people that were allowed to vote on this issue were the five heads of the family. The underbosses had no voting rights this time. If anything should happen to go wrong, it would be the head of that particular family that would be held accountable for what went wrong. He and he alone, would stand responsible.

The vote was taken and as my grandfather had predicted, only he and Uncle Paul voted no. The decision to allow narcotics to flow freely throughout the United States was passed. The next hour was spent deciding who would control, who would enforce, who would supply political protection, who would supply the drugs, how the money would be divided up among the families, and how much would be spent to pay off police and government agents. The meeting was now over as everyone stood up and began to shake hands and hug one another. It was all business, and no matter what the outcome of any family vote, it stayed business and never became personal.

Looking over at both Don and Andy, no words were needed. Walking quietly over to the opposite side of the room, I slowly slid my right hand gently into the inside of my suit jacket. Slowly, I pulled out my .9mm Beretta automatic pistol. Both Don and Andy moved a little closer to my grandfather, who was now smiling and laughing as he talked with all of his old time friends. John Gotti was talking to his personal friend and had his back turned to me as I walked up behind him. Reaching up, I tapped John on his right shoulder. "Excuse me," I said calmly, as I released all of my anger at one time with the full swing of my right hand that held the Beretta in it. As John turned his head to the right to look over his right shoulder, I hit him full force with the butt of my gun. Hitting him just above his right temple, I grabbed him by the hair with my left hand and hit him quickly a second time as he staggered backwards. The second blow to the head took the wind out of the big man as he dropped down to one knee.

"Freeze, Sammy," I heard Andy yell as John's friend and bodyguard had begun to pull out his handgun from under his jacket. From the corner of my eye, I could see that Don had stepped completely in front of my grandfather to shield him from any trouble. Andy, on the other hand, stood in front of both Don and my grandfather with both of his Colt .45 automatic handguns drawn. Andy was pointing both weapons at Sammy. The look in Andy's eyes was dangerous, cold, and very frightening. I just saw a side of Andy that I had never seen before.

Still holding John by his hair with my left hand, I pressed the cold barrel of my Beretta against the right side of his nose and cocked the hammer back. "If you ever disrespect my grandfather or any of the men in this room ever again, I'll kill you," I whispered calmly as I bent over slightly and looked John in the eyes.

Holding both of his hands out in front of him, with his fingers slightly spread apart, John spoke. "I meant no disrespect to my Godfather or to any of my elders who stand in this room," John explained as a trickle of blood ran from the small cut on his head.

"Remember what I said," I replied as I let go of John's hair and backed away. Sliding my Beretta back into my shoulder holster, I walked back around the large table and stood next to my family.

"Don't think that because I am young, that that makes me weak, gentlemen," I said calmly as I addressed the room. "Don't ever insult my grandfather or any member of my family. Remember gentlemen—we are all LaFamilya and that makes each one of you a part of my family. Business is business. Don't ever make it personal as that man did," I explained as I pointed to John, who was now standing up and pressing a handkerchief against the right side of his head. "If anyone ever insults my grandfather, my family, or any of you ever again, I'll kill them. There will be no warning, I'll simply do it," I explained as I looked at Don and nodded in the direction of the door for us to leave.

Looking at Andy, who still had both weapons pointing at John and his bodyguard, I said, "Andy," as I reached up and gently touched his right shoulder. "Andy," I said again quickly, in an attempt to break the trance-like stare he was directing at both John and Sammy. "It's over, my dear friend, put your guns away," I explained with a straight face and a serious look, raising both of my eyebrows at once. Nodding his head in agreement, Andy placed both of his handguns back under his suit coat and into they're holsters.

"I must go now, my friends," my grandfather explained. "I promised my Helen that I would try to be home tonight. Her brother, Hagop, is with her, but it's not the same. I wish you all good fortune with this new expansion," he said with a smile and a gentle wave of his hand.

The men all lined up to say their goodbyes. Some kissed the ring on his left hand, some kissed him on the cheek; they all called him Godfather as a show of respect to the man who had built them into the powerful businessmen they now were.

It caught me be surprise when Gotti walked up to my grandfather. "I meant no disrespect, Godfather," he said as he lifted my grandfather's left hand and kissed it. "Please, forgive me," he continued in a soft voice.

"Johnny, there is nothing to forgive. Run a good business and be safe," my grandfather answered with a half smile on his face.

Saying our goodbyes to everyone, we left the St. Regis Hotel, got into our limousine, and drove away. Once it was just us and we were alone, my grandfather was the first to speak.

"I thought it was the Miami family that was pushing to expand the drug business. It wasn't until this afternoon that I realized it was Paul's underboss, John who was behind this move all along. Paul must be very careful now," my grandfather explained. "This young man, Gotti, is a power hungry man and that make him dangerous. The stronger the profits from this drug business make him, the more of a threat he will become to Paul. You, David," my grandfather explained as he patted his hand on my knee, "you must be careful now. You made John look weak in front of the other families. You were right in doing what you did, so he won't attempt to strike back at you. But he won't forget what you did either. One day John will make his move against you. He is afraid of you now and so are all of the men who saw what you did. I saw it in all of their eyes. Now, David, they fear you and respect you. Today, you have made your mark in LaFamilya."

Dropping my grandfather and Don off at the airport, we stood next to the limo and watched as his private Learjet took off and flew back to Michigan. It was Friday night, we were in New York, and Uncle Sam told me just before we entered the conference room that his daughter Gina had invited me to a private party. How could I say no to an offer like that.

Pulling up in front of Spark's Steak House where we were suppose to meet Gina, our driver got out of the car and opened the door for us. Stepping out of the limo, I looked up and saw Gina walking out of the restaurant toward me with her arms out and with a big smile on her face.

"Hello, cuz," Gina said as she gave me a hug and a kiss on the side of my cheek. Gina stood five-feet, ten-inches tall, had long brown hair, big, drop dead gorgeous brown eyes and an Italian body that any sane man would kill for. Gina was also the same age I was.

"Hey, cousin, what's up?" I replied with a grin.

"Daddy said that you were coming into the city. So why is it that you didn't call me?" she asked as she slipped her arm through mine and walked me into the restaurant.

We spent the next two and half hours eating prime rib, lobster, baked potatoes with sour cream, and hot fresh garlic bread. The meal was superb. The bottle of vintage red Italian wine made it simply perfect. Catching up on the times, Gina told me about a friend of hers and this new nightclub that he had just opened in New York called Studio 54. She explained that it was packed seven nights a week and the latest 'Hot Spot' where all of the big Hollywood stars, celebrities, and big money 'who's-who' people go. Pulling up to the front entrance of Studio 54 was like watching the stars on Oscar night. People of all ages were lined up and waiting to get into this new 'Rave' club.

"Damn, Gina, these people are lined up for at least two city blocks," I said in awe as we got out of our limousine and walked right up to the four huge doormen that were making the decision as to who got in and who didn't.

Seeing Gina, the men smiled and opened the large red velvet rope that was used to block the front door. "Ms. Gina G., how are you tonight?" the man, who was obviously in charge, asked with a smile.

"Hello, Pete," Gina replied. "I'm doing pretty good. This is my cousin David and one of his bodyguards, Andy. They're in for the weekend from Michigan. If they ever show up without me, let them in Pete, they're family," Gina explained with a smile.

"You got it, Ms. G." Pete answered as he looked at Andy and I, smiled, and extended his large right hand out for us to shake. "It's a pleasure to meet you both," he said as we shook the big man's hand.

"Is it always like this?" I asked as I looked at the crowd of people waiting to get in.

"No, sir, this is a slow night so far. Things will pick up at about eleven," he answered calmly.

"Try not to catch anything, Pete," Gina said with a grin as we walked passed them and into the club.

"Pete loves working the front door," Gina explained as she leaned closer to my ear to talk. "He gets more pussy and blow jobs now than he ever did before. The women out there standing in that line will do anything, and I do mean anything, just to get in this place," Gina explained in a louder voice.

The music was booming, the strobe lights were flashing and the large round-mirrored bulbs that hung from the ceiling were reflecting rays of light in all directions at once. It was almost like a laser light show. The place was packed with beautiful women. Some were dancing; some were sitting around chatting with drinks in their hands.

"My friend who owns this place calls this a disco club," Gina explained as she pointed up toward a young deejay, who was talking into a microphone and telling everyone what the next song was going to be. Placing another 45-record onto the turntable the Bee Gees latest song began to play through the speaker system.

"There's no band, no juke box, just one man spinning the record," Gina explained with a smile and a twinkle in her eyes. "Pretty cool, huh?"

Walking me through the club, Gina introduced me to almost everyone inside, including her friend who owned the place. I met Hollywood movie stars, pop and country music singers, millionaire businessmen, and beautiful professional models. It was the one brown haired fella that was surrounded by well-dressed young black men that had caught my attention. He had been watching us from the time we walked in. He looked to be about twenty-eight years old, was good looking in a rough way, stood six-feet tall, and looked to weigh about one hundred and eighty-five pounds. Seeing him sitting at his private table, he quickly smiled at Gina and waved at her to come over and join him at his table.

"Ah, there's Frank. Come on cuz, I want you to meet him," Gina said as she grabbed me by the arm and began to pull me through the crowd of dancing people to the other side of the large room. Stepping up and off of the large dance floor, we moved up to Frank's table. It was Frank that spoke first.

"Gina, you look lovely as always," he said with a large smile on his face. He then looked over at me.

"Frank, I want you to meet my cousin. He just came in from Detroit to meet with my father," Gina explained. "Frank, this is David. Cuz, this is Frank White, also known as 'The King of New York'. Isn't that right, Frank?" Gina said with a grin as we sat down at the table. Shaking Frank's hand, I introduced him to Andy and he in return introduced me to several of his close associates. One of which was a pretty female who was also his attorney.

"Detroit, huh?" Frank said with raised eyebrows as he looked over at his partner who sat off to his right. "I hear that's a real rough city."

"Only if you're weak," I replied calmly with a grin.

Taking a second, Frank lost his smile and tilted his head slightly to the right. He was trying to size me up, but I wasn't sure why. Looking over at his black partner who was wearing a nice Italian made black Fedora hat, he then looked back at me. Smiling once again, he pointed his finger at me and said, "Okay, okay."

We spent two hours sitting with Frank at his table. Andy drank a couple of Budweiser's, I drank two Pepsi's, Frank drank Scotch straight up, and Gina drank Crown Royal whiskey and Coke. Looking at his gold Rolex watch, Frank whispered something into the ear of his partner and then looked at me.

"You hungry?" he asked.

"Yeah, I could eat. Why, what do you have in mind?" I asked in a loud voice so he could hear me over the sound of the disco music.

"Hot dogs," he said with a straight face, never taking his eyes off of mine.

"Hot dogs?" I replied in a questioning tone of voice.

"New York City is famous for their hot dogs. Didn't you know that?" Frank asked.

Looking at my watch, I saw that it was after 1:00 a.m.

"I hear that the city streets are dangerous this late at night," I questioned with a straight face.

"Only if your scared of the dark and weak," Frank answered with a gleam in his eye.

Smiling, I said nothing. Getting up we left Studio 54 and climbed into our limo. Frank rode with us along with his girlfriend. The other three limousines that tailed right behind us were his and filled with all of his close associates.

"Driver, take us to the Rutt's Hut in Clifton," Frank asked as his lady friend reached over and kissed him on the left side of his neck.

"Clifton, is that in the East Village?" I asked.

"New Jersey, cuz," Gina explained. "You've never had a real hot dog until you've had one at the Rutt's Hut, " Gina said with a laugh.

"We're going to Jersey to eat pig snouts and assholes?" I asked with a grin, looking over at Andy. "I love it!"

"Sounds like you and Frank have a lot in common, Dave," Andy explained.

"Yeah? How's that?" Frank asked as he looked around at everyone in the car.

"You're both crazy," Andy replied. "David just bought 500 boxes of Girl Scout cookies from a Brownie Scout, just so she could become a full fledged Girl Scout," Andy explained as he slapped his right hand on top of his right leg and laughed out loud.

"You did that, cuz?" Gina questioned with a female awe in her voice.

"Yeah," I said slowly. "She was a nice kid," I explained as I looked over at Frank. "I like kid's, Frank, I used to be one," I said jokingly.

"Gina, I like this guy. I really do like this guy," Frank explained with a serious look on his face and a touch of a grin.

Clifton, New Jersey's famous Rutt's Hut was everything you would expect. It was a small restaurant located in a small brick-front building. They served deep-fried tube steak, which is a strip of bacon wrapped around each hot dog, then deep-fried. Andy and I ate ours smothered in chili with extra hot jalapeno peppers. As Frank said, New York was famous for their hot dogs and he was right. Rutt's Hut was an old school wiener joint that first opened in 1928. It was a haven for the late night crowd. Gina called what we were eating 'colon-Drano-in-a-bun', but it didn't stop her from eating two of the great tasting deep fried hot dogs herself.

Returning back to the city, Andy and I spent the night at Gina's place. We slept in the extra bedroom, but, as usual, we were lucky to get a full two hours worth of sleep. We spent all day Saturday walking around the city and taking in the sites. New Yorkers were a fast paced people and their cab drivers were stone cold crazy! Gina took us to a private party that was held in Manhattan at an art gallery. It was a fundraiser for a new hospital project that some of the local politicians were supporting. Frank White was there with his people. I was caught by surprise when he handed the party's host a cashier's check for ten million dollars to get the project started. The TV news reporters loved it.

"Exactly what does Frank do for a living, Gina?" I asked, whispering in Gina's ear.

"Do you mean when he's not killing off all of his competition?" she replied with a stare.

"Oh, now I understand," I said softly. "The King of New York."

After talking to Frank, the Mayor, and a handful of Senators for a while, Gina, Andy, and I left the party and went back to the Steak House for a late night dinner. It was really great seeing Gina again, but I felt uneasy inside about this big time drug dealer, Frank White. Over dinner, Gina had explained to me that Frank White had just gotten out of prison several weeks ago. He had served almost eight years in New York's toughest prisons. Just before his release his black friends that were die-hard loyal to him, killed off six of the city's most powerful drug dealers. Even though they had come into power after Frank had gone to prison, they were in the way now. So, the men known as Frank's posse eliminated the competition in true 'Frank White' style.

Saying goodbye to Gina, Andy and I caught a flight back to Michigan. It was almost 2:00 a.m. early Sunday morning as our plane lifted off. Looking out of the side window of the United Airliner, I watched as the glittering lights of New York faded away into the darkness.

"So, what did you think of Frank White?" Andy asked with a yawn.

"Interesting fella, Andy, but I'm more concerned about Uncle Paul's underboss Gotti," I explained.

"Yes, well the Commission all knows now where you stand. In this family business, as we call it, the only way to sit in the big chair like your grandpa does is for all of them to respect and fear you. No one has ever assaulted another family member at a meeting of all of the family Dons like you did Friday, David. You got their attention now, brother. You just stepped in line to take over your grandfather's seat if anything should happen to him, David. Now they all know that," Andy explained as he reached over and patted me on my left forearm.

"I'm not interested in any of this, Andy. Plus you're wrong, brother," I said.

"Wrong? Wrong about what?" Andy asked.

"About nobody ever hitting another family member at a meeting of all the five Dons," I answered.

"Who did that before?" Andy asked with a curious look.

"Al Capone did. He took a baseball bat and crushed the skull of one of his top enforcers, and he did it in front of everybody as they sat at the big table," I explained.

"No shit. I didn't know that. Did the guy die?" Andy asked.

"Yup, he died right there at the table," I answered calmly.

Little did I know, as Andy and I flew back to Michigan, that I would indeed see both Frank White and John Gotti again. One would be a friend, the other an enemy. The final result would be bloody.

Chapter Eight
Trinette

The voice of the Viet Cong soldiers drew near. The voices became louder and louder and then, before I knew it, one of them was standing right next to my hole. Reaching up with my left hand, I grabbed the bamboo lid to keep it secure. My heart raced with fear, pumping adrenaline through my entire body. Slowly, I reached up and very quietly slid my Kabar survival knife out of its sheath. Looking up at the side of the hard packed dirt, I saw the ground start to break away.

"He's standing right next to my lid! Damn, he's going to fall in on top of me," I thought to myself as I let go of the bamboo lid and placed my left hand flat against the dirt trying to keep it from falling into the hole...

Sitting up quickly, my body trembled. Covered with sweat, I looked over at the clock sitting on the nightstand next to my bed. Realizing I was home and in my own bed, I let myself flop back down on my back. Reaching up with my right hand, I wiped the sweat off my forehead and face and tried to calm myself down. I could still smell the dry stale dirt from the hole I was hiding in when Butch, Chopper, and I had gone into Cambodia to kill three NVA Generals.

Reaching underneath my pillow, I pulled out my .9mm Beretta. Looking at the cold blue steel, 15-shot weapon, I placed the barrel of my pistol against the left side of my head at the temple.

"I can't do this anymore, God," I whispered in a trembling voice as a tear ran from both of my eyes and down my cheeks. "Forgive me, Father, for the sins I have committed against you. If you don't want me to do this then stop me now. If you don't stop me, then I'm coming back home to you." Pausing for a second, I waited for an answer from God. No answer came. "He must be busy," I whispered as I cocked the hammer back on the pistol. "Forgive me, God," I said softly as I pulled the trigger of my handgun.

The loud boom, followed by two crackling sounds and another loud boom, startled me. Sitting straight up in my bed, I quickly reached up and felt the right side of my head. Looking around the bed and then at both of my hands, I couldn't find my Beretta. Another bolt of lightning rippled across the sky outside causing the quick flash of light to illuminate my bedroom. Another boom echoed in my ears as I slid my hand under my pillow and felt the cold steel of my pistol that was still lying there.

"Oh, shit," I whispered as I stood up and walked over to my bedroom window to look outside. It was almost 5:00 a.m. and there was a real nice storm brewing outside. "Two nightmare kind of dreams, one right after the other, you're losing it, David. Damn, you used to be such a nice carefree guy," I said to myself as the rain outside continued to pour down harder and harder. "Just like in Vietnam," I whispered out loud. "Oh shit, now you're talking to yourself, David. This can't be good," I told myself as the telephone began to ring. Scratching the right cheek of my butt, I walked over and picked up the telephone on my nightstand. "Hello?" I said softly into the receiver.

The telephone continued to ring as I pulled the receiver away from my ear and looked at it. "What the..." I started to say and then it dawned on me, the phone that was ringing was the private phone in my den with the scrambler box attached to it. Running to my den, wearing only my underwear, I grabbed the red phone that was a direct line to the CIA headquarters in Langley, Virginia. Feeling the phone's receiver vibrate in my hand, I reached up with my left hand and pinched myself on my left cheek. "Ouch," I said softly as I picked up the receiver of my telephone and placed it against my ear. I had pinched myself to make sure I hadn't fallen back asleep and was dreaming again.

"Hello?" I said cautiously.

"David?" the voice on the other end asked.

"Yes," I replied as my mind became fully alert once again.

"You alright?" the voice asked carefully.

"Yes, dear, I'm just peachy," I answered. Kathy had a way of making me feel good. Just the sound of her voice was refreshing and had a soothing affect on me.

"Asshole," she muttered softly under her breath. "You sounded different, David, I thought that something was wrong with you," Kathy explained in a concerned tone.

"Other than the fact that I am slowly losing my mind, I feel just fine," I explained.

"You need to get to the VA Hospital, David. Weren't you supposed to have gone straight there as soon as you got home from Vietnam?" Kathy asked in a concerned tone.

"Yes, I was," I answered.

"Then why didn't you?" she asked sharply.

"Because if I would have gone to the Veteran's Administration Hospital right after I had gotten home, I would have missed your phone call. And if that had happened, I would never have met you. Then where would I be?" I asked.

"Good point," was all that Kathy said.

"What are you doing up this early?" I asked.

"Yeah, right, what are you kidding? I'm just getting home," she explained with a yawn in her voice.

"Late night date?" I asked

"Are you kidding, I haven't gone out on a date since I took this new job assignment. Anyway, I have my hands full just keeping an eye on you," she replied with some humor.

"We could always move in together. Then you would always have direct access to me," I said hoping to get a different kind of more personal response.

"Now that's an idea," Kathy answered. "Hey listen, meet me at the Pontiac Airport. No, better yet, you come to Langley and I'll send the plane to pick you up. We have something very important we need you to do for us. Plus, you have to qualify at the range and Marge has some really neat stuff she wants you to look at. It's all brand new and our Black Op's agents get to have first pick of any of the new stuff before anyone else does. Call me when you land and I'll meet you at headquarters. Until then, I'm going to bed," Kathy explained. "Oh, I'll have the plane there to pick you up at 9:00 a.m., so don't fall asleep," she said as she hung up the phone in my ear.

"Well, goodbye to you too, Kathy," I said into the receiver of the telephone that was now humming in my ear. "Boy, she must be real tired," I thought as I went to take a cold shower.

* * * * * * *

I spent three days in Virginia. First, I went to the training center to qualify with my handgun, shotgun, and high-powered rifle. Kathy had been overly tired when she told me that I had to qualify. I was told I could use the training facility anytime I ever wanted to. However, because I wasn't a duly sworn agent and I was a Black Operations wet work agent, I didn't fall under the same government set of training rules as the licensed agents did. To make it up to me, Kathy took me out to Virginia Beach for dinner. This was the first time we had ever gone out together without it concerning company business. Even though Kathy had a beautiful four-bedroom home in Virginia, I stayed at the Hyatt Regency Hotel.

Day two was spent looking at a variety of brand new, high-tech equipment and weapons. I felt like a young kid in a candy store. The Kevlar Company had just brought out a brand new bulletproof vest. It was an ultra-thin, lightweight model that could be worn underneath a dress shirt without looking bulky. The warning notice in the box said "experimental use only." It was supposed to stop a .9mm, .357 magnum, .45 caliber, and .44 magnum round fired at point blank range. It looked cool, so I took two of them, one for me and one for my friend Andy. After my run in with

Paul's underboss, John Gotti, I figured it was better to play it safe than be sorry.

I also picked up a new .45 caliber Colt, Gold Cup automatic pistol with an extended barrel. The barrel was Magna Ported. The new, lightweight .22 magnum automatic pistol had a built-in silencer. This silencer was built right inside the barrel! The clip held twice the amount of bullets than the older heavier model did. What impressed me the most were the new bullets that were being offered to all Field and Black Op's agents. They were called Rhino-rounds. They came in two models, white or black Rhino, and were guaranteed to cut through the best-made bulletproof vest like a hot knife cuts through butter.

Looking at the new lock pick handgun, I smiled. This was a brand new hand held gun. You slid the tip of the gun into the open face key section on any lock, pulled the handle three or four times until it was snug, and then you simply turn the entire gun like a big key. The gun wasn't that big at all. It fit into the palm of your hand. After what happened at Big Jim Brown's apartment, this would be a huge blessing over the old, pick-and-rake handpick set I was trained with. Loading all of my new toys into an Agency suitcase, I thanked Marge and went to the meeting that was scheduled between Kathy and I. Sitting in the open air of the park, I looked at Kathy and smiled.

"This is nice, Kathy. I thought we would be talking about this in one of your offices," I explained.

Opening her briefcase, Kathy pulled out a manila envelope and handed it to me. "I like it out here, it's peaceful and quiet. That, and the fact that if I am the only one directly involved in briefing you, the Agency won't end up with egg on its face if something should happen to go wrong. I'm the only one that can be burned," she explained calmly.

"I would never do that to you, Kathy. I give you my word," I said as I sat the envelope down on my lap without opening it.

"You're not going to look at that?" Kathy asked with a curious look on her face.

"I'll read it on the plane on my way back to Michigan. It will give me something to do," I explained.

"Well, for the record, our intelligence has confirmed that Syria is up to something and the man in that envelope is their direct contact person here in the United States. We think they're planning a terrorist attack of some sort on either us or one of our allies. He just bought a new house, so it shouldn't be to hard for you to get in. Take this guy out of the picture, David, and see if you can find an address book or any paperwork that might lead us to whoever he is working with here in the States. They picked you for this because they want his death to look natural, so it won't set off any alarms in Syria or with anyone in they're terrorist network," Kathy explained, as she sat back on the park bench and looked up at the clear blue sky above.

"Your heart's really not into this kind of stuff is it?" I asked.

"No, not really, but someone has to keep America safe, and that's us," she replied. "I guess this is just boring to me. I'd like to get into the action. You know, do the kind of heart pumping stuff like you do," Kathy explained with a look of excitement as she turned to face me with a smile.

"Why don't you?" I asked.

"They won't let me. I gather intel, David. That and they're catching a lot of heat right now because there aren't enough women in the Agency. That has some of the top brass upset. They're old school in their ways of doing things and they don't think women can cut the mustard," Kathy explained.

"Yeah? They should have spent some time in Vietnam. The women there would have changed the minds of these dinosaurs real quick," I answered.

"So what do you think of the new poisons and gasses that Marge showed you?"

"I loved it; but, Kathy, sometimes you have to think fast and even do it on the run. If you don't have it with you at the time, you better be able to make something work on your own. I did take some of the new stuff though. I'll lock it in my safe just in case I ever need it," I explained. "Hey, when this hit is over with, what do you say we go and see this new Godfather movie that's out? It sounds like it might be pretty good," I asked. My heart raced with anticipation as I waited for Kathy to respond. I really wanted to get closer to her, but wasn't sure how to do it.

Smiling, Kathy sat forward and looked down at her feet. "The Godfather, huh? Vito Corleone You know that movie is based on a true story, don't you?" she asked.

"Really?" I asked.

"Yup! It's based on the Andolini Family. The Godfather, Vito, has a godson that sings and is also an actor. Guess who that is in real life?" she asked with a grin.

"Who?" I asked, waiting for her to say Frank Sanatra.

"Old blue eyes himself, Frank Sanatra," she explained with a grin.

"How do you know all of this, Kathy? I think you're dreaming. There's no such thing as Mafia," I explained with a straight face.

"Oh, really?" she replied with a taunting look. "Who do you think killed President Kennedy? Oswald?" she said with a laugh.

The thought of the family I was now a part of, being involved in the murder of John F. Kennedy made me sick to my stomach. Kennedy was a great President! "I'm a sniper, remember, Kathy? I know for a fact that it wasn't Oswald. It was a triangulated hit, three snipers. I always thought that it was the FBI," I explained calmly.

"Yeah, the FBI, Secret Service, and Sam Giancana," Kathy explained sadly.

"What?" I replied. Sam was like an uncle to me. Even though I didn't want to hear anymore, I continued forward. "Why would the mob want Kennedy dead, Kathy?" I asked.

"The old man, Joe Kennedy, David. He made his millions in bootlegging and slave trading, back in the old days. Joe Kennedy paid Sam Giancana and the Mafia six million dollars with the agreement that the mob would help get John elected President. The deal was that if Giancana helped to get John elected, then Joseph Kennedy promised that his son would back off the Mafia. As President, young John Kennedy would be able to do it. Damn, David, Joseph Kennedy had already hired Sam Giancana to hit Castro in Cuba, but Castro found out about it before Sam could pull it off. Anyway, after John was elected and sworn into office, his dad Joe goes to the White House and tells John about the deal he had made with Sam and the mob. John blows up and has a big falling out with his father over it. John then calls his little brother Bobby Kennedy and tells Bobby what their father did. Now the Kennedy boys are scared to death that if the press finds out about it, the public will call for John to resign as President. They already have problems with J. Edgar Hoover. Hoover's not only a cross dressing faggot who loves little boys, but he is also the director of the FBI and he hates the Kennedy's!" Kathy explains laughingly.

"No shit, that's a losing situation," I reply.

"John tells Bobby to attack organized crime. So Bobby goes after Teamster President Jimmy Hoffa, of all people, and he does it on national television using a Senate Hearing," Kathy explains. "And Hoffa strikes back fast!"

"I remember that. Hoffa got mad and picked up the telephone that was sitting on his table and ordered the Teamsters to stop every truck in the United States. I remember that within a half an hour the TV news was reporting that semi-tractor trailer trucks were stopping everywhere and refusing to deliver their cargo," I explained.

Now it made sense to me. I remember sitting in my grandfather's front room as a young teenager, with my grandfather, Sam Giancana, Paul Castellano, Tony Provenzano, and several other men, who I didn't know, watching the Senate Hearing. It was a personal war between Bobby Kennedy and Teamster President Jimmy Hoffa. I remember Tony Pro kept whispering, "Back off, Jimmy. What are you trying to prove?"

My grandparents owned a beautiful red brick home that sat facing Telegraph Road. Across from us was the Oliver Supply Building, the Savoy Lanes Bowling Alley, and next to it was the Savoy Motel. My grandfather told both Don and Andy to go across the road and rent all of the rooms at the Savoy Motel, and then tell my Uncle Jack to expect a large crowd at his restaurant. My Uncle Jack owned the Eat More Restaurant on the corner of Telegraph Road and Huron Street, right next to the Cunningham's drug store.

Within minutes, semi-tractor trailer trucks began to pull over all up and down Telegraph Road. The drivers had to have a place to sleep and eat, and my grandfather made sure they did. Jimmy Hoffa had just flexed his muscle and now the entire world knew that Jimmy Hoffa had the power to shut down the trucking supply lines across the United States, and that organized crime was a very real and powerful organization.

"I'm surprised that the mob hasn't hit Hoffa yet. But then again, it's only a matter of time. They killed Bobby Kennedy. We all know that Jimmy is next on their list," Kathy sighed.

"The mob hit Bobby?" I asked with a tone of curiosity in my voice. These were my people that she was talking about.

"Oh, yeah. When Senator Kennedy got shot giving his acceptance speech, his wounds weren't that bad. When they moved him into the kitchen area, a uniformed police officer walked up toward his head; people heard two shots as the cop walked by and left the kitchen. Bobby had now been shot twice in the head at point-blank range and was dead," Kathy explained sadly.

"All because of the Hoffa ordeal?" I asked.

"That, and nobody wanted young Bobby Kennedy to become the next President of the United States," Kathy answered.

"Why? He would have made a good President," I explained.

"David, Joe Kennedy knew that if John was elected President he would have ran for two terms. That's a total of eight years. He also knew that Bobby Kennedy would be next in line and that he would be President for two terms, that's another eight years. Then Teddy Kennedy would run, and by no doubt win, and be President for another two terms. That's another eight years! Hell, David, had Joseph Kennedy's plan worked, the Kennedy boys would have been in control of the White House for a grand total of 24 years. But you also have to remember that once John was assassinated in Texas, President Johnson took over. Johnson ordered all files in the Kennedy assassination to be sealed under Presidential orders for sixty years! Johnson was making damn sure no other President would be allowed to look at or reopen the Kennedy files until everyone who played a part in it was long gone. Johnson was part of it," Kathy explained.

"He was?" I questioned.

"Hell, yes. Kennedy refused to get involved in the Vietnam War. John agreed to send a handful of Special Forces troops to help train the South Vietnamese Army, but that was it! As soon as Kennedy was killed in Dallas, Johnson was sworn into office while he was on board Air Force One. As soon as he lowered his hand from taking the oath of office, he committed two hundred and fifty thousand American troops to Vietnam and opened up the draft," Kathy explained.

"Why? That doesn't make any sense, Kathy," I said in a confused tone.

"David, Johnson owned a lot of stock in two very big corporations; both of which supplied our military and were ready to file Chapter 13 bankruptcy. One of the corporations just happened to build helicopters. Guess who got all of the billions of dollars in contracts to supply our military troops with helicopters and supplies?" Kathy asked calmly, with a look of disgust on her face.

"That dirty bastard. My brother Nick died over there just so they could turn a profit?" I said defiantly.

"Sad but true, my friend, sad but true," Kathy explained as she reached over and patted me on my right leg. "The next time you're in the Pentagon, just go to the Situation Room and pull it all up on the computer. You have Q-clearance; you have complete access to a lot more than you know about. Come on," Kathy explained with a grin as she put her sunglasses back on and stood up. "You can buy me lunch before you go out and kill Mr. Hassimi for your country."

I took Kathy out to lunch and then flew back home to put away my new toys. My mind was racing with everything Kathy had told me. I felt both sad and angry inside, but not surprised. After everything I had learned in Vietnam about the American Government Agents I had killed for betraying us; I felt more anger than anything else, and some of it was now directed toward my Uncle Sam Giancana. I liked John Kennedy; I liked him a lot!

* * * * * * *

CIA Black Operation
Code Name: "Trinette"
Sitting in my den, I carefully looked at all the documentation and photographs that Kathy had put together on the man the Agency believed was about to plan a terrorist attack on the United States. Kathy's intel package was impressive. It was just as accurate as the package the family put together on one of their hits. The target was a thirty-one year-old man

named Mohamid Hassimi. He was from Pakistan but now lived in the United States. He had just bought a brand new four-bedroom home in Los Gatos, California. It was a brand new subdivision being built just off Los Gatos Saratoga Road. The homes located across from, and on both sides of, Mr. Hassimi's home were still under construction or brand new, and were sitting empty and for sale. Mohamid had only lived in this house for six weeks. He worked at the Los Gatos Brewing Company on North Santa Cruz Avenue. This was going to be a piece of cake.

Packing a few of my things, my mind raced with my plans on how I was going to kill Mohamid. I felt troubled deep inside with the news about Sam and his involvement in the deaths of both John and Bobby Kennedy. What troubled me even more was what Kathy had told me over lunch, just before I had left Virginia. Kathy had explained to me that Sam Giancana had secretly been working with the CIA and that the CIA was also involved with Sam in the conspiracy to kill Castro.

* * * * * * *

My flight from Michigan to California took about four hours. Renting a car from Avis Ford, I drove to Los Gatos and took a quick look at the subdivision of new homes on Saratoga Road. Something kept bothering me about the information Kathy put together on Mohamid. Mohamid had a brother named Murta who lived in Syria. If Mohamid was from Pakistan, why would his brother be living in Syria?

Walking into the Black Watch Bar at 141 North Santa Cruz Avenue, I called Kathy at Langley Headquarters. It was Tuesday night. Using my voice identification code, it took three minutes for me to get Kathy on the phone.

"Working late again?" I asked sarcastically.

"Anytime you're out of pocket and on an assignment I have to be here in case you call and need something," Kathy answered.

"Is that policy?" I asked.

"No, it's the way I do things. Why, dear, do you miss me?" Kathy asked jokingly.

I couldn't believe it. This was the first time Kathy had ever played around with me in a joking manner.

"Well, now that you ask, yeah," before she had time to respond, I continued. "Do me a favor and punch-up the name, Murta Hassimi, in the computer. When was the last time he was in the United States? When did he use his passport last?" I asked.

"Hang on," Kathy replied.

Standing at the pay phone, I ordered another Pepsi and waited. Looking at my watch, ten minutes passed when Kathy finally returned to the phone.

"You're onto something, kiddo. Murta used his passport to enter the United States on Saturday and then left Monday from LAX International Airport. He was here and gone in less than 24-hours. What's going on, David?" Kathy asked in an almost paranoid tone of voice.

"My line's not secure. Get on the Company Learjet and meet me tomorrow at twelve noon. Come to Los Gatos and meet me at a place called Billy Jones Wildcat Railway. It's at the Oak Meadow Park," was all I said as I quickly hung-up the telephone.

* * * * * * *

It was a sun shiny, beautiful California day as I sat at the Billy Jones Wildcat Railway and waited for Kathy. There's an old mini-train that runs through Oak Meadow and Vasona Parks. You sit in it, and a guy points out stuff like the Big Creek. For kids it would be a lot of fun. Looking at my watch, it was two minutes to twelve when I saw Kathy walking toward me. She was wearing a three piece, pin-stripe suit, and carrying a briefcase. Her dark Ray Ban Aviator sunglasses concealed her eyes. Sitting down next to me on the park bench, she smiled.

"What's going on?" she asked in a very serious tone of voice.

"You look like an attorney. Well, maybe more like a mob hitwoman," I said with a smile. "Either way, you look great."

Smiling, Kathy reached up with her right hand and pulled her sunglasses down to the tip of her nose. "Well, thank you. You really like this?" she asked in a flattered tone.

"Kathy, if you weren't my supervisor. Boy, oh boy," I said softly as I looked into her deep blue eyes. A few moments passed as I leaned forward slightly to kiss her. Catching myself, I stopped. Taking a deep breath of air into my lungs, I let it out slowly and turned my head to look at the mini-train that was now pulling into it's parking area. "I'm hungry, let's go have lunch," I said quickly as I stood up and looked at my watch. Out of the corner of my eye, I saw Kathy as she shook her head very slightly and smiled.

Taking Kathy to the Los Gatos Brewing restaurant, we ate lunch. The brewing company, on 130 North Santa Cruz Avenue served good food and also made thirteen of there own beers. It was a little noisy but a nice place to have lunch. Opening her briefcase, Kathy showed me the complete file the CIA had on Mr. Murta Hassimi. After finishing our lunch, we stepped outside. We were in the Silicon Valley and off to the southwest we could see the Santa Cruz Mountains.

Reaching up, Kathy gently grabbed me by my right arm. Turning to look at me, she asked, "David, be honest with me. Why did you ask me to come out here?"

I knew Kathy had just opened the door for me. All I had to do was tell her I was attracted to her and I wanted a more serious relationship with her. Opening my mouth, I tried, but deep down inside I knew she deserved a lot better than me.

"I need you to do something for me, Kathy, it's very important," I explained with a serious look on my face.

"Really?" she responded anxiously. "You really need my help?'

"Yup," I said as I looked at my watch. "It's one-thirty, we need to take a ride. I need to show you something," I explained.

Locking the briefcase into the trunk of my rental car, Kathy and I drove to Saratoga Road.

"Just tell me what you need me to do, David, and I'll take care of it for you," Kathy explained with a serious look on her face.

"I appreciate it, Kathy. You're the only one I trust, other than Marge, and I know she can't go too far from headquarters. So you're it," I explained.

"Name it, David. What do you need me to do?" Kathy asked. "Oh, my God," she said as she thought about it. "Murta is still here isn't he? You need me to keep an eye on him while you go after his brother, don't you?" Thinking for a second, the look of excitement left Kathy's face. "Damn it. I have to call someone in to help you. They won't let me do this kind of work, David. I'm not a field agent, shit!" she explained sadly.

Pulling into the driveway of the new, but empty, house two homes down from Mohamid's, I turned off the car and turned sideways in my seat to face her.

"Do you remember when I was at Langley the other day and you asked me about the new poisons and gasses I had picked up?" I asked.

"Yes, I do, but what does that have to do with this?" she asked.

"Remember, I told you that sometimes when you're out here and all alone, you have to think fast and make things work for you while you're on the run. Remember? I told you that sometimes you don't have what you need so you have to improvise on the run. Remember?" I asked with a serious look. Handing Kathy a pair of thin leather ladies driving gloves, I said, "Put 'em on."

"Okay," Kathy answered with a confused look on her face, looking at the gloves.

"I didn't bring any poison, all I have is my silenced .22 magnum pistol and you. Follow my lead, don't think, just move and move now or we're both dead!" I explained quickly as I jumped out of the car and placed a drop of Methadrine under my tongue.

Kathy had said she was bored and wanted to do what I did. Well, I was now going to give her that chance and test her at the same time. I knew for the moment we were completely safe. Telling her if she didn't move now and fast was only my way of scaring her a bit to psych her up. I knew from experience that right at this particular moment Kathy was experiencing the combination of fear and total excitement. Her adrenaline was pumped up to the maximum.

Walking down the road and up the driveway of Mohamid's new home, we moved up beside the garage and opened the side gate of the fence connected to it. The home was a four-bedroom model with a two and half car garage attached to it. The house had white aluminum siding with red brick front trim. It was a nice home by all means.

Closing the side gate behind us, we moved to the backdoor of the garage. Reaching into my suit coat side pocket, I pulled out the new lock pick gun and loosely held it at my side. Reaching up with my left hand, I grabbed the doorknob and turned it. It wasn't locked. Opening the door, I smiled.

"After you, dear," I said as we both stepped quickly into the garage and closed the door behind us.

"How did you know the door wasn't going to be locked?" Kathy asked.

"Very few peopled ever lock the backdoor of their garage. Growing up as a kid we never did. None of my friends' families ever did either," I explained calmly. "But remember this and learn from it. I had the lock pick gun ready just in case. Pay close attention Kathy and feel free to ask questions. Remember, there are no stupid questions. Now, listen and listen very carefully," I said as I turned the doorknob on the wooden door that goes from the inside of the garage to the house. It was locked. Placing the tip of the lock pick gun into the key section of the doorknob, I pulled back and squeezed the hand lever three times until it wouldn't move. Turning the entire hand-held device, the lock clicked open. Taking the lock pick gun out of the lock, I quickly put it back into my coat pocket. Turning the doorknob, I opened the door and stepped inside. I already knew no one was home because I had called the house while we were getting ready to leave the restaurant. Our intelligence report confirmed that Mohamid was allergic to animal hair, so I knew there was no dog in the house. Pulling out my silenced .22 magnum automatic, I smiled as I watched Kathy pull her .9mm model 59 Smith & Wesson automatic out from under her suit jacket.

"We clear the house first. Check every room, behind every door, in every closet, and under every bed. Move quickly and don't disturb or move anything out of its original place or position. Understand?" I explained softly.

Nodding her head yes, we moved quickly throughout the entire home checking everywhere until we felt safe knowing no one was home. Sliding my gun back into my shoulder holster, I looked at Kathy and smiled. She was breathing fast and wide-eyed. She was excited and listening to my every word.

"Remember this and don't ever forget it, Kathy. Always expect the unexpected, and never forget the Golden Rule: Everything is subject to change at any given moment. So, be ready for it. Got it?" I asked.

"Yes," she answered.

"How do you feel?" I asked with a smile.

"Oh man, David, this is a total head rush. I feel unbelievable. Now I know why you do this kind of stuff," she answered with a fascinated look on her face as she turned her head from side to side to quickly look around.

"The best is yet to come, pretty lady, wait and see. Okay, for now we need to get ready for Mohamid. Hang on a minute," I said as I walked out and looked in the garage. Walking back into the kitchen, I had a smile on my face as I held up the battery jumper cables.

"Jumper cables?" Kathy asked curiously. "The Sandman is coming to pay Mohamid a visit, isn't he," she said with a grin and excitement in her voice.

"We'll see, let's go into the basement and wait," I said as I looked at my watch.

"Let's search the house and see if we can find any names, addresses, phone numbers, or anything that will lead us to his terrorist-ass friends," Kathy suggested.

"If I went into your home and moved something on your bedroom dresser, would you notice it when you got home?" I asked.

"Of course I would. I know exactly where...Ah, I get it," Kathy said as it dawned on her that if we searched the house, it might tip off Mohamid we were inside. "Dumb, huh?" she asked with an embarrassed look on her face.

"No, it's not dumb. It's how we learn. Your perfume might tip him off. So we go downstairs and wait and give the air up here a chance to clear itself out," I explained as I turned and walked toward the basement stairs. Stopping for a brief moment, I reached up and locked the door going into the garage.

Once down stairs, I walked over to the main fuse box and looked up and to my left at the ceiling.

"What are you looking for?" Kathy asked.

"Holster your weapon," I explained. Kathy put her handgun back into its holster. "Our people want this to look like a natural death. You're intel report says that he comes home at three-fifteen, goes to the bathroom to take a crap and then takes a hot bath. After that he makes something to eat, right?" I questioned with a serious look.

"Yes, that's exactly what he does, why?" Kathy asked.

Opening the fuse box, I secured one end of the jumper cable to the main power inlet section of the fuse box. "This is a direct feed from the outside power line of the telephone pole to the house. By hooking up to these two leads, we bypass the main breaker system. As soon as Mohamid climbs into his bathtub full of water, you're going to touch the positive end of the cable up against this steel drainpipe on the bathtub drain," I explained as I pointed at the steel drainpipe with my right hand. Grabbing the opposite negative end of the jumper cable, I grounded it on a different pipe that ran from the bathroom sink. As soon as you touch the positive end to that drainpipe, Kathy, you count to three and pull it off. If you keep it on for five seconds or more the medical examiner will know, just by looking at the body, that he was electrocuted. Three seconds and you will blow his heart out. It will look like a heart attack, case closed," I explained.

"You want me to do it?" Kathy asked with a shocked look on her face.

"Only if you want to, Kathy. But if you do, you're life will never be the same. You said you were bored and wanted in on the action. Well, here's you chance. Make damn sure you're ready to live with it though. It will either make you sick and you'll throw up, or you'll really get off on it. It could almost be orgasmic," I explained. "Let me warn you though, Kathy. As soon as you touch that cable tip to that pipe, you're gonna feel Mohamid's body jerking out of control in that bathtub. You're gonna feel it and hear it. You're gonna be a part of it. You're gonna feel his life slip right through your hands. You're going to become death. Is that what you really want to experience?" I asked with a very serious look on my face.

"Yes," she answered with a strange look in her eyes. "Are you sure this is going to work?" she asked.

"Yes, I'm sure. I have used this method to hit someone once before," I explained. I looked at my watch then back at Kathy. "He'll be home in thirty-four minutes. You've got thirty-four minutes to change your mind," I explained.

* * * * * * *

Looking at my watch, I knew that Mohamid would be home any minute now. Kathy and I hadn't said a single word to each other for the past thirty minutes. The look in her eyes and her body movements all told me she was really looking forward to killing Mohamid. Reaching into my pocket, I pulled out a penny and handed it to her.

Looking confused at the penny she asked, "What's this for?"

"A penny for your thoughts. I would really love to know what's going on in that pretty little head of yours," I explained.

"You have no idea what you're doing for me right now, David," Kathy explained. "If they find out I am out here and doing this, the director will fire me. But, my God, David, I am so pumped up right now. I'm scared to death and excited beyond belief, all at the same time. I know you're going to think I'm crazy, but, David, I used to fall asleep at night and fantasize about killing people. Now, all of a sudden, completely out of the blue, you're giving me a chance to fulfill my wildest fantasy. I only wish I could actually look him in the eyes as I take his filthy terrorist life. Oh well, this is better than nothing at all, right?" she asked with a wide smile on her face.

"It was the opposite for me. The first time I killed anyone was in Vietnam. I was with a guy named John LaMadlin. He was testing me to see if I was Black Op's material, but I didn't know it at the time. My first time, I killed two young Viet Cong soldiers with one shot. I was using a Winchester bolt action .300 magnum. I blew the one kids head completely off. I fought with my demons over it for a long time. Hell, Kathy, I'm still fighting with them. I can't sleep at night anymore. Their faces still come back to haunt me. I'm only telling you this, pretty lady, because it could happen to you too, and I don't ever want to be responsible for doing anything to hurt you or cause you any pain," I explained.

"You're making my dream come true, David. When I joined the CIA, I signed up for this. I wanted to be an assassin. You should have seen the looks on their faces when they interviewed me and saw that written on my application," she explained laughingly. "They never had a female apply with the Agency and ask to be trained to kill someone."

"Interesting," I said with a grin.

"Can I ask you a very serious question, David?" Kathy asked.

"Sure," I replied.

"Be honest with me, David. Promise?"

"Always," I answered.

"Back at the park you started to kiss me. Why didn't you?" she asked with a serious female look in her eyes.

Taking a deep breath of air into my lungs, I let it out slowly and looked Kathy in the eyes. "To be very honest with you, Kathy," I started to say.

The sound of the garage door opening cut my statement short. Hearing the car pull into the garage, I raised my fingertip to my lips and signaled Kathy to be quiet. Hearing the car door open and then close, we heard Mohamid as he pulled the garage door closed and open the side door to the house.

Pulling out my .22 magnum pistol, I cocked the hammer back. Placing another drop of Methadrine under my tongue, I handed the vial to Kathy. Now, with a serious look on her face, she shook her head no, and pulled out her handgun. Cocking the hammer, she looked over at the basement stairs, raised her gun, and pointed it at the top of the stairway.

Just as Mohamid's profile said, he came in and tossed his mail on top of the kitchen table and headed straight for the bathroom. We then heard Mohamid turn on the bathtub water, lower the toilet seat and sit down.

Quietly, we both stood up. Kathy holstered her weapon and then bent over to pick up the battery cables that were on the cement basement floor. Walking over to the main fuse box, I unhooked the cables from the power feed and gently closed the door to the fuse box. Taking the set of jumper cables from Kathy, I rolled them up, walked over, and placed them underneath the basement stairs. Nodding at Kathy to come over to where I was standing, I heard the toilet flush as Kathy now stood next to me with a confused look on her face. Looking up toward the area of the bathroom, we heard Mohamid turn off the water to the tub, take off his clothes, and step inside of the tub. Reaching into my inside suit pocket, I pulled out the small glass vial of Methadrine. Handing it to Kathy, I leaned forward and whispered into her ear. "This is pure liquid Methadrine, one-hundred percent. I'm going to question him. When I'm done, all you have to do is make him drink it. It will blow his heart out. You can look into his eyes while it happens," I explained as Mohamid began to sing in the tub.

Walking upstairs, I quietly put the jumper cables back in the garage and joined Kathy as she waited in the kitchen.

"Do you want to wait until he is done and dressed, or go after him now while he's naked and in the tub?" I asked in a whisper.

"Let's wait for him to get dressed," Kathy explained softly.

"No, we go after him now. Listen, Kathy, if we let him get dressed he'll have the freedom to move on us. He's going to be scared and that is going to make him extremely dangerous. If we move on him now, we have him naked, contained, and sitting in a wet slippery bathtub. See the difference?" I asked softly.

Nodding her head 'Yes', we made our move. Waking down the hallway, we stepped right into the bathroom as Mohamid continued to sing. Seeing us scared him so badly that he began to scream at the top of his lungs.

Moving straight to the bathtub I quickly shoved the end of my gun barrel into Mohamid's widespread screaming mouth.

"Shut the fuck up!" was all I said.

The screaming quickly stopped. Pulling the gun barrel out of Mohamid's mouth, I turned slightly, reached over, and flushed the toilet. I then sat down on the toilet seat, crossed my legs, and looked at Mohamid.

"Did you see how easy it was for me to flush this toilet?" I asked.

"Yes," Mohamid replied in a trembling voice, as he quickly realized he was sitting in the bathtub completely naked and in front of Kathy. Placing both of his hands in the water, he covered his penis.

"Listen to me, Mohamid. If you lie to me, I am going to flush your life away, just as easily as I flushed your toilet. If you tell me the truth, you will then get dressed, and come with us. We will give you protection, just as we have given your brother Murta protection and asylum. Do you understand?" I asked calmly with a smile.

"Murta? My brother and I have diplomatic immunity. What asylum? We are diplomats," he explained in broken English.

"You're a diplomat and you're working in a beer factory, bottling beer?" Kathy asked as she leaned up against the bathroom wall.

"Yes, yes. In my pocket, go look, on the bed in my pants pocket. Go look," he explained anxiously.

"Keep an eye on him, Kathy," I explained as I stood up and went into Mohamid's bedroom to get his wallet. Taking Mohamid's wallet out of his pants pocket, I opened it up, looked at it, then went back into the bathroom and sat back down on the toilet seat. Handing the wallet to Kathy, she opened it and looked at Mohamid's diplomatic identification credentials.

"Get out of my house! Now!" Mohamid shouted defiantly.

"Oh, my God, how did I miss this?" Kathy asked in a paranoid voice as she looked over at me for an answer.

"Get out, God damn you, get out of my house," Mohamid shouted once again, more bravely this time.

"Mohamid, if you yell at us one more time, I will cut out your tongue and make you eat it. Where are the chemicals your brother Murta brought to you from Syria? If you don't tell me, and I mean right fucking now, then I am going to start snipping your teeth up and into your gums. The pain will be so bad you will beg me to kill you," I explained calmly as I stood up and raised the wire cutters in my right hand for Mohamid to see. "Mohamid, your brother Murta is with us. We grabbed him at the airport Monday when he tried to leave. He told us everything. That is why we are here right now. Tell us where the chemicals are and you will live to be deported back to your country of Pakistan. If you don't tell me, then I will simply kill you where you sit. We will then tear this house apart piece by piece until we find what we are looking for. The choice is yours. Live or die," I explained as I tucked the wire cutters into my back pants pocket and pointed my .22 magnum directly at his left eye.

Raising his right hand up with his palm facing the barrel of my gun, he closed his eyes tightly and begged, "No, no, please no. I tell you, I tell you. Please no shoot me, please."

"Where are they, Mohamid?" I asked calmly.

"Drying machine, down in basement, drying machine for clothes. Please, no shoot me. I want asylum," he said as he slowly opened his eyes and faked a smile.

"Go check it out, Kathy, and be careful," I explained never taking my eyes off Mohamid.

"I'm on it," Kathy said quickly as she turned, holstered her weapon, and headed for the basement.

It took Kathy about three minutes before she returned to the bathroom. Opening the briefcase she held in her hands, my eyes widened as I began to count the large glass vials safely secured to the inside of the briefcase. Pulling out a handwritten list of names, addresses, and phone numbers from the briefcase, Kathy looked over at Mohamid.

"Are these the people you're suppose to deliver these chemicals to?" she asked calmly, showing no emotion.

"Yes, yes. I am to call them this weekend and they will come here to my home to pick these liquids up. Honest," he said as he raised his left hand as if he were taking an oath.

"What is this other list, this one here, on the back of the paper with the names on it. This is written in your country's language, yes?" Kathy asked.

"Yes, yes, that is the places they are suppose to go to and release the chemicals," Mohamid explained. "You give me asylum like you give Murta, my brother. I work with you, yes?" Mohamid asked with a smile.

Putting the paper with the list of names back into the briefcase, Kathy gently closed the case and snapped the locks shut. Setting it down next to the door, she turned, looked at me, and smiled.

"Alright, Mohamid, here's how were going to do this," I explained with a smile.

"We are going to give you something to drink. It will make you a little tired. This is so you don't try to escape. Once you drink it, you will then get up, towel yourself off, get dressed, and then we will fly you to Washington, D.C. so you can have asylum in America. Okay?" I asked. Reaching into her suit pocket, Kathy pulled out the small vial of Methadrine and walked toward Mohamid.

"No, no, this is a poison. You are going to kill me," Mohamid said quickly, as he tried to slide backwards and away from Kathy.

"Wait, Kathy," I said as I reached out and took the glass vial of Methadrine from her hand. Opening my mouth, I placed a drop of the liquid speed under my tongue. "It's not poison, Mohamid. See?" I asked.

A look of relief spread across his face as I pulled a piece of paper off the toilet paper roll, wrapped it around the thin glass eye dropper and snapped it off. Tossing the broken tip of glass wrapped in paper into the toilet, I handed the vial of speed back to Kathy.

"Please open your mouth, sir, and tip your head back. I need to give you all of this," Kathy explained calmly.

"Yes, I will do this but then you must leave. I am Muslim; women have no rights in my country. It is insulting to me for you to see me this way," he explained as he tilted his head back and opened his mouth to accept the liquid he thought would make him tired.

Walking up to Mohamid, Kathy asked, "Please raise your tongue, sir, it works faster if some of it gets under your tongue."

Raising his tongue as he kept both hands over his penis to cover it, I watched as Kathy poured the entire bottle of liquid speed into Mohamid's mouth.

"Say goodnight, asshole," I said as Kathy sat down on the edge of the bathtub.

"Look at me," she said sternly. "I said look at me, you terrorist piece of shit," she said quickly, as she grabbed Mohamid by the right side of his face with her left hand, and by the hair on the top of his head with her gloved right hand. "I just killed you, mother fucker. Me, a woman, I just killed you," she explained as Mohamid's eyes got wide and his mouth opened.

Grabbing his chest with both hands, Mohamid gasped for air and began to thrash around violently, splashing water all over the sidewall of the tub, Kathy, and the bathroom floor. I was impressed with Kathy. She sat on the side of the tub and held Mohamid's head in her hands, forcing him to look into her cold blue eyes. It took almost a minute and a half and then Mohamid's eyes rolled up and back in their sockets. He gasped one last deep breath of air and let it out slowly with a gurgling sound as his body fell limp in the tub.

Letting go of Mohamid's head, Kathy stood up, walked over to the bathroom sink, and bent over slightly as she placed both of her hands on the front of the sink to steady herself. Taking three fast breaths of air into her lungs and letting it out quickly, she spoke, keeping her eyes closed.

"I think I just had an orgasm," she said softly. Standing up, I walked over, stood behind Kathy, and gently rubbed her shoulders. "Oh God, that feels so good," she said in a whisper.

"The orgasm or my rubbing your shoulders?" I asked calmly.

Raising her head, she looked into the bathroom mirror at me as I continued to rub her shoulders. "Both," she said with a smile.

"Life will never be the same for you now, pretty lady. Welcome to my world. Welcome to Black Op's," I explained.

"How do I thank you, David?" Kathy asked as she turned around to face me, with a soft sexy look in her eyes.

"Well, first you can toss that empty glass vial into the toilet and flush it. Make sure it goes down. Then put Mohamid's wallet back into his back, left pant pocket. I'll put the wire cutters back and we'll get out of here," I explained as I turned, picked up the briefcase, and headed for the garage to put the wire cutters back where I found them.

"You asshole," Kathy whispered with a chuckle. "You had your chance and you blew it," she added, waiting for me to respond.

Smiling, I didn't say a thing. Leaving the home with the doors all locked and Mohamid's dead body inside, we returned both of our rental cars to Avis Ford and boarded the Agency Learjet. Once in the air, Kathy used the secure line to call our director personally. He knew she had flown to Los Gatos to deliver the intelligence information to me on Murta Hassimi, but that was it. She then explained that I had discovered what appeared to be biological chemicals and a list of names, addresses, and locations where they were to be released in our country. The director told Kathy that the Agency would be waiting for her to land and that a biohazard team would be there to take charge of the unknown vials of chemicals. The list of names was to be delivered directly to him and to him only. He would be waiting for her at his office.

Hanging up the phone, Kathy sat back down next to me. "It will take seventy-two hours or less for our lab boys to find out what's in these vials. I'll call you and let you know as soon as I find out, okay?"

"Please do. What do you think the director will do about it?" I asked.

"We'll go Code Red and pick up everyone on this list. Then we'll wait for Murta to fly in to pick up his brother's body to take back home to Pakistan. We'll grab him too. We have a private place we will take them to so we can get all the information out of them that will lead us to their associates, and then they'll simply vanish from sight," Kathy explained with a smile.

"You did a good job back there, Kathy. I'm proud of you," I explained.

"Really? Does this mean you're going to take me out on another mission with you?" she asked in an anxious and excited tone of voice.

"Boy, I don't know," I said softly.

"David, teach me. Teach me how to be like you. You're the best assassin the CIA has. Everybody I know talks about you," she said.

"Really?" I asked surprised to hear what Kathy had just said.

"Please, David, will you be my mentor. Will you teach me everything you know, so I can be as good as you?" she asked.

"What if the Agency finds out?" I asked.

"They'll never know, David. I'll be the first female American assassin. Please, David, will you teach me?"

"Maybe," I said with a chuckle as I looked out the side window of our plane.

"What's so funny?" she asked.

"I was just thinking. If we ever had children, the world would be in serious trouble, huh?" I said jokingly.

"You had your chance, kiddo, you blew it," Kathy said in a seductive voice.

"Maybe, we'll see," I replied calmly.

I knew that killing Mohamid had turned Kathy on sexually, as well as emotionally. She was one of a kind, that was for sure. I just didn't know how far I should take this. How far was she willing to go? How far was I willing to go. I was involved very deeply now with two very deadly organizations. The CIA and the Mafia. I was walking the razors edge. I felt alive again. I was back in the jungle, except this time it was a different kind of jungle. It was in my own backyard, in America.

Chapter Nine
The Neanderthal

Sitting on my front porch, I looked across the street at my neighbor's house as he picked up his little girl and gave her a big hug and butterfly kisses. He had just gotten home from work. He was a computer programmer for one of the new high-tech companies in Gross Point, Michigan. His wife had just stepped out onto the front porch of their home; smiling, she kissed him on the cheek as they went inside and vanished from my sight.

"Damn, you're so lucky. What I would give to be able to come home everyday after work and be greeted by my wife and child," I thought to myself as the blue Ford van pulled into my driveway.

Seeing Mrs. Carlson and little Tara brought a big smile to my face, as they got out of the van and walked up to where I was sitting. Little Tara was wearing her brand new Girl Scout uniform and smiling from ear to ear.

"Hello, David," Mrs. Carlson greeted. "Tara insisted that I bring her over here so she could show you her new Girl Scout uniform."

"Hi, Mr. David," Tara said with wide eyes and a big smile.

"Tara, I am so very proud of you," I answered.

"Really?" she replied.

"Yes, I sure am. I'll bet that your mom and dad are real proud of you too, huh?" I asked with a smile. My smile quickly vanished when I saw Tara's big happy smile leave her face. "What's wrong sweetie, did I say something wrong?" I asked as I looked up at Mrs. Carlson.

"My mommy's real proud of me," Tara explained as she looked down at her feet.

"David, Tara's daddy died in Vietnam in 1967," Mrs. Carlson explained with a sad look on her face, as she reached over and gently touched little Tara on the back of her left shoulder. "Her daddy was a hero and God needed a hero in heaven, so he took Tara's daddy up to heaven to be with him. Isn't that right, Tara?" Mrs. Carlson asked.

My heart sank in my chest as my mind took me back to the jungles of Vietnam and the men who lost their lives there.

"I was in Vietnam, Tara," I said gently.

"Really? Were you a hero like my daddy?" she asked with a curious look on her face.

"Gee, I don't know, honey, I never thought about it like that before."

"You were a soldier?" Mrs. Carlson asked with a surprised look on her face.

"Yes, ma'am," I answered, never taking my eyes off of Tara. "I was there for two years," I explained. "Would you like to see some pictures of me and my teammates, Tara?"

Looking up at me, Tara nodded her head up and down saying yes.

"Well, lets make sure it's alright with your mommy first, okay, honey?" Mrs. Carlson explained with one eyebrow raised as she looked over at me.

"I'm sorry. I wasn't thinking. Of course, you should make sure it's okay with your mother first. If your mommy says it's alright, then I'll show you my pictures okay, sweetie?" I explained to Tara, who was now half smiling.

"Okay, Mr. David, I'll ask my mommy when I get home," Tara replied.

"Yes, but for now we must go. After selling all of her cookies and doing it so quickly, Tara's first task as a Girl Scout is to find one of the Girl Scout mom and dads that will let us use their home for a Scout meeting and overnight camp out, huh, Tara?" Mrs. Carlson explained as little Tara began to perk back up and smile.

"Yup," Tara answered quickly.

Crossing my arms, I raised my head slightly. "You hurt my feelings, Tara," I said as I rolled my bottom lip as if I were about to pout.

"Huh?" she said with a wide-eyed look.

"How come you didn't ask me? My house isn't good enough for you?'

Looking up at her Scout mother she asked, "Mrs. Carlson?"

"Well, I don't know. Our rules require a parent or relative of one of our Girl Scouts own the home. Plus, having a wife helps too," Mrs. Carlson explained.

"Well, that's not fair. I'm Tara's friend and I have a very special lady friend that I'll bet would love to be here for a camp out. Besides, Tara's daddy was in Vietnam. That makes him my brother. So in a way, that makes me her adopted uncle, huh, Tara?" I explained.

Tara's eyes got big and her smile huge. Full of newfound excitement she blurted out, "Really, you want to be my uncle, really?"

"Yes, but only if its alright with your mommy. Tell your mommy that she can spend the night here with Mrs. Carlson and my friend Kathy. I have lots of room and your mommy can sleep in one of my guest bedrooms. What do you say, Mrs. Carlson? Can you make this work? I'll pay for everything. It won't cost the Girl Scouts a penny," I explained with a grin.

"Well, a lot of our girls live here in this neighborhood. Some of the parents will want to stop by to meet you, plus there are three other scout mothers that will be required to be here for the meeting and the over night camp out," Mrs. Carlson explained.

"Sounds good do me," I said with a smile. "It's a big house with a huge backyard. I have a deep fryer and restaurant style grill in the basement. There is a bathroom down there with a shower that the girls can use. As you can see, the entire backyard is fenced in. I'll call the Michigan State Police and the Oakland County Sheriff's Department to let them know we have minor children on a camp out staying here. They'll patrol every half hour that way. Plus, I have two older male friends that will also be here to cook and help run security. All I will need to know is what do Girl Scouts like to eat?" I asked as I looked at young Tara and winked.

"We have a total of thirty-two Girl Scouts, David, plus three scout mothers and myself. Do you think you can handle a total of thirty-six females in your home all at one time?" Mrs. Carlson asked with a large grin on her face, as she crossed her arms and tapped her right foot gently on the ground.

"Piece of cake!" I explained smiling.

"Alright then, remember I tried to warn you. We will be here next Friday at 6:00 p.m. for our scout meeting," she explained.

Mrs. Carlson and I exchanged phone numbers so we could make the necessary plans, then she and little Tara left to go tell the rest of Girl Scout Troop 220 that they had found a place to meet and camp out. Hearing the phone ring, I went down into the den and picked up the telephone that was my direct line to CIA Headquarters.

It had been two days since Kathy and I had gotten back from Los Gatos, and I was expecting her call. "Hello, dear," I said softly into the receiver.

"Well hello, lover," came the reply with a laugh.

Smiling, I knew I had just been had. "Hello, sir. How are you?" I asked, as I waited for the director to reply.

Laughing, he answered, "And some people don't think I have a sense of humor."

"I'm glad that you do, sir," I answered. "I'm going to kill Kathy for this," I thought to myself.

"I just wanted to call to tell you congratulations. You hit the jackpot, son."

"Really, sir, what was in those vials?" I asked.

"I'll let Agent Eckland explain. Good job, son," the director said once more before he handed the telephone over to Kathy.

"David?" she asked carefully.

"Yes, Agent Eckland," I replied calmly, not knowing if we were on the open speaker box or not.

"Are you scrambled on your end?" she asked.

"Yes, my scrambler box is on and working. Are we on the speaker box?"

"No, I am on a closed line," Kathy answered calmly.

"So what was it? What was in those vials?" I asked.

"Total panic, fear, and death," she answered. "We tested them all and confirmed the following. Each vial contained four fluid ounces. Ten vials were full of cholera, eight vials contained Botulin poison, but the other twenty vials contained enough VX Nerve Agent to wipe out most of New York City. It was targeted for the White House, Pentagon, six major cities, and the CIA Headquarters here at Langley, Virginia. Scary thought, huh?" Kathy asked.

Taking a deep breath of air into my lungs, I let it out slowly. "Whoa! That is scary. Are we going to sweep these assholes up?" I asked.

"Oh yeah, its personal. You did a good job, David. I wish I could have been there to see the look on Mr. Hassimi's face," Kathy explained.

I knew the director was still sitting in the office with Kathy so I kept it professional. "Well good, I'm glad it all worked out. Call me on another line as soon as possible would you?" I asked.

"Absolutely. I'll talk to you soon. Goodbye and good job, David," she said as she hung up the telephone.

Hanging up the telephone on my end, I sat back in my black leather recliner chair and waited for Kathy to call back. I knew it wouldn't take more than a few minutes. As soon as she left the director's office, she would head straight to her office and call me back. Four and a half minutes went by when my phone rang once again.

"Hello?" I said.

"David, it's me. You're not mad at me are you?" Kathy asked with a half laugh to her voice.

"No, I'm not mad. I'm just glad I didn't answer the phone and say, Kathy, I think I'm falling in love with you," I knew by saying that, I could cut her off short and really surprise her!

"What?" she said in a very surprised and soft voice.

"Hey, I need a favor. You said you owed me one. Can you come over here to my place next Friday and spend the night?" I asked in a timid tone.

"Spend the night? What's going on, David?" she asked.

"Something big, Kathy. I can't explain it right now, but I really do need your help. You said you wanted to learn from the best, now is your chance. You coming?" I asked.

"Absolutely. I'll be there. This is great; it's another hit, isn't it? What do you want me to bring?" she asked in a very serious voice.

"Dress casual, and bring clothes for at least two days of work. It might get rough, Kathy. You sure you want to help me out with this one?"

"After the rush I got on the Hassimi hit, shit, I wouldn't miss this for anything in the world," Kathy explained anxiously.

"Hassimi was an easy hit, Kathy. This is going to be dangerous. It's going to require your full attention. You sure?" I asked again.

"I'll be there. Thanks, David. What time do you need me there?"

"Between noon and two o'clock. I've got to go, I'll see you Friday unless something else comes up before then," I explained calmly.

"You can count on me, David. I'll be there," Kathy said with a serious tone of voice.

"See you Friday, kiddo. Be ready and psych yourself up. It's going to be big," I explained as I quickly hung up the phone.

Smiling, I sat back and picked up my regular telephone. I called both Andy and Don and explained what I had gotten myself into. They both thought I was completely nuts until I told them that Tara's father was killed in Vietnam. At that point, they were one hundred percent with me. Both Don and Andy loved kids just as much as I did. That would make it even more fun. I put Don in charge of finding seventeen real nice tents. I figured that two Girl Scouts could sleep in each tent and once the camp out was over with, I would simply give the portable tents to Scout Troup 220. It would be a good tax write off at the end of the year.

I put Andy in charge of food and snacks. I told him, hamburgers, hot dogs, potato chips, potato salad, and ice cream for Friday night. Eggs, bacon, hash brown potatoes, and toast for breakfast Saturday morning, and lots of Pepsi, milk, and orange juice. But no horse or dog meat! Andy got a kick out of that.

If nothing happens between now and next Friday, this should be fun. Well, it was wishful thinking anyway...

* * * * * * *

Hearing my doorbell ring, I opened the front door of my home and smiled. It was early Thursday morning, and so far, everything was going according to my plans for the Girl Scout Troop 220 camp out tomorrow night. Don had gone to the Pontiac Mall and purchased twenty brand new waterproof tents from Sears. Of course, with Don, nothing is simple. He also bought thirty-five Coleman lanterns, forty Thermo sleeping bags, forty Sony radios with batteries (color pink), and just to be safe forty battery-operated camping lanterns and forty flashlights.

When I asked him why forty and why not thirty-two, he gave me a serious look and mumbled, "What do you know?" Can't argue with that, can you? Don was now in the backyard putting up the portable tents and having the time of his life.

Andy was down stairs already. He hung pink bed sheets over the bottles of vodka, rum, whiskey, and assortment of other booze that I had behind my bar. He then decorated it with plastic flowers and stuffed animals. For food, he bought everything I had told him to get and then went overboard with Hostess cupcakes, Twinkies, cookies, and of course six different flavors of Hostess pies. Baskin & Robins would deliver the five, one-gallon, restaurant size containers of ice cream Friday evening around 7:00 p.m.

I, on the other hand, wasn't going to be out done by my two elders. I called the Waterford Chapter of the Michigan Jaycee's and explained to their Chapter President what I had going on with Scout Troop 220. They suggested that I hire the members of their chapter to run a kid carnival. The Waterford Jaycee's would supply all of the carnival equipment and run all of the games, which would include a full-size water dunk tank. The girls would get a chance to throw balls at the small round target. If they hit the metal disc target, whoever was sitting on the seat inside the water tank, would fall down into the water. Along with all of the other games and the cost for the prizes that the girls could win, it cost me a donation of $700.00. The Jaycee's, who are a non-profit organization, would then donate the money to a worthy charity. The Jaycee's would arrive this afternoon and begin the process of putting the carnival equipment up in my front yard.

"David, I couldn't wait any longer," Kathy explained as she walked past me and into my front room, suitcase in hand. "I know I'm early but I am dying to find out who it is that we are going after!"

Kathy was wearing a blue T-shirt that had 'Woodstock' written on it, a pair of Levi jeans and black leather, low-cut, slip-on dress shoes.

"Multiple targets," I said calmly, trying hard not to smile.

"I knew it, this is so great!" she said in an excited voice, as I closed the front door and walked her over to the sofa.

Sitting down next to her, I smiled. "Thanks for coming, Kathy. God, you look great," I explained.

"Well, thank you," she replied and then remembering something, she continued. "Oh, I almost forgot," she said quickly as she leaned forward and opened her neatly packed and well-organized suitcase. Pulling out the dark wood grained box, she handed it to me. "Marge asked me to give this to you. She only has two of them. The other one is still locked in her security vault. After what you discovered in Mr. Hassimi's home, she wanted to..." pausing for a moment, "well, its our way of saying thank you, David. If we would have killed him without questioning him, we may never have recovered what was in his dryer downstairs. I wish I could have told everyone how smoothly you talked Mohamid into revealing where the chemicals were hidden, but I was never there," she explained with a grin. "Anyway, open that up, kiddo, you're gonna love it."

Setting the wooden box on my lap, I flipped up the two gold clasps and opened the box. "Whoa," I said softly as I picked up the brand new Beretta and looked at it. "This is so light!"

"Marge wanted me to tell you that what you are holding in your hands is the first experimental prototype weapon of its kind. Beretta Corporation made two of them just for our Agency. It's a 15-shot, .357 magnum, David. It's made out of the highest grade of aircraft quality aluminum, Number 7075. It has a built in silencer, so you will never have to hand screw a silencer onto the end of the barrel ever again. We're all so very proud of you, David. You not only saved the lives of millions of Americans, you also saved us," Kathy explained as she reached over and gently kissed me on the right side of my cheek.

Turning to look at Kathy, I said, "Tell Marge I said thank you, I really love this," I explained as I looked back down at my new prototype weapon.

"What about me?" Kathy asked softly as she leaned slightly forward to look into my eyes.

Reaching up with my left hand, I gently slid my palm across the side of her face and pulled her toward me. "You had me when you first said hello to me at the Pine Knob Ski Lodge," I whispered softly. Closing her eyes, I could feel her breath on my face. The time had finally come.

"Hey, brother, I need...oops," Andy said loudly as I pulled my face back and away from Kathy. "Sorry, David, I didn't know that you had company," Andy said quickly.

"Kathy, this is my dear friend and brother, Andy. Andy, this is..." I started to say as I turned to look at Kathy. Our eyes met and I could tell that she was waiting to hear me say something special. "And this is Katherine. The girl of my dreams," I introduced with a serious look deep into Kathy's eyes. Her smile was enough.

Turning to look at Andy, Kathy extended her right hand and said, "Hello, Andy. It's nice to finally get to meet you. David talks about you all of the time."

Shaking Kathy's hand, Andy responded. "Its nice to meet you too, Kathy. You're pretty, would you like a cold beer?" he asked.

"No, thank you, its a little too early for me," she answered with a smile. "Do you always drink beer at 8:30 in the morning?" Kathy asked as she looked at her watch.

"No, I usually get started at about 4:00 a.m., but with all of these Girl Scouts coming tomorrow, I figured I better take it easy. I must be on my best behavior for all of these young ladies, ya know," Andy said with a grin.

"Girl Scouts?" Kathy asked with a look of surprise on her face, as she turned to look at me. "Girl Scouts, David? This weekend is about Girl Scouts?" she asked a bit louder.

Before I could answer, Andy cut back in, "You know that Don is digging a big hole in the middle of your backyard, right?"

"What!" I snapped as I jumped up and ran into my dinning room and looked out through the dinning room window into my backyard.

"Yeah, he said that it's for the campfire," Andy added with a laugh. "This is going to be so much fun. I'm really glad you thought of it, brother."

"That's Kentucky Blue Grass sod," I whimpered sadly as I watched Don dig up more and more of my beautiful lawn.

Walking up next to me, Kathy chuckled. "I was a top honor-winning Girl Scout when I was young," she explained proudly. "Look at all of those tents! Are you paying for all of this?" Kathy asked.

Looking at Kathy, I smiled, "Yeah" as the doorbell rang once again.

"Hey, David, its Tara's mother," Andy explained as he walked Tara's mom into the front room.

Smiling, I walked up and shook her hand. "Hello, I'm David, this is Andy, and this is Kathy."

"Hi, I'm Amy, Tara's mother. So you're my daughter's new Uncle David, huh," Amy asked with a smile.

"I'm really sorry, Amy. I should have talked to you first," I explained.

"No, no, its perfectly alright. Marie Carlson told me that you're a very special man. You are all Tara talks about, David. She really needs a male figure in her life right now," Amy explained as the doorbell rang once again.

Opening the front door, I smiled, "Hello, Marie, come on in."

Hello, David, is that Amy's car..." Marie started to ask as she saw Amy sitting on the sofa. "Amy, hi. I was just at your house," Marie said as she walked over to Amy and sat down next to her on the sofa.

As I introduced Kathy to Marie Carlson, Don walked into the front room, covered with dirt. "Grand Central Station?" he asked jokingly.

More introductions were made as I carefully slid my Beretta back into its box and took it into my bedroom with Andy and Don following right behind me.

Andy made lunch for us as the women talked and made plans. We explained about the Jaycees and the carnival, talked, laughed, and had fun. Kathy fit right in and for the first time since I had met her, she let the female side of her personality shine through. Everything was going great. Hearing the phone in my den ring, I went in and picked it up.

"Are you available, sir?" the voice asked.

I looked at my watch; it was 2:00 p.m. Thursday afternoon. "The girls will all be here for their scout meeting in twenty-eight hours," I thought to myself as I looked out through the double wooden doors of my den and into the front room at Amy, Kathy, and Marie. "Who are you trying to kid, David?" I asked myself as my heart began to ache.

"Yes," I said into the receiver of my phone and then hung it up.

I wanted to be a husband and a dad so badly. "How did you get so screwed up, David?" I asked myself as I headed to my front door and opened it just as the older lady was reaching up to ring the doorbell.

"For you, sir," she said with a straight face showing no emotion whatsoever as she handed me the shoebox from the Payless shoe store.

"Thank you," I said as I closed the door and turned to look at Andy and Don. Motioning with a slight nod of my head for them to follow me, we headed upstairs to my bedroom and closed the door behind us.

"Is that a hit?" Don asked with a look of confusion on his face.

"It sure looks like it. Lock the door, would you, Don?" I asked.

Opening the shoebox, I pulled out the manila envelope that was rolled up inside of it. Dumping the contents of the envelope onto my bed, I reached down and picked up the stack of money that had dropped out of the envelope.

"David, you've got a house full of kids coming for the weekend. What were you thinking?" Don asked.

Picking up the piece of paper that had the information about the target on it, I began to read. "Who's Pete Catranus? I've heard that name before," I asked as I looked up at both Andy and Don.

"What?" Andy said quickly with a shocked look on his face. "Pete? No, it can't be. He's one of Carlo Gambino's boys."

"Holy shit!" I said loudly. "It says here they received information that Pete killed Joshua Door."

"Joshua Door? Who in the hell is Joshua Door?" Don asked as he sat down on the bed next to me.

"You know, Joshua Door, the guy that's got all of those commercials on TV," I explained. "They always sing, 'You've got an uncle in the furniture business, Joshua Door, Joshua Door'. Remember?" I asked as I continued to read.

"Why would Pete do that? He knows that Joshua is connected to Tony Jack's people in Detroit," Andy explained.

Picking up the photograph of Pete, I looked at it. "Damn, this is a big dude."

"Pete isn't going to go down easy," Andy explained. "He's as strong as a country ox and just as big!"

"It says here that Joshua Door never made it home last night and that his Cadillac is still parked out in front of his main furniture store. Hell, they don't even know if he's dead or not," I commented as I looked up at Andy.

"Trunk?" Andy asked with raised eyebrows. "Can you pick a car trunk lock?" Andy asked with a serious look on his face.

"Oh yeah. Wanna go take a look?" I asked with a smile as I reached into my shirt pocket and pulled out my vial of Methadrine. Placing a drop under my tongue, I felt a genuine feeling of excitement rush through my body.

"We're gonna be cutting it real close, David. We've only got until 6:00 p.m. tomorrow to get it done and get back here," Andy explained. "You don't want to disappoint little Tara."

"We?" I asked.

"Hell yeah, I'm going with you. It's going to take two people to take Pete Catranus down," Andy explained with a sinister look in his eyes.

"Don, keep an eye on things here. Kathy can sleep here in my room. Amy and Marie can sleep in the guest bedrooms. I'll show them where they can sleep before we take off. We'll leave here at about 5:00 p.m., Andy, get ready," I explained.

Taking the information package into the bathroom that was in my bedroom, I put it all in my sink and lit a match to it. Watching the photographs of Pete and the paperwork about him burn, my mind began to race with all of the different possibilities of what could happen in the next twenty-four hours. I couldn't help but wonder if Joshua Door was lying dead in the trunk of his own car. Looking at my watch, I knew Andy and I would find the answer to my question in just a few hours.

* * * * * * *

Looking at my watch, I saw it was 7:30 p.m. as both Andy and I sat in my Corvette and watched Joshua Door's main furniture store warehouse. We had been sitting across the street and watching for over an hour. Michigan State Police and Southfield Police Detectives had both been looking at Mr. Door's new Cadillac, which had been parked by the front entrance of the huge furniture store for the past twenty-four hours. Its owner, Joshua Door, had been missing since early yesterday morning.

"What kind of last name is Door?" I asked as I looked over at Andy.

"A very rich one by the looks of that store. Hell, that's just one of his stores, David. He has a bunch of these furniture stores," Andy explained.

"It's about time," I said as I pointed across the street at the police detectives who were getting back into their cars to leave.

It was a beautiful summer night out. I had the T-tops off of my Corvette and there was a small cool breeze blowing across our faces.

"How long will it take you to pick the lock on the trunk of his car?" Andy asked as we both put our black thin leather gloves on and I started the engine of my Corvette.

"About three seconds," I explained as I looked both ways up and down the four-lane road, and quickly drove across it into the parking lot of Joshua Door's main furniture store. "The place is empty, Andy. If anyone shows up while I have that trunk lid open, kill 'em!" I explained as I pulled up behind the pretty red Cadillac.

"What if they're cops?" Andy asked as we got out of my car and stepped quickly up to the rear of the Cadillac.

"Especially if they're cops," I said as I slid the tip of my lock pick gun into the lock of the trunk. Pulling the handle of the lock pick gun twice, I felt it snug up inside the lock. Turning it to the right, the trunk lid of the new Cadillac popped open. Pulling the lock pick gun out of the lock, I reached down with my left hand and raised the lid of the trunk.

The smell of dried blood and death quickly reached out to us as I looked at Andy. "Does he look dead to you?" I asked.

"Oh yeah," Andy replied as I slammed the trunk lid shut and climbed back into my car.

Joshua Door had been forced to get into the trunk of his car and shot. His car keys were lying on top of his body.

"Another day or two in the sun and the police won't have any trouble finding his body. Let's go see if we can find your old buddy Pete," I explained.

Andy and I spent the next seven hours driving to Pete's favorite bars and stripper clubs. We finally found his car at 2:30 a.m. early Friday morning.

"What are you gonna use?" Andy questioned.

"I've got a 15-shot, .9mm Browning automatic. I figure even Pete Catranus won't be able to take fifteen hits, if worst comes to worst," I said with a grin looking over at Andy.

"Wanna bet?" Andy asked with a worried serious look on his face. Reaching down toward the floorboard of the car, Andy pulled up his right pant leg and pulled a revolver out of the ankle holster secured to his leg. "Use this, brother," he said as he handed the pistol to me and pulled his pant leg back down. "Its a .357 magnum, six-shot Smith & Wesson, two-inch snub nose. It's loaded with hollow-point bullets. It's a throwaway piece so don't worry about it. It can't be traced."

"Watch my back, brother. As soon as he comes out and gets in his car, I'm going to light him up," I explained.

Pulling a Colt .45 automatic out from under his nylon windbreaker, Andy pulled back on the guns receiver and chambered a live round into the firing position of the gun.

"Don't take this guy lightly, David. He's as dangerous and tough as they come. He's also a hit man for the family, so he'll be on his toes and ready for anything. Don't shoot him once or twice. You dump all six of those hollow-point rounds in him and do it fast. Don't hesitate, do it fast, David. Do you understand me?" Andy asked with a worried look on his face.

"He's that tough?" I asked.

"He's a fucking Neanderthal," Andy explained. "While you're shooting him, David, Pete will be pulling his own gun out on you."

"Get behind the wheel, Andy. I'm going to go over there and get closer to his car so he won't see me coming."

"Good idea, now you're starting to think," Andy explained nervously, as I got out of the car and moved closer to Pete's car.

Standing in the shadows, I looked down at my watch. "Damn, it's almost 3:30," I thought to myself as I heard the front door of the building open and saw Pete walk out.

Now I understood why Andy was so concerned. This guy wasn't big; he was a full size rhino. Pete opened his car door and climbed behind the wheel, he never heard me coming until it was too late. As he reached out to pull the car door closed, I walked up fast with my gun pointed at his chest.

"Pete!" I said as I pulled the trigger. Our eyes met but this guy didn't panic. He simply reached for his gun as the first two .357 hollow-point bullets tore into his chest. The impact of the bullets hitting him at 1,850-pounds of pressure per square inch and pushing him slightly back only made him mad.

I don't know if it was the booze he had been drinking, the coke he was snorting, or the adrenaline now surging through every pore of his body, but this guy snorted at me like a raging bull and said, "You, mother fucker," as the next four magnum rounds tore through his upper chest and neck. Pete then slumped over slightly to the right; and then to my surprise, he forced himself back up into a straight sitting position and looked right at me. He was in a rage as I slammed the car door shut and walked back over to my Corvette, climbed into the passenger's seat, and closed my door. Looking over at Pete, who was still watching me, I watched as he slowly lowered his head and slumped over. Andy slowly pulled out of the parking lot and drove away.

"Now do you believe me?" Andy asked as I pulled out my handkerchief.

"You were right, Andy. Pete Catranus was a Neanderthal!" I explained as I empted the six spent shell casings from the pistol, wiped them clean of any fingerprints, and tossed them out the side window of my car.

"You hungry? There's a Denny's restaurant up ahead. Wanna stop?" Andy asked.

"Hell yeah, I'm starving," I answered as I wiped off the handgun. Pulling into the Denny's parking lot, we heard police sirens as the patrol cars flew past us and down the street toward the direction we had just come from. Pulling toward the back of the restaurant, I got out and walked up to the trash dumpster and tossed the gun inside. Taking off my leather gloves, I reached in, set them onto the front seat of my car, and smiled at Andy.

"Looks like we'll be home in time for the Girl Scout meeting," I said with a grin.

"Looks like it, but what I want to know is what are you going to do about the pretty blue eyed gal that's sleeping in your bed tonight?" Andy asked.

"To be honest with you, brother," I said as we opened the door and stepped into the air-conditioned restaurant. "I have a feeling that Kathy is more dangerous than Pete."

"They say that the devil is a blue eyed lady. You better be careful, boy," Andy said laughingly as he patted me on the back.

"Boy, if you only knew, Andy," I said to myself. "If you only knew!"

* * * * * * *

Friday nights Girl Scout meeting and overnight camp out went extremely well. I'm not sure who was having more fun, thirty-two Girl Scouts or Andy and Don. I do know this much, thank God for Dana, Kathy, Marie, Amy, and Ashley. These were the Scout mothers of Troop 220 and they had their hands full. Not so much with the girls, but more so with Don and Andy.

The Jaycees' carnival was such a big success that even the parents of the children in the neighborhood came down to see what was going on. It was little Tara that impressed me the most.

"Uncle David," she said as she looked across my front yard and watched as the neighborhood kids stood out on the street watching the Girl Scouts play all of the carnival games with Don in the water dunk tank.

"Yes, sweetie. Are you having fun?" I asked as Tara's mother stood next to me.

"Yes, Uncle David, but what about all of those little kids standing out there with their parents?" Tara asked with a look of concern on her face.

"What about them?" I asked as I looked at Amy and grinned.

"They should be able to play too. They're just children and we're Girl Scouts. Can they come and play the games too?" Tara asked with a serious look on her face.

"I'll tell you what, Tara. Let's get your entire Scout Troop together and we will vote on it. That's the fair way to do it. Tell Mrs. Carlson what it is you want to do and then let me know how the vote turns out. How does that sound?" I asked smiling.

"Great! Thank you, Uncle David," Tara said as she ran over to talk to her Scout mother.

Feeling Amy's arm slide through mine, she gave me a friendly little nudge. "I don't think that these girls have ever had this much fun. Thank you, David," Amy said.

The vote was taken by the entire scout troop and all thirty-two girls agreed. The neighborhood children were invited to play, and the excitement level rose one hundred and eight-five percent. After talking to the Scout mothers and Kathy, who the girls voted in as an honorary Scout mother of their troop, a second vote was taken. It was agreed that we would let the Jaycee carnival run until 5:00 p.m. and the girls would spend another night camping out in my backyard.

"Tara shows a lot of character, Amy. You should be very proud of her," I explained as Kathy walked up next to me.

Smiling, Kathy looked at Amy's arm that was now holding on to mine. She then looked at me with slightly raised eyebrows. "You're gonna need more food and a bunch of towels so they can take showers tonight," Kathy explained as she looked over at Amy and smiled.

"You're right. Don, Andy, and the Scout mothers can handle everything here. Why don't you come with me and we can go and pick up some towels," I suggested as I slid my arm away from Amy.

Amy stood five-feet, seven-inches tall. She had long blond hair, big blue eyes, and a body that was a good eight and a half on a scale of one-to-ten with ten being the highest rating.

Walking over to my Corvette, Kathy and I climbed in and headed for Hudson's at the Pontiac Mall to buy soap, shampoo, and towels for the girls.

"Amy's looking real hard at you to be Tara's new daddy," Kathy explained with a jealous look in her eyes.

"She just gave me a hug to say thank you, that's all," I explained carefully. "Besides that, if I had a chance to have children, I already know who I would want to have them with. I think she would make a great mommy," I explained as I reached over and held Kathy by her left hand.

* * * * * * *

It was now 10:00 p.m. Saturday night as I stood behind the bar in my basement and watched as the delivery boy from Pizza Hut sat down the last stack of pizza boxes onto my oak wood bar.

"That's twenty large pizzas, sir," he said smiling as he looked around at all of the girls who were now eating pizza and watching Magnum P.I. on the television set. Looking back at me, he handed me the bill as Kathy slipped up behind the bar and stood next to me.

"That will be ninety dollars, sir," he explained. Handing the delivery boy one hundred and ten dollars, I thanked him and told him to keep the change. I had just been placed on the Pizza Hut most preferred customer's list.

"You really love this kind of stuff, don't you?" Kathy asked in a soft voice as she slipped her arm in through mine.

"Yeah, I really do. Look how innocent they are. They have no idea how nasty the world they live in really is. I look at all of these kids and then it makes doing what we do worthwhile. People like Mohamid Hassimi don't belong on this planet," I explained as I ran the fingers of my hand through Kathy's and squeezed.

"Were you serious about what you said earlier this afternoon, you know, about having children with me?" Kathy asked as she turned me slightly to my left and looked deep into my eyes. "No one has ever said anything like that to me before. You really meant it, didn't you?" she asked tilting her head slightly to the right.

"Yeah, I think so. We certainly have a lot in common," I said, smiling in a whisper so the kids wouldn't over hear us. "Did you really mean what you said about fantasizing about killing people?" I questioned.

"Pretty sick, huh?" she answered as she lowered her head slightly.

"No, its not. To be honest with you, watching what you did to Mohamid had me so sexually aroused, I had to fight my emotions so I wouldn't do something stupid and have you slap me," I said with a half smile.

"I don't believe it," Kathy replied as she looked up into my eyes. "I've been fascinated with true crime and serial killers all my life. It's this really sick side of me. I'm not into that slasher crap, that's sick and cheesy. But if something is realistic and I'm actually the one doing it, my God, David, it's scarier than anything else and that to me is sexiness. It's a total turn on to me. Remember when I leaned on the sink and fought to catch my breath?" Kathy asked.

"Yeah," I answered as I leaned in closer to Kathy's ear. "You said you thought you had an orgasm," I whispered softly into her ear.

Turning to look at the girls, Kathy looked back at me. "I did have one. You should have made your move. I've never been that turned on before. God, I was so hot, so excited. Too bad, kiddo, you blew your chance," Kathy said as she slipped past me and patted me on my butt with a giggle in her voice.

"Damn," I thought to myself. "I'm going to have to take her out with me on my next hit."

"You should have never told me what you just told me," I said with a big smile on my face as I grabbed a piece of pizza, a cold Pepsi, and sat behind the bar and watched Magnum P.I.. I was a big fan of Tom Selleck and a bigger fan of his new hit TV series, Magnum P.I..

* * * * * * *

Staying up all night with Don and Andy, we stood guard watching over the girls who were fast asleep in their tents. This would be a weekend we would all remember, that was one thing for sure. We woke up the girls at 6:00 a.m. and by seven we all sat in McDonalds on Dixie Highway in Drayton Plaines, eating Egg McMuffins, Big Mac hamburgers, and having a great time.

After thanking Don, Andy, and I, the girls of Scout Troop 220, along with their Scout mothers, said their goodbyes. Kathy left at 9:00 a.m. to return to Virginia. This left Don, Andy, and I with a house that was littered with fast food boxes, empty pop bottles, and dirty towels.

Looking around at the total carnage, I scratched my head and sighed. "Well that was fun," I explained calmly.

"It sure was, brother. Let's get some sleep and we'll clean this mess up later," Andy suggested.

"Good idea," Don added with a yawn.

Closing the door to my bedroom, I climbed into my bed. I could still smell the scent of Kathy on my blanket and sheets. Sliding my hand under my pillow, I felt something just as I had closed my eyes. Pulling out the piece of folded paper, I unfolded it and began to read: "David, what if we were just two normal people, like everyone else. Wouldn't it be great? Thank you, for letting me see the real side of who you truly are. I will hold the memories of this weekend close to my heart, where I hope you will one day be. Now, if I could just meet the Sandman my dreams would be complete." Setting the note from Kathy on my nightstand, I closed my eyes.

The smell of her scent quickly faded as I drifted off to sleep. It was now the smell of the jungles of Vietnam that would return and the memories of my past would once again sweep me away into the shadows of the darkness of my mind.

Chapter Ten
Vixen Seven

It had been three days since Scout Troop 220 had spent the weekend at my home. Don had taken down all of the tents and picked up the mess in my backyard. The Waterford Jaycees had taken down all of their carnival equipment and helped to straighten up the front yard. Andy and I were blessed with the task of picking up the house, washing all of the sheets, pillowcases, and blankets in the guest rooms, along with all of the towels we had purchased for the girls to use. Loading all the trash into Andy's Ford pick-up truck, we took it to the Pontiac dump and disposed of it. We then folded all of the towels and placed them into a clean, large plastic bag. Putting the towels, along with all of the tents, into the bed of Andy's truck, we delivered them to Mrs. Carlson at her home. This took two trips, and the look on her husband's face was worth every penny of what I had paid for the entire weekend. His name was Scott Carlson and he was a real nice fella. He was an attorney who worked for a law firm in Birmingham, Michigan. I carefully explained to Scott that with all of his college education, I was quite sure he would figure out where he was going to store all the tents, lanterns, and camping accessories. He simply grinned, scratched his chin with his finger, and sighed.

Going back to my place, Andy and I watched as the Lawn and Garden men from Sears stood in my backyard with their arms crossed. They were trying to figure out how to repair the hole that Don had dug for the late night campfires.

"Sorry, David, I wasn't thinking about the damage I was causing when I dug the hole," Don explained as he took a sip of his cold Budweiser.

"Forget about it, I had a great time," I explained with a smile. "Hey, brother, check this out," I explained to Andy and Don as I walked over and turned up the TV set.

Channel 7 Action News was reporting that police officers had found the body of furniture Mogul, Joshua Door. Employees of the furniture store reported a rancid smell coming from the trunk of his car, which was parked in front of his furniture store.

The shooting death of Pete Catranus went unmentioned, or at least we didn't see it on the news. People being shot to death in Detroit was a common thing and not very news worthy. We also had a house full of giggling girls at the time, and didn't have time to watch.

I paid the men from Sears in advance, and said goodbye to Don and Andy. They needed to take care of a few things of their own and I was getting a tiny bit of a headache. Locking both doors of my house, I went upstairs to my bedroom to lie down. "What next?" I asked myself with a grin on my face as I closed my eyes and drifted off to sleep.

* * * * * * *

Following the trail of broken plant stems and disrupted ground foliage, we moved deeper into the thick green jungle. Moving almost two hundred and fifty yards, my heart pounded in my chest as the force of adrenaline and anger raced through me. Taking a moment to look beyond a fallen tree, I saw the tiny bare foot of a child.

"Over here," I said softly as I waved at Butch to get his attention.

Running toward the long fallen tree, my emotions exploded inside of me as I jumped over the tree and set my drop-pack and rifle down on the ground floor. There lying on the ground in front of me was the tiny body of the child from the tribe. Her long, black hair was filled with leaves. Her naked body was trembling as blood ran from her torn vagina. Her big, brown eyes stared at the treetops as I quickly sat down beside her. They had raped her and left her alone in the jungle to die. Reaching over to try and help her she tried to scream, but her voice was hoarse.

"It's okay, it's okay," I said softly as I pulled her broken, bleeding body up onto my lap. "It's alright, you're safe now," I whispered to her as I reached down between the child's legs and cupped my hand over her vagina and applied pressure, hoping to stop the bleeding. I was a young American and did not realize that the hemorrhaging was coming from deep within the child's body, something I could not stop.

Smiling at the child, I said, "Shhh, don't be afraid, I won't let anyone hurt you anymore, I promise."

The child must have sensed I was trying to help her. She slowly began to calm down, turned her head slightly toward me, and reached up with her little hand and gently pulled on my big handlebar mustache. She must have never seen a mustache that big before. She pulled a second time and then smiled at me and in a whisper said something in Vietnamese.

Looking up at Chopper, who was now standing across from me with Nick and Butch, I said, "I can't stop the bleeding."

"She said that she thought your mustache was a big caterpillar," Chopper explained as a tear fell from his eye and ran down his cheek.

Feeling the child's body quiver in my arms, I looked down at her and kissed her on the forehead and smiled. Looking back up at me, the little girl smiled again, took a deep breath of air and let it out slowly. Her tiny body became limp in my arms as her big, brown eyes stared into mine.

"She's gone, David," Nick said softly as his voice broke and he began to weep.

Pulling her body closely to mine, I began to rock her back and forth in my arms. Startled, I sat up quickly and looked around the bedroom. I was trembling as I placed my face in the palms of my hands. Covered with sweat, I couldn't stop shaking as the telephone continued to ring.

"Shit, oh shit," I whispered softly as I reached over toward the night table next to my bed. Picking up the phone, I quickly shook my head from side to side, trying to clear my mind. I could still smell the jungle as I placed the telephone to my ear. "Hello," I said softly in a still shaken voice.

"You alright?" Kathy asked.

"Yeah, I'm okay. Just a bad dream, that's all," I replied as I began to regain my focus. As I looked at my gold Tag Heuer watch, I realized it was 11:00 a.m. and I had only been asleep for two hours.

"We have a 'Dull Sword.' You're needed at the Pentagon. There's a plane waiting for you at the Pontiac airport. Hurry, David, there's not much time," Kathy explained as she hung up the phone.

"Shit!" I said out loud as I jumped out of my bed and ran into the bathroom to take a thirty-second shower.

Kathy had just given me a top-secret code name, which meant that something of a nuclear nature had just taken place. Climbing into my black 1970 Chevelle Super Sport, I was at the Pontiac airport within ten minutes. Waiting for me there was the private Learjet that belonged to the CIA. In less than two hours, I was walking into the front entrance of the Pentagon in Washington, D.C.

"Hello, David," Kathy said calmly as she greeted me at the front desk. Grabbing me by my right arm, Kathy pulled as we both began to run.

Two military policemen were running in front of us yelling, "Make way!" with two more MPs bringing up our rear. All four military policemen were armed. Everyone else in the hallway placed his or her backs up against the wall to clear a path for us. Standing at the elevator with the door held open were two more military policemen. Scrambling into the elevator, the ranking officer pushed the button and then turned a silver security key he had placed into the key section of the front panel board. When he did, we headed downward. Getting off of the elevator, Kathy walked next to me.

"I can't go in with you, David," she explained as we approached a guarded door at the end of the long hallway. "It's top secret and a need-to-know basis. Be careful and good luck," she whispered.

Showing the Secret Service agent my Q-clearance identification card, he quickly opened the door allowing me to enter the Situation Room.

"Have a seat, son, and thank you for getting here as quickly as you have," the two-star general said as I sat down in the only empty seat at the table.

Saying nothing, I simply nodded my head. Sitting at the solid oak wood table was the Director of the Defense Intelligence Agency; my boss, the Director of the Central Intelligence Agency; the National Security Advisor to the President; another young man I did not know; and the President of the United States, Richard Nixon. It was the two-star General that spoke first.

"We don't have a lot of time, people, so I am going to cut right to the chase. At 3:48 a.m. Eastern Standard Time this morning, one of our keyhole-13 spy satellites fell out of orbit. NORAD thinks it may have been hit by space debris. It came back into the earth's atmosphere at 4:18 a.m. and crashed on the top of Dandong Mian Jiang Mountain in the Peoples Republic of China. Normally, this wouldn't be so serious of a problem. However, this particular satellite was equipped with heat shields, its main body did not burn up upon re-entry. Our problem is that this satellite is equipped with a state of the art computer brain cell system, CBCS, and is powered by a Uranium core power cell system. The Uranium is weapon grade material."

"Yes," my boss, the Director of the CIA added, as he interrupted the two-star general and took over, allowing the general to sit down. "The Chinese do not know it came down and crashed on their turf. Their people were probably asleep on the job, as usual. The big threat to us is that Syria, Iraq, and Iran were not asleep last night. Our contacts with Kuwaiti Intelligence and the Israeli Mossad confirmed they are picking up a lot of chatter from Iraq and Iran. They're both sending agents from their countries into China to try to recover the satellite. If they get to it first, they will sell the computer brain cell system to either the Chinese or the Russians. That would set us back ten years in our spy technology. If they get their hands on that Uranium core they will then have what they need to build a nuclear weapon."

"A nuclear weapon in the hands of known terrorist countries is a direct threat, not only to the United States but also to our allies, gentlemen," the National Security Advisor added.

"What we need, gentlemen, is two people that are Halo Jump qualified to jump in, retrieve the brain cell and Uranium core, and get out without getting caught," added the two star general.

"Isn't this a job for the Navy Seals, sir?" the young man sitting next to me asked.

"Yes, it is, but if any American military personnel gets caught in China, it could be considered an act of war against them if they bitch loud enough to the United Nations," the general replied, "especially if its us."

"But, sir, with all due respect, I'm a Captain with the United States Marines," the young man sitting next to me explained.

"Not if you get caught, you're not. If you two get caught, our government will deny any knowledge of knowing you," the CIA Director responded. "And you, David, if they catch you over there and find out who you are, after your run in with them in Cambodia, I don't even want to think about what might happen," my boss said in a serious tone with a worried look on his face as he leaned forward.

"If it's a threat against America, sir, I'm in," I answered with a worried feeling deep in my gut.

"Me too, sir," the young Marine Captain added, looking over at me he smiled. "My friends call me Oliver. My partners call me Ollie," he explained as he reached over with his right hand to shake my hand.

Shaking his hand, I smiled, "Turn on some James Brown, Ollie, it's time to rock and roll. You can call me Dave," I said with a grin.

"Good," the President said as he stood up and headed for the door to leave. "Let's get this done," he added in a softer voice as he motioned with his right hand for the Secret Service agent, who was standing guard at the door, to open it. Without saying another word, the President and his bodyguards left the Situation Room, followed by the National Security Advisor.

"Alright, boys, listen up," the general explained. Seal team Ten is standing by. They will supply you with your Halo Jump gear and anything else you will need. We're running out of time, boys. There is a Navy helicopter outside waiting for you. You need to get airborne, and I mean right now. Good luck," the general explained as he shook our hands.

"David, Oliver, take these with you, just in case," the CIA Director explained as he handed each of us a glass Cyanide poison capsule.

* * * * * * *

CIA Covert Operation
Code Name: Vixen Seven
Location: Dandong Mian Jiang - China
Target: CIA Spy Satellite
Time: 4:10 a.m.

"We'll be over the target area in twenty two minutes, fellas. Boy, I wish we were going in with you," the Seal team Master Chief shouted with a grin on his face.

Double-checking our gear and oxygen mask for the tenth time, I looked over at the Master Chief, "How high are we, Master Chief?"

"Thirty-two thousand feet," he answered.

"What if my chute doesn't open?" I asked. I had just begun the Seal team Halo Jump favorite joke.

"Pull your backup chute," came the reply.

"What if my backup chute doesn't open, Master Chief?" I asked with a grin.

"Why hell, son, bring it back up here and we'll give ya another one," the Master Chief shouted as we all began to laugh out loud.

The rest of Seal team Ten gathered around Ollie and I, and knelt down. "Seals don't die, we fly," shouted one of the teammates.

"Hoo yah," we all yelled with pride.

Leaning in closer to Ollie and I, the Master Chief explained, "Grab it fast and get to the beach. Seal team Four will be waiting for your call. From there they'll get you to the sub and you're home free. Understand?"

"Two minutes to target," the voice yelled over the intercom.

Walking up to the back of the plane, we watched as the back ramp lowered, exposing us to the cold air.

When the green jump light came on, the Master Chief shouted, "Go! Go! Go!" as he pointed outward into the blackness.

Running side by side, Ollie and I dove out the back section of the plane and vanished from sight. My heart raced with the full pump of total fear as I began my descent into the darkness of the night. I've always had a deep fear of heights and today was quickly becoming a total nightmare for me! To make it even worse, a halo jump is the most dangerous jump of all. If your oxygen tank lines or face mask fail, you're dead! If you should happen to fall through a flock of birds, ducks, or geese, you're dead! If you should happen to fall into the path of a plane, 'splat', you're dead! Above and beyond all that, we were jumping at night to avoid being picked up on Chinese radar and our target is the top of a mountain that is covered with trees. Very large trees, I reminded myself as I fell, head first, through the clouds.

Skydiving has a reverse drug effect. You get a total high on the way down.

Looking to my right, I could see Ollie. Both of us had our small pop chutes held tightly in our left hands. All we had to do was let it go, it would catch the wind, and automatically deploy our main chutes.

Looking at my altitude gauge, I watched as the numbers told me the rate of our descent, 30,000, 27,000, 24,000-feet. We were picking up speed at a rapid pace, 20,000, 17,000, 15,000-feet; faster and faster and then at 12,000-feet they came out of nowhere. Within a mega-second, three

Chinese attack fighter jets shot past us directly in our path of descent. The massive heat from the jet wake of these fighters was unbelievable. I shot through the wake, faltered for a second, and quickly regained control of my descent. Ollie, however, had just missed the tail section of the farthest fighter. He was spinning out of control.

"Oh shit, oh shit, oh shit," I shouted into my breathing devise as I stabilized my fall and quickly spread my arms and legs to slow down my rate of descent, 9,000, 8,000, 7,000-feet. Turning my head, I watched in awe as that crazy Marine bastard regained his composure, twisted his body, and shot back into his original line of descent off to my right.

"Oh, thank you, dear God," I whispered to myself. I thought Ollie had blacked out from the pressure and intense heat of the jet wake. I was wrong; the young Marine had recovered in true Marine fashion. "Hot damn, you bad ass Marine!" I said as I looked back down at my altitude gauge, 4,000, 3,000, 1,000 and then at 850-feet, I released my chute. It was picture perfect as my chute caught wind and quickly snapped me backwards. Looking down toward the ground, I smiled when I saw the small clearing directly beneath me. Landing on an angle of descent, I took off running, turned, and quickly began to pull off the nylon harness that attached me to my chute. I began to very quickly pull in and roll up the nylon cords and parachute. Rolling them up into a tight ball, I ran and stood under one of the large trees off to my left. Within a minute, Ollie was standing next to me. We were both breathing fast and heavily from the surge of adrenaline and fear that filled every pore of our bodies.

"You bad ass mother fucker! Man, I thought you had bought the farm, brother," I said softly as I bent over trying to catch my breath.

"Piece of cake," Ollie replied as he lowered his trembling body to a sitting position onto the ground. "Hoo yah," he said softly.

"Hoo yah," I replied as I dropped to my knees and spread my body out onto the firm ground of the forest floor. "Oh, thank you, God, thank you, thank you, thank you," I repeated slowly as my body trembled.

"You alright?" Ollie asked.

"Just give me a minute, I'm scared to death of heights," I answered in a shaken voice.

"What!" Ollie said loudly. "You're halo qualified. How can you be scared of heights and jump out of a perfectly good airplane at thirty-two thousand feet?" he asked.

Pulling off my gear, I rolled over onto my back. "In Vietnam, I wanted to be Black Op's so bad I was willing to do anything. Every time the Seals took me up, they had to throw me out of the plane. Master Chief Jeff Mareno used to shake his head from side to side and laugh at me because I refused to ring out. I earned their respect and kept going back up. But

I'm not in Vietnam anymore and I'm not going to jump ever again!" I explained sternly.

"Yes, you will. That's why they picked you for this mission," Ollie explained.

"Oh yeah, and why is that?" I asked as I sat up and began to pull out some of my gear.

"They were out of time and they knew you wouldn't say no," Ollie explained with a grin.

"Well, it's your job to find the satellite and my job to take it apart. Think you can find it?" I asked.

"No, I can't," Ollie, answered.

"What?" I replied in a shocked tone as I turned my head to look at the young Marine.

"Nope, I can't, but this will track it down within a matter of minutes," Ollie explained as he pulled the small black plastic box out of his pant leg cargo pocket. "It's a locator box that is tuned into the computer brain cell. If the brain cell is still active, this will take us right to it." Pulling out the small antenna, Ollie turned on the CIA locator box, *beep-beep-beep*, rang out from the tiny device. "Oh yea, hoo yah," Ollie whispered with a grin on his face.

"Hoo yah," I answered. "Unpack your gear and I'll bury these parachutes and our halo gear. The sun is coming up fast, so lets get ready to move," I explained as I grabbed all our jump gear and looked for a place to bury it.

Within a matter of minutes, we were on the move heading in a northwest direction. Looking at my watch, it was 5:30 a.m. and the sunrise at this altitude was breathtaking. The quicker we moved, the faster the beeping sound rang out. The forest was beautiful and the large trees were in full bloom.

"Look, David, over here," Ollie said as he pointed in the direction of some broken pieces of satellite. Looking up toward the top of the forest canopé, I stood in awe.

"Look at that, Ollie. These pieces of metal tore the shit out of the tops of some of these trees," I explained as I pointed up toward the large broken branches. Some of which hung loosely, being held to the main trunk of the tree by a thin layer of tree bark and wood.

Moving the locator box slightly, it gave a loud and constant beep. "Over here, Dave, its right over here," Ollie explained as he took off running into the direction that was littered with metal parts and debris.

We ran for about fifty yards and then we saw it. It was lying on its side, next to a fallen tree and a large rock boulder.

"Holy shit," I whispered softly. "Look at how big that thing is."

"Yeah and this is one of the smaller ones," Ollie explained as he turned off the locator box and placed it back into his left pant leg cargo pocket and secured it. "I found it, buddy, now it's your turn to work your magic," Ollie said as he took off his small backpack and pulled out a Mack-10 machine gun. Loading a clip into the weapon, Ollie pulled back on the action of its receiver and loaded a live round into the chamber.

Opening my small backpack, I pulled out my black nylon pouch containing the tools I would need to remove the computer brain cell and the very toxic Uranium core.

"I'll pull out the Uranium power core first, Ollie," I explained as I began to unscrew the first of twelve security screws that held the faceplate to the main body of the satellite. "Then I'll try for the brain cell, if I can get to it."

"No kidding, the face access plate to the brain cell is pressing up against that boulder. This thing is too big and heavy for us to move by ourselves, David. What do we do if we can't get to it?" Ollie asked with a concerned look on his face as he looked around the woods to make sure we were alone.

"Always expect the unexpected, Ollie. That's what Master Chief Jeffrey Mareno used to always tell me. Don't worry about it; I'm trained and ready for this. Just cover my six while I work on getting this damn faceplate off," I explained as I quickly removed all twelve of the screws that secured the faceplate to the main body of the satellite.

Reaching into my backpack once more, I pulled out two white candles, my biohazard material waste gloves, and a half gallon plastic bottle that had double seals on the top.

"Have you got the hazardous material container?" I asked.

"Right here," Ollie answered as he unscrewed the top of the nuclear waste container. "What are the candles for?"

Setting a candle at each side of the faceplate cover and about two feet away from the main body of the satellite, I quickly lit both of the candles.

"Put your oxygen mask back on," I said as I turned to grab my mask. "Oh shit, I buried them with the parachutes," I said softly as I dropped my head and began to try to clear my thoughts.

"That's bad, huh?" Ollie asked with a concerned look on his face.

"No, we're still good, put the container right next to the hatch. Keep the top in your hand and back up a few feet. I'll pull out the nuclear core and slide it into the container. When I say 'now', you put the lid on it and secure it. Watch the flames on the candles, Ollie. They'll show us which way the breeze is blowing, so stay up-wind. If the flames shift direction, move fast and don't hesitate, the fumes from this core, as you already know, are radioactive. They'll kill you if you get a big hit of it. Ready?" I asked.

"Lets do it, brother, I'm ready," Ollie replied with confidence in his voice.

"Whatever happens, Ollie, don't touch the glove I grab the core with. My right hand glove is going to be hot, real hot," I explained as I pulled on the long thick gloves. "Let's do it," I whispered as I pulled the metal faceplate up and off the body of the satellite.

Watching the flames, we were careful to stay up-wind of the light breeze that blew gently through the forest trees. Grabbing the handle that held the nuclear power core, I pulled. "Shit," I whispered out loud as I stood closer and jerked the handle fast and hard. "It's stuck." Standing right over the top of the core, I placed one knee onto the body of the satellite as I grabbed the handle with both hands.

"Back away, David," Ollie shouted. "You're exposing yourself."

Jerking hard for a second time, the toxic core gave way and slid out of the satellite. Carefully, I slid the hot core into the nuclear waste container being careful not to let it touch the top or sides of the biohazard receptacle. Backing away quickly, I held my gloves out in front of me, and down wind.

"Cap it, Ollie, cap it, watch the flames," I said quickly as I pulled off both of my gloves. It took Ollie less than six seconds to secure the top onto the container.

"Secured," Ollie said quickly.

"Put that in your backpack and back away. That container is clean, so you're safe," I explained as I moved to the other side of the satellite and began to unscrew the top six screws that held the cover faceplate over the computer brain cell.

"There's no way that you're going to get that open, David. The bottom section is pressing up against the rock boulder. You can't even get to those screws," Ollie explained with a worried look on his face.

Removing the top four screws and one screw at each side of the top of the faceplate, I reached over and picked up the large flat tip screwdriver that was in my tool pouch. The sound of two Chinese jet attack fighters flying low and right over our heads scared me; I quickly looked up at the treetops.

"Think they saw us?" Ollie asked.

"I doubt it, that canopé of tree tops is too thick. But I'll bet you ten bucks they found out something's up here," I explained as two more jets passed by just off to our left. Placing the flat tip of the screwdriver in between the faceplate and the body of the satellite, I jammed down hard with both hands forcing it between the faceplate and the body of the

130

satellite. Pulling back hard with both hands, I pried the faceplate open about one inch.

"That should do it," I explained as I reached over and picked up the plastic half-gallon container. Pulling off both of the safety seals, I quickly and very carefully twisted off the plastic cap. Standing back, I began to pour the liquid into the open part of the computer brain cell storage area. The hissing, bubbling, and popping sound was followed by a rancid smell of melting computer components and melting metal.

"What the hell?" Ollie uttered with a surprised look on his face.

"Sulfuric acid," I said with a grin as I emptied the entire half-gallon into the hole, "Eats everything, even metal."

Looking down at the satellite, we watched as the faceplate and section of the satellite it was still screwed too begin to bubble and hiss. Tossing the plastic container off to the side, I quickly grabbed my backpack, pulled out my .22 magnum automatic pistol, and loaded a full clip of Cyanide filled bullets into the butt of the deadly weapon. Pulling the small backpack onto my shoulders, I pulled back on the receiver of the gun and loaded a round into the chamber. Reaching into my left pant leg pocket, I then pulled out the long slender silencer and screwed it onto the barrel of my handgun.

"My job is to retrieve the core and computer cell and to protect you. I'm going to kill anybody and anything that gets in our way, Ollie. Your job is to find the satellite and get us to our pick-up point. It's your turn, brother. Get us the hell out of here. This mountain top is going to be crawling with Chinese soldiers any minute now," I explained with a very serious look on my face.

"Follow me, David, I've got my end covered. Let's go," Ollie explained as we both began to move quickly through the woods and off the top of the mountain known as Dandong Mian Jiang.

"Ollie, there's something you need to know if I start to get sick."

"What's that?" Ollie asked.

"They lied to us, Ollie. That's not Uranium it's Plutonium. I'm sure of it. I guess it really doesn't matter though. It's weapons grade, that's for sure," I explained.

Moving for almost three hours, we stopped to catch our breath. "How ya feeling?" Ollie asked.

"Fine, maybe I didn't get any of the radiation on me," I replied as I reached into my top left shirt pocket and pulled out my tiny vial of liquid Methadrine. Placing two drops under my tongue, I handed the tiny vial of liquid speed to Ollie. "Methadrine?" I asked. It took less than thirty seconds for the liquid speed to kick in as I felt my body tingle and my heart begin to race.

"No thanks, I don't use that stuff, I'm on a natural high," Ollie responded with a smile.

"Do you think this stuff happens a lot, Ollie? You know, satellites falling out of the sky with weapons grade material in it?" I asked.

"Shit, this is nothing, David, compared to some of the stuff I know about. When you have a Q-clearance like you and I have, you have open access to the Situation Room, and that's where all the big, top secret stuff takes place," Ollie explained.

"You mean it gets worse than this?" I asked as I scanned our surroundings to make sure we were still alone.

"Man, brother, this is child's play compared to some of the real nuclear warheads that have been lost by us, the Russians, the Chinese, and the British," Ollie explained.

"Are you kidding me?" I responded, not wanting to believe what I was now being told.

"Nope, the USS Scorpion and its warheads have been 10,000-feet beneath the Atlantic since 1968, and the Russians are leaving atomic litter everywhere. The Komsmolets leaked Plutonium at the bottom of the Norwegian Sea. The Russian K-8 sub sank southwest of the UK in 1970. They've got a Russian Sentinel ship guarding the Uranium-rich wreckage. We monitor that with our spy satellites," Ollie explained with a grin.

"You've got to be kidding me, Ollie. Do the American people know about any of this?" I asked.

"Man, please. Hell, in 1961, a spiraling American B-52 Bomber dropped a nuke over North Carolina. The bomb shattered but failed to detonate. Its Uranium core is still sitting somewhere in waterlogged farmland. We lost two nuclear cores from a B-47 when it disappeared over the Mediterranean Sea in 1956. We never recovered those either," Ollie continued to explain. "Then, of course, there is the A-4-E Sky Hawk Jet that accidentally rolled off one of our aircraft carriers near Japan in 1956 and sank with a nuclear baby on board. There's also the C-124 transport plane that jettisoned two, still unrecovered, nukes over the sea just off the east coast in 1957. But the best one is the eleven-foot Mark-15 that is one hundred times more powerful than the bomb that we dropped on Hiroshima, that's been lying off our coast since a midair crash in 1958. Guess where it's at?" Ollie asked.

"Where?" I asked with a sick feeling in my stomach.

"You're gonna love this, David. It's classified as 'Irretrievably Lost' by the military. But it sits in shallow waters near Tybee Island, just off the coast of Georgia. The authorities claim its safe, but I read reports from not only experts, but also a report from the guy that loaded the bomb onto the plane; they all say the bomb is very much alive and its Uranium filling is there for anyone who wants to go get it," Ollie explained.

"Yeah, well it won't be me," I responded in disgust.

"Those are not the worst of it, David. We're still missing ten suitcase nukes that were designed to be carried by one person. They came up missing in Europe at the end of World War II. We have just recently gotten a lead on a couple of those. Our boys are following up on that lead as we speak," Ollie explained.

"I was trained on those weapons," I commented. "You can detonate one of those in less than thirty-minutes. The Seals call them Samsonite Gorillas," I explained with a grin on my face.

"Yeah, I read a CIA report on the ten that were missing, but you don't know about the one-hundred-plus suitcase nukes that the Russians are missing, do you?" Ollie asked with a serious look on his face.

"Holy shit! Does the President know about that?" I asked.

"Sure does, but what's he gonna do about it? Not a damn thing," Ollie explained. "The Russians promise all their bombs are accounted for."

"Come on, Ollie, let's get moving. We've been standing here way too long," I explained as I quickly applied more of my black and gray camouflage face paint to my hands, face, neck, and ears. Moving slowly, we began our long trip down the mountain.

Day Two:
Looking at my watch, it was almost 4:20 p.m. Ollie and I had built ourselves a hiding spot that covered us with brush, ground foliage, and tree branches.

It happened early this morning, at almost 7:30 a.m. Chinese ground troops equipped with military helicopters and gunships began to secure the top of the mountain. They were now moving by foot up the sides of the Dandong Mian Jiang Mountain. There was no doubt about it. They were searching for either debris or for us. Either way it was impossible for us to move without being seen. So we hid, waiting for the cover of nightfall to aid us in our escape.

* * * * * * *

Day Two, 9:30 p.m.:
Giving Ollie a small nudge on the shoulder, I nodded my head. Nodding back at me, acknowledging that he understood, we both very quietly stood up and began our descent down the mountain once again. Helicopters had been flying around us all day long, while some Chinese patrols had walked

within several feet of our hiding spot, never knowing we were right under their noses.

If nothing else, the Chinese had a lot of soldiers. It was a big mountain and they were covering most of it. Their campsites were spread out all over as we weaved our way, ever so quietly, past them. Everything was going well until 2:12 a.m. It was then things took a turn on us for the first time.

Ollie was walking about twenty-yards ahead of me, through the trees. The moon was full, which gave us light to maneuver. I heard someone speak in Chinese, I saw Ollie freeze and slowly raise his hands in a gesturing manner. I was surprised when I heard Ollie say something back to the unarmed soldier in Chinese. Moving quietly and off to the right, I carefully crept up on the soldier who was moving closer to my partner. The Chinese soldier, who was now close enough to see and realize that Ollie was not Chinese, grabbed what appeared to be a whistle that hung from his shirt pocket and quickly put it in between his lips to blow.

I could barely hear the shot as I fired my silenced .22 magnum automatic. The Cyanide-filled round struck the Chinese soldier in the left side of his head close to his temple. Staggering for only a second, his lifeless body fell straight to the ground.

Moving up next to Ollie, I whispered, "Move out, we're almost at the base of this mountain. Get us out of here before someone finds this body."

Without saying a word, the young Marine Captain never lost his composure. He simply nodded his head in agreement and moved out.

* * * * * * *

Day Three, 4:22 a.m.:
Reaching a small dirt road, we stopped.

"This is it," Ollie explained as he pulled off his small backpack and took out the walkie-talkie radio that was inside.

"This is what?" I questioned. "We're still a good mile and a half from the base of this mountain."

"Do you smell that?" Ollie asked.

"Yeah, what is it?" I asked as I began to look around in the darkness to make sure we were alone.

"Chicken shit," Ollie whispered softly.

"What?" I whispered back.

"There's a large chicken farm here. You're smelling chicken shit. Tourists come here and shoot chickens. That's what this mountain is best known for," Ollie explained as he keyed the microphone button on the side of the small radio and whispered something in Chinese. Waiting about ten seconds, Ollie tried again and spoke into the walkie-talkie. Within a few seconds, a voice spoke back to Ollie. Ollie turned off the radio and put it back into his backpack. "Our ride is on its way," Ollie explained.

"Our ride?" I questioned.

"Yes, our ride. They work for us, and believe me the Agency pays them very well," Ollie explained.

"Do you trust these people, Ollie?" I asked as my stomach began to feel queasy.

"Yes I do. I've worked with them once before. It's okay, Dave. Don't worry about it. Just trust me," Ollie explained as he tried to reassure me. "You alright?" he asked as he moved closer to my face and put his right hand on my forehead.

"I'll be alright," I explained as I placed a couple of drops of Methadrine under my tongue and took a long drink of water from my canteen.

"Man, you're getting sick," Ollie started to say as the small truck, loaded with vegetables and fruit, pulled up toward us. Waving his arms in the beams of the truck's headlights, the truck came closer to us and then stopped. "Come on," Ollie ordered.

Running up to the back of the truck, the driver jumped out and pulled a canvas tarp up and backward from the bed of the old pick-up. Jumping in, we both lay down as the old man, who looked to be in his early seventies, covered us up with tarp and began to cover us with fruits and vegetables. The old man then climbed back behind the wheel and turned the old truck around, taking us back out the same way he had come in.

It took us about ten minutes before the old truck came to a full stop. We had run right into a roadblock. Staying completely motionless, the Chinese soldier began to question the old Chinese farmer. He walked to the back of the old truck and began moving some of the bushels of vegetables around. Tightening my grip around the butt of my silenced .22 magnum, I placed my finger gently onto the trigger and waited. My heart raced with the combination of fear and adrenaline as the old farmer began to speak in a more angry tone to the Chinese guard. A few seconds later we heard the sound of the soldier's boots as he walked on the gravel dirt road and got back into his Jeep, laughing at the old man. Listening, I heard the truck door close, the gears in the stick shift transmission grind slightly as we began to move forward once again. A few minutes later, we felt the truck bouncing around on the dirt road, stop, and a smoother ride began as the old truck picked up speed. We were now on the paved highway at the base of the mountain. The sound of traffic and smell of exhaust fumes filled the air.

"Boy, that was close," I whispered to Ollie, who was lying right next to me with a grin on his face.

"Not really," Ollie whispered. "The old man is real good at this kind of work. The guard asked him what he was doing out here this early in the morning. The old man told him he was doing the same thing he has been doing every morning for the past forty years," Ollie explained with a laugh in his voice.

"Yeah, what's that?" I asked.

"Delivering feed grain to the farmer that owns the chicken ranch!" Ollie explained as we both began to relax a bit, now that we were off Dandong Mian Jiang Mountain.

"You're sweating real bad, David. You getting sick?" Ollie asked.

"How far is the ocean from here?" I asked as I tried to avoid Ollie's question.

"Not far, about an hour, maybe a bit longer," Ollie explained. "You're real good at avoiding questions," he continued.

"Really, I'm okay. I just feel sick to my stomach. It's probably too much Methadrine. I haven't eaten anything for almost five days now. Things moved pretty fast for me once I got the call to move and get to the airport," I explained.

"Yeah right, anything else?" Ollie asked, raising one eyebrow slightly.

"China," I said softly as my mind took me back to Cambodia and the POW camp. "I had a bad experience with a Chinese Major once," I explained.

"I know," Ollie explained as he shifted his weight to his right side to face me. "Major Dinh. I read about it while we were waiting for you to arrive at the Pentagon. It took a lot of guts for you to volunteer for this mission," Ollie explained. "I'm glad you did, though. You saved my ass back there when that Chinese soldier stood up out of nowhere and began talking to me," Ollie said with a sigh.

"No big deal. I wonder what he was doing out there alone and with no weapon?" I asked.

"He was taking a shit!" Ollie answered quickly.

"You serious?" I asked.

"Sure am. He was pulling up his pants when I walked by. Plus, I could smell it," he explained with a laugh. "Thank God you had that .22 magnum silenced," Ollie added with a more serious look on his face.

"It's a good weapon. I used it a lot in Vietnam. You ever use one?" I asked.

"No, not me. I'm more into the intelligence part of the Agency."

"Oh really, and what do you call a guy like me, stupid?" I asked with a grin.

"No, I call you dangerous. You've got big cojonés. That's why we leave all of the Cloak & Dagger stuff to guys like you. Thanks, David. I thought I was dead meat. I knew I couldn't use the mac-10. It would have been way too loud and that would have gotten us both captured," Ollie explained.

"Not me, brother," I responded with a grin as I moved my left arm slightly, so Ollie could see the Cyanide capsule that was still taped to my wrist.

"You would have taken it, wouldn't you?" Ollie asked.

"You bet I would have. The Chinese are not very nice when it comes to torture. But then again, neither was I," I explained as the truck made a full stop, and then made a sharp right hand turn.

Looking at Ollie, we both smiled at the same time. The smell of the ocean and the sound of her waves coming onto the shore was music to our ears. We were both Seal team trained. Once in the water, we would disappear from sight. The truck came to a full stop. The old Chinese driver got out of the truck and spoke softly in his native tongue. Saying something back to the old man, Ollie whispered to me.

"We're at the ocean, but there are too many people around. We'll have to wait for nightfall. He said he is going to set up his fruit and vegetable stand right here to maintain his cover. So relax, brother, we're almost home," Ollie explained.

Early Morning, Day Four, 12:01 a.m.:

I had to give the old Chinese farmer credit. He had been out here at the beach now for thirteen hours straight selling almost all of his fruits and vegetables. He also talked his way through five different policemen and three different military patrolmen. All of who stopped to question the elderly farmer, asking why he and his truck were still parked out here at this late hour of the night. Once he explained that his wife of fifty-three years had died this morning and that his heart was broken over the loss of his beloved wife, they would pat him on the back and tell him they were sorry. They would then leave him alone to grieve. It worked each and every time over the past eight hours. The old man was slick. There was no doubt about it.

Pulling back the canvas tarp after the old man had given us the all clear signal, Ollie thanked the old man for his help and we quickly ran across the sandy beach to the large sharp rocks at the water's edge.

Pulling off our backpacks, Ollie quickly pulled out the small two-way radio he had used at the mountain to call the old man. Pulling the antenna out, Ollie quickly unscrewed it, reached into the top flap of his backpack, and began to cut away at the stitching with his Kabar survival knife.

Pulling the thin aluminum sheet of round metal out from between the two layers of nylon, Ollie set the center of it on his knee and pushed the metal, gently forming it into a half-dish shape. He then took the wire that was attached to the back of the metal dish and pushed the male end of it into the hole that once held the antenna.

"What the fuck?' I asked as I watched the intelligence officer work his magic.

"The Navy has a sub about three miles off shore. There are Seals in the water about a half-mile offshore. They come out every night around eleven and wait until just before sunrise before they go back to the safety of their submarine. They're waiting for our signal to come pick us up," Ollie explained, as he faced the cone section of the metal dish out toward the water and began keying the microphone button, sending a Morse code signal to the Seals letting them know we were ready for pickup.

"Hot damn," I whispered as I looked around in the dark to make sure our position was covered. "I'm teamed up with James Bond!"

"Why do you think they call us the Central Intelligence Agency?" Ollie asked with a broad smile on his face. "Key word, my friend, is intelligence. That's why we're in the spy game, remember?" Ollie asked.

Turning to my left, I rolled over onto my knees and threw-up. My head was beginning to throb, my stomach was on fire, and I couldn't hide it from my partner any longer.

"You're contaminated with radiation! You lying mother fucker. I'll signal the sub so they'll be ready to put us into decontamination. Why did you lie to me, David? We're suppose to be partners," Ollie asked as he moved closer to me and began to rub my back and shoulders.

"I really don't think its radiation poisoning, Ollie. But it's better to warn them now, so we don't contaminate the whole sub," I explained as I regained my composure.

Hearing the Morse code clicking sound come through the speaker of the radio, Ollie pulled out his small pen-light flashlight and cupped his hand around the bulb end of it, and blinked the light out toward the ocean three times. Waiting ten seconds, he repeated the signal once again. Seeing a tiny light flash back at us from out in the vast darkness of the ocean, we sat quietly and waited.

"They're on their way to pick us up, brother," Ollie explained. "They've got our location now."

"Secure that biohazard container onto your body, Ollie. For God's sake don't lose it out there in the ocean," I said as I gave him a friendly nudge with my right arm.

"Wouldn't that be a real bitch to explain?" Ollie asked with a chuckle.

Within two minutes, four members of Seal team Four ran their rigid inflatable boat up onto the sandy beach, right in front of us. Two of the camouflaged Seals jumped out of the rubber raft with fully automatic assault weapons ready to defend us if a Chinese patrol should happen to pass by. One Seal kept full control of the outboard motor engine and the fourth Seal jumped out to help us get on board.

"Where's the Uranium?" the Seal team leader asked.

"Right here," Ollie said quickly as he patted the hazardous material container that was secured to his lower back, in a nylon harness. "We're contaminated," Ollie said quickly as we climbed into the inflatable boat and sped away into the blackness of the night.

"We expected that. So don't worry, our medical officer is standing by to treat you," the team leader shouted back so we could hear him over the sound of the outboard motor.

Bouncing up and down in the boat as each wave hit the bow caused me to throw-up once again. There wasn't much coming out of me, but what little did come out, was liquid and rancid tasting.

"He's the one that pulled the core out?" the team leader asked.

"Yeah, we couldn't get to the brain cell though," Ollie explained.

"What!" came the response from the Seal team leader. "You guys left it behind?"

"Yeah, but don't worry, my partner dumped a half gallon of Sulfuric Acid in the computer brain cell compartment," Ollie shouted.

"Hoo yah," was all that was said by the team leader.

Three miles off shore we reached the Navy's nuclear powered submarine that was waiting silently for us in the darkness. Watching it pop up to the surface from the cover of the sea was nothing short of awesome. Coming to the surface caused such a big wave to form and rush toward us, that it almost overturned our small boat.

This was the first time I had ever seen a real submarine up close and this one was huge. She was the SSBN-601 Robert E. Lee. It was one of the first five George Washington Class Nuclear Submarines ever built. She carried 16-Polaris nuclear missiles on board, each with a range of 1,500-miles. She and her crew were now risking their lives to save ours. Pulling up to her side, we quickly climbed up the rope ladder that was thrown down to us.

Climbing to the top, the Seal team leader spoke first. "They think they may be contaminated, sir," he said quickly to the captain of the ship.

Seal teams are never on board a nuclear sub. Once a nuclear submarine leaves port, it never ever comes back up to the surface until it reaches port once again. They have a ninety-day patrol cycle and never surface for the full ninety days they are out to sea. It was obvious the captain of this sub was very uneasy about bringing his ship to the surface and having the seven-man Seal team, Ollie, and I on board.

"Sink the raft, Master Chief. Strip down completely naked, men, and leave everything you have on deck, that includes weapons. Where's the Uranium core and brain cell?" the captain asked quickly as we stripped down naked.

"Right here, sir," Ollie explained as he pulled off the nylon harness and set it down on the deck of the sub.

One of the Navy corpsmen carefully picked up the harness and quickly placed it into a larger biohazard container. As soon as he did, he took it below deck.

"We couldn't get the brain cell out, sir," Ollie explained as we ran toward the hatch and began to climb down into the submarine.

"And?" the captain asked calmly.

"Melted it, sir," Ollie answered.

"Good, down the hatch people, move, move, move!" the captain shouted as we climbed down and into the top hatch that was located in front of the coning tower.

"Secure the hatch! Take us to 350-feet XO and get us the hell out of here. Get these men to sickbay so Mr. Decker can check them out," the captain ordered as we felt the Robert E. Lee descend back into the depths of darkness.

As I followed two of the Navy sailors to sickbay, my naked body trembled from being on top of the sub in the cold night air. It felt good though because inside I was burning up. Once in sickbay, Ollie and I lay quietly in the medical examination room as the hospital corpsman began to examine me.

He was Chief Petty Officer Ray Decker. He was twenty-eight years old, had brown hair, stood five-feet, ten-inches tall, and was a slender 160-pounds. Looking up at the ceiling, I could hear the mild humming sound of the submarine's hull and engine system. My head was pounding.

"Oh, man," I whispered to Ray Decker as he tried to talk to me. "Just shoot me will ya, Doc, and get it over with," I muttered as my eyes closed. The darkness came quickly as I drifted off into the gray haze of my inner mind.

* * * * * * *

Day eight, 8:36 a.m.:
Opening my eyes, I blinked several times as I tried to focus my thoughts and clear my head.

"Welcome back," Ollie greeted as I turned my head to the left and saw him sitting next to me.

"Hey, partner," I replied as I began to sit up. "What time is it?" I asked.

"You mean what day is it?" Ollie answered as he reached up and gently pulled me back down onto my back. "You don't want to try to get up just yet, my friend. Let Ray get all of those IV tubes out of your arms first," Ollie explained.

"Who's Ray?" I asked as I raised my arms and looked at the IV tubes taped to them.

"Ray Decker, he's the medical corpsman and the only medical officer on board this ship. You asked him to shoot you and get it over with when they first got us on board. These sailors are lucky to have him on board as their hospital corpsman. He really cares about the health of every man on board. He sat right here in this tiny room with you for two days until he was sure you were going to be alright," Ollie explained.

"He must have been in Vietnam," I said with a smile. "How bad was it? I'm feeling pretty good right now," I explained.

"Well, you were right, it wasn't radiation contamination. Ray said he's shocked you didn't get a good dose of it, climbing over top of the core like you did. That little trick with the candles worked. What you had was something called the Swine Flu. Doc said the only thing that kept you on your feet was all of the Methadrine you're always taking," Ollie explained.

"Yeah, well I feel pretty good right now. I am thirsty though. I wonder if they have any Pepsi on board?" I asked just as the medical officer and captain walked in.

"Good morning, gentlemen. How are you feeling?" the captain asked with a smile.

"A lot better, sir. Thank you for your help. I was feeling pretty rough for a while," I explained.

"Well, you look a lot better now than you did when you first came on board. My medical officer kept you under a pretty close watch," the captain explained proudly.

"Yes, sir, there's a real bad outbreak of the Swine Flu in the United States right now. From what we hear, a lot of people are dying from it. You're a very lucky young man. Another day or two and you probably wouldn't have made it without immediate medical attention," the Chief Petty Officer explained with a serious look on his face.

"The good Lord takes pretty good care of me, sir. I really do appreciate your help, Doc," I explained once again.

"As the hospital corpsman and Chief Petty Officer of this ship, it's my duty to warn you, if you keep taking that Methadrine like its candy, you're going to end up killing yourself," Ray explained with a very serious look on his face.

"Understood, sir, thanks again for your help," I answered as I reached out and shook his hand.

"You're welcome," he answered with a firm handshake. "Feeling hungry?" he asked with a grin.

"Yes, sir, more thirsty than hungry," I replied with a smile.

"Well then, let's get you unhooked and see about getting some good ole Navy submarine chow into you. That should perk you up," Ray explained as he began to remove the IV tubes and catheter from my body.

"Got any Pepsi, sir?" I asked.

"No, that we don't have. But we will get you fed. I'm sorry, boys, but you'll be with us for another twenty-eight days. You're lucky we picked up the message from the Pentagon to break our patrol cycle and pick up the Seal team from the Carrier USS Coral Seas. You're stuck on board with us now until we reach port at the end of our ninety-day patrol. We have plenty to do, so welcome to the Navy, boys," the captain explained with a grin as he turned and left the medical station.

"He is kidding, right?" I asked as I looked at Chief Petty Officer Decker.

"Nope, he was real upset when we dropped our wire to pick up our messages and found out we had to surface for this operation. We never surface once we leave port. Once we submerge, we stay under until we return to port. But hey, don't worry, I've got a lot for you to do," Ray explained with a grin. "Ever clean a nuclear warhead?" he asked jokingly.

* * * * * * *

Debriefing was held in the Pentagon. It took five hours and ten minutes to complete. It was then my boss, the Director of the Central Intelligence Agency, told me the President of the United States had raised my status. I was an Elite Covert Black Operations Agent now.

"Now," I thought to myself as I boarded our Agency Learjet for my flight back to Michigan, "Thing's might get a little more interesting." Boy was I right...

USS Robert E. Lee SSBN-601
1971 Photo courtesy of Raymond Decker

Chief Petty Officer Raymond "Doc" Decker (right)
receiving his "Submarine Dolphins"
from Captain aboard the USS Robert E. Lee

Chapter Eleven
Bent Spear

Sitting in the Situation Room, I tried to figure out how to gain deeper access into the Pentagons top-secret computer system.

"Hello, David, what are you doing here?" Ollie asked as he turned on the heavy-duty paper shredder and began to shred a bunch of documents that were stamped, "Top Secret."

"I'm trying to learn more about a Russian Colonel that I had a run-in with in Cambodia. I just can't figure out how to gain deeper access into this system," I explained as I tapped gently on the keyboard.

"Let me show you," Ollie offered as he set down the stack of documents and walked over to where I was sitting. Reaching over my shoulder he typed in the words, "Sandman, The Haunted Storm." As soon as he pressed the Enter button a whole new computer network opened up to me.

"Sandman, the Haunted Storm?" I questioned with raised eyebrows as I looked up at Ollie.

Patting me on the shoulder, Ollie smiled and went back to shredding his stack of papers. "Yeah, your team named you Sandman, but here at the Pentagon, the big brass in the War Room gave you the second code name. It's fitting," Ollie explained with a grin.

"Funny," I said as I searched for the name Colonel Kalashnikov. "Son of a bitch," I whispered as I read the information that had just popped-up on the computer screen.

"What?" Ollie asked as he finished shredding the last handful of documents and walked back over to see what I was looking at.

"It says here that my old buddy Boris is more than a KGB Colonel. His family owns and manufactures the Kalashnikov assault rifles. I never put his name together with the AK-47 rifle," I explained.

"Yeah, his family is big in Russia. They're at the top of the food chain in our books. Look at this baby," Ollie explained as he touched a computer key and a three-dimensional picture appeared on the screen. "That's their latest model assault rifle. The AK-74-M complete with grenade launcher," Ollie explained. "You planning on seeing old Boris again, are you?" Ollie explained with a curious expression on his face.

"One day, Ollie, one day I'm going to look him in the eyes and kill him."

"Really? Well, then you're gonna really love this," Ollie explained as he gently tapped the computer key again. Looking at me, Ollie waited for my reaction.

Trying hard not to show any emotion I looked over at Ollie. "That's my name," I said calmly, as I began to feel sick to my stomach.

"He talks about you a lot. You, my dear friend, are the only one that ever got away from him. He's taking it real personal, even though it was Major Dinh and Colonel Ky that you actually escaped from. We have at least a hundred hours of tape-recorded phone conversation of Boris talking to high-ranking KGB members and government officials. Your name always seems to come up in most of his conversations. You've become his best adversary. Now that you know about it the betting will begin," Ollie explained with a smile that went from ear to ear.

"Betting?" I asked.

"Yeah, the people here, and some of them at Langley, place bets on us when we go out on covert operations. Not just you or me, but any of our Black Op's people. I think that it stinks myself. I would never bet against any of our people, but these wanna-be desk jockeys have nothing better to do. Anyway, I'll catch you later, David. I've got some things that I have to attend to. Take care, partner, I'll see you later," Ollie said as he got up, patted me on the back, and left the room.

Turning my attention back to the computer screen, I couldn't believe what I was being made privy to. I spent the next six hours reading about Fidel Castro, the Hong Kong Triad, German War Criminals, Area 51 in Nevada, but the most frightening was what I had spent the last three hours reading. Al Qaeda and Taliban Terrorist splinter cells were growing stronger around the world. The Russian's however, had made their move against us right after World War II. Soviet espionage had already placed over 250 Russian spies in American Federal Government Agencies, in Hollywood, and into our news media. KGB Major General Oleg Danilovich Kalugin was a key player in this well planned move against the United States.

"Excuse me, young man, but would you like some coffee or something? You've been in here all day," Carla asked with a smile.

Carla stood five-feet, ten-inches tall, had graying brown hair, brown eyes, and was in her mid-forties. She was a very sweet, no-nonsense lady, who spent countless hours locked away in this small, top-secret office. Looking at my watch, I looked at Carla and sighed.

"I didn't realize how long I had been in here, Carla, I'm sorry," I explained.

"Oh heavens no," she responded in a motherly tone of voice. "David, you can stay in here for as long as you want. I was just getting worried about you, that's all."

"Carla, it says here that Russia has over 250 spies that are already working in our Federal Agencies, media, and in Hollywood. Why don't we do something about this?" I asked.

"Honey, if we knew who they were, we would. We're working on it, but they're dug in really deep. That's why we call them Moles," she explained as I switched off the computer and rubbed my eyes. "You, young man, need to take some motherly advise from this old mom. Because of who you are and what you do, be very careful who you trust. If you slip, if you make one mistake, you're dead! Understand?"

"Yes mom," I said smiling. "It's just a real scary thought to think that they know most of our moves before we even make them," I explained as I stood up and stretched my body that was aching from sitting for so long.

"Would you do me a favor?" Carla asked with a straight face.

"Name it, pretty lady. If I can do it for you, then I'll do it."

"You can do things that the rest of us can't. If you should happen to find any of these Moles or if you even think that someone is spying against us, do what the Sandman does best and put 'em to sleep, would you?" Carla asked calmly.

Walking up to Carla, I leaned forward and gently kissed her on the forehead. "Count on it, pretty lady, count on it," I answered coldly.

"David, I'll send you a very special computer system and have our people deliver and install it at your home. You're gonna need to do a lot of research into our files, so that you're up to date on what's going on behind the scenes. I will also download and encrypt a lot of our up-to-date material and data, so you can read it at home. You can decrypt it by putting this code next to your password," Carla explained as she went back to her small office to write down my new password. Handing me the piece of paper with the two new code words written on it, she smiled and then got serious.

"Only you and I know this code word. Do not, and I mean never ever, tell anyone else what you're decryption code is. Don't tell Ollie, Special Agent Eckland, not even the President of the United States. That decryption code word is between the two of us, for our eyes only. Also be very careful when you use it. Don't let anyone see it when you enter it into the computer to decrypt a disc, understand?" Carla asked.

"Yes, ma'am, I understand. Can I ask you two questions?" I asked.

"Anytime, David, what do you need to know?" she asked.

"Ollie told me that a lot of people here, and at Langley, bet on some of us. You know, whether or not we'll fail or succeed on a mission, do you bet on us?" I asked seriously as I looked into Carla's eyes.

"Never!" she answered sharply. "You're not the only one that is out there risking your life, son. We have people doing 'wet work' and covert operations all across the globe. I take keeping my country safe very seriously. You men and women are like my own children, and we are family, David. I don't bet against my own family," she explained without taking her eyes off of mine. She never looked away as she replied. That told me she was telling the truth.

"We have women doing what I do?" I asked, remembering that Kathy had told me she applied with the Agency to be an assassin and was told women were not allowed into that area of Black Op's.

"Yes, and what's the next question?" Carla asked now smiling once again.

Holding up the piece of paper with my new decryption code on it, I asked, "Where do you guys come up with these code names? First the big boys added 'The Haunted Storm,' to my name and now you come up with this one."

"Listen, young man, we try very hard to come up with code names that no one else would ever think about, especially someone who is a spy from another country. We also try to find or pick a name or series of names that fit the profile of the person it's being given to."

"President Johnson was in the War Room when Black Operation Team One, your team David, had just successfully completed a mission in Laos. As I recall, you were the youngest member of Team One and they picked you as team leader. When the War Room was notified that your operation had been successfully completed, one of our military generals looked at the President and asked, 'so what do you think of this young kid now, sir?' The President whistled softly and said, 'there's a storm brewing inside that young boy from Michigan.' The Major, who was also in the room with them added, 'the kid's haunting those commie bastards'. So there you have it, 'The Haunted Storm' became the Sandman's Pentagon code name," Carla explained.

"No kidding? Johnson was there, huh? Okay, I'll go for that, but how about you and your choice?" I asked holding the paper between my two fingers and waving it back and forth.

"Are you telling me that it doesn't fit you, Mr. Sandman?" Carla asked as she raised her eyebrows and crossed her arms across her chest in a motherly fashion.

Thinking about it for a minute, I handed Carla the piece of paper. "I would rather not have this laying around my home. I'll remember it," I answered.

"Well?" she asked again.

"Yes, I guess it does fit. See ya later, Ma," I said with a grin as I left the Situation Room and headed back home to Michigan.

The flight from Washington D.C. back to Michigan was a quiet one. I used the Agency Learjet, but couldn't help but wonder, did these people really like me as a person or were they simply using me because they were afraid of me? Did Kathy deliberately lie to me or did the Agency simply lie to her so they could put her talents to work in the intelligence gathering area of the CIA?

"I guess it will all come out in the wash sooner or later," I thought to myself as I laid my head back on the headrest of my seat and looked out through the side window of the plane at the ground below. "God, I hate heights," I whispered out loud as I closed my eyes and felt a sudden chill run up my spine.

* * * * * * *

I had only been home from the Pentagon for 72-hours when I heard my doorbell ring. Walking to my front door, I looked at my watch and smiled. It was 12:00 and a beautiful Michigan fall afternoon. "I'll bet that it's Tara," I said out loud to myself as I opened the front door of my home.

"Hello, sir, I'm Special Agent Brandi Trautner, Central Intelligence Agency," she explained as she opened her leather wallet to show me her credentials. "Carla sent me to install your new computer system. May I come in, sir? I will need you to show me where you will want the system set up," Brandi explained smiling.

"You can come in, only if you call me Dave," I answered.

"You got it, Dave," Brandi replied as I took her to my den and showed her where my large oak wood desk was. Brandi had jet-black hair, brown eyes, and stood five-feet, eleven-inches tall. She was tall for a woman, and appeared to be in her late twenties, but she had a slender-frame build. She also had no trouble carrying the new Apple computer system into my den, all by herself.

"Which one of these telephones is your direct line to the Agency? I will need to use that phone line to tie this new system into," she explained as I pointed out which telephone to connect to.

Brandi was sexy in a plain sort of way. She wore very little make-up and her coveralls with the Radio Shack logo on the back made my mind wonder as to what she really looked like underneath.

It took Brandi almost four hours to get the new system up and running. "David, this system has a lot of fail safe, special security, and self destruct equipment built into it. On the outside it looks like a regular everyday computer system. I can assure you that it is not. It is loaded with our state of the art technology. If someone tries to access this system without the proper security codes needed to do so, it will automatically shutdown. If anyone tries to tap into it, it will automatically burn its own circuit board out and render itself useless. If anything happens to it, do not call Langley or your supervisor Agent Eckland. Call Carla and Carla only. She will contact me and I will come back here right away to either fix or replace it.

This system gives you direct access to the data bank system in Langley and also serves as a direct line to the Situation Room, and to Carla," Brandi explained in a now more serious manner.

"Okay, so do I have computer discs that have the information stored on them or how exactly does this work? I'm kind of new at this," I explained.

"Dave, with this system you can send e-mail letters, notes, memo's, or simply type in whatever it is that you're looking for," Brandi explained.

"Here, let me show you. What is it that you would like to get data on?" she asked as she turned on the system and looked at me.

"Lets try Chechen Rebels for starters," I asked as I looked at the computer screen.

"What is your access code, Dave, I will need that before I can gain access," Brandi asked as she looked down at the keyboard to type it in.

Pulling my new .357 Baretta out from in between my lower back and my belt, I cocked the hammer as I pointed it at Brandi's face.

"On the floor, belly down, right now or I'll blow your brains all over that computer," I ordered coldly.

"Wait a minute, Dave," Brandi said in a panicked voice as she raised her hands into the air and lowered herself to the floor of my den. "Whatever I did wrong, it's a mistake. I can correct it," she explained in a now more paranoid tone of voice.

Placing my Beretta at the base of her head I quickly patted Brandi down to make sure that she wasn't armed.

"Roll slightly to your left and keep your hands stretched straight out and above your head," I explained as Brandi turned slightly to her left.

Popping open all of the snaps that held the front of her coveralls closed, I reached inside and pulled out the Browning automatic pistol I had felt secured to her waist.

"You have three seconds to tell me who sent you here or I swear to God I'll cut out your liver and show it to you before you die," I explained coldly as I looked deep into Brandi's eyes.

"Please don't kill me, I swear to God Carla sent me, please, please don't kill me," she begged as her eyes filled with tears and her body began to tremble.

Rolling Brandi completely over and back onto her stomach, I smiled. I knew that she was one of ours, but she should have never asked me for my security code access numbers. It would be a good lesson for her and I was actually enjoying this. Sitting down at my desk, I picked up my Agency phone and called Carla at the number that she had given me a few days earlier. Using my voice recognition code, Carla got on the line.

"Hello, David, did my girl get you installed all right," Carla asked cheerfully.

"Hi, Carla, I have a pretty young lady laying spread eagle on the ground next to me. She said that you sent her, but then she asked me for my computer access code numbers to show me how to boot-up the new system. You didn't send her, did you?" I asked trying hard not to laugh.

"Oh my, David, she's one of my girls, is she alright?" Carla asked in a concerned tone of voice.

"Awe damn, I knew it, she's a spy," I said quickly looking over at Brandi for a response.

"Oh shit," Brandi said softly as she lowered her hands and covered her face with them.

"Don't scare her, young man, do you hear me?" Carla scolded.

"Brandi, mom wants to talk to you. You can get up now, it's okay," I explained laughingly, as I handed Brandi the telephone.

Placing the telephone receiver to her ear, I stood back and listened to the one sided conversation.

"Hello, ma'am, I screwed up... yes, ma'am... yes I know, ma'am... no ma'am, I'm alright... I think that I wet my pants though, when he threatened to cut out my liver and show it to me," Brandi explained as she placed one hand over her face in embarrassment. "No, ma'am, I don't know who he is. All that you said was to install the new system at this address."

Now I felt like a total jerk! What started out to be fun, didn't seem funny any more.

"Yes, ma'am, here he is," Brandi explained as she handed me the telephone.

"Hello, Carla," I said calmly as I looked at Brandi, feeling like a total piece of shit.

"You threatened to cut out her liver?" Carla asked with humor in her voice.

"Can I tell her now?" I asked.

"Tell her, tell her what? The poor girl sounds scared to death," Carla explained.

"Yes, ma'am, she passed the test," I said, as Brandi looked up at me with her mouth open. "No, Carla, she showed absolutely no signs of being afraid and she never once mentioned your name or any sensitive information. My report will show that she passed this part of her security test with a one hundred percent rating," I explained with a professional look and a smile as I looked over at Brandi and winked.

Brandi now had both hands on her cheeks and was smiling as she whispered, "This was a test?"

"David, you're something else," Carla said as I nodded my head 'yes' in answer to Brandi's question. "I owe you one, kiddo, she is a good agent. I'd sure hate to lose her. You gave her back her dignity. I owe you one, I'll talk to you soon," Carla explained as she hung the phone up on her end.

"No, she was joking about wetting her pants," I said as I continued to talk into the empty phone line. "I'll make her dinner while she shows me how to use the new system, and then I'll send her on her way. Yes, ma'am, I'll talk to you soon," I explained to an empty phone as I hung it up and smiled at Brandi.

"You lied to keep me from being fired. Why did you do that?" Brandi asked with a slight tilt of her head.

"Did you learn anything?" I asked calmly.

"Boy, did I," Brandi replied with a strange look in her eyes.

"Well then, that's all that matters. Come on, you can use my shower to get cleaned up. I've got some clothes that will look great on you," I explained as I walked Brandi up to my guest room and showed her where the shower was.

While she was in the shower cleaning up, I laid out a pair of my camouflaged army jungle pants, a brand new pair of my Fruit of the Loom underwear, a new pair of socks and one of my blue pullover Navy T-shirts that had Seal team One written in gold on the left front chest section of the shirt. Going back down stairs, I pulled two Porter House steaks out of my refrigerator and went downstairs to my basement to fire up my grill.

I was just finishing cutting up the lettuce for our salad when Brandi came walking down stairs with a smile on her face.

"How do I look?" she asked jokingly as she struck a pose for me.

Looking at the Special Agent, I noticed that the coveralls covered up a lot of Brandi's assets.

"Want to know the truth?" I asked as I looked at her and shook my head from side to side.

Nodding her head 'yes' she said, "Be honest."

"Alright then, you look good enough to eat!" I answered with a grin, as I turned around to flip the steaks over on the grill. "What would you like to drink?" I asked without turning around.

"Got any Pepsi?" Brandi asked.

Smiling, I stepped over to the refrigerator that was behind my bar and pulled out two bottles of cold Pepsi. Opening them up, I gave one to Brandi, along with a glass of ice.

"Listen, no matter whatever happens, or how scared you may feel inside, never ever show the enemy that you're scared. If you do, he will use your own fears against you. Remember this, no matter how bad it gets, what is going to happen, is going to happen anyway, no matter whether you're crying, begging, or spitting in their face in defiance. Besides, there's always a guy like me that's going to be called in to rescue you," I explained as I smiled at Brandi and winked.

"Thanks for the advise, I'll remember it, I promise. Now I understand what Carla just told me on the phone," Brandi explained as she took a drink of her Pepsi straight out of the long neck bottle.

"You lost me, what do you mean what Carla told you?" I asked with a curious look on my face.

"Carla asked me if you really did have me spread eagle on you floor? When I said 'yes ma'am,' Carla said, 'you're lucky, young lady, you've been screwed by the James Bond of our elite Black Operations Team'," Brandi explained smiling. "Are you really that dangerous, Mr. Navy Seal?" Brandi asked as she reached up with the first finger of her left hand and ran it across the section of her shirt that read, Seal team One, and then down her left breast, causing her nipples to pop up and press into the tight material of the shirt.

Looking at both of Brandi's firm breasts, I took in a deep breath of air and slowly let it out.

"Catsup or A-1 Steak Sauce?" I asked calmly as I looked up and into Brandi's eyes.

"How about whipped cream," she answered as she placed her lips over the end of the Pepsi bottle in a seductive gesture, and smiled.

"This was going to prove to be a long night," I thought to myself as I turned to pull the steaks off of the grill.

* * * * * * *

"There, that should do it," I said to myself as I tightened the last screw on my new dead bolt lock. I had just finished installing the new lock on the doors of my den. "Better to play it safe than be sorry later," I told myself as I looked up at the computer system that was now beeping.

My lustful thoughts toward Brandi were quickly shattered last night while we were eating. Finding out she was married brought me back to reality fast. That was the one thing I would not do. I was a lot of things but I would never mess around with a married woman, even if she was into 'whipped cream sex.' After we ate, I did get Brandi to explain to me how the new computer system worked. Explaining it down to each and every last detail. Of course we used her access code. She got a real laugh out of that.

Walking over to the computer, I sat down, picked up the telephone, and called Carla.

"Well, that was quick," Carla said, as she answered her end of the phone.

"You rang?" I asked jokingly.

"I'm sending you some data on a possible target. Memorize it, David, you might be the one going after this guy. I'll get back with you as soon as we know for sure. Please, David, stay close to the telephone. You'll understand once you read what I am sending you," Carla explained.

"I'm ready, Mom, I won't go anywhere until I hear from you," I replied as I hung up the phone and typed in my new access code: Sandman, the Haunted Storm, Death's Gatekeeper... pressing the Enter button three times, I smiled when I saw a picture of the Grim Reaper wearing his hooded cloak sitting on his Pale Horse.

"Boy, Ma, you're something else," I said out loud to myself as I began to laugh. The Grim Reaper had just pulled back his hood and revealed his face for the first time. It was my face that Carla had somehow programmed into the computer system. Pulling up his long black hood cloak, he then pulled out a silenced Beretta automatic pistol, pointed it at the screen, and pulled the trigger.

"Whoa!" I said softly as a whole new three-dimensional program appeared on the screen right before my eyes. It started with a map of Germany and then went to the town of Mannheim and the estate of a man named Klaus Gruber.

"Look at this," I said as I touched the key to move forward. Klaus Gruber was a self-made billionaire philanthropist, who was deeply involved with Islamic Militants, Chechen Rebels, and a terrorist group known only as Red Cell. His bank records showed that he was sending millions of dollars to groups that have been confirmed by the CIA, British MI6 Intelligence, and Israeli Mossad Intelligence, as terrorist.

"Holy shit!" I said out loud as I continued to read on. The Israeli Mossad captured a known Syrian terrorist who told Mossad Secret Service Agents, that Gruber was selling two suitcase-size nuclear weapons to the highest bidder. The weapons were American made.

"Son-of-a-bitch, these must be two of the ten weapons that came up missing right after World War II. Ollie told me about these and said that we were following up some real good leads," I reminded myself.

Getting up, I went to the kitchen and grabbed a cold Pepsi. It was going to be a long day. I have a lot of reading to do. "God, I love this shit! Butch, Chopper, where are you guys?" I said with a sigh as I headed back to my den to read.

* * * * * * *

153

It had been 76-hours since I had received the information on Gruber. Sitting at my desk, I drank Pepsi and ate Chocolate Mint Girl Scout Cookies while I watched Magnum P.I. on my new wide screen Sony television. I loved the way that Tom Selleck always managed to get under Higgins' skin. Frank Sinatra was also starring in this episode. He was playing the part of a New York Police Detective after the man who had raped and killed a little five-year old child, who just happened to be his niece.

"Get him, Frank," I said out loud to myself as the suspense began to build. Hearing my computer beep startled me. Looking at my computer screen, I waited for the message that Carla was about to send to me.

"Just received a message from PEOC. We have a green light. Meet me at my office ASAP – Scorpion One." was all that the message said.

"This is huge. Yes!!!" I shouted as I called my grandfather to let him know that I would be gone for a few days.

"PEOC, the White House, Presidential Emergency Operations Center! Hot damn, the President is ordering a hit, you just got to love him," I said as I shut down my computer system and headed to the Pontiac Airport, where I knew our Agency Learjet was waiting for me.

* * * * * * *

Sitting down at the Special Operations Group table, I looked at Carla and smiled.

"Scorpion One huh?" I asked with a grin on my face.

"President Johnson gave me that tag," Carla explained. "It was shortly after he had taken over the office of the President. There was a rumor going around the White House that said I was the one who ordered the hit on Oswald and Jack Ruby. Johnson was overheard telling the Secretary of Defense, 'that Bitch Carla is a fucking scorpion, she bites your ass and you're dead.' Of course, he was drunk at the time; he usually was," Carla explained calmly.

"A rumor can be far worse than any truth," I replied.

"Who said it wasn't true?" Carla asked as the Secretary of Defense and the CIA Director walked into the room and sat down across the table from us.

It seems as though Mom Carla was a lot more dangerous than I had anticipated.

Opening her briefcase, Carla pulled out some 8x10 photographs and handed them to us. "Gentleman, we received these photos less than an hour ago from the CIA Analysts that runs our GSES," Carla explained as she saw the look of confusion on my face. "That's our Global Satellite

Elimination System, David," she explained with a motherly look. Nodding my head, I said nothing.

We have been watching Klaus now for eight days. The one thing we know for certain is that he is usually at home and alone from Friday nights at 8:00 p.m., all the way until Monday morning at 6:00 a.m., at which time his housekeepers, cooks, maids, lawn and garden servants return to the villa to work. Our operative in Germany has been using a new system we call Bloodhound.

It's a small hand held dish scanner that looks for a flux in gamma radiation. This would indicate a high probability that a small nuclear weapon might be at the Gruber Estate. So far, we have picked up no sign that either of these weapons are at the Gruber home," Carla explained as the closed door to our security room opened up.

"I'm sorry to interrupt, but we haven't been able to contact Amanda for over 48-hours now."

"Ollie, please come in and have a seat," the CIA director asked. Closing the door behind him, Ollie walked over and sat down.

"Congratulations, I see that you've been promoted," I replied.

"So what are you saying, Major?" the Secretary of Defense asked.

Pausing to gather his thoughts for a moment, Ollie answered, "David may be going in alone. He also doesn't speak German, nor does he know his way around the area. I've worked with this man once before as you all know. He's real good, sir, but..."

"But what, Oliver?" Carla asked in a now concerned tone of voice.

"Ma'am, with all due respect, he will be walking around out there with his dick in his hand. Get him to Gruber's home and I know for a fact that the Sandman will do his thing, but getting him there may be a problem," Ollie explained as he looked over at me.

"What about Agent Eckland? She speaks four different languages, one of which is German?" my boss asked.

"Out of the question," Carla responded quickly as she looked over at Ollie.

"How long will it take for you to change your clothes Major?" Carla asked.

"Ma'am?" Ollie asked as he looked across the table and at the Secretary of Defense.

"What about El Salvador, Major?" The Secretary of Defense asked.

"No problem, I'll juggle it. It's a matter of guns or nuclear weapons, sir," Ollie explained.

Looking over at Carla, the Secretary of Defense sat back in his chair and crossed his arms. "Make the call, Carla," he said calmly.

"Alright, here is how we're going to do this. David, your job is to go with the Major to Germany. Go to your designated location and try to meet up with your contact there. If for some reason she does not show up, then you are to take Oliver with you. Stealth in and penetrate into the estate of Klaus Gruber. Use whatever means necessary and try to retract the information from Gruber; we need to know where those weapons of mass destruction are. Retrieve them if at all possible, David, and leave no witness behind that could link us to the invasion into Gruber's home.

Oliver, David is in charge. He will get you inside and protect you once he has secured the home. If Amanda doesn't show up, then it falls on you to access Gruber's mainframe system and get us a direct feed into it. We will download its entire data bank and then put this disc into the system that he may be connected to. Don't activate the virus until I tell you that we have downloaded successfully and our system is disconnected. God," Carla said as she looked around at all of us. "I can't imagine what would happen if we virused our own system," she said as she began to laugh out loud.

"Should we check on Amanda, ma'am?" Ollie asked.

"Hopefully, she is all right and you won't have to go in. If she does not show up, then it falls on you, Oliver, to download the system. Do not go to Amanda's home. It could be compromised and under surveillance. Do not jeopardize this mission. We will check on her through other means if she doesn't show up, and only after this operation is complete," Carla explained.

"David, draw whatever you're going to need and lets get this done. Good luck, gentlemen," the CIA Director explained as they all got up to leave.

"David, let me speak with you a moment, would you?" Carla asked. Waiting for everyone to leave the small conference room, Carla closed the door and looked at me in a serious way.

"Oliver is being groomed for a very special spot in our government. If Amanda fails to show, and Oliver has to go in with you, please keep a close eye on him, will you? He isn't trained the way you are," Carla explained. "Oh, by the way, kill Klaus Gruber, he must not escape!"

"Ah yes, Bond, James Bond, right?" I asked with a grin.

"Brandi told you, that little shit."

* * * * * * *

CIA Elite Operations
Code Name: Bent Spear
Target: Klaus Gruber
Location: Mannheim Germany

Taking the Agency Learjet, Oliver and I flew to Germany and landed at Ramstein Air Base. We were greeted there by Military Intelligence Officer Captain Neil Ford. Ramstein's Air Base was a focal point for our Agency in Europe. Ollie knew it like he knew the back of his hand. He had spent a lot of time here during the early part of his military career as an intelligence officer.

Dressed in pullover shirts, dress slacks, black slip on shoes, and a nylon wind breaker, Ollie and I got into the silver two-door BMW that was hidden under a tarp in one of the airplane hangers, and drove off the air base.

It was early morning Friday. I was suppose to meet with my German counterpart at noon. We had 4-hours to get there. I could only hope that Amanda Swisten was alright.

* * * * * * *

Sitting on the park bench of the Leipzig Zoo, I watched as Ollie stood off in the distance and threw shelled peanuts to the monkeys.

"I hate Germany," I said to myself. "This is where my Uncle Tommy and two of his teammates were killed during World War II. The only thing good about this place is that they have Pepsi," I muttered as I took a drink from my bottle of Pepsi, and looked at my watch. It was five-minutes to twelve and a beautiful, early fall day.

Acting as if I was reading the newspaper, I couldn't help but notice the beautiful blue eyed blonde, slowly making her way towards the bench I was sitting on. I couldn't help but feel sorry for her. She was walking with crutches and appeared to be in a lot of pain.

Sitting down next to me, she groaned and then leaned the two long wooden crutches down next to her, against the metal bench.

"I love it here," she explained as she looked across the sidewalk at the monkeys. "It is so peaceful."

She had just given me the first part of the code words that would identify us as agents to each other.

"The phone booth is leaking water," I replied as I looked over at her. "Are you alright? The Scorpion is worried about you," I explained.

"It was an accident, I went to cross the street and a young man on a scooter bike ran the red traffic light. He ran into me. I am glad he was not riding on a full size motorcycle," Amanda explained with a laugh and a long groan as she reached up to grab her right side.

"Ouch," I said with a sympathetic look.

"Yes, ouch is correct," she said in broken English. "I have a broken leg, five broken ribs, all on my left side, and a mild concussion. But I am here," she added with a pretty smile.

"Is there anything that I can do to help you?" I asked.

"No, no, I am fine now that I am out of that damn hospital. Four days there is five days too many, if you know what I am saying to you. Just get me into the Gruber home. I will get my job done," she explained with a determined look on her face.

Looking over at Ollie, I motioned for him to come over and join us. Walking over to us, Ollie sat down next to Amanda and smiled.

"Oliver, I did not recognize you. How are you my friend?" Amanda asked cheerfully.

"I'm well. Are you alright?" Ollie asked as he looked at Amanda's left leg in a cast.

"I will be fine, just help me to get into the house. I can take care of my end," she said with confidence.

"No, Amanda," I explained in a soft tone of voice so as to not draw any attention to us.

"Change of plans, you'll sit outside of the Gruber home, and back us up in case of any trouble. I will take Ollie in with me. He will work his magic on the computer system. How far is the Gruber home from here?" I asked.

"Not far. Come, I will show you," Amanda explained calmly.

Taking our BMW, Ollie drove us to the Gruber Estate. Growing up to hate the German people, I began to see them in a different light. Germany was indeed a beautiful country. The Autobahn was nothing less than an over size NASCAR racing track. If you were driving less than 100 miles-an-hour, you were going to slow. I was a long way from home, but I quickly began to realize that these people weren't any different than us. It wasn't there fault that Hitler was a madman.

"Up ahead, turn off here, Oliver," Amanda explained as she pointed at the exit up ahead. "Turn left and we go four more miles into the country."

Doing as Amanda directed him to do; Ollie pulled off at the exit and turned left. Four-miles down the road we made a right turn and drove into a wooded section of Mannheim, Germany.

Driving for another mile, we made a left turn onto a hard packed gravel road. "Up ahead, there are six estates, Gruber's is the last home on this road," Amanda explained with a very serious look in her eyes.

"Are you alright, Amanda?" I asked as I turned to look at her.

Reaching into her purse, Amanda pulled out a .22 magnum automatic pistol and screwed the long slender silencer on the barrel, cocking the hammer back, she answered, "This man is sick in the head. He wants to start another war! He does not need the money, yet he tries to sell these weapons that will start another war. We do not need men like Klaus Gruber in my country. One madman was enough," she explained.

Looking at my watch, I then looked up at Ollie.

"Pull into the driveway," I explained calmly as I reached into my jacket side pocket and pulled out my tiny glass vial of Methadrine. Placing two drops under my tongue, I looked over at Ollie and smiled. "Shall we see if he's home, partner?" I asked as Ollie pulled up to the tall, black cast-iron gates at the front of the driveway.

"It's your call, partner," Ollie answered, as he looked down the long driveway.

The big metal gates to the estate were already open. The long driveway snaked its way in through the forest of trees that sheltered the old rock mansion.

"Pull in and drive right up to the front door. I've got a plan," I explained.

"The gates were wide open. Klaus Gruber wasn't expecting any trouble," I told myself as we drove through the wooded trees and up to the large estate. The home was impressive. Its outer structure was made out of large rocks. It had white metal awnings and an old-style tile roof. Looking up I saw smoke coming out of the chimney. Pulling up to the front door, we opened our car doors. Looking at Amanda, I smiled.

"Watch our back, pretty lady. We'll be back shortly," I explained as I got out of the car.

Stepping to the back of the car, Ollie opened the trunk. Reaching in, I opened one of the suitcases we had placed inside.

Handing Ollie a 35mm Pentex Camera, I explained, "You're a photographer for People Magazine. Play along until we get him to a point that I can get close to him. As soon as that happens, I'll hit him with the stungun and then I'll check the house to make sure that we're alone."

"I'll follow your lead, partner. Just tell me when it's time for me to make my move," Ollie explained.

Grabbing my briefcase out of the trunk, we closed the trunk lid and walked up to the front door. Pushing on the gold button next to the large solid oak double doors, the doorbell rang.

"Nervous?" Ollie asked as he looked at the camera that now hung around his neck by a nylon black strap.

Pushing the doorbell once again, I replied, "I'm pumped."

Pushing the doorbell a third time, we heard footsteps and then the door opened. I was caught by surprise when I saw the young woman's face that had just answered the door. Smiling, I made my move.

"May I help you, gentleman?" she asked politely.

"Yes, ma'am," I replied calmly, as I reached up and handed her my business card. "I am David Hilton and this is my photographer Ken Wilson, we are here to do an interview with Mr. Gruber for the feature story of the up-coming December issue of People Magazine."

"People Magazine? From America, People Magazine?" she asked in a surprised tone of voice. "Mr. Gruber never mentioned this to me. Please come in and I will go and speak with him, he is in his study."

Stepping inside, the maid closed the door behind us and then went to go and talk with her employer.

"She isn't suppose to be here," Ollie whispered calmly.

The maid had sandy blonde hair, green eyes, stood five-feet, seven-inches tall, and was medium built. She couldn't be more than 27-years old. The inside of the house was unbelievable. It had crystal chandeliers, large wood beam ceilings, and was breathtaking to say the very least.

Looking straight ahead, I smiled and extended my right hand out when I saw Klaus walking down the long hall toward us.

"Mr. Gruber, it is such an honor to meet you, sir, you were expecting us, weren't you?" I asked politely.

"No, I wasn't," he said with a smile, as he reached out to shake my hand. Klaus Gruber wasn't a very big man. He stood five-feet, ten-inches tall, had blonde wavy hair and blue eyes. He was in his early fifties and medium built.

"Oh, sir, I'm sorry. We will leave and come back when you have the time. Our publisher had just hired a new public relations assistant. She must have confused our assignment with someone else's, it's too bad though, and we were going to put you on the cover of the December issue. We will try again later, sir, at another date. Maybe June or July," I explained calmly.

"Heavens no, come, come in and sit with me in my study. I have nothing to do today anyway. Besides, only a foolish man would turn away People Magazine," he said laughingly.

Walking down the long hallway, we went into the large study room. It had a leather sofa, two black leather recliner chairs, a small bar, and a large fireplace with a fire burning inside.

The left side of the room was lined with a bookshelf that was full of books. His large wooden desk sat at the back of the room and on top of the desk was a very large computer system.

"Please, gentlemen, have a seat. Would you like something to drink?" he asked politely.

"No, thank you, sir, maybe later. Are these paintings Picasso?" I asked as I looked up at the paintings hanging on the wall behind him.

Turning to look at his collection of priceless artwork, he began to point at each painting and explain who the artist was for each painting. Reaching into my back pants pocket, I quickly pulled out my stungun, pushed it into the side of his neck, and pulled the trigger. Counting to three, I pulled the gun away from his neck as he fell to the floor.

"In my briefcase, Ollie," I said quickly, as I pulled my .357 magnum Beretta out of my shoulder holster and cocked it. "Grab the roll of duct tape."

Leaving the study, I went straight up stairs. Starting at the back of the hallway, I worked my way forward checking each room one by one. Seeing that it was clear, I went back downstairs and then to the far back side of the house. Moving forward, I began my sweep, room to room. "So far, so good," I said to myself as I walked into the kitchen.

The maid was sitting at the kitchen table facing me, peeling potatoes. Looking up as I moved toward her, her eyes got wide, her mouth opened, but it was too late.

Pulling the trigger one time, all that she saw was the muzzle flash. The .357 magnum Rhino round bullet struck the maid in the mouth and blew the back of her head off. Pieces of her skull, hair, and flesh splattered a crimson red design onto the wall behind her as her hands flew upward and her body fell backward, forcing her chair to fall over with her and onto the marble floor below.

Turning quickly, I headed to the basement to check it. Reaching up, I grabbed the doorknob of the basement door and turned it. Nothing happened, it was locked. Feeling that the house was now secure I moved fast and went back to the study where Ollie was waiting on me with our boy Klaus Gruber.

"We're clear, brother, do your thing," I explained as Ollie turned and stepped up to the large desk. Picking up the telephone, he dialed a number and waited for someone to answer on the other end.

Ollie had duct taped Gruber and put him into a seated position in one of his leather recliner chairs. Reaching into my briefcase, I pulled out the plastic medical kit and removed the syringe from it. "I don't have time to play games with you, Klaus," I explained as I pulled the red plastic tip off of the long needle. Finding a good vein in his arm, I slipped the needle into it and slowly pushed the plunger.

"Yes, we're in, get ready to begin downloading," Ollie explained into the receiver of the telephone. Putting the receiver of the phone into the phone cradle that was wired into the computer system, Ollie then started to type on the computer keyboard. "Come on, come on, come on," Ollie said nervously. Waiting a few seconds, he then said, "Yes, we're in. They're downloading." Looking at me, Ollie then looked at Klaus and then back up at me. "Do I dare ask what that was?"

"Sodium Penathol," I explained with a grin.

"Ahhh, truth serum. Very good," Ollie responded.

"It will take a few minutes to take hold. Then he'll tell us anything that we want to know," I said as I walked over and closed the door to the study.

"What's this doing?" I asked as I pointed at the computer screen.

I hooked this system directly into the system that we have in the War Room at the Pentagon. They're downloading everything inside of this system now. See that red line?" Ollie asked as he pointed at the computer screen.

"Yeah," I responded.

"As it disappears, it is telling us how much of the system is downloaded so far. We're half way there," Ollie explained nervously.

Looking over at Klaus, I reached up and pulled the strip of duct tape off of his mouth. He took a deep breath of air into his lungs and let it out slowly.

"You have two or more A-pack suitcase nuclear weapons. Where are they, Klaus?" I asked as I looked at my watch. Enough time had passed for the Sodium Penathol to have taken a good hold on him.

"No, yes, yes," he said softly as he shook his head from side to side, trying to clear his mind. Klaus was fighting the effect of the truth serum, but it wouldn't work. He was fighting a lost cause.

"Where are they?" I asked again.

"Sold them, I sold them Wednesday," he said as he began to laugh out loud. This was part of the effect of the Sodium Penathol.

"Who did you sell them to?" Ollie asked as he looked up at me and raised his eyebrows. He was guessing and it was a good one.

"Hilfiger..Fagermeifter..Gruber," he said in perfect German.

"Is all of this information in your computer system?" Ollie asked.

"Yes, yes, everything," he said calmly, as he began to laugh once again.

"Say goodnight," I said coldly. His speaking in perfect German reminded me of my Uncle Tommy and six million innocent Jewish people murdered during World War II.

"Goodnight!" he replied proudly.

"Sleep time, ass hole," I whispered as I looked Klaus Gruber in the eyes and pointed the barrel of my gun at his liver and pulled the trigger. The Rhino round hit Gruber with such a violent force, that it blew a section out of the back of his chair, spraying blood and pieces of his back onto the wall and carpet behind him. Even though he was high as a kite, from the effect of the Sodium Penathol, he still cried out in agonizing pain. I wanted him to suffer, and a liver shot was a horrible and painful way to die.

Hearing the computer beep, both Ollie and I turned our attention to it. Typing on the keyboard, Ollie sent them another message. "I just told them that the Iranian Embassy had both of the A-pack weapons and then I sent them the decryption code that Klaus just gave us," Ollie explained as he carefully watched the computer screen for a reply.

"Alright, they've got everything that they need," Ollie explained as he took the telephone receiver out of the computer cradle and hung it back up.

Taking the computer virus disc out of his jacket pocket, Ollie slid it into the computer system. "Watch this, David, you're gonna love this," Ollie explained smiling.

The computer screen went crazy and within a few minutes, the entire system was wiped completely out. Removing the CIA virus disc from Gruber's computer, Ollie quickly placed it back into his jacket pocket.

"Let's go, Ollie, we've got to get out of here," I explained as I tossed the duct tape and empty syringe back into our briefcase, locked it, and handed it to Ollie.

"What about him?" Ollie asked as he looked over at Klaus.

Raising my pistol, I pointed it at Gruber's chest and pulled the trigger. Gruber's body fell limp in his chair.

"What about who?" I asked with a grin as Ollie and I walked across the room and to the door of the large study room.

Looking at Ollie, who was now smiling, I opened the door to the study room and said, "After you, partner."

Just as I said it and pulled the door open, Ollie lost his smile as a very large, brown-haired man stepped into the doorway, raised the double barrel shotgun up, and pointed it at Ollie's chest. In one cat-like move, I stepped in front of Ollie, grabbed the shotgun with my left hand and jammed the barrel of the gun into my chest. It seemed as though everything had gone into slow motion as I raised my Beretta and pointed it at the German. His eyes were filled with hate as both of our weapons fired at the same time.

The impact of the shotgun blast, firing point blank into my chest, sent me flying backwards. My nasal passage was filled with the smell of gunpowder and burning cloth from my shirt. I felt as though I had just been hit by a semi-truck traveling at 200 miles-an-hour! The pain was more than I could bare. I tried to scream but couldn't. I fought hard to breathe but no matter how hard I tried, I couldn't get any air into my lungs. Staggering backwards about ten-feet, I saw the ceiling and large oak wood beams come into view as I felt myself falling backwards and felt my body hit the floor.

Seeing Ollie lean over me, I could see his mouth moving, but I couldn't hear him. The sound of the double-barreled shotgun blast was so loud that it was ringing in my ears. I couldn't move my body, I couldn't breathe, and the pain was too much to bare. I could see a gray cloud descending down over me, as everything turned dark and I slipped away into the darkness of my soul...

Chapter Twelve
The Bayou

Opening my eyes, I felt confused as I looked up at the white ceiling.

"Hello, partner, try to lie still," Ollie explained as he stood up from the chair that was next to my bed, and looked down at me with a smile. "I owe you my life, David. I don't know what to say."

Trying to sit up, I quickly remembered what had happened. Moaning out loud, I laid back down and tried to reach up with my right hand to remove the tubular breathing apparatus that was in my nasal passage. That was also a big mistake, as the movement of my arm caused me to cry out even louder. The pain in my chest was excruciating.

"Man, partner, stop moving around. All your ribs are broken. Your whole chest and abdomen are bruised. Man, kid, you're black and blue from the esophagus to your testicles," Ollie explained with a concerned look on his face.

"The pain is excruciating! I can't expand my chest it hurts so bad," I explained in a soft whisper of a voice.

"I know, buddy, you lost consciousness as soon as your body hit the floor. I was in shock, David, I couldn't believe what you did!" Ollie explained.

"Dumb, huh?" I said with a grin.

"Didja know that he pulled both triggers at the same time? That shotgun was a 12-guage, and to make it even worse, it was loaded with 3-inch magnum, 00 buck shot!" Ollie explained as he shook his head from side to side in disbelief.

"Yeah, that feels about right," I replied in a whisper.

"That new Kevlar bulletproof vest is one bad ass serious piece of material. I called Carla at the Situation Room as soon as we got you here. The Kevlar Company wants to see the vest. They'll probably make you their new poster boy," Ollie explained as he began to laugh.

"Amanda? Is she alive?" I asked.

"Yes, she's fine, David. You would have been proud of her. She heard the shotgun blast and came running into the house without her crutches. She actually ran with that cast on her leg, shot the German fella three more times in the head as she ran past him, and then gave you mouth to mouth to get you breathing again. That blast knocked the wind out of you big time!" Ollie explained.

"Where are we?" I asked.

"Ramstein Air Base, we're secure and safe," Ollie said smiling.

"How long have I been out?"

"Not long, maybe three hours. You would come to and then pass out again. They ran an EKG on your heart and said that you have some heart problems, but all in all you're gonna be just fine once those ribs heal up," Ollie explained with confidence.

"Where's Amanda?" I asked as I tried to look around the room for her.

"She's getting her leg reset and her rib cage retaped. She tore everything loose when she came running in to back us up. She is one hell of an agent," Ollie said in a complimentary way.

"No kidding, I don't think that I could run on a broken leg, with broken ribs on top of that. Mouth to mouth, huh?" I asked smiling.

"Yeah, too bad you weren't awake to enjoy it," Ollie said with a smile as he moved his eyebrows up and down quickly.

* * * * * * *

It took two days before the military doctor's at Ramstein would release me. They were concerned about my heart, but I assured them that I felt fine.

Ollie flew all the way back to Pontiac with me and wouldn't leave my side until Don and Andy came to pick me up at the airport.

Ollie then went back to the Pentagon for debriefing, while I went home and lied to Andy and Don about falling from a rock ledge while I was mountain climbing with a friend of mine in Aspen, Colorado. I didn't like lying to them but when you lead a double life, like I was, sometimes you had no choice.

Carla had Brandi deliver four cases of Pepsi along with an extra large pizza with everything on it as her way of thanking for saving Oliver's life. After Brandi had gone Carla sent me a message on the computer. All it said was: "Let's see James Bond top that!"

I spent the next four weeks being babysitted by Andy, Don, and Tara's mother Amy. Of course, little Tara had to tell the rest of the scout troop that Uncle David was hurt. So some of the girls just had to stop by to help take care of me.

By week six, I was feeling great and moving around on my own. I was back to my normal self again or so I thought.

Andy and I were sitting in my den playing a game of chess when the phone rang. Watching Andy make his next move, I picked up the telephone as Andy smiled and said, "Checkmate!"

"Hello?" I asked as I looked at the chessboard in disbelief.

"Are you available, sir?" the voice asked.

"Yes," I said as I hung up the phone and stood up to go to the door. "You cheated," I said as I walked out of the room smiling.

Answering the door when the doorbell rang, the mail lady handed me an envelope marked United States Postal Services.

"Thank you, ma'am," I said as she smiled and walked back to her small mail delivery truck.

Closing and locking my front door, I went back into the den, sat down, and opened the envelope.

"A hit?" Andy asked as he took a sip of his Budweiser beer, and looked over at the envelope I was holding in my hands.

"Sure looks like it," I said as I pulled out the contents of the envelope and began to read it.

"Have you ever been to the Garden District in New Orleans?" I asked Andy as I picked up the 8x10 photograph of Sean Tibideaux, and looked at it.

"Sure have, I used to date a little Cajun girl that lived out there," Andy explained grinning.

"Still wanna go to New Orleans for a little vacation?" I asked.

"No," Andy replied as I looked up at him with a surprised look on my face. "But I'd love to go to N'awlins with yah," he added with his best Cajun accent.

* * * * * * *

New Orleans, home of the famous Mardi Gras and the French Quarter. Everywhere you look you'll see that New Orleans is rich in unique French-Creole culture. The French Quarter is one square mile in actual size. It has a total of twelve strip clubs within that square mile. It is famous for it's cheap booze and even cheaper women.

A lot of people think that New Orleans is the home of voodoo, but the CIA computer told me that only fifteen percent of the population actually practices it.

New Orleans is a full eight-feet below sea level and still sinking. As a result of this, since the Eighteenth Century, when flooding sent coffins popping up and out of the ground, New Orleans stiffs or dead people have been interred in ornate above-ground mausoleums.

Renting a car, Andy takes me to what he calls his favorite place to stay. We rent a suite at the Royal Sonesta. However, now that I have access to the agency computer, I pick up the telephone and call 504-200-6523 and quickly book a room at Loft 523, which is the best hotel in town.

It's almost noon and Andy looks at me with that 'feed me' Indian look in his eyes.

"You like oysters?" he asks.

"I've never had 'em before. Why?" I asked.

"Damn boy, you never ate oysters before? They're an aphrodisiac. Makes your pecker hard. Come on, son, I'll show you the best place to eat," Andy explains proudly.

Walking into a place called Acme Oyster House, we were greeted at the door by self-proclaimed 'bad-mothershucker' Michael 'Hollywood' Broadway, who shucks 1,100 oysters each and everyday. Andy pigs out on oysters, but I'm not eating anything that looks and tastes like snot!

"Eat up, boy," Andy says as he squirts some super hot Cajun hot sauce on an oyster and slurps it down right out of the half shell.

"I'll pass, thank you. Listen, Andy, it says that this Sean Tibideaux spends most of his time playing Black Jack on the riverboat. Think that we can use that to our advantage?" I asked.

"Maybe, I've got his address. Let's just go to his house and knock on the damn door," Andy suggested as he slurped down some more oysters.

"The contract said to make him disappear. Know where there's any gators?" I asked with a grin.

"The gator to human ratio is two to one in St. Charles Parish. I got an old friend out there that runs an airboat. You get this Sean fella into the car and I'll show you how to make 'Gator Bait' out of him," Andy explained as he washed down the last of his oysters with the last half of his Budweiser beer.

"That's disgusting. I can't believe that you actually ate that shit," I taunted as we got up and left the Acme House.

Sean Tibideaux lived in what was called the Garden District of the city. Looking around, I could see that there was little separation out here between the rich and the poor.

"God, this place is hot and humid," I explained as I checked my .22 magnum automatic to make sure that it was ready to fire.

"That's it right there, that's his house and his car is parked in the driveway," Andy explained calmly as we drove by Sean's home.

"Go to the end of the street and turn around. Then come back up here and pull into his driveway," I explained as I looked at my watch.

"You gonna try to grab him right now? Damn, David, it's only 1:15. It's still daylight out," Andy pointed out with a look of surprise on his face.

"The most obvious is the least obvious, Andy. He's a professional gambler so he works at night. That means that he'll either still be asleep or will have just woke up and that gives me the edge. Once I get him in the car, I'll zap him with this," I explained as I held up my stungun and pulled the trigger. The bolt of light blue electricity jumped across the metal electrodes and made a snapping, crackling sound that even scared me when I heard it.

"Holy shit, where did you get that?" Andy asked as his eyes widened at the sight and sound of the 150,000 volts of electricity that had just shot out of the stungun.

"You mean you don't have one of these?" I asked with a serious look on my face.

"No, and I don't want one either. My luck I'd zap myself with it," he chuckled as we pulled into the driveway and came to a stop.

"Wait here, I'll see if he's home," I explained as I got out of the car, tucked the stungun into my back pocket, and stepped up onto the front porch.

The homes in this neighborhood were well kept. Some had aluminum siding, some were red brick, some had a chain link fence around them, some didn't. All were clean with fresh cut lawns.

Knocking on the door, I waited. Looking over at the new Chrysler LaBaren, I knocked on the door once again and then looked back at the car. "What the heck?" I said to myself as I stepped off the porch and walked over to the driver's side of the dark blue Chrysler.

Sean Tibideaux stood six-feet, three-inches tall, had dark brown hair that he combed straight back, brown eyes, and weighed two hundred and fifty-eight pounds. Every bit of which was now laying passed out cold in the front seat of his car.

Reaching in through the open side driver's window, I carefully picked the .357 magnum pistol up off the dashboard and tucked it into my belt. Looking over at Andy, I smiled, and then opened the driver's door of the dark blue Chrysler.

"Wake-up pal," I said loudly. "Come on, Mr. Tibideaux, I'm not going to tell you again, wake-up!" I said sternly as I shook him by the shoulder. Sean was laying across the front seat of his Chrysler. The smell of whiskey coming from his mouth with every breath that he took almost made me dizzy.

"Huh? What?" he mumbled as I helped him out of his car and walked him the few steps to where we were parked right behind him. "What's going on?" he asked as he staggered slightly and tried to clear his thoughts by shaking his head. "Awe, son-of-a-bitch," he mumbled as he rubbed his big hands across his face.

Opening the backdoor of our silver four-door, Ford Ltd, I gently helped Sean into the backseat.

"I'm detective Jim Beatty and this is my partner, Joe Reynolds. We're with the St. Lafitte Sheriff's Department," I explained as I looked around quickly at the homes that surrounded us, reached into my back pocket and pulled out the stungun.

"Him, ben draken' 'gain, huh?" the little girl asked as she walked up to see what was going on.

Slipping the stungun back into my pants pocket, I smiled. The little girl came out of nowhere and startled me.

"Him in big trouble, little miss, ya all gaw on now, cuz him going to jail," I explained in my best made-up version of Cajun talk.

"Bout time," she said as she turned and walked away.

"Hey, what's go'n on here," Sean asked as he started to regain his focus and thinking.

"You were involved in a hit and run accident last night, Mr. Tibideaux. You're gonna have to come with us and answer a few questions," I explained quickly as I placed my hand back on the stungun.

"No, mon, that nevuh hapun, no," he started to explain as he looked at Andy.

"That man standing right over there, say he see you hit that woman," I explained as I pointed my finger through the inside of the car and out the opposite side window.

"Huh, who say that?" he asked as he turned his head to the left to look out through the window on that side of the car.

Jamming the live end of the stungun into the now exposed fleshy part of Sean's neck, I pulled the trigger. The jolt of electricity caused Sean to jerk wildly as I counted to three and pulled the gun away from his neck.

"Holy shit," I said out loud as Sean shook his head slightly and tried to regain his composer. He was stunned, but not out by a long shot!

Hitting him with a second jolt, I counted to seven, and then stepped back and slammed the backdoor shut. Climbing into the front seat, I looked at Andy, "Your turn, brother, show me some gators," I said calmly as we backed up and drove away.

* * * * * * *

Every time that I would hear Sean moan, I would reach back and give him another seven second jolt from my stungun. I had made no plans to grab Sean like this, which meant that I was ill prepared and had nothing to tie his hands and feet together. Andy, however, couldn't stand the sound of the stungun or the faint smell of burning flesh that was coming from Sean's neck. So he stopped and bought a roll of duct tape and we bound Sean's hands and feet together.

Looking at my watch, it was almost 4:30 p.m. when Andy pulled into the dirt driveway of the man that he called his old Cajun hunt'n partner. It was an old cabin that looked as though it had been built back in the forties. It was well kept and sat about eighty-yards up from the waters edge of the swamp. Andy went up to the cabin, knocked on the door and walked inside. We were deep in the Bayou of St. Charles Parish.

Looking over at Sean, who was laying across the backseat of the Ford, I reached down and pulled the strip of duct tape off from across his mouth so he could speak.

"Where are we? What you gonna do to me?" he asked in a calm voice that was almost shocking to me.

"Six weeks ago you met a high class lady at the Coyote Ugly club. She was a tourist, blonde hair, middle aged, a real nice lady, remember her?" I asked as I looked over the back of the front seat and down at Sean whose eyes were now a bit wider with surprise.

"I remember," he answered curiously.

"You took her out to the riverboat to do some gambling. Then you raped her, robbed her of all of her money, and beat her half to death, remember?" I asked.

"No, mon, that was no me who done them things," he replied as he looked up and to the left. His eye movement had just told me that Sean was using the creative side of his brain. Something that I was taught to look for while I was at the Farm. He was lying to me!

"Then you pushed her over the side Sean. You were hoping that the gators would get her or that she would simply drown. Guess what, Sean, it was dark out and you were drunk, kinda like you were when I found you this afternoon. You didn't see the young black fella that works on the riverboat, but he got a good look at you, just before he jumped into the water and saved the lady. She was in the Charity Hospital for three days, Sean. She told the police that she didn't know who assaulted her. You want to know why she said that, Sean?" I asked calmly.

"Why?" was all that he said.

"Her husband is a United States Senator, Sean," I explained. "He is also a friend of mob boss, Sam Giancana, who just happens to be my uncle," I said with a cold stare and a broad smile on my face, as I reached down and put the strip of duct tape back across Sean's mouth.

Looking up, I saw Andy as he came walking out of the old cabin, followed by the biggest black man I had ever seen in my entire life! Damn, I thought Chopper was big, but this man was huge! He stood seven-feet tall, and had a baldhead. He wore his old denim coveralls with the top half hanging down and tied around his waste. He was the same age as Andy, but this guy had a stomach that looked like a washboard, muscles that were bigger than large rocks, and was a very dark shade of black. Getting out of the car, I smiled.

"David, this is my brother and best friend, Keanu Greta. Keanu, this is my friend and son, David," Andy introduced with a smile.

"Keanu, it's a pleasure to meet you, sir," I said as we shook hands.

"Same with me to you; you call Keanu, Jaba. All my friends call me Jaba," he said smiling as he turned to look into the backseat of our car. "This him?" Jaba asked coldly.

"Yes, him be the one," Andy replied.

"Come, we go now, while sun still shine," Jaba explained as he opened the backdoor of the Ford Ltd and pulled Sean Tibideaux out with one hand.

Sean was a big man, but he was no match for Jaba, who picked him up as if he were a small child and carried him to his airboat at the edge of the swamp.

"Andy, this guy is going to be a witness to a murder. You sure that you trust him?" I asked carefully, so as to not offend my dear friend.

"You know that young kid you were in Vietnam with. The one you call Chopper?" Andy asked as we walked across the back of Jaba's property and down to the lake.

"Yeah," I replied.

"I met Jaba when I was ten-years old. I grew up out here in these Bayou's, David. Jaba's family and my mom and dad were best friends to each other. Hell, son, we've put more bodies into this swamp than you could shake a stick at! Jaba is an ole Creole swamp man. He would cut his own throat before he would ever betray a friend. Let me put it like this, Jaba is to me, as Chopper is to you," Andy explained with pride.

"Enough said, brother," I replied with a smile as we stepped up onto the large airboat and sat down in one of the front seats.

After putting in the earplugs that Jaba handed Andy and I, Jaba started the engine of his craft and away we went, deep into the marshy Bayou Wetlands of the famous New Orleans swamp!

We went from the waterways into the denser forest. It was beautiful in its own way. The large trees were covered with moss and were a rich dark green in color. The airboat was insanely noisy, but the ride was smooth as we skimmed across the surface of the water.

We traveled deep into the swamp and then stopped. Turning off the engine of the airboat, I pulled out my earplugs and sat in awe. Everything was silent!

Looking around, I couldn't believe how beautiful this area of moss-covered trees really was. Hearing something cry off to my left, I turned to look out into the dense swamp.

"That's just a Nutria, David," Andy explained calmly as he looked over at Jaba and smiled.

"What's a Nutria, a bird?" I asked as I looked out to my right and saw a large Cottonmouth snake sunning itself on a log.

"Swamp rat, they average about twenty-pounds. Damn things are destroying the wetlands. Feel free to shoot 'em if you see 'em. They're in season late winter," Andy explained as we floated on top of the surface of the water.

"Look," Jaba explained as he pointed his large finger out and off to our right. There were six of them. They looked like log's floating calmly in the water. The only difference was that these logs had eyes.

"Ever see a gator take a man down before?" Andy asked as he looked over at Sean and grinned.

"No, sir, I can't say that I have," I replied as I looked at Sean, who was sobering up quickly and beginning to panic, but unable to do anything about it. Jaba had hog tied Sean to the metal rail at the back of the boat.

"They'll hit him and then start to roll him around and around. They call it the Death Roll. It will make him dizzy and disorient him. Then they'll take him down under and drown him!" Andy explained as he looked over at Jaba and smiled.

"That's it?" I asked as I looked around to make sure that no snakes were trying to climb onto the boat. I hated snakes and the sight of that Cottonmouth made my skin crawl.

"Gators can't chew, they rip and gulp down chunks of meat or whatever they're eating at the time. It may not look like it from up here, but this area is deep water. Underneath this calm surface of water, you'll find caverns and fallen trees. They'll take him down and tuck him under a log or in one of those caverns. They'll leave him there for seven, maybe ten days. Once he starts to bloat-up and rot, then they'll come back and eat the rotting meat," Andy explained.

"Him go down, him no come back-up," Jaba added as he stood up and began to untie Sean from the metal brace.

"If we cut his hands and feet loose, will he be able to capsize this boat and put us in the water with him?" I asked as Jaba pulled the tape off of Sean's mouth and he began to beg for his life.

"Please, mon, no, not like dis," Sean cried out in a frantic voice as he looked at me for help. Sean still had his feet taped together and his arms secured to his back as Jaba turned him around and grabbed him by the thumb.

'*Snap!*' The sound of his thumb breaking was almost as loud as Sean's scream. '*Snap, snap, snap,*' continued until Jaba had broken all of the fingers on both of Sean's hands.

Handing Andy the small Cannon 35mm camera, I explained. "Take pictures, brother, but be careful not to get any of our faces in the photos.

The Senator wants pictures to show his wife and that's exactly what he's gonna get. Maybe seeing you die Mr. Tibideaux will give his wife some comfort. Now you know how she felt," I explained as I cut the duct tape loose from around his ankles and wrists.

Sean's screams were almost deafening as the combination of fear and total paranoia began to over power him.

"Shoot me, mon, please shoot me, God no, mon, please I don't deserve dis. Please shoot me, mon, shoot me," Sean begged as fear over powered him, and he began to struggle.

Grabbing Sean by the hair and the back of his belt I whispered in his ear. "That lady was innocent, you're not."

His body was covered with sweat as the big man trembled in my hands. Looking over at Jaba, he started the engine of his airboat and began to slowly back the boat up in the water.

Seeing the large gator's as they slowly swam closer, I looked into Sean's eyes. "Sandman is here, say goodnight, asshole," I said loudly as I pushed Sean into the water.

The swamp water was too deep for Sean to do much as he lashed out wildly with both of his arms. The gators came in fast and with a vengeance as Sean screamed and tried to fight them off. The largest Gator disappeared from sight, went low and underneath the water, grabbing Sean by the leg. One of the other gators quickly grabbed Sean by the left arm. Both gators began to spin the big man around causing the water to churn and splash wildly.

Watching the gators as they put Sean into the Death Spin sent a chill running up my spine. You could hear him scream every time his face appeared above the water. As Andy continued to take pictures, I heard muscle, flesh, and tendons tearing away as one gator twisted and pulled Sean's left arm completely off, ripping it out of its socket. Watching the gator swim away with his newfound meal, the larger gator pulled Sean Tibideaux under the water. As quickly as it all started, it ended!

"Him no hurt woman now, him won't" Jaba said loudly as he turned the airboat around and headed back to his home.

Once back at Jaba's home he asked Andy and I to come in and visit with him. He lived a very simple life. Even though he had very little education, he was one of the most decent men that I had ever met before.

Reaching into my pocket, I pulled out five thousand dollars in brand new hundreds and handed it to Mr. Keanu Greta. Looking at the money with a confused look on his face Jaba asked, "This you give to Jaba, why?

Handing Jaba the .357 magnum pistol that I took from Sean's car, I explained. "You my friend now Jaba, you are brother to Andy, that make you my brother now too. You do most of the work, Jaba. You get pay too, mon," I explained in a feeble attempt at Cajun slang.

Nodding his head, Jaba accepted both the money and the gun and took them into his bedroom.

"Think Jaba will go out to dinner with us?" I asked.

"No, David, he doesn't go into town very often. When he does, it's only to get supplies. He told me earlier, when we first got here, that he has a woman he is going to go see tonight. They're both Creole Cajun. He said that he wants to marry her. With the money that you just gave him, he probably will now," Andy explained with a broad smile on his face.

We spent the next two hours with Jaba, and then left the Bayou to head back to Bourbon Street. However, before we left, Jaba made it perfectly clear that we could use his swamp and gators' anytime that we needed them. It was a comforting, yet scary thought!

Andy and I spent the next three days spending money and acting like fools. We went bowling at a place called Rock 'n Bowl and then rented a limo from, Niccol's Limo Service 504-468-1787 and spent the rest of the day driving around looking at some of the old Civil War mansions and plantations. New Orleans is rich with historical sights.

We ate lunch at Rene Bistrot 504-412-2580 and hung out with the strippers at Coyote Ugly. The best strip club in N'awlins was by far a place called Rick's on Bourbon. Following the advice that I got from the CIA computer system, we went to Ruth's Chris Steak House, where the booze, babes, and steaks were all excellent.

Following a tip from our limo driver, we then went to a place called Ampersand, located at 1100 Tulane Avenue. We called 504-587-3737 first and for five hundred dollars, Andy, our limo driver, and myself owned the entire second floor of the Ampersand, another hot club in town. There's a full bar, a kitchen, two 'bedrooms' and a window that overlooks the dance floor. The best part is the girl-on-girl show that we bought; it's hidden from the riffraff by a steal door, manned by two huge bouncers!

Even though this is a book of fiction and none of this ever really happened, if you're going to N'awlins with your buddies for a full-service bachelor party call, Bachelor Blowout at 877-226-7278. These boys will make all of the arrangements for you. Well, if any of this was true they would...

Saying goodbye to our limo driver, Andy and I headed back to the airport, turned in our rental car, and mailed the roll of 35mm film to the Senator at his home in Washington D.C., which he will have to have developed on his own.

Boarding my grandfathers Learjet, I looked over at Andy as we took off and headed back to Michigan.

"We should have brought Don with us," I commented.

"Fuck him," Andy replied as he popped two aspirin into his mouth and took a drink of his cold beer.

"That sure was a hell of a way to die, wasn't it?" I asked as I looked out through the side window of the plane and my mind took me back to the Bayou. I could still hear Sean screaming and the sound of flesh, muscles, and tendons tearing as the gator twisted and ripped his arm completely off his body. Thinking about the Senator's wife and the pain and horror that she must have felt on that dark, hot, summer night, I shook my head from side to side. "Shit!" I said in a soft voice.

"What? What's wrong?" Andy asked as he looked over at me.

"We let that piece of shit off easy. Remind me to make the next one suffer," I said calmly, as I closed my eyes and relaxed in my seat.

Chapter Thirteen
Star Burst

Saying goodbye to Andy, I went inside for a rest. The past four days had moved fast. As usual, I had gotten little to no sleep. New Orleans, along with its great food and spicy hot women, has that affect on you.

Unlocking the doors to my den, I went in to check my computer. There I found four urgent messages from Marge in Langley, and two more from Carla at the Situation Room at the Pentagon.

"Damn, I forgot to tell them that I was going away for a few days, oops," I mumbled to myself as I read one of eight other messages that Kathy had also left on my computer. Turning on my scrambler box, I called Kathy first.

"Hello," Kathy said softly into the mouthpiece of her phone and into my ear.

"Hello, pretty lady," I responded in a soft and sexy voice.

"David? Is that you?" Kathy asked a bit more loudly.

"Yes, dear, it's me," I replied.

"Are you alright? I've been worried sick about you!"

"I'm...." was all that I was able to say before Kathy cut me off and began to ream me out!

"Who in the hell sent you out on a mission without getting my permission first? I have to hear that you've been shot, by some paper-pushing secretary for Christ sakes! I'm your direct supervisor God damn it, you don't do a fucking thing unless I'm involved. When it comes to you, I am never left out of the loop! You got it?!!!!" Kathy shouted angrily into my ear.

"Kathy?" I asked calmly, even though I was now upset at her for yelling at me in such a way.

"What, damn it!" she responded sharply.

"Click, m, m, m, m," was all that she heard as I hung up the telephone in her ear!

Picking the phone up again, I called Marge at her office in Langley. Using my voice recognition code, I was talking to Marge in less than thirty seconds.

"David, how are you feeling, are you healing up all right or are you having problems?" she asked in a concerned voice.

"I'm fine now, but Marge I've got to be honest with you. It hurt like hell, fire, and brimstone for the first two weeks," I explained with a touch of a chuckle in my voice.

"I read a top secret report that said you shoved both barrels of the shotgun into your chest and took the hit point blank. I couldn't believe it until Carla sent me your bulletproof vest. No agent has ever done anything like that before, David. You have a lot of powerful people looking at you now," Marge explained with a touch of excitement in her voice.

"Yeah, well it seemed like the right thing to do at the time. Besides, it was that or Ollie would have been killed and that was not part of my plan," I explained calmly.

"Oh hey, Marge, I need a new vest. Do you think that the Kevlar people will cough up another one for me?" I asked even though I knew that Marge would remember that I signed out two vests.

"And you lost the second vest, right?" she asked giving me a way to justify not having it anymore.

"No, I gave it to a good friend of mine. He does some pretty dangerous bodyguard work," I explained honestly.

"Well, that's honest enough." Marge said laughingly. "Hell, son, you can have as many as you want. Kevlar Company loves you, David. They no longer list the vest as experimental. It's now rated to be proven one hundred percent guaranteed effective at point blank range!"

"I can vouch for that," I said in agreement.

"Listen, kiddo, I have some really neat stuff that just came in for Carla. She said to have you look at it first and see if you want any of it. So get your butt over here and take a look at this new equipment. You might even get this old gal to take you out to dinner. Of course I'll use the government credit card, but that is what its for, right?" Marge asked with a snicker to her voice.

"I'm on my way, Marge. Oh, before I forget, I'm going to need some new ID's. I don't like using the same ones twice. Can you help me out?" I asked.

"I'll have them ready for you by the time you get here. Any particular names that you want on them?" Marge asked.

"Yes, give me Secret Service Special Agent credentials that have the name James Bond on it. It's for a joke that Carla is trying to tag me with," I said cheerfully.

"Ahh, now I understand. When Carla sent your vest to me, so we could see it, there was a note in the box that said 'Look at what our boy just did to save his partners life. The Sandman makes James Bond look like a bitch!' "

"On second thought, Marge, forget the James Bond credentials. I'm a lot of things, but I'm no bitch!"

* * * * * * *

Passing the security gate at CIA Headquarters, I went straight to see Marge at her office. When I got there she was all smiles.

"Hello, Dave, its good to see that you're up and about once again. Close the door and lock it would you please?" she asked politely.

Locking the door, I walked over and sat down in the seat next to Marge's desk.

"So, what's going on, Marge? You really didn't call me all the way to Virginia just to see some special gadgets did you?" I questioned with raised eyebrows and a grin.

"Partly," she said as she walked over to her vault, opened it, and stepped inside.

"Does everybody have walk-in vaults in this place?" I asked.

"Only those of us who are important," she explained as she came walking out with a suitcase in her hand. Sitting the suitcase down on her desk, she opened it and pulled out the first item.

"This is an optic cable camera, David," she said as she pulled out the long tubular cable and handed it to me. Taking me to the outer door of her office, that was now locked, she explained, "Let's say that you need to breach the security of a room but you don't know if anyone is inside of that room or not. You slide this end under the door like this," she said as she slid the small end under the door and into the outer hallway. "Then you look into the eye piece on this end and you can see everything that is happening in the other room, without them knowing that you're outside watching them."

Looking into the eyepiece, I reached down and moved the opposite end of the cable with my hand. "Woe, I can see everybody out there."

"Yes, and they don't even notice that there is a small pencil size object under the door, do they?" she asked.

"I'll take it," I replied with a smile.

"I thought so. When you walk into a room now, you'll know exactly which direction to point your gun to shoot it, which brings me to this little baby." Pulling out the small weapon, my eyes widened with excitement. "This is so brand new that it's still not even listed as experimental. It's a .9mm PK-9 machine pistol. It's made by H&K. They are also in the prototyping stage of an H&K MP-5. They say that this little baby here will fire faster on fully automatic than the Mack-10 we're using now on our covert operations. It may even replace the Mack-10 with the Secret Service agents who bodyguard the President. However, the Secret Service won't touch it until we've tested it out. They love their Mack-10's and hate the thought of having to give them up," she explained.

"I'll test it out for 'em, no problem," I explained as I took the new weapon and set it down next to the cable camera.

"This is called a sticky camera. If you're on an operation and you have a partner with you, you put on this Seal team headset and go into the building; you then stick these mini cameras to the hallway walls or wherever you see fit to put 'em. While you're moving in on your target, your partner is outside watching the hallways to make sure that no one is coming up behind you. Pretty cool, huh?" Marge asked smiling.

"I'll be damned," I said as I took one of the tiny cameras and held it in my hand to look at it. "I don't know Marge. When I go into a room, it's usually with my weapon firing," I explained with a smile.

"Take it anyway. Trust me, David, you're being considered for some very special covert operations. That little stunt that you pulled with the shotgun to save your partner caught the attention of a very special group of people," Marge explained.

"Who, what people?" I questioned.

"Need-to-know basis, kiddo, and right now you don't need to know. Besides, it's too early to talk about it. Now then, this is a voice stress analyzer, you face the back end of it toward whoever you are talking to, and it will tell you if they are lying to you or not. You'll probably never need it, but take it anyway, you just never know when you might need it. Now then, last but not least are these night thermal goggles, put these on and you can see in the dark. They're also being issued to Navy Seal teams along with the PK-9 machine gun. Take it all with you and let me know what you think," Marge explained smiling.

"I need to ask you something, Marge. I used the Rhino-round at the Gruber Estate. It blew a hole out of his back, went through his recliner chair, and then went right through the wall behind him. What is it made out of, Marge?" I asked.

"Ahh, the White and Black Rhino bullets. They have small thin rods in the tip of the bullet. The rods are made out of depleted Uranium, some are Titanium, and all of them are super nasty. We are calling them 'Cop killers,' and are going to try to stop the company from selling them to anyone other than law enforcement personnel.

"I'll tell you what, I'll bet you I could actually shoot through the fender of a car and blow the engine block out with a Rhino round," I explained with a very serious look on my face.

"I have no doubt about that. Our people are making some .50-caliber bullets out of depleted Uranium. The whole bullet projectile will be depleted Uranium. We're going to give them to the Seal team snipers. They'll be able to shoot right through the front, side, or back of a tank with it. Should prove to be interesting, don't you think?" Marge asked.

"I'd sure say so," I answered.

"Well then, go into the vault and grab yourself a couple more of those Kevlar vests and let's get out of here. I'll buy you dinner before you leave for Washington D.C.," Marge explained as we both stood up.

"Yeah, I promised Carla that I would be in her office no later than 9:00 a.m. tomorrow morning," I explained as I packed everything back into the suitcase and went into the vault to pick up a couple more vests.

"I'm suppose to tell you to stop by Agent Eckland's home before you leave for Washington. Kathy said that she needs to talk to you about something," Marge explained as she closed the vault and locked it.

"Oh boy, I hung the phone up on her yesterday. She's probably real upset with me."

"Go easy on her, kid. Kathy has been at home sick for the past four days. If she jumped on you its only because she cares about you. We were all shocked when we heard that you had been shot. I found out right away from Carla after Oliver called in from Ramstein Air Base. Agent Eckland, however, found out about it when a couple of the secretaries were talking about it and she just happened to be walking by and over heard them. She must have been on her period or PMSing really bad, because she went right into the office of the big boss and raised holy hell about how they kept her out of the loop," Marge explained as we left her office to go to dinner.

"So, Kathy was really worried about me," I thought to myself as I carried my suitcase full of new toys out to the car. "Things are looking up, David, things are looking up."

* * * * * * *

Kathy had a beautiful five-bedroom home in the elite outer suburbs in Langley, Virginia. Pulling into her driveway, I saw that the double gate of her chain link fence was open. Getting out of my car, I went into the backyard to see what was going on.

"Damn," I said in a low voice as I walked up to the side of the full size swimming pool and stood next to Kathy.

"Hello, pretty lady," I said with a smile, as I watched the pool maintenance people drain the water out of the pool.

"David, hi, thanks for stopping by. Hey, I'm sorry about yelling at you the other day. It's been a bad week and I took it all out on you, sorry," Kathy explained as the pool man walked up to her.

"That should do it, young lady. We drained out all of the water and secured the tarp cover over the pool. That will keep the kids, pets, and leaves from falling into it over the winter. If you'll sign right here next to the 'X,' I'll get my truck out of your backyard, and we'll see you in the spring. How's that sound?" he said as he handed Kathy the clipboard to have her sign the bill for their services.

Looking around, I was impressed at how nice Kathy's home was. Looking up at the roof, I noticed a tall, short-wave radio antenna attached to the roof and what looked like a small satellite dish that was almost completely hidden from sight. It was secured to the roof where they came together on three different angles. Watching the pool man get into his truck and drive away, I closed the gates behind him, snapped the large Master Lock shut in the gate handle, and followed Kathy into her home.

She was wearing a blue pull over sweater, blue jeans, and Nike tennis shoes. The inside of her home was breathtaking. She had leather furniture, crystal end tables with gold legs, large paintings hung on the walls of almost every room, and leaded glass crystal lamps, vases, and nick-knacks were neatly organized throughout the home.

"Man, Kathy, the Agency sure does take care of you," I commented as I walked up to look at the large painting hanging next to the full size glass mirror on the front room wall. "Van Gough," I said in a whisper to myself as Kathy walked up and handed me a glass of cold Pepsi in a leaded crystal glass. "Thank you," I said as I took a sip of the cold Pepsi.

"The Agency doesn't have anything to do with this home, David. This is all mine, along with the mortgage payments. Only guys like you have all the trimmings free of charge," she said jokingly.

"Rich family?" I asked with a smile.

"Something like that," she answered. "Come on, let's go sit in my den, it's my favorite room in the house, plus I have to check to see if I have any messages," she explained.

Walking into her den, which was also a beautiful library study, I was amazed at the deep, dark oak wood beams, Picasso paintings, classical music that was playing on the reel to reel tape stereo system, and the large computer and short-wave radio set-up located at the back of the room inside a hidden section of the slide away mirrored wall.

"Now I am impressed," I said as I walked over to look at her short-wave computer system.

Looking at the frequency setting number 4287, I picked up the mike, keyed it, and said, "Calling all car's, calling all car's, this is Dick Tracy."

Reaching in front of me, Kathy quickly turned the frequency setting and then turned off the radio receiver transmitter set.

"It's a hobby of mine. On a real clear day I can pick-up China and Japan. It's kinda neat; you can talk to total strangers in other countries. Most of the time we become friends and talk to each other off and on throughout the week," Kathy explained.

"The frequency setting that you had it on, who was that? What country?" I asked out of curiosity.

"I'm trying to find Saudi Arabia, but I think that I'm way off of my mark. It's all hit and miss. I don't even know if they have short-wave radios out there," Kathy explained as she checked her computer for messages and then slid the mirrored wall back into place, hiding the entire system.

I spent the next two hours telling Kathy about the Gruber hit and how we had missed recovering the two nuclear suitcases by a matter of a few days. The two hours went by quickly and then I had to leave.

"Well, boss lady, I've got to go. I'm suppose to meet with Carla at 9:00 a.m. sharp and my plane takes off in two hours, so I best get back to the airport and turn in the rental car," I explained as I caught a light scent of her perfume.

"Listen, David, do me a favor and call me if they send you out on anymore spur of the moment, last minute missions and I'm not there, will ya?" she asked.

"You've got it, Kathy. Like I told you, I thought that you knew, sorry," I answered. Leaving Kathy's home, I placed a drop of Methardine under my tongue and headed for the airport. "She's pretty, she has a great body, and she comes from an extremely rich family. I might just have to marry this girl," I thought to myself as I drove down the road and remembered the look that Kathy had in her eyes when she killed Mohamid while he sat in his bathtub. "But then again, maybe not!"

* * * * * * *

Walking into the Situation Room of the Pentagon, I was surprised to find only one person there manning the telephones and computer systems.

"Hi, is Carla here?" I asked with a friendly smile.

"Are you, David?" he asked.

"Yes, sir," I answered.

"Down the hall and to the right. She said for you to meet her at the War Room," he explained calmly.

The War Room is full of satellite communication systems. Three dimensional imaging, large screen TV systems, and one complete wall that has a fully digital screen that will allow you to see any section of any country in the entire world with the press of a computer key button. To put it in simple terms, it is a Global Satellite Elimination System, known as GSES.

Showing my Q-clearance to the military guards who were standing outside of the door, they opened the door for me, allowing me to go inside. Stepping inside of the large room, I found Carla standing next to the

President of the United States. Also in the room were the directors of the CIA, NSA, and DOD. The man sitting at one of the computer system consoles was talking to the Captain of the USS. Coral Seas, one of our aircraft carriers. From this room, we could be in constant touch with Navy Seal teams, CIA covert operation teams, and Delta Force Special Operations group. We can pull up geographical terrain mapping systems and talk directly to the men on the ground risking their lives. It's high tech and has other systems in it that cannot be mentioned for reasons of national security.

Stepping up next to Carla, I gave her a gentle nudge with my elbow.

"David, hi, I'm glad that you could make it," Carla explained as she watched with intense interest as the controller talked to the skipper of the Coral Seas.

"What's going on?" I whispered into Carla's ear.

"The Iranian Embassy has their diplomatic Learjet in the air and in route to Iran. We believe that our A-pack weapons might be on board that craft. We're going to have one of our pilots from the USS. Coral Seas, shoot it down," Carla explained.

"That's dumb," I said calmly, catching the attention of everyone in the room and a nasty glare from my boss, the Director of the Central Intelligence Agency.

"And what would you suggest, son, we should just let them fly away with two nuclear weapons and then let them send them back to us, once they have figured out how to arm the weapons?" the President asked.

"No, sir, I didn't mean it like that. What I meant was, if one of our attack fighters lock their weapons system onto that diplomatic plane, they're going to radio it in to Iran that we are trying to shoot them down," I explained calmly.

"Your fucking right, we're the ones shooting it down! They have nuclear weapons on board that plane, and they're our weapons!" Nixon snapped back with a glare of anger in his eyes.

"You don't know that for sure, Mr. President. Call off the fighters and have one of our submarines lock onto it and fire a heat-seeking missile at it from below the ocean's surface. The pilot of that Iranian jet won't ever see it coming. He can't radio in what he can't see. The diplomatic plane simply disappears from the radar screen and nobody except those of us in this room and the men on that sub will know the truth. Then, send a Seal team or Deep Sea Diving Team in to check the crash site. That way we'll know if we need to search for the weapons or if they were actually on board. At which point we've got them back in our possession," I explained quickly.

"He's right, sir," Carla explained to the President, as she took over control of the operation at hand.

"Neil, abort the Navy Fighter and tell it to return to the Coral Seas. Find our nearest sub, one that is in the pathway those bastards are heading in. Tell their captain to go to Red Alert and shoot that Iranian jet out of the sky!" Carla explained as she stepped up behind the controller and gently placed her left hand on the back of his right shoulder. Turning her attention to the young lady sitting at one of the other computer control stations, Carla continued. "Diane, find our closest underwater team and dispatch them to the crash site as soon as we get a satellite fix on it. Tell them what we're looking for and tell them to move fast! I don't want any mistakes made on this one, people. Let's do it!" Carla explained as she stepped back and stood next to President Nixon and I.

Watching both Neil and Diane as they ordered a very covert strike and recovery action against the embassy Learjet of Iran was almost mesmerizing in itself.

Watching the large digital clock on the wall, we waited anxiously as every minute ticked by. The captain of the American sub was as cunning as an old silver haired fox watching the hen house. He was waiting quietly under the surface of the ocean for the diplomatic jet to pass through his radar screen and directly overhead. He wasn't going to allow any room for the Iranian pilot to escape the pending attack on his plane.

"Eagles Nest, this is Stalker. We are half a mile from land base 74-A-21-L. Will strike once the plane is over the island – over," the captain of the sub explained.

"Copy, Stalker, that will sure make searching the debris a lot easier – Eagle's Nest out," Neil replied.

"Diane, find out what the name of that island is and get a Seal team deployed there ASAP. Cancel the underwater search team," Carla explained calmly.

"We're in luck, ma'am. Seal team five is aboard the USS. Coral Seas. They can reach the island by helicopter, right from their ship. I'm notifying their captain now," Diane explained.

Thirty-three minutes later, we stood in awe and watched as the submarine fired a satellite guided missile at the Iranian plane.

"Keep a satellite lock on that plane, Neil," Carla explained.

"I've got him painted, ma'am," Neil replied as we all watched the large screen.

Neil was using one of our satellites to paint a target on the Iranian diplomatic plane. The Cruise Missile has a computer brain that will lock onto that target, as the satellite guides the missile straight to it. The satellite picture was perfect as we watched the missile hit the Iranian jet and turn it into a huge ball of flames.

"Hoo yah," I whispered under my breath as I felt Carla nudge me with her elbow and smile. "God, I love this shit!" I explained as Carla turned to talk to the President.

"Richard, I'll let you know what we find as soon as Seal team Five searches the debris."

"Thank you, Carla, good job," the President said as he walked out of the War Room. "Good job everyone."

"David, that was fast thinking. Good job, son. Come with me, I have something that I need to ask you. Neil, Diane, everyone, thank you for a job well done. Neil please let me know right away if they find our weapons," Carla explained as we left the War Room and went down the hall back to the Situation Room.

Walking into her personal office, Carla closed the door and locked it. "Have a seat, David," she said as she sat down behind her desk and pulled out a file folder that was marked "Top Secret – Eyes Only" and handed it to me.

"His name is Morimoto Soba. He's fifty-two years old and a powerful figure in the diplomatic world for the People's Republic of China. We have very good intel that he is the one that sold the two nuclear weapons to Klaus Gruber," she explained calmly.

"Okay," I replied as I looked at his pictures and began to read the personal data information package on him.

"There's a high level diplomatic party being hosted by a billionaire banker. It's being held at his private estate in the Swiss Alpine Mountains. Mr. Soba is going to be there. Do you think you can figure out a way to kill him while he is at the party and make it look like a natural death?" Carla asked with a serious look on her face.

"How am I going to get into a party like that? At my age? Without security getting in my way?" I asked.

"If I can get you in, can you kill Soba?" she asked once again.

"No problem," I answered as I handed back the papers and photographs. "I'll put him to sleep for you."

"Good. I've been invited to attend," Carla said with a smile as she pulled open her top desk drawer and waved the gold trimmed invitation at me. "You're going as my escort and personal bodyguard," she explained. "You know, we older women just love you younger men," she added with laughter in her voice and a big smile on her face.

"You're dangerous," I said with a grin as I waved the first finger of my right hand toward her face.

"What? Little old me? Naaah," she added with a chuckle.

"I noticed that the President took a backseat along with the rest of the fella's while you blew-up a diplomatic plane," I explained as I stood up.

"The party is a week from this Saturday. Wear a tuxedo. If you don't have one I'll have you fitted for one. We have a great German tailor here that everyone uses," Carla explained as she avoided my statement in a professional manner.

"Wouldn't Ollie be more suited for this, Carla?" I asked.

"You're the one that we're interested in, David, not Oliver. Besides that, you're the one that I would like to get to know better. What better way to do it than at a diplomatic party with you on my arm," she said in a sinister way with a grin on her face.

"We're interested in me? We, who, and for what?" I asked.

"Lets see if you can pull this off first. I want to see the Sandman put Soba to sleep. I want to see it with my own two eyes. Your good, David, but can you kill someone in a room filled with over 200 diplomatic people from 38 different countries, all of whom will be watching?"

"What do you think?" I asked.

"I think that you and I are a lot alike, that's what I think," Carla answered with a more serious look in her eyes this time.

"Good, you can buy me lunch then," I explained as I opened the door and waited for her to join me.

"You got it, kid," Carla answered as she got up and walked toward me. "By the way, how are you feeling, are you okay?" she asked. "How are your ribs?"

"Well, we younger men love older more experienced women. So, I'm feeling pretty frisky right about now!" I explained as we walked out of the Situation Room and closed the door behind us.

* * * * * * *

Elite Operation
Code Name: Star Burst
Target: Morimoto Soba
Location: Switzerland
Status: Termination

Meeting Carla at the airport, I boarded the Agency Learjet and found her already waiting inside. Securing the side door of our plane, the pilot had us airborne in less than ten minutes. Carla was on the secure phone talking to Neil at the War Room. Thanking him for his help, she hung up the telephone and turned her attention to me, as I sat down across the aisle from her.

"Bad news, David," she said with a troubled look on her face.

"The nuclear suitcases weren't on the plane, were they?" I asked.

"You never did think that they were on that plane did you? I could see it in your eyes last week when we were together in the Elite Operations Room at the Pentagon," she explained calmly.

"Want me to explain?" I asked.

"Please do. I am very interested in hearing what you have to say about all of this," she replied with interest.

"Gruber was very clear about having sold both weapons on a Wednesday. The Iranian people aren't the smartest people in the world, but they're also not the dumbest either. Those weapons were airborne on that same Wednesday they were picked up. Hell, Carla, would we wait all of that time to move weapons?" I asked.

"No, we would transport immediately," she answered.

"I was looking at that map, just before the sub fired on the plane. He shot it down over Tierra del Guego. Damn, Carla, that's north of Cape Horn in the South Atlantic Ocean near the Antarctic Peninsula for Christ sakes. That's a long way from Iran, kiddo," I explained.

"So where do you think they are?" she asked.

"God only knows, but sooner or later you'll pick up some chatter. Someone, somewhere will feel safe enough to talk about it over a telephone. Delta Force, NSA, CIA, someone monitoring it will pick it up and we'll get another shot at retrieving them. Until then, remember this old saying: 'There was a wise old owl who sat in an oak. The more he saw, the less he spoke. The less he spoke, the more he heard. Why can't we all be like that wise old bird?'" I explained with a small grin on my face. I knew that Carla was frustrated at the loss of those two weapons. But I also knew that she was more dangerous and powerful than she wanted me to believe.

"Okay, I'll sit back and keep my eyes open and mouth shut and we'll wait and see what happens," she said with a half hearted smile on her face. "So tell me, David, have you figured out how to kill Mr. Soba, yet?"

"We'll see," I replied smiling.

"I'll bet that I'll spot it when you do it," she said.

"I'll take that bet," I replied quickly before she changed her mind.

"Alright, what do you want to bet?" she asked with confidence.

"I'll write down how I'm going to do it and I'll leave the paper locked here in our safe. If you can tell me how I did it, I'll do whatever you want me to do."

"Anything? Anything that I want from you, you'll have to do it. No matter what it is?" she questioned with a look of mischief in her eyes and a smile on her face.

"That's right, anything, no matter what it is, I'll have to do it. However, if you lose you'll have to do whatever I ask you to do, no matter what it is. No argument no hesitation, you have to do it. So, is it a bet?" I asked.

"It's a bet, young man, and you're going to lose. Would you like to know why?" she asked with confidence.

"I'm all ears, tell me why?" I asked sarcastically.

"Because I am the best there is at the 'Cloak & Dagger' game, kiddo. You just lost a bet and remember, I warned you," she said with a sexy look on her face as she sat back and crossed her legs.

"Warned me?" I asked.

"Yes, sir. We older ladies prefer younger men," she replied with a smile and a laugh.

"Hoo yah," I said smiling. "Too bad you're gonna lose."

* * * * * * *

An hour before we landed in Geneva, Carla and I changed into our formal wear.

"Wow," I said as I looked at Carla who was now wearing a long evening dress with a diamond necklace, ring, and earrings.

"How do I look?" she asked being critical of herself.

"If I win, I know what I'm asking for," I said smiling.

"Well, thank you. I'll take that as a compliment," she answered.

"You look rather sophisticated yourself."

"Well, thank you, my dear. Shall we join the party?" I asked.

"I wouldn't miss it for the world." she answered as we sat down and waited for the pilot to land.

* * * * * * *

Landing at the Swiss International Airport, we were immediately taken to one of six privately owned helicopters and flown to the dinner party we were invited to attend.

"Who owns this place?" I asked as Carla looked into the small mirror of her compact to check her make-up.

"A man named Pavel Malenkov. He is a very powerful executive that sits on the board of directors and a decision maker for the World Bank," Carla explained.

"A Russian?" I asked.

"Oh yeah. And a very powerful one at that. There is a lot more going on in this world than you know about. Keep heading in the direction that you're moving in now, and you may very well end up a player in a whole new ball game," Carla explained as she put away her compact. "His pilots are under very strict orders. They are not allowed to let the helicopter engine run, when we board, the engine must be completely off and the helicopter rotor blades must be at a full stop before we can leave the helicopter. Wanna know why?" she asked.

"Okay, why?" I asked.

"He doesn't want his helicopters to mess up anyone's hair. After all, we are the 'Elite Group,' you know," she answered with a laugh. "He also has a beautiful young daughter who loves to attend these diplomatic parties. Her name is Sasha. She is your age, so keep an eye out for her. Look, David, there's the estate," Carla explained as she nodded her head toward the window next to me.

Here, nestled in the quiet valleys of the Alpine Mountains of Geneva, was the most incredible sight that I had ever seen before.

"Holy shit," I whispered, as I looked over at Carla. "This looks like something you would see in a major motion picture."

"Believe it or not, it was built in the late 1800's by Pavel's great grandfather. It's a four-story structure, it also has four watchtowers that sit at each corner of the estate. Two outdoor water fountains, elevators in the home, and a vintage wine cellar that is estimated to be worth over a billion dollars all by itself," Carla explained calmly as she checked the small palm size .380-automatic handgun that she wore in a holster attached to the inner thigh of her left leg.

"Nice legs," I commented with a sinister smile as the helicopter landed and turned off its engine.

Smiling back at me, all that Carla said was "Thank you," as she pulled her long evening gown back down.

After waiting for the large rotor blades to stop, Carla and I stepped off the helicopter and walked across the large flat rock foundation of the outer courtyard. The entire complex was lit with bright lights. Looking across the compound, I could see the Alpine snow-capped mountains.

Entering through the front door, Carla gave the gentleman, who was standing just inside and off to our right, her gold-laced invitation. Thanking us for attending, he announced our presence as we walked in and began to mingle with the other guests. Carla introduced me to the power elite diplomats of the Philippines, Hungary, Turkey, Australia, France, Thailand, Germany, and the Netherlands. Most of who were drinking fine, vintage wine and who obviously knew each other on a first name basis.

Walking over to a Chinese gentleman, who stood about five-feet, seven-inches tall, Carla said, "Mr. Soba, how are you, sir? Its good to see you once again, as always."

"Ms. Silverman, how are you? I see that you are looking most stunning as always," Soba replied as he smiled and turned his attention to me.

"Mr. Soba, this is my friend Mr. Damian. David, this is one of my closest and dearest friends, Morimoto Soba," Carla introduced as Mr. Soba and I shook hands.

"It is a pleasure to meet you, David. You look young. How old are you?" he asked smiling.

"Well, sir, I'm old enough to know better but still too young to resist," I replied with a grin.

"I like this young man, Carla, is he one of yours?" Mr. Soba asked in a very cunning way.

"No, David is the grandson of Mr. Onassis, the shipping tycoon. I thought you would have known that, after all, your bank handles most of their money."

"I knew that, my dear. I just wanted to see if you were going to be honest with me," Soba explained as he turned his attention over to me. "Carla can be mysterious at times," he added jokingly.

"I wouldn't know, sir. My grandfather forced me on to Ms. Silverman. He insisted that I meet with the people I will one day be involved with when I inherit his empire," I said as if I had no real interest in the Onassis' billions.

It was then that we were all called into the main hall for dinner.

"We should talk later, young man," Mr. Soba implied as we all went to our assigned seats at the table.

Leaning close to Carla's ear I whispered, "Onassis?"

"You look Greek," she responded as the table man filled our water glasses.

Looking down the long table, I saw a beautiful dark haired young lady. She saw me look at her, smiled, and then looked in the direction of the older gentleman who was sitting at the head of the table.

"That's Sasha Malenkov," Carla whispered softly.

"You don't miss a thing do you," I asked as I looked over at Carla and smiled.

"Not very often. That's Pavel sitting at the head of the table, her father," Carla explained as the servants began to serve us our meal.

Pavel Malenkov welcomed everyone to his home and then explained how important it was for the world to seek peace and harmony with each other. I was impressed with this man and was buying into all of what he was saying, until Carla leaned over and whispered in my ear, "Did you know that Colonel Boris Kalashnikov was promoted? He is now General Kalashnikov, of the KGB," Carla explained as she took a sip of her water and waited for my response.

"So I've heard," I replied.

"Boris and Pavel are first cousins," she added cunningly. "Glad you came now?" she asked.

"Absolutely! How close are they?" I asked curiously as the memory of the POW camp in Cambodia and Colonel Kalashnikov began to make me bitter.

"They're closer than brothers," she whispered as the servant's poured soup into our bowls.

We spent two hours eating exotic foods from all around the world. Sasha continued to look over at me every few minutes. We flirted with each other with our eyes and facial expressions and stuffed ourselves with the best-cooked food the world had to offer.

One by one, people began to get up and go into the other large sitting rooms in the huge estate. Reaching into my shirt pocket, I pulled out my tiny glass vial of liquid Methadrine, and placed two drops under my tongue.

Excusing myself from Carla, I went to go look for a bathroom. Asking one of the servants, I was directed to the open faced elevator and went to the second floor of the home. Stepping off the elevator, I was in awe at how beautiful this home was. Even the hallways of the upper floors had crystal chandeliers hanging from the high ceilings. The floorboards and room doors were made of hand polished wood.

Turning the solid gold doorknob, I stepped into the bathroom, checked to make sure that I was alone, and then locked the door. Moving over to the marble sink, I reached into the inside pocket of my tuxedo and pulled out two hand rolled Cuban Cohiba cigars. Reaching into my pants pocket, I pulled out the small glass bottle I had hidden there. I knew that Mr. Soba loved exotic wines and expensive cigars. The Cohiba was the most expensive Cuban cigar that Fidel Castro had to offer. It was also banned in the United States because of the tension that our country had with Cuba.

Setting the thick, long, hand rolled cigar onto the marble countertop next to the sink, I unscrewed the top of the small glass bottle, being very careful not to touch any of the deadly poison within. I pulled out the small eyedropper and ran a thin line of the liquid poison from the tip of the cigar up about one-inch along its side. Screwing the top back onto the glass bottle, I placed it back into my pocket and waited for the deadly liquid to quickly dry.

In Vietnam, we called the poison Coo-da-day. It comes from the glands of a very small frog found in both Brazil, but mostly in Colombia. It is known as the Colombian Poison Arrow Frog. One adult frog has enough of this toxic poison in it to kill one thousand humans. Jungle tribesmen rub the tips of their wooden arrows on the frog and then let it dry. When they shoot their prey, which is mostly monkey, wild boar, or jungle cat, it will kill the animal in thirty seconds or less, no matter where they hit it with the arrow. With this very deadly poison, even a flesh wound will kill the animal. If it touches human flesh, anywhere, you're dead!

In the case of Mr. Soba, if I can get him to take the cigar and put it in his mouth, the wetness of his lips along with the smoke passing through the poison will kill him. Placing the cigar back into its tube container, I slid the poisoned cigar back into my inside jacket pocket and then put the other cigar into my right pant pocket. Checking to make sure that I hadn't left any trace evidence of any wrong doing on the countertop, I used the bathroom, washed my hands, and rejoined the party. Stepping off the elevator, I was pleasingly surprised when Sasha walked up to me smiling.

"Hello, I am Sasha. You are?" she asked.

"David," I answered as I looked deep into her big green eyes. "I'm sorry for staring at you during dinner. I did not expect to see such a beautiful young lady as yourself," I explained.

"Come, I will show you around my father's home," she suggested with a smile as she ran her arm through mine. "It is very beautiful, do you not think so?" she asked as she walked me around as if I were her newfound prize, showing me her home.

"It has little beauty compared to you," I said calmly as I turned on the charm.

We spent the next hour and a half walking around the estate. Sasha introduced me to more people who were arriving late; I drank Pepsi, while she drank crystal clear champagne.

"Sasha, where have you been? Your father wishes to speak with you for a moment," the middle aged lady explained.

"Cecilia, this is my friend, David. David, this is my Aunt Cecilia," Sasha introduced.

"It is very nice to meet you, ma'am," I said with a slight nod of my head.

"Yes, it is nice to meet you too, David. I am afraid, however, that I must take my niece away from you for just a little while though, will you excuse us?" she said as she placed her hand gently on Sasha arm.

"Yes, ma'am," I said smiling. "I was just going to step outside for a bit of fresh air anyway. I will see you later, yes?" I said looking at Sasha.

"Yes, David, I will look for you," she answered as her aunt walked her into the other room.

Walking out into the large back courtyard, I noticed Mr. Soba standing by the waterfall that had water running from the top, down the rocks, and into the large pool of water at its base below. Reaching into my pant pocket, I pulled out my Cohiba cigar and the gold trimmer designed to snip the tip of the cigar you put into your mouth. Walking up to Mr. Soba, I smiled.

"Hello, again, sir. It is such a beautiful evening out, don't you think?" I asked as I raised the Cohiba and placed the end of it into the trimmer and snipped it off.

"Yes, it is lovely here in the Alps. Is that a Cohiba?" he questioned.

"Why, yes it is, sir. Do you smoke?" I asked as I looked at him as if I didn't know.

"Oh, my yes. But unfortunately my wife forgot to pack my cigars. She is hoping that I will quit," he said smiling. "I think that she does it on purpose."

"Nonsense, please, sir, join me in an evening cigar," I insisted as I reached into my jacket pocket and pulled out the thin gold tube, that held the other cigar in it. Handing Mr. Soba the cigar and trimmer, he smiled as I put my cigar between my lips and lit it with my solid gold lighter.

"I see that your grandfather has taught you well, my young friend," he said as he trimmed the tip of his cigar and handed me back the trimmer and cigar case.

"Life is too short to enjoy anything less than the best," I explained as I snapped the lid back on my solid gold lighter and struck a flame. Holding the lighter up toward Mr. Soba, my heart raced with excitement as he placed the end of the cigar with the poison on it into his mouth and began to puff as I lit the other end.

Taking a deep breath of smoke into his lungs, he let it out slowly. "Excellent, a superb cigar," he said as he placed it back into his mouth and smiled.

"Do you believe in fairy tales, Mr. Soba?" I asked.

"No, my friend, I do not. Fairy tales are for children. Why do you ask?"

"My friends call me the Sandman, because they say that I put people to sleep. But I believe that death is something you should not fear," I explained, as I looked over at Mr. Soba and smiled. Nodding his head in agreement, he had a confused look on his face as he tried to figure out what in the hell it was I was talking about. Taking another puff of his cigar, I tossed my cigar into the pool of water, knowing that the churning water at the base of the pool would destroy any evidence of it.

Looking back at Mr. Soba, I reached up and took the cigar out of his hand, being careful not to touch the end that had the deadly poison on it. Tossing in into the pool of water, I looked him in the eyes. He had a confused look on his face as he started to have trouble breathing; he then reached up to wipe the sweat that was forming on his forehead.

"It wasn't my grandfather that taught me, sir. It was the CIA," I said calmly. "Carla Silverman sends her regards," I continued as Soba grabbed at his chest and fought to catch his breath with a paranoid look on his face.

"Look at me, look at me," I said as I looked into his eyes. "You're looking into the eyes of death. Say goodnight," I whispered as I turned and walked away.

Hearing his body as it fell to the ground, I didn't turn around. Walking in through the servant's entrance, I smiled as the chef and his work crew looked at me. They were preparing the deserts of chocolate, cakes, pies, and pastries for the evening snack.

"It is such a big house, I am afraid that I have become lost," I explained, as I raised my hands and smiled.

"That direction," the chef explained as he smiled and pointed to the opposite side of the kitchen.

Thanking him, I headed across the kitchen and back into the main dining room. Crossing the dining room, I walked up to the bar. Seeing me coming, the one bartender smiled at me. "Pepsi?" he asked with a laugh.

"Yes, please," I answered as he poured my drink into a crystal leaded champagne glass and handed it to me.

"David, there you are. I thought I had lost you," Sasha said as she walked up to me smiling.

"Is everything alright with your father?" I asked.

"Yes, he is fine. Without me, sometimes he looses things. But I always know where to look," she explained as she picked up a glass of champagne and walked with me back into the sitting room. Sitting down on one of the large chairs, Sasha sat next to me and began to talk.

Looking across the large room, I saw Carla who seemed to be in a very intense conversation with the diplomats from Turkey and Australia. We had been sitting for almost fifteen minutes, when the ambassador of Hungary and his wife rushed into the room.

"Mr. Soba has fallen outside. Please, someone call a doctor," his wife explained in broken English.

Everyone emptied the room and went out into the back courtyard. Looking at me, I noticed that Carla had a confused, yet curious look on her face.

Our host, being a man of insight, had several doctors at the estate; all of whom were his friends and attending the party. Looking around, I realized that there were at least a hundred people here.

"Let me through please, let me through," Mr. Malenkov asked as he and his daughter made their way through the crowd of people who had gathered outside.

"Doctor, what has happened?" Pavel asked with a true look of concern on his face.

Checking the body of Morimoto Soba, the doctor looked up at Mr. Malenkov and sadly shook his head from side to side. "I am sorry, Pavel. Morimoto is gone," he explained as some of the guests gasped saying "Oh no."

"It appears to be a heart attack. Everyone please, go back inside. There is nothing that you can do here. Please go," the doctor asked delicately, trying hard not to upset the guests.

It caught me by surprise when I saw Carla place her hands over her mouth as she began to cry. "Oh, that's very good. You devious, bitch, you," I said to myself as Sasha looked at me with tear filled eyes.

"This is so sad," she said as I put my arms around her to console her.

"Yes, it is, but life is too short to waste. We should enjoy it while we are here," I explained as I walked Sasha back into the house.

I thought that the party would break up, but it didn't. Instead, people drank, ate, and told stories of their times with Mr. Soba.

"Are you alright, Sasha?" I asked as I looked deeply into her pretty green eyes.

"Yes, I am fine," she said as she paused and looked down at my lips and then back up into my eyes. "Did you know him well?" Sasha asked.

"No, I only met him today. My father and our friend Carla knew him very well though. They were very close friends. Carla is crying, it is sad. I only wish that I could call my father to tell him. This will upset him, he should hear about if from me," I explained.

"I can do this for you, come," Sasha explained. "I will take you to my fathers special room. From there, you can call anywhere in the world," she explained as we stood up and walked to the elevator.

"Are you sure your father won't mind?" I asked.

"If he knew, maybe yes. But I have a key that he does not know about," Sasha said smiling. "I call my friends from there all of the time," she explained.

Taking the elevator to the third floor, we went down the long hallway to Sasha's bedroom. "Wait one minute. I will get the key," she explained as she went into her bedroom and closed the door.

It only took Sasha a moment and she returned with a key in her hand and a smile on her face. "Come," she said as she grabbed me by the hand and took me back to the elevator and up to the fourth floor of their estate.

Walking all the way to the end of the hall, Sasha unlocked the door to one of the rooms. Stepping inside, she turned on the light and quickly closed the door behind us, locking it shut.

"What if we get caught?" I asked, looking at the beautiful young Russian.

"Never, no one ever comes up here. This room is for emergency only. In case the snow comes and we are snowed in," she explained as she took me by the hand and walked me into the back room. Opening the other door, she turned the light on.

My eyes widened as I saw the large computer system, three separate telephones, and the very large short-wave radio sitting at the far side of the room.

"Go ahead, David, you use this to call your father, while I wash my face and fix my make-up. My tears have made my face look ugly," she explained as she closed the door to the room and went into the bathroom.

Walking over to the computer system, I turned on the computer and opened the desk drawer. Seeing the computer discs, I smiled. Opening a new disc, I put it into the computer and set the computer to download. I was sure that it had nothing in its memory, but my training at the CIA Spy Farm made me curious anyway. Pressing the button, the computer began to download itself onto the new empty disc. Pausing for a moment, I listened. I could still hear the water in the bathroom sink running.

Looking at the short-wave radio, I sat down and picked up a pencil and began to copy the list of the radio frequency numbers that was listed on a piece of paper next to it. I paused when I saw the number 4287. "Where have I seen that number before?" I asked myself as I heard the water in the bathroom turn off.

Folding up the piece of paper, I placed it into my pants pocket and looked at the computer. "Come on, come on," I said as my words made me think of Ollie and how he had said the same thing when he was downloading the Gruber computer. "Yes," I said softly as the computer screen read, 'Download Complete.' Removing the disc, I put it back into its hard cover plastic case, tucked it into my jacket pocket, turned off the computer, and moved quickly to the telephone. Hearing Sasha as she opened the door, I picked up the telephone receiver and placed it up against my ear.

"I know, Dad. I'm really sorry to have to be the one to tell you. I just thought that you should hear it from me first," I said into the phone that was humming in my ear. "I love you, too, Dad," I said as I hung up the telephone and acted surprised when I turned to find Sasha standing in the doorway looking at me.

"He is okay, your Father?" she asked politely.

"Yes, he will be fine," I explained as I stood up and walked toward her.

"Come, let's take the key back to your room. I don't want you to get into trouble because of me," I explained with a tender smile.

Leaving what I now called the 'Communications Room,' we went back to the third floor and to Sasha's bedroom to put away the key. To my surprise, this time she didn't ask me to wait out in the hallway.

Walking into the bedroom with her, I closed the door behind us and watched as she opened the dresser drawer and hid the key under a stack of very sexy lingerie.

Realizing that I was standing next to her and looking at her underwear, she closed the dresser drawer and placed her hands over her face.

"I am embarrassed now," she said softly.

"You're too beautiful to be embarrassed," I said tenderly as I pulled her hands away from her face.

Turning her head slightly to the left, she asked, "Really? You think that I am pretty?"

Our eyes met once again. This time, there was nothing left to say as our lips touched tenderly against each other's.

* * * * * * *

Looking at my watch, it was almost midnight as Sasha and I walked back into the main dinning room, where everyone had gathered for a late night snack. We had exchanged telephone numbers with the promise that I would show her the United States and she would take me to Russia to show me her motherland. Saying our goodbyes while we were still in her bedroom, Sasha went to sit with her parents, while I sat down next to Carla.

"I would ask where you've been, but I can smell her perfume on you, so I'll let that speak for itself," Carla explained with a grin.

"You have such a nasty mind," I replied calmly in a low voice so the other guests wouldn't hear. "She was very upset over the death of Mr. Soba. I held her in my arms to comfort her, nothing more," I explained. "So tell me, Ms. Silverman, have you figured it out?" I asked with a grin.

"I didn't even know that you had left the damn room. Smooth, David, very smooth. I guess I owe you one," she explained with a touch of disappointment in her voice.

"It's a very beautiful home," I said as I took a bite out of my German chocolate cake.

"Yes, it is," Carla replied as she ate a piece of her pie.

"Did you know that Pavel has a very large 'Communications Room' up on the fourth floor of his beautiful home?" I asked.

Turning her head to look at me, I could see I had caught Carla by surprise.

"Oh really, we didn't know that," she explained with a look of intense interest on her face.

"Shall we step outside for a breath of fresh air?" I asked.

Nothing else was said as we walked out to the back courtyard and up to the water fountain where Mr. Soba had died. Looking around to make sure that we were alone, I picked up the conversation once again.

"He has a very large computer system, which has a phone line that is directly connected to the main frame."

"Oh, really," Carla replied with raised eyebrows.

"Three telephones and a very large short wave Hamm radio," I explained as I looked around at the water to make sure that the cigars had broken apart and disappeared from sight.

"Boy, what I'd give to find out what is in his computer data storage system," Carla said softly. "We might be able to gain some very critical information out of this man's personal system. Damn," she said with a look of disappointment on her face.

Pulling the computer disc out of my pocket, I waved it carefully in front of my face as if I was fanning myself with it. Carla was in such deep thought that she never even noticed it in my hand.

"How hard would it be to breach that room and download his system? Is it heavily secured?" she asked as I slid the disc back into my jacket pocket.

"Boy, I don't know. It's secured with the best security system available. Plus, no one is allowed on the fourth floor. I doubt that James Bond could even get in there," I explained with a serious look on my face. I knew I was lying but I was hoping that Carla would say something to me that would show that she had faith in my being able to breach the system.

"I don't give a rat's ass about Bond. What I want to know is can my boy get the job done?" she asked with a very serious look in her eyes.

"Who's your boy? I didn't know that you had a boy?" I said jokingly with a grin.

"You may not understand this right now, David, but I have my entire reputation bet on you, and your natural ability to get the job done. Can you do it? Can you get in and download that system?" Carla asked once again.

Pulling the disc back out of my pocket, I smiled and handed it to Carla. The look of total shock on her face was payment enough. I knew now that this special lady trusted me as a person and as a friend.

"Holy shit!" she said out loud. Realizing that her outburst may have attracted attention from some of the other guests that were walking around with us, Carla looked around and smiled. "Tell me that this is from his computer," she asked in an anxious tone.

"It's the complete download, but I don't know if there is anything on it, it may be empty. Pulling the piece of paper out of my pants pocket, I handed it to Carla. "This is a list of the short-wave frequency codes that were written down on a piece of paper next to the radio. There was stuff written next to each individual number, but it was written in Russian. Those bottom three numbers are the numbers that were on each phone line. I thought that you might want to monitor those. Look carefully at those numbers, ma'am. There is only one number at the end of the number that is different. They're in order. That tells me that the telephone number, to the phone line that is connected to his computer is one digit up or down from the sequence of numbers. What do you think?" I asked in a low voice.

Shaking her head from side to side in amazement, she looked at me and became serious. "I don't know what to say, David. You didn't come here for this, yet you had the instincts to do it. What can I do to repay you for this?" she asked sincerely.

Turning my right cheek towards her, I smiled and said, "A kiss on the cheek will be enough."

Reaching up Carla kissed me on the cheek, placed both of her hands on the sides of my face and turned my head to face her. "There is a small elite group working at the international level, David, they are watching everything you do. This, my dear friend, is going to impress the hell out of them. It's forbidden for me to say any more at this time. Be patient and continue to follow your instincts. I am pushing to bring you in," she explained. "Now, how did you kill Mr. Soba?" she asked smiling.

"Ahh, Mr. Soba, I told him that I was CIA and that you sent your regards. I wish that you could have seen the look on his face," I explained.

"You told him that I was the one that ordered his assassination?" Carla asked with a look of disbelief.

"Yes, ma'am," I said smiling.

"How did you do it?" she asked again.

"Its going to take more than a kiss on the cheek for me to tell you that. Besides, the best-kept secrets are the secrets that keep themselves, I whispered softly into her ear.

"If I were only twenty-years younger, David, oh what I would do to you," Carla explained in a seductive voice as she slipped the computer disc and piece of paper into her small hand held clutch purse and walked back toward the party.

"Are you kidding? With the legs you've got? Hell, don't let my age stop you," I said jokingly as I stepped up my pace to catch up with her.

Chapter Fourteen
Battery Power

Looking at my empty box of Chocolate Mint Girl Scout cookies, I burped and let out a sigh. "I can't believe I ate the whole box." Taking a sip of my Pepsi, I went up to my bedroom to pick up my tuxedo so I could put it in the front room. Andy was going to pick it up and drop it off at the dry cleaners for me.

I had been home from my trip to Geneva for almost three days. Picking my pants up from the bedroom floor, I checked to make sure the pockets were empty. Then I picked up my suit jacket, pulled out the solid gold lighter, the cigar trimmer, and the two cigar tube holders and tossed them onto my bed. "Oops," I forgot to turn those back in when Carla and I had gotten back to the United States.

Reaching into the left outer pocket, I found it empty. I then placed my hand inside the coat, and checked the hidden inside pocket. Feeling something inside, a puzzled look crossed my face as I pulled out what was inside and took a close look at it.

Sitting down on the side of my bed, a smile crossed my face as I looked at the 5x7 picture of Sasha and the pink and silver lace garter she had put inside the pocket. Looking at the back of the photograph it read:

'Remember me. My heart
has gone to America with you'
Love, Sasha

Taking a breath of air into my lungs, I let it out slowly. Placing the garter to my nose, I could still smell her scent on it. Lying back on my bed, I closed my eyes and remembered the two hours I had spent alone with this special young lady in her bedroom.

"I'll see you again, Sasha, I'll see you again. I promise," I whispered softly to myself.

* * * * * * *

My arm and hand was covered with blood from the girls' leg wound. I needed to find a place to rest; someplace where I could stop her bleeding. My heart raced with the combination of fear and adrenaline. I could hear the Viet Cong soldiers as they drew closer to us. "Oh, God, no!" I whispered softly to myself.

"Kate!" I shouted out loud, as I sat straight up in my bed. My body was covered with sweat. I could feel my heart pounding in my chest as I placed my trembling hands over my face. "Calm down, David, calm down," I repeated as I tried to slow down my heartbeat and erase the memory from my mind.

Looking to my left, I saw the picture of Sasha and picked it up. As I looked at it, I began to calm down from the nightmare of my past. Placing both the picture and garter on the top of my dresser, I went into my bathroom to take a cold shower.

After my shower, I put on a T-shirt and pair of jeans, went to my kitchen, opened the refrigerator, and pulled out two ice-cold bottles of Pepsi. Opening the first bottle, I tipped it up and emptied the whole bottle with one long gulp. Burping three times out loud, I smiled. "Now I feel better," I told myself as I went into my den to check the computer. Sitting down, I opened the second bottle of Pepsi and tossed the can opener onto my desk next to the phone. Just as I did, the telephone rang.

"Hello?" I said.

"David, its me, Andy. The boys are having a meeting at your Uncle Jack's restaurant around 9:30, after its closed. We need you to be there. Can you make it?" Andy asked.

"I'll be there around nine. What's going on?" I asked.

"Aw, Tony Pro and Tony Jack are all up tight. They want to whack Hoffa, so there's going to be a pow wow about it. It's no big thing," Andy explained.

"Tony Pro is a real piece of shit!" I said calmly. "Hell, Andy, Jimmy said he would give him the damn money out of the teamsters' pension fund. He just wants Tony to pay it back with interest. How does that make Jimmy the bad guy, for crying out loud! Jimmy is loyal to his teamsters; he's trying to turn a profit for his drivers. That's honorable, brother," I commented.

"Yeah, I know, but what are you going to do? I'll be there at 8:20, I'll see you tonight," Andy said as he hung up the phone.

Hanging up my phone, I sent Carla a very detailed message on the computer. All it said was, "Well?" I was curious as to whether or not they had found anything on the disc I had downloaded from Pavel Malenkov's computer.

Turning on the TV, I opened another box of Chocolate Mint Girl Scout cookies, and watched Magnum P.I..

* * * * * * *

My uncle owned the Eat More restaurant located on the corner of South Telegraph Road and Huron Street, next to the Payless Shoe Store. It was a very nice restaurant that catered to the hard working middle class people. Being true to its name, my uncle made sure that if you ate at his restaurant, your plate would be full and you would definitely eat more. He felt that if he fed you more than any other restaurant in town, you would always come back to eat at Jack's restaurant because the food was delicious and you got lots of it! Walking into my uncle's restaurant, I saw that it was packed, and it was 8:45 p.m. I guess he was right. Seeing Don and Andy sitting at the corner booth next to the front windows and door, I slid in next to them and ordered a Pepsi.

* * * * * * *

Looking at my watch, it was 10:12 p.m. as the last couple finally paid for their meal and walked out the door. Locking the door behind them, my uncle looked at me, smiled, and then went back into the kitchen to clean things up.

Taking a chair with him, Don and two of Tony Pro's people went to the backdoor of the restaurant, checked to make sure that the backdoor was locked and then sat down. Closer to the kitchen, was a big round table. There, sitting at the table was my grandfather, Tony Pro from New Jersey, Tony Jack from the Detroit enforcer family, Tony's brother Vito, and another man named Baines.

Drinking coffee, they listened as Tony Pro explained exactly how the murder of Teamster President Jimmy Hoffa would take place. Walking over to the round table, I handed my grandfather a glass of ice water and then sat down next to him. It was here that the details of the Hoffa hit were laid out and finalized.

Tony Provenzano would send three men from the Teamsters' Union Hall in New Jersey. Two of these men would be brothers; all three would be hit men. They would drive a black 1975 Lincoln Continental four-door. It would be registered with New Jersey plates. Inside the car, riding with them, would be Jimmy Hoffa's stepson Chucky.

Tony knew that Jimmy would be nervous about this meeting and worried that it might be a possible set up. Jimmy trusted his stepson Chucky. So Chucky would play a key roll in keeping Jimmy calm. Jimmy would be told that Tony pro and Tony Jack, wanted to meet with him to make the peace between Jimmy and Tony Pro. Jimmy would be led to believe that both Tony Jack and Tony Pro would meet with him at the Macus Red Fox Restaurant on Telegraph Road in Bloomfield Hills, Michigan. They knew this detail would relax Jimmy even more. The Macus Red Fox was well known for being a mob restaurant where a lot of top-level meetings took place over lunch or dinner.

Chucky's job would be to convince Jimmy to come with them and travel less than one mile south, on Telegraph Road, to another mob spot called the Raleigh House. It's a banquet hall that can cater to four banquets at one time. What few people knew, however, is that near the backdoor is a small room. In that room is a trash grinding system. This system cuts everything up into two-inch chunks; paper plates, plastic cups, cardboard boxes. But what it was originally designed for is the disposal of human bodies. This system would grind-up a body, bones, shoes, belt, wallet, everything quicker than you could say 'Bada bing – Bada boom.' Jimmy Hoffa was going to take a one-way ride to the Raleigh House.

Tony Pro and Tony Jack would both be there. They would try to make the deal their way, one last time. If Jimmy said 'no,' then the two brothers would shoot him once he got back into the backseat of the Lincoln Town Car. Then they would run his body through the trash grinder. Once this was done, a garbage disposal truck would pick up the trash dumpster and take it to the dump. Instead of dumping it with the rest of the local trash, it would be placed in the new incinerator that had just been built there. They would incinerate everything in the container, not once, but twice to ensure that no trace of Jimmy Hoffa would be left. This would fulfill the promise that Tony Pro had made to Jimmy Hoffa, when they served a small prison term together. Tony told Jimmy, 'I'll make you a very powerful man. But if you ever cross me, they won't find so much as your fingernail.' Tony had meant what he said.

The incinerator would then be dismantled. The black Lincoln Town Car would be driven to the local scrapyard, which was owned by Tony Jack's close friend. Once there, it would be put into the car crusher and compressed into a small metal cube. Jimmy Hoffa, along with all of the evidence, would vanish without a trace.

Once the investigation into Jimmy's disappearance began, two Federal agents would take it out of the hands of the local authorities. Mr. Baines would then come into play, by having mob connected friends call in 'Tips' saying that Jimmy was on a boat; in a 50 gallon drum; in the Florida Everglades; at the local garbage disposal dump; buried under a football field; so on, and so on. This would keep the real agents busy, while both Tony Pro and Tony Jack made fools of them.

The meeting broke up at 12:18 a.m. and everyone went their separate way. However, it was agreed that they would wait just a little longer, to give Jimmy time to change his mind.

Walking out to my Corvette, I got in and headed home. I found three things very interesting. Vito would be there for the hit on Jimmy, but his brother was nervous and said that he would be at the local health spa. He was going to ask people what time it was to ensure they would remember him being there at the time Jimmy disappeared. They were also willing to dismantle a 1.6 million dollar incinerator to make sure that no trace of

Jimmy could be found. What puzzled me was how two FBI agents were going to be able to convince their supervisor to take over the investigation? There would be no evidence of a kidnapping, a murder, or Jimmy being taken across the state line. The FBI, or someone high up, would have to be in on this. They would have no legal jurisdiction giving them the authority to take over the investigation and remove it from the Bloomfield Police Detectives. The Bloomfield Police had a reputation of being real good at solving crimes. Tony Jack and Tony Pro weren't going to give them a chance to solve this one. But who was it in Washington D.C., that would authorize the FBI to take over the case?

Laughing out loud, I smiled. They had all the bases covered except one. They forgot about the trash-grinding machine. It would have 'trace evidence' of blood and hair on, and in it. In there haste, they forgot about that.

Tony Pro was a real piece of shit. He was bringing in four hit men, knowing that he was going to kill them once he got them back to New Jersey.

"I'll have to put Tony on my list of things to do. The next time I'm in Jersey, I'll stop by and kill him. Yeah, that's what I'll do. It will even it all out," I said to myself as I pulled into my driveway and turned off the engine.

Walking into my house, I heard the computer beeping in the other room. Unlocking the door to my den, I turned on the light and walked over to my desk and sat down. I had a message from Carla. All that it said was: "Do the words, Gold Mine, mean anything to you?"

"Yes!" I said out loud in excitement. They found something in Pavel's database. Looking at my watch, I realized it was almost midnight, so I sent Carla a message: "Bond sleeps with his women. Does this mean that I get to see more than one leg?"

Breaking out in laughter, I couldn't help but wonder what it would be like, to actually have an affair with Carla. She was very pretty, had a firm well-built body, and was as deadly as a scorpion!

"Well, it's fun just to be able to tease each other. I'll settle for that. Why blow a great friendship over something stupid like sex?" I told myself as I placed a drop of Methadrine under my tongue. "I'll fly out to see Carla first thing in the morning," I thought. as my telephone began to ring.

Picking up the receiver, I placed it to my ear, "Hello?"

"Are you available, sir?" the deep voice asked politely.

"Yes," I replied as I hung up the telephone and went to the front door.

Hearing my doorbell ring, I opened the door, "Hey, dude, you dropped this at the mall earlier this evening. Like, it was real hard trying to find you, man!" the long haired, bearded, hippie explained as he handed me the manila envelope, turned, and walked back to his yellow van painted with 'Peace' symbols and large multi colored flowers.

Closing my front door, I smiled and locked the door. It was never the same person who delivered the envelope.

"Amazing," I said to myself as I went back into my den to check out the information in the envelope. Dumping the contents of the envelope out on to the top of my desk, I picked up the 8x10 photograph and looked at the man the family wanted me to kill. Picking up the personal information sheet, I began to read.

Jack Manetti was a thirty-eight year old corporate attorney for one of New York's biggest law firms. He was a Yale graduate, stood six-feet tall and weighed 200-pounds. He plays racquetball on Wednesday night, and was full-blooded Italian. He ate supper on Friday at a placed called The Beer Garden at Bohemian Hall in Queens, New York, where he meets with his girlfriend. He had just finalized his divorce with his wife, Kay, of whom he was married to for twelve years. He had two daughters now in Jr. High School, but living with their mother. He has a multi-million dollar suite in Manhattan; his office is in the Empire State Building. However, he spends Friday night at this place called The Beer Garden. Parties until midnight there, with his girlfriend Laura, and then spends the night at Laura's place.

Turning on my computer, I checked the CIA databank on this place called, The Beer Garden in Queens. Looking at the information that just appeared on my computer screen, I began to read. Bohemian Hall, the city's last remaining European-style beer garden, is a walled-in oasis where you can drink beer all day long without being bothered by the neighbors. The 25,000-sqaure foot beer garden opened in 1919 as a Czech community center, but now caters to the younger crowd wanting to party and relive the backyard kegger days of Yore. They serve Goulash with frosty Staropramen while an 'Oompah' band plays in the outside back courtyard. The backcourt is lined with picnic tables.

"Hot damn, this sounds like fun," I said to myself as I wrote down the address and phone number. "Bohemian Hall, at 29-19 24th Avenue, Astoria, New York. I clicked on Queens and then zoomed in on the address 29-19 24th Avenue, Astoria. "This place is in the middle of freakin' nowhere Queens! Laura lives right down the road from the Beer Garden. "That's his weak spot," I said to myself. "I'll hit him at Laura's or the Beer Garden, and I'll use his brand new Mercedes to do it."

* * * * * * *

Calling my grandfather, Kathy, and Carla, I explained that I was going to be gone for a couple of days.

I locked up my house and flew to New York to meet with my cousin, Gina. Getting off the Northwest Airlines flight, I saw Gina standing at the 'off boarding' area smiling at me.

"Hello, cousin," she said with a smile as she walked up to me and gave me a big hug.

"Boy, pretty lady, if you weren't my cousin, what I would do to you," I whispered in her ear, as I smiled.

"Well, gee," she said teasingly as we walked through the terminal and out to the parking lot. "We're not real blood cousins, so what are you trying to tell me?" she asked in a sweet and sexy voice as she fluttered her eyelashes at me.

"Girlfriend, you are one beautiful Italian lady. Want to spend the night with me?" I asked boldly knowing that she was going to say 'no.'

Climbing into her brand new Lincoln Mark V, she started the engine and then turned in her seat to look at me.

"Are you being serious?" she asked with a straight face.

"Wow, man, don't get mad at me, cuz. Damn, I'm sorry Gina; I thought you were being serious. I'm really sorry," I said apologetically.

"No, David, I'm not upset." she explained as she looked down at the black leather seat, ran her hand across it nervously, and then looked back up at me. "I've had a crush on you ever since we were little. Yes, I would sleep with you, as long as you promise it won't ruin our friendship," she explained shyly.

Laughing, I shook my head from side to side. "I can't believe it. I've had the hot's for you since we were six-years old, and trust me, Gina, nothing, and I mean nothing and no one, will ever tear apart our friendship. I give you my word on that," I explained as I looked Gina in the eyes.

"Promise?" she asked seriously.

"I promise, cuz, you got my word on it, No matter whatever happens, remember one thing and never ever forget it," I explained.

"What?" she asked.

"I love you, cuz, nothing can ever stop that," I explained as I leaned over and kissed her on the forehead.

Smiling, she put the car in gear, "Alright, lets get out of here."

"Were you able to get the things I asked you for when I called to have you pick me up?"

"Oh yeah, piece of cake. New York, Chicago, hey these are my towns," she explained smiling from ear to ear. "Do I dare ask what you need that stuff for?" Gina asked, as we drove into the city.

Taking a deep breath of air into my lungs, I grinned and let it out slowly. "Don't ask, its better that you don't know. Hey, have you ever been to The Beer Garden in Queens?" I questioned hoping to change the subject.

"Oh yeah, lots of times. It's a great place to go and have fun, and if you're hungry, you won't be when you leave there. They feed the shit out of ya there," Gina explained.

Looking at my watch, it was almost 9:00 a.m. Friday morning. I had all day to check out the Queens area, especially where this girl Laura lived. Then I would go to The Beer Garden, have dinner and wait for Mr. Manetti. If all went well, I would make my move on him tonight.

* * * * * * *

The Bohemian Hall, or better known as The Beer Garden at Bohemian Hall, is something you simply have to experience to understand. From the street it has a small brick front look to it. It's surrounded by old four-story apartment buildings with fire escapes, just like you would see on TV. The brown front door sits to the left of the bar front and a small window off to its right. The sign on the door had an arrow taped to it that points to the left as you walk up to the door. Walking to the left, there is a large brick wall. Walking in through the front entrance of the wall, I smiled!

"Check this out, would ya," I said out loud to myself. The large courtyard had picnic tables lined up all over the place, large square cement floor and a closed in structure that looked almost like a small garage with an open face.

Inside, the Oompah band was playing old Czech style music. The place was full of people. Smiling, I went inside the bar, through the back doorway, and found it full of people who were buying plates of food and large jugs of Staropraman beer. The bartender was middle-aged with brown hair that was slightly balding on the top front, but covered his ears and touched his shirt collar. The younger kid next to him was filling pitchers of beer right from the tap.

"Man, I wish that I would have brought Andy and Don with me. They would love this place," I thought to myself as I made my way through the long line and picked up a plate of Czech style goulash and a cold Pepsi. Finding a table to sit at, I listened to the band, ate two huge plates of goulash, and relaxed.

Looking at my watch, it was almost 7:00. Jack and Laura were late. This place was nothing less than one big neighborhood party. It was seventeen minutes after seven when the overhead lights came on and Jack and Laura came walking in.

Jack had olive skin, Italian jet-black hair, which was combed back, brown eyes, and stood six-feet tall at about two hundred pounds. I could see the tan line on his left finger where his wedding ring used to be. Laura, however, was a whole different story. She was built like Gina; was about five-feet, seven-inches tall, had a body to die for, the face of a super model with flaming red-hot hair!

"No wonder he divorced Kay," I thought to myself as I watched them go into the bar and come back out with two large plates of food and mixed drinks. To my surprise, they walked directly toward me and sat down at my picnic table.

Within a matter of minutes, another couple sat down with us. We introduced ourselves to each other and spent the next two hours laughing, eating, drinking, and having fun. Jack was sitting with and looking death in the eyes, and he would never know it.

At 10:00 p.m. I bought a round of drinks for Jack, Laura, and the other couple. Then I said goodnight and left The Beer Garden. Driving down 24th Avenue about two blocks, I pulled my car over to the side of the road, turned off the ignition, and waited for Jack to bring Laura back home to her apartment.

* * * * * * *

Looking at my watch, it was seventeen minutes past midnight. I checked my rearview mirror and smiled when I saw Jack pull up to the curb and park his brand new 450XL Mercedes Sport Coupe. Getting out of the car, Jack took Laura upstairs to her two-bedroom apartment, at the opposite side of the building.

Placing a drop of Methadrine under my tongue, I sat back and waited. I wanted to give Jack enough time to have sex with Laura, clean up, and go to sleep. I also wanted to wait until most of the traffic and movement of people was over with for the night.

* * * * * * *

Looking at my watch it was 4:00 a.m., and the streets were quite as I opened the car door to my Chevy Impala, pulled out my black leather doctor's bag and closed the car door. Snugging my leather gloves up a bit tighter on both of my hands, I walked up to the front of Jack's car and opened the hood.

Setting my leather bag on top of the silver air cleaner, I could smell the fresh scent of a brand new engine. Opening my bag I pulled out my pliers and small flashlight, turned on the flashlight and quickly pulled the battery cable off of the negative post of the car battery and set it off to the side of the battery.

Putting the small set of pliers back into my bag, I then removed all the round caps from the top of the battery and placed them off to one side. I then pulled out an empty plastic jar and turkey baster. Putting the turkey baster into the first open hole of the battery, I began to withdraw the battery acid from the battery and put it into the empty jar. Removing about an inch worth of the battery acid, I shined my light into the battery and could see the 'Fins' of the inside of the battery. It was still full of acid, but the very top section was empty. I then did the same thing to the other chambers of the battery, screwed the top back onto the plastic jar now full of battery acid, and put the jar back into my leather bag.

Looking up, I casually looked around to make sure no cars were coming or that anyone was watching me. Seeing that the coast was clear, I reached back into my bag and pulled out a brand new plastic bottle of bleach. Using the turkey baster, I carefully filled the battery back up with bleach and then put the round caps back onto the top of the battery. Putting the top back onto the bottle of bleach, I put it and the turkey baster into my bag, pulled out a small rag, and wiped off the top of the battery. Looking around one more time to make sure I was still clear, I put the rag back into my doctors bag, zipped the top closed, picked up the bag and closed the hood of the car. Smiling, I went back to my car, put the doctors bag away and drove down the street. Turning the car around, I parked it against the curb on the opposite side of the street, turned off the engine, and sat back and relaxed.

* * * * * * *

It was 9:04 a.m. when Jack walked out of Laura's apartment building. The sun was shining and a few people were up and about, but not many.

Jack got into his car, put the key into the ignition and turned it. Nothing happened. Seeing the look of confusion on Jack's face, I smiled. He was trying to figure out how a brand new car battery could have gone dead. Getting out of the car, Jack opened the hood and looked at his battery, while I watched him from 100-yards away. Even though his back was turned to me, I could almost read his mind He saw that the negative side of the battery cable was unhooked. He was thinking that some young kid must have tried to steal his car battery. "Damn kids!" Picking up the battery cable, Jack leaned slightly over the top of the battery, with the cable in his right hand.

"Say goodnight, asshole," I whispered to myself as Jack pressed the battery cable back onto the negative side post of the battery.

By touching the cable to the post, Jack completed the circuit of electricity to the battery. The combination of battery acid and pure bleach causes a chemical reaction. It's harmless all by itself. But once you touch an electrical charge to it, it becomes highly explosive.

When Jack touched the negative cable to the battery, it activated and completed the electrical circuit. The explosion was not only very loud, but the battery blew-up with a vengeance! The left front section of the Mercedes, the grill, headlight, and left front corner of the fender, turned into flying shrapnel; most of which hit Jack in the face, neck, and chest. Jack's body flew through the air a good fifteen-feet before it slammed back down again onto the asphalt street. People began to come out of their apartments to see what had happened. Seeing Jack's body laying in the street and covered with blood, they rushed to his aide.

I started my car and drove away. The one thing that I knew for sure was that Jack Manetti was dead before his body hit the ground!

* * * * * * *

Driving back to Manhattan, I couldn't help but wonder why Jack would deliberately lose a multi-million dollar civil suit? The insurance company paid Jack five hundred thousand dollars to throw the case. Jack was already worth ten million all by himself. One of the senior partners had found out that Jack had betrayed their law firm. They were about to win a hundred million dollar judgment against a major insurance company. Now the client who was injured would spend the rest of her life sitting in a wheel chair. Jacks betrayal cost him his life.

The police and medical examiner would file their reports in the case of Jack Manetti's death as an 'accidental death,' caused by a faulty battery.

Kay Manetti, who still had life insurance on her now ex-husband, for the sake of her minor children, would not only collect double indemnity from the insurance company; she would also receive a multi-million dollar settlement from the company that manufactured the battery.

As for me, I spent the afternoon hanging out with Gina. We went to Studio 54 that night and once again ran into Frank White and his boys, and partied until 2:00 a.m.

I spent the night at Gina's place and slept on the couch. Even though we talked about having a sexual relationship, we didn't. We were too much like brother and sister to each other to actually cross that line.

My flight back home to Waterford, Michigan gave me time to reflect on my past. I missed Chopper and Butch and the action of Vietnam even more now.

"Damn," I whispered to myself under my breath. "I'm still in the business of Death, only at a different level, and business is real good!"

Chapter Fifteen
Whip Lash

Sitting in the Situation Room, I scanned the computer with the hope of getting a location on Chopper. I knew he wasn't at the waterfall where I had taken Kate. He was back in Vietnam working as an agent for the CIA. Agent Eckland told me they recruited Danny before they approached me. "Where in the hell are you, big brother?" I asked myself quietly.

I was waiting for Carla. She had called me and left a dozen messages on my computer over the weekend. I, however, was in Queens, New York killing Jack Manetti for the family. I knew there was something Carla wanted to give me. I could hear it in her words, 'Top Priority Important.' So, here I sat waiting, while she attended a meeting with the big boys at the White House.

One of the other agents, working here at this office, called her to let her know I was waiting for her. So, I didn't expect it to be too long before she arrived at her office.

Scanning through the data bank, I continued my search for the man who had become more than my friend; he had become my big brother. His name was Danny McBride, but to me, he would always be Chopper. Hearing the door open behind me, I turned to look at who was coming into the room.

"David, thank you for coming so quickly," Carla said, as she closed and locked the door behind the man who had just walked into the room with her.

"Please, join us, David," Carla asked as she motioned for me to leave the computer and join them at the conference table. Turning off the computer, I moved over to the long wooden table and sat down.

"Henry, I would like you to meet the young man I have been telling you about. This is David. David, say hello to Henry, the Secretary of State," Carla said as she introduced me to President Nixon's number one, right hand boy. Henry was a pretty good size man with graying hair and a deep scraggy voice. He was the power behind the President of the United States, and everybody knew it!

"David, it is nice to meet you. Ms. Silverman has been telling us a lot of good things about you. She says that you are a young man that refuses to fail at anything you do. She also says that you are a fast thinker. I was reading some classified top-secret documents about some of your Black Operations missions in Vietnam. You were the youngest member of your team, yet your seasoned team members chose you as their team leader on most of your missions. Because of all this, we would like to discuss something with you and ask you for your thoughts. Carla?" Henry said as he turned the meeting over to her.

"David, as you know, we are tracking a number of missing A and B pack suitcase size nuclear weapons. Two of these weapons are ours. We believe the other two may be from Russia. There is a lot of, shall we say, tension between the United States and Russia right now. What we didn't know was just how bad that tension really is. The computer disc that you downloaded from Pavel Malenkov's Communications Room was nothing less than shocking! There are terrorist groups in the Middle East that are recruiting new members everyday. They are also trying to buy Plutonium or Uranium with the hope of building nuclear weapons."

"We can't allow that, no!" Henry said, interrupting Carla. "I am sorry, Carla, please finish what you were saying."

"We have agents, spies as you would say, that have penetrated deep into these countries. Our Delta Force boys are monitoring phone conversations from top ranking military leaders, and up to some Presidents of these countries. Russia, China, Iran, Syria, just to name a few. The threat against us is very real and now we know that it is a lot worse than we once thought. It's against international law to assassinate Presidents of other countries or their diplomats. We have a few ideas, but we would like some input from a guy like you that has been there and done that. How do we do something like that and protect the President at the same time?" Carla asked.

"Yes, your team never failed in Vietnam. What was it that made your team so good at what they did?" Henry asked as he leaned forward and rested his arms on top of the table, with a curious look on his face, waiting for an answer.

"Loyalty and trust, sir. Captains Bell and Mosier, Lieutenant Joe Knight, Cookie, Butch, Nick, Chopper, and I; we were family. We could look at each other and without saying a word we knew what the other person was thinking or going to do. We protected each other, without question. We never lied to each other, not ever. Once the Deputy Director of the CIA, Mr. Crock, or the Deputy Director of the Defense Intelligence Agency, Mr. Putnam, issued the order for a mission, they backed off and let our team decide on our best plan of action. One time Mr. Joseph Peterson, Deputy Director of the National Security Agency, came with Mr. Crock to one of our mission briefings. Mr. Peterson and some of his pencil pushing bureaucrats had already put together a plan on how they thought we should go about the mission to accomplish it. I was cocky at that time..."

"Some things never change, huh?" Carla added with a smile, as she interrupted me in mid-sentence.

"As I was saying, sir, I was the cocky one in our team. I told Deputy Director Peterson that if he thought he knew how to get into Laos and kill the Mayor, then he should go and do it his own damn self. I then told Mr. Crock that we would accept the mission and that we would do it our way and only our way without anyone from the outside knowing what we were going to do, or how we were going to do it. Mr. Peterson started to get upset with me, but Mr. Crock cut him to the quick and told him that we do it my way. He then told Peterson that if any of his people should have happened to leak the information about our mission and we walked into an ambush... Well, sir, to put it plain and simple, Crock told Peterson that he would kill him.

Give us the mission, give us what we need to accomplish it, no matter what we ask for, give it to us, then step back and let us do our thing. For Mr. Crock we were actually protecting him. The less he knew, the safer he was. If something went wrong and he was called into a Senate hearing, he had plausible deniability and we were on our own. Expendable, as you would say here in Washington. You need to put together another Black Operations Team One, like ours. One person here on this end gets the order from you, Henry. The President never speaks to anyone but you. You give the order to lets say Ms. Silverman, she gives it to, in our case, Captain Bell or Mosier, they give it to us, and we go do our thing, our way. If we succeed, you win. If we get boxed in, we kill ourselves. It's that simple.

Now then, if you want to make it even better, you give my guy a computer and he gets the mission profile over that or directly from Carla. But that person is never, ever told about who Carla gets the order from. It's hard, sir. In our case, when they made me discharge and leave Vietnam, the whole team quit and went home. You're going to need to find a team or a couple of people that have been through hell with each other before. Putting total strangers together will be hard work. So, you'll have to start them out on small, simple missions until they get used to working with each other. Once they're tuned in to each other, turn them lose. Then you've got the Band of the Hand, and that's what you're looking for, sir," I explained.

"Interesting, very interesting," Henry said as he nodded his head up and down slowly and looked over at Carla. "Now I have some thoughts to work with. David, thank you, young man. Keep up the good work," Henry said as he reached across the table to shake my hand. "Carla, call me later, I have something I need to discuss with you," he added as he got up and left the room.

Waiting for the door to close behind Henry, Carla turned to look at me. "Would you really kill yourself to protect us, rather then be captured?" she asked with a dead serious look on her face.

"Damn straight I would. I spent 89-days as a special guest of the Chinese and Viet Cong, in Cambodia. I lost my best friend Nick on that mission and got myself captured at the same time. You know what makes it worse?" I asked sadly.

"What?" Carla asked in a soft whisper.

"I was so emotionally upset at seeing Nick shot and in so much pain, that I completely forgot we both had a cyanide capsule taped to our wrists. I could have put his capsule in his mouth; he would have bitten into it and have died all on his own. I could have then escaped with the rest of my team."

"Why didn't you?" Carla asked as she reached over and gently placed her hand on top of mine. "David, did you really forget or are you lying to yourself to justify a deeper reason?"

"Nick was Catholic by faith. Suicide is against his beliefs. That would have been suicide." Pausing a moment to gather my thoughts, I asked, "So, what did you want to see me about?"

Seeing that I was uncomfortable with the first subject, Carla answered, "I'll be right back." Leaving the room, she was gone about ten minutes. As she walked back into the room, I smiled. She had two cans of cold Pepsi in her hands. Handing a can, to me she smiled and sat back down.

"Hoo yah," I said softly, as I opened the can and took a drink.

"Feel better?" she asked.

"Yeah. Sorry, Carla, sometimes its hard to keep the pain and guilt inside," I explained. "Hey, it took you ten minutes to go for two cans of Pepsi?" I asked curiously.

"No, it took me seven minutes to use the bathroom and three minutes to go down the hall to the vending machine to get the soda," she explained with a grin.

Looking at the top of my pop can, I asked, "You did wash didn't you?"

"No," she said with a laugh as she reached into her pocket and pulled out the small device and handed it to me.

"This is a brand new item, David. It's called a Sky Pager. With this we can contact you anywhere in the world. It will give you a digital read out of the number you are to call or we can send you a written message with it through our satellite system. We also have a hand held telephone coming to us any day now. It's battery operated, so you'll have to keep it charged up. I'll have Brandi deliver it to you as soon as it arrives," Carla explained proudly.

"This would be worth millions on the open market," I commented as I looked at the new satellite paging system.

"Within a few years, David, everyone in the world will have one. The phone companies are working on it right now. Its state of the art technology and we're giving it to the elite few now. Guys like you, Delta Force, Seal teams, and officials here at the Pentagon and the White House, are all getting one. That download you did on Pavel's computer was a real wake-up call for us. I'll give you my pager number before you leave," Carla explained as someone knocked on the door.

"Come in," Carla said loudly as she looked over at the door to see who was opening it.

"Excuse me, ma'am but you've got a phone call that's top priority urgent," the older gentleman, whom I had never seen before, explained, "Line two, ma'am," he continued.

"Thank you, Benny," Carla said as she reached over, picked up the telephone, and pressed the square button at the bottom of the phone to connect her with line two.

"Hello?" she said in a firm, professional voice. "Yes, sir, he's still here.... yes, sir... Really?... It's been confirmed then?" taking a deep breath into her lungs, Carla let it out slowly and rubbed her temples with her right hand. "Who, sir?... Agent Eckland?... Are you sure that you want to do that, sir, I mean, is that a wise decision?... Yes, sir... She's on her way here now?... Yes, sir, if you say so, I'm sure our boy will keep an eye on her... Yes, sir, goodbye, sir," she said as she hung-up the phone and stared at it with a deep thoughtful look on her face.

"So, what did Henry want?" I asked.

"How did you know that was Henry?" Carla asked as she looked over at me. She looked like she was dazed by the phone conversation she had just received.

"Duh," I responded sarcastically with a grin on my face. "You alright? You look like you just lost your best friend," I asked with a look of concern.

"I'll be fine. The Malenkov disc just confirmed that one of our closest people is selling secrets to both Russia and China."

"A mole?" I asked.

"Not only him, but his wife and two oldest kids are all part of it. We're sending you after the whole family, and they want Agent Eckland to be close by in case something happens and you need an alibi," she explained.

"Bullshit, boss, what's the real reason they're sending Kathy with me?" I asked.

"I think it's their way of making up for not telling her about the Gruber hit in Germany. Kathy has been pushing to get in on the action for a long time. I want you to keep an eye on her, and evaluate her on this mission. Who knows, they may use her more as back up for you," she explained.

"I thought that was Ollie's job?" I asked.

"Oliver is walking in dangerous waters for us right now. He's selling weapons to the Contras. We need his complete attention right where he's at and doing what he's doing," Carla explained. "Come on, I'll buy you lunch while we wait for Ms. Eckland."

* * * * * * *

It was almost 3:00 p.m. by the time Kathy arrived at the Pentagon. Because she didn't have a Q-clearance, we met with her down the hall in a secure briefing room. Carla and I were waiting for her when she walked into the room. Kathy was wearing a three-piece women's business suit that was dark blue with silver pin stripes. I could detect a slight bulge under her left arm. If you weren't looking for it, you would never notice it.

"I'm really sorry if I have kept you both waiting. Traffic was a bitch," Kathy explained as she sat down across from us at the table.

The Briefing Room was an average size room. It had a coffee maker with sugar, Sweet & Low, and coffee creamer just off to your right as you first walked into the room. The long table sat in the center of the room. It was a dark solid oak table with six leather chairs on both sides. The small bathroom was off to the back far left corner of the room.

"Agent Eckland, thank you for coming on such a short notice," Carla explained.

"Please, call me Kathy," Kathy asked politely.

"Did they tell you why you're here, Kathy?" Carla asked.

"No, ma'am, all I was told was that it was urgent I meet with you as quickly as possible. To be honest with you, ma'am, I thought something had happened to David," she explained as she looked at me with a shy smile. "But I should have known better, shouldn't I?"

"Well, I don't know about all that. David has had his mission status elevated to Elite Counter Measures Covert Operations Only Agent," Carla explained with pride as she looked over at me.

"Am I being removed as his direct supervisor?" Kathy asked.

I could see it in her eyes. She was beginning to get angry, but remaining calm on the outside.

"Oh no, not at all. In fact your status is being altered slightly also. You're going with him on this next mission," Carla explained as we both watched to see what Kathy's expression would be.

"I am? I mean, yes, ma'am," Kathy replied anxiously.

"Let's make sure that the three of us have a complete understanding here. You're still the field supervisor for David, but you are in no way a wet work agent. You're going along to observe and be an alibi for him should something go wrong. You are in no way to be directly involved in causing harm to anyone, not even to save David if his life should be threatened! Do I make myself clear on this, young lady?" Carla explained sternly.

"Absolutely, ma'am," Kathy replied calmly.

"Now then, off the record, you're being considered for... well, let's say more hazardous duty, Kathy. We're going to bring you into it slowly. This is your first step, young lady, so don't screw it up. Watch what he does, how he prepares for the mission. Ask questions. In time, if David feels that you've got what it takes, you may even be sent to the Farm for Special Advanced Training. But for now, we start slowly with your request to do wet work," Carla explained.

"I won't let you down, ma'am," Kathy replied as Carla reached down and picked up her briefcase. Setting it on the table, she opened it and pulled out the envelope, which read "Top Secret Eyes Only" on it and handed it to me.

Neither Carla or Kathy spoke while I opened the envelope and began to look at the 8x10 photographs. There were at least a dozen of them. The targets were the husband, wife, and both teenage children.

"Any problem?" Carla asked, being worried that I may not want to kill the women and her two children.

Looking at the profile individual data information sheets, I began to read them. I hadn't answered Carla yet. I was feeling an adrenaline rush as it began to build up inside of me.

"Son of a bitch," I said softly, "consider it done."

"May I see that?" Kathy asked as she reached her hand out to me.

"No, you can't," I explained as I placed the contents back into the envelope and put them back into Carla's briefcase. "Mind if I use your briefcase?" I asked.

"Not at all, we have a storage room full of them," Carla explained.

"We're going to need two sets of Secret Service credentials, one for me, and one for Agent Eckland," I explained.

"You'll have them by 9:00 a.m. tomorrow morning. I'll call Marge personally," Carla replied.

"Excuse me, but if I'm still your supervisor. I'm going to need to know who the target is in case there is any trouble," Kathy explained with a touch of bitterness in her voice at my telling her no when she asked to see the photographs.

"Let's make one thing very clear between us," I said as I looked across the table at Kathy. "I don't like having you around on this mission. I do my job well; I don't have time to babysit you. You don't have the killer instinct Kathy. You're living in a little girl's fantasy. If you interfere or screw-up this operation, I'll kill you and I won't think twice about it. You don't need to know who these people are. You didn't need to know about Gruber either, but you went crying to your boss about that. A real team player wouldn't have said a thing. Damn bureaucratic bullshit!" I said as I got up and left the room with the briefcase in my hand. Kathy had her mouth half open and looked stunned. Carla was smiling. "Well are you coming?" I asked as I opened the door and looked back at Kathy.

Moving down the long hallway of the E-wing of the Pentagon, Kathy caught up with me quickly, "Let me tell you something, asshole," she began to say until I cut her sentence off short.

"Shhhh, don't say anything until we get outside," I whispered as I pressed the button on the elevator. Glancing down the hall, I could see Carla standing outside of the briefing room door watching us.

"You're not really mad at me, are you?" Kathy asked quietly. Stepping into the elevator, I waited for the doors to close.

"Nope, I'm not mad. I love it," I said smiling.

"Okay, now I'm confused. What's going on? Why did you blow-up on me like that in front of Ms. Silverman of all people?" Kathy questioned.

"They want me to evaluate you, Kathy. If I act as though you and I are friends, they'll suspect that I favored you and didn't really judge you by your ability to get the job done professionally. If they think I am upset with having you tag along, whatever I tell them about you has rock solid credibility," I explained calmly as we stepped off the elevator and headed out of the building and into the parking lot.

"You were protecting me? Damn, David, thank you," Kathy said as we both put our sunglasses on and headed for our cars.

"I'm going to tell you this, Kathy," I said as I unlocked the driver's side door of my rented Buick Limited. "I'll train you to be one of the best in the business, but you better start telling me the truth. There's more going on with you than you're telling me. I'm no brain surgeon, but I'm no fool either," I explained as I got into my car and closed the door. Putting the key in the ignition, I started up the big Buick, pressed the power window button, and lowered the side window as Kathy walked up and leaned forward, resting her arms on the window ledge.

"How do we play this one out?" she asked with a serious look on her face.

She had avoided my question. I gave her a chance to come clean and she didn't. "Why?" I asked myself. "Well, we're not going to go anywhere until Marge sends us our new ID's. Let's get rid of this car. I'll turn it back in and we'll use yours. Then we will have to rent a couple of rooms and study the material that Carla gave me. Let's get this stuff done, secure these documents, and go and grab a nice dinner. After that, we have work to do," I explained smiling.

"You're taking me out to dinner?" she asked in a sexy voice.

"Hell no, you're taking me. You're the one with the company credit card," I said jokingly.

"Me? You've got unlimited spending on yours," she started to say as I smiled and pressed the button once again, closing the window in her face.

* * * * * * *

Elite Covert Operation
Code Name: Clean Sweep
Target: Marcus Guillo Family
Location: Paris, France

"Have you got this all memorized?" I asked as I looked over at Kathy and held up the envelope with all of the information on our target and his family in it.

"Yes," Kathy replied calmly.

Getting up from my seat next to Kathy, I walked to the back of the Agency's plane and ran all of the documentation through the paper shredder. Sitting back down next to Kathy, I looked at my watch.

"We'll be landing in Paris within the hour. Double check to make sure that you have your diplomatic credentials and passport ready. Remember to follow my lead, Kathy. Just flash your ID. at the customs agent and keep moving. All diplomats are arrogant. Do not talk to them unless they talk to you first. We are already two days behind schedule. Waiting for the extra sets of credentials cost us time, but it will be worth it in the end," I explained.

"Do you really think they're going to buy our being diplomats from Italy and me being your wife? I don't speak Italian," she added as an after thought. Speaking to Kathy in Italian, I saw that it caught her by surprise.

"Hey, that's good," she explained as she got a confused look on her face. "Hey, wait a minute. Your CIA profile doesn't say anything about you being bilingual."

"I told you before, kid, the best kept secrets are the secrets that keep themselves. Never let anyone know everything about you. One day they may become your enemy, and then they will know everything about you. Always expect the unexpected, remember?" I asked.

"I got it," she replied.

"You sure that you're up to this? Marcus is 41 years old. His wife Bella is 38. His son Marcon is only 15 and his daughter Sura is 14. The kill order says to make it messy, so that it looks like a terrorist hit on the family, which would be against the United States.

If you get to the kids first, Kathy, you're going to have to butcher them alive. Are you sure that you're up to this? You can pass on this one, Kathy, and I'll let you get in on the next one," I explained trying to give her a way out.

I didn't like the idea of having to kill children, however, these two were flying on their own to China and Russia to deliver documents and film about our country to our enemies. Vietnam had changed me. I was becoming even colder now, with a growing attitude of, I really didn't give a damn anymore. But Kathy, what was in her head? What was it that I felt deep down inside, that she was keeping from me? What was she thinking?

"Are you kidding? I'm in," she answered as our plane began its decent and prepared to land. Our pilot had already radioed in to the control tower that we were a diplomatic aircraft with two diplomats on board.

Stepping off the plane, we were greeted by Airport Security Customs Agents and given a ride to the limousine waiting for us in front of the airport. The driver of the limousine was one of ours. He was CIA and would supply us with anything that we might need. However, that was all he would do. He had no knowledge of what we were in Paris for, or what our assignment was. Driving to the Safe House that we had in Paris, Kathy and I changed clothes and climbed into the new BMW. We drove away, leaving our counterpart behind.

Marcus Guillo, was the American Ambassador on the United Nations counsel as the representative to the President of the United States. He was American born and a traitor to the American people. I felt sick inside at the thought of how many Americans I already killed because they betrayed our country. First in Vietnam, now here in my own homeland of the American dream. Remembering what I had read on the CIA computer in Carla's office about the assassination of President John F. Kennedy and Vice President Johnson's involvement in the wrongful death, I became even more bitter.

Marcus had a beautiful villa on the southern coast of France overlooking the ocean. He and his family had been living out here for almost eight years. How many Americans had lost their lives because of his treacherous acts against our country? How many secrets had he already sold to our enemies? How much damage has he already caused to the National Security of the United States and to my people? And for what? Money?

"You alright?" Kathy asked as she took her eyes off the road for a moment to look over at me.

"Yeah," I replied as I stared out through the passenger's side window of the cherry red BMW.

"What's wrong, David? I can see it in your eyes. Is the Sandman coming out to play?" she asked with a touch of excitement in her voice.

"No, I'm just sick of this shit, Kathy. My Uncle Tommy died defending our flag in World War II. My brother, Nick, died in Vietnam, and for what? So this French piece of shit and his wife and kids can sell us out and collect on our deaths?" I said bitterly. "What happened to American pride, faith in the words, 'In God we Trust?' There's no men of honor anymore. John Kennedy, Bobby Kennedy, Martin Luther King – all great men. Men who would have changed the course of history, only to be assassinated by the same people we're suppose to be protecting. They weren't saints, Kathy; they were simple men, but they were men that you could look up to and trust not to betray us.

One of the reasons they killed John and Bobby Kennedy was because these race hating, sick bastards wanted to kill Martin Luther King. Did you know that? They knew that John and Bobby stood for equal rights for all people. People of all races, colors, and creeds. The Kennedy's would never have stood by and let anyone kill Dr. King. Their father would have," I explained, "but not John or Bobby."

"What, you mean Joseph Kennedy was a racist?" Kathy asked with a surprised look.

"Hell yes, he was a racist. He made the Kennedy fortune by bootlegging liquor during the prohibition years and slave trading. Hell, Kathy, he was very outspoken about how he thought that Hitler was on the right track by killing off the Jewish people. Joseph Kennedy hated the Jews and was pro-Hitler for Gods sake!"

"I didn't know that," Kathy explained, "that's disgusting."

"Oh, it gets even better than that, kiddo. Jack Ruby kills Oswald on national television, and then turns around and tells the American people that he did it to save the Kennedy family the pain and anguish of a public trial," I explained angrily.

"You don't believe him?" Kathy asked.

"Jack Ruby was a Jew, Kathy!" I explained sarcastically.

"What?" Kathy asked in surprise.

"Yup, a Jew and a professional hit man," I explained.

"There it is, David, there's the home of Marcus Guillo," Kathy explained as she pulled the car over to the side of the road. "Remind me to finish this conversation about Ruby being a professional hit man later. I want to know how you know that," Kathy added.

"The proof is all on film. The most obvious is the least obvious. It's right in front of the American peoples eyes, but they don't know what they're looking at. I'll explain it later. For now lets go kill some traitors," I said as I looked over at Kathy, who seemed to be getting excited at the thought of it.

Placing two drop's of Methadrine under my tongue, I handed the tiny glass vial to Kathy. I was surprised when she took it. "Under the tongue?" she asked as she looked at me.

A big smile broke out across my face, she was going to try a hit of speed. "You go, girl," I joked. "One drop under your tongue. It takes about 15 to 30 seconds to kick in. Then you'll feel it," I explained as Kathy placed a drop of Methadrine under her tongue.

Handing the tiny glass vial back to me, I placed it into my pocket and turned around. Reaching into the backseat, I opened the dark brown suitcase and pulled out two long stainless steel knifes. Both were made in Syria, the blades were ten-inches long, slender, and razor sharp. Handing one to Kathy, I reached back into the suitcase and pulled out two silenced .9mm Smith & Wesson fifteen shot automatic pistols. The CIA was beginning to use this new Model 59 handgun because it was shorter and double action. Handing one to Kathy, I couldn't help but grin. The speed had just taken effect on her.

"Whoa! Oh my God! Oh shit! I like this. Can you get me some of that?" she asked with wide eyes.

"I'll think about it," I said as I checked both guns to make sure they were loaded and ready to fire. Both weapons were fully loaded with hollow-point bullets. It was a common round and available to the Syrian government. "I'll buy you dinner tonight," I added with a grin.

Kathy and I had an extra change of clothing with us just in case we got blood on us. Handing Kathy a pair of thin black leather gloves, she put them on, as I looked up at the old French built villa that sat high up on the side of a beautiful section of land overlooking the ocean.

I looked at my watch then over at Kathy. "It's 6:12 p.m. They've already eaten supper so they'll probably be all throughout the house. Now listen, we start at the front door and move forward. One quick, clean, sweep. Don't let anyone get behind you, or out of the house. Understand?" I asked. "As soon as we get into the house, lock the front door behind us."

"One clean sweep. Got it. Shit, I feel so fucking pumped right now. I can feel every muscle in my entire body tensing up, David. Shit, I can feel the blood running through my veins. No wonder you love this shit," she explained excitedly.

"Don't leave my sight, Kathy. I don't want you hurt. Alright, lets get this done. Pull straight up to the front door when we get there," I explained. It took us another twelve minutes to actually get to the house from where we were parked on the side of the highway.

"Damn, look at that," Kathy said as we pulled up to the front entrance of the home. It had a circular driveway with a waterfall that was spraying water up and back into a cement pool in front of the home. Silver Cloud Rolls Royce's were parked out front of the home. Putting the car in park, I looked at Kathy, then got out of the car. There was nothing left to say as we walked up to the front door.

Opening the wooden designed hand carved door, we stepped inside quickly, and quietly locked the door behind us. The inside of this beautiful French Villa was immaculate. It had fine art paintings hanging on the walls of every room. Chinese and Russian vases and statues were throughout the home. Russian leaded glass crystal was everywhere. Moving forward we looked quickly into the front room and then the dining room, nothing. I could hear music upstairs as we checked the kitchen and den. Again, we found nothing.

"Wait here," I whispered as I moved quickly down the basement stairs and took a quick look. Going back upstairs, I looked at Kathy. "They're all upstairs," I explained as Kathy looked at me wide eyed and breathing heavily.

Walking over to the spiral staircase, we moved upward as the French music became louder. Moving to the first bedroom, I tightened my grip on the handle of the long slender Syrian knife. Opening the bedroom door with my left hand, we moved in quickly. Sura, the fourteen-year-old daughter had long brown hair that reached her waist. She was standing with her back to me, facing her bed as I moved up behind her quickly.

"Marcon, you never knock," she started to say as she turned to face who she thought was her brother. The look of total fear was on her face as she tried to scream. With one violent thrust of my right hand, I felt the stainless steel blade of my knife enter her throat and cut its way through the tender flesh and muscle of the young girl.

Grabbing her by the hair with my left hand, I looked into her eyes as she urinated onto the carpet. She was frozen stiff with the shock of what was happening to her, but still very much alive as I whispered into her ear. "Say goodnight, you American traitor," I said as I pulled the knife back slightly, dropped the handle down, and shoved the blade of the knife upward and into her brain. Twisting the knife in my hand, I quickly pulled it out and pushed her over and onto her bed. The flow of blood gushed out through her mouth and neck with a sickening sound. Turning to leave the room my eyes got wide. "Kathy," I said as I pulled my pistol out of my belt.

Kathy was so engrossed in watching me as I killed young Sura, that she didn't hear or see Sura's brother, Marcon, as he was walking into the room behind her. Turning slightly, Kathy didn't hesitate. With one cat like move she thrust her knife in a backhanded motion, and drove it straight into young Marcon's right eye, and deep into his brain. Grabbing him by the hair with her left hand, she quickly pulled him forward into the room, twisting the handle of her knife twice in both directions, scrambling his brain, and then pulled the knife out as the young boy's body fell lifelessly to the floor.

Taking several deep breaths of air into her lungs, Kathy looked at me. Our bodies both surged with a steady flow of fear, adrenaline, and excitement as we left the room and moved down the hall to the next bedroom. Opening the door, we found it empty. Checking the next two bedrooms, they, too, were empty. Moving to the end of the hallway, all that was left was the master bedroom and the large bathroom. I could hear water running in the sink of the bathroom as I reached for the door handle.

"Watch that door," I whispered as I looked at Kathy and nodded at the master bedroom door. Nodding her head back at me, she turned her attention to the bedroom door as I opened the bathroom door and stepped inside.

Bella Guillo was standing, facing the sink. As was with her daughter, she had long beautiful brown hair and a firm well built body. She was bent over lathering her face with soap. Because the water was running, she didn't hear me when I came into the bathroom. Turning to look at Kathy, I smiled as I waited for Bella to rinse the soap from her face. As she did, she stood up to reach for a towel with her right hand.

Grabbing her by the elbow of the right arm with my left hand, I spun her around to face me as I thrust the blade of my knife, blade pointing upward, into her belly button. As I did, I grabbed her by the throat with my left hand and tightened my grip.

Her big green eyes were wide with shock and fear. Her mouth was open, her lips were moving, but no words would come out. She looked like a fish out of water. Looking into her eyes, she kept blinking as her eyes filled with both pain and fear.

"The President sends his regards. Say goodnight, bitch," I whispered into her ear quickly, as I pulled the knife upward. The sound of muscle and flesh being cut open brought with it a funny smell, as the knife blade also cut through her intestinal track. Pulling quick and hard, I felt the knife hit her rib cage. Pulling the handle up, I pointed the blade down, turned it sideways inside of her, and pulled it out through the long cut in her belly. As I did, I pulled most of her intestines out with it, then I let her go. She was still alive as she fell to the floor and onto her own pile of blood and guts.

Walking out of the bathroom, I tossed my knife on top of Bella's body, and closed the door. Pulling out my silenced .9mm, I leaned up against the wall, facing the door of the master bedroom. Just as I did, Marcus opened the bedroom door to step out into the hallway. He was fixing his necktie. Before he could see me, Kathy stepped in front of him and stabbed him in the stomach. Grabbing the handle of her knife with both hands, she pushed Marcus backwards and back into his bedroom, pulling the knife upwards. As she did, Marcus Guillo grabbed Kathy by the throat and cried out in pain. He regurgitated his supper and dropped his hands down to his sides.

Leaving the knife in Marcus, Kathy let go of the handle and backed up and away from Marcus as he starred at Kathy and dropped down to his knees. He was trying to speak but all that could be heard was a gurgling sound as he began to choke on his own blood. Falling forward, his body made a wet, slushing sound as it came to rest on the beautiful oriental carpet of his bedroom floor.

Breathing heavily, Kathy walked over to the long dresser and bent over, resting her forearms on top of the dresser.

Walking up behind her, I pressed my body up against hers and ran my arms around her waist. "You okay?" I asked breathing heavily, as she placed her hands over her face.

"Oh God, David," she whispered as I felt her move her body tenderly up against mine. Reaching down, I slowly unfastened her belt.

"Ohhh," she moaned softly. Unfastening the top button of her pants, I then slowly unzipped them. Feeling her breath even more heavily, I then reached up toward her hips, grabbed the sides of her pants and pulled her pants and underwear both down at the same time.

"David," she whispered, in a hushed voice, as I slid my body tenderly into hers. Raising her head up, Kathy looked into the mirror for the first time. Our eyes met as our passion for each other had finally taken over.

* * * * * * *

Two hours had passed by the time Kathy and I were ready to leave the Guillo Estate. Picking up the telephone, I called the French police and reported that I had heard gunshots coming from inside the Guillo home. This was absurd because the Villa sits all alone overlooking the ocean. I never figured that the French authorities would even figure it out, and they never did.

Once the local authority arrived at the home and found the crime scene, they would call the Central Intelligence Agency because Marcus was a United States Representative. Once our people got there, they would conduct a thorough investigation and seize all documentation in the home. This would include computers, safes, everything. This is why we didn't try to get Marcus to tell us the combination of his safe or computer codes.

Hearing the knock at the front door surprised us. I was just reaching for the doorknob and French police were on their way to this address. Opening the door, I smiled politely, "Hello, may I help you?" I asked.

"Yes, we are here to pick-up Marcus and Bella, are they ready?" the man asked. He was in his mid-fifties and was with his wife who looked to be about the same age. Their limousine driver was standing outside next to the car.

"They will be with you in just a moment, sir. Please come in," I explained as I stepped back and opened the door completely so that they could enter the home.

Closing the door behind them, I directed them into the large front room. His wife was saying something to her husband in their native tongue, as I pulled out my silenced .9mm Smith and Wesson and quickly shot them both in the back of the head. Their bodies fell to the floor and lay beside each other; they never knew what hit them.

Sliding my gun in between my belt and the small of my back, Kathy and I left the Guillo home. Walking up to the long, white limo; I looked at the driver and noticed that he was wearing a gun in a shoulder holster under his dinner jacket.

"Nice car," I said as I smiled and looked past him at the long stretch limo.

Smiling back at me, he said nothing as he turned to look at his hand polished limousine.

Pulling my weapon, I fired one silenced shot that struck the driver in the back of his head. The hollow-point bullet went straight through his head and sprayed blood, flesh, teeth, and brain matter all over the hood, left front fender, and windshield of the vehicle. His body bounced off the fender and fell to the ground with a thumping sound.

Climbing into our BMW, Kathy started the engine, put it in drive, and floored it.

"Whoa, no, no, don't do that," I shouted "Calm down, baby, and drive away as if nothing had ever happened," I explained as we pulled out calmly and drove away.

"I hear sirens," Kathy said as she looked over at me.

"Uh huh," I replied.

"That limousine had diplomatic plates on it from the country of Turkey," she explained as we left the long driveway and pulled out onto the main road.

"Yeah, I know," I said with a smile. "They can consider that a down payment for what they did to my people in 1915, when the Turk's invaded Armenia and massacred over three million Armenian men, women, and children," I explained as my memories took me back to the stories that my grandparents had told me. They were survivors of that holocaust.

"Boy, you really hate the Turk's, don't you," Kathy asked as two French police cars raced past us with their lights and sirens blaring.

"Yes, ma'am. I hate the Turk's more than I hate the Viet Cong," I explained as I looked out through my side window and thought of my great grandparents, Vector and Sophie Negoshian; my grandfather, John Godoshian; and my grandmother, Helen Gopigian.

Kathy and I spent the next two days seeing Paris and enjoying the sites. As promised, I took her out to dinner that night. I didn't know that the French had McDonalds restaurants. They do, and yes, I did take her there to dine. Believe it or not, she loved it!

Chapter Sixteen
Hands Off

Sitting on the floor of my den, I laughed out loud as Magnum set the fire extinguisher system off in Robin Masters wine cellar by accident. Higgins was in the cellar with some very high-class guests conducting a wine tasting at the time. "Magnum!!!" Higgins shouted as they went to a commercial break.

I had been home from France for six days and nothing was happening. Little Tara and two of her Girl Scout girlfriends, Meghan and Jessy, had decided to come over and baby-sit me, while their mothers went shopping. It was a pleasant surprise to see how badly I needed company when they needed somewhere to hang out. I looked down at the two pizza boxes, eight empty bottles of Pepsi, and three empty boxes of Girl Scout cookies and burped out loud. That made the girls laugh, and start a burping contest. It was only a matter of time before someone would fart, then the war would really begin.

I made it very clear at the beginning – relax, have fun, and do whatever you want, especially the stuff your moms won't let you do at home. Never say that to young girls, they have some very creative minds.

We hung out, laughed, and had some young girls to Uncle David talks about school, boys, and how badly I needed an in-ground swimming pool, so I could swim in it during the summer and stay cool. I really liked these girls. They had a way of getting what they wanted. They were cute and in ten years would be to die for dangerous. It was when ten-year old Jessy got up to go to the bathroom; I noticed she favored her right leg a little.

"You alright, Jessy?" I asked with concern.

"I'm alright, Uncle Dave. I hurt my leg a little bit on the swing set at school," she explained.

"You want me to take you down to the Clarkston Clinic and have Doctor Hamilton take a look at it for you?" I asked.

"No!" she said quickly. "I mean no, its okay, its just a bruise that's all," she explained as she and Meghan went to use the bathroom. Waiting for the two girls to get into the bathroom and close the door, I looked at Tara who was staring at me intensely.

"She didn't get hurt at school, did she?" I whispered as I looked at little Tara. She didn't answer. "You can trust me, Tara," I said calmly.

"We made a promise never to tell, Uncle David," Tara explained with a very serious look on her face.

"Honey, listen to me. Sometimes you make a promise, but deep down inside you know that you need to tell someone you know, someone special, like me. I won't tell anyone, Tara, I promise. But I can't help Jessy if I don't know what's going on," I explained.

"Promise?" she whispered.

"I promise, cross my heart and hope to die, stick a needle in my eye. I promise," I swore, raising my right hand and crossing my heart.

"Her daddy hits her a lot," Tara explained as she looked over at the bathroom on the other side of the room.

"Does her mommy know?" I asked.

"Yes, but he hits her, too. Last night, Jessy said that her daddy came home drunk and tried to touch her down here," Tara explained as she pointed toward her crotch. "Jessy kicked him and he hit Jessy in the leg with his fist. Jessy's mommy ran into Jessy's bedroom when she heard Jessy scream. But then he hit Jessy's mommy in the breasts and stomach," Tara explained as the toilet flushed.

"Don't worry, sweetie, bad things happen to bad people like that. God doesn't like people who hurt little girls and their mommy's," I explained. "Shhhh, here they come. Its our secret, cupcake," I whispered as the girls came out of the bathroom giggling and went behind my bar to grab some candy bars and more Pepsi.

We goofed off for the rest of the afternoon. I took the girls to the Pontiac Mall and let them buy some girl stuff. They had a blast and enjoyed embarrassing me by showing me the girls' underwear section. Kids, you gotta love 'em. While I smiled on the inside, deep inside I was planning the solution to Jessy's problem.

The girls left around 5:00 p.m. when their mothers came to pick them up. Amy, Dana, and Michelle were very beautiful women and the mothers of these three young children. I became angry inside at the thought of some sick piece of shit hurting any of them. Saying goodbye, and accepting a kiss on the cheek from each of the ladies as payment for watching the kids, I memorized the license plate number of Dana's car.

Closing my front door, I went to my den and turned on my computer. Pulling up the CIA data information section, I typed in the license plate number. Jessy's father, George Hellman, lived in Drayton Plains, Michigan, just down the road from my home about a mile and a half.

"Sandman's coming, George," I whispered softly under my breath. "Count on it!"

Hearing my doorbell ring, I looked at my watch. It was almost six o'clock; I walked to my front door and opened it. I was caught completely by surprise!

"Uncle Sammy, hey, come on in," I said as I welcomed Sam Giancana into my home for the very first time. Looking out at my driveway, I saw two of Sam's bodyguards standing next to his car, smoking cigarettes. "Uncle

Sammy, have your boy's come in, please. I have a full bar downstairs. They're welcome in my home," I explained calmly as I watched Sam sit down on my sofa.

"Thank you, David, but no, I can't stay," Sam explained. I could see by the look on his face that something was bothering him as I closed the door and sat down next to him on the couch.

"What's wrong, Uncle Sammy?" I asked.

" I don't like to ask, but I need a favor and I need it fast," he explained as he looked up into my eyes.

"Name it," I replied quickly.

"I came to you, David, because I know I can trust you," he explained as he patted my left knee with his right hand. Nodding my head in agreement, I said nothing. "I have a very close friend, my eyes and ears in the New Jersey family. He keeps me informed whenever Tony Pro is up to no good," he said as he looked at his watch and then back up at me. "In less than two hours, Tony Pro, is flying in and meeting with Tony Jack and old man Baines at the Pontiac airport. I also believe one of the Tocco brothers, from Detroit, is going to be meeting with them. I called your Uncle Pauly in New York and we both agree we need to know what is being said at that meeting."

"They're going to have dinner in the restaurant at the airport. We have a close friend that works there who is going to put a listening device in the flowers on the table. They have already made reservations for five people, so we know which table they will be sitting at," Sam explained as he opened the metal briefcase he had brought in with him. "I need you to go and have dinner at the Pontiac Airport tonight, David. Set this briefcase down next to you, and when you see them come in and sit down at their table, pull this antenna out like this," Sam explained as he pulled the small thin antenna out from the side of the briefcase to show me. "Then push this button. Let it run until the meeting is over," Sam explained as he pulled the white envelope out of the briefcase and handed it to me. "There's five thousand dollars in there, its for you, David," Sam explained with a sad smile on his face.

"What are you talking about?" I said as I leaned over and placed my left hand on Sam's right cheek and kissed him on the left cheek, as a show of respect. "I don't want this," I explained with serious heart-felt emotion in my eyes and voice.

"I know you don't, but this is business, David. Learn a lesson by this. Always pay people for the job they do for you. Then they can never come back to you one day and say, 'Hey, remember when I did this for you, well now you owe me," Sam explained. "Tonight put this briefcase on the front seat of your grandpa's car. I'll have someone pick it up and bring it to me," Sam explained as he stood up. "I need to hear what they are saying."

"Does my grandfather know about this, Uncle Sam?" I asked.

"No, David, it breaks my heart to see him and your grandmother in such poor health. I'm going over to their home to spend some time with them. Ahh, what happened to the old days? They know John is old and out of the business, so now they make plans to kill Jimmy," Sam explained sadly.

"You want me to hit all of them while they're at the airport?" I asked.

"No, no, that's bad business, David. Your Uncle Paul, John, you and I, we are still men of honor and respect," he explained as he walked to the front door and opened it.

"Hey, I come to your home, how come you never come to my home, huh?" Sam asked with a grin.

"I'll come and see you soon, Uncle Sammy, I promise."

"Good, call before you do and I'll show you how to make the best Italian sausage in the world. I have a nice little kitchen in my basement that I cook at," he explained as he raised his left hand to say goodbye. "Oh, before I forget," he said as he motioned at his bodyguard to bring something to him. Sam's bodyguard was a big man who didn't say much. Walking over to Sam, the bodyguard brought him a small box from the flower shop down from my home, Dixie Flowers. "Wear this in the lapel of your suit. That way our girl at the airport will know who you are, okay?" Sam explained. "Make sure you call me soon, David. We'll make sausage and drink Italian wine," he said as he waved goodbye once again and walked back to his car with his bodyguard.

Closing the door, I opened the small box and looked at the baby red rose with white babies breath. Looking at my watch, I moved quickly and went to my bedroom to change. For now George Hellman would have to wait.

* * * * * * *

The Pontiac Airport is a small airport that faces the M-59 highway in Pontiac. Walking in through the front door of the restaurant part of the building, I looked at my watch, "7:58, damn, that's cutting it close, David," I said to myself as the cute red headed waitress walked up to me smiling.

"Hello, Mr. Armani, we have your table right over here," she said politely as she walked me to my table to be seated. Her nametag read, Laura. So, I thanked her.

"Thank you, Laura. I won't need a menu. I'll have the Prime Rib, baked potato, Italian bread, and a tossed salad with extra tomatoes and

Italian dressing. Also, may I have a Pepsi, please, and a slice of cheese cake for desert," I asked with a polite smile.

"This is refreshing," she commented as she wrote my order down on the hand held order pad. As she did, Tony Jack and three other men walked into the small restaurant bar and stood over to the right by the cash register.

"What's refreshing?" I asked.

"To see a man who knows what he wants for a change. Most people come in here and take thirty-minutes looking at the menu while they try to figure out what they want," Laura explained, while a different waitress took Tony Jack and his friends over to the larger round table facing the glass windows and the landing strip of the airport runway, and seated them.

As Laura smiled and left to go place my order, I slowly reached down and pulled the small antenna out of the side of the briefcase. Opening the top of the case, I pressed the play button and plugged in the small ear bud. Pressing the tiny speaker into my left ear, so I could listen to what was being said, I closed the lid of the briefcase. I listened and smiled as Laura returned with my Pepsi, salad, and bread.

"Here you go, sir, it will be about fifteen to twenty-minutes for your steak to be ready. How would you like your steak cooked, sir?" she asked.

"Medium well, please," I replied with a smile.

"Alright, sir, enjoy your meal," she said as she walked away.

"Thank you," I replied as I took a sip of my Pepsi and listened to the conversation that was taking place five tables away.

The table that Laura had given me was perfect. My back was against the wall. To my right, left, and front were windows that faced the parking lot, front entrance, and runway. Looking to my left, I watched as a white Learjet touched down, making a perfect landing on the runway outside.

"There's Tony Pro," Tony Jack explained as I watched his mouth move.

"Man, guys, isn't there any other way to do this?" the heavier set, younger, brown haired fella asked.

"Relax, Chucky, just do what you're told to do and your debt is wiped clean. Plus, you make a ton of cash ta boot."

"Mr. Tocco, he's my dad," Chucky replied as I began to eat my salad.

"Yeah, well your dad's gonna die. You wanna join him?" the other medium built man, who I now knew only as Mr. Tocco, explained. Mr. Tocco was in his late forties to early fifties. Turning his head slightly to the right, Chucky looked at the other shorter man who sat next to him.

"Don't look at me Chuck," he said as he raised both of his hands slightly in a keep-me-out-of-it gesture. "I'm only along for the ride. Hell, my boy says for ten grand he'll cut off your old mans head and shit in his neck!" the guy explained, as Tony Jack and Tocco began to laugh out loud.

"Baines, your boy's an animal. Hey, his boy said the same thing to an FBI agent one time," Tony explained as he looked over at Chucky and patted him on the back of his left shoulder. "Relax, Chucky, everything's gonna be just fine. When its over and the heat dies down, you'll move to Florida and live like a fucking king. What do you think about that, huh?" Tony Jack asked, as Tony Pro walked into the restaurant, using the see through glass door that was close to their table at the far corner of the building. Walking up to them, Tony Pro, from New Jersey, sat down. They didn't talk until the waitress brought them another round of mixed drinks and took their order.

"I can't stay long, fella's. I don't want the Feds to know I'm here," Tony Pro explained. "Chucky, I came a long way just to look you in the eyes and ask you one fucking question," he said as he looked at Chucky. "You in or not?" he asked calmly.

Hesitating for only a moment, Chucky responded, "Yeah, I'm in. Just tell me what I need to do."

Turning to look at Tony Jack, Tony Pro smiled. "You got everything covered on your end?" he asked.

"All we got to do is set the date, then Jimmy disappears. I got my people ready with the car crusher. I got a real nice motor home we'll have waiting for us at the Raleigh House. We meet in there, but we leave Jimmy's car in the parking lot at Macus Red Fox. That keeps the cops looking there. If Jimmy doesn't play ball, we have your boys do him as soon as he gets back into the car. We wait about ten minutes and then your boys can carry his worthless ass into the backdoor of the Raleigh House and run him through the trash mulcher. I got a truck coming at 3:00 p.m. sharp to pick-up the container. So, we got to have Jimmy ground-up by 2:45. They'll take the container to the Dearborn Trash Disposal and we'll run everything through the incinerator. Say goodbye to the evidence," Tony said with a laugh as their main course arrived.

"What if those Bloomfield Dick's go snooping around that incinerator?" Tony Pro asked.

"No problem, we're going to have it dismantled," Tocco said as he began to eat his meal.

"What about the EPA, won't they question why you dismantled a 1.6 million dollar incinerator?" Pro asked cautiously.

"Nope, we got that covered. Forget about it," Tocco explained.

"I told you, Tony, we're ready on this end. Just pick a date, and try to make it a weekday. That way there's only a couple of people working at the Raleigh House. If anyone is there at all," Tony Jack explained in a whisper, as Tony Pro pulled a pocket calendar out of his back pocket and looked at it. "I'll give Jimmy till the end of June. I want that money. After that, there's no more talking, its over. And you, Chucky, don't you cross me. I swear to God that if you do, I'll have your fat ass put into a crab trap and tossed into the Florida Keys," Tony Pro explained with a cold look in his eyes.

"I'll get him there, don't worry about that. Dad trusts me. He'll come if I tell him that Tony wants to meet with him to help him make the peace with you," Chucky explained.

Taking the earpiece out of my ear, I set it down next to the briefcase and smiled as Laura brought me my dinner.

"This was old news," I thought to myself. "But Sammy, you call yourself a man of honor and respect, and still you help to kill John Kennedy. What a bunch of two faced people," I thought to myself. "I'll play along until its time not to play along. Then I'll decide what it is I want to do about all of this."

By 9:42 p.m. Tony Jack and his people left the restaurant. Tony Pro was airborne by 10:00 p.m. and on his way back to New Jersey. Finishing my second glass of Pepsi, Laura cleaned off the round table and put the tiny bugging device into her top left shirt pocket. Five minutes later she laid the bill for my meal down in front of me. It was on a small shinny stainless steel tray. On top of the bill was the small bugging device.

"Will there be anything else?" she asked with a smile.

"Yes," I said as I pulled out my money clip and pulled three brand new one hundred dollar bills out of it. Placing the money on the tray, I picked up the tiny bug and slipped it into my suit coat pocket. Picking up my briefcase, I stood up. "That's for you, keep the change and thanks for the help," I explained.

"Wait a minute," she said as she picked up the silver tray and saw her tip. Smiling she turned and looked at me. "Thank you," she said. "You said 'yes' that there was something else that I could get for you?" she questioned.

"Yes, ma'am, there certainly is, but if I told you what it was, you might slap me," I said as I winked at Laura with a smile on my face and turned to walk away.

"Maybe, maybe not," she replied in a sexy voice.

Leaving the Pontiac Airport, I went to my grandfather's home and put the briefcase with the tape in it on the front seat of my grandfather's car.

Looking at my watch it was almost 11:00 p.m. It was getting too late to go after George now. "I'll have to plan this out right," I said to myself as I drove back to my home. "I'll get him tomorrow and I think I know just how to do it."

* * * * * * *

Calling Andy, I told him I needed him to drive to Detroit and find a young, pretty hooker and hire her for the whole night. I also explained to him that I needed a girl that was clean, dressed well, and expendable. Filling Andy in on what I had found out about little Jessy and her mother, Dana, Andy was more than willing to make the drive to Detroit and go shopping for a hooker. I needed someone who had never been seen in this area before, and who would not be missed if she should have to be disposed of later on down the road.

Punching the name, date of birth, driver's license number, and social security number of George Hellman back into the CIA computer, I found out that he worked at the General Motors Truck and Coach Plant, in Pontiac. He was a union representative there. That explained his love for drinking. His union hall always met on Wednesday nights around 6:00 p.m. and then after their meeting was over, went down the road to the local bar. His love for the bottle was his weak point. His passion for sex, once he had gotten drunk, would be the hook I would use to lure him into the spiders web. Why he would desire some other women, when he had a beautiful wife like Dana at home, boggled my mind. But then again, wanting to have sex with a ten-year old child, who was also his own daughter, was unthinkable to me.

For now, I waited for Andy. Looking at my watch, I put a drop of Methadrine under my tongue, opened a box of mint Girl Scout cookies, and went to the refrigerator to grab a cold bottle of Pepsi. It was Wednesday afternoon. "Andy should be here in a couple of hours," I thought to myself. "If all goes as planned, tonight will be the night that George takes his last drink of booze."

* * * * * * *

Shortly after six o'clock, Andy arrived at my home with a cute little blue eyed, blonde named Ginger. I was going to ask him why it had taken so long for him to find Ginger and get back here to my place. However, when I saw the big smile on his face, I figured out the answer to my question.

"David, this is Ginger. Ginger, this is David," Andy explained as he introduced us and sat down with Ginger in my front room.

"Hello, Ginger. How are you?" I asked politely.

"I'm fine, how are you?" she replied with a cute little smile. Why a young girl this pretty would choose to be a whore for a living made absolutely no sense to me.

Taking Andy and Ginger downstairs, I poured them both a drink and showed Ginger a computer printout of George Hellman's drivers license, complete with picture.

"Ginger, I'll give you a thousand dollars, in cash, if you'll do a job for me," I explained as I reached under the bar, opened my small safe, and placed one thousand dollars in front of Ginger to see. Closing the safe, I caught a glimps of a smile and then a look of concern on Ginger's face.

"I don't do S&M or animals," she explained.

"Good, that means you're the right young lady. I would never ask you to do anything like that anyway," I explained with a smile. "See the guy in that picture?" I asked.

"Yes," she replied as she downed a full eight-ounce glass of rum and Pepsi.

Making another drink, I continued. "Ginger, I need you to go into a bar tonight and pick him up. Let him make the move on you. He'll be pretty much drunk, and as hot as you look, trust me, he'll make a move on you. I need you to get him outside, alone. He's going to be with some of his buddies, so do it slow, and make him think that he's going to go outside for a quickie. He's going to want you to fuck him in his car. Tell him it's too nice of a night out, and then tell him you want to do something different. When he asks what? Rub your hand on his dick and tell him you want to suck it, but you want to do it out back, behind the bar, so nobody sees you. I just need you to get him to the back of the bar. I'll take it from there, and then Andy will drive you home. Can you do that for me?" I asked.

"Sure. That's all you want me to do?" she asked as she looked at both Andy and me.

"That's it, I just need to get him alone. Then, pretty lady, you leave with a grand in your pocket," I explained as I watched Ginger down her second drink.

"You gonna hurt him or kill him?" she asked as she handed me her empty glass for another refill.

"Neither, I just need to talk to him alone, that's all," I explained.

"You're a gangster aren't you? You look like a mob wiseguy. You a Mafia wiseguy?" she asked with a wide-eyed look of excitement.

"How old are you Ginger?" I asked as I began to get a bit frustrated.

"I'll be 19 in two weeks." she replied with a perky smile on her face as I handed her, her third drink in less than five minutes.

"You won't be if you keep asking me stupid questions," I explained calmly as I looked Ginger in the eyes and pulled my .45 caliber Colt automatic out from under the bar and set it down on top of the bar in front of her. Patting the gun gently with my right hand, I smiled.

"You want a blow job?" she asked nervously.

"No, thank you," I answered. "But I'm sure that my friend here would love another," I explained as I nodded in Andy's direction.

* * * * * * *

The small bar faced Woodward Avenue and sat next to Treene & Carmen's Mexican Restaurant. Just down to the left, was Saint Joseph's Mercy Hospital. Looking at my watch, it was 7:32 p.m. as Ginger got out of Andy's car and went inside to buy a drink.

It was already dark outside as Andy walked over and climbed into the passenger's side of my car.

"How many times did you screw her?" I asked with a concerned look on my face.

"From the time I picked her up in Detroit, four times, why?" Andy asked.

"Just wondering is all. Make sure that I spray you down with Lysol disinfectant before you go home tonight," I said jokingly.

"Ahh," Andy said with a wave of his hand.

"You know what you gotta do with her right?" I asked, concerned that Andy may have gotten a little to attached to Ginger. Sex has a way of making men careless.

"Don't worry about it," Andy answered as he took a sip of his long neck bottle of Budweiser. "Hell, why do you think I fucked her so much? I knew that I was really going to fuck her tonight!" Andy explained as he broke out laughing. Reaching into my backseat, I grabbed my brand new aluminum baseball bat and set it down beside me. "Good thing for him that he's going to be drunk, that's going to hurt," Andy commented as we sat back and waited.

The traffic on Woodward Avenue was steady, business at Treene & Carmen's was exceptionally good. They were the only authentic Mexican restaurant in all of Oakland County. That I knew of anyway. The bar parking lot was gravel and had about twenty cars parked in it. About twenty-four minutes had passed when I saw Ginger as she walked out of the bar with good old George.

"Holy shit, Andy," I said in a surprised voice as I tapped him on the left arm and pointed at Ginger and George. "That was quick."

Waiting for Ginger to get George safely to the back of the bar, both Andy and I got out of the car and went back to join them. Carrying the ball bat in my left hand, I checked my pants pocket to make sure that I still had the small brown paper lunch bag I had folded up earlier and put there. Looking around to make sure the coast was clear and nobody was watching us or pulling into the parking lot, I pulled out my silenced .9mm Beretta and stepped behind the bar. Ginger was already on her knees. George was standing in front of her with his dick in her mouth. Ginger was struggling as George held her by the sides of her head, by the hair, and was trying to force all of his dick down the young girls throat!

"Take it all, you fucking bitch. Swallow, damn it," he said loudly in a brutal manner. He then punched Ginger in the left side of her face with his right fist.

Walking up fast, I dropped the baseball bat behind George, grabbed him by the hair on the back top section of his head with my left hand, and pushed the cold metal of my gun barrel tightly into his right cheek.

"Don't move," I said in an angry voice as I tried to maintain a calm composer in front of Ginger.

"Come on, baby, let's go," Andy said as he grabbed Ginger by her left arm and helped her to her feet.

"You fucking piece of shit," Ginger muttered at George as she tried to control her coughing. Taking a full swing, Ginger connected with a real nice right hook and punched George in his left eye. Pulling Ginger away, Andy got her back to his car and left the parking lot.

"On your knees, now!" I ordered as I forced George down.

"Okay, okay, take it easy man," he said in a drunken stutter.

Pulling the paper bag out of my pocket, I opened it and handed it to George. "Empty your pockets, asshole, I want it all. Your wallet, keys, watch, rings, gold chain, all of it, now!" I said sternly as I jerked his head back with my left hand.

"Okay, okay, you got it, stay cool man," George said in a low tone of voice as he emptied all of his pockets and put everything into the paper bag. Taking off all his jewelry, George dropped it in the paper bag and handed the bag to me.

Rolling the top of the bag tightly shut, I set it down on the ground and picked up the baseball bat. Putting my gun back into its holster, I snapped the thin leather snap shut across the hammer of the gun to secure it.

"You really enjoy hurting women, don't you?" I asked as I pulled both of my leather gloves up snuggly onto my hands.

"What?" George said as he looked straight ahead and confused.

"You beat up your wife Dana the other night, remember George?" I said quickly.

"Oh, wait a minute, I was drunk," he started to say.

"Remember what you did to Jessy," I asked.

"Who?" he questioned.

"Your daughter, remember her, George?" I asked as I bent down to whisper in his ear and look around to make sure we were still alone.

"You tried to feel her up. Your own daughter, George. You wanted to fuck her real bad, didn't you? But then your wife came running into the bedroom to stop you, so you beat her up instead," I said angrily.

"I was drunk, man, I was drunk," George said frantically.

"I've got a message for you, George, its from God," I explained as I tightened my grip on the bat and looked down at him.

"God? What message?" he asked, now totally confused.

"God wants you to know that when you hurt one of his little children, he's going to send a guy like me to put you to sleep. Say goodnight, asshole," I whispered as I swung the bat.

George started to respond, but my first swing caught him in the right side of the jaw, shattering both the jaw and most of his teeth. The second swing caught George full force in the right side of his head, at the temple. The sound of his skull splitting open, sounded like someone had dropped a watermelon onto the cement floor.

George's body fell sideways onto the ground next to the large metal garbage dumpster. Blood was pouring out from his mouth and the side of his head in a steady flow as I turned and walked away. There was no doubt in my mind, that the second blow to the head had killed George.

Climbing into my car, I started it and took one last look around to make sure that no one had seen me walk out from behind the bar. Putting the car in gear, I drove away.

Spring Lake is on Maybe Road, in Clarkston, just down from where I had grown up as a child. It was a spring fed lake, and from what everyone always said, was bottomless. Someone had just purchased all of the land on this side of the road. The new Spring Lake Country Club golf course was under construction. At the time though, no one was there as I pulled in close to the lake and put my car in park.

Reaching down next to me, I picked up the long white striped sport sock and put all of George's belongings into it. Opening the door to my car, I got out and picked up four nice golf-ball size rocks and put them into the sock. Tying the top of the knee high sock into a tight knot, I walked down to the lake and threw the sock as far as I could, trying to get it as close to the center of the lake as possible. It wasn't a big lake. But its water was cold and deep as the sock made a splashing sound and quickly disappeared from sight.

Walking back up to the gravel section where my car was parked, I couldn't help but wonder how the death of George would effect both Dana and Jessy. Getting back into my car, I drove away and headed back home. The police will write it up as a robbery gone badly. George's friends will identify Ginger as a pretty little blue eyed blonde that left with George. The case will go into the unsolved dead file of the police department within two weeks. Dana will collect his life insurance and hopefully will find happiness with a decent fella. If not, what the hell, I'll get rid of him too.

"Damn, I was born 100-years too late," I thought to myself. "Western justice, fast and simple. Live fast and die young. Now that would have been the life."

Placing a drop of Methadrine under my tongue, I headed home. "Wednesday night and there's nothing to do. Maybe I'll get lucky and I'll have a message waiting for me at home. What I need is a little excitement in my life." By the time I got home, that's exactly what I got.

It was 11:00 p.m. Wednesday night when I pulled into my driveway and found a long, black, stretch limousine waiting for me. Getting out of my car, I knew something was up when the driver of the limo got out and opened the backdoor of the limousine.

"Sir, you have someone who would like to speak with you," the driver explained politely. Looking inside the car, I saw a great pair of legs and knew right away who had come to see me.

Climbing into the backseat, I smiled as the driver closed the door behind me. "Hello, pretty lady, I'd know those legs anywhere," I said surprised that Carla had come all this way to see me. Something must be up that she doesn't want to talk about at her office, I thought to myself as Carla began to speak.

"You really think I have nice legs?" she asked.

"Oh yeah," I replied with a smile.

"I always thought you were kidding about that," she answered. "David, if I asked you to kill the President of the United States, would you do it?" Carla asked as she looked deep into my eyes waiting for an answer.

"Yes, ma'am," I answered calmly without a moments hesitation.

"Even if it had nothing to do with protecting our country? What if I was asking you to kill him for my own personal reasons with absolutely no authorization to support it?" Carla asked as she continued to search my eyes with hers.

"Listen, Carla, you're my friend. If you want the President dead, say the word, and I'll put him to sleep for you," I explained seriously.

"How would you do it?" she asked quickly.

"That's none of your business. Plausible deniability, Carla. I already know exactly how I would do it. Do you want him dead? Yes or no?" I asked looking her in the eyes.

"No, of course not. I just needed to know if I could count on you, no matter how serious the threat might be," she explained as she opened her briefcase and handed me a used passport and new set of fake credentials.

"Can you get away for a few months? I need you to go somewhere at which time a friend of mine will train you and teach you some very special tricks of his trade. This is the first time that he has ever been willing to let anyone see his face. I am one of the very few people who knows who he really is, what he does, and can identify him. Because I have asked, he is willing to teach you the art of his trade," Carla explained calmly.

"Who is he?" I asked.

"Will you go and learn from him?" she asked, avoiding the question.

"Of course I will. I just need to call and let my grandparents know that I'll be gone for a while. Plus, I need to let Agent Eckland know that I'm going to be out of pocket for a few months," I explained.

"No! Don't tell Kathy anything. Let your grandparents know you're leaving for a while, but do not tell them or anyone else where you're going. Understand?" Carla explained sternly.

"Understood. Now then. Can you at least tell me where I'm going?" I questioned.

"Venezuela. You're going to go meet the Master," Carla explained with a grin.

"The Master? Can we cut to the chase here, please?" I asked as I began to get a bit frustrated.

"You're going to meet Carlos the Jackal," Carla explained.

"Carlos the Jackal! Are you serious? He's wanted by law enforcement from all around the world. He's a terrorist!" I replied.

"Carlos is a very dear friend of mine. He is responsible for killing over eighteen political people throughout the world. They call him the Jackal because that's exactly what he is. He is a master at disguise and extremely deadly. He has never accepted a contract that was less than forty million dollars and he has never killed in the United States. Would you like to know why?" she asked.

"Yes, why?" I questioned with an intense interest.

"Because I won't let him," Carla replied with a sinister tone of voice as she looked at me and smiled.

"Who are you, Carla? Seriously, who are you really?" I asked in a dead serious tone of voice as I looked deep into Carla's eyes.

"I am your friend, David. America needs a Jackal of its own and you have proven to me that you've got what it takes to be my Jackal," she explained as she closed her briefcase.

"Oh really, and what's that?" I asked out of curiosity.

"You've got the heart to get the job done no matter what the cost. You've got the courage to do it. You love the hunt, David, it excites you. I also know that I can trust you. Now then, here are your airline tickets. When you get to the airport, get your luggage and sit down. Carlos will find you. Never tell him anymore about you other than your first name that we have placed on your passport and identification. Never ask him what his last name is. Do what he tells you to do and do not carry any weapons on this trip with you. Do not take your personal papers or identification with you. You travel only under the name that is on the credentials I have given you. Understood?"

"I thought that you trusted this guy?" I asked.

"I do trust him. This is how we play the game. This is also how we've earned each other's trust. By the way, before I forget," Carla explained as she reached into her purse. Handing me a small hard plastic device with the gold chain on it, she continued, "This is the sky pager that I told you about. You can set it to beep or vibrate. Keep it in your pocket and out of sight so people don't see it and ask you what it is. With this devise, I can page you from anywhere around the world. It's satellite operated and battery powered. If the numbers on the digital readout start to fade that means you need to replace the battery. Take these," she explained as she handed me twelve small round batteries sealed in plastic. "These are your replacement batteries," she explained as she took in a deep breath of air and let it out slowly. "No one in Washington or anywhere else knows that I know Carlos," she explained with a touch of worry on her face.

"Carlos? Carlos who?" I replied.

Smiling, the look of worry quickly disappeared. "I've been waiting for a young man with your qualities for a long time, David. Enjoy your vacation, and please be nice, will ya," she asked with a grin.

"Yes, mommy. I'll be nice as long as Uncle Carlos is nice," I said jokingly.

"You two are going to love each other," Carla said with laughter in her voice as I got out of the car and went into my house to pack my bags.

"She really does trust me. I'm going to go and meet with the world's most feared assassin, Carlos the Jackal. You're in the big time now, David. Don't slip. If you do, you're a dead man!" I told myself as I packed my bags and called my grandfather.

* * * * * * *

My flight to Venezuela went well. Getting off of the United Airlines Flight, I picked up my baggage and sat down in one of the chairs close to the boarding area. About five minutes had passed when I noticed a lady walking up to me, smiling. She was in her late fifties and had graying, brown hair.

"Hello, you are David, yes?" she asked as she extended her hand out for me to shake.

"Yes, ma'am," I replied as I shook her hand and smiled politely.

"Please come, I will take you to where you are going," she said as she turned slowly and walked away.

Picking up my bags, I followed her out to the parking lot to her car. I placed both of my suitcases into the trunk of her dark, blue Volvo, and then I got into the backseat as she had asked me to. The weather was hot outside. It was a beautiful, sunshiny afternoon as we drove away and headed out of the city. Venezuela was a poor but beautiful country. Leaving the city, we headed northwest to the higher hill country. It was then that the woman pulled the car over, put it in park and turned to face me. Handing me a black cloth bag, she spoke, "Please, put this over your head and lay down in the seat. Will you do this for me?" she asked kindly.

"Yes, ma'am," I answered as I placed the cloth bag over my head and lay down, as I was instructed.

I knew that this was their way of protecting Carlos. If I couldn't see where I was going, then I wouldn't be able to find his home again if I ever came back looking for him. It was a smart move and I respected it. "Hell, with it. I'll take a little nap," I said to myself as we pulled back out onto the dirt road.

It took us another hour and a half to get to the beautiful ranch home that sat high up in the hills and valleys of Venezuela. What I didn't know at the time was that the woman who was driving me wasn't really a woman at all. It was Carlos the Jackal himself, dressed in one of his many disguises.

I spent the next seventy-two days learning the fine art tricks of the Jackal's trade. Some of what Carlos taught me I had already learned at the CIA Farm. Most of what he had taught me, I didn't know, and to my surprise, I was able to teach Carlos a few tricks that even he didn't know. Because of my promise to him, I will not discuss anything that he had told me or taught me. I told him about some of the new poisons and gasses that were made available to me through the agency.

By the time I left Carlos, we had set-up a way that we would be able to communicate with each other through three different major newspapers. In doing so, I was able to send him a number of different poisons, gasses, a Kevlar vest, and a lock pick gun that he really didn't need but found amusing. He taught me so many valuable lessons that it made me sad, when years later, I would be told that a man named J. Cofer Black would finally catch Carlos the Jackal. By then, Carlos would have over thirty high profile assassinations from around the world to his credit.

For now, however, we said our goodbyes. This time, Carlos was dressed as a nun when he took me back to the airport. Flying home to Michigan, I found myself a wiser, more cunning young man...

Chapter Seventeen
Time Click

After I returned home from Venezuela, I went straight to Washington D.C. and checked in with Carla. We spent the afternoon together and watched the computer as a fresh batch of intelligence information began to come in.

A counter revolutionary group of Cubans had been discovered in Miami. The agency had been watching these Cubans for quite some time. But this was the first time they had made an attempt to purchase a large amount of weapons and explosives from within the United States.

They had made contact with a man named Luis Enrique Villablobos, who was suspected, by Ollie, as being one of the people who were running guns for the Contras. This by itself was not a big deal; Ollie had that under control. What he didn't have under control was the direct connection that Luis had with the Ayatollah in Iran. This connection might be the link we needed to help us locate our two missing suitcase-size A-pack nuclear weapons. The problem was that Luis, for some reason unknown to us, had a contract put out on him by none other than Fidel Castro himself. Even though Luis Villablobos was a low-level dirt bag, he could be useful to us. The Cubans, on the other hand, were classified by our Agency as terrorists. We needed to infiltrate them and find out just how deeply they were rooted into Miami.

Carla took me to dinner while Neil monitored telephone conversations taking place between Fidel Castro, the Russians, and Fidel's terrorist group in Miami. After dinner we went back to the CIA's Covert Operations Room, which I called The War Room.

"Anything happening, Neil?" Carla asked.

"Yes, ma'am," Neil replied as he turned in his chair to face us. "You're gonna love this, Carla. The man we believe to be the leader of this Cuban group, who goes by the name Patron, is trying to put together a meeting with the local Miami crime boss."

"What? They're trying to go to bed with the mob?" Carla asked with a surprised look on her face.

"What else would they have to talk about?" Neil asked, with raised eyebrows and a smile on his face.

"Did you catch the conversation?" Carla asked.

"Only one side of it, ma'am. Our local wiseguys had their end scrambled," Neil explained.

"Walter Shaw, Sr.," Carla replied with a shake of her head. "Stay on it, Neil. Have someone monitor this communication 24-7, around the clock, will ya?"

"You got it, ma'am," Neil replied as he turned back to face his computer.

"Who's Shaw," I asked as Carla and I left Neil to do his spying and went back to Carla's office. Sitting down at Carla's desk in her private office, I asked again, "Who's Shaw?"

"Walter Shaw, Sr. is without a doubt the most brilliant man alive. He's also the greatest jewel thief that ever lived! He is of Sicilian ancestry and the man who invented the Cheese Box or what we now call the Black Box," Carla explained.

"That's what we use?" I asked softly with a curious look on my face.

"That's right. Walter has also come out with several brand new inventions that are in the patent office right now. Call Conferencing is one of them. This is the genius that invented the Red Phone the President uses in the Oval Office to call the President of Russia. The problem is that every time Walter invents something, the bureaucratic powers that sit high up in our government steal it from him," Carla explained with a sad shake of her head.

"Gee, why doesn't that surprise me?" I said sarcastically.

"Yeah, no shit. So now his son, Walter Shaw, Jr., has put together his own wrecking crew of jewel thieves. We call them the Dinner Set Gang. They hit the homes of the elite rich and do it at dinner time while the victim is at home eating dinner!" Carla explained with a chuckle.

"That takes some real big balls!" I replied. That impressed me.

"No shit. I wish Walter was working for us. Walter Jr. was recruited and trained by a mob wiseguy named Pete Salerno. Get this, Pete was trained by the Secret Service back in the day and worked for us at one time," Carla explained.

I had heard the name Pete Salerno many times in the past. But this was the first time that I had ever heard the name Walter Shaw, Sr., and his son. I had heard Sam and Pauly talk about the Cheese Box. Mob bookmakers used it to make toll free, untraceable calls. Now I knew who the genius was that invented it.

"Well listen, Carla, I'm going home. I need to make sure my house hasn't burned down. I've been gone almost three months now," I explained as I stood up to leave.

"I've had Brandi stopping by your place once a week to check on it. By the way, did you know that she's getting a divorce?" Carla asked.

"No, I didn't. That's too bad," I said on the outside as I made a mental note to invite her over to dinner once her divorce was final.

"Yes, it is. It's hard to be married and do what we do. She puts in long hours and her husband gave her a choice to either quit the Agency or quit the marriage. She told him goodbye, and filed divorce papers on him," Carla explained laughingly. "God, I love that girl."

"If he gives her any problems let me know, I'll take care of it. I'll see ya later, ma. Call me if you need me or if anything breaks with those Cubans," I explained as I left Carla's office and headed back home to Michigan.

* * * * * * *

I had been home for six days. Four of which I had spent at the hospital with my grandfather. He had what the doctors called hardening of the arteries, which caused him to hallucinate due to the fact that he wasn't getting enough oxygen to his brain. My family took shifts sitting with him at the hospital. We wanted to make sure that whenever he woke up, there would be a familiar face in the room so that it would help to keep him focused. He had been in the hospital for two weeks already. By the time I got home, with the help of blood thinners, he was back to his normal self and back home as of yesterday and resting comfortably.

Hearing my Agency telephone ring, I picked it up and turned on the black scrambler box. "Hello," I said as I looked at the black box and thought of Walter Shaw, Sr.

"Hello, David. How's your grandfather?" Carla asked politely.

"He's doing a lot better," I began to say. "How did you know about my grandfather being ill?" I questioned, surprised by her question.

"You're my personal number one operative, David. It's my job to know. Is there anything that I can do to help him?" Carla asked sincerely.

"No, ma'am. He's getting old and the doctor said that his body is simply starting to shut down on him. Thank you for asking though. Hey, I wanted to ask you a question about Walter Shaw and his son," I said curiously.

"Sure, what is it?" Carla responded.

"If you know what they're doing, why don't you stop them?" I asked.

"Why? They're not hurting anyone for starters. Plus, it's none of our business. Right now they're reeking havoc in Florida. Especially Florida Palm Groves, Las Olas Isles, Palm Beach, and the north west corner of the private communities of the privileged in the Hamlets of Opa Locka, Florida. They never carry guns and they don't hurt anyone. Besides, one day I might need young Walter Shaw, Jr., to do a job for us. He'd kind of owe me one, wouldn't he?" Carla explained with a chuckle.

"He would probably tell you to go screw yourself," I replied with some humor.

"Yeah, probably. Listen, I need you to do something for me," Carla asked.

"Sure, what's up?" I replied as I reached into my shirt pocket and pulled out my tiny vial of Methadrine and placed two drops of liquid speed under my tongue.

"We're setting up a meeting with this Patron fella in Miami. We're posing as mob wiseguys. He wants to buy weapons, so we're going to be the ones to sell them to him. If the sale goes well, it could help us to penetrate deep into their organization. The problem is the Cubans are very highly wired people. I don't want to risk Oliver by putting him into play with them," Carla explained as I cut her off.

"Oh, but you'll risk me, huh?" I said teasingly.

"You're a gun fighter, kiddo. If anything should happen to go wrong, I know you're the one that will walk out of the room," Carla explained calmly.

"When and where?" I asked as my adrenaline began to pump blood throughout my body. The thought of this was exciting to me. We'll set it up for this Saturday. I doubt that Patron will meet with you at first. He'll send his dealmakers to check things out, and to make the gun deal. If all goes well, they'll take you to Tampa, Florida. Patron is big in the racing business down there," Carla explained.

"Horse racing?" I questioned.

"Greyhounds. The Cubans love dog racing and cock fights. It's a big money business in Florida and growing quickly in popularity. We'll set the meeting up at the Holiday Inn in Miami and make it for, ahh, lets say 4:00 p.m.," Carla explained. "If all goes well, you'll be at the racetrack by 7:00 p.m., meeting Patron and betting the dogs. Try to get inside of these people, David. Become Patron's best friend if at all possible. We need to know where their main underground headquarters is and who all of their contacts are. We can only monitor so much by telephone. I really believe now is the time to put you into play," Carla explained.

"I'll need a list of the weapons available that you're willing to sell to them. But listen to me, Carla. If I give these people my word and my handshake that it's a deal, you damn sure better come through on your end. I take giving my word to someone very seriously," I explained.

"That's one of the many reason I respect you, David. You're a lot like me. I'll have up to two million dollars worth of weapons and explosives delivered to Patron within twenty-four hours of the time you make the deal. Anywhere in Florida, but only in Florida," Carla explained. "I'll also have one of my people meet you at the airport to back you up. I'm not leaving you out there by yourself," she explained.

* * * * * * *

Elite Covert Operation
Code Name: Time Click
Target: Danny Patron
Location: Miami, Florida

It was Friday afternoon when my plane landed at the Miami International Airport. I was caught off guard but pleasantly surprised when I saw Kathy and two other young men walk up to greet me.

"Hello, David, welcome to Miami," Kathy said as we shook hands. "I'd like you to meet Matt and Adam. Fellas, this is David," Kathy introduced as I went to claim my luggage. Leaving the terminal, we went to the parking lot and climbed into a brand new silver limousine. Driving away, Kathy asked, "How are you feeling? Carla said that you've been in the Veteran's Hospital. Everything okay?" she asked.

"I'm fine. They wanted to run a bunch of tests to check on my heart and stuff. It was a bunch of bullshit, no big deal," I answered. I didn't like to lie to Kathy, but I also couldn't tell her that I was really in Venezuela hanging out with Carlos the Jackal either.

"Matt and Adam are both ex-Special Forces, also," Kathy explained.

Both Matt and Adam looked to be in their late twenties. Matt stood six-feet, three-inches tall, weighted a good 245-pounds, all of which was muscle, and had jet-black hair. Adam, stood six-feet tall, had brown, wavy hair, and looked to be a good 200-pounds of solid muscle.

"Really? That's good, I'd prefer brother Vietnam veterans watching my back than some draft dodging punk," I explained with a smile as I looked over at Kathy and winked.

"Don't worry about your six, bro, we'll have it covered. If something jumps off with these inbred pieces of shit, we won't hesitate, count on that," Matt explained as he drove the car.

"Oh yeah," Adam said coolly. "To be honest with you, we're hoping that they do something stupid. We could use some action right about now."

"Boy, I know Force Recon Marines when I see 'em," I said with a smile, as I watched their expressions to see if my guess was right.

Turning to look at me, Adam smiled, "How did you know?" he asked.

"I did a lot of work with Marine Special Forces in Vietnam. I was Black Op's. I could always count on the Force Recon boys to watch our six when my team was down and dirty," I explained with a grin.

"Black Op's, hell yeah, we're killing Cubans this weekend," Adam said smartly, as he and Matt began to laugh out loud and slapped each others hands in agreement.

"Be nice boys," Kathy said smiling. "We're not here to kill 'em, we're here to make a deal with them and penetrate their organization." Turning to look at me, she added, "However, if they make one wrong move, kill 'em all, and my report will say, 'Justified'."

We went to the Holiday Inn in downtown Miami and rented four rooms on the seventh floor. room's 707, 708, 709, and the room directly across the hall from room 707, room 714. Our plan of action was now being put into play.

I would meet with the Cubans in room 707. Matt would be in room 714, armed with his Mack-10, just in case things went wrong. If they did, as soon as the Cubans tried to leave the room, they would walk right into Matt and his machine gun. Adam and Kathy would be next door to me, in room 708, listening and tape recording everything being said as I made the arms deal with the Cubans.

While Matt and Adam wired the room for sound, so they would be able to tape record everything from room 708, I was busy putting a back-up plan together. The room was a nice one. It had a large bed, bathroom, and a television set. You could open the sliding glass doors and walk out onto the balcony. From there, you had a beautiful view of palm trees, girls in bikinis, the in-ground swimming pool that was part of the hotel, and the ocean. Just inside and next to the sliding glass doors was a round dinner style table.

Opening my suitcase, I pulled out my small tool kit and began what I called my back-up plan. Turning the table upside down, I took my extra leather holster and secured it to the bottom of the table with four small wood screws. Placing the table right side up again, I set the table on an angle so I could sit with my back against the wall facing room 708. The gun holster would be under the table, right in front of me in case I needed a weapon fast. Taking my back-up gun, a .9mm Smith & Wesson model 59, I loaded it with 15-rounds of hollow-point bullets and slid it into the holster that I had secured under the table. Sitting down at the table, I tested the holster to make sure that the gun would slide out easily. It did. Smiling at Kathy, I winked, "I hate Cubans," I said calmly.

"Be nice, I don't want to screw anything up, David. If I screw this up, I'm back on information gathering detail," Kathy explained.

"Don't worry about it, pretty lady. If anything goes wrong its my call, not yours," I explained as Matt and Adam walked back into room 707 and closed the door behind them.

"We're all set, boss. This room is wired for sound. From next door, you'll be able to hear everything that is said in here," Matt explained with a smile as he talked to Kathy.

"How do we play it, David? It's your ball game, we're just here to back you up," Kathy said as they all sat down to hear what I had planned.

"We're gonna need three bottles of Bacardi Rum. Get Bacardi Superior 151 proof, glasses, a bucket of ice, and some Coke," I explained.

"Coke?" Kathy responded with a look of surprise on her face. "The Pepsi Man, is asking for Coke?" she added jokingly.

"Cubans drink rum, straight up with ice, or rum and Coke as a mix drink. Pay attention and learn something. This isn't about me. It's about making them feel comfortable and making this deal. Now then, no matter what you hear on that tape, do not come into this room," I explained as I looked at Matt, Kathy, and Adam.

"What if we hear gunshots?" Matt asked with a serious look on his face.

"If something jumps off, listen to what's being said in this room. If I'm dead, you'll hear them say that. If not, I'll call for you and tell you to get in here. If you hear gunshots Matt, and I don't call for you, do me a favor will ya?" I asked.

"You got it, brother, just name it," Matt answered as he looked intensely into my eyes.

"Kill 'em all, as soon as they open the door to this room," I asked coldly. "They'll have already killed me."

"You got my word on that, brother. Consider 'em dead!" Matt answered, as he looked over at Adam and nodded his head.

"Thank you," I said as I looked at my watch. "We're running out of time. Kathy, call Carla and tell her where we are. She's suppose to call Patron by 3:00 p.m. and set the meeting place. One of you other fella's, hit the party store and pick up the rum. Hell, grab a bottle of Tequila too, just in case they want some of that instead," I added as an after thought. Our plan was in motion, the question now was – would it work?

* * * * * * *

It was exactly 4:00 p.m. sharp, when I heard the knock on the door of my room. I was wearing a black silk T-shirt, black dress slacks, black leather belt, and black slip on low-cut dress shoes. I was dressed like this because it was comfortable and so the Cubans would be able to see that I was not armed.

Placing two drops of Methadrine under my tongue, I put the tiny vial of liquid speed back into my front pants pocket, opened the door, and smiled. There were three of them. All three were dressed nice and wore a lot of gold jewelry. They all stood roughly five-feet, ten-inches tall. All three had black hair, and looked to be in their early thirties. It was the one fella with the gold teeth that made me feel a surge of excitement; he was the dangerous one.

"You da pizza man?" the one with the suit coat asked with a smile.

"No, man, I sell taco's," I answered. "Come on in fella's and make yourself at home." I explained as I welcomed them into the room and walked over toward the table. The words, pizza and taco, were the code words we were given, that would let us know we were in fact the right people that were meeting for the gun sale. Turning to face them, I extended my hand and smiled. "I'm David, from Detroit."

Smiling, the thinner clean-cut Cuban shook my hand. "I am Julio, this is Mr. Cruz," he said as he introduced me to the man with the gold teeth. The third man had locked the front door to the room and stood with his back up against it. There was no introduction to him.

"I have some rum and tequila, come in fella's, help yourselves," I said as I sat down at the table and took a drink from my glass. Mr. Cruz had been drinking heavily already. I could smell the booze on his breath as Julio sat down at the table across from me. Mr. Cruz kept staring at me and stood behind and just off to the right of Julio. This told me that Julio was the man running the show, at least for now. No one touched the drinks.

"I am told dat you have sometings dat we might be looking to buy," Julio said in broken, but decent English. My briefcase was on top of the table already. Reaching up to open it I noticed that Cruz quickly put his right hand behind his back and whispered something in Spanish. Whatever it was, it caught the attention of the man who stood guard at the door.

"Tranquilo, brother, Tranquilo," I said as I opened the lid of the briefcase and pulled out a list of the weapons and explosives I had for sale, along with pictures of each item. When I said, Tranquilo, I was telling him to take it easy. Handing all of the paperwork and photographs to Julio, I put my right hand on my lap and picked up my drink with my left hand to take a sip.

Keeping my eyes fixed on Julio, I could see Mr. Cruz was ready to go at any given moment. It then dawned on me that I wasn't wearing my Kevlar vest. This meeting was going to go bad. Cruz was going to blow it; I could feel it in the air.

"Dis is nice, I like dis," Julio said, as he looked intently at the photographs. Nodding his head up and down.

"I have two semi-trucks loaded and not far from here, Julio. You can have it all for two million or I'm willing to break it up and sell you whatever you need for a cheaper price," I said calmly. As I did, I noticed that Cruz tensed the muscle in his right arm.

Before Julio could speak, Mr. Cruz made his move. I was impressed. He was fast, real fast, and real stupid. In one fast, cat like move Cruz pulled a .380 automatic pistol out from behind his back, lunged forward, and pointed the gun in my face. As he did, he cocked the hammer and began to yell loudly. "FBI, FBI, you fucking FBI," he shouted, as the knuckle of his trigger finger began to turn white. He was applying pressure to the trigger.

Julio looked up from the paperwork and pictures, right into my eyes. He had a look of surprise on his face, as I looked him straight in the eyes and remained calm. Leaning slightly forward, I put my right hand on the butt of my gun and held it tight. I never looked at Cruz or the gun that was no more than six-inches from my face. I kept my focus directed into the eyes of Julio, showing no fear. After what I had gone through in Cambodia as a POW with Major Dinh and Colonel Ky, this didn't scare me.

I found myself excited as the combination of speed and adrenaline surged through every poor of my body. Looking Julio in the eyes, I spoke, "Our people know each other, that is why we are sitting here today. If you think that I am an FBI agent, then tell Mr. Cruz to pull the trigger. If not, then tell him to put the gun away. I don't want to be late for the first race, it starts at seven," I explained calmly as I continued to stare into the eyes of Julio.

It took about ten seconds, then Julio smiled and said something to Mr. Cruz in Spanish. When he did, Cruz smiled, showing me all of his gold teeth. He then relaxed his grip on his handgun, and tucked it back into his belt, behind his back.

Now smiling, Cruz spoke, "Okay, you okay, I like you. You have balls, big balls," he explained as he turned his head to look at the man standing guard at the door. As he did, the man at the door smiled and lowered his right hand and pointed the gun he held down toward the floor. When he did, I made my move. Standing up quickly, I pulled my gun out from under the table and pointed it over the top of Julio's head at the man standing by the door. His eyes got big as he tried to raise his gun, but it was too late.

Firing two quick shots, my hollow-point bullets struck him in the throat and upper chest. The impact of the bullets forced his body backwards, slamming him up against the door. His gun fell from his hand and made a thumping sound as it hit the floor. His body slid down against the door. As it did, it left a wide bloodstain against the inside of the white door.

Even though everything was happening fast, it seemed as though it was all happening in slow motion. Mr. Cruz was now turning back to face me with an angry look on his face as he reached behind his back for his weapon. I fired one quick shot, which struck Mr. Cruz in the face just below the nose. The bullet hit him in the center part of his upper lip and mushroomed as it went in. His head snapped backward so violently from the force of the bullet, that I could actually hear the neck bone snap as his body flew backwards spraying blood, hair, and what little brain he had all over the floor and carpet behind him.

Turning the gun quickly, I pointed it at Julio. To my surprise, Julio had remained calm. Turning his head to look away from the gun, he raised both hands up and pointed the palms of his hands at me. Moving them slowly from side to side he spoke.

"Easy Heffa, easy," he said in a low soft voice. This time, however, he spoke in perfect English. "I'm a Federal agent, man, you don't want to do this," he explained.

"Can you prove that?" I asked calmly.

"I sure can, my Federal ID is in my shoe," he explained, keeping his hands in the air.

"Real easy, bubba, get it," I said keeping the gun pointed at him. "Which Agency?" I asked as he pulled off his left boot and reached inside.

"ATF," he said as he pulled out his Federal credentials and handed them to me.

"Damn," I said in a whisper.

"Yeah, no shit. You're one of us, aren't you?" Julio asked keeping his hands in the air.

"Yup," was all that I said.

"Man, I've been working undercover trying to get Patron for five months now. It took me all this time just to get him to trust me enough to take me to his home. I've been snorting his Cocaine and fucking his women. I've been waiting for this gun deal and now I find out you're the fucking FBI!" Julio explained.

"Julio?" I said as I lowered my gun and smiled.

"Yeah?" he answered as if I was about to ask him a question.

"Say goodnight, asshole," I said calmly as I quickly raised my gun and shot him in the face. Julio flew backwards onto the floor. His arms and legs were moving in all directions wildly as if he was kicking and swinging at someone. As a sniper in Vietnam, I saw it before. Sometimes a bullet in the brain caused the body to react this way; we called it the Death Dance. He was dead, his body just didn't know it yet. It took about thirty-seconds, then Special Agent Julio Garcia's body came to a rest.

"Matt, Kathy, Adam, get in here," I shouted as I walked over and picked up the telephone.

Running into the room, Matt, Kathy, and Adam had their guns drawn. Closing the door behind him, Adam locked the door and spoke. "Which one was the Federal agent?" he asked as they put their weapons back into their holsters.

Calling the agency in Langley, I gave them my voice recognition code and waited. I didn't answer Adam's question. It took about twenty-seconds, then the voice on the other end of the line said, "Yes?"

"I need some laundry cleaned," I replied calmly.

"Location?" he asked.

Giving them the name, address, and room number of our hotel, I hung up the telephone, and looked at Kathy. "The Agency will send someone to clean this mess up and dispose of the bodies. Pack up the recording equipment and let's go. We've got a dog race to go to," I said as I smiled and winked at Kathy.

"David, we'll never get close to Patron now," Kathy explained with a disappointed look on her face as she looked around the room at the three dead bodies.

"Watch and learn, pretty lady," I said as I grabbed her by the arm and headed toward the door. "Watch and learn. I have a plan!"

* * * * * * *

Making the drive from Miami to Tampa, we arrived at the Tampa Florida Greyhound Race Track a few minutes before seven. Paying our one-dollar admission fee, Kathy, Matt, Adam and I went in to look around and see if we could find Patron.

To my surprise, the place was packed with people of all ages. From inside, I looked out through the large glass windows of the inside section of the building and watched as the gates opened releasing the slender greyhound dogs. They would chase a mechanical white rabbit around the 5/16-mile track. The crowd was going crazy yelling for their favorite dog to run faster. This was a multi-million dollar business!

Looking out through the windows, I spotted Patron as he stood up from the long bench seats in front of the racetrack. Smiling, he walked back inside to cash in his ticket. His dog had won!

"There he is," I said as I pointed at Patron from the safety of the building. Looking in the direction I was pointing, Kathy and Matt saw him.

"How do you want to do this, David?" Kathy asked.

"Watch my back, I'm going to go and tell him that I just killed his friends," I explained with a cold sinister smile on my face.

"You're kidding me, right?" Kathy asked in a concerned tone of voice.

"Stay back and don't be too obvious that you're watching us," I said as I walked over to the bar to get a cold bottle of Pepsi.

Waiting for Patron to cash in his winning ticket, I watched as he walked to the bar with two of his lady friends and bought some mixed drinks. As soon as he did, he sat down at a table inside where a few of his friends were sitting.

Patron stood a good six-feet tall and weighed about 185-pounds. He looked to be in his late twenties, early thirties. He had dark brown hair, and was dressed nicely. Watching how everyone treated him at the table, there was little doubt that this man, Danny Patron, was the boss.

Seeing me walking toward their table, two other Cubans who were sitting at the table next to Patron, said something and quickly got up to intercept me.

"Very good," I thought to myself. "He's got bodyguards."

Raising his hand to stop me, the smaller of the two bodyguards spoke, "Can I help you?"

"Tell Mr. Patron that I'm the guy from Detroit. Then tell him that he has one minute to talk to me or my play toys go to the Chinese Triad in New York," I explained calmly as I looked at my watch.

Stepping up to Patron, the smaller fella whispered in his ear while his partner kept an eye on me. Looking over at me, Patron said something to his friend and then spoke to the young ladies at the table.

"Follow me would you," the smaller bodyguard asked as he tried to lead me in the opposite direction.

"I don't take orders, my friend, I give them. Tell your boss that he just lost his chance to buy my guns," I said calmly as I turned to walk away.

"Wait a minute, sir, there seems to be a little misunderstanding. Please, wait one more minute," the smaller man asked as he walked back over to speak to his boss. This time things were different. The girls got up and went to the bar with the two other men that were sitting at the table. Walking up to the table, Patron smiled at me. "Please, sit down," he said as I sat down across the table from him. "Do I know you?" he asked politely.

"No, let me introduce myself to you. I'm the guy that just killed your three boys!" I said calmly as we stared each other in the eyes. The look on his face told me that he was real upset with the news that I just delivered to him. I didn't give him anytime to react. I followed up with more. "I hope that Julio didn't know a lot about you. He told me that he fucks your women and snorts your cocaine. That was after I killed Cruz and his partner." Patrons face was turning red with anger, so I continued. "You insult me by sending two of your flunkies and a Federal agent to make a deal with me. Is that how you do business?" I asked.

"Impossible!" he said bitterly in a low tone of voice as he slammed his left fist down hard on the top of the table.

"Really?" I replied as I reached into my back left pants pocket and pulled out Julio's Federal ATF ID and tossed it across the table to Patron.

Looking down at the credentials, I thought that Patron was going to pass out. He was in total shock. I knew now that I had him, so I drove one right into his heart. "I was told by my people that Danny Patron was a man that could be trusted, a man of respect. Let me tell you something, Danny," I said as he looked up at me. "If I find out that you're a cop, I'll gut you alive. Now then, I usually charge twenty-five thousand to kill a Federal Agent. But I'm not going to charge you, Danny. You owe me big time, brother. Julio was ready to take you and your crew down, all the way down," I explained calmly as I took a sip of my Pepsi. Handing his bodyguard the Federal ID, the bodyguard looked at it and whispered something in Spanish.

"I don't know what to say. I can't trust anyone in this country. Not even my own people," he said bitterly.

"Your boy Cruz pulled a gun on me and stuck it in my face. Then called me the FBI. That's why I killed him. Don't ever make that mistake with me or my people. If you do, it will be the last mistake you make," I explained.

"I can see that," he said with a slight grin on his face.

"You and I, do we have a problem between us? Do we have issues to settle?" I asked as I stared Danny in the eyes.

"No, like you said, I owe you. At least I know you ain't no cop!" he said as he looked at his bodyguards and laughed. "You still want to sell your stuff?" Danny asked.

"You trust these guys?" I asked as I nodded towards his bodyguards.

"With my life. They're my first cousins. They came from Cuba with me," Danny explained proudly.

Handing Danny my briefcase, I watched as he opened it. Glancing at the pictures, he quickly closed the briefcase.

"I have a private room upstairs. Let's go talk up there where it's quiet," Danny suggested.

"Sounds good. You sure that Julio didn't bug it or your home and car?" I asked.

"Shit," he said as he muttered something angrily in Spanish.

"I've got my limo parked outside, Danny. Let's go out there and talk. I'll introduce you to my partner. If you want our help, we have all the equipment that is needed. We can sweep your home, car, and any other place that Julio had access to. If there are any bugs planted in your stuff, my partner will find it," I said as we left the building and went out to our limousine.

I spent the next hour with Danny Patron. He bought both semi-trucks full of weapons and explosives for a cool two million dollars in cash. The weapons were delivered the next day. We parked both trucks in the same large parking lot of the local food store on the night that I had made the deal with Danny. I took Danny to the trucks personally. He looked everything over and was very pleased with what he saw. Paying for the weapons, Danny had his people drive the trucks away. What he didn't know was that we were watching both trucks by satellite from the Pentagon. Neil is very good at his job.

I then put both Matt and Adam into play and introduced them to Danny as my most trusted friends. Danny asked for our help, and wanted to know if we could check out his homes and vehicles for bugs. I had planted the seed and it worked extremely well for us.

Using high tech equipment, Matt and Adam swept both of Danny's homes, his yacht, nine of his cars, three of his night clubs, and his private viewing rooms at both the Tampa and Pensacola Greyhound Race Tracks.

We knew that Julio was trying real hard to gain Danny's trust. This would prevent him from bugging Patron's home. However, we gave Danny fifteen listening devices known as bugs and told him that we found them all throughout his personal property. In reality, it was out-dated material that the CIA didn't use anymore.

It all worked to our advantage. Danny Patron now trusted us one hundred percent. It had also given us a chance to plant our own high tech, CIA, surveillance bugs all throughout Danny Patron's personal property.

As I had expected, Danny Patron was a very smart fool. I had spent three days in Florida with Danny. I kept Kathy away from everyone so they wouldn't be able to recognize her if anything should happen to go wrong.

Saying goodbye to Danny, I left Matt and Adam in Miami with the agreement that if Danny or his people should need anything else, he would come to us to buy it. Using the two million dollars we had made on the gun sale, I instructed Matt and Adam to find a nice home in West Palm Beach and buy it. They could use that as their base of operations and monitor Danny Patron and his people from there.

Our Agency had sent people to the Holiday Inn to clean up the mess that I had made. Within five hours, you would have never known that three people had been killed in room 707. They did that good of a job. Flying back home to Michigan, I found myself feeling cold and empty inside.

Walking into my home, I closed the door behind me and locked it. Standing in the quietness of my home, I suddenly felt all alone. Walking into my den, I turned on my television set. There was a Special News Bulletin on every channel.

"Oh no," I sighed as I watched and listened as the news broadcaster explained that a janitor, working in the Watergate Office Building, found a piece of tape on the door lock of the Democrat National Committee

Headquarters office. The place had been bugged and all eyes were on our President. It was then that my telephone rang.

"Hello," I said as I watched the news on my set.

"You got your TV on?" Ollie asked.

"Yeah, how bad is this?" I questioned, knowing how close Carla was to the President.

"We're trying to do damage control now. The White House and Camp David also have secret listening devices installed in them," Ollie explained nervously.

"Did the President know about this?" I asked curiously.

"Yes, we're looking for Russian moles and traitors, but we can't say that publicly. I just called to tell you to stay away from the White House while the damage control team tries to down play this," Ollie explained.

"Yeah, no kidding. This happened all because someone forgot to pull the duct tape off a door lock?" I questioned.

"Yup, someone got careless and now all hell is going to break loose over it. Listen, partner, I have to go, I have a lot of things I need to clean up, if you know what I mean. I'll talk to you later," Ollie explained as he hung up the telephone on his end of the line.

Hanging up my telephone, I sat back and watched the news report.

"We're trying to catch spies and in doing so it might cost the President his job. Boy, this really sucks," I said to myself as I headed to my refrigerator to grab a cold Pepsi.

Chapter Eighteen
A Message Sent

"Hang on, buddy, you've got to hang on, don't give up! Help is on the way," I whispered in an attempt to give him hope. My words fell on deaf ears. The American in the tiger cage was shivering profusely and dripping with sweat at the same time. He was sick, real sick. It was plain to see that this man was malnourished and had malaria. Looking up at the soldier's face, I could see the tell tale signs of the one thousand yard stare. It was the stoic expression on a face that had seen its fill of too much combat, pain, and horror of torture and war. This man had given up hope and retreated into himself; this American wasn't going to make it much longer. His body fell limp, but the pressure of the bamboo poles, pressing against his body on all four sides, kept him from sliding down. Looking down, I saw blood dripping from the bottom of his torn feet.

"His name is Jerry," the soldier with his feet tied to a tree whispered. "Jerry's not here anymore..."

"No!" I shouted out loud as I sat straight up in my bed. I could still smell the blood and dirt as I fought hard to regain my focus and calm myself down. My entire body was covered with sweat and was shaking almost to the point that I couldn't control it.

"Oh shit," I muttered under my breath as I looked around at my bedroom in the dark. "Get up, David," I said to myself out loud as I stood up quickly and rubbed the sweat from my face. "Don't go to sleep, don't ever go to sleep again," I said as I searched for my tiny vial of liquid Methadrine. Finding it on my dresser, I placed a tiny drop of the liquid speed under my tongue. Within a matter of thirty seconds I felt every pore of my body come alive as my blood surged through my veins. Placing the vial of speed back on my dresser, I turned on my light and went to take a shower.

I had been home from Miami for two days. I had spent all day yesterday talking to Amy, Tara, Dana, and little Jessy. They came over to find out where I had been for the past three months. Dana told me about what had happened to her husband. As she did, I could almost sense a sigh of relief on her face.

I made barbecue chicken on my grill downstairs and Amy made one of the best potato salads I had ever eaten. The only potato salad I ever had that was better than Amy's was the one Cookie used to make for our team in Vietnam.

It was 2:14 a.m. when my telephone rang. Picking it up, I smiled; I needed something to do. "Hello," I said.

"Are you available, sir?" the woman's voice asked.

"Absolutely," I replied as I hung up the telephone and walked to the front door. It took two minutes before the doorbell rang, which surprised me. It usually took less than a minute. Opening the door, my heart stopped for a second as I looked into the eyes of a Pontiac Police Officer. He was wearing his full uniform and was driving a patrol car.

Handing me a large manila envelope marked Police Evidence in big letters across the face of it, he turned and walked away. Closing my front door, I quickly locked it and leaned my back up against the door.

"Holy shit. I wonder if he's a real cop?" I asked myself as I took a deep breath and let it out slowly. Turning off the front room light, I went to my kitchen, opened my refrigerator door, and grabbed a cold bottle of Pepsi and plate of cold leftover chicken. I closed the refrigerator door and headed for my den to see who was so important the family would call this early in the morning to put a contract out on.

Opening the seal on the first envelope, I was surprised to find a second envelope inside that was also sealed. Opening the second envelope, I dumped the contents onto the top of my desk. The first note was short and to the point, it read: 'Don't worry; the cop is one of ours. He's not real.' Feeling better, I took a bite of chicken and picked up the photograph to look at it. I then picked up the personal information sheet and began to read.

The hit was on a thirty-one year old Italian named Joey Piore. He stood six-feet, two-inches tall, weighed 241-pounds, had black hair, brown eyes, and was sent to Nashville by none other than Tony Pro, from New Jersey. His mission for Tony was to muscle into the country music industry, and force recording studios to pay a percentage of their gross net to the New Jersey crime family. What Tony Pro didn't know, was that some of the studios and record company's stood in high favor with the enforcer family out of Detroit. After all, Detroit is the home of Motown Records and the best soul music ever produced.

What made this hit nice was the person putting out the contract, didn't care how Joey was killed. They wanted to deliver a message to Tony Pro in New Jersey. They were going to make it clear that Tony Pro wasn't welcome in Nashville. The country music people weren't afraid of him, and were heavily connected to the Mafia.

Flying into Tennessee, I rented a car and headed to Nashville. As I drove into Nashville, the first thing I saw was the very tall Bellsouth Building. I couldn't help but smile when I saw the two long spikes that stuck out and pointed upward at the top of the building. "Looks like my stungun," I said out loud as I turned off the car radio. Kenny Rogers was singing 'Coward of the County,' and I needed to focus my thoughts.

Pulling off Highway 40, I headed straight to Westgate Circle. Joey had a home there, just down from a restaurant ironically called Joe's Crab

Shack. The information package was very clear; Joey hung out at a bar called Bar Nashville located at 114 2nd Avenue South. He was dating a cute little blonde who worked at the Exxon Building. Hopefully, he won't be with her when I find him.

Looking at my watch, it was almost 6:30 p.m. so I rented a room at the Sheraton Hotel. After taking a shower, I placed two drops of Methadrine under my tongue and headed for the Grand Ole Oprey House to listen to the legend himself, Mr. Roy Clark.

The Grand Ole Oprey House was packed with people. Most of who were tourists, and I could see why. Roy Clark is, without a doubt, the best guitar player that ever lived. Mini Pearl did her comedy act, and Barbara Mandrel stole my heart with a song that was about eating crackers in her bed anytime. It was a great night.

After leaving the Grand Ole Oprey House, I headed for Bar Nashville. It was Friday night, 11:00 p.m., and Joey might just be there. As I walked into Bar Nashville, I couldn't help but smile. The place was rocking with country music. Some of the young ladies were dancing on top of the bar and pulling their skirts up showing their pretty little butts. The bartenders started lifting up their shirts; the crowd loved it.

Ordering a Pepsi, I sat down and waited to see if Joey would show up. It was 1:30 a.m., early Saturday morning, and Joey was a no show. Leaving the bar, I headed past 2nd Avenue South, across Lafayette Street. It only took me a few minutes to find Westgate Circle. From there, finding Joey's home was simple. It was right down the road.

Driving past Joey's house, I thought about walking up and knocking on the door. His solid white Cadillac was parked in the driveway. Right behind it was a dark blue Ford Ltd. "Must be his girlfriend," I thought to myself as I drove past. "You get a break tonight, Joey, but tomorrow your ass is mine," I whispered to myself as I began to look for a gas station. My Lincoln Mark was low on gas.

Driving to the corner of 2nd Avenue and Broadway I found a place called the Exxon Tiger Market, which was the only gas station still open this late at night. Filling up the car, I had the attendant check the oil. Even though the car was a rental, I always played it safe. The last thing I needed was for the car to break down right after I hit Joey. Remembering my Seal team instructor, I tried to live my life by some of the things he had taught me. Always expect the unexpected, and everything is subject to change at any given moment. They were good rules to live by. I would live by them for the rest of my life. In my line of business, if I didn't I might not live long enough to see the sunrise in the morning.

With nothing left to do, I went back to my hotel room and laid down. "They wanted to deliver a message to New Jersey mob boss Tony Pro," I said to myself as I lay down on my doublewide bed. I didn't like Tony Pro. Smiling, I came up with the perfect plan.

* * * * * * *

It was Saturday, noon, as I walked into Joe's Crab Shack to eat lunch. I liked this restaurant; it had a very relaxed atmosphere. Ordering my meal, I smiled when I saw one of the young waitresses as she brought out a birthday cake with all of the candles lit. The birthday girl was 24-years old; if it's your birthday and your eating at Joe's Crab Shack in Nashville, Tennessee, they make you ride on one of those little stick ponies. This 24-year old girl was riding away as we all clapped our hands and sang Happy Birthday.

I spent the next hour drinking Pepsi and eating some of the best, fresh, crab legs I have ever eaten before. "Boy, would Andy like this place. I'll have to bring him here to eat one day," I thought to myself as I ordered another glass of Pepsi.

After paying for my bill, I left the crab shack and went down Lafayette Street to the local hardware store. Once there, I bought a roll of heat duct tape and a box of heavy duty, industrial strength, plastic trash bags. Paying for that, I left the hardware store and went to Jerry's Sporting Goods Store. Here I bought a Rubber Maid ice chest and a razor-sharp filet knife used for cutting gourmet meats. From there, I went to the A&P Food Store and gave one of the high school aged bag boys five dollars for five brown shopping bags. Putting everything in the trunk of my car, I smiled. "Boy do I have a surprise for Tony Pro," I said out loud to myself as I started my car and drove away.

I spent the next six hours driving around Nashville and taking in the sights. It was a beautiful clean town. All that I needed to do now was wait for it to get nice and dark. Then, I'd go pay Joey a visit.

* * * * * * *

Looking at my watch, it was 10:00 p.m. Saturday night as I parked my car in the parking lot of Joe's Crab Shack, opened my trunk, took out my small ice cooler that had all of my equipment in it, and closed the lid of my trunk. Locking my car doors, I began to walk east on Westgate Circle heading to Joey Piore's home.

A half hour ago I had stopped at Bar Nashville and found Joey there with two of his friends. I didn't know if they were from the New Jersey crime family or not. I didn't like staying in one spot for too long. Tonight, with or without his friends, Joey Piore was going to die.

Walking up the driveway of Joey's four-bedroom home, I walked to the backyard and knocked hard on the backdoor. The information sheet said Joey didn't own a dog, but I wanted to play it safe. Knocking on the door of a home usually will get a house pet to bark. Hearing nothing, I slid the tip of my lock pick gun into the key section of the backdoor lock, pulled the finger lever three times until it was snug, and turned the lock pick gun to the right. Hearing the lock click, I pushed the door open slightly, removed the lock pick gun and slipped it into my back pants pocket.

Pulling out my lightweight .357 Baretta, I cocked the hammer back, and stepped inside closing and locking the door behind me. Standing in the darkness I waited a few seconds for my eyes to adjust to the dark. As I walked down the stairs, I pulled out my small mag flashlight and took a quick look around to make sure that the basement was empty. I had learned a very valuable lesson in Germany during the Claus Gruber hit. The basement door was locked; so I didn't go down to check it. Amanda had gone back to the house after the hit and reported that the basement door was open. The man with the shotgun was downstairs working on some hot water pipes. He had locked the basement door to ensure his privacy. When he came back upstairs, he found the maid dead in the kitchen. Because he worked for Klaus at his home, he knew exactly where to go to get the shotgun. My mistake almost cost Oliver his life. It was one mistake that I would never make again!

Moving quickly, I made a quick sweep of the entire house to ensure I was alone. Walking back to the kitchen, I put my gun back into my shoulder holster and picked up my ice chest. Opening the refrigerator door, I smiled when I saw the six-pack of Pepsi. As much as I wanted to take one and drink it, I didn't. When Joey came home tonight, if he went to his refrigerator and saw anything missing, it might alert him to the fact that I was in his home. Closing the door to the refrigerator, I went down the hallway and put my ice cooler on the floor of the guest bedroom and then went to the bathroom to take a leak. Keeping my thin leather driving gloves on at all times; I went back to the guest bedroom and sat down in the chair at the opposite end of the room. Placing two drop of Methadrine under my tongue, I sat back and relaxed.

Hopefully, Joey wouldn't stay out too late tonight. But even if he did, it wouldn't matter. I'd be sitting right here waiting for him.

* * * * * * *

Hearing the key as it unlocked the front door, I quickly looked at my watch. It was 1:18 a.m. early Sunday morning as Joey Piore walked in through the front door of his home. Sitting quietly, I listened patiently from the guest bedroom as Joey locked the door behind him, walked down the dark hallway, and headed right for the bathroom.

Walking into his bathroom, he didn't even close the door behind him. Standing in front of his toilet, he began to take a leak as I moved quietly from the bedroom and snuck up behind him. His bladder must have been killing him. It took almost a minute and a half for him to finish. Just as he zipped up his pants, I pressed the electric spikes of my stungun into the back of his neck and pulled the trigger. Counting to five, I stepped back and watched Joey as he fell helplessly to the floor.

Moving quickly, I checked the front door to make sure it was locked and then picked up my ice chest from the guest room. Walking back to the bathroom, I duct taped Joey's hands behind his back and then taped his ankles together. Pulling his body over to the bathtub, I pulled him upward and rolled his body into the tub. As I did, I watched his head slam against the side of the tub with a thump!

"Ouch, I'll bet that hurt," I said out loud, as I walked to the kitchen and opened the refrigerator. Pulling out two bottles of cold Pepsi, I headed back to the bathroom to wait for Joey to wake up. Sitting on the toilet seat cover, I sipped on my Pepsi and smiled as Joey slowly regained consciousness.

"What the fuck," he said, as he tried to move but bounced his head off the side of the bathtub once again. "Ouch," he muttered as he shook his head and looked over at me. "Who in the hell are you?" he asked as he began to struggle, trying to free his hands. "Do you know who I am, you fucking punk? I'll hunt you down and cut your balls off for this, mother fucker!" he shouted in anger. He was so mad that his face turned a beet red and the veins of his neck began to bulge. "Untie me, right now, you son-of-a-bitch!" Joey barked loudly.

"Do you eat out of that same mouth?" I asked with a grin.

"What? I'm going to kill you, mother fucker," Joey threatened.

"I don't think so, Joe," I replied calmly.

"I'm Joey Piore, from the New Jersey crime family. Who the fuck are you?" he asked, as he tried once again to free his hands.

"I'm the guy your mother warned you about when you were a little kid, Joey," I explained as I set my bottle of Pepsi down on the side of the sink. Bending forward, I reached into the ice cooler and pulled out the long stainless steel meat knife.

Holding it in my hand, I turned my head slightly and smiled as I waved the razor sharp knife back and forth in my hand. "Sandman's here, Joey. Say goodnight," I whispered softly as I stood up slowly and walked over to the bathtub.

"Wait a minute! Wait a minute!" Joey shouted, as a look of total fear spread across his face and his eyes widened. "My boss will pay you. He's the head of all the families. Just name your price. Please, man, wait," he begged as sweat ran down his forehead and into his eyes.

Grabbing Joey by the hair, I pulled his head back and looked deep into his eyes. "Tony Pro is a coward and a punk! My grandfather is the head of all the organized crime families, Joey." I explained as I reached down and touched the razor sharp edge of my knife to Joey's throat.

"Wait, wait, why me? Why you killing me?" Joey asked with a paranoid look on his face.

"The people you're trying to extort are connected to our family in Detroit. You're not welcome here, Joey," I explained as I applied a bit more pressure to his throat.

"What? Tony never told me that!" he shouted in a panicked tone.

"I told you your boss was a punk!" I replied with a grin, as I pushed hard on the handle of my knife. The razor sharp blade cut deep into the muscle under Joey's right ear. He struggled and kicked his feet begging, "No, please, no!" as I pulled the blade of my knife across his throat, cutting through his esophagus. I didn't stop until the blade severed the artery under Joey's left ear. Blood squirted out of the veins at both sides of his neck. His eyes blinked and stared up at me, while his lips moved. He looked like a fish out of water. The sound coming out of his sliced throat was almost nauseating. Reaching over, I turned the hot water on and ran it through the showerhead down onto Joey's face.

Stepping back, I sat down on the toilet seat and opened my second bottle of Pepsi. I knew it would take Joey about two more minutes to die. The lack of blood and oxygen to the brain was a slow tedious way to die. The hot water would help Joey's body bleed out quicker and would wash most of the blood down the bathtub drain. Once that was done, I would finish what I came here to do. I was going to send a message to big bad Tony Pro in New Jersey.

Taking my second drink of Pepsi, I noticed that the gurgling sounds Joey was making had stopped. Looking over at the bathtub, Joey's lifeless eyes stared into mine.

"Oh, don't look at me like that, Joey," I said, as I stood up and turned the water off. "You knew what the rules were when you joined the family." Just as I finished my sentence, I heard the front door as someone keyed the lock open. Turning off the bathroom light, I pulled my silenced .357 Baretta out of its holster and cocked the hammer back. Waiting silently in the darkness, I listened as the door opened.

"Joey," the female voice called in the darkness. Hearing the front room light click on, my heart raced with the full surge of excitement and adrenaline.

"Yo, Joey," the male voice shouted. Laughing, I heard them close the front room door. "I'll bet that drunk bastard fell asleep on us, Fran," the man explained.

"See if he has any beer in the fridge, Hank, and I'll go wake my baby up," Fran explained as she walked down the hall toward Joey's bedroom. Standing in the darkness, I watched as Fran walked up to the bedroom door across from the bathroom. Just as she stepped into the bedroom and turned on the light, she said, "honey."

I moved quickly across the small hall with my gun pointed toward the front room and grabbed Fran from behind, cupping my gloved hand over her mouth. Pressing the barrel of my gun up against the right side of her head, I whispered, "Shhh, not a sound or you're dead."

She stood frozen stiff, as she acknowledged me by nodding her head up and down slowly. She had the combined smell of cigarette smoke and alcohol. Her long blonde hair was combed straight down on her short slender body. She stood five-foot, four-inches tall. Her body trembled as I pulled it tightly up against mine.

"Call for Hank. Tell him you're having trouble waking Joey up," I whispered. Nodding her head up and down, I slowly removed my hand from her mouth.

"Hank, come here, will ya? I can't get Joey to wake-up," Fran yelled.

Hearing bottles rattle and the refrigerator door close, I put my hand back over Fran's mouth, turned her body to face the bedroom door, and pulled her backwards. I wanted to back away from the bedroom door a bit to give Hank room to step inside.

"Beers cold as a witches tit, Fran," Hank said loudly as he came down the hall and walked into the bedroom.

Hank was a heavyset man that stood five-feet, ten-inches tall and weighted a good 260-pounds, most of which was fat. He had blonde hair that was combed straight back, blue eyes, and wore a well-trimmed goatee. He was holding one bottle of Budweiser beer in front of him, probably for Fran, and was taking a drink out of the other bottle. Just as he swallowed, I raised my right hand and fired! The .357 hollow-point round shattered the bottle Hank was holding in front of him. My bullet entered his body just above the waist. The impact of the bullet made Hank's body fly backwards, slamming him up against the wall at the far side of the hall. As he flew backwards, he spit beer in a spraying fashion into the air.

Pushing Fran to the side and onto the bed, I moved into the doorway as Fran began to scream! My second shot hit Hank in the upper chest blowing most of his heart out through the softball size hole my bullet made as it exited his back.

Turning toward Fran, I looked coldly into her pretty blue eyes. As I did, she stopped screaming. "Please don't kill me, please," she begged as I held my gun down at my right side. "You can fuck me. I'll let ya. You wanna fuck me?" she asked in a pleading voice.

"Yeah, sure, okay, I'll fuck you," I said with a smile as I raised my gun and pulled the trigger.

My bullet hit Fran in the face, just to the left of her nose, blowing the back of her head off, spraying blood, brains, and hair all over the gold bedspread behind her. Her body flew backwards and bounced off the side of the bed, coming to its final resting spot on the floor next to the front of the bed. "There, Fran, now you're fucked," I explained to the dead woman, as I holstered my gun, turned off the bedroom light and walked into the front room. Locking the front door, I turned off the lights and walked back down the hallway. Stepping over Hank's body, I went back into the bathroom to finish what I had started.

"Sorry, Joey, we had company," I started to say out loud to Joey's dead body. "Damn, David, you're losing it. Now you're talking to dead people. Shit, now you're talking to yourself!"

* * * * * * *

I spent Sunday eating crab at Joe's Crab Shack and watching TV. Sunday night I spent four hours at the Grand Ole Opery House. Mel Tillis, Grandpaw Jones, Tammy Wynet, and Glen Campbell were performing. Then Charlie Daniels took front stage with The Devil Went Down to Georgia. To keep it simple, they were awesome!

* * * * * * *

Looking at my watch, it was 8:30 a.m. Monday morning, as I paid the lady at the post office to mail my package wrapped in brown paper bag material and taped tight with duct tape to Tony Pro in New Jersey. The return address was from Mr. Joey Piore, 1462 Westgate Circle, Nashville, Tennessee. Turning in my rental car, I flew back to Michigan on United Airlines Flight 418.

Rumor has it the package arrived at Tony's home in New Jersey marked Special Handling on Thursday. His wife, seeing it was from Joey, took it into their kitchen and opened it. They say she screamed so loudly that people in Manhattan heard her. When Tony arrived home, he found his wife being treated by their family doctor. Walking into his kitchen, he saw the Rubbermaid ice-chest and looked inside. Picking up the heavy-duty industrial strength trash bag that was inside of the cooler, he screamed in agony as he looked at the head and both hands of Joey Piore. Dropping the bag back inside the ice chest, he sat down at the kitchen table and placed his hands over his face.

"There's a note here, boss," his bodyguard said sadly as he picked it up from the top of the kitchen table, where Tony's wife had set it, and handed it to Tony. Unfolding the piece of plain white paper, Tony read: "Stay in New Jersey and out of Nashville! If you don't this will be you."

I never knew that Tony Pro's wife's maiden name was Piore and that she had a younger brother named Joey. But then again, I didn't give a damn either. When death calls and you look into the eyes of the Sandman, life, as you know it, will be over. Born into this world, you know one thing is guaranteed, sooner or later, one way or another; you're going to meet death face-to-face. When you do, you're going to die.

Chapter Nineteen
Time Kill

I had just walked into my house returning home from my trip to Nashville, when my sky pager went off for the very first time. Taking it out of my pocket, I looked at the digital read out on the face of the pager. It said, 'Urgent.'

Using the bathroom I washed up then went to my refrigerator to get a cold bottle of Pepsi. Opening the bottle, I took a drink and noticed my left over barbecue chicken had turned green. Closing the refrigerator door, I left the green chicken inside; I went to my den to call Carla at the Situation Room.

I sat down at my desk, put my bottle of Pepsi down, and opened the jar of Valasic Kosher Pickles that I had brought with me. Taking a bite out of my first pickle I picked up the telephone, turned on my black scrambler box, and called Carla. She picked up the phone on her end and said "Hello."

I answered, "Hello, pretty lady, you rang?" I said jokingly.

"Ever been to the Shetland Islands in Scotland?" she asked.

"Nope," I replied.

"Is your computer system on?" she asked.

"Nope," I replied as I took another bite of my crunchy pickle and turned on my system.

"Would you turn it on please?" she asked with a touch of frustration in the tone of her voice.

"Yup," I replied as I watched my screen and typed in my security Q-clearance code number.

"Are you ready?" she asked sharply, now fully frustrated.

"Yup," I answered, waiting for her to yell!

"David," she said as she took in a deep breath of air, paused, and let it out slowly.

"Yes, dear," I answered softly, with a grin on my face, as I took another bite of my pickle.

"This is not the time to play with me," she said slowly.

"Darlin', if I was playing with you, you would be having the best orgasm of your life right about now," I replied, as I took another pickle out of the glass jar and bit into it. As I did I looked at my computer screen. Carla typed in the words, "Promise?"

"Oh yeah," I typed back. "Are you PMSing today?" I asked trying to get her to relax a bit.

"Yup," she typed back. "What are you eating?" she asked over the telephone receiver.

"Kosher dill pickles," I replied as I took a bite out of my second pickle.

"Pregnant," she asked, now joking around a little.

"Maybe," I replied.

"Mine?" she asked.

"You wish," I answered as I watched the personal data information appear on my computer screen.

"Asshole," she whispered under her breath. "Are you getting the information?" she asked, now acting a bit more normal.

"We're getting a ton of information from the Gruber and Malenkov downloads. This man's name is Kevin O'Donald. He's a very high-ranking member of the IRA in Ireland. He's also highly trained in explosives. Guess where he got his training?" Carla asked.

"Oh shit," I whispered into the mouthpiece of my telephone. As I read the data on Kevin O'Donald, "It says here that my old buddy Boris Kalashnikov trained Kevin personally at his home in Russia."

"That is correct," Carla replied. "Now, click over two pages to Future Terrorist Target," Carla directed.

Clicking over I began to read. "This guy is responsible for bombings in Ireland, England, Columbia, and one in Israel. Damn, he's killed thousands of people. He blows up school buses full of kids, and buildings and restaurants that are heavily populated with customers of all ages. What a total piece of shit!" I said angrily.

"Drop down two more paragraphs. We just picked this information up by monitoring his short wave frequency number. It was one of the numbers that Pavel Malenkov had written down next to his set. It's on that list you discovered and brought to us with the Malenkov downloaded disc," Carla explained.

Reading on, my mouth fell open when I saw where Kevin's next target was. "When do I leave?" I asked as anger began to over ride my common sense.

"Kevin has a beautiful old fashion, Scotch built home on the Shetland Islands. He is scheduled to leave there in ten days. You've got eight days to kill this man, David. I don't care how you do it, just do it!" Carla said coldly.

"Does the President know?" I asked.

"No. Only you, Ollie, Neil, and me. If you fail to stop him and he reaches the United States we'll have to notify all law enforcement agencies throughout the U.S.. David, at midnight December 31st, Time Square will have a million people packed in that one small area. At midnight he is going to blow something up there. Whatever it is, with his training, he could easily kill and seriously injure, a half a million Americans, all who came there to watch the Big Apple come down and celebrate the New Year. Our plane is on its way to the Pontiac Airport as we speak. Take a look at the computer map, David. You're the fast thinker. How do you get to the island without drawing any attention to yourself?" Carla asked in a very concerned and serious tone.

Clicking over to the map, I began to use my Seal team and CIA Farm training. "Give me a minute to look at this, ma'am," I said as I studied the map. It took me about thirty seconds to find my entry point. "Okay, I got it. Your pilot has to get me to Denmark," I explained.

"Denmark?" Carla questioned.

"Yes, Denmark, from there I'll charter a boat and sail west to the Shetland Islands in Northern Scotland. Just get me to Denmark, I'll take it from there," I explained as I reached into my pocket and pulled out my vial of Methadrine. Placing two drops under my tongue I sat back in my leather chair.

"Good luck, son," Carla said as she hung up the telephone.

"It's not about luck, Carla," I said to myself as I turned off my computer system and headed to my bathroom to take a shower. "It's about hunting the hunter!"

* * * * * * *

Opening the door to my security safe, I began to look through my passports, fake identifications, and credentials. I would need a reason to be in Scotland. Marge had put together a number of fake IDs and business cards, for a variety of different organizations. Finding the one I wanted, I smiled. "National Geographic Magazine. This will do it. I'm going to the Shetland Islands to shoot a cover spread for the magazine," I said as I packed my gear and grabbed two different 35mm cameras and ten rolls of film. Grabbing my backpack I used for deer season, I began to plan my next move.

Driving to the Pontiac Airport I waited in the lounge for the Agency plane to arrive. When it did I was surprised to find Kathy on board.

As I climbed on board, she greeted me. "Hello, David," she said as she looked at the way I was dressed. Kathy was dressed in a woman's business suit and looked great as always. I was wearing my red and black squared plaid hunting shirt, blue jeans, brown high top, leather boots, and had my winter coat with the lambs wool collar.

"Which one of us isn't dressed right?" she asked with a disappointed look on her face. Kissing her on the cheek I laughed as I tossed my backpack and coat onto one of the seats and sat down so our pilot could take off again.

Sitting down next to me Kathy looked at me with a sad expression on her face. "Please don't leave me behind on this mission," she begged.

Taxing out on the runway, our plane took flight. Looking at Kathy I smiled. "We'll get you outfitted in Denmark. It should be chilly there this time of year," I explained with a grin.

"Denmark?" I thought that we were going to the islands?" Kathy questioned with a confused look on her face.

"We are. This guy is a professional terrorist. He'll spot trouble a mile away. We're going to land at Denmark International Airport. We'll get you outfitted and then charter a boat to take us to the islands. Once we get to the island we'll hike across country to Kevin's home. We're going to have to move fast, Kathy. The clock is ticking on this one and Kevin may decide to leave early," I explained calmly.

Kathy was an unexpected surprise. She would slow me down and I couldn't afford to waste time on this mission. Remembering Master Chief Jeff Mareno, "Always expect the unexpected, everything is subject to change at any given moment." I needed to live by these valuable Seal team lessons and codes. This is what made the difference between life and death.

* * * * * * *

Black Operation
Code Name: Time Kill
Target: Kevin O'Donald
Location: Scotland

We landed in Denmark; I was in awe at how clean and beautiful this country was. The people of Denmark were unbelievably kind and courteous to Kathy and I. Once we had passed through customs and left the airport, CIA Special Agent James Maruca took us shopping so we could grab some supplies and get Kathy outfitted.

"God bless Carla Silverman," I thought to myself as I handed Kathy two sets of thermal underwear, tops and bottoms. James would save us a lot of time. He had lived here for almost four years working undercover for the Agency. He knew where everything was and also had all the right contacts to help us charter the boat we would need to get us to the island.

To my surprise, Carla had already instructed James to have a boat chartered and ready for us. James did, and it was a nice one.

After we picked up everything we needed for Kathy, James took us to his home. There he supplied us with silenced .22 magnum pistols, a pound of C-4 plastique explosives, two electric blasting caps, an old school 45-

second fuse, and an authentic Greek meal. He was full-blooded American born Greek, and he cooked like one too. We spent the night at Jim's home. It was 6:30 p.m. and even though she wouldn't admit it, Kathy was tired.

* * * * * * *

Pulling up to the docking port I looked at my gold Tag Heuer drivers watch. It was 8:00 a.m. right on the money as we got out of Jim's car, opened the trunk, and pulled out our backpacks.

"That's him over there, Dave," Jim explained as he pointed in the direction of where our Captain and his boat were waiting for us. Closing the trunk lid we all three walked over to meet Jim's friend.

"Derek, this is David and Kathy from National Geographic Magazine. Dave, Kathy, this is my friend," Jim explained as he introduced us to the Captain of the ship.

"Welcome to Denmark, National Geographic," Derek said with a smile as he extended his hand out for us to shake. Shaking his hand I spoke.

"Derek, I'd like to take some photographs if you don't mind," I asked as I grabbed the Pentex Camera hanging around my neck.

"Pictures of me? Me and my boat? For the magazine?" he asked. Derek was an old seaman. He stood five-feet, eleven-inches tall, and weighed a good two hundred pounds. He was in his mid-fifties and had brown, wavy hair that was just starting to turn gray. He was a good and honest man. A man that I respected.

"Yes, sir," I said with a smile as I backed up. "Lets get one of the three of you first, then I want to take some of you and your boat, Derek. That is, if its okay with you?" I said with a smile.

"Absolutely. I'm going to be in the big magazine. By golly what a surprise this will be for my wife, Martha," he said as he smiled and posed for the first picture.

We spent the next half hour taking photographs and stowing our gear. Saying goodbye to Jim, we told him Derek would call him on the boat's, Ship-to-Shore radio to let him know when we were on our way back to port. This way Jim could meet us when we docked to give us a ride back to our plane.

It was 9:30 a.m. by the time we actually left dry-dock and headed to sea. It was a beautiful early winter day. The weather was cool but not cold. There was no snow falling. I could only hope we wouldn't run into any bad weather or storms.

Steering his 48-foot inboard, long-keeled Albin Vega boat west, Derek told Kathy and I that he was going to take us to the Shetland Islands by using the old Viking routes. We were now headed to Northern Scotland by sea.

We spent two days listening to Derek as he told us stories of how he began his life as a sailor at the age of fifteen when his grandfather had given him his very first boat. "I didn't want to work in an office," he said. "I wanted to fill life with life." This was one of the first routes he had ever taken to the Shetlands Islands. He would later sail to Ireland and Europe, down the coast of Africa and eventually crossed the Atlantic Ocean to South America.

For two days we listened to his tales and enjoyed scenery few people – other than sailors – would ever encounter. We became sea hands for Captain Derek. He laughed as Kathy and I staggered around trying to get our sea legs.

I had brought a map with me and showed Derek the exact spot where I needed him to drop us off. Neil had sent it to me via computer, by using the Pentagon's CIA Global Satellite Mapping System. From this spot of the Shetland Island, it would be a simple two-mile hike to Kevin O'Donald's home. Derek, however, found it by compass.

Because of the location, Derek dropped anchor and took us to shore on his small dingy. Handing us a flaregun and four flares, he told us he would look for us at the top of every hour. If it was dark all we would have to do is pop a flare at the top of the hour. From 11:00 p.m. to 6:00 a.m. however, Derek would be asleep on his boat.

Saying our goodbyes, Kathy and I headed southwest on foot. We needed to catch Kevin before he decided to leave the island and head to the United States. If Kevin left before we got to him, we would have no way to alert Carla at the Situation Room. We would have to get back to the boat and call James by short-wave radio. If Kevin made it to the U.S., a lot of innocent American's were going to die.

This island was absolutely beautiful. Even though it was early winter it had meadows and valleys that were only seen in magazines.

We had traveled about five hundred yards when Kathy asked, "David, would you ever consider leaving the United States and living in another country. You know, some place pretty and peaceful like this?"

"Yeah, I might. I guess it would depend on if I had a good enough reason to leave and do it," I explained, "Why? Why are you asking?"

"My biological clock is ticking. I love my job, especially now that they're letting me go out with you. But I'm still a woman, David. I still think a lot about having a baby. I don't know, forget it, I'm just thinking out loud," she explained.

Stopping to take a break I turned and took a picture of Kathy. "You're my friend, Kathy. If you're asking what I think you're asking me. Yeah,

I would. But right now in my life, I've got a lot of problems. I don't sleep very well at night. I'm hooked on Methadrine because my nightmares come back to haunt me every time I close my eyes. It scares me to death. I've been studying metaphysics, its called Lucid Dreaming. My dreams are so real that when I wake up, I can actually still feel the pain if I got hurt in my dream. Or I can still taste whatever it was that I was eating at the time of my dream. I don't know, Vietnam screwed me up. I spend most of my nights downloading data information about dreams and nightmares out of the Agencies computer. I'll figure it out sooner or later. But for now, I've got to kill this terrorist," I explained as I reached down and gently raised Kathy's chin. As our eyes met, I kissed her tenderly on the lips. "Your a stone cold fox, Kathy. You could have any man you wanted. You could do a lot better than me, kiddo," I explained.

Our time at Marcus Guillo's home in France had stirred up Kathy's female emotions. It was our first and only time of making love to each other. It was a night I would never forget. Now it gave me something to think about.

"Come on, lets get moving. We've got a ways to go yet," I said as I placed two drops of Methadrine under my tongue and looked at my watch.

Moving another two hundred yards I heard Kathy cry out in pain. "Ouch, shit!" she yelled as she fell to the ground and grabbed her right ankle. She was only a few feet behind me and off to my right.

"You okay? How bad is it?" I asked as I knelt down beside her to look at her leg.

"I stepped in that damn hole," she said as she nodded her head at the gofer hole that was next to her. "I think I twisted it," she explained as she reached down to rub it.

"Let me check it out, just relax," I said as I untied her dark, brown hiking boot. "Its my fault, Kathy. I thought you were right behind me. I should have told you to stay right behind me and follow my path. I constantly look at where I'm walking, its part of my Seal team training."

"David, leave me, go. You have to get this guy," Kathy explained.

"I don't leave my partners behind, Kathy," I replied as I pulled off her boot. When I did, she winced in pain.

"Just get me up to those trees, I'll be alright there," she said as she pointed to a small group of white birch trees about fifty yards off to our left.

"I'm not leaving you behind, Kathy, forget it," I replied as I pulled her wool sock down and off of her foot.

"I'm giving you a direct order, David. Leave me and go, now!" she said sternly with a look of anger on her face.

"I told you. I don't leave my partners behind. Not ever," I said once again. This time I had a cold dead serious look on my face. "Never!" I said sharply. The look on her face said a lot. She wasn't expecting me to snap at her like that.

"Calm down, David, we'll figure this out," she explained with a fake smile.

"You twisted it. It's starting to swell already," I said as I pulled off my backpack and unzipped it.

"Am I seeing the Sandman?" she asked with a half smile and a curious look on her face.

"No, you're not. You don't ever want to look into the eyes of the Sandman, Kathy. You don't understand. I live by a code. Not because I was trained to, but because I believe in it. Brothers and friends, throughout life and into death, till the end. I stayed with my brother Nick and spent eighty-nine days in a POW camp being tortured because of it. I wouldn't hesitate, not for one second to do it again, Kathy. I don't leave my partners behind, not ever. If you can't accept that, then you need to get the fuck out of my life!" I explained harshly as thoughts of my brother and friend, Nick, filled my mind.

Taking a bottle of Codeine painkillers out of my backpack, I handed them to Kathy along with my canteen. "Take two of these, would you? It will ease the pain and help to slow down the swelling." Taking two of the pills, Kathy handed the bottle and canteen back to me.

"I'm sorry, David, I didn't mean to upset you," she said in a timid voice.

"It's okay, forget about it, I just miss my friends that's all. I guess you had to be there to understand. Chopper, Butch, Nick, Cookie, Joe, Mosier, and Bell, we were family. It was so special. Damn, I miss 'em so much," I explained.

"I can see that. The pain is written all over your face," she said kindly.

"Well, we need to get moving," I explained in an attempt to change the subject. "Looks like I'm going to have to carry you, and both backpacks," I said with a grin.

"I'm sorry, David," Kathy said as she sadly lowered her head.

"You still don't get it, do you? You're my partner and my friend. You're on this mission with me. I'm not complaining, Kathy. If your going to do this kind of job then you better get used to this. Don't you remember what I taught you in France?" I asked.

"Always expected the unexpected. Everything is subject to change at any given moment," she said as she looked up at me and smiled. "Right?" she asked.

"Hoo yah!" I answered as I helped Kathy to stand up on her good leg.

I was carrying a small lightweight pack. Because of this it was easy to secure it to Kathy's backpack. Once I did, I looked at her and grinned.

"Wanna ride?" I asked, as I turned around. Climbing onto my back, Kathy wrapped her arms around my neck and placed her chin on the top of my left shoulder. Grabbing her around the legs just behind the knees, I moved out once again. I had gotten about a hundred yards when I thought of something and laughed out loud.

"What? What are you laughing at?" she whispered in my left ear.

"Your light as a feather. I was thinking, thank God you're not my big brother Chopper. He's huge!" I said with a smile and another laugh.

"He's really that big, huh?" Kathy asked.

"He's the second biggest black man I've ever met. The only guy I've seen bigger than him is a friend that I made recently. He's from New Orleans. His name is Jaba. He's the size of a small tank," I explained as I thought back to how easy it was for Jaba to pick up Sean and carry him to his airboat.

"Is this Jaba a nice guy like your friend Chopper?" Kathy asked.

"Yes. They are both gentle giants, as long as you don't get them mad at you. If you piss either one of 'em off, life as you know it, is over."

It took me all day to carry Kathy the mile and a half needed to get to Kevin O'Donnell's home. Kathy took pictures of the scenery as I carried her through the woods, down the valleys, and across the meadows. It was 5:12 p.m. when we reached the top of a small wooded crest that looked down across the grassy meadow into the small valley where Kevin's home was nestled.

"That's it," Kathy said in a whisper as I set her down. Helping her to sit down, she took off her backpack and leaned her back up against one of the trees. Kneeling down, I took another look at her ankle. It was swollen and had now turned black and blue.

"Wiggle your toes," I asked as I reached into my pack and handed Kathy the bottle of painkillers.

"Ouch," she said under her breath as she wiggled her toes.

"Can you move it up and down and side to side?" I asked.

"It feels like a balloon that's about to burst," she said as she moved her foot slightly.

"Okay, that's good. If it was broken you wouldn't be able to do that without screaming. When we get back to Denmark, we'll get you to a hospital so we can get it X-rayed and have a doctor take a look at it. Just to be safe," I explained as I reached over and unzipped my pack.

Taking out my small pair of high-powered camouflaged binoculars, I handed them to Kathy. "Take a look and see if anyone appears to be home," I asked. Pulling my electric blasting caps, C-4 plastique explosives, 45-second old school fuse, and remote detonator out of my backpack, I put them in my pockets. Taking my small glass vial of liquid Methadrine out of my shirt pocket, I looked down the valley at Kevin's home, and placed two drops of the liquid under my tongue.

"See anything?" I asked as I gently lifted Kathy's leg and placed my backpack underneath it to elevate her swollen ankle.

"Thank you, that feels better. No, it looks like we missed him. "Damnit," Kathy replied as she lowered her binoculars from her face and looked at me. "Now what do we do?" she asked with a frustrated look on her face.

"We aren't doing anything. You're staying here. As for me, I'm going down there before it gets to dark to see," I explained calmly.

"David, he's gone," Kathy said once again.

"It took two days for us to get ready and actually get to Denmark. We were with Jim for one day. It took two days for Derek to get us here by boat. It took another day to get here and get a visual look at Kevin's home. That's six days. We had a ten-day time frame to take him down. If he left, then he left four days early. If he did, there is nothing we can do about it now. My money says he is probably in town drinking beer with his friends," I explained as I pulled my .22 magnum out of my shoulder holster and checked it to make sure it was fully loaded and ready to fire. "Get your weapon out," I said to Kathy as I fired two shots into the trunk of the tree next to us.

"What are you doing?" Kathy asked.

"Fire two shots into that tree," I said with a serious look. Firing her weapon twice she looked at me with a confused look on her face.

"Listen, never trust or take for granted, that a weapon that was given to you by someone else, is going to work. Always, and I mean always, double check it to make sure it not only works, but that its also fully loaded. Your life depends on it, Kathy. If your gun doesn't fire when you need it to, and it's your personal weapon, then you died because you screwed up. But if its a gun that your partner gave you or in this case a fellow agent, and it doesn't fire when you need it to, then you died because you were stupid enough to trust someone else with your life," I explained.

"What if it was you that gave me the gun?" Kathy asked sarcastically with a smile on her face.

"Then you damn sure better check it! It doesn't matter who gives it to you. It's your life at stake. Always double-check your weapon to make sure it's ready to fire. Understand?" I asked.

"I understand. Seal team training, right?" Kathy asked.

Looking down at her I smiled. "Hoo yah," I said softly as I put my gun back into its shoulder holster. "That's why the United States Navy Seals are the best of the best. It's also why we never leave our partners or friends behind. Not ever!" I explained as I knelt down next to Kathy and kissed her on the forehead.

"Now listen closely. If anyone walks up to you while I am gone, kill them. Even if it's a small child. Don't think about it. Don't hesitate. Smile until they get close enough to you and then kill them. If you don't you'll be dead before I get back up here to you. Understand?" I asked as I looked Kathy in the eyes.

"Oh yeah. That I can do," she answered with a cold stare.

"This shouldn't take long. I'll be back shortly," I told Kathy as I stood up and left the safety of the tree line, and walked out into the open meadow and headed down the small valley to Kevin O'Donald's home.

* * * * * * *

It took about forty-minutes for me to walk down the valley to Kevin's home. It was an old, but well kept home. It had a large round rock foundation with a large oak wood timber structure, firmly built on top of it. Just off to the back of the home, was a smaller storage area that housed a gas operated, electric generator; which was used to supply electrical power to the home through a large battery bank in the same room.

Stepping up to the large oak wood front door, I knocked. I couldn't help but wonder if Neil was watching me by satellite, as I looked up at the sky and smiled. Turning my attention back to the front door, I knocked once again.

Kevin O'Donald was in his late forties, stood five-feet, ten-inches tall and weighed one hundred eighty-seven pounds. He had sandy, blonde hair, hazel eyes, and was well known for keeping himself well groomed. He was a lady's man, who loved to drink good Scotch whiskey. He was single and had no children, as far as we knew.

Trying the front door I turned the brass doorknob. It was locked. Walking to the back of the home I stepped up to the backdoor and tried it. When I did, I smiled, it was open.

"Thank you, dear God," I said out loud. In my hurry to get here I had forgotten to bring my lock pick gun. "Hello, is anyone home," I shouted into the house as I pulled my pistol out of its holster and held it in my right hand down at my side.

"Hello, I need help," I shouted once again as I stepped inside and closed the door behind me. It was a one floor home that was an easy three thousand square feet in size. It must have taken his great grandfather years to build this home back in the late 1800s. It was built out of all raw natural materials and appeared to have been up dated and modernized as the years went by.

Moving through the home quickly, I double-checked to make sure I was alone. Walking into the kitchen I turned on the faucet and was surprised when the battery operated electric pump, kicked on. Out came water. "I'll be damn. This place has a well and septic system for the bathroom. I'm fucking impressed, Kevin," I said to myself as I began to look around the home.

It was very well kept and clean, with everything put in its place. Walking into the bathroom I opened the medicine cabinet. "Basic stuff," I thought to myself. Then I smiled when I saw the Remington Electric Razor that Kevin used to shave. Thinking back to the computer data information on Kevin O'Donald, it said he was well groomed, a lady's man. I'll bet he shaves at least once a day.

I couldn't risk getting killed or hurt on this mission. Kathy was hurt and two miles from Derek and any help. Without me she would be in even more trouble than she already was.

Taking out the electric razor I went to work. Using Kevin's round tip tweezers I removed the four small screws from the back of the electric razor and set them on the shelf under the bathroom mirror. Pulling the hard plastic back off, I took a close look at the inside.

Picking up Kevin's toenail clippers, I cut the end of the red and black wires that went from the 'on/off' switch, to the small electric motor inside the razor. Using the tweezers I removed two more small screws from the inside of the razor that secured the small motor. I then carefully pulled out the small electric motor and set it on the shelf, along with the tweezers. Using the nail clippers I bared the plastic insulation of the two wires. Setting the electric razor back down, I then reached into my coat pocket and pulled out, one electric blasting cap and my pound of C-4 plastique explosives.

I peeled the plastic wrapper back away from the C-4, and pulled a golf ball size piece of the high explosive off the one-pound brick, and then put the C-4 back into my pocket. Picking the blasting cap back up, I pushed its thin slender metal body into the golf ball size piece of C-4. Picking the razor up, I pressed the C-4 explosive, along with the blasting cap, into the inside of the electric razor, where the electric motor once was. I then attached the two wires from the 'on/off' switch to the end of the two wires on the electric blasting cap. I put the back onto the electric razor, tightened the four tiny screws into place, and checked to make sure the 'on/off' switch was set in the 'off' position. Smiling, I put the electric Remington razor, tweezers, and toenail clippers back into the medicine cabinet, exactly as it was when I first opened it up.

I walked into the bedroom, pulled out my small electric detonator, and the rest of the brick of C-4 plastique explosive. Pushing the blasting cap all the way into the pound of plastique explosive, I attached the detonator to the wires of the blasting cap and pressed the electronic detonator into the end of the putty substance of the C-4.

Walking out of the bedroom and down the hallway I stopped when I saw the linen closet door. Opening the door I saw it was full of sheets, pillowcases, blankets, and towels. Grabbing one blanket, I put it under my arm and closed the closet door. Walking back into the kitchen I was caught by surprise when I heard a key slide into the metal lock of the front door.

"Shit!" I said softly. Moving fast I opened the backdoor and stepped out into the darkness.

This house was built so solid I didn't hear Kevin coming, or the car door when he closed it. Seeing the light come on in the front room, I very carefully peeked in through the corner of the kitchen window. "Holy shit," I said to myself as I watched Kevin O'Donald and a second man. The second man had long, brown hair and wore a beard. He stood six-feet tall, and was at least two hundred and forty pounds. Kevin was armed with two fully loaded Israeli made Uzi .9mm machine guns. The other man was also carrying an Uzi and a large box full of explosives.

Setting down their weapons and the box of explosives Kevin locked the front door. As they walked into the kitchen and turned on the light, I moved quickly and walked around the side of the house and went directly to Kevin's four-wheel drive Ford Bronco. Dropping the blanket from under my arm, I opened the front drivers door, reached under the driver's bucket seat and pressed the pound of plastique explosives down onto the floor under the seat. Feeling for the metal toggle switch with my finger, I pushed it into the 'On' position. The battery operated remote detonator was now armed. Closing the driver's door, I picked up the blanket and ran back up the small valley toward Kathy.

It took about fifteen minutes for me to make the run in the dark. There was a full moon out, which made it easy to see once my eyes adjusted to the darkness of the outside. Very close now to the tree where I had left Kathy sitting I said, "Kathy, its me. Don't shoot. Do you hear me?" in a normal voice.

"Yes, its okay, I'm all right, come on up," she responded in an excited voice. It made me smile when I heard her voice. I don't think she felt very comfortable sitting all alone in the darkness of the night. Walking up to her I could see she was happy to see me.

"I brought you a blanket to help keep you warm," I explained as I unfolded the blanket and tried to catch my breath.

"Are you alright? You're breathing pretty hard," she asked.

"I'm okay, I ran all the way back," I explained as I wrapped the blanket around her.

"Did you get him? I saw his truck headlights pull up to the house, but it was dark out. Once he turned off his headlights I couldn't see very much. It looks like he had someone with him," she said quickly.

"No, I didn't get him. Thank God I didn't try to hit him in the house," I explained as I sat down next to her and tried to slow my heart rate down a bit.

"What? What happened?" she asked.

"They were both heavily armed with Uzi machine guns. They also had a box loaded with high explosives. "Miss me?" I asked.

"Yes, I don't know how you guys did it in Vietnam. Sitting in the swamps, jungles, and forests at night. God, David, I was getting scared out here all by myself," she explained in an anxious tone.

Reaching over I put my right hand on the right side of her cheek, turned her head toward me, and gently kissed her on the lips. "Its alright, I'm here now, calm down."

Reaching for my backpack, I gently lifted up Kathy's leg. "How's your ankle?" I asked as I unzipped my backpack and pulled out my remote control detonator. Pulling the antenna up from the top of the detonator, I reached into my shirt pocket and pulled out the small key that was needed to activate the box.

"It hurts, but I'll be alright," Kathy explained as I turned on my small pen light flashlight. Shinning it onto the face of the box, I slid the key into its slot, turned it to the right and watched the small green light come on. "Good, Jim has new batteries in this unit," turning the key to the left, I turned the box back off.

"Why did you turn it off. Aren't you going to blow up the house?" Kathy asked in a curious voice. Reaching into my coat pocket, I pulled out the small electric motor I took out of the electric razor. Shinning my penlight on it, I handed it to Kathy.

"What's this?" she asked.

"A small motor," I replied.

"Gee, really, I'd have never figured that out all by myself. Duh! What's it go to?" she asked. I was going to play around a bit with Kathy, but I knew she was in pain, so I didn't.

"His electric razor. Either tonight or tomorrow morning, if he shaves, he will blow his own head off," I explained with a smile as I took the small electric motor from her hand and tossed it out into the darkness of the night.

"And what if he decides not to shave?" Kathy asked as she leaned forward slightly, trying to look into my eyes.

"I've got a pound of C-4 under the front seat of his truck," I explained as I raised her leg back up and put my backpack back under her calf.

Using my small penlight I took a close look at her ankle, "This doesn't look to awfully bad. It's a good thing you were wearing that high-top hiking boot. It helped to support your ankle. Have you eaten anything?" I asked as I shinned the small light on Kathy's face. I wanted to see the expression on her face.

"Oh my, yes. I ate peanut butter, cheese, and dry crackers, not only for lunch with you, but also for supper. Yum, my little tummy is full," she said sarcastically. As she said it I broke out laughing.

"You find this funny?" she asked as she crossed her arms across her chest and stared at me in the dark. Turning off the small penlight, I handed it to Kathy.

"Here you hang on to this, and yes, I do find it funny. You were expecting, what? Steak and eggs? You're a cold-blooded killer when it's easy. But you don't have what it takes to do it the hard way. Listen closely. Peanut butter, cheese, and crackers is a high protein, high carbohydrate energy meal. A real sniper lives on it for days on end. Its lightweight, easy to carry, and doesn't make your body smell," I explained.

"Smell? Thank you for reminding me. I had to use leaves to wipe my butt. I guess you never considered bringing a roll of toilet paper along, did you?" she asked.

"No, and guess what?" I asked.

"What?" she snapped back at me.

"I never thought about bringing a toilet along with me either," I said as I broke out laughing again.

"Asshole," she said as she hit me in the chest with her right fist.

Sliding up close to Kathy I put my arm around her and pulled her close to me. Resting her head on the left side of my chest, she sighed. "God, David, I'm so glad you're here with me."

"Where's the binoculars?" I asked softly.

"Right here," she said as she reached down to her left side, picked up the small pair of binoculars, and handed them to me without taking her head off of my chest.

"Thank you. Now try to get some sleep. It's going to be a long night," I said as I reached over and snugged the blanket up tight around her.

Reaching into my coat, I pulled my vial of Methadrine out of my shirt pocket and placed two drops under my tongue. Putting it back into my pocket I picked up the binoculars and looked down at Kevin's home. The lights were still on, but I doubted he was going to go anywhere else tonight.

Holding Kathy close, I set the binoculars on my lap and pulled out my pistol. It was going to be a long night. Turning my head slightly to the left I smelled Kathy's hair. "Had she not hurt herself, this would have been a great night," I thought to myself.

* * * * * * *

Looking at my Tag Heuer gold watch, I picked up my binoculars and took another look at Kevin's house. "Its 6:12 a.m., I thought you would be up by now, Kevin," I whispered to myself as I set my binoculars back down beside me, and placed two drops of Methadrine under my tongue.

Turning my head, I looked over at Kathy. She had fallen asleep quickly last night. When she did, I laid her down, put her backpack under her head for a pillow, and tucked the blanket in around her. She had a restless night due to her injury, but at least she got some sleep.

The first explosion went off at 6:16 a.m. Turning quickly I picked up my binoculars and took a look at Kevin's house.

"What happened?" Kathy asked as she sat up and rubbed her eyes, awakened by the sound of the first blast. The window at the far left of the house was blown out. The window curtain was now hanging out through it, blowing slightly in the breeze.

"I believe that Mr. Kevin O'Donald has just blown himself up," I said with a chuckle in my voice.

"Here, take a look," I said as I handed the binoculars to Kathy who was sitting behind me and slightly to the left.

"Look at the far left window," I explained.

"Was that the bathroom?" Kathy asked quickly as she looked through the binoculars at the house.

"No, that was the bedroom right across from it," I explained as I picked up the remote control unit for the detonator.

"The other guy is coming out, David, he's carrying a box," Kathy explained as she kept the binoculars on her eyes and watched the house. "Boy, he looks scared and in a hurry!"

Looking down into the valley I could see everything clearly. The house really wasn't that far away from us. I watched as Kevin's friend, with the long, brown hair, ran back and forth from the house to the truck.

"Look at that," I said to Kathy as Kevin's friend made his third trip to the truck with an arm load of assault rifles. Placing them on the floor of the truck, behind the driver's seat he ran back into the house for another load.

"You didn't see any of that?" Kathy asked.

"Nope, but then again, I wasn't looking for any of it. I just want this guy dead, and now he's dead. As soon as that idiot jumps into the truck I'm going to put his terrorist ass to sleep too," I explained calmly.

"What about all of those weapons and explosives?" Kathy asked as she continued to watch the house through the binoculars.

"The blast should destroy most of it, if not all. If my pound of C-4 causes that box to explode, believe me, it will be a sight you won't want to miss," I explained as Kevin's friend ran back out to the truck with more weapons and an armful of paperwork.

"Boy, does he look scared. Maybe we should let him go so he can tell the rest of his friends what happened to Kevin. What do you think?" Kathy asked, as the man with the long, brown hair climbed into the Ford Bronco and closed the door.

Looking down at the box that I held in my hands, I turned the silver key to the right. When I did the small green light came on. Underneath the small green light there was a word written on the box. It read, 'Armed.'

"Never let a terrorist go, Kathy. If you ever have a chance to kill one, do it. Kill him," I said as I raised the box up, pointed the antenna at the truck and waited.

On the face of the box, there is a small metal cover that protects the round red button you push to detonate your explosive. Using the tip of my right thumb, I flipped it up. Placing my thumb on the button, I waited.

"What are you waiting for?" Kathy asked anxiously as she continued to watch the truck through the small pair of camouflaged binoculars.

"He might have forgotten something. He's panicked and running scared right now. I want all of their dirty little toys in that truck when it blows," I explained.

The man sat in the truck for another two minutes. Getting back out of the truck, he opened the hood and began to look around the engine compartment.

"What's he doing?" Kathy asked curiously.

"He's scared. He's looking for explosives. He's worried that whoever blew-up Kevin, may have also wired the truck to blow as a back-up plan," I explained calmly with a smile.

Closing the hood of the truck he got down on his knees and began to search underneath the bottom of the vehicle.

"What if he finds it?" Kathy asked.

"He won't. The most obvious is the least obvious. That's what my Seal team instructors always taught me. It's right under his nose. Its so obvious he won't look there," I explained with a smile.

Watching as the man checked the entire bottom of the truck, I sat patiently and waited with my thumb still poised on the red button. Climbing back into the truck, the man with the long, brown hair closed the driver's door.

"Now what are you waiting for?" Kathy asked.

"He's still worried. He doesn't want to turn the ignition key on. I'm going to let him sweat for a little bit. Its not so funny now that I'm hunting him," I explained.

"He started the truck, David, I can see the exhaust coming out of the tail pipe. Boy, he just sat back in the seat and put both of his hands over his face. He's scared to death," Kathy said as she began to laugh.

Just as the truck started to back up, I pressed the red button. There were two explosions that occurred back to back. My pound of C-4 plastique explosives caused the explosives in the box behind the drivers seat to also explode. The first explosion was big, the second one came one second after the first one. It was massive! The first explosion caused the truck to buckle in the center and fly straight upward in the air. As it did, the second bigger explosion tore the truck completely to shreds, sending tiny pieces of sheet metal flying in all directions, along with a bloody spray of body parts.

"Whoa," Kathy shouted out loudly as excitement raced through her. "Look at that, David, it blew a section of the front of the house off. It looks like something inside the house has caught on fire," Kathy explained.

"That's to bad, it was a nice house," I explained as I picked up my backpack and put the remote detonator back inside it.

"Put your backpack on, Kathy, its time to go," I said as I helped my injured friend put her pack on and get ready. After getting Kathy situated comfortably on my back, we left the crest over looking the small valley that was once the home of a terrorist, known as Kevin O'Donald.

I thought our two-mile trip back to where Captain Derek had his boat anchored would have been quicker, but it wasn't. With every step I took it caused Kathy discomfort. Her ankle was swollen and completely black and blue. We needed to keep her foot elevated to keep the flow of blood to the ankle and foot at a minimum rate of pressure. Because I had to carry her on my back her foot was pointing downward, which caused her blood to flow stronger in that direction. I loaded her up with pain medication and walked as fast as I could.

It was almost five o'clock in the afternoon by the time we reached the beach and signaled Derek. Seeing us waving at him, he smiled, waved back, and came to pick us up in his small outboard engine dingy boat.

Very carefully, we got Kathy back on board. As soon as we got her settled in, Derek started his powerful inboard engines and raised anchor.

Our trip from the Shetland Islands of Northern Scotland back to Denmark took a little over two days. Using Derek's medical kit, I took out a wide ace bandage and with a figure-eight motion, wrapped Kathy's ankle. About three-hours from docking back in port at Denmark, Derek radioed James and told him that Kathy had twisted her ankle and be ready to pick us up.

The last three-hours of our trip went by quickly. Seeing James standing on shore with a wheel chair, we waved. Derek being a true seaman had his boat docked and tied off quickly. Seeing the look on Jim's face I had an uneasy feeling that something was wrong. After helping Kathy off the boat we got her seated in the wheel chair. As we did she smiled and gave out a sigh of relief. Turning to look at me, Jim, with a worried look on his face, spoke, "David, I've got bad news."

"My grandfather died?" I asked sadly as my heart began to hurt at the thought of losing the man that was like a dad to me.

"No, David, its your friend Danny from Vietnam," Jim started to explain.

"Danny McBride? Chopper? My big brother?" I asked with a confused look.

"David, I got the call yesterday afternoon from Carla. Your brother, Danny, has been captured in North Vietnam," Jim explained.

"What?" I shouted out loud in total shock.

"My orders are to get you two back on board your plane ASAP. Carla needs you at the Pentagon, David, right now!" Jim explained as he grabbed the handles of Kathy's wheel chair and pushed her quickly to his car.

It took us an hour to get to the airport and get Kathy on board. Our pilot and copilot were ready and waiting for us when we got there. As our plane took off from Denmark International Airport I felt sick to my stomach. I loved Danny like a brother. I needed to get back to Vietnam before the North Vietnamese found out who Danny was. I needed to get to him before then or my best friend would be tortured to death. The memories of being a POW came rushing back into my mind and sent a cold chill up my spine.

"I'm coming, Chopper, no matter what I have to do, no matter who I have to kill, I'm coming," I whispered softly under my breath as I turned to look out the side window of the plane.

I could feel my eyes as they began to fill with tears. My heart felt as though it had just been torn out of my chest. Pain, anger, fear, and rage had now started to overwhelm me, as I remembered Colonel Ky, Major Dinh, and the death hooch of the POW camp in Cambodia. The smell of urine, blood, dirt, and my own burning flesh filled my sinuses.

All of a sudden I heard a tiny voice as it whispered in my ear. "I knew you would need me again. I'm always with you, I never leave you, I'm here," it said as I felt David leave and the Sandman return. Suddenly, I felt revitalized, alive once again.

"I'm back...." I whispered as a smile slowly crossed my face.

Chapter Twenty
Lost Star

The flight from Denmark to Washington D.C. seemed to take forever. The thought of my brother and friend being held captive by the North Vietnamese, and knowing, from my own personal experience as a POW, of how brutal they were to American prisoners, was unthinkable to me. Kathy, knowing how upset I was at the news of Chopper being captured, hadn't spoke to me for the entire trip.

As our pilot announced we were about to land, she spoke for the first time. "David?" she asked as she leaned forward in an attempt to look into my eyes.

"Yes," I answered, as I turned to look at my friend and field supervisor.

"There's a lot I would like to say to you right now, but I won't. I don't know what's going on in your head right now or what you're planning to do. Whatever it is, David, please be careful and good luck," Kathy said as she pressed her lips tightly together.

"Would you do me a favor, Kathy? A personal favor," I asked, as I looked deep into Kathy's eyes.

"Name it," she answered sincerely.

"Contact Danny's mother, she lives in New Orleans. Tell her that Danny's been captured. Don't sugar coat it. Tell her straight out, just like it is. Tell her I'm going back to Vietnam; I'm going after my brother. Would you do that for me?" I asked.

"I'll do my best to find her, David. Danny's file is classified 'Eyes Only'. I don't know if my security clearance is high enough to access it, but I'll try," she replied with an honest look.

Taking a piece of paper and an ink pen off the small table in front of me, I wrote down two telephone numbers. "The first telephone number is to Mrs. McBride's home. If for some reason, you can't get through to her, then call the second number. That second number is to my brother Andy's home. I've already called him and my grandfather from the telephone on the plane. I told them what happened and that I would be gone for a while. Tell Andy to find Mrs. McBride and fill her in on what's going on. Please do that for me, will you?" I asked again as I tried to hold my emotions inside.

"I'll do it, but don't you think maybe it would be better if she doesn't know her son is in extreme danger right now?" Kathy asked as she tapped the small piece of paper with the numbers on it with her fingernail.

"No. She will have already sensed it. She's very close to her son. She's also like a mother to me. She's one of the strongest women I have ever met. It will give her comfort to know I'm going back in to try and find him," I explained as our plane began its descent heading toward the long airport runway.

"I'll call her from here, David, as soon as the plane comes to a stop," Kathy answered as she looked back over her right shoulder at the computer and telephone system located at the back of the plane. "They should have a car waiting for you as soon as we stop," Kathy went on to explain.

"Yes, they will. I called the Situation Room a few hours ago. They said Carla was busy working on this, so she wasn't available. They did say she had military police waiting to escort me from the airport back to the Pentagon," I explained as the plane's wheels touched down.

"You look troubled, what's wrong?" Kathy asked.

"She should have been waiting by the telephone for my call. That bothers me that she wasn't. It doesn't make sense, Kathy, what can Carla do from here to help Danny?" I asked.

"I don't know Carla as well as you do. At least not yet. But I do have some friends that tell me she is very protective of her operatives, no matter who they are. Maybe she's trying to call in some favors. Trust her, David, I know she trusts you. Besides, we're all partners, teammates. Like you said, we have to trust each other with our lives. Look what you did for me on this mission, David. You carried me on your back for a total of four miles. You even brought me a blanket. Partners, right?" Kathy asked with a broad smile as she reached out to shake my hand. Shaking Kathy's hand, I stood up as our pilot brought our Learjet to a complete stop.

"Partners," I said softly as I reached over and raised Kathy's chin gently to look in her eyes. "To be honest with you, I really enjoyed squeezing that firm little butt of yours during the whole trip," I explained as I bent down and kissed Kathy tenderly on the lips.

"I know, I enjoyed letting you do it," she answered with a sly little grin and a chuckle.

"That's it, lets go," our copilot shouted as he unfastened his seatbelt and moved quickly to the exit door of the plane.

"David, be careful," Kathy shouted as I moved toward the door.

"Listen, Dave," the copilot explained as he quickly unlocked the side door of our Learjet and pushed it open. "Ms. Silverman will be waiting for you at the front doors of the Pentagon. Good luck, buddy," he said quickly as he reached out and shook my hand.

"Thank you, get Kathy to a hospital and have them X-ray that ankle, will ya?" I asked as I began to run down the steps of the plane toward the two military police officers waiting patiently for me by their car.

"I'll take care of her, go, go!" he shouted back.

"David?" the military police staff sergeant asked in a shout as he opened the backdoor of their four-door Ford.

"Yeah," I shouted back as I jumped in the backseat. Closing the door behind me, both military police officers climbed quickly back into their vehicle and sped away with their emergency lights and siren on.

*   *   *   *   *   *

CIA Covert Operation
Code Name: Lost Star
Location Target: Hanoi-North Vietnam
Mission Status: Green
Security Level: Eyes Only – Top Secret
Mission Profile: Penetrate deep into enemy territory of capital city, Hanoi – North Vietnam. Find POW camp Strong Hold known as the Hanoi Hilton. Hostage POW reconnaissance critical. Locate CIA operative Daniel McBride, retrieve and extract POW. Strike with surgical precision by using stealth intelligence.

Technology available: Black Operation, Elite Group, War Room, Pentagon.

Time frame for mission status: None.

Unconventional warfare: Yes.

Day One:

Running up to the front door of the Pentagon I saw Carla. A team of military police were waiting with her. One of them held the door open as I ran inside. Carla had a look of fatigue and stress on her face as she grabbed me by my right arm and yelled, "Go!"

"Make way, make a hole," the two larger MPs shouted as we all ran down the hall and to the elevator on the right. As the MP yelled, Pentagon employees stopped what they were doing, looked at us coming, and stood with their backs up against the walls of the long hallway until we ran past them. Once we did, they went back to their normal routine. Stepping into the elevator being held open for us, Carla reached up, turned a silver security key located in the face of the elevator control panel and pushed button number five.

"I've assembled a team of people, David. They're in our Satellite Operations War Room right now. We are trying to come up with a plan on how to get Danny back. We know where they are holding him. We just haven't figured out how to get him out yet," Carla explained as the elevator came to a complete stop and the elevator doors began to open.

"You're going to need trained people on this one, ma'am, not a bunch of desk jockeys. How long have they had Chopper?" I asked as Carla ran her arm through mine.

Walking at a slower pace she explained, "I need your expertise on this, David. You were a POW for eighty-nine days. You know how the enemy thinks. I also know that no matter what I do, I won't be able to stop you from going back to Vietnam after your teammate, your brother, Danny. So, with that in mind I assembled a team of desk jockeys that I think you'll approve of," she said as we reached the door of the War Room. Opening the door Carla Silverman looked at me and smiled. "Meet my brain storming team of desk jockeys," she said as we walked into the satellite communications room and closed the door behind us.

Everyone stood with their backs to me as we walked into the room. They were all looking at the computer screen wall and the map and data information displayed on it. All of the communication computer counsels had people sitting at them talking to people through their light weight head sets. Neil was manning our counsel, pointing to the large satellite digital wall display and talking to the team of men that Carla had assembled to help us find Danny.

"Gentleman, I believe you all know each other," Carla said loudly. As she did the men talking to Neil turned around to look at me.

"Hello, youngster," Cookie said loudly with a big smile on his face, as he walked toward me with his arms held out.

"Cookie!" I shouted with excitement as my heart raced with joy from seeing my mentor and dearest friend. Hugging Cookie we both whispered, "Hoo yah!"

"Hey, little brother, what about us?" I knew the voice, my eyes almost filled with tears of joy, I turned to look, it was my brother and teammate Butch. Next to him stood Lieutenant Joe Knight our helicopter pilot and other teammate.

"Butch, Joe! Oh sweet Jesus, I missed you guys," I explained as we all hugged each other.

"Gentlemen, I'd like to give you some time alone but time is the one thing we're running out of. Neil, bring David up to speed on this, would you, please?" Carla asked as she stood next to me with her arms crossed and listened intently.

Turning around in his leather swivel chair, Neil smiled as he reached out to shake my hand. "David, good to see you," he said as we shook hands. "Good job in the Shetlands, buddy. We saw the explosion via satellite. What in the hell did you use, a two thousand pound war head?" he asked with a curious grin on his face.

"No, I'll explain later. Is all of this for Chopper?" I asked. Neil knew I wasn't fully aware of how the different computer stations worked. So he quickly explained it to me.

"No, its not. I was just telling your fellow teammates that we have eight different covert operations going on all at one time right now, in eight different parts of the world. Six of these operations are based on information we have put together from the Malenkov and Gruber data you brought back from your missions," Neil started to explain.

"Yeah, good job, youngster," Cookie said with a broad smile as he patted me on the back.

"We're assassinating high ranking terrorist officials. The plan is to hit all six of them at one time around the globe or at least within an hour of each other. The other two stations are monitoring one Delta Force Operation in Baghdad and one Seal team covert operation in North Korea. Its the Seal team operation that we are the most worried about right now," Neil explained.

"Why's that?" I questioned.

"They're not actually in North Korea. Our Seal team is on an island in the Pacific that belongs to China and is the home of a North Korean nuclear project. Our team went in to steal the plutonium China insists they never gave to their communist friends, North Korea." Just as Neil was explaining it the young woman from the National Security Agency monitoring the Seal team swore out loud.

"Shit! Seal team Eight is taking fire!" she yelled.

"Go to external speaker, punch them up on the global satellite mapping system," Neil shouted as he gave the young lady a direct order.

"We're taking fire, where do we go, Ops? Which direction?" the Seal team leader shouted as he tried to talk over the sound of all of the gunfire.

"Hold, team leader, I'm checking the system?" she replied, as she keyed in the global satellite mapping system and focused it on the team.

"There they are," Neil said as he stood up and walked over to where the young female agent's station was.

"Carol, magnify to eighteen hundred-percent so we can see them better. Eliminate the big picture and focus the satellite directly on the team and surrounding area," Neil said calmly as he tried to calm the young agent down.

"Talk to me, Ops! Where the fuck do we go?" the team leader shouted as the automatic gunfire intensified. As the new satellite picture appeared on the large full-wall screen, Carol took a quick look and with an untrained eye she gave them bad advice.

294

"Go to high ground, team leader. We see you, go to Grid 7842," she said in a worried tone.

"No," I said in a whisper.

"What's wrong, David?" Carla asked quickly.

"Not the high ground, ma'am," I explained as I walked up next to Neil, followed by Cookie, Joe, Butch, and the Deputy Director of the CIA who had just walked into the room as everything began to go bad.

"What?" the Seal team leader shouted back over the sound of intensifying gunfire.

"David, take over, Carol, give David your headset, now!" Carla shouted angrily. Jumping up out of her seat, Carol quickly took off her headset and handed it to me.

"What am I looking at here, Carol?" I asked as I put on the headset.

"That's Seal team Eight," she said quickly. Then she froze as more automatic gunfire erupted and intensified.

"Neil, who's their extraction?" I asked.

"Hang on," he said as he sat down at Carol's computer station and began typing on the computer keyboard.

"They're trying to flank our guys, Sandman," Cookie explained as we watched a crystal clear picture of the action from above.

"The USS Coral Seas. It's a flat top aircraft carrier. They're just off the Coast," Neil explained.

"Can we talk to the team and the captain of the Coral Seas at the same time?" I asked quickly.

"Ops, it's getting hot down here!" the Seal team leader shouted over the external speaker.

Typing in a few code numbers Neil yelled out, "Go, David you're live." Looking at the satellite map, all of my Seal team and Black Operations training, quickly took over.

"Team leader, you've got new eyes on deck. Position point to your twelve o'clock. Disregard your last instructions," I said as I walked up closer to the wall to take a better look at the terrain. Move now to your two o'clock. Go, go, go, move now! Your going five hundred yards, move out!" I shouted.

"Moving now to our two o'clock!" the Seal team leader shouted back over the sound of gunfire as he returned fire.

"Team leader, when you get there, you're going to find a small ravine, get your team in it, go to your twelve o'clock. It will take you down into a small wooded valley. It's not very wide, so stay tight and use the cover of the trees. As you get into the tree line, break hard to your ten o'clock and follow the small valley. It will take you directly to the ocean," I explained calmly.

"Roger, Ops, we're on the run!" the team leader replied.

"Captain, this is Ops One, sir, do you copy?" I asked.

"Talk to me, son," the Captain replied calmly.

"Team Eight is in trouble, sir. There's a cliff at Coordinate 225487-22558. Can you blow the top of that shelf off for us, sir? There's about forty plus tangos (enemy soldiers) now stationed there. They're going to ambush our team from the high ground as soon as team Eight leaves the cover of the tree line. Do you copy, sir?" I asked calmly.

"Copy that, Ops One, I have Danger Seven in flight already. Danger Seven, adjust to Coordinates 225487-22558. Take out the top of the cliff," the Captain of the USS Coral Seas ordered his attack jet fighters that were already in the air.

"Roger that, 225487-22558. We're four-miles off shore, and in route," Danger Seven responded.

"Team leader, this is Ops One, do not stop. I repeat do not stop your movement. Air support is one-mile from your twenty. Heavy tango movement is on the top of the cliff at your nine o'clock. They'll be toast in forty-five seconds," I explained into my mouthpiece.

"Roger, Ops One, we're almost there," the team leader answered. He was breathing heavy into his Seal team headset but he was following orders and wasn't stopping.

"Alpha One, get your extraction team in now, team Eight is ready for extraction," the Captain explained over the airwave.

"We're right behind Danger, sir," Alpha One's pilot replied. Smiling, I looked at Cookie who was looking back at me.

"CH-46?" Cookie asked.

"Sure sounded like it," I answered.

"What's a CH-46?" Carla questioned with a curious look on her face.

"CH-46, Sea Knight helicopter, ma'am. Its a marine transport helicopter," Butch answered.

We could hear the team leader breathing heavily into the mouthpiece of his headset as they continued to run for the beach. Then, we heard multiple explosions and the sound of debris falling down onto Seal team Eight.

"Hoo yah! Take that, motherfuckers!" the Seal team leader shouted into his headset. "Ops One, this is team leader, we see the water, two-hundred yards out. I can hear our extraction slick. We see it, we see it," he said in a calmer but stressed voice as they continued to run out to the beach so the marine helicopter could pick them up.

"Thanks for your help, brother, man, thank you," he said again as we heard him stop, and breathe even heavier into his headset.

"Hoo yah, team leader," I said with a smile as we watched the big CH-46 Sea Knight helicopter land on the beach from our satellite TV screen.

"I thought so, hoo yah, brother, and thanks again. Team leader, out," he said as we watched the seven man Seal team board the slick and lift off into the air from the large digital satellite television screen on the War Room wall.

"Hoo yah!" Cookie, Butch, and Joe all said loudly as they began to pat me on the back.

"Quick thinking, youngster," Cookie said with a proud smile. "I see you haven't lost your touch," he added.

"I don't understand," Carol said with a completely confused look on her face. "The helicopter would have picked them up from the top of that cliff. That's why I told them to go to the high ground," she tried to explain as she looked over at Carla for support with her hands held out at her sides.

"David, why did you send them in the other direction?" Neil questioned with a truly curious look on his face.

"They're Seals," I said with a proud smile. "Never send Navy Seals to high ground if there's water near by. Get them to the water and they'll disappear. They're trained for the water that's why President John Kennedy created the Navy Seals and named them Seal. Kennedy was a Navy Officer on PT-109, a small navy assault boat. Had they gone to high ground you would have left them with no way to retreat. Those Korean soldiers would have had them boxed in with their backs up against a cliff. At that point a helicopter extraction would have been a total disaster. They would have shot the helicopter and its crew out of the air," I explained as I looked over at Cookie.

"That's right, youngster. Damn I've missed you and your quick thinking. I still haven't figured out where you get it from," Cookie said as he looked over at Carla, as she sat down on Neil's seat.

"Carol, you're clearly not ready nor are you trained for this. Report back to your supervisor, young lady," Carla ordered as she rubbed her tired face with her left hand.

"I'm sorry, ma'am," Carol said sincerely.

"Tell that to the families of those Navy Seals had you gotten them killed by sending them to high ground," Carla said coldly. Picking up her purse, Carol left the room without saying another word; her eyes filled with tears.

"Are you alright, Carla?" Deputy Director Richard Crock asked as he walked up to Carla and placed his right hand gently on her shoulder and rubbed it.

"Hello, Richard, thank you for coming on such short notice."

"No problem, after all, these are my boys. Hello, fella's, its good to see the legendary Black Ops Team One back together again," Deputy Director Crock said with a smile as we all said hello and shook his hand.

"Well, not quite, sir," Cookie said quickly. "We would need Captain's Mosier and Bell to make it right. Plus without Chopper, Team One is not the original Team One."

"Well let's see if we can fix all of that. Where do we stand so far, Carla?" Richard asked.

"Neil was just bringing David up to speed when Seal Team Eight encountered trouble. Neil would you get Danny back up on the big screen for us and bring us all up to date on his situation?" Carla asked politely.

"Yes, ma'am," Neil answered.

"How can you get Danny up on the big screen?" I asked totally confused at the thought of it. "You mean the location of the area you think he is being held in, right?" I asked.

"Hang on, youngster, Neil was explaining all of it to us just as you and Ms. Silverman walked in. Go ahead, Neil, finish telling us exactly how this chip works," Cookie explained.

Reaching into his top left shirt pocket, Neil pulled out a very tiny plastic bag. As he handed it to Cookie, Neil explained. "This micro chip is the size of a grain of rice. We implant it just under the skin, somewhere in the scalp or upper area of the shoulders. It's not only state of the art technology but also highly classified and top secret. With this chip, we can track you anywhere in the world by satellite. Danny agreed to let us put one of these chips on him for experimental reasons," Neil explained as Cookie handed the small plastic bag to me to look at.

The chip looked exactly like a piece of thin slender rice but was clearly a microchip. Looking at it I handed the plastic bag to Butch so he would be able to check it out also. Tapping on his computer keys a clear picture of North Vietnam appeared on the full-size wall screen.

"North Vietnam, gentlemen. Now I punch in the satellite tracking code for Danny's microchip and wa-la. See that white dot?" Neil asked as he raised his right hand and pointed at the small white dot that clearly appeared on the screen.

"Yeah, that's our boy? That's Chopper?" Cookie asked as we all took a very close look at the screen.

"That's Danny. Now I magnify to eighteen hundred percent and type in global satellite elimination mapping and our GSEM system locks directly onto Danny's exact location," Neil explained proudly.

"See the computer read out where it says Target Acquired Ident Positive: Daniel McBride and right next to it the computer screen gives us Danny's exact global satellite position where it says, Lock Coordinate:

42871-69542, see it?" Neil asked in an excited voice with a broad smile on his face.

"Yeah, we see it. But where in North Vietnam is that?" Joe asked.

"It says Target Status: Locked. So we press this one key and the satellite zooms in on Danny's exact location," Neil explained as he pressed the computer board key. As he did the satellite zoomed in at eighteen hundred percent magnification. The picture of the heavily guarded large cement structure made me feel bad enough, but when the satellite identified the building and read what it said on the visual screen, my heart sank.

"Awe shit!" Cookie said softly.

"Boy oh boy," Joe whispered under his breath as he shook his head from side to side and placed his right hand on the end of his chin, as he studied the picture on the screen.

"The Hanoi Hilton, gentlemen. It's their most secure prison located right in the heart of the capitol city of North Vietnam, Hanoi. See the white dot, right there toward the back of the building?" Neil asked as he once again pointed at the large screen.

"Yeah, is that Danny?" Butch asked.

"That's him, that's his exact location," Neil explained as he turned in his chair to look at us.

"How do you know he's alive?" Joe questioned.

"Two ways. Every so often the dot moves ever so slightly. That's him moving around in his prison cell," Neil explained as he looked up at Carla. "Ma'am?" he said as he raised both of his eyebrows and pressed his lips together tightly.

"The reason I called all of you in out of your assigned duty areas," Carla began to say when she saw the look of surprise on my face.

"David, Cookie, Joe, and Butch were recruited by Deputy Director Crock as soon as they were discharged from the United States Army and had returned home to the States. Your teammates are all CIA agents, duly sworn," Carla explained as she watched the expression on my face.

"Why didn't you tell me, ma'am?" I questioned feeling a little betrayed by Carla.

"We needed to watch you for awhile after you had come home. You were a POW, which meant you were traumatized by that experience. There are things I just can't tell you right now, David. I really need you to trust me, please. I will say this much. You're the only one of your team that has Elite Operative Covert Status. You're the only one that trained at the Farm and you're also the only member of your team that has a Q-clearance security level status. I'm sorry that I didn't tell you, but you do have to admit, you have been busy," Carla explained.

"No problem, ma'am. I'm not upset, I'm happy. At least I have access to my brothers now," I said as I smiled and said, "Hoo yah!"

"Hoo yah!" Cookie, Joe, and Butch responded.

"Now the news goes from bad to worse," Carla explained.

"With the information, telephone numbers, and radio frequency codes we now have access to, from the Gruber and Malenkov disc's, we have agents assigned around the clock who are monitoring every word that key players are saying. Neil, please tell these men what you overheard," Carla asked with a worried look on her face.

"Three nights ago a North Vietnamese Major that we have identified as Major Lai Bui called the Kremlin in Russia. Major Bui has identified Danny McBride, through photographs, as one of the Black Operation intelligence team snipers from Bien Hoa. We believe those are the same pictures you saw, Dave, when they identified you with them in Cambodia," Neil explained. "Major Bui is in charge of the Hanoi Hilton prison."

"That's why I called you men in and asked Deputy Crock for his help," Carla explained with a very nervous, worried look on her face.

"What's wrong, Carla?" Cookie asked when he saw the worried look on Carla's face.

"They called General Boris Kalashnikov and told him they have Danny," Carla explained as she looked over at me.

"What did Boris say, ma'am?" Joe asked, as I closed my eyes and tilted my head slightly backwards. I felt like throwing up. If they took Chopper to Russia we would lose him, possibly forever, just like our Iron Hand pilots.

"The General has ordered Major Bui to hold Danny and not let anything happen to him. Boris has just had some long overdue stomach surgery. He is in the hospital in Moscow as we speak. He told Major Bui that he will be there to personally pick up Danny, in eleven-days, as soon as the doctors release him from the hospital," Carla explained.

"Yes, and that's not the worst of it. Major Bui has also placed a call to the Chinese Consulate telling them he has Danny. The Chinese government called Boris yesterday. They want to use Danny as a trading chip," Neil explained carefully as he looked up at Carla and Deputy Director Crock.

"Well that's good news, what do they want in trade for our brother?" Lieutenant Knight, now Agent Joe Knight, asked. Placing her hand over her mouth, Carla looked at Mr. Crock and then at me.

"They want the Sniper with the big handlebar mustache that killed their Chinese Major Dinh, in Cambodia. They want to trade Danny for David!" Deputy Crock explained as everyone in the room slowly turned their heads to look at me. All of a sudden, the room fell silent.

"How can they make such a demand?" Butch asked as he looked from me to Carla.

"They are trying to say that David committed a war crime. They are alleging that David snuck into Cambodia assassinated Major Dinh, with Cambodia being a neutral country," Carla explained. Turning to look at the big TV screen, I listened to the conversation that was taking place and began to focus my thoughts back on how to rescue my brother Danny.

"What did Boris say?" Cookie asked in a pissed off voice.

"He loves the idea. They could try David as a war criminal and then execute him in Russia. Boris has a very bitter hatred for David," Neil explained.

Looking at the satellite picture of the prison, I smiled when I saw the tiny white dot move. "Hang in there, brother. We'll think of something," I thought to myself.

"How about a full out assault just like we did when we rescued Kate," Joe questioned.

"That's an idea," Butch added. "They would never expect it. Its a daring move."

"I don't give a damn what we have to do, I want my boy out of that fucking camp," Carla said sharply as she sat back down and looked over at me.

"Remember your training, David. Damn it think," I said to myself as I stared at the screen and watched the heavily armed guards as they moved around in plain sight of the satellite.

"Always expect the unexpected. Everything is subject to change at any given moment," Master Chief Jeff Mareno used to repeat to me, over and over again.

"We could come in by air from the ocean and hit 'em so fast and so hard they'll never know what hit 'em," Joe explained as the brainstorming session continued.

"If you see something low, look high. If you see something high, look low," I remembered as I closed my eyes trying to focus deeper into my memory. "Never eat anything that a monkey won't eat. If a monkey can eat it, then so can you. The most obvious is the least obvious," I thought to myself as I remembered our last mission together. Butch, Chopper, and I had just assassinated three high-ranking North Vietnam Generals in Cambodia. I had committed a sniper's sin and my shot had given up our location. We were on the run and ran right into a small Viet Cong village. With enemy soldiers right on our heals, I told Butch and Chopper to put their black headbands on. We walked right into the small Viet Cong camp and had a cup of Beatle Nut coffee with the old man that was squatting down next to the campfire. Old popason thought we were deserters fighting for the NVA. We then left the village and got into the safety of the tree line on the other side of the small village, just as the enemy troops came into the village. We had tricked that old man into thinking we were one of his, and it saved our lives. The memory of that incident brought a smile to my face and made me laugh out loud. "The most obvious was the least obvious, you were right, Master Chief," I whispered to myself as I saw the small white dot move again.

"Damn, that's awful risky. We'll lose a lot of men trying to rescue Danny that way," Cookie said. "What do you think?" he started to ask as he turned thinking I was still standing just off to his right. Cookie hadn't noticed that I had walked up to the satellite screen and was staring at it.

"The most obvious is the least obvious. If you're on the run, hide right in front of them and they'll never know you're there. The most obvious is the least obvious," my Master Chief, Seal team instructor, use to always tell me.

"Give him a few minutes, Cookie. I think the news of swapping him for Danny has upset him," Carla explained to Cookie as they both looked over at me. Even though I was looking at the picture screen and thinking, I could still see Carla and my friends out of the corner of my right eye, through my peripheral vision.

"You don't know David as well as you think you do, ma'am. He'd trade his life for Chopper's in a heartbeat," Butch explained as he looked over at me and began to walk toward me.

"He's not upset, Carla," Cookie said in a whispered voice as he began to walk toward me also. "He's planning something."

"Yeah, and whatever it is," Joe added as he followed behind Butch and Cookie, "It will be awesome. He always came up with the craziest ideas, but they always work," Joe explained.

Cookie walked up to me and stood close to my right side. Butch was now standing on my left and Joe was standing right behind me. All four of us were watching the satellite screen and staring at that tiny white dot that was our brother, Chopper.

"You've got an idea don't ya, youngster?" Cookie asked never taking his eyes off the screen.

"Yup," I answered in a soft whisper.

"I'm in," Butch said without knowing what it was I was thinking.

"Me too," Joe added.

"Fella's," Carla began to say until Deputy Director Crock stopped her.

"Shhh, I've seen these men work. Don't say a word," he whispered in Carla's ear as the entire room remained silent.

"I'm with ya, youngster," Cookie added calmly as the small white dot moved slightly on the board once again.

"That's our brother, Danny out there. We swore an oath," I said as the thought of them torturing Danny began to fill me with rage. "Brothers and friends," I said calmly.

"Throughout life," Cookie added.

"And into death," Butch continued.

"Until the very end," Joe concluded as I turned around to face them.

"Anybody speak Russian?" I asked with a cold deadly look on my face. I was caught completely by surprise when Cookie responded to my question in perfect Russian. Then Joe spoke in Russian. Joe's Russian wasn't as good as Cookies, but it was damn close.

"Shit! I didn't know you guys could speak Russian?" I said with a look of surprise on my face.

"I speak four different languages, youngster. Vietnamese, German, Russian, and Chinese," Cookie explained proudly. "Not bad, huh?" he added as he winked at me.

"No kidding, not bad. I'm impressed!" I replied with a smile.

"I speak two. Vietnamese and Russian," Joe added.

"I only speak one, Vietnamese," Butch also explained. But I shoot real good, that speaks for itself," he said with a grin as he winked at me.

"Oh God, Richard, their going to do something crazy, aren't they?" Carla asked as she looked up at the Deputy Director of the CIA.

"Probably," he said as he walked over and stood by us. "I'm in, what's the plan?" he asked catching us totally by surprise by using the words I'm in.

"We'll pose as Russian's and fly into Hanoi, walk right smack dab into the center of that POW camp and take Danny out. The most obvious is the least obvious," I explained with a serious look on my face as I looked around at the faces of my friends and teammates. "What do you think?" I asked. No one spoke for almost fifteen to twenty-seconds as they thought about what I had just said, and wondered if it would actually work.

"I love it!" Cookie said as he looked at Crock and then back over at me. "What's your plan, youngster?" he asked.

"Mr. Crock, can you get us high ranking Russian uniforms and Russian documents?" I questioned.

"It will take a few days, but yes, I can do that. No problem," he replied with an interesting look on his face.

"Now the hard part. We'll need Russian assault rifles at least four Israeli made Uzi machine guns, and a Russian helicopter," I explained as I looked over at Cookie for support.

"A Russian helicopter?" Deputy Crock asked.

"Without a Russian helicopter, my plan won't work, sir," I explained as I started to lose hope at the way Richard had responded to my request.

"Major Bell still has that large Russian helicopter he brought back from that village when you boys killed that Russian Colonel and his diplomat wife. Remember that mission?" he asked with an anxious tone.

"Yeah, they were with that American piece of shit traitor. Damn, what was his name?" Butch asked as he looked over at me.

"Benson. His name was Benson, he was selling out our Iron Hand trained pilots," I said bitterly as I remembered his face.

"Yeah, that's him, Benson. Sandman shot him in his right knee first and then shot him right between the eyes. It was a beautiful thing to see," Butch said proudly with a smile on his face.

"Major Bell?" I asked with a smile as I looked at Mr. Crock.

"That's right. Both Captain's Bell and Mosier were promoted to Majors right after your team returned home to the States. They could have both came home and had a cushy desk job but they refused. When they refused to come home, your other teammate, Johnny, decided to stay also. It took almost a year but they put together a brand new team. They're still running their Black Operations Team Four, out of Bien Hoa. Nothing's changed just the team. Bell kept that damn helicopter. He swore that one day we might need it. I'll be damned if he wasn't right! That Russian bird is suppose to still be at the Bien Hoa Air Base. Neil, open a secure telephone line to Major's Bell and Mosier intelligence command would you?" Crock asked as he looked at his watch.

"What's the plan, Richard?" Carla asked as she stood up and walked toward us.

"I'm authorizing full access to these men, Carla. They're my boys and they have my complete confidence. If they say they can walk into the Hanoi Hilton, I believe them. I want you to assemble a team here, Carla. I want your best global satellite communications people operating this system, around the clock, until this mission is completed," Crock explained.

"That would be Neil, sir," I said quickly. "We would like Neil to be the one running the show here in the War Room. He has earned my trust, sir," I explained. When I did, I could see it caught Neil by surprise, he turned to look at me with a sincere look of gratitude on his face.

"Carla?" Richard said as he looked at our other boss.

"David is right. I wouldn't trust the lives of these men in the hands of anyone other than Neil. He's a computer genius. This is his satellite system. He knows it inside and out. Neil, you on board?" Carla asked as she turned to look at Neil who was calling Major Bell for us.

"Yes, ma'am. It would be an honor," he answered as he looked from Carla over to me and smiled.

"I'm going to need to put a satellite GPS chip in each one of your teammates, Sandman," Neil explained.

"You got it, brother, tell Major Bell that we are going to need him to get that Russian helicopter operational and flight ready. We also need him to find us one more person that speaks perfect Russian," I explained.

"I'll call the President and let him know what we're about to do," Carla explained as she walked over and picked up the red telephone that was secured to the back wall of the room.

"I see one very serious flaw, David," Deputy Crock said loudly as everyone, including Carla, stopped what they were doing and turned their total attention to him.

"What's that, sir?" I questioned.

"They've got your face burned in their memory. They also have your 8x10 photograph and wanted posters out on you. What if one of them recognizes you?" he asked with a serious look of concern on his face.

"He's right, youngster. They've got pictures of both you and Butch," Cookie added.

Looking over at Carla I saw her smile and remembered that she had told me she had a closet full of Hollywood make-up kits. With that in mind, and the tricks the master of disguise, Carlos the Jackal, had taught me, they would never recognize us.

"Don't worry, sir, I've got a surprise for 'em," I answered with complete confidence in my training as I turned around to look at the large satellite screen and the tiny white dot that was our teammate and brother, Danny.

"Sir, I've got Major Bell on the line," Neil said as Deputy Director Crock walked over to him and placed the telephone to his ear.

"Major Bell this is Deputy Director Crock, Black Operations Team One, as you once knew it, has been reclassified by the President of the United States. They are now Covert Elite Black Operations Team One! They've come up with a plan on how to extract Agent McBride from Hanoi. Both you and Major Mosier along with your Black Operation Team Four, will oversee this operation from Bien Hoa. We will run it from the War Room. Your boys are coming back to Vietnam, Mr. Bell. Here's our plan..."

* * * * * * *

It took Mr. Crock two days to get us the authentic Russian uniforms we would need to disguise ourselves and most of the second day to have them fitted to form. After all Russian KGB officers were well known for being clean-cut, clean-shaven, and well uniformed.

Major Bell had given us the uniform size of one other person he knew of that spoke fluent Russian. So we took along with us another uniform for this unknown individual.

We received our Russian identification credentials, complete with pictures of us wearing our uniforms, and the forged documents we would use to get the North Vietnamese Major to release Chopper to us. We were told that the forged signature of General Kalashnikov would have made the general proud, had he been working for our side. I asked the Agency lab boys to give me six Cohiba cigars and three packages of Lucky Strike cigarettes. I wanted four of the expensive cigars and two packs of the cigarettes laced with the deadly poison I used to kill Morimoto Soba with in Switzerland.

My thoughts were that the Vietnamese love to smoke. If anything went wrong and we didn't make it out alive, I knew they would strip us down and steal all of our clothing, weapons, and personal item. As they took turns lighting up my cigarettes in victory of killing us, I'd take a whole lot of them with us.

We received our glass cyanide capsules around midnight, and were in flight to Southeast Asia on Delta International Airlines Flight 412 by 9:00 a.m. on day three.

We asked to sit at the back of the plane together. From there we found some humor in the fact that this plane, full of soldiers, were just as scared as we once were when we flew to Vietnam our very first time. That humor quickly faded when we looked at them and remembered that some of these young men would never see home, or their families and loved ones ever again.

It took twenty-two hours for the big Delta airliner to touch down on the hot asphalt runway of the Bien Hoa Air Base in Vietnam.

Looking out through the side window of our plane, Cookie nudged me with his shoulder and pointed out through the side window of the plane. "Look familiar?" Cookie asked with a broad smile on his face.

Looking through the window, I felt my heart pounding with excitement as I placed two drops of Methadrine under my tongue. There, off in the distance, on the First Calvary Division side of the Air Base, sat our Black Operation snipers hooch. It was just as we had left it several years ago, nothing had changed, and we were back home, once again.

"Hoo yah," I whispered softly as Cookie held his left hand out, palm facing upward.

Slapping my hand gently on top of his, he replied, "Hoo yah, youngster, we're back."

My mind raced with the memories of my two year tour of duty, living in that hooch with Butch, Nick, and Chopper. The long fatherly talks I used to have with Cookie, when he would find me sitting on top of our bunker all alone and troubled. All the jokes and horse playing around. All of the good times when I would pick at my commanding officer Captain Mosier, knowing that it pissed him off. The laughter, the tears, the joy, the sadness all came rushing back at one time as our plane came to a full stop. When it did, I looked around at a plane full of wide eyed soldiers who now sat in complete silence.

We waited for all the soldiers to off board before we stood up. Pulling our suitcases out from the over head compartments we walked to the front of the plane. Butch and Joe were the first two to step off of the plane and walk down the ramp.

Turning to look at me Cookie spoke, "You okay, youngster?"

"I'm fine, pop. Let's go get our brother," I answered as Cookie nodded in agreement and stepped out through the door and walked down the ramp.

Stepping through the door behind Cookie the intense heat of Vietnam almost took my breath away. The sound of helicopters from the First Calvary Air Mobile Division, and the jet fighters from the Air Force, filled the air. The smell of jet fuel and heat filled my nostrils, as a sudden surge of adrenaline filled my being.

I walked down the ramp and smiled when I saw my old commanding officer, his new rank of Major displayed proudly on the lapels of his faded camouflaged uniform. He had just finished hugging Butch, Joe, and Cookie as he turned to look over at me, with a big smile on his face.

"Dad, can I have my favorite meal for supper tonight?" I asked jokingly as I remembered Captain Mosier serving me a plate of white rice with a full-size, cooked rat laying on top. It was our last meal together as a team and the first time that Captain Mosier had ever joked around with us like that.

"You better be careful what you ask for, Sandman. Your dad's waiting for you at our office!" he said with a big smile as we hugged each other. "How have you been, you alright?" he asked out of concern for my health.

"I'm fine, sir. I'll be even better when we get Chopper back," I replied with a straight look.

"Hoo yah, come on, lets get to my office, we don't have a lot of time," Major Bell explained as he introduced us to Billy his eighteen-year old clerk. Climbing into the two jeeps he had waiting for us we made the short drive across the Air Base to our intelligence office on the First Calvary side of the Air Base.

We got out of our jeeps, picked up our suitcases, and stepped inside our old command office. My heart was racing with excitement at the familiar sights and smells of being back on my old stomping grounds. I couldn't believe how excited I actually was to be back here with both of my commanding officers once again. I had missed them both so very much.

I was the last one to walk into the second room in our small intelligence office. As I did, young Billy pulled the door closed behind me. Setting down my two suitcases, I watched as Major Mosier shook hands, hugged, and laughed loudly with Cookie, Butch and Joe.

"Remember this guy, sir?" Cookie asked as he turned and nodded his head at me.

"I remember him. Isn't that the youngster that ate rat meat while everyone else ate prime rib?" he questioned with a straight face as he rubbed his chin with his left hand.

"That's him," Cookie responded.

"Yeah, I know this little prick. He's the one that gave me all of this gray hair," Mosier said as he broke out smiling and walked up to me with his arms extended.

My heart was about to explode as we hugged each other tightly. "I never forgot you, boy, I swear," he whispered in my ear as he gave me an extra long hug.

"I've missed you, sir," I whispered back as we both whispered "Hoo yah," to each other.

"Men, I want you to meet the Black Operations team that made history here," Major Bell said loudly as he began to introduce us to the other five men who were now standing up to greet us.

"This is Cookie, Joe, Butch, and David. This is Black Ops Team One. Men, these are the young men that replaced you when you left. This is Ron, Bob, Glen, and Alan, Black Ops Team Four," Captain Bell introduced with a proud smile as we all shook hands.

"Boy, you fella's are all we hear about around here. You're a hard act to follow," Ron explained with a smile as he shook our hands.

"We were no act, son, we were deadly serious," Cookie answered with a grin on his face as he looked over at the fifth man that was still sitting down and watching us.

"No shit, check this out," Alan said with a nod of his head as he directed our attention to the wall behind Major Mosier's desk. There, hanging on the wall, were seven large picture frames with pictures of Cookie, Joe, Nick, Johnny, Butch, Danny and I, wearing our black berets. They were hanging in a circle with an eighth picture hanging on the wall in the middle of them. The center picture was a picture of Butch, Nick, Chopper, and I. We were posing with our M-40-A-1 Remington Snipers Rifles and wearing our Ghillie suits. Our faces were camouflaged with black and dark green grease face paint.

"If you don't mind, sir, may I have the privilege of reading this to them?" Glen asked as he walked behind the desk to read what was engraved on the bronze plate that was right under the center picture.

"Go ahead, son," Major Mosier replied as he pressed his lips together firmly and looked down toward the floor.

The men of Black Operations Team One: Butch, Nick, David, and Danny. Mission success rate, 100%. These are the men that rode the Pale Horse of Death deep into enemy territory. They feared nothing. To excel with excellence is what they strived for and achieved with valor and honor.

"I read this every time I get a chance, one day Team Four is gonna have their pictures up on this wall too," Glen said with certainty.

"Were you guys really that good?" Bob asked.

"They were. If they weren't, I wouldn't be here right now willing to join this mission," the fifth older man said as everyone turned to look at him. As he stood up out of his chair and walked toward us smiling, I fought hard trying to remember his face.

"You two don't remember me do you?" he asked as he walked up to Butch and I grinning. He had a tint of gray hair and wore his hair high and tight on the sides. He was in his early forties and wore sun bleached camouflaged fatigues. His face was tanned and looked like leather. He was a warrior, there was no doubt about it.

"I know the face," I said softly as I tried hard to remember.

"What makes you think that Charlie is in that tree line, son?" he asked grinningly.

That's all it took to help me remember. "Gunny Sergeant Tom Burke. Now I remember!" I said proudly as we shook hands vigorously.

"Yeah, hot damn, Gunny, are you the one that's coming with us?" Butch asked smiling as he shook Tom's hand.

"If you'll have me along for the ride. I'd sure love to be part of this operation and I speak Russian real well. Besides that, I like that big man they've got hemmed up over there. The Major said it's entirely up to you men. What do you say, am I in with you?" he asked as he reached out his leather hand to shake ours once again.

"Welcome aboard, Gunny," I said proudly as we shook each other's hands. "There is a little catch though," I explained.

"There usually is," he replied with a smile.

"We've got a small satellite micro chip that we're going to have to put under your skin. You mind?" I asked.

"Major Bell told me all about it. I don't mind at all. Whatever it takes. I want in on this mission real bad," he explained with a serious look in his old Marine eyes.

"You understand that we're probably not going to make it out of there alive don't you, Gunny?" I asked.

"I understand that," he answered calmly showing no fear.

"Mind if I ask why you want to risk your life like this, Gunny? I mean, don't take me wrong, I'm glad you're coming along. I'm just curious is all," Joe explained with a look of interest on his face.

"I'm a professional soldier, boys. I'm a die hard Marine. How often do you get a chance to walk right into the enemy's kitchen and shit in his stew! And to do it with the legendary Black Ops Team One. Shit, I'm in," he said with a wide serious smile on his face.

"I've got a uniform in that suitcase for you, Gunny," I explained as I looked over at both Bell and Mosier.

"We've killed four days just getting here. We're running out of time, sirs," I explained. "Where's Johnny?" I asked.

"Billy!" Mosier shouted out loud to his clerk.

Opening the door to our inner office Billy stuck his head in. "Sir?" he asked wide-eyed.

"I need you to fire up the coffee pot, son. Keep it hot and full, we've got a lot of work to do and not very much time to do it in," Mosier explained.

"Yes, sir. John Wayne style, sir?" Billy asked as Mosier looked over at Cookie and smiled.

"Damn straight. John Wayne style, Billy. Thick as mud and black as sin," Moser said as we all shouted, "Hoo yah" and began to laugh out loud. We were back for one last and very dangerous mission. This time Chopper's life depended on it and the odds were completely against us.

* * * * * * *

It was day five as I sat in our intelligence office going over our plans with Cookie, Joe, Tom, Butch, and Johnny. Team Four was busy setting up the new satellite dish we had brought with us. With this new system both Mosier and Bell would have a direct line to Carla and Neil in the CIA's War Room at the Pentagon. Stealth intelligence and teamwork would be the ultimate weapon that would either make the mission a success or a complete failure. Direct communication was a must between, Neil, Mosier, and our helicopters.

As Neil watched our every move via satellite through the computer chips in our shoulders, another team would be monitoring the telephone and radio communications between General Boris Kalashnikov in Russia and Major Lai Bui in Hanoi at the prison.

We were going to fly in using two Russian made helicopters. A Mi-17 model and the large gunship we captured during one of our missions when team one was running at its peak.

Both of these helicopters had been stored right here at the Bien Hoa Air Base and hidden under camouflaged netting. With the loan of a couple of staff sergeant crew chiefs from the airmobile division of the First Cavalry, we would have them primed and running perfectly within another twenty-four hours.

Doctor Dave Pari came to our intel office and carefully placed the tiny satellite chip under Tom's skin, at the top rear of his left shoulder.

Opening the inner door to our conference room, Billy stuck his head in. "Sir, Johnny's friends are here," Billy explained with a smile.

"Yes, let them in," Mossier said as Johnny got up with a big smile on his face and went to greet them, "Now we're in business. Boy, have I got a surprise for you," he whispered under his breath. Watching the inner door of the office my heart almost stopped when I saw the two North Vietnamese high-ranking officers step into the room. One was a Colonel and the other was a General. Both were dressed in full NVA uniforms.

"Thanks for coming my friends. You both look perfect," Johnny said with a smile as he turned to face us.

"Remember Mr. Twe and Mr. Doc, fella's?" Johnny asked as I remembered his two South Vietnamese Ranger friends and the day they fed me the snake meat causing me to throw-up.

"Oh hell yes! Hoo yah!" I said with a smile as we all shook hands and said hello.

Both Mr. Twe and Mr. Doc were small in size but as deadly and professional as it gets when it came to killing the enemy.

"Mr. Sandman, Mr. Butch, how are you?" Doc said in broken English, with a huge smile on his face.

"Great, Mr. Doc, its good to see you both again," Butch answered as he shook Doc's hand.

"You still got that big gun?" I asked Doc, remembering that I had given him a brand new 12-guage Winchester riot gun during one of our missions.

"Oh yes, Mr. Sandman. I kill many Viet Cong with big gun," he said smiling with pride.

"Fella's, Doc and Twe insisted that they come along with us when we go in after Chopper. They're like brothers to my guys, I can't say no," Johnny explained with a serious look on his face.

"Of course they're coming along. They're part of our family," Cookie said loudly.

"Hoo yah," we shouted out loud. The odds had just shifted slightly in our favor. Major Bui would be hard pressed to deny us dressed as high ranking KGB Russians and Twe and Doc dressed as they're superior officers."

"Satellite system is up and running, sir," Bob explained as he and Alan walked into the room to join us. "Hey, Twe, Doc, what's going on, fella's?" Alan said to the men that now helped team four just as they had done with us.

"We look how?" Mr. Twe asked as he patted his uniform and pulled out some documentation and handed it to Cookie. Reading the paperwork Cookie whistled in agreement.

"This is nice, real nice and it's authentic too," he said as he handed the credentials to Bell.

"You look great Mr. Twe. You know we might not get out of there alive, don't you?" I asked knowing that both Twe and Doc were married and had families depending on them.

"You go, we go. Family must fight together to be family that is number one," he answered. "Number one meaning the best."

"Johnny, why don't you and Cookie bring our brothers up to speed on our plan to rescue Danny," Major Bell explained as his telephone rang. Picking up his phone he spoke into the receiver. "Hello, this is Major Bell... Yes, Sergeant Major... Awe shit, we need that bird up in the air, Sarge, our whole operation depends on it... Alright, Sergeant Major, keep me posted. Thank you, goodbye," Bell said as he hung up the telephone and rubbed his eyes with the fingers of his left hand.

"How bad is it?" Major Mosier asked.

"They've got a problem with the turbine engine on the Soviet gunship. They're trying to figure it out, but it doesn't look good," Bell explained sadly as he looked at all of us and shook his head from side to side slowly.

"Damn it, that's the bird we need the most. All of the Russian big shots fly in those gunships. The North Vietnamese brass know it," Mosier responded in frustration.

"May I use your phone, sir," Gunny Sergeant Burke asked.

"Absolutely, Tom, you got an idea?" Bell asked with renewed hope.

"I know an old Master Gunnery Sergeant that can fix anything. I've got a months pay that says if anyone can fix that Russian bird, he can!" Tom said as he picked up the phone and began to dial it.

"Hello? Who is this?... This is Burke, put Charlie on the line, tell him its an emergency," Tom explained.

"Hello, Charlie?...Yeah, this is Tom. I've got a Russian frog with an engine problem. We need it up in the air to rescue an American POW and the Army dogfaces can't fix it. Now my question to you, you old

Bushwhacker, is simple, what are you gonna do about it?" Tom asked in a challenging tone of voice. "Yeah... Yeah... I hear you talking Master Gunnery Sergeant but I don't see your sorry ass here doing anything about it. Grab your tools and your best crew, partner, I'm at the Army side of the Air Base. Come to the Intelligence Division Office. Hurry, Charlie, we're running out of time. The clocks against us on this one... All right, bye-bye," Burke said as he hung up the telephone and stared at it for a few minutes. The room fell into complete silence. We could hear each other breathing, then Tom raised his head and grinned. "The Marines are on their way. We'll show your boys how to fix that Russian frog," Tom said with confidence.

"What is frog?" Mr. Doc whispered as he looked over at me.

"That's what the Marines call a helicopter. We call 'em slicks or choppers in the Army. The Marines call 'em frogs," I explained as we all sat down to fine tune our plans and test out the new satellite telephone system

* * * * * * *

Two days had now passed since Tom had called his buddy Charlie. Sitting on a small clump of grass I sipped on a bottle of Pepsi and watched Marine Master Gunnery Sergeant Charlie Dane and his four-man maintenance mechanical helicopter repair crew.

Charlie had pulled the engine of the Soviet built helicopter gunship completely out of the helicopter and had torn it completely down. Parts were scattered all over the ground.

"Damndest thing I've seen," Charlie said as he chewed on the stub of a two-day-old cigar. Looking at one of the engine parts Charlie tossed it over his shoulder. Watching it bounce on the ground and land next to a pile of engine parts, I turned to look at Butch, who was sitting next to me.

"We're screwed," Butch whispered trying hard not to let Charlie hear how frustrated he was getting. "We've only got three days left, Sandman. What do we do if they can't get that bird up and running again?" Butch asked with a worried look on his face.

"We go on day ten, Butch, one way or the other. We've still got the Russian Mi-17 helicopter that Team Four captured. Tom says Charlie will get it fixed. I believe him, brother," I explained calmly.

"Dale, where's Rick? How long does it take to mill a damn rotor plate for Christ's sake," Charlie asked as he began to show signs of frustration himself.

Major Bell had called the Air Force base supervisor. They gave us full access to their milling machine and anything else we might need to fix this damaged bird. That was the one good thing about this war. When the chips were down, it didn't matter what branch of the service you were in. Everybody pulled together to get the job done. The young Marine Private named Rick was with the Air Force milling the part that Charlie swore was causing the problem.

"Give me a pound of C-4 explosives and a forty-five second old school fuse and I'll show you how to fix this Russian piece of shit! Where in the hell is Rick?" Charlie shouted once again.

"Please, God, we could sure use some help down here right about now," I whispered softly.

"Amen," Butch added as we continued to watch Charlie and his team tear apart the helicopter.

"How's it going?" Gunny Sergeant Burke asked as he walked up toward us looking at his watch.

"Not to good, Tom," Butch answered as he looked up at Tom.

"Charlie," Tom shouted as he held both hands out to his sides.

"I can make an old broken lawn mower fly if I have to. Just leave us alone, we'll fix this broken piece of shit, you crusty old fart!" Charlie shouted back to Tom. "Where's that damn kid, Dale?" Charlie asked as he looked over at his Line Sergeant.

"Come on, boys. Cookie just called from the mess hall and said that supper's ready," Tom explained as I looked up at him.

"Charlie's never failed me yet, Sandman, have some faith," Tom explained as he reached out his hand.

Grabbing Tom's hand he helped me to my feet.

"Faith is all I have left, Gunny," I answered.

"Its all you need, son. Come on, boys, I'm buying," Tom explained with a friendly wink and a pat on my back.

* * * * * * *

Standing in our old snipers hooch I watched as the rain came down by the buckets. As I looked out through the side window my mind brought back the pleasant memories of the two years I had lived in this small black operations hooch with Butch, Chopper, and Nick.

"It's going to be okay, youngster," Cookie explained as he walked up and stood next to me. Handing me a cold Pepsi, Cookie took a sip of his Budweiser beer.

"I really missed all you guys, Cookie. I was going crazy back in the States. I missed the action that much," I explained as I took a sip of my soda.

314

Taking a deep breath he let it out slowly. "Yeah, I know what you mean. I wasn't home three days and I was climbing the walls. I couldn't believe it when the Agency called and asked me if I was ready to get back in the game. It was an answer to my prayers. I could never get this place out of my head. The smell and sounds of jets and helicopters flying in and out all day and all night long. Mind if I ask you a sensitive question?" Cookie asked as Butch walked up and stood next to us.

"Not at all, what's up?" I questioned as I turned to face both Butch and Cookie.

"Did you ever get a chance to go see Nick's mom and dad?" Cookie asked solemnly.

"Yes, I did. I got home on Christmas Eve and went to see them the very next day," I explained.

"Was it pretty rough? You know, keeping your promise to Nick and all," Butch asked.

"I was scared when I first got there but his mother was so sweet. His dad was super. When his mom went to put together some snacks, Nick's dad and I had a serious talk. The Honor Guards at the funeral home opened the casket so he could see with his own eyes that his son was really in there," I explained as I looked down at my boots.

"Oh shit," Butch whispered softly.

"Yeah, no kidding. I guess they had cleaned up Nick's body before they shipped it to his family. His dad said that he saw the spine shot and the bullet wound to his temple," I explained sadly.

"Oh boy, I'll bet that was real bad for his father to experience," Cookie commented with a look of concern for me on his face.

"Man, Nick is an identical copy of his dad, just younger. Chopper had sent them a letter," I said.

"Really?" Butch responded with a surprised look on his face.

"Yeah, but it was cool. All he said was we were all together when Nick died and that I got captured because I wouldn't leave him alone. His dad figured it all out after he saw Nick's body. It was a real good visit. You guys should go and see them when this is all over with and we get Chopper back. My visit with them was a real healing for us. You owe it to his mom and dad to go and pay them a visit," I explained as I looked up at my two partners, hoping that they would say yes.

"They probably wouldn't even know us," Butch commented.

"Oh, they'll know you," I answered with a smile. "They have our pictures all over the place. I finally got to see what Carl looked like, his pictures were there too," I said proudly.

"Yeah, maybe I will go and see them," Cookie replied as he looked out through the window of our hooch. "I wonder what Chopper is thinking right now?" he said as an after thought. Turning to look out through the window, I stared at the rain.

"He knows we're coming; he has that satellite locater chip in him," Butch answered.

"He doesn't know if anyone knows that he's been captured. He doesn't know if the chip is working or if it works from inside a cement building. He doesn't know we know or that we're here. He's scared right now and he's probably hurt," I explained with a sick feeling in my stomach as my mind began to recall my dark and lonely days as a POW.

"Danny will fuck 'em up. He'll fight," Butch explained as he stepped up beside me and began to stare out into the rainstorm.

"That's why they'll hurt him. They'll be afraid of his size, so they'll hurt him, to slow him down."

All of a sudden, all we could hear was the sound of rain as it fell outside our window, just a few inches from our faces.

* * * * * * *

I have to say one thing about the Marine Corp, they simply refuse to give up. It was early evening of day nine. Master Gunnery Sergeant Charlie Dane and his men had worked all day yesterday in the pouring rain. The rain had finally stopped around midnight. By then their young private had made three more trips to the Air Force side of the base to use their metal milling machine.

"Come on Marines, you've never failed your country yet. I know you can do this, you leather necked old bastard," I said to myself as I looked at my Russian made watch. I told all our team to wear the watches the CIA had given us to match the Russian uniforms. Everything on the face of the watch was written in Russian. Knowing that, we continued to wear them so we would be use to them by the time we reached Hanoi tomorrow.

"Hey, Sandman," Butch hollered as he, Cookie, and Joe walked up to join me. "How come you didn't come eat?" Butch asked.

"I'm not hungry. I just want this damn thing to start up," I explained.

"Bell called Carla, General Kalashnikov called Major Bui. Bui wasn't there at the time so he left a message, said he would be in Hanoi day after tomorrow to pick up Danny," Joe explained as Gunny Sergeant Burke walked up to join us.

"How's it going?" Tom asked as he opened a can of Budweiser beer and took a sip out of it.

"We're out of time, Gunny. Either way, with or without that bird, we go tomorrow," I explained as I looked over at the large Soviet gunship.

The helicopter was almost as big as a Marine CH-46 Sea Knight Transport helicopter. This gunship was heavily armed with mini-guns and rocket launchers. Its rotor blades were so long and heavy, that they hung limp and bowed downwards toward the ground. After Charlie finished tightening what appeared to be a bolt on the large turbine engine, he climbed down from the top of the helicopter, rolled his cigar stub around in his teeth, and looked over at his long time friend, Gunny Sergeant Burke.

"Told you I'd get it fixed," he said proudly with a smile as he wiped the sweat off his face with an old greasy rag.

"Fixed?" Tom shouted back in a challenging manor. "You old bucket of pig shit, I don't see it running," he responded sarcastically.

"Oh really?" Charlie shouted back. "Dale, start this pile of shit up, will ya?" Charlie asked as he crossed his arms and continued to look at Tom without looking back at the Soviet gunship.

Climbing into the pilot's seat, Dale flipped up some switches and hit the ignition key. When he did my heart began to race with excitement and the hope it would fire up all right. The turbine engine slowly began to turn the long heavy rotor blades at the top of the helicopter. As it did the engine let out a loud back fire through its exhaust and started!

Letting it run for a few minutes Charlie looked at us, smiled, and asked, "Want to take her for a test drive?"

"Hell, yes!" Cookie and Joe both shouted as they walked up to the helicopter and climbed into the pilot and copilot seats; the work crew also climbed in to take their first ride in a real Russian helicopter. Watching the bird lift off, Cookie took flight and began to circle the large air base. It was running perfectly! We were now back in business.

"Thank you, dear God," I whispered as I watched Cookie and Joe fly Charlie and his men around the air base of Bien Hoa. "Now if you could just help us to get Danny out of that prison tomorrow without any of our guys getting hurt, I'd be very grateful," I said as I looked up at the sky above.

Joe, Cookie, and Charlie spent the next two hours double checking both helicopters and topping the fuel tanks off with as much fuel as they could possibly get into each tank. When they were finished we all took showers and gathered in our intelligence office for one last planning session before we left for Hanoi in the morning.

* * * * * * *

We were all to excited to sleep. Our minds raced with excitement, fear, and doubts as we mentally planned out what might go wrong on this rescue mission. The big concern was Danny and how he might react if he recognized any of us. The wrong facial expression from him could possibly blow the entire mission and get us killed.

Opening one of my suitcases, I began to pull out the Hollywood special effect make-up kits and stack them on top of the planning table in our snipers hooch.

"Who's first?" I asked as I looked at my watch. It was 10:01 p.m. and I had a lot of work to do.

It was Cookie that stepped forward first. "I hope you know what you're doing, youngster," Cookie said with a grin as he sat down in the wooden chair.

"How are you going to fix a face that looks as bad as that one?" Butch asked with a chuckle.

"Cookie, Joe, and Tom will be easy. It's your face and mine that they've got pictures of. Ours are going to take some time, brother," I explained to Butch as I held up my brand new set of electric barber clippers and turned on the switch.

"Hey, you didn't say anything about cutting my hair," Cookie began to say as I made my first pass up the back of his head. "The things we do for our friends," Cookie whimpered as he looked up at Tom.

"Oh yeah, high and tight, now you've got the idea, Sandman," Tom said in true Marine fashion with a broad smile.

"Somebody grab me a Pepsi, would you?" I asked as I began to laugh when I saw the expression on Cookie's face; I continued to cut his hair off. "Its gonna be a long night..."

* * * * * * *

The plan was simple, we were going to leave the safety of the Bien Hoa Air Base and head directly to the ocean. The Air Force was going to supply us with four of their attack fighter jets to escort us. We didn't want any American troops thinking we were really Russian. If they did, they might attempt to shoot us down. This was also one of the reasons we were flying straight to the ocean. To fly straight north across country to Hanoi would have every NVA and Viet Cong soldier radioing in to their command headquarters that Russian helicopters were spotted flying through South Vietnam. If that happened the enemy would know we were not really Russians.

Once we got to the ocean we would fly north, being careful to stay as far away from land as possible so enemy troops would not detect us. Once we were past Da Nang we would continue to head north over the water. Once we knew we were north of Hanoi we would then fly west back over land and enter North Vietnam between China and the capital city of Hanoi.

Coming in from the north would make it appear that we had actually came in from Laos or China, which would be the natural route General Kalashnikov would take.

Five minutes before take off we got the satellite transmission from the War Room at the Pentagon. It was Carla Silverman.

"Kalashnikov tried to take off twenty minutes ago," Major Bell explained as he hung up the telephone and looked over at all of us who were standing in the intelligence office with him. "Damn, looking at you men sends a chill up my spine. You look just like Russians and NVA commanders. I know you men, but I can't tell who's who," Bell explained as he took a sip of his coffee.

"What about Kalashnikov, sir?" Cookie asked in perfect Russian with a serious, mean, Russian look on his face.

"Do that again you Commie bastard and I'll shoot you," Bell responded with a smile as he put his right-hand on the butt of his holstered Colt Army issued automatic pistol.

"Let me rephrase that, sir," Cookie answered quickly with a chuckle. "What about Kalashnikov, sir?"

"There's a Delta Force team that is in Russia, they've been watching the General for quite some time now. They anticipated he might be anxious to go and pick up Danny, so they went in several nights ago and tampered with the General's gunship. Their actions were actually meant to buy you boys some time, but we're out of time now, gentlemen. They'll have that gunship fixed by tomorrow. If we don't get Chopper out of that prison today, we stand a damn good chance of losing our brother, forever," Major Bell explained as he sat back down behind his desk, and looked over at his long time partner and friend, Major Mosier.

"Sandman, its your plan and you're team leader, how do we play this hand out?" Major Mosier asked with an intense look on his face.

"Did Boris call Major Bui today to let him know that his helicopter is busted?" I asked.

"No, not yet. Carla doesn't think he'll call now until tomorrow morning," Bell answered.

"We wait," I explained as I sat down and rubbed my new looking face gently with my left hand.

"What?" Alan from Team Four said sharply with a surprised look on his face. "You don't have time to wait! I realize you guys are the legendary Team One, but would you please explain your logic about waiting to me, so I'll understand?" Alan asked as he looked over at his teammates with a confused look on his face.

"You're out of line, Alan," his teammate Ron told him. "That's the Sandman you're talking too. He's also team leader on this mission. We never question our team leader. Did you forget that lesson during Seal team training?" Ron asked as he kept his loyalty true to the code.

"Its okay, Ron," I said quickly as I looked over at Cookie who nodded his head in agreement. "Master Chief Mareno taught me some very valuable lessons when I trained with the Seals to become a Black Operations Sniper. But when I got home and was recruited by the Agency to do wet work, I went to a place called the Farm. It's where they train you to become a spy. They taught me some real eye opening stuff while I was there. We don't know if Boris is going to call Bui or not. If we're about to land in the Bad Lands and he makes that call to Bui, then I just got us killed," I explained as I sat forward and looked down at my feet.

"I didn't follow my instincts once when we were in Cambodia searching for a Marine pilot named Captain David B. Williams. Because I didn't follow my instincts we lost our brother Nick. I'm not making that mistake ever again. I love Danny with all my heart. If we lose him and they take him to Russia, I'll go after him. But I will not endanger your lives or jeopardize this mission for any reason unnecessarily.

We'll leave at noon, by the time we land in Hanoi we'll have two things going for us. We'll know that Boris hasn't called Bui yet to let him know he's coming, and it will be getting dark. Bui should have already gone home. If not, he'll be tired and caught by surprise with our popping in on him unexpectedly. I don't speak Russian or Vietnamese. Cookie and Tom's rank and uniforms show that Cookie is a General with the regular Russian Army and Tom is a KGB Colonel. Tom, you and Cooke will do all of the talking once we land.

My uniform shows that I am a KGB Brigadier General, Joe and Butch will pose as my bodyguards. My rank will make me arrogant so I won't have to talk to them. If they should speak to me, Cookie, Tom, or Joe will cut them off. See this scar that I put across my throat at the esophagus?" I explained as I raised my chin and pulled down my thin nylon scarf. "If they try to talk to me tell them that I had surgery on my throat and I am here strictly to make sure the American Intelligence Sniper doesn't get away." Reaching into my pocket I pulled out my hand size stungun and pressed the trigger.

"Holy shit!" Butch said as he backed away a bit from me.

"I might have to use this on Chopper, so be prepared for it if I do. Now listen closely, if I do shock him with this, I want everyone to start laughing. Find humor in it. Then I want one of you to explain that you're glad you're not the American, because I love to use electricity on my prisoners just before I begin to skin them and pack the wounds with salt. That should scare them.

We're not going there to show off, fella's. We need to get in and out as quickly as possible. One last thing, remember your training, always expect the unexpected, and everything is subject to change at any given moment. If it does, adjust, and move forward, don't back up," I explained.

"Who flies with who?" Joe asked.

"Joe, you're going to fly the Russian Mi-17 helicopter. You'll take Butch, Mr. Twe, and Johnny with you. Cookie will fly the big gunship. Tom, you, and Mr. Doc will fly us in that one," I explained as I reached into my pocket, and pulled out my tiny bottle of Methadrine. Placing a drop under my tongue, I put the tiny vial back into my pocket and pulled out the small plastic medicine bottle Carla had given me. Taking out a glass capsule I passed the bottle to Cookie and picked up the roll of heat duct tape that was sitting on the corner of Major Bell's desk. Tearing a piece of the duct tape off I passed the roll to Cookie and taped the glass capsule to my left wrist.

"One way or the other, we get Danny out of there or we all die trying," I explained as I looked over at my mentor and friend Cookie.

"Brothers and friends, throughout life and into death, till the very end," I whispered.

"Till the end, hoo yah!!!!" they all shouted out loud.

* * * * * * *

We left the Bien Hoa Air Base at 1:15 p.m. and headed straight to the coast surrounded by our Air Force fighter jet escort. Once we reached the ocean our escort dropped off and we were on our own.

The combination of fear, excitement and adrenaline surged its way through every pore of our bodies as I placed two drops of Methadrine under my tongue and handed the tiny vial to Cookie, who was piloting the craft.

The last time this kind of mission was ever attempted was during World War II. This was unconventional warfare at its best. It was also crazy, insane, stupid, and suicidal, which is why it actually had a chance of working.

We were running on radio silence. Cookie and Joe as pilots did have direct contact, via our Seal team radio system, with both Major's Bell and Mosier. An open line between Bell and Mosier was established with Carla and Neil at the Pentagon at Noon. It would stay open via satellite until this mission was over. Everything was going fine, we had past the border of North and South Vietnam just north of Da Nang. Charlie and his men had done a great job fixing this huge gunship.

"About another twenty minutes and we'll bank west and head inland. We're deep in Indian territory now, boys," Cookie explained as I reached over and felt my left wrist to make sure that my cyanide capsule was still there. The memories of being a POW still haunted me and were vivid enough to remind me that I would rather be dead than face being a POW again.

Looking at my watch it was 4:34 p.m. when Cookie broke radio silence and began talking quickly into the mouthpiece of his headset.

"Oh no," Gunny Sergeant Burke said in English.

"What' s wrong, Gunny?" I asked when I saw the worried look on Cookie and Tom's face.

"Joe's losing oil pressure in the Mi-17. Butch and Johnny are trying to stabilize it," Tom explained as he listened to Cookie as he talked to Joe.

"Tell them to abort, abort now!" I shouted as I grabbed Cookie by his right shoulder to get his attention.

Cookie turned to look at me and asked, "You sure?"

"Tell them to try to get it back to Da Nang and land it. If not, mayday an emergency distress call and bail out into the water. They abort now, damnit. They're no good to us dead and dead is what they'll be if that bird drops out of the sky this far north. Tell them to turn it around now. Tell them we're going in alone!" I shouted as I looked out through the side window of our gunship and saw a hint of smoke as it began to come out of the engine exhaust system of Joe's helicopter.

Cookie quickly gave Joe the order to abort the mission and turn his craft around. As he did I saw Agent Joe Knight look at me and mouth the words, "Good luck," as he banked his helicopter to the right and broke away from us. Cookie then radioed Major Bell and told him I had ordered Joe to abort due to mechanical failure of his aircraft and we were going in to get Danny on our own. As he finished talking to Major Bell, Cookie banked left. "We're going in," was all he said.

"Good call, Sandman," Tom said as he patted me on the shoulder. "You sure you ain't a Marine?" he asked with a smile on his face.

"Looks like we're on our own, Gunny," I said as I looked at Mr. Doc. "I'm sorry, Doc, its just the four of us now," I explained.

"No problem. We four are to much for all of them," Mr. Doc explained with a proud look on his face as he patted his Israeli made Uzi machine gun.

Smiling I looked back over at Tom. "I think Doc's the Marine, Tom," I explained as I tried to control my inner emotions. I was so very proud to call these men my friends.

We had lost half our team and half our strength. Deep down inside I knew it was the right call; Joe, Butch, Johnny, and Mr. Twe were no good to us in a broken bird. My Seal team instructor was absolutely right. "Everything is subject to change at any given moment," and it just did, we were now on our own.

Looking out through the windshield and side window of our helicopter I saw the plush green canopy of treetops and squared rice paddy fields as we flew over top of them. Vietnam was a beautiful country. Had I been the President of the United States, I would have nuked North Vietnam right away. In doing so it would have saved everyone a lot of time and trouble in the long run. Adjusting the radio frequency on the Russian radio to the numbers Neil had given us, Cookie began to speak Russian to someone at the prison in Hanoi. We had caught them off guard. The North Vietnamese Captain, who was now in command of the second shift, would meet us at the landing pad just off from the prison. With a little luck he wouldn't call Major Bui. Flying into the capital city of North Vietnam we saw the Hanoi Hilton right away. It was right in the middle of the city. Cars and motorcycles were driving all over. To look at it you would never know there was a war going on in this country this far north.

"Damn, why don't they send in some B-52 bombers and blow the shit out of this place?" Tom asked as Cookie began to set our helicopter down on the landing pad.

"Mr. Doc, you go first. They're not expecting to see you. Its show time, fella's," I said as Cookie switched off the engine of our helicopter.

The North Vietnamese Captain was waiting for us as promised. He was in full uniform and had four armed men standing with him all of whom were also wearing North Vietnamese uniforms and carrying AK-47 assault rifles.

As Tom pulled open the side door of our helicopter, my mind flashed back to Major Dinh and Colonel Ky and the POW camp where I was held in Cambodia.

Just as Doc started to exit the helicopter, I grabbed him by the arm, "Doc, leave the Uzi in the helicopter," I said.

"Why?" he questioned.

"You're an NVA General. Officers carry pistols not automatic weapons. Leave it, you've still got your .9mm automatic pistol," I explained quickly.

Leaving the Uzi behind, we all stepped off the helicopter. Doc was great. He immediately began to chew out Captain Min. General Doc was mad because Captain Min had not brought the American prisoner with him. It would be dark soon and we did not want to have to fly at night. Doc told him that we, the Russian's, had a jet plane waiting for us in China to transport the American to Russia.

Captain Min was no longer smiling as he began to yell at the men he had brought with him, calling them incompetent for not bringing the prisoner as he had told them too. Of course he had never told them to bring the prisoner, but it was his way of shifting the blame to someone else so Doc would stop yelling at him. Doc, posing as a North Vietnamese General had them scared. Cookie then spoke to Captain Min in Vietnamese, "Take us to the prisoner, Tywe. We will bring him out, I want my Comrade General Mulovich to see him," he explained as he turned to me and spoke to me in Russian. Tywe is Vietnamese for Captain.

Acting as if I were about to speak, I cleared my throat and removed the silk scarf that I had around my neck. Rubbing the scar that I had placed across my throat, I started to speak. Cookie raised his hand to stop me and explained to Captain Min that an American POW had stabbed me in the throat when I had gone to Cambodia to interrogate him. He then told Captain Min that the American prisoner was DuK'ich. The sniper that escaped two and a half years ago. The sniper that was the teammate to the sniper that Captain Min was now holding in his prison. DuK'ich is Vietnamese for sniper.

"Ahhh," Captain Min replied as a wide smile spread across his face. Saying something to his guards we climbed into the jeeps and drove the short distance to the Hanoi Hilton. Walking through the front gates of the prison, we went directly to the cellblock where Chopper was being held. As Captain Min opened the large steel door, a rancid smell escaped into the outside fresh air. As we stepped inside we tried to maintain our composer.

Walking down the long, poorly lit hallway we stopped to look into each steel door that secured the cells. The building was made of cement and steel. It had a foul smell of urine, mold, mildew, dirt, blood, and human feces. The guards inside were Viet Cong. They didn't wear NVA uniforms. Instead they wore their black silk pajamas and sandals.

Cookie had made a good call by telling Captain Min we wanted to go in to see the American prisoner. It gave us a chance to check the cells to see if any other Americans were being held in this cellblock. So far, we found none, only Vietnamese prisoners.

Just as we reached the cell where Chopper was being held, Captain Min ordered one of the guards to unlock the thick steel door. As he did, we heard a commotion and what sounded to me like two Vietnamese arguing with each other. Turning to look down the long hallway I saw six uniformed NVA soldiers walking toward us. Four were carrying fully loaded AK-47 assault rifles; one carried a hand full of papers. It was the shorter mean looking fella, which caught my attention. He was smoking the butt of a Vietnamese made cigarette. In his right hand he carried a pair of thick leather gloves. As he walked toward us he was slapping them angrily into the palm of his left hand. There was no doubt, it was Major Bui and he was pissed.

Walking directly up to us, Major Bui took a good look at Tom, Cookie, and I, as he began to speak to Captain Min. He then turned his attention to Mr. Doc, our South Vietnamese ranger friend posing as a high-ranking NVA General. Mr. Doc tongue lashed Major Bui in their own language.

As they argued, I couldn't help but notice that the one NVA guard who came in with Major Bui, looked awfully familiar. It took a moment and then I remembered him and that rat looking smile he had on his face. He was the soldier that liked to urinate on me when I was a POW in Cambodia. He was that piece of shit guard that brutalized the American prisoners along with Major Dinh at the POW camp.

If Captain Min mentioned I had been stabbed in the throat at that camp, this fish head and rice eating piece of shit would know that had never happened. It was Gunny Sergeant Burke that stepped in and began to speak to Major Bui, the commandant of the prison.

Reaching into my pocket, I pulled out a pack of Lucky Strike cigarettes and tapped it against the palm of my left hand. As I did, I glanced down at the bottom of the pack to make sure it didn't have a small red dot. The red dot would indicate it was one of the packs I had our CIA lab boys, lace with the deadly poison I had used to kill Morimoto Soba. Seeing it was a good pack, I opened it, and pulled out a cigarette. Placing it in my mouth I pulled out my silver Zippo lighter.

Bui was upset at the fact he hadn't been told we were coming a day early. He also wanted to know why General Kalashnikov wasn't with us. Tom explained to the Major that Boris was taken back into the hospital because of some minor bleeding in his stomach, the general asked me to come in his place, as a show of respect to Major Bui. As Tom explained this, I tapped Major Bui on the shoulder and offered him an American made cigarette. Seeing the American brand name, Bui quickly accepted it. Rolling my thumb across the striker on the lighter, I held it out for the Major to light his cigarette. Bui was starting to calm down as I then lit my cigarette and took a puff on it. Handing the pack to Tom, I nodded with my head for him to pass a cigarette to the captain and all of the guards. As Tom passed the pack of cigarettes around, he, Cookie, and Doc continued to talk to both Major Bui and Captain Min.

Stepping up to the steel door of Chopper's cell, I reached up and pulled the sliding metal plate used as a cover for the small square opening in the door to the left. It was a sickening smell that filled my nasal passage. It made me feel nauseated and angry.

Looking in through the open window slot, I saw my brother and friend, Chopper. He was sitting on the cement floor and was covered with sweat and dirt. All he had on was a pair of striped, worn out, prison pants. He had no shoes or shirt. He was bare footed and the bottom of his feet were badly bruised and bleeding. He had been severely beaten and tortured. His ankles were chained together with a short chain. His hands were shackled together behind his back. His hair had grown out longer than when I had seen him last and was all matted down tight against his head, it was soiled with blood and dirt.

Chopper's left eye was swollen almost shut and he was breathing heavily. Every muscle in his large body was bulging and rippled as he stared back at me from where he was sitting. Choppers eyes were filled with rage and hate. He was mad, real mad, and even with his hands and feet chained together, he was more dangerous than ever, especially now.

Pulling the stungun out of my pocket I held it up next to my face and looked at it. Pressing the trigger twice, its angry blue electrical current, danced across the two metal spikes at its front. Both the sight and sound of the crackling surge of fiery electricity made Major Bui and his men step backwards in awe.

Looking at Major Bui, I smiled. Cookie told the Major that it was going to be a long and painful flight for the American. They all loved it and laughed as the Major ordered his man to unlock and open the door to Chopper's cell.

Standing outside the cell door with my back up against the wall I listened, as Cookie and Tom stepped inside followed by Major Bui and Captain Min.

"Russians, I should have known it," Chopper said in an angry tone of voice. It was working Danny didn't recognize Cookie or Tom.

"You are, this man, Sergeant Danny McBride, you are the sniper from American Intelligence Division at Bien Hoa Air Base, yes?" Cookie asked as he held up the 8x10 photograph Major Bui had brought with him.

"Fuck you, you Vodka drinking, communist piece of shit," Chopper snapped back as he tried to kick Cookie with his chained feet.

"So, you wish to test your strength, yes?" Cookie asked in broken English.

"Take these chains off of me, boy, and I'll fuck you so hard that your mama's asshole will bleed!" Chopper snapped back as both Tom and Cookie grabbed him by the chains binding his feet together.

"We have a surprise for you, nigger!" Tom explained as they began to drag Danny out of the cell and into the dimly lit hallway.

"You will come to Russia with us. There, we will execute you for war crimes. But first, I want you to meet KGB General Mulovich. He has a new toy he wants to show you," Tom explained in Vietnamese so the Major and his men would understand what he was saying. As big as Tom and Cookie were, they were struggling as they pulled Chopper out of his cell.

As he fought, I could hear him wheezing and coughing. "You couldn't break my little brother, motherfuckers. You'll never break me either," Chopper shouted.

"Tomorrow you will die by public hanging," Cookie explained.

"My team will hunt you down. They'll avenge me," Danny countered as they pulled him out into the hallway.

Turning quickly, I knelt down and pressed the spikes of my stungun into Chopper's stomach. As I pulled the trigger I noticed that he was coughing up blood. He was hurt and bleeding internally. The snap of electricity jolted Chopper so hard his back bowed. At the count of seven I released the trigger and Chopper's tense muscle structure relaxed. He was out cold. As we had planned, Tom, Cookie, and Mr. Doc all began to laugh out loud, so did Major Bui and his men. My heart sank in my chest. I had just hurt my best friend but I had no choice. He was struggling so much it would have taken us forever to get him out of the prison; and forever is time we didn't have.

Two of the guards grabbed a cheaply made gurney and with the help of their friends, they rolled Chopper's limp body onto it. It took six of the Vietnamese guards to carry Chopper's big-framed body out through the camp and out the front door. Standing back we watched as the guards secured the gurney across the backseat of one of the jeeps. Chopper was starting to come out of being stunned. His head was turned to the side as he began to moan and cough up more blood.

Tom and Cookie thanked Major Bui as I leaned over and whispered into Mr. Doc's ear. Looking at me with a surprised look on his face, Mr. Doc smiled, and walked over to Major Bui, As Doc began to talk to Bui, I reached into my shirt pocket and pulled out a brand new pack of Lucky Strike cigarettes. Looking at the bottom of the pack I kept my facial expression calm and cold as my heart began to race with excitement. It had a red dot on the bottom of the pack, it was deadly.

Climbing into three of the jeeps we drove back to our Soviet gunship as Major Bui rushed back into the prison. It was Captain Min and his men that drove us the two hundred yards to the helicopter landing pad.

Seeing the huge Russian gunship, Chopper who had now regained full consciousness, was madder than a full-size bull that had just had its nuts cut off. As he began to kick and fight the best he could, the cheaply made gurney snapped in two at the center.

Moving fast I stuck the stungun in Chopper's neck as he stared up into my eyes and spit in my face.

327

"I'm going to kill you, motherfucker," he shouted as I gave him another seven-second stun, which caused him to black out again.

It was now dark outside as we carried Chopper to our helicopter and tossed his limp body into the back. Seeing Major Bui drive up in his jeep, with the guard that always urinated on me when I was a POW, brought a smile to my heart. Bui was carrying with him a freshly pressed military uniform that he had gone to get out of his office.

Thanking Captain Min and his men for a job well done, Cookie and Tom climbed into the pilot and copilots seat of the helicopter and fired up the big Soviet engine. As the big rotor blade began to turn I handed one pack of the red dot Lucky Strike cigarettes to Captain Min and the other unopened red dot pack of cigarettes to the guard that always urinated on me and abused the American prisoners in the POW camp that I had been held in.

Shaking their hands, Doc thanked them, and then told Captain Min he was placing him in charge of the prison camp for the next few days. He explained that Major Bui was flying back to Russia with us to receive an award from the President of the motherland for his excellent work on capturing and securing the American Intelligence prisoner. Major Bui was all smiles as he climbed into our helicopter and buckled himself into the seat next to Mr. Doc.

Climbing into the Russian built Soviet gunship, I slid the side door shut behind me and locked it. Sitting down next to Major Bui, I looked down at Chopper who was out cold and seriously injured. Turning my head I smiled as I saw both Captain Min and the NVA soldier I had promised to one day kill, opening their packs of poisoned cigarettes. As we began to power up and lift into the air I spoke in English for the first time.

"Make a wide sweep around the area and come back by this spot as we head out Cookie, I need to see something," I said as Doc pulled his .9mm Chinese made automatic pistol out of his holster and placed it at the left side of Major Bui's head. As he did, Doc told him in Vietnamese that he was now a prisoner of war. The look on Major Bui's face was worth all the gold in the world. Pulling Major Bui's pistol out of his holster I handed the gun to Tom as Cookie spoke.

"We're coming back around, youngster," he said as I looked out through the side window of the helicopter.

The Vietnamese soldier that I hated and one of his friends were already laying on the ground dead. Captain Min was holding his throat and had just dropped to his knees as we flew past.

"I told you I'd kill you, you rotten son of a bitch," I said coldly. "Get us out of here, Cookie. Tom, give me the bolt cutters from under your seat, then tie Major Bui up. Use the duct tape," I said quickly as Marine

Gunny Sergeant Tom Burke handed me the bolt cutters and grabbed the roll of duct tape.

Using the large set of bolt cutters, that Master Gunnery Sergeant Dane recommended we take with us, I cut the chains loose from Chopper's hands and feet. Tossing the bolt cutters and chains off to the side I quickly pulled Danny's upper body into my lap as he began to regain consciousness once again.

"My brothers will come, they'll avenge me, they'll come," he mumbled as I hugged him in my arms.

"We're here, big brother, we got you," I whispered into Chopper's ear as he began to cough up clots of blood. As he did, our teammate and brother passed out again. "Break radio silence, Cookie. Use the Seal team satellite set and tell Bell we've got him. Tell them to contact China Beach Hospital in Da Nang and let 'em know we're coming in with a wounded American. Tell him to get some Cobra gunships out in our direction to escort us in so our own troops don't shoot us down," I shouted out loud as Tom bound Major Bui's hands and feet together and then came to my aide with Mr. Doc.

Breaking radio silence, Cookie called Major's Bell and Mosier and relayed the message. Help was on its way and we weren't far away from China Beach Hospital. The question was, would we get there in time to save our friend's life.

* * * * * * *

Four army Cobra gunship helicopters were waiting for us halfway between Hanoi's eastern coast and Da Nang. To our surprise, so were two Phantom II Marine fighter jets to ensure our safe passage.

China Beach Medical Trauma Care Hospital in Da Nang hadn't changed much at all since I was treated here some two and a half years ago. Only the faces were different. Landing on the helicopter pad with the big red cross on it, we found a medical trauma team standing by and waiting for us to arrive. Once they saw Danny and the clots of blood he was coughing up, they knew his condition was a lot worst than even we had imagined. The trauma surgeon and his medical team quickly rushed Danny inside. We were not allowed to go in for reasons of sterile conditions, so we walked out to the beach where the other Mi-17 Russian helicopter had landed. Seeing Joe, Butch, Mr. Twe, and Johnny, we all smiled and yelled, "Hoo yah!" for a mission we once again had completed successfully.

Upon landing, Danny was taken inside, Army military policemen picked up Major Bui to secure him until the military intelligence interrogators arrived to pick him up. Because he was the commanding officer of the

Hanoi Hilton prison, he was in for a real surprise. He would have a lot
to answer for. We didn't take kindly to the inhumane treatment of our
prisoners.

Walking onto the beach we all sat down in the dark and waited for
Major's Bell, Mosier, and the men of team four to arrive.

"I can't believe we actually pulled if off," Gunny Sergeant Burke said
as he rubbed his face vigorously with both hands.

"They weren't expecting it," Cookie explained. "Mr. Doc, that was a
brilliant idea. Fella's, Mr. Doc invited Major Bui to come with us so he
could receive an award from the President of Russia," Cookie explained to
Joe and his team who didn't make it in.

"No shit, outstanding Mr. Doc," Joe said as he shook Doc's hand.
"That's fast thinking, brother."

"No, no, I no do. Mr. Sandman, tell me. He whisper in my ear and
tell me how to do," Mr. Doc explained in broken English as he smiled and
looked over at me.

"Damn, youngster," Cookie said with a smile as he shook his head
from side to side.

"Yeah, plus he killed Captain Min and at least three of his guards on
the way out the door," Tom added. "There's no doubt about it, son, you're
a Marine," he said proudly.

"The cigarettes?" Butch asked with a curious look on his face.

"Yeah, they love American cigarettes. Don't they know smoking will
kill ya?" I asked with a straight look on my face.

"If they didn't, they do now," Johnny answered. As he did everyone
became very quiet. Our thoughts were of Chopper, our brother, and dear
friend.

"Think Chopper will make it?" Butch asked as he looked over at me.

"I hope so," I answered in a whispered voice. I felt as though someone
had torn my guts out. I felt real bad that I had to use my stungun on
Chopper, not once, but twice, just to calm him down.

"As hurt as he was, that boy continued to fight. But I'll tell you this,
I've seen and experienced a lot over here, but I've never been so proud of
a man," Tom told us.

"Why's that, Tom, what did Chopper do?" Joe questioned.

"He spit right in the Sandman's face and continued to tell us his
teammates would hunt us down and kill us. He said, 'My brothers will
avenge me!'" Tom explained as he picked up a hand full of sand and
sprinkled it back through his fingers. "That's a special kind of bond. I wish
I had a bond with men that loved each other like that. You boy's came back
from the States just to rescue or die with your brother. There's no greater

love or loyalty than that," Gunny Sergeant Burke explained as he looked up and stared out at the ocean that was in front of us.

"We would have done the same for you, Tom," I explained.

"Hell, I'm with the Marine Corp, Sandman," Tom replied.

"When I was captured you broke all of the rules, Gunny. You came looking for me. You disobeyed direct orders from your superior officers and risked a court marital to go deep into Cambodia looking for me. Why did you do that, Tom?" I asked as I looked over at Tom waiting for an answer.

"I respected you boys. You were young and had more guts, more heart, and more love for your brother Americans than I had ever seen before. I respect that, that's why," Tom explained.

"You may not have known it, Gunny. Maybe we should have told you this before, but we adopted you as part of our family along time ago. Why? Because you've got more guts and love for God and country than we do. That, and you jumped in to look for one of us when you didn't have too. Hell why do you think that Bell and Mosier made a personal request that the Marine Division loan you out to us for this mission? He could have used anyone of those new men from Team Four. They didn't, Tom. They stayed true to our team, to Team One, and called all of us in personally. That's why you're here, brother. Because like it or not, you're part of Team One!" Cookie explained proudly as we all yelled, "Hoo yah!"

"Well, I'll be damn, I thought they just didn't want to risk any of their boys," Tom explained with a surprised look on his face.

"They did risk their boys, Tom. You just didn't know you were one of their boys, that's all," Butch explained with a chuckle as he slapped Tom on the shoulder.

"Yeah, welcome to the family, brother," Johnny added. As he did, our old Black Operation's helicopter landed off to our left on the beach.

It took Mosier and Bell a few minutes to reach us. The look of concern on their faces said it all.

"How bad is he?" Bell asked.

"It's bad, sir, can you go in and find out how he is for us? They won't let us in," I explained.

Without saying another word they both ran across the beach and went into the main emergency entrance of the hospital. A few minutes later a Navy helicopter landed on the landing pad.

Opening the side doors of the Navy's medical helicopter, it took two more minutes, then they wheeled Danny out on a hospital gurney, put him in the Navy bird and flew him away into the darkness of the night. Looking across the sandy beach, we saw the hospital surgeon as he stood out in front of the emergency entrance and talked to both Major's Bell and

Mosier. Our hearts sunk with a dull sick feeling as we waited in the dark to find out what was going on with our brother. As we waited Ron, Bob, Glen, and Alan walked up and stood beside us.

"That can't be a good sign," Bob said in a low voice as Bell and Mosier walked toward us, both men looked beyond upset.

"Where's Major Bui?" Bell asked in an angry voice.

"MP's are holding him, sir. What going on with Danny?" Cookie asked.

I'd seen that look in Bell's eyes before on several occasions when he was my commanding officer. He wanted revenge and he wanted it now!

"They shaved up bamboo. They powder it up. Then just before they fed Danny, they mix it in with the rice," Bell explained then he simply couldn't compose himself any longer.

"Motherfucker! I'm going to cut that bastard's liver out of his fucking chest and shove it down his cock-sucking throat. I'm going to kill that communist cocksucker with my own two hands!" Major Bell shouted out at the top of his lungs into the darkness of the night.

"How bad is it, sir?" Cookie questioned as he turned to Major Mosier, realizing that Major Bell was beyond talking to.

"You eat rice. You don't taste the bamboo at all. But once you drink some water those tiny powdered pieces of bamboo begin to swell up. It's like having swallowed a thousand tiny pins. It literally tears your guts out. The doctor said they had to have fed it to him sometime today. Otherwise he would have been screaming or dead by now. They flew him to the Navy hospital ship, the USS Repose, for help. They've seen it before, the Navy doctors have a way to dissolve the bamboo and flush it out of the stomach and digestive track, if they catch it early enough. This is a very slow and painful way to die," Mosier explained.

Walking up to me, Major Bell stood a foot away from my face and asked, "I need the Sandman, is he still around?"

Placing two drops of Methadrine under my tongue, I put the tiny glass vial of liquid speed into my shirt pocket. "Oh yeah, the Sandman is always close by," I answered calmly.

* * * * * * *

Even though we needed the information that was stored away in Major Bui's head, our desire to torture him seemed more important. Taking Major Bui with us, we all flew back to our restricted area at the Bien Hoa Airbase. Once there and secure, where no one could interfere with us, we explained to Major Bui that we knew about what he had done to our brother and friend Danny, with the bamboo.

332

Bui denied it, telling Mr. Doc and Mr. Twe that kind of mistreatment of a prisoner was against the Geneva Convention. After two three-second jolts of electrical shock from my stungun, Major Bui decided to clear his conscience and confess to us that he had given the order to poison Danny in such a fashion. He then spent the next two days telling us everything he knew about the locations of prison camps where American and South Vietnamese prisoners were being held. Names of American prisoners he had personally talked to, some of which he had also killed, and then he gave us all the telephone numbers and radio frequency codes he possessed of all of his high ranking NVA friends, to include his Chinese and Russian friends.

In exchange for all this information Mr. Twe and Mr. Doc stayed true to their promise they would not kill him. I however, had never made that promise. I did however, promise both Major's Bell and Mosier and Ms. Silverman that I would make Major Bui scream so loud that Carla would hear him all the way at the Pentagon.

Taking Major Bui into our sandbagged bunker we stripped him completely naked and tied him securely to a sturdy piece of flat wood, four-feet wide and six-feet long. He was facing up looking at us as I added some warm, coffee temperature water to a glass bowl filled with rock salt.

Major Bell explained to the men of Black Op's Team Four that under the CIA's Phoenix Project we were allowed to use any means of torture we deemed fit, to get the information we needed from a prisoner during this war. Filling my syringe with the pure salt solution I injected the whole syringe full of liquid salt into the muscle tissue of Major Bui's left hip. I then did the same to his right hip and my third syringe, full of salt, was injected directly into his penis. His screams were deafening.

Placing a piece of duct tape over his mouth to quiet his screaming, we went into our snipers hooch to have a cold drink. Two hours later I returned and injected Bui in his testicles and lower stomach. This injection process continued for the first twenty-four hours of Major Bui's stay with us.

It was noon of day two when I went into the bunker to check on our prisoner. Seeing me, Major Bui became paranoid. His body was covered with sweat and trembled almost to the point of being out of control. Each spot I had injected with liquid rock salt was swollen red.

"Mr. Doc, tell Major Bui I have a little surprise for him," I explained calmly. Lifting up the board at his feet, I placed two cement bricks under it and then set it back down. His feet and body were now at a higher angle than his head.

Doc told Major Bui what I had said just as Butch walked into the bunker with the small saucepan and turkey baster. Everyone else was already in the bunker waiting to see what I was going to do next.

"Gentlemen, this sauce pan has a bottle of Coke Cola in it. I had Butch put it on the stove and heat it up until it began to boil," I explained as I put the tip of the turkey baster into it, pressed on the rubber end, and released the pressure on the rubber bulb which filled the basting tube with the boiling hot, sugar filled, cola.

Major Bui became frantic and tried to fight but it was useless. We had him secured to the board with duct tape and nylon rope. He wasn't going anywhere. Sticking the tip of the turkey baster into his left nostril I pushed it in snuggly and filled his nasal cavity with the boiling Coke Cola. As I did the hot sugary liquid ran all the way into his sinus membrane cavity.

He couldn't scream or breath through his mouth because I had it taped closed. His only option, if he wanted to breathe, was to suck it all in. His pain, was now far more than even he could tolerate. The boiling hot syrupy liquid felt like hot lava as it burned and stuck itself to the inside of his sinus passage. Filling the turkey baster one more time, I pushed it up into his right nostril and repeated the process. His eyes were bulging as he fought and tried to scream.

"Tell him we'll be back in four hours to do this again, would you, Mr. Doc?" I asked as Doc delivered our message.

On day two, I used this method of torture on the Major a total of three times. Seeing he was about to go into shock I gave him an injection of morphine to prevent him from going into a coma.

On day three, we stood Major Bui in an upright position while we kept him secured to the board. We fed him meat, potatoes, and lots and lots of water. Even though he didn't want to drink anymore we made it very clear if he didn't, we would go back to the hot Cola in the nose treatment. So, he continued to drink even more water.

When I was sure Major Bui could ingest no more water, I pulled a long piece of nylon string out of my pants pocket, wrapped it around the shaft of his penis and tied it off tightly. When I did he cried out in pain and begged both Doc and Mr. Twe for mercy.

"You're never gonna pee again, motherfucker!" I said as I got real close to Major Bui's face and looked deep into his eyes. As I did, his eyes rolled up into his head and he passed out.

On day four we walked back into the bunker to check on our prisoner. His breathing was heavy and labored. He had become dysfunctional. The pain in his body, nasal passage, and now kidney's and bladder had become so excruciating that he simply couldn't take it any more. He was falling into a coma.

"How long do you think he'll last?" Major Bell asked.

"He'll be dead in less than thirty-six hours. He can't pee. Because of that his urine will poison his own body. It happens to old people sometimes. They get so old they can't pee or shit anymore. Their body becomes toxic and they die a painful death. That's what is happening to Major Bui," I explained calmly.

"Fuck him!" Gunny Sergeant Burke said coldly.

"When he dies just fly him out over the jungles and slide him, board and all, out of our helicopter. It will give the animals something to nibble on," I explained as Major Mosier walked into the bunker with a smile on his face.

"It's a wonderful thing to see isn't it, sir?" Butch asked as he looked over at Major Bui.

"Yes, it is, but that's not why I'm smiling. I just got a call from Naval Intelligence. They've got Danny stabilized. In two days they're going to fly him to Japan. He'll be in the hospital there for a while but they believe he will have a complete recovery. They said he's awake and talking to everyone and he's hungry. The doctors said that's a real good sign the damage to his stomach and intestine is minimal and should heal all by itself, but they still want to send him to Japan so they can take a closer look at him," Mosier explained smiling.

"Well, that's the best news I've heard all month," Bell added with a wide smile.

"What's the deal with our guest?" Mosier asked as he nodded his head in the direction of Major Bui.

"He's not happy with the treatment he has been getting here. Just before he passed out he told Mr. Twe that we were violating the Geneva Convention and his rights to humane treatment," Gunny Sergeant Burke explained.

"Imagine that," Mosier replied. "When the shoe is on the other foot he doesn't like it. Boy, his face is a mess."

"His nose and nasal passages are all burned inside from the hot Coca Cola," Johnny explained.

"Sandman, where did you learn that nasty little trick?" Mosier asked.

"Master Chief Mareno, Navy Seals. He taught me a bunch of neat stuff like that, sir," I replied.

"Well, lets call the Pentagon and see about getting you men back to the States," Mosier explained.

"Hell, this news about Danny has made me hungry. I'm buying, anyone want to join me?" Cookie asked with a big grin on his face.

"Yeah, I could eat. Do they still serve rat meat and white rice at your old chow hall?" I asked with a serious look on my face as I looked over at Major Mosier.

"And to think I missed you," Mosier replied as he put his arm around my shoulder and walked me out of the bunker.

We spent the next week teaching our brothers from Team Four some of our old tricks. Now that we were all back in country, we didn't want to leave Mosier or Bell behind. Carla, however, wanted us back in the United States. More and more information was coming in from the Klaus Gruber and Pavel Malenkov computer discs.

Saying goodbye to our friends we boarded a United Airlines flight and headed back home. With us on the flight, were a bunch of American soldiers who had finished their tour of duty and were headed home to their families and loved ones. They made it out alive and so did our brother and teammate Danny.

"That's what its all about," I thought to myself as I looked through the window of our airliner. "Survival, no matter what the cost. Freedom isn't free, its paid for with the blood of young Americans like Danny and the young men on this plane. Damn, I'm proud to be a part of all of this."

Chapter Twenty-One
Dull Sword

Upon arriving home from Vietnam, Cookie, Joe, Butch, and I spent most of the day at the Pentagon debriefing. Carla had pulled out all the stops and assured us that Chopper would receive the best care available. It was then that she made the call to the Defense Intelligence Agency and the Department of Defense. When she did she vigorously urged them to immediately promote both Major's Bell and Mosier to the rank of Colonel and promote Gunny Sergeant Tom Burke and Sergeant First Class John Lamadlen, to the ranks of Master Sergeant.

Deputy Director Richard Crock took the telephone from Carla and said, "I'm not asking you, I'm telling you, promote all four of these men and cut their order to return to the United States, immediately. I want all four of those men reassigned to the Pentagon. They've served their country well. Now promote them and bring them home before something terrible happens to them." Mr. Crock hung up the telephone and sat down at the conference table, "At this particular moment in time, the President of the United States is doing back flips in the Oval Office. He is over joyed. Take advantage of it while you can," he explained smiling.

"I don't know if they would want it or not, but if its possible could you get Mr. Twe and Mr. Doc, along with their entire families American citizenship and bring them to the States?" I asked. "If they want to come?"

"Yeah, and Master Gunnery Sergeant Charlie Dean. We owe him and his men, big time. They worked around the clock for three days, one of which was in the rain, to get that Soviet gunship flying for us," Joe added.

"I'll make the calls first thing in the morning," Mr. Crock replied. "Now, what do you boys want? You pulled off the impossible mission and killed the enemy, captured Major Bui, and successfully extracted valuable information that may very well save the lives of a lot of American POW's," Crock explained.

"I'd be happy with a cold Pepsi. Other than that, I don't want anything, sir. We were going in for Danny, with or without your help. We don't leave ours behind. We appreciate everything you and Ms. Silverman did to help us accomplish our mission. Thank you, both," I explained.

"You men don't want anything for yourselves?" Carla asked with a surprised look on her face.

"Nope," Cookie answered.

"Not me," Joe replied after Cookie answered.

"I want one thing," Butch said.

"Finally, someone that makes sense. What would you like, Butch?" Richard asked.

"I just want to know one thing. How did our boy, Boris, react when he got to Hanoi and found Danny gone and his comrades dead?" Butch asked with a wide smile.

"Right now General Kalashnikov is demanding answers from the Chinese. He thinks that Major Bui took Danny to China. By the time he got to Hanoi, early the next morning, they had discovered twenty-two dead North Vietnamese guards. I guess they were to stupid to figure out that the cigarettes were poisoned. So they just kept passing them around to each other. Boris is back in the Kremlin raising holy hell. We're monitoring him, the Chinese, and high ranking officials in Hanoi. I'll keep you men posted on how things turn out," Richard answered.

"Also, men, just so you know, I've talked to Danny's mother and have made arrangements to fly her to Japan to see her son. She'll stay with one of our people while she is in Japan. That way we'll know she is okay and will be seeing the sights of that magnificent country all at the same time. It will be a nice vacation for her," Carla explained as she looked over at me, smiled, and winked.

"Well, men, if you don't want anything I'll say once again, thank you for a job well done. Now then, I'm hungry and Ms. Silverman is buying. Care to join us for supper?" Richard asked as we all said, "Hell yes, let's eat!"

We only spent a few more hours, with Mr. Crock and Carla then went our separate ways. Now that I knew Danny was going to be all right and I would see all my teammates again, I suddenly felt tired.

My flight back to Michigan was a short one. Walking in through my front door, I locked the door behind me, striped off all my clothes and took a hot shower. In my bedroom, I turned off the light, flopped down on my bed, and smiled. "Thank you, God, for keeping us safe and for healing Danny. I owe you one," I said softly as I yawned and closed my eyes.

* * * * * * *

When I opened my eyes I found myself covered with sweat, as I turned my head to look at the clock on the nightstand beside my bed. It was 9:30 a.m.; the bright morning sun was shinning in through my bedroom window, I found myself lying in bed confused. My body was covered with sweat, but I didn't have any nightmares of my past sins. At least none that I could remember anyway.

Getting out of bed I went into my bathroom, took a hot shower, shaved, and got dressed. I actually felt good for the first time in a very long time. I went downstairs, turned on my television, and grabbed a bottle of Pepsi out of the refrigerator. Switching the station over to CNN News I felt my mouth fall slightly open when I saw the date. I had gotten home on Monday. It was now Thursday morning. I had been asleep for three days straight. I hadn't slept like that since I had come home from Vietnam. Turning off the TV, I went to my den to see if there were any messages for me and found only one. It was from Kathy asking me to call her when I got home.

I spent the next two days with my grandparents. Being around them made me feel good, yet sad when I saw how their age was starting to catch up with them. I knew one day they would both be gone and all I would have left of them would be my memories of happier childhood days.

Sunday morning I caught a flight to Virginia and drove to Kathy's home. I wanted to surprise her and see how her ankle was coming along. Stopping at the A&P Food Store I picked up a couple of bags of goodies. I knocked on her front door holding the two bags of groceries in my arms.

"David!" she said out loud, in an excited voice, when she opened the door.

"Hello, sexy lady, I came all this way just to see how you're feeling and to make you dinner," I explained as I raised both bags in my arms.

"Oh my God, this is great. I've been so worried about you, are you alright?" she asked as she let me in, closed the front door, and followed me to her kitchen.

Kathy was on crutches and seemed to be moving around pretty well. Her ankle was wrapped in an Ace Bandage. It wasn't quite as swollen but still black and blue. She was on medical leave and would remain on it until she was back to perfect health.

I spent the next couple of days with Kathy at her home. It was quality time spent for me. We laughed, joked around, and had long talks that went well past midnight and into the early morning hours. I cooked for her and filled her in on all the details of our rescue mission on Danny.

I flew back home on Wednesday and called Carla to get an update on Danny's condition. Simply put, Chopper was mad and wanted to go back to Vietnam so he could kill every Viet Cong and NVA piece of shit in the country. That told me Chopper was going to be all right.

Then Carla explained to me that Danny was confused. He remembered being taken out of his prison cell by a team of high ranking Russians, but couldn't remember anything about how he had been rescued and taken from them. Carla said it was a good thing his mother was with him when she explained that those Russians were his teammates disguised as Russians.

"My brothers came back for me?" Danny asked Ms. Silverman.

"Yes, Danny, there was no way anyone could have stopped them. When they found out you were in trouble they were back in Vietnam with a rescue plan in less than four days," Carla explained in a motherly tone.

"They came back after me, mama?" Danny asked his mother.

"Yes, honey. David sent a message to me, telling me you had been captured and that he was going back to get you. I didn't know all of your teammates had gone back for you until after you had been rescued and flown to the Navy hospital ship. That's when Ms. Silverman called me and told me to pack my bags and that you were headed here to Japan," Mrs. McBride explained to her son.

"My brothers came back for me," our gentle giant of a brother whispered softly to his mother as she smiled and held her son's hand.

"Cookie said that David held you in his arms during the whole flight from Hanoi all the way until they got you to China Beach. He feels real bad he had to use his stungun on you twice to calm you down," Carla explained.

"That old Russian with the scar on his throat was the Sandman? He's the one that electrocuted me?" Danny asked in a calm voice.

"Yes, it was, that was your brother, David," Carla replied.

"I'm going to beat that boys butt, mama. I knew they would come, mama," Danny said softly as his mother put her arms around him and held him close to her breast.

Wiping the tear that fell from his eye, Mrs. McBride explained. "You lost your older brother in Vietnam, baby, God took him to heaven to be with him. Then, the good Lord gave you eight more brothers to replace the one he took."

"They came back for me, mama. They came back for me."

* * * * * * *

"Checkmate!" Andy said as he took a sip of his Budweiser beer and grinned.

"You cheated!" I snapped back at him as I took a closer look at the chessboard.

"He didn't cheat, Uncle David, he got you fair and square," little Tara explained.

"Oh yeah, stick up for him," I answered with a smile as I stood up and tousled Tara's hair with my left hand. "Sit down and see if you can beat him then. I need a Pepsi," I explained as Tara sat down in my place and began to reset the pieces on the chessboard.

Amy and Dana had a baby shower to go to, so the girls decided to come over and hang out with Uncle David for the afternoon.

"Magnum P.I. is coming on, Uncle David," Jessy yelled out as I grabbed a bottle of Pepsi out of the refrigerator and sat down on the floor in front of the TV next to her. I noticed that both Dana and her daughter, Jessy, looked a lot more relaxed and at ease now that Dana's husband was out of the picture. Dana smiled a lot and little Jessy laughed, giggled, and acted more like a ten-year old girl should. She wasn't afraid anymore and that made me feel good inside. I still remembered growing up as a young child Jessy's age and having a stepfather that would come home everyday after work, and beat the hell out of me. Just hearing his car pull in the driveway would make me so sick to my stomach that I would almost throw-up. But to be a little girl and experience that kind of fear would have to have been a hundred times worse.

"How come you don't have a Ferrari like Magnum, Uncle Dave?" Jessy asked, as she took a sip of her soda, and burped in my face.

Seeing her start to giggle at me Andy yelled, "Hey, brother, that computer thing-a-ma-jig is beeping in the den."

"I'll get it," I yelled back as I answered Jessy's question about the Ferrari, "I like Corvettes better than Ferraris, but I'll think about it. If I buy one you could drive me around in it, huh?" I asked. Just as little Jessy started to answer with an excited look on her face, I stood up and farted.

"Oh man, that's gross," little Jessy started to say in retaliation.

"Wow, Jessy, I didn't think a little girl could fart that loud," I shouted out. "Hey, did you guys hear Jessy fart?" I asked as I moved quickly past Andy and Tara and headed to my den.

"Yeah, Jessy, you're a pig!" Tara yelled out to her best friend.

"Jessy, go change your underwear. It smells like you pooped in 'em," Andy added as they both started to rib Jessy.

"It wasn't me! Uncle David you better tell them," Jessy replied in a squeaky voice as she walked toward Andy and Tara pinching her nose closed with the fingers of her left hand.

Closing and locking the doors to my den, I walked over to my computer. I was laughing so hard that I almost had tears in my eyes. "She's going to find a way to pay me back and with those two girls, it will be a doozy," I said to myself as I sat down and typed in my security code.

As I watched the computer screen, the phone rang. Picking it up I placed it to my ear and switched on my scrambler box.

"Hello," I said softly.

"God, you have a sexy voice," Carla answered.

"Well, thank you. I'm looking at a computer screen that has a church pictured on it. Why am I looking at a church?" I questioned.

"That church is St. Paul's in New York. It's down from the World Trade Center, Twin Towers. We just got word from Amanda in Germany, the Priest that runs that parish is making a deal to sell an A-pack suitcase size nuclear weapon to a man named Rasheed Murtaza who lives in Pakistan. You should be getting all of their pictures on your screen any minute now," Carla explained.

"It's coming through now," I answered as I took a careful look at the faces and information now coming across my computer.

"The man on the left is Rasheed, the man on the right is Father Antonio Giovanni, the Priest who is selling the weapon," Carla explained.

"So where is the weapon and how do you know he has it?" I asked.

"A Chinaman from the Ling Yuem Company here in the States had it. One of our agents picked up gamma radiation signatures all over their building. Another one of our agents checked the church at the ground floor level. She found more gamma radiation. The A-pack devise is somewhere in that church. Our plane is on its way. I have one of my boys on board. Find the devise and he'll take it from there," Carla explained.

"Your guys name?" I asked.

"John Mitchell. John will disarm it and transport it to a secure location," Carla replied.

"There's a nuclear weapon in downtown New York. Why don't we just send in every cop in the city?" I asked.

"Have you ever seen what happens when you panic two million people? We keep this kind of stuff secret, David, you know that," Carla explained.

"Well at least we've got a good chance at recovering one of our ten missing weapons this time," I explained as I placed two drops of Methadrine under my tongue.

"Its not one of ours. The radiation signature tells us that its Russian grade plutonium," Carla explained.

"Now I understand why your sending John to secure it," I answered. "It's unstable."

"Unstable and leaking. Get that damn thing out of there, before it goes off, David, then put that Priest to sleep!" Carla ordered.

"I'm on it," I answered.

"You've got a couple of hours before John and our Learjet get to the Pontiac Airport. By the way, Neil said you gave him a bunch of radio frequency codes and telephone numbers to check out, but you didn't tell him where they came from. Anything I need to know?" Carla questioned.

"No, not really. I'm just curious about something, that's all," I answered.

"Let me know as soon as you secure the weapon. As soon as you have it, call me. I've got thirty-three Federal agents standing by to raid the Yuem Company and all of their homes and offices. Their Hong Kong Triad and the Yuem Company brought a nuclear device to the United States. We're going to take them all down," Carla explained.

"The President is going to let you go public with this?" I asked in surprise.

"This is a 'Dull Sword', Top Secret operation. We're not going public. Nobody brings a nuclear weapon to the United States and endangers the lives of our citizens. We're killing all of them. Those are my orders. Find the weapon, kill the Priest, and call me as soon as Johnny has his hands on the nuke. We hit the Triad here in the States as soon as you make the call to me," Carla explained.

* * * * * * *

Covert Operation
Code Name: Dull Sword
Target: Antonio Giovanni
Location: New York, USA

CIA Special Covert Agent John Mitchell was a nuclear weapons containment specialist. He stood five-feet, ten-inches tall, had brown hair with a medium build. He was in his mid-twenties, and carried two, Colt-45 automatic pistols. In all reality he was born a hundred years to late. Without a doubt, this young man was the reincarnation of Billy the Kid.

Meeting John on the plane we found out that we had a lot in common. We both loved to shoot our guns, we both loved our country, but didn't trust any of the Federal Government Agency's, we both loved children and women, we both were walking the razors edge, and were both border line crazy.

"How do you want to handle this, Dave?" John asked as our plane began its descent heading toward the runway of New York's International Airport.

"I'm not sure, John, I don't usually plan things out. I just go with what feels right at the time. I'm sure there will be people in the church. If there is, I'll have to get this phony bastard somewhere by himself. Then we'll simply take it one step at a time. Look at these pictures," I explained as I showed John the pictures of the Catholic Church where we were headed. "It's a big church, the nuke could be hidden anywhere inside. I just hope we get there before he sells it to this Rasheed fella."

"We will, Amanda, hit pay dirt with this one. Carla told me how you and Ollie just missed those two suitcase nukes at that Gruber fella's estate. That's fucked up! We're not going to miss this one, brother," John explained as he held up one of his .45 caliber pistols and chambered a round into the firing position. Looking at me John smiled. "Can I kill the Priest?" he asked with an excited look on his face.

"No, John, you can't kill the Priest. I'm killing him. But if anyone else poses a problem you can kill them. How's that?" I answered with a grin as our pilot opened the door of our plane.

Looking at my watch, it was almost 10:00 p.m.; we walked past our pilot to get off the plane. "Good luck, fellas," he said calmly.

"Thanks, hopefully this won't take to long. We'll meet you at the St. Regis Hotel when we're done. Reserve us a couple of rooms, will you?" I asked as I placed two drops of Methadrine under my tongue.

"Carla already took care of that. I'll refuel and then secure the plane. You sure you guys don't want me to come along as back-up?" Ben asked.

"No, brother, thanks for offering. You're married, Ben, and you have two small kids at home that are depending on you. Sit this one out, brother. This could get messy," I explained as I headed down the steps of our plane with John following right behind me.

Renting a new Oldsmobile, we quickly headed for St. Paul's Church. Driving toward the old church, I could see its three, tall steeples, reaching up toward the darkness of the night, like three slender fingers. I parked the car and pulled out my silenced .22 magnum and double-checked it to make sure it was loaded and ready to fire.

"What's up, Dave? Carla won't let you play with adult size weapons?" John teased as he looked at my slender weapon of death.

"I may not even shoot the Priest," I answered with a serious look on my face as I holstered my gun and opened the driver's side door.

"Oh really? Got something else in mind do you?" John asked as we closed the car doors and began walking toward the front of the church.

"Maybe," I replied with a grin.

"Do you believe in God, Dave?" John asked as he looked upward at the tall steeples of the church.

"Yes, sir, I sure do. He's the only one that truly loves me, John," I answered as we reached the front of the church and began to walk up the cement steps heading toward the large wooden front doors.

"Do you think God will be upset with us for killing one of his Priests?" John asked in a whisper as two elderly women left the church and walked passed us.

"God has warrior angels, John. How do you know God didn't send us here to do exactly what we're about to do, kill this Priest?" I questioned with a grin as I opened one of the wooden doors and stepped inside.

"Whoa, I like that answer," John said softly as he crossed himself with his right hand.

"Nothing in this life can happen without God's permission, brother, remember that," I explained as we stepped into the main chapel and sat down. The church was huge. It had stained glass windows and wooden pews. It was your typical Catholic church.

Looking around, I saw eight women and two older men sitting in the pews toward the front of the church waiting for their turn to step into the confessional booth to confess their sins.

Looking around, John looked at me. "How are we going to find it? Look at this place," he said with a concerned look on his face.

"I got a plan, so relax, will you," I whispered as a young female hooker stepped out of the confessional booth and looked toward the alter. As she did she knelt slightly and crossed herself with her left hand. Then another person went in and closed the door.

"Mind if I ask what it is?" John asked with a curious look on his face.

"The most obvious is the least obvious. Just watch and let the Sandman teach you something," I answered as I sat back in the pew. We were going to be here a while waiting on these last ten people. Hopefully no one else would show up.

* * * * * * *

It was midnight when the last person stepped out of the confessional and headed toward the doors to leave.

"Go lock the front doors, John. I'm going to go confess," I whispered as I got up and headed for the confessional.

Opening the door on the right, I stepped inside, closed the door, and sat down. Because of my Christian faith I refuse to call anyone Father except for God himself. I had never been in a confessional before so I wasn't sure what I was suppose to do. It was when the small wooden divider slid open that I figured it out.

"I'm looking for Antonio Giovanni, is that you, sir?" I asked as I tried to see through the cloth that separated us.

"I am Father Giovanni, what is your confession?" he asked.

"I confess that I have a lot of money in a suitcase that I am suppose to give to you in exchange for the Russian made suitcase you have for sale," I said calmly as I pulled my pistol out of its holster and held it in my right hand.

"I'm afraid I do not understand, my son. Do you wish to make a donation to the church?" he questioned cautiously.

I am here from Pakistan, my uncle sent me to purchase the weapon, Racheed Murtaza. Now do you understand?" I asked.

"You are early," he explained curiously.

"I've had enough of this," I said softly as I stood up and opened the door. Seeing John standing right outside of the confessional holding both of his .45 caliber Colt automatic pistols in his hands, made me smile. Opening the other door of the confessional I raised my .22 magnum, pointed it at the priest, and cocked back the hammer.

Father Antonio Giovanni was pure Italian. He stood about six-feet tall, was medium built, had jet-black hair, and bushy eyebrows. Looking at me with his big brown eyes I could see a look of worry start to show on his face.

"I am Mohamid Murtaza, my uncles name is Rasheed Murtaza. I have flown along way to get here. I am hungry, tired, and a Sunni Muslim, which means I have no problem killing you, Priest, if you have lied to us. I am here early because Saddam Hussein is sending two of his Mukhabarat Intelligence Secret Police here tomorrow to steal the nuclear device. Because of this, I do not have time to play this cat and mouse game with you. Do you have our weapon or not?" I asked coldly.

"Yes, yes. Come with me," the Priest said as he stood up and I lowered my weapon. "Its upstairs." Following the Priest I holstered my weapon and picked up my pace to keep up with him. Leaving the main chapel we walked across another smaller room and headed up the dark oak wood stained stairway.

"The Mukhabarat? This is not good. How did Saddam find out about this?" Antonio questioned nervously.

"I don't know. You must have said something to someone other than my uncle," I replied as I turned to look at John who was smiling at me in disbelief.

Walking down the hallway of the second floor we stopped as the Priest reached into his pants pocket and pulled out a set of keys. Sliding his key into the lock of the door, he unlocked it, and invited us inside as he walked into the room and turned on the light.

Looking around quickly, I could see that this room was his living quarters. The Priest walked over to his large wooden framed bed and knelt down. When he did his knees made a small popping sound. Reaching under his bed he pulled out a brown leather covered suitcase.

"Here, this is it," he said as he picked up the heavy suitcase and set it down on his bed. As he did the mattress indented itself slightly from the weight of the suitcase. It looked like it was leather, but it had a strong metal frame.

"John, check it out then we'll pay the Priest," I said quickly as I walked over to the nightstand next to Antonio's bed. "May I use your telephone?" I asked politely.

"Yes, of course you can," the priest answered.

John pressed on the two metal latches that held the suitcase closed; they didn't open. "Where's the key?" John asked.

"Oh, I am sorry, here it is," Antonio replied as he lifted up his large golden crucifix hanging from around his neck. Turning it over the Priest pulled the small silver key off the back of the crucifix, where it was taped. Handing the key to John, John carefully unlocked the suitcase and opened the top.

"Oh yeah, this is it. It's nuclear," John explained without looking at me. Reaching into his back pocket John pulled out a small nylon tool pouch, untied it, and began to disarm the Russian made nuclear weapon.

Picking up the telephone I called Carla at the Pentagon on the open, unsecured line. "Hello," she said in an anxious tone.

"We've got it," I replied.

"What? Already?" she answered with a surprised tone as I hung the telephone up in her ear.

"What are you doing?" Antonio asked as he walked up closer to John who was now removing a small metal plate from the face of the weapon.

"He's disarming it so it won't go off by accident. We don't want to blow ourselves up on our flight back to Pakistan," I explained.

"Oh, I see," the Priest answered as he watched John work.

"If you know anyone that has anymore of these for sale, I'd like to buy them," I commented casually.

"Well, I do have two more, but I would need more money for those," Antonio explained as John and I turned our heads quickly to look at him. We were caught by complete surprise. Our information was that the Priest only had one weapon for sale. I was fishing, hoping to get the name of someone else who might have another weapon. It had never dawned on me that the Priest might have more than just the one.

"How much more will it cost me to buy the other two?" I asked the Priest as he turned to face me. Pressing the tips of his fingers against each other on both of his hands, he paused to think for a moment.

"Well, I told your uncle he could have this one for four-million dollars. But I would need at least seven-million for each of the other two suitcases," he explained cunningly as he looked up slightly to see what my response was going to be.

"I can have fourteen-million dollars here, in cash, within the hour. The question is, how long will it take you to get them here?" I asked calmly.

"Within one hour?" he asked.

"All I have to do is pick up the telephone. My cousin will bring it here from Manhattan. One hour, no longer," I explained with a confident look on my face. Nodding his head one time, he looked at me and smiled.

"Make the call, the other two are also under the bed," he explained with a broad smile.

"What? You've got to be kidding me," John said loudly as he knelt down to look under the bed.

"Well, I'll be God damned. There's two more of 'em under here, Mohamid," John explained as he pulled them both out from under the bed and placed them on top of the mattress next to the first one.

Picking up the telephone I dialed the telephone number to my house. I knew no one was there so I waited a few seconds and began to talk into the mouthpieces as the phone rang in my ear.

"Hello, cousin... Yes, it's me, Mohamid... Yes we have it. We are with the Priest. Bring me another fourteen million dollars... Yes, bring it to St. Paul's Church... Yes, right now, I am buying two more. Uncle will be pleased... Yes... Yes.... Good, I'll meet you at the front door of the church in forty-minutes. Okay, goodbye," I said as I hung up the telephone. "The money is on its way," I explained with a smile.

"Good, this is good," Antonio replied joyfully. Now I understood why there was so much gamma radiation at the warehouse and here in the church. Three nuclear weapons would most certainly do it especially if they were leaking radiation from their cores.

A half an hour passed when John finally closed the top of the last suitcase and locked it shut. Turning to look at me he smiled, rolled up his nylon tool pouch, and placed it into his back pocket. "That's it David, we're ready to go," he explained.

Calling me David caught Antonio by surprise, "David? Why does he call you, David? You are...," the Priest began to say as I raised my left hand to stop him.

"My name is David, Mr. Giovanni. And my friends name is John. We work for the Central Intelligence Agency," I explained as I snugged my thin black leather gloves up a bit tighter on my hands.

"Oh no," the Priest said with a shocked look on his face, as he began to look back and forth at John and I quickly.

"Calm down, Antonio. Your not going to jail," I explained calmly in an effort to calm the panicked Priest down.

"I'm not? What will happen to me?" he questioned as he began to back up a few steps.

"You're going to work for us now. We want Rasheed Murtaza. You're a real fucking idiot. I mean how stupid are you terrorists, anyway?" I asked as John began to laugh.

"Grab two of these, John, lets get 'em downstairs and to wherever you need to take them," I explained as I grabbed the third suitcase nuclear weapon with my left hand. As I slid it off the bed I felt that it wasn't really as heavy as it first appeared to be. "Come on, Priest, you're going back to your confessional to pray for the sinners," I said smiling as we left the bedroom and began to walk down the hallway toward the stairs.

"Can you get anymore of these weapons for us?" I questioned as John headed down the stairs; Antonio and I stopped at the top of the stairway. Turning to look at each other the Priest dropped his head slightly and shook it from side to side, sadly.

"No, this was all that I could get. They will come for me if I don't have their money," he explained.

"They? They who?" I asked.

"The Chinese Triad. They will kill me," the Priest explained as he puckered his lower lip and looked down at his shoes.

"Hell, don't worry about that, Priest. My partner's going to kill you," John explained as he reached the bottom of the stairs, stopped, and turned around to look up at us. As he did, the Priest raised his head to look at me. With one quick move I twisted my body slightly and struck Antonio at the base of his nose with the open flat palm of my hand. It's called a Quick Kill. To make it work you actually use the bone of your forearm where it meets the meaty part of the hand at the wrist. The strike must be clean, fast, and straight, which mine was.

As the base of my palm hit Antonio's nose I felt the cartilage inside his nose snap and move upward. As it did, the cartilage entered the Priest's brain, the force of the blow caused his head to snap backward. His brain hemorrhaged as his head returned to its normal position. When it did, I grabbed him by the hair and quickly jerked him forward. The Priest was already dead as the mass amount of blood gushed out of his nose and his lifeless body tumbled down the stairs.

"Whoa, you've got to teach me that one. Shit that was awesome," John said excitedly as I walked down the stairs, stepped over the body of the dead Priest, and joined him at the base of the stairs. "You should have shot him in the nuts!" John said as he began to laugh out loud. "That was so cool. One hit and he was dead as a doornail and still standing on his feet. Shit that was fucking great!" John continued as we walked through the church and headed to the front doors.

"This way it will look like he tripped, fell down the stairs, just a tragic accident. No scandal, no fuss, no muss," I explained as we unlocked the large wooden doors and looked outside to make sure no one was waiting to get inside. We were lucky, the coast was clear. Moving quickly we went to our car, put the three suitcases into the trunk, and drove away.

"Look at how tall those two building are," I explained as I pointed out through the front windshield of our vehicle.

"The Twin Towers. They say they're 110 or 120-stories tall," John explained.

"Would you work in an office that high in the air?" I asked as I stopped for a red light.

"Hell no, that's to tall for me. I'm afraid of heights," John explained as he looked over at me.

"No kidding. So am I. No wonder we get along so well," I said smiling. Moving forward again we pulled into a Shell gas station.

"What's up? We don't need gas," John explained as he looked over at the gas gauge on the dashboard.

"I know. I'm going to call Ben and tell him to meet us at the airport. We're not spending the night in New York. I'll feel a lot better once you get these three baby gorilla's tucked away somewhere safe," I explained.

"Yeah, no shit. I'll drop you off at the Pentagon and then fly these babies to Nevada and get 'em stored away, underground. You don't mind doing the debriefing by yourself, do you?" John asked.

"No problem. I hope we get a chance to work together again, John. You're alright. If I ever need back-up for a gun fight I'll request you, how's that?" I asked as I opened the car door.

"Hell, yeah, I haven't had a good shoot out since I came home from Vietnam," John explained as we both got out of the car and closed the doors. Resting my forearms on the roof of the car I looked over at John.

"When were you in country?" I asked. I should have known by the way he was acting that he was a Vietnam Veteran but my mind was occupied on the mission at hand.

"Sixty-nine and seventy, got shot twice in my second tour so they made me come home. Boy, that really pissed me off," John explained.

"What pissed you off, getting shot twice?" I asked.

"Fuck no, that was fun. It pissed me off when they made me come home. So I didn't re-enlist, I discharged and told 'em to kiss my white ass. Shortly after that the Agency recruited me. Now here I am," John explained with a smile as he extended his arms out from his sides.

"I was a Black Op's Sniper. Who were you with?" I asked as I walked around the front of the car and headed inside to call Ben.

"Army 82nd Airborne Special Forces and damn proud of it," John explained proudly.

"Hoo yah," I replied as I remembered Sergeant Tom McBride who died a horrible death in the POW camp I was in. He was a young man of honor, a wild thing, never once having felt sorry for himself.

We called Ben, met him at the airport, and was in flight by 4:00 a.m. We got lucky this time, real lucky. I could only hope our luck would continue and I would be able to work with John again. After all, he is Billy the Kid.

* * * * * * *

Debriefing took three hours and shocked everybody in the room when they found out we had recovered three Samsonite gorillas and not just one. Had even one of those weapons exploded we would have lost New York City and then some. One would have set off the other two and that would have been disastrous to say the least.

My flight back home to Michigan gave me time to think about things. Millions of Americans lay asleep in their beds every night thinking they're safe, when they're not. But thanks to people like John, Carla, Ollie, Neil, Kathy, and the rest of the men and women who work for the CIA, Americans will sleep soundly never knowing that their American brothers and sisters are risking their life's everyday, to keep them safe and free.

John Mitchell (left) with author in South Carolina, 2004.
"Brothers and Friends, till the very end."

Chapter Twenty-Two
Mystery One

There it was again; it sounded like something moving in the leaves. Maybe it was a wild animal, or, oh shit, I thought as I slowly reached up with my right-hand and slid my finger onto the trigger of my snipers rifle. It's another cat, it must have picked up my scent and was now stalking me. The sound of movement would start and then stop, start and then stop, as it came closer and closer towards me. Moving only my eyes, I held my breath, as I saw the arm and then body of the sniper slowly moving up and around the tree I was leaning against.

Startled, I sat up quickly and shook my head. The memories of Vietnam continued to haunt me in my dreams. Wiping my hand across my sweat covered face, I heard the constant crackling sound of my television set. Looking at my watch it was 4:32 a.m. I had fallen asleep watching an old James Cagney movie. The TV station had gone off the air for the night. All that was left was the blank, white snow covered screen as it hissed softly at me in the darkness of the night.

I went into my bathroom and took a shower. I put on a clean set of clothes, went into my kitchen, grabbed a bottle of cold Pepsi, and tossed a two-inch thick porter house steak into the broiler of my oven.

Opening a bottle of Valasic dill pickles, I pulled one out, and took a bite. "This is crazy," I whispered softly to myself as I looked down at my right hand and flexed my fingers several times. I could still feel the flesh of Antonio's nose as my palm drove the cartilage of his brain exactly one quarter of an inch into his brain, causing his brain to hemorrhage. His death was instant. He was dead before his knees buckled. Now, I would add his face to the list of many that came back to haunt me in my dreams.

Taking another bite of my pickle and a sip of my Pepsi I couldn't help but wonder what had happened to me. I used to be such a good kid. Now I kill people and it doesn't even bother me anymore when I do.

The sound of my telephone ringing sent me to my den. Sitting down at my desk I turned on Walter Shaw's black scrambler box and picked up the receiver.

"Hello," I said calmly into the mouthpiece.

"Don't you ever sleep?" Carla asked jokingly.

"Not without having nightmares. Besides if I would have been asleep, I'd have missed your call. What's up?" I asked as I took a sip of my Pepsi and hoped that she had something for me to do.

"I noticed that you keep trying to access the computer data information on Area 51 in Nevada. Why is that?" Carla asked with a curious tone.

"Trying is right, hell the computer doesn't say much about it," I answered.

"Why are you so curious about our forbidden Area 51?" Carla asked once again.

"I don't know. I'm not like a lot of other people who walk around wearing blinders and have tunnel vision. I have always believed that we're not the only ones living in this universe," I explained wondering why Carla was so interested in my thoughts at this early hour of the morning.

"Do you believe in aliens? You know, people from other planets?" she questioned.

"Yes, I do. God talks about it in the book of Genesis, but most people don't catch it. I believe we are a lower, more violent form of life. I also think they fly by once in a while to check on us to see how we're progressing. But believing and seeing are two different things, right?" I asked.

"Yeah, I guess so. What happened that has you so curious now? Did you see a flying saucer?" Carla asked.

"No, I wish I did. It was in Vietnam after I had escaped from the POW camp in Cambodia. I was wondering around in the forest, I was dying; I have no doubt about that. I had sat down next to a large tree. It was over and I knew it. I simply couldn't go any farther. That's when it happened," I explained as my mind took me back to that point and time.

"What? That's when what happened, David?" Carla asked.

"I closed my eyes to sleep and just as I did I heard a voice telling me to open my eyes. When I did I saw both my uncles, plain as day. I could see through them, but it was them, there's no doubt about it. My Uncle Tommy was killed in World War II and my Uncle Sammy was killed six months later when a drunk driver hit him and his buddy while they were riding on his new scooter bike," I explained remembering what I had seen.

"You sure that you weren't hallucinating?" Carla asked.

"That's what the doctors at China Beach Medical Hospital in Da Nang said. But no, Carla, I saw 'em, it was them. No one will ever tell me anything that will change my mind. I do know this, ma'am. There's a lot more going on around us than we can actually see with the naked eye. I pray and ask God to let me see more than I have so far, but I haven't got an answer yet," I explained with a bit of chuckle in my voice.

"Maybe he has heard you. I'm flying to Groom Lake tomorrow. Wanna take a ride and see more?" Carla asked in a mysterious tone.

"Area 51's Groom Lake, in Nevada?" I questioned as a surge of newfound excitement began to build up inside of me.

"The one and only," Carla answered.

"How can you get me in past all of the security?" I questioned.

"David, you have Q-clearance. You're allowed in there. You'll have to take a medical examination and some allergen tests, but once the medical team clears you, you'll be able to look at everything. Personally, I think you're ready. So I'd like you to come along. I also have someone there I would like you to kill," she added with a laugh.

"Just tell me what time you want me to be at the airport," I explained with a smile as I placed two drops of Methadrine under my tongue. Just as I did, I smelled smoke. "Damn, my steak!!!!"

* * * * * * *

CIA Elite Covert Operation
Code Name: Mystery One
Target: Risa Tansiri
Location: Tonopah, Nevada
Coordinate: GSP Classified Area 51, Groom Lake

Carla handed me the information data package; I opened it up, and pulled out its contents as our Agency Learjet neared Tonopah, Nevada. My target was born in Thailand, her name was Risa Tansiri. She stood five-feet, one-inch tall, had short, black hair, brown eyes, and weighed one hundred, eight pounds. She was a small young woman, twenty-nine years old, and had an IQ of 281. She was a scientist who specialized in nuclear fusion. She was one of the elite group chosen and cleared to work at our top secret forbidden Area 51 in Nevada.

Area 51 is a large area of desert and mountains located to the east of Tonopah, Nevada. To the east of Area 51 is the small town of Carlin, to the north of Carlin is another small town called Pahrump, to the north of Pahrump is another small western town called Ely. Highway I-50 runs through Ely and is north of Area 51. I-95 comes down the western side of Area 51 and runs into the small town of Tonopah and then cuts to the southeast and passed the top-secret nuclear test facility known as the Mercury Test Sight. It then goes into Las Vegas. The Mercury Test Sight Facility is three hundred miles south of Area 51.

Both Area 51 and the Mercury Test Faculty have a No Fly Zone status. If you attempt to fly over either of these areas, your plane, no matter who you are, will be shot down without notice, without warning. Both areas are completely fenced in. If you attempt to cross the fence at either facility, you will be shot without notice, without warning. Your body will simply disappear. Some of our government's best kept secrets are hidden at both of these top-secret areas.

Our pilot radioed Area 51 well in advance of our coming close to their airspace, and then gave them all of the proper top-secret security identification codes needed to enter their airspace and approach for landing at Groom Lake. He then reached under the dashboard of the plane and turned on the small transmitter box that sends another set of codes to them verifying who we say we are. If our pilot would fail to turn on the transmitter box we would still be shot down even though our first set of verbal security codes were correct.

Our landing strip is in the center of what was once known as Groom Lake. Now nothing more than dry, hard, desert land sits out in the middle of nowhere. I couldn't help but wonder where all of the water had gone as our plane touched its wheels down onto the hot runway.

"Excited?" Carla asked as she looked over at me and smiled.

"You have no idea how excited I really am, ma'am. This is an answered prayer for me," I replied as I placed two drops of Methadrine under my tongue and then put the tiny glass vial back into my pocket.

"All that's out here is a small guard shack?" I asked as I looked out through the side window of our plane.

"Oh there's more than that out here, David. You'll see. The time consuming part is when you first arrive. You have to take a complete physical exam. They're mostly concerned with what you might be carrying. If you're sick or even have a minor cold, you can't come in. The allergen testing and blood work up takes most of the time. But once that's complete, you're good to go," Carla explained.

"What's the big deal? I don't understand," I said as I shrugged my shoulders and looked at Carla.

"Lets save the mystery for the big surprise," Carla replied with a grin as our plane taxied to a stop.

Stepping off the plane we were greeted by a dozen heavily armed men, with them were four jeeps, two of which had M-60 machine guns mounted on a steel pipe just behind and between the front seats. The other two jeeps had .50 caliber machine guns mounted in the same spot. All of the men were in plain clothes and wore dark sunglasses. They were all ex-military, special forces, and had no problem killing who ever they needed to if the situation called for it.

"Credentials," was all that the first man said as he extended his hand out toward us. Handing him our Q-clearance identification credentials he looked at them, then at us, and then returned them to us.

I was impressed, these men and their vehicles weren't anywhere to be seen when we first landed. They appeared out of nowhere like the ghosts of the desert.

"I've never seen you before, is this your first time at this facility?" the man asked.

"Its his first time, he'll have to go in for an exam," Carla explained as she put her sunglasses on.

"Ms. Silverman, you two can ride with me," he explained as he pointed toward his jeep.

Our first stop was a small white building. Once I was in there the medical personnel asked a bunch of personal questions about my past medical history. They drew blood and then began the process of sticking hundreds of tiny needles into my back and arms to test and see what I might be allergic to.

As Carla had explained, it took several hours to complete the entire process. Once it was over and I was medically cleared, I was photographed and given an entirely different identification card. With this card I could now pass in and out of any of our forbidden area facilities.

Leaving the building, two of the Groom Lake security men drove Carla and I north in their jeeps. It was a long, bumpy ride down a pothole filled gravel road that ran at the base of the mountains. We were headed to what is known as Area S-12, which was a good twelve-mile drive from where our plane had first landed. The security men never said a word during our drive. As our jeep drove around the base of one of the mountains, Carla nudged me lightly with her left leg and nodded her head toward the side of the mountain.

As I looked, my eyes got wide and my heart began to race with excitement. There at the base of the mountain were nine very large airplane hanger style doors. Parked out front were a number of different vehicles. Using his mobile hand held radio, the security guard that sat in the passengers seat radioed to whoever was inside. Within a matter of a few seconds a man who appeared to be in his mid-forties came out to greet us.

He stood about five-feet, ten-inches tall, had thick, wavy, brown hair, brown eyes, weighed about 185-pounds, and wore gold, round shaped, wire frame glasses. He wore a white medical style coat and had his picture ID clipped to the tip of his collar. His shirt pocket had a pocket protector in it, which held different types of ink pens. Getting out of the jeep he smiled and extended his hand out to Carla.

"Carla, its good to see you again, as always," he said in a rich Australian accent.

"Rex, its good to see you too. How are things progressing?" Carla asked, as she shook his hand.

"Slow but good. And who is this?" he asked as he looked at me and shook my hand.

"This is David, he is the one I called you about," Carla explained with a pride filled look on her face.

"Ah yes, the quick thinker," he said with a curious look on his face. "Come, let me show you around. We'll start with Hanger One and work our way quickly to Hangers Seven, Eight, and Nine. Where we are doing our more serious research."

Hangers One, Two, and Three had pieces of metal debris carefully placed on the cement floor. In reality these were huge building size areas that were cut into the side of the mountain. The large steel hanger doors were all that kept it hidden from the outside.

These first few hangers had no one in them. It was just a small amount of metal scattered around on the floor. The inside of Hanger's Four, Five, and Six held the frame structure and more pieces of what appeared to be some type of spacecraft.

"We've pretty much torn these down to the bare frame. Our research teams are trying to study and learn as much as they can about these alien crafts," Rex explained as we headed for Hanger Seven.

Looking at Carla I couldn't help but smile. I knew it; I've always felt it deep inside. We're not alone in this universe.

Hanger Seven and Eight had full teams of research scientists working on both of the disc shaped spacecrafts that were secretly secured inside of them. I was allowed to look but not touch the crafts. They weren't what I would call huge, but they were big. Moving into Hanger Nine caused me to stop dead in my tracks and stare in awe.

"What do you think?" Carla asked as she nudged me with her left elbow.

"Wow, that's a big spaceship. What happened to it? It doesn't appear to be damaged like the other ones," I noted.

"That's the mystery of it. It came down all on its own," Carla explained as a pretty blonde female walked up to us smiling.

She stood five-feet, seven-inches tall, had blonde hair that was pulled back tight on her head and formed into a bun at the back. Her gold-framed, wire rim glasses accented her pretty blue eyes. She looked to be about thirty-four years old and had a smile that highlighted her sparkling white teeth.

"Hello, ma," she said joyfully as she walked up to Carla.

"Hello, Jeni. I'd like you to meet David. David, this is Doctor Jennifer McFadden," Carla said as she introduced the two of us to each other.

"Hello, David, mom tells me that you're a quick thinker," Jennifer said with a smile.

"Well I don't know about all of that. But I am impressed. This is surreal," I explained as I looked at the silver colored spacecraft. It was in the form of a perfect disc saucer.

"Yes, it is but it has Rex and I stumped, as well as the others," Jennifer explained as she turned to look at it.

"What is it that's so baffling?" Carla asked.

"We can't figure out how to start it up. Pretty crazy, huh?" Jennifer explained.

"How hard can it be?" Carla asked. "You have an IQ of 202."

"Being smart doesn't always mean you can figure everything out," Jennifer explained with a sigh.

"Lets take David and Carla inside of this baby and see what they think," Rex explained.

"Of course, I'm sorry, follow me and take a look at some master craftsmanship," Jennifer invited.

There were six large landing pods that extended downward from the bottom of the ship like legs. Walking to the center of the craft I reached up but couldn't touch the underneath of the craft.

Exactly dead center in the belly of the spacecraft was a perfectly round opening, a doorway, so to speak. There were a set of steps coming down at an angle from the inside of the opening. As we walked up to the steps I couldn't help but make an observation. Stopping I looked up at the metal craftsmanship of this unique spacecraft.

"Amazing isn't it?" Carla said to me as Rex began to climb up the steps.

"Its more than that. Look at this. This porthole opens into the metal structure. It's not a door like we would make. Its all part of the body and opens into itself," I explained as I looked up at the craft.

"Good observation, I wasn't paying any attention to that," Carla explained as she took a second look.

"What else do you notice?" Jennifer asked with a look of curiosity on her face.

"There's no rivets or welding seams. Its all one perfectly made piece of metal," I explained.

"Bingo, very good, David," Doctor McFadden commented as we all began to walk up the steps and enter the main body of the spacecraft.

Once inside, I could feel my jaw drop open as I stood in complete awe of what I was looking at. It was an all-metal spacecraft that had no visible windows that could be seen from the outside. But now that I was standing on the inside of the craft I could see out through the metal as if it were a solid piece of glass.

"Whoa...." I said softly in a whisper. "How in the hell..."

"Its metal, you can't see in but you can see out. We can't burn it, torch it, cut it, or shoot through it. We've never seen anything like it before. It's not like the other eight spacecrafts. This one is much bigger and far more advanced. Yet it came down, why? That's what we can't figure out. Why would they land it and let us get our hands on it?" Jennifer questioned in frustration.

"Makes entirely no sense," Rex added.

"Maybe they wanted us to get it," Carla commented.

"But why, mom, why?" Jennifer asked.

"To show us what we're up against. Maybe it's their way of scaring us," Carla explained with a questioning look.

"No, they're not trying to scare us. They're far more advanced than us. That means they've got us out gunned. They have nothing to prove. Whatever it is, its right in front of our eyes, we're just not seeing it," I explained as I walked over to what appeared to be the pilot's seat. It was sleek and all metal. The control panel was smooth. It had no buttons or switches on it. Everything was written in a weird looking hieroglyphic print. "Can I sit down here?" I questioned.

"Absolutely," Rex replied as he turned to look at Carla.

"The most obvious is the least obvious. That's what my Seal team instructor used to always tell me," I whispered as I touched the control panel.

Even though it was smooth to the eyes, it had the feel of a thousand very tiny pin tips to the touch. Nothing that poked or hurt, but just enough to feel it.

"I wonder what your Seal team instructor would say about this," Jennifer asked in a joking tone with a smile.

"Shhh," Carla said softly as she looked at Jennifer and Rex and placed her finger over her lip.

"What?" Rex questioned as he looked over at Carla and Doctor McFadden.

"He's on to something. I've seen him do this before in the War Room. I'll bet he figures it out," Carla said in a soft tone.

Sitting back in the chair I placed my arm on the armrest and cupped my hand over the end of it. The whole chair including the armrest had that tiny pinhead feeling to it.

"I'll bet you a months pay he doesn't" Rex said to Carla as he turned his attention back to me.

"That's a bet," Carla whispered.

Looking down at the metal floor I reached down off to the right of the pilots seat. The metal was polished to a smooth finish. Leaning forward,

I touched the floor by my feet. Again, it had that pinhead prickly feeling to it.

Sitting back in the seat I whispered to my self as I tried to clear my thoughts. "Everything is subject to change at any given moment. Always expect the unexpected. The most obvious is the least obvious," I thought to myself.

"Boy, its to bad you couldn't talk to the pilot," I commented as I tried to figure out the mystery. "I'd sure like to see what his flight suit looked like."

"They weren't wearing any. They had no clothing on what so ever," Rex explained.

"You saw them?" I asked with a look of surprise on my face.

"Better than that, we've got 'em here," Jennifer added.

"What!" I shouted. "You have aliens that are alive?" I questioned as I quickly stood up to face them. "How many are there?" I asked.

"There were four total. Two were dead; the other two appeared to be sick. We've got them in a containment area."

"Can we see them?" I asked in an excited tone of voice.

"Sure. Isn't that what you came here for?" Rex asked with a broad smile on his face.

"Yes, it is," Carla, said quickly. "Where are they?" she asked.

"Area S-2," Rex replied.

"Of course. Well lets go and say hello to our guests," Carla said anxiously as she grabbed me by the arm.

* * * * * * *

Climbing into Doctor McFadden's all black, four-wheel drive Chevy Blazer, Carla, Rex, Jennifer, and I headed for Area S-2.

It was a four-mile drive across the dry sun baked earth of Groom Lake. Arriving at our location I had a puzzled look on my face as I stared through the windshield of our vehicle.

"You're keeping aliens in that?" I asked in a cynical tone of voice.

There, sitting in front of us, was a small white storage looking structure. It was twelve-feet by twelve-feet in size. There were some old fifty-gallon barrels next to it several of which were lying on their sides. It was a cement structure with a tin metal roof. It had a front door but no visible windows.

Turning to look at me Jennifer adjusted the glasses on her face and smiled. "We don't allow to many people to see this. Come with me and I think you'll understand," she explained.

360

"I can see why you don't let many people see this. Its a dried out shack," I said jokingly as we all got out of the air conditioned blazer and stepped back into the Nevada heat.

Stepping into the building I saw it was empty. The cement floor was covered with a light coat of sand. The paint on the inside of the walls was pealing and faded.

Closing the door to the shack Carla explained. "You can never discuss anything you are about to see, David. Even I couldn't protect you if you do. I know that you never will, but I still need to warn you. Even the President doesn't know about this," she explained.

"He doesn't know about an empty shack in the middle of the desert?" I joked with a smile.

"No. He doesn't know about this," Carla explained as she placed the palm of her right hand up against a small metal plate in the cement wall inside the building. As she did I felt the cement floor start to move downward.

Stepping into the center of the floor I stood in awe as a flat steel plate came up out of nowhere and sealed all four walls of the small room. As they reached the ceiling the cement floor began to lower itself. The small shack was a simple disguise that held within it an elevator shaft that took us down into the earth.

We descended downward into an all stainless steel shaft for about 100-feet. Then the elevator stopped. To the north of us a metal security door unlocked and then opened. As it did a heavily armed plain clothed man greeted us.

Stepping into the small area on the other side of the metal security door; I found myself in a more modern day looking elevator. As the security guard sealed the thick stainless steel door, he turned to look at Carla.

"Where to, ma'am?" he asked politely.

"Take us to Medical Containment, please. How have you been, Roger?" Carla asked.

"They're keeping me busier than a one-legged man in an ass kicking contest, ma'am," Roger, the security guard, answered as he reached up and pressed the button Numbered 21.

As we all smiled at his joke the elevator took us downward. I couldn't help but wonder how they had constructed something like this. We were going down 21-stories into the earth. It was mind boggling to me. Reaching the 21st floor, the door opened and Roger turned a silver key in the face of the control panel. As he did, security locks secured the elevator into place. Removing the key from the face of the control panel, Roger tucked it into his pants pocket and grinned. "Its a long climb to the top," Roger whispered as we stepped off the elevator.

"No kidding," I replied jokingly as I looked at the sterile medical containment room. I couldn't believe what I was looking at. This area was huge. It had two long hallways that formed outward in a V-shape from the main lobby room we were standing in. Twenty-one floors below the surface of the earth it looked like an actual medical center. "Does everything look this nice?" I asked as Carla slid her arm through mine and walked me down the west wing of the facility.

"Yes it does. We could withstand a nuclear blast down here and not only survive but live out our lives. I'll show you everything before we leave, but for now, I need you to meet Ms. Tansiri, our scientist from Thailand. I also want your input on these aliens," she whispered to me in a soft voice.

"Carla, I have an IQ of minus zero compared to these people. What could I possibly tell you that would be of any help?" I asked as we reached a door toward the middle of the long hallway.

"You have a gift that you don't realize. I hope this experience helps you to expand that gift," Carla explained as Rex slid his identification card into the locking system. When he did I could hear the security lock click open.

Grabbing the doorknob with his left hand, Rex turned it and pushed the door open. Stepping inside, the door locked shut behind us.

Walking up to greet us was the young scientist from Thailand. "Hello, Ms. Silverman, what a pleasant surprise," she said as she and Carla shook hands.

"Hello, Risa, I'd like you to meet my confidant, this is David. David, please say hello to our Nobel prize winner, Ms. Risa Tansiri," Carla said with a smile.

Saying hello to Risa I couldn't help but be amazed at how smoothly Carla operated. She had brought me here to kill Risa because Risa had stolen a videotape of the autopsy that was performed on one of the aliens. Yet at the same time she introduces me to her and brags proudly about her achievements.

"What a cold hearted bitch. No wonder we got along so well," I thought to myself as Risa and I shook hands.

"Hello, Ms. Tansiri, Carla has told me a lot about you and the excellent work you do here," I explained.

"Well thank you, that is so nice to hear. It's nice to meet you, David. Are you a doctor?" Risa asked with a slight tilt of her head.

"Yes, I am. I'm a doctor of metaphysics. I am anxious to see your guests. How are they? I am told two have died," I replied with a curious look of confusion on my face.

"With your permission, Ms. Silverman, would you like to see them?" Risa asked.

"Absolutely," Carla replied as Risa led us into the other room.

"They are very interesting beings. The autopsy showed that they have two hearts. Two internal systems. They have a large dark colored lens that covers the actual eye that is underneath it. Try not to be startled when you see them, and please don't touch the glass window," Risa explained as we stepped up to the large observation window.

"Is that fog?" I asked as I looked into the dark room that had a foggy appearance inside of it.

"Its vapor. They seem to breathe better in it," Risa explained.

"Why can't we touch the window?" Carla asked.

"Because we don't know what will happen. They were unconscious when their spacecraft landed. They didn't regain consciousness until after we had placed them into this containment cell. They always place their hands on the glass. Its almost as if they are trying to draw us in. You know, trick us," Risa explained as one of them stepped out of the vapor and looked at us through the glass security window. The being was only five-feet tall, it had a large head. Its skin was a pale green. Its eyes were black.

Seeing it made me feel sad inside. It was in a POW camp so to speak. They had lost their freedom to move around. Even though they appeared to show no outward emotions, I couldn't help but feel that they felt afraid inside.

Stepping closer to the glass, the alien being placed its hands up against the glass, palm facing outward toward me. Stepping up closer to the window I raised my left hand.

"No, don't do that!" Risa shouted. As she did, I placed the palm of my hand against the glass and pressed it firmly against the alien's hand on the opposite side of the glass. At first I felt nothing. Then I felt a warm tingling sensation. As I did I looked into the dark lenses of the beings eyes and smiled.

"Hoo yah," I said softly as I did, it was then that everything flashed through my mind. When it did it startled me causing me to step backward, thus breaking the connection between us.

"What happened? Are you alright?" Jennifer asked.

"He was communicating with me," I said in a mesmerized tone as I looked at my hand.

"What?" Risa said excitedly as she pressed her hand up against the glass directly across from the aliens. As hard as Risa tried, she felt nothing. Then Rex and Jennifer both tried but nothing happened. "That's not funny," Risa scolded thinking I had played a joke on them.

"It wasn't meant to be funny," I said as I stepped back up to the glass and pressed the palm of my hand up against the aliens once again. This time it was instant.

I could see everything they had seen on their trip to earth. Galaxy after galaxy, entire solar systems, it was the most beautiful experience of my life. I could see colors that we didn't even know existed. Then without moving his mouth he spoke to me. By using what I assumed was mental thought projected energy. He was telepathic.

"Why do you hold us?" he asked. Without saying a word I simply thought it in my mind hoping that he would hear me.

"They're afraid of you," I responded.

"Why?" he asked.

"Ignorance. Fear of the unknown," I replied.

"We protect you," he replied.

"From what?" I asked.

"David, what are you doing?" Carla asked as she stepped up next to me, noticing that something wasn't right.

"He's talking to me," I explained. "They're telepathic."

"What? How?" Risa asked excitedly.

"ESP," Jennifer replied. "They're using mental energy."

"How can we help you?" I asked.

"Let us go," he answered.

"Will your ship fly?" I questioned.

"Yes," he replied.

"Why did you land?" I asked.

"Malfunction in hydrogen containment cell," he replied.

"You landed for repairs?" I asked.

"No," he replied.

"Why then?" I asked.

"We were sick," he replied.

"Your body is part of your craft. Without it, it won't fly. You complete the circuit don't you?" I asked.

"Yes, where are my friends?" he asked.

"Two of them were dead. Their bodies are in cold storage."

"They are not dead, they are regenerating," he explained.

"I am sorry, we didn't know that. Our doctors cut them open with the hope of finding a way to help you," I explained sadly.

"Let us go, we must leave now," he explained. Turning to look at Carla I explained everything he said.

"Are you crazy, we're not letting them go," Risa said coldly as she interrupted me.

I had kept my hand on the glass hoping they would be able to hear what I was saying on their behalf. As I did, Carla called for security. Turning to look at the alien being, I spoke again.

"Why do you come here to earth?" I asked.

"To check on you," he answered.

"Why? You're far more advanced than we are. Why waste your time?" I asked with a curious look on my face.

"We put you here," he replied.

"What? When?" I asked.

"Long ago, when the planet that you call the Moon was destroyed. We put you here to save you," he explained.

"Were we friends?" I asked.

"We are the same beings. You haven't evolved yet," he explained.

"Who do you protect us from?" I asked.

"A race that wants this planet," he explained.

"Can we defeat them in a fight?" I asked.

"No," he replied.

"Can you?" I asked.

"Yes, that is why you still exist," he answered.

"Thank you. Will we ever evolve like you?" I asked.

"In time," he explained.

"Let me talk to my friends," I explained. Turning to face Carla, I explained everything. I then lied and added a little about how the other beings would destroy earth if these beings didn't get a message back to their solar system for help. That was all it took to convenience Carla that it was time for our guests to leave. For some unknown reason, Risa was extremely upset over Carla's decision to release the aliens.

"They didn't land here to be held captive by us, Doctor Tansiri. Their bodies act as part of the circuit that powers their ship. When they became sick it forced them to land because they needed to regenerate and repair their craft. It won't fly if they're sick. With their bodies being sick, it broke the circuit that kept the ship flying," I explained. "That's why I told you I wished I could have seen what their space suits looked like. The pilots seat and control panel that navigates the craft have a tiny pin like texture to it. I knew that it had something to do with the circuitry of the ship. I thought that it ran through the suit, but it doesn't. It runs through them. Without them the ship is worthless," I explained.

"Genius, pure genius," Doctor McFadden said as she looked at Carla. "What are we going to do, Mom?"

"What do you think, David? We killed two of their people by mistake," Carla explained.

"He said they put us on earth long ago to save us when the Moon was destroyed," I replied.

"What if it's lying," Risa asked sarcastically.

"Let 'em go, Carla, they're family," I explained.

"Bullshit! I'm no family member to that," Risa snapped back at me.

"No you're not, Doctor Tansiri. You're to fucking stupid to be related to anyone intelligent," I replied. "I was going to enjoy killing this bitch," I thought to myself as I placed my hand on the glass once again.

"What are you doing?" Rex asked.

"I'm telling him that we're letting them go. Hopefully they'll understand and forgive us for what you did to their two friends," I explained as I looked at the alien being again and smiled.

"There is nothing to forgive," he said to me.

"You heard me without touching the glass?" I asked.

"Yes, we have heard all of you. We choose to communicate with only you," he replied.

"My name is, David," I explained with a smile.

"I am Ap. You're not like these others. Why is that? Why are you not afraid of us?" he asked.

"Why should I fear you? I am a child of the God of Abraham," I explained.

"He is the all mighty one," Ap replied.

"Yes, do you know him?" I asked as my heart raced with anticipation waiting for an answer.

"Yes, he is our Father," Ap replied.

"Mine too," I answered.

"Interesting," he commented.

"Can you breathe our air?" I questioned being concerned for them.

"Yes, we have some of our people who live here with you," Ap explained. "They look like you humans, not like us."

"I won't tell them that," I replied as I turned to look at Carla.

"Tell them that on behalf of the President of the United States of America, I am sorry for their mistreatment," Carla explained.

"He can hear you, ma'am," I explained.

"As soon as the personnel and vehicles get here, we'll get them back to their ship. Do they want us to bury the bodies of their friends?" Carla asked.

"No, ma'am, they want to take the bodies with them," I explained.

* * * * * * *

It took eight hours to assemble the security team and make the decision how to move the aliens back to Hanger Nine and their craft. The fear factor was high because no one knew what to expect from Ap and his friends. During that eight-hour period I would learn from Ap that their planet is a lot like ours. It has some differences. Its cleaner, there is no disease or sickness there. There is no violence or wars. Everyone is at peace with each other.

What I found to be most interesting was the fact that there people look just like we do. When I asked Ap why his friends didn't look like us the answer was simple. Ap and his friends are a separate race of people that are time travelers. Their bodies are designed to travel at high rates of speed. Their ship travels so fast that if a human, such as one of us, were to be on board, our body would implode, from the inside out. Their bodies are more fluid like, which allows the molecules to float at speeds unimaginable to our way of thinking on this planet.

The thick dark lenses of their outer eye acts as a shield, much like our jet pilots wearing dark visors to protect them from the sun. In much the same way their outer lenses protects their more sensitive inner eye from bright light and radiation. In short, they are pilots, whose bodies are designed for space travel.

When I told them that some people, here on planet Earth, say they were abducted by aliens and taken away in spaceships, Ap was quick to say that was nonsense. A human body such as ours would have to be contained in fluid to keep it from blowing up. The pressure of space travel is something we could not endure at a high enough rate of speed that would actually get us far enough away to see anything. With a room full of scientists that had IQs of no less than 260, I was amazed at how stupid they actually were. Finally, after eight-hours of listening to their ignorance I spoke out.

"Listen, why don't we just put them in a helicopter and fly them back to Hanger Nine? This way if they try to harm anyone the helicopter will crash and kill them too. Does that make you feel better?" I asked as I looked over at Carla in disgust.

An Army troop transport helicopter was brought in. Ap, and his friend, who never spoke a word the entire time, and the bodies of their two friends were flown back to Hanger Nine at gun point.

I was embarrassed to see how we, as American's, actually treated them. We were indeed violent and ignorant people.

It was almost midnight when Ap and his friends boarded their spacecraft. As soon as his friend sat down in the pilots seat, everything on board lit up like a Christmas tree. Opening a hidden compartment, Ap gave Carla four items, and told her to figure them out. One item was a piece of cloth looking material that was one foot square in size. One item was something that looked like a piece of cable, one item looked like a hand held weapon of some sort, the forth item I have no idea how to describe.

Carla would later turn these items over to an Army Colonel named Corso. Colonel Corso would be given twenty million dollars, which would act as a down payment that would be given to a California research laboratory along with these four items. Their task would be to try to figure out what these items were.

Within a short period of time we would begin testing out our new pulse weapon, microwave weapon, and fiber optic cable systems. We would learn that the cloth couldn't be cut, shot through, or burned. It was a material that was unknown to us. Its weave design was what amazed us. What made it so unique was the fact that it gained its strength and durability because it was the same weave design as a spiders webbing. The most obvious was in fact the least obvious in all cases. When Colonel Corso would inquire as to the cost to replicate it, the research company would quote a price of one hundred thousand dollars, per square inch.

Opening the hanger doors we all went outside and waited for Ap to start his spacecraft. When he did I couldn't believe what I was seeing. It was quiet. It had a small humming sound as the large spacecraft floated out of hanger nine and passed us. He went out across the dry sun baked earth, about 400-yards, hovered about 700-feet in the air and then simply vanished from sight. We would never know if it was a cloaking devise or simply a speed that was so fast that the human eye couldn't track it. Whatever it was they were gone in an instant.

"You lied about our planet being attacked by aliens if we didn't let them go, didn't you?" Carla asked as she ran her arm through mine and looked up at me in the darkness of the Nevada night.

"Yup, I sure did," I responded as I leaned forward and kissed my boss on the forehead.

"I thought so," she replied as Rex, Jennifer, and Risa walked up to us.

The mass security of Area 51 began to disappear as Doctor McFadden spoke. "Would anyone ever believe this? We made friends with aliens," she said in an excited voice.

"Unbelievable, simply surreal," Rex added.

"Your all a bunch of fucking idiots. We could have learned from them and advanced our race," she shouted out in defiance.

"They gave us keys to figure out," Carla responded calmly as she glanced over at me.

"Keys? They gave you nothing. How could you be so stupid?" Risa answered bitterly.

"They'll be back, and when they return they'll land right here on this spot, because they now know we won't harm them. You don't enslave people because of how they look or because you're afraid of them. They kept reaching out their hand to communicate with you and you were to blinded by fear to understand," I explained.

"Oh yeah, like you really knew that when you touched the glass," Risa snapped back angrily.

"He offered his hand and I took it. That's what we, the people of the United States of America, do. We accept each other and seek peace. But then again, you wouldn't know anything about that would you?" I asked.

"Fuck you, asshole!" Risa responded bitterly.

"Its the first step of our evolution, and it was the right decision, to seek friendship, to seek peace," I tried to explain calmly.

"And if they had killed us, then what?" Risa asked sarcastically.

"Then you would be dead and it wouldn't matter anymore," I explained jokingly as Rex and Jennifer began to laugh at my statement.

"Well, what do you say, how about I buy everybody dinner?" Carla invited.

"Sounds good to me, I'm starving," Rex replied.

"My gosh, with all of the excitement I completely forgot, I haven't eaten since breakfast," Jennifer answered as they all turned to walk back over to the vehicles.

As Risa turned to follow them I stepped up behind her. Reaching over her left shoulder with my left hand I grabbed her by the chin, I put my right hand against the top upper part of the back of her head. In one quick, cat-like move I pulled upward on her head and pushed her chin slightly to the right. Reaching up with her hands she grabbed my left arm and tried to resist the pressure by pulling her chin to the left. She did exactly what I wanted her to do. It was to the left that I wanted to snap her neck. As she resisted I quickly pulled my left hand fast and hard to the left as I pushed the top of her head to the right. It happened so fast that Doctor Risa Tansiri was dead within a matter of seconds. Her tiny, thin neck snapped silently in the darkness of the Nevada night. Her brainstem severed, death at that point was instant. Both of her hands slid off of my left forearm and fell lifelessly to her sides. Her body quivered for only a second.

Looking up I saw Carla, Rex, and Jennifer as they continued to walk toward the vehicles and talking to each other. Slowly, I lowered Risa's body to the ground and let go of her head. Stepping over her body I moved forward quickly and caught up with Carla and the scientists. Still a few feet behind them, I spoke.

"So, are you going to come with us, Doctor Tansiri? I'd love to continue this discussion with you over dinner," I said calmly as I moved closer behind Carla and her friends. "Well, Doctor, are you coming with us?" I asked again as I stopped and turned around. "Carla!" I shouted loudly. Just as Carla, Jennifer, and Rex turned around I began to run back toward Risa. "Something happened to Risa," I shouted as I reached Risa's body, knelt down, and checked the side of her neck to see if I could find a pulse.

"Oh my god!" Carla shouted as they ran up to where Risa was laying on the hard dirt ground.

Clearing her airway, I began CPR. I knew there was no way to revive Doctor Tansiri. But it looked good and would make both Jennifer and Rex feel better knowing that I had at least tried to revive her. I continued CPR for about five minutes and then checked the side of Risa's neck for a pulse one last time.

"She's gone," I said sadly as I sat down on the ground next to Risa's dead body. "Why? How could this happen?" Jennifer asked in a whisper of a voice as she placed both hands over her mouth.

"She had a heart condition. She didn't want anyone to know about it. Getting all excited and angry must have agitated it and gave her a massive heart attack. How sad. How very sad, what a waste of a brilliant young mind," Carla explained sadly as she looked down at Risa.

"It happens. At least she got to see real aliens before she passed on," Rex commented sadly.

"Rex, would you please call security and tell them we will need them to contact Ms. Tansiri's family and make the proper arrangements to ship Risa's body back home to Thailand," Carla requested in a sad tone.

"Yes, of course I will," Rex replied as he began to walk toward Hanger Nine.

"Jennifer, there's nothing you can do here. Why don't you go with Doctor Rhoads. David and I will meet you inside as soon as security gets here," Carla recommended. Without saying a word Doctor McFadden nodded her head in agreement and followed behind Rex. This was the first time Carla had mentioned his last name.

As we watched Rex and Jennifer walk in through the open doors of Hanger Nine, Carla spoke, "Smooth, David, real smooth. And you did it right in front of everyone. How did you do it?" Carla asked with a slight grin.

"Do what?" I replied as I looked up at the full moon shinning in the midnight sky.

"Okay, I know. The best kept secrets are the secrets that keep themselves, right?" Carla asked as security guards began to walk out of Hanger Nine.

"That's what they say, ma'am," I answered. "Were you serious when you said that the President doesn't even know about this place?" I asked.

"President's come and go, David. They know that Area 51 is out here. They're just not allowed to see it and one day write a book about it. We on the other hand are here to stay. We run this country, not the President. He's just a figure head for the world to see," Carla explained as several guards walked up to us with their flashlights in their hands.

"We'll take care of this, ma'am," one of the guards said.

"Thank you, gentlemen," Carla replied as we began to walk toward the open door of Hanger Nine.

"How did they build all of this without anyone knowing about it?" I questioned.

"This whole area is full of tunnels and mine shafts, David. Nevada used to be a big mining state. It was rich with gold and silver. When the gold and silver ran out the miners left. We brought in Japanese work crews. Housed them in Mexico and flew them in everyday to build it. All of the materials and supplies were shipped in by air and army trucks. In ten years Area 51 won't be that much of a secret anymore. We're building two new sites in two different areas as we speak. Now those new sites will be state of the art, underground, and top secret. We're far more advanced than we let the world know, David. We release things to certain companies a little at a time and let them take all of the credit. We, in return get huge kick backs in profits from them," Carla explained.

"Like the sky pagers and cell phones that only we have. That's where all the money comes from to fund these top secret projects?" I questioned.

"Some of it. Most of it comes from Congress. You don't really think we pay eight hundred dollars for a toilet seat for the military do you? We pay ten dollars for the toilet seat. The other seven hundred and ninety dollars goes to our special project fund, that's us. You'll see more as time goes on," Carla explained as she ran her arm through mine and gave me a hug.

"Why me, Carla? That's the one thing that I don't understand. Why did you pick me?" I asked as I stopped walking and turned to look at Carla.

"At first, I was looking at Danny, but then you caught my eye. Why you? Because you're a quick thinker and you're unpredictable. I never know what you're going to do, but I can always count on the fact that you'll get the job done. Danny is more muscle, you're more cunning, and that's why. Hell, you even teach me things. My best scientist couldn't figure out in two weeks, what you figured out in ten minutes. It was their body that was part of the system that makes the spaceship operate," Carla said proudly as she looked up at me. "We can use that to our advantage in the military."

"It was a lucky guess," I replied.

"Lucky guess my ass. You've got a gift, David. Right away you put your hand on the glass, and when you did the entire situation changed. We became friends with Ap and his people and then let them go. We would have never understood had you not thought through the problem so quickly," Carla explained as she looked up at me.

"What did you do with all the water from Groom Lake?" I asked with raised eyebrows and a wide grin.

"We rerouted it. It's all underground now. Lets go and get something to eat and tomorrow I'll show you everything that's here, some of the projects we are currently working on, and an underground world that has a beautiful lake in it," Carla explained as we walked into Hanger Nine.

* * * * * * *

Staying true to her word we spent the next two days at Groom Lake. Carla showed me everything, much of which I will not reveal in the writing of this book.

On July 20, 1969, astronauts Neil Armstrong and Edwin "Buzz" Aldrin became the first persons to step on the moon. Now in my mid-twenties, I would stand at Area S-4 in Nevada's forbidden Area 51 and look at the exact spot Mr. Armstrong made his one large leap for mankind. Once again, it was one of America's biggest lies. It was a staged event just so America could say they beat the Russian's to the moon.

Within a few weeks I would go to the Pentagon and watch that historical film footage once again. This time I was older and trained to see what was right in front of my eyes but once hidden from my sight because of my lack of understanding. Taking a more careful look at the film, I now noticed that there was no moon dust on the landing pods of Neil Armstrong's space capsule. With his space rockets blasting downward to ease his landing, there should have been a small crater size hole underneath the capsule and dust all over it from the landing, yet everything was clean and no crater was there. The American flag was already up when he tells America that he is now opening the hatch to step outside. If he just opened the hatch, who put the flag up? Why was the flag blowing freely in the wind? There is no wind on the moon. How did his land rover get there and why was it so clean?

Sitting back as I watched the film, I would shake my head in disgust as I saw for the first time that the shadows of Armstrong and his space capsule were going in two different directions at once. This was impossible unless the large stage lights that were used to film the event were pointing in from two different angles of Area 51.

As I did a little more research, I would find out that two people of the original team of Apollo astronauts would threaten to expose the lie to the American people. Their conscious was bothering them. Just before they were scheduled to go public on national television, three of our NASA astronauts would burn to death while sitting in their spacecraft just before it was launched on national television. People would say, "What a tragic accident," I would say, "What a great assassination."

The moon is five hundred thousand miles from earth. Between us is a radiation field that is one thousand miles long. It is impossible for us to travel through it with the technology we had available to us at the time. The Russians could never figure out how we got through it without it killing our astronauts. The answer is simple, we never made the trip.

However, I will say this much, Area 51, Groom Lake, showed me that we are a lot more advanced than we let other countries of the world know. Beneath Area S-12 of Area 51 is a vast open cavern. Within it are trees, artificial sunlight, birds, plants, and a beautiful lake that is called, Mystery Lake. There is a fresh air and water system down there. The technology of which came from the two spacecrafts that are hidden in Hanger's Seven and Eight of Area S-12, Groom Lake.

On day four we headed back to the Pentagon. Within six months many people living around the area of Tonopah, Carlin, Pahrump, and Ely, Nevada would begin to report strange sightings of fast moving objects and glowing lights from the area known as 51, Groom Lake. Within eighteen months our government would expand the Off Limits – Restricted Area of Area 51. They would expand the area out another full mile in all directions to keep those Americans with inner vision from seeing the truth. Ap and his friends would return frequently.

Some information would be leaked in a subtle way to Hollywood movie producers. This would spark a number of major motion movie pictures and television science fiction series about aliens and other worlds. It would be done with the hope of slowly programming the minds of the American people. The more you see aliens on television, the more likely you will be willing to accept it when you find out that its real. This will cause less of a panic when the truth is finally known for all to see. Crop circles would begin to appear in England, Ireland, and then in limited areas of the United States. This again is another way to bring awareness of alien life through the means of mystery.

Eventually a man will surface that is not afraid to search for the truth. Because I do not have his permission to use his name in the writing of this book or anyway to reach him to get his permission, I will simply call him Mr. Bell. His radio broadcast program will become very popular throughout the United States and even into other countries. He doesn't understand what it is inside of him that drives his curiosity to search for the truth of aliens, space travel, the quickening of time, and the phenomenon of ghosts, poltergeists, and life beyond this plain of existence as we know it. Some of it frightens Mr. Bell, as it would with most people. But it doesn't stop him from searching for the truth. Eventually he will come to realize that he was sent here for a purpose. His wife is a good woman who is also a witch that holds within her the power of white light energy. She is a good witch with the power to protect him. He lives in a trailer out in the middle of the desert of Pahrump, Nevada. Close to the forbidden Area 51 of Groom Lake. In time he will figure it out. When he does he will no longer be afraid.

For now however, as the author of this book, I would advise you to search for the truth. See what is right in front of you, and when you do, "See with seeing eyes," and don't be afraid. They are out there, they are watching us, and they are helping us, because they are part of us.

Special Note to the Reader

I have been asked, does the government have a plan in case of an alien invasion?

My answer is this. There are undercover projects that you will never hear about. A group called the MJ-12, composed of both government and military officials, studies the hardware of downed alien spacecraft to create defenses against attacks.

President Reagan's Star Wars program wasn't intended to shoot down soviet missiles. It was designed to obliterate ET. Our government feels that most aliens are hostile. Ap was the exception. This is part of the reason for the cover-up. I also believe we now have particle-beam weapons we use to shoot down alien spacecraft, technology that came from them.

On July 3, 1947, in Roswell, New Mexico, Rancher Mac Brazel discovered pieces of what appeared to be an alien spacecraft. They are now in Hanger One at Groom Lake.

On January 7, 1948, Air National Guard pilot Thomas Mantell tailed a metallic, teardrop-shaped figure across the Kentucky sky. When Mantell pulled up for a closer look, he crashed and died. The Louisville Courier printed that he was shot down by aliens.

To date over 10,000 crop circles have appeared all over the world. On August 12, 1972, in Wilshire, England, two farmers watched as a thirty-foot circle of wheat laid down all by itself.

September 1967, a filly was found in Colorado's San Luis Valley. Its brain had been carved out, burn marks were found on the ground nearby, and the carcass smelled like medicine.

On March 13, 1997, hundreds of Phoenix residents report a giant v-shaped UFO flying over the area at a reported speed of 400 mph.

As the author of this book I find it very interesting that after serving eight years as one of our most loved presidents, that Ronald Reagan would become ill. A brand new disease would surface called Alzheimer's. It works on the neurological system of the brain and causes you to lose all your memory. President Reagan was the only president that had ever seen, with his own eyes, our hidden secrets in Area 51. Knowing that there are indeed aliens that could pose a threat to our great nation, he tries to create a Star Wars program. Using key words, Star Wars, he was trying to tell the American people that we were, and still are, at risk of an alien invasion. All of a sudden, President Ronald Reagan can't remember who he is. Strange how that happened, isn't it?

I would say that the most obvious is the least obvious, if you know what you're looking for, and it happens right before your very eyes. But then again this is a book of fiction, isn't it?

Chapter Twenty-Three
Samurai One

Opening my eyes, I laid flat on my back and stared at my bedroom ceiling. I had been home from Area 51, Groom Lake for three weeks. Ever since my encounter with Ap I hadn't had any nightmares.

When I had touched the glass and communicated with Ap I had felt a tingling run through my body. But once he and his friends were removed from the containment area and we actually shook hands physically, I felt a strange sensation run through me. I can't explain it but I just felt different inside, more at peace with myself.

"I can't believe this. I'm not covered with sweat, my body isn't trembling, I'm not emotionally upset, the bad dreams are gone," I thought to myself as I got out of bed slowly, walked through my house, went outside, and into my backyard.

Looking at my watch, it was almost 3:30 a.m. Placing my eye onto the eyepiece of my new telescope I looked out across the darkness of the clear, vast sky and smiled when I saw the full moon shinning brightly out in the darkness. I had purchased the powerful telescope as soon as I had gotten home from Nevada. My excuse was that it was for Tara and her friends to help expand their minds. The real reason I had bought it was because I had a newfound interest in space and who was out there.

"What's up, Ap," I whispered with a grin as I turned and headed back inside to get a cold Pepsi.

Opening my refrigerator door, I scratched the right cheek of my butt and smiled, "Oh yeah," I said out loud to myself as I pulled out a long neck bottle of Pepsi, a half eaten large pizza from Pizza Hut, and a bottle of Valasic pickles.

I sat down at my bar, opened my Pepsi, and took a drink. Out of the corner of my eye I saw Kathy walking down the steps. She was wearing her black, bikini underwear and nothing else. Scratching her head she looked up at me and yawned. "Are you okay?" she asked still half asleep.

"I'm sorry, I tried to be quite, I didn't mean to wake you," I explained as I pointed at my pizza. "Hungry?" I asked with a broad smile.

"Oh God, you're not really going to eat that are you?" Kathy asked as she walked up behind me, slid her arms around my waste and nestled her body up against my back. Resting her head on the back of my shoulder she yawned again. "Come on baby, let's go back to bed," she said tiredly.

"You go ahead, I'm going to check the computer for messages and then I'll be right behind you, okay?" I explained as I took a big bite out of my cold pizza.

"Okay," she replied as she let go of me and headed back upstairs to bed.

The girl scouts had invited Kathy to a special girl Scout meeting last week. They all gathered at my home to decide what kind of swimming pool I was going to have installed in my backyard. It took them ten-hours. The decision was finally made; it would be a full size in ground pool, with two diving boards at two different heights and a water slide in the middle toward the deeper end.

Even though I had both Don and Andy with me as backup, we had no say in the matter. The girls knew what was best for Uncle David's needs. It also just happened to be exactly what they wanted.

It was Kathy's last week of sick leave, so she decided to spend it with me, at my place. That alone was worth the cost of the swimming pool. Her ankle had healed up real well from her injury in the Shetlands when we went after Kevin O'Donald. Tomorrow Kathy would have to fly back to her home in Virginia and get ready to go back to work in the spy game. Eight weeks of being on crutches was driving her nuts. She was definitely ready to get back into the game.

Finishing my snack I checked my computer and went back to bed. Feeling Kathy cuddle up next to me I could smell the scent of her body. "I could get used to this," I thought to myself as I yawned, closed my eyes, and drifted back to sleep.

* * * * * * *

Licking the chocolate off of my fingers I looked at my empty box of Girl Scout mint cookies. Setting the empty box down on the floor next to me, I placed both of my hands on my stomach, lay back on my carpet, and groaned. Kathy had left three days ago and I was all alone and board to death.

I closed my eyes and listened to my home. It was quite. "My god this is nice," I thought to myself as I lay still in the peaceful stillness.

It was the smell of dirt and blood that caused me to open my eyes. Turning my head slightly to the left I saw the little six-year old Vietnamese girl that the Viet Cong had raped and left all alone in the jungle to die. She was naked, her long, black hair had dried leaves in it. Her inner thighs were covered with blood. The smell of her body was the same as it was when I held her in my arms at the time of her death.

"Hi," she said in a soft whisper.

"Hi," I replied as a chill ran up my spine.

"It hurts," she explained.

"I know," I answered as I looked down at my right hand and saw that it was covered with blood.

"I want to see my mommy," she explained as a tear ran down her cheek.

"I know," I replied as my heart broke inside at the thought of this child being afraid and all alone.

"I'm afraid," she said as she began to cry.

"Don't cry, little one, don't be afraid. I'll protect you," I explained as I stood up and reached my arms out to her. Just as I did, she reached out her little arms, and ran to me. When she did, her tiny body vanished as it entered into mine.

Startled, I sat up quickly, and began to look around the room. My nose was filled with the smells of blood, jungle leaves, and dirt. "Oh shit," I muttered to myself. Looking at my hands they were trembling so badly that I could barely control them as I placed them over my sweat covered face.

My heart raced with the combination of fear and adrenaline as I tried to calm myself down.

"Focus, David," I said to myself as I fought hard to catch my breath. "It was a bad dream, a nightmare, that's all, nothing more," I said as I tried to convince myself that I wasn't losing my mind. "Damnit, the ghosts of my past are back. I knew it was to good to be true," I whispered to myself as I stood up and headed to my bathroom to take a shower.

* * * * * * *

Two days had passed since my last nightmare. I continued to find myself unconsciously rubbing my right hand in an attempt to get the young child's blood off of it, even though there was no visible blood to be found. The memory of holding her small broken body in my arms so long ago in the jungles of Vietnam was still as vivid in my mind as ever.

"You couldn't save her, David, there was nothing that you could do. It wasn't your fault, stop blaming yourself," I continued to tell myself over and over in my mind, as I sat at my desk in the den and stared at my computer screen.

My telephone rang; I turned on the black scrambler box, and put the phone to my ear.

"Hello, Wong's Bar and Grill," I said jokingly into the mouthpiece.

"I would like to order two dozen egg rolls, a plate of ham fried rice, and bring it along with your young ass to the Situation Room. Our plane is on its way. On second thought, just get your butt to the Pentagon and be ready to do your thing. I need the Sandman right now," Carla said calmly as she hung the phone up in my ear.

"Oh yeah," I shouted out loud as I placed two drops of Methadrine under my tongue, smiled, and began to lock my house up.

* * * * * * *

Looking at my solid gold Tag Heuer divers watch, I opened the door to the Situation Room and stepped inside. It was almost 11:00 a.m. Inside I found Carla, Ollie, and Deputy Director Richard Crock waiting for me. Sitting down next to Ollie I nudged him with my elbow, "What's up, partner," I whispered with a grin. Staring back at me Ollie didn't say a word. I knew then some thing was wrong.

I set the bag of Chinese take out food on the table then slid it over to Carla, keeping a straight face.

"What's this?" Carla questioned as she opened the bag and peeked inside.

"It's your order, ma'am. Two dozen egg rolls and an order of ham fried rice," I replied. "That's why it took so long for me to get here. The Chinese cook had to hand roll the egg rolls," I explained with a serious look on my face.

"You are such an ass!" Carla said with a smile.

"Yes, ma'am, that's what Agent Eckland, Major Bell, and Major Mosier are always telling me," I explained calmly as I sat back in my chair and looked at Ms. Silverman.

"We have just received information that this man and this young lady are planning a terrorist strike against America sometime in the very near future," Carla explained as she slid the 8x10 photographs across the table to me.

"His name is Walter Chang, he's a high ranking member of the Chinese Triad who happens to be living in a monster Italian villa nestled in the hills of Orange County, California. Her name is Chantel Cafarelli; she lives in Milan, Italy and just happens to be the owner of the estate where Mr. Chang is living.

I want you to fly to California first, breach, and clear the estate that Mr. Chang is living in and find a way to get us into his computer system. We need you to crack that computer system, gentlemen, and find out what it is that Mr. Chang is up to. If its as bad as we're being led to believe it is, you, David, will be flying to Italy to introduce the Sandman to Ms. Cafarelli. Neil is waiting in the War Room to give you a bird's eye view of the estate in California. You might want to take some back-up with you, David. Neil tells me that Mr. Chang is well protected with heavily armed men," Carla explained with a serious look in her eyes.

"I thought you guys swept the Triad up after we found those weapons in St. Paul's?" I questioned.

"We did, David, these are a completely different group of people. We just found out about them no more than twenty-one hours ago," CIA Deputy Director Crock explained as he looked at his watch.

"Time is against us on this one, gentlemen. We have no idea as to what they're up to. What we do know is that its something big. Draw what you need from here and we will have people standing by to assist you with anything you need if you should happen to call for it," Carla explained.

Turning to look at Ollie I kept a straight face. "Last time I teamed up with you I got shot!" I explained.

"Yes, and you did it so well," Ollie joked back at me, as we stood up to go and meet with Neil.

* * * * * * *

Elite Black Covert Operation
Code Name: Samurai One
Target: Walter Chang
Target Status: Green
GSP Coordinates: 81642-99741
Mission Profile: Breach and clear the estate of Walter Chang. Take down and eliminate any and all threat against us or allied interests. Crack computer system. Secure hazardous weapons and turn them over to Delta Force if found.

"What time is it?" I asked as I looked through my small pair of high powered binoculars.

"Almost 5:00 a.m. Sun should be coming up any minute," Ollie replied as he sat next to me in the darkness. We were sitting almost twelve hundred yards away from the estate of Walter Chang.

Perched on the side of one of California's beautiful mountains we watched down into the valley and took a head count to see how many guards we were going to have to encounter in order to breach this massive estate and get inside the large heavily armed home.

"How do these people get away with this for Gods sake. I count sixteen heavily armed guards so far. Who knows how many more are on the inside of that home. This is California for crying out loud, not China," I said in bewilderment.

"He's a diplomat and that estate you're looking at is protected under diplomatic international policy," Ollie responded as I placed two drops of Methadrine under my tongue and looked over at him.

"Bullshit. That's not an embassy it's a Triad strong hold. Everyone of those guys is tattooed from their neck to their toes. Man, I wish Chopper and Butch were here right now," I explained.

"Sorry, partner, I know I'm not very good at this kind of stuff but I'll do my best," Ollie said with a sigh.

"Oh no, Ollie, I didn't mean it like that. Your job is to crack the computer. All I meant was that sixteen people are a lot for one man to take out. I have to figure out how to do it without any of them noticing what's going on. If I shoot ten of them and one guy sees his buddy laying there dead, he's going to set off the alarm and we're screwed," I explained as I looked down at my Remington .308 caliber, silenced match competition rifle with its twenty-power scope.

"I hear your really good with one of those," Ollie said with a serious look on his face as the first rays of sun light began to shine their slender fingers of light across the California mountain tops.

"I better be. I just don't understand why Carla didn't let the Navy Seals or Delta Force hit this estate, that's all," I answered not understanding the logic of it all.

"Can you imagine what would happen if the news media found out we had to use our elite commando teams to secure a hostile enemy in our own country? The American people would panic, they would never feel safe again living in their own suburban homes," Ollie explained.

"And if I screw this up? Then what?" I asked as I took a sip of water out of my canteen.

"It goes down as bad guys shooting it out with bad guys from China. The American people are used to stuff like that happening in this country," Ollie explained with a smile.

"I've never seen you worried like this before. Are you okay?" Ollie asked in a kindly way.

"Yeah, I'm alright. I'm just feeling wired I guess," I calmly explained.

"Still having those nightmares?"

"Yeah. They went away for about two weeks but then they came back with a vengeance," I explained sadly.

"I know where there is an ancient Shaolin Temple hidden deep in the mountains of China. I have a friend that could help to get you in there. It would be rare for them to help a westerner, but my friend could get you in. I'm sure of it. If anyone can help you, partner, those old monks can," Ollie explained as the sun began to brighten up the entire valley in front of us. "Just let me know if you're interested."

"I'll think about it, partner, thanks. But for now lets get out of here. I need to get some different weapons if I'm going to pull this off. We'll come back and hit this place tonight," I explained as we prepared to withdraw from our hidden position.

* * * * * * *

"How do you want to play it, partner?" Ollie asked in a serious tone of voice as he chambered a live round into his silenced .9mm Smith and Wesson, model 59, automatic pistol.

Loading my brand new Smith and Wesson automatic pistols, I paused for a moment before I answered. My mind took me back to Vietnam and some of the missions that Nick, Chopper, Butch, and I had gone out on. Placing two drops of liquid Methadrine under my tongue, I put the tiny glass vial back into my pocket and watched as the sun set in the west causing darkness to descended upon us once again.

"There's really no way to plan something like this out, Ollie. I've learned from experience that my Seal team instructors are one hundred percent correct. Always expect the unexpected, everything is subject to change at any given moment, and the most obvious is the least obvious. I'm going to wait for all of the bedroom lights to go off. Then I'm going to put on these night vision, thermal goggles, and go in shooting.

There's a twelve foot high security fence around the entire property. They're not expecting any trouble, so its not electrified and there is no motion sensor wire running through it. So I really believe I can simply breach the fence by cutting through it.

From what we saw last night, there are two armed guards that are on the roof, but their not doing their jobs. They just stand around smoking cigarettes and talking to each other. Four guards walk the property close to the estate itself and the other ten sleep in that building at the rear of the estate. They switch off in shifts every three hours.

I'll use my rifle to take out the two guards on the roof first. Then I'll breach the fence and take out the four that are on foot. Once I've got the direct threat terminated, I'll hit the guard house with cyanide spray. That will kill everyone inside.

If I survive that, then I'll enter the house and secure it," I explained as I put on my Kevlar bulletproof vest.

"Sounds good, I'll stay directly behind you and cover your six," Ollie explained calmly as he looked out toward the massive estate.

"Not this time, partner, I go this one alone. Your not going anywhere until I get this place secured," I replied.

"But," Ollie began to say as I cut him off before he could say another word.

"No my friend. I'm expendable, Ollie. My life sucks. You on the other hand have a bright future ahead of you. I do the 'wet work', you do the computer," I explained as I pulled my black knit top on and began to put on my shoulder and belt holsters.

"You're team leader, I don't like it with you going solo and all, but I trust your instincts, your carrying four handguns at one time?" Ollie questioned as I checked all four of my automatic handguns and secured them in their holsters.

"Each gun fires fifteen shots. I won't have time to reload, so I'll simply drop the gun when it's empty and grab a fresh one. If I can't get this done with sixty shots I'm in real trouble," I explained with a grin.

"You'll get it done. The Sandman always puts 'em to sleep," Ollie replied with confidence.

"I hope so, I just wish that I knew how many people there are in that damn house. If anything happens to me, you abort this mission and call it in to Carla. Don't cross the fence, Ollie. She'll activate Plan B automatically."

"Plan B? I didn't know that there was a Plan B," Ollie answered with a surprised look on his face.

"There's always a Plan B, partner," I explained as I leaned my back up against a large walnut tree to wait for everyone inside of the estate to go to sleep. I knew that there was no Plan B. I hated to lie to my partner, but I also knew that if they killed me I didn't want this crazy die hard Marine to get himself killed trying to save me. Ollie had become a good friend. I wasn't gong to risk his life, not even to save mine.

* * * * * * *

When the last light went off in the upstairs bedroom section of Walter Chang's estate, I looked at my watch; it was 1:21 a.m. I waited patiently for two of the guards to walk past the east section of the estate and disappear around the back corner of the house.

I was fifty yards from the outer perimeter of the fence when I stood up, raised my silenced .308 caliber Remington rifle, and took careful aim at the first of the two men that were standing guard on the walkway of the estate roof.

"Say goodnight, asshole," I whispered as I placed the cross hairs of my scope onto the left side of the first mans head. Taking in a deep breath I let it out slowly as I stood in a free style stance. Releasing half of the air slowly from my lungs, I held my breath as I applied pressure to the trigger of my competition match rifle.

The first guards head exploded, sending with it a crimson red spray of blood, flesh, and brain matter in all directions, most of which sprayed directly into the face of his friend who was lighting his cigarette and standing right next to him. Quickly, I chambered another round into the firing position of my rifle, aimed, and pulled the trigger a second time.

Feeling the butt of my rifle kick backward into my right shoulder for a second time sent a surge of excitement and adrenaline through my entire body. My second shot hit the second man in the chest blowing his heart out through his back. His body flew backwards and disappeared from sight.

The head shot of the first man caused the second man to freeze in shock from what he had just witnessed. It gave me the extra few seconds needed for me to reload and take aim once again on my second target.

I set my rifle down onto the leaf covered ground, ran up to the security fence, pulled out my small pair of bolt cutters, and quickly cut my way through the chain link fence.

Ollie didn't understand why I had brought with me the hand size bolt cutters instead of the traditional wire cutters. Once I explained that a chain link fence is a lot tougher to cut through than you would think, he realized that he shouldn't always believe its as easy as it looks in a Hollywood movie.

Sticking the bolt cutter back into my leg pouch, I slipped through the thin slice in the fence. Pulling my first two pistols out of my belt holsters I cocked the hammers back and moved quickly across the plush green lawn toward the house.

My heart was pounding in my chest. My senses were on full alert. The smell of freshly mowed lawn filled my nose as I drew near the east side of the red brick estate.

I felt alive again for the first time in along time. "I might as well get use to it," I thought to myself as I placed my back up against the wall of the home. Pointing each gun in opposite directions, I paused to catch my breath with the hope of calming down a bit. I was on a full adrenaline rush, I was excited and scared to death, all at the same time. "God I love this shit," I thought to myself as I moved toward the southeast corner of the home.

Sixteen feet from the corner of the home I stopped. Raising my head slightly, I smelled the warm California breeze that was blowing gently in my face. It was then that I caught it. "Aftershave," I said to myself as I quickly but very quietly laid down on the ground and pressed my back and legs up against the side of the house.

From this angle I pointed the pistol, in my right hand, chest high at the corner closest to me. With my left arm extended out along the side of the house I pointed my left pistol in the direction that I had just came from.

I knew that someone was coming toward me. I could smell him. I also had both zones covered in case someone came back around from the other side by surprise. I could hear the cloth material of his pants as it brushed up against itself as he moved closer toward the corner of the house and to where I was laying.

"He's not talking to anyone, he must be alone," I thought to myself. Just as I thought it, the bodyguard appeared and stepped around the corner of the house.

I knew he wouldn't be able to see me right away in the position I was in. I paused for a second and was glad I did. A second guard stepped around the corner of the house, paused, and lit his cigarette. When he did I fired. My first shot hit the man closest to me. I was worried about him. He was carrying a fully loaded Israeli made Uzi .9mm machine gun. It hung from a leather strap over his right shoulder.

The .9mm Rhino round hit the first guard in the face and blew most of his head off. As his knees buckled and blood began to squirt out of the top of what was once his head, I fired two more quick shots into the upper chest of the second guard who was now trying to reach for his weapon. His arms lashed out wildly as his body flew backwards and toppled to the ground.

Jumping up to my feet I looked behind me to make sure the coast was clear and then peaked around the corner of the large home. Seeing no one, I moved quickly toward the front of the home.

My thermal night vision goggles were working great but felt bulky on my face. I reached the front of the estate. There were two large round cement pillars that stood in front of and off to the sides of the front entrance of the estate. There was a walk in archway of red brick that led up to the large dark oak wood, double doors at the front of the home. A big crystal chandelier hung from the center of the archway that was used as the front door light. The light was off as I stepped into the archway.

There was a large circular driveway in front of the home. Several cars were still parked out in front. An all black Bentley two-door sedan, a red two-door Ferrari sports car, and a brand new two-door Rolls Royce, silver-cloud, convertible, which still had the convertible top down.

Listening carefully I heard nothing. "Oh shit," I thought to myself. "What if they come back around the other way and find the bodies of their friends laying on the ground." Moving out of the safety of the archway I started to head to the other side of the house. As I did I heard two men talking to each other.

Stepping back quickly I returned to the safety of the cement archway and pressed my back up against the side that the men were walking towards. I could hear their voices more clearly now. They had rounded the corner of the estate and were headed toward me. I had noticed as I moved across the front of the estate that all of the window curtains had been pulled shut on the front of the home. "Thank God that the Chinese like their privacy. The only problem that I've got now, is if someone comes walking out through the front doors," I thought to myself as my heart raced in my chest. Tightening my grip on my pistols I waited in the darkness of the front door archway as the voices drew near. I could smell the smoke from their cigarettes now. With every step they took my senses peaked.

Then without even thinking I stepped out of the archway turned to face both of the men and walked quickly towards them. Seeing me, the look on their faces told me they were caught completely by surprise.

"Draw," I said calmly as I raised both of my weapons and opened fire.

The two Chinese guards wore regular clothes; I fired two shots from each of my weapons. The high velocity impact of the Rhino round bullets cut through their upper bodies as easy as a hot knife cuts through butter. Both men tried to grab for their weapons but it all happened so fast there wasn't much they could really do. The high impact of the bullets drove both men backwards so fast that their feet flew upwards almost a foot off the ground as their bodies dropped backwards. These bullets were so lethal that they were both dead before they hit the ground beneath them.

"Now that was real fucking stupid," I said out loud to myself in a whisper. "I could have let them both walk by and shot 'em in the back from the darkness of the front door archway. Yeah, but this was definitely more fun. Draw!" I said again to myself. "Don't get suicidal, David, and stop talking to yourself," I said as I began to smile.

Moving around the estate I headed out back, to my left was a long garage full of vehicles; to my right was a full size in-ground swimming pool. A hundred yards past that and to the far left was the small sleeping quarters for the rest of the security guards. I could hear a mild humming sound that was coming from the back of the small structure. Walking to the back of the small guesthouse I smiled when I saw what it was.

"A central air conditioning unit," I said to myself as I moved up to the round metal cover that housed the unit. It sat on top of a cement slab on the ground in back of the house. It was an expensive unit that drew air from the outside, chilled it, and sent it into the guesthouse through the floor vent system.

Placing both of my weapons back into their holsters, I felt around the sides of the air conditioning unit with my hands. I was looking for the spot where the unit pulled the air into it. Feeling the spot that was sucking the air in, I reached into my left, cargo pant leg pocket and pulled out the black, aerosol canister of the deadly cyanide poison. I set the canister of deadly poison next to the intake vent; I held my breath and pulled the metal pin out of the top of the canister. As I did I let go of it and very quickly stepped back away from the entire unit and moved back toward the estate as the canister hissed. The air conditioner would spread the deadly gas throughout the entire guesthouse. As it did, it would kill everyone inside within five seconds.

"So far so good," I thought to myself as I moved across the back lawn and up to the home once again. Moving toward the west wing of the home I reached into my back pocket and pulled out my lock pick gun with my left hand and my silenced .9mm pistol out of its holster with my right hand. I stepped up to the door of the service entrance, put the lock pick gun in my mouth, and held it with my teeth. Reaching for the doorknob I turned it. Hearing the door lock click I smiled. It was unlocked. But then again it should be. They weren't expecting any trouble. I put the lock pick gun back in my pocket, opened the door, and stepped inside. Quietly, I closed the door behind me and adjusted my thermal night vision goggles. The house was dark but I could see everything clearly. Moving through the small service entrance I stepped into the room next to it.

It was a huge kitchen and the smell of oriental food filled the entire area. It had a walk in cooler, a large butcher block cutting table in the center of the floor, and an assortment of pots and pans hanging from a rack above the large marble countertop to the right.

Just as I started to move forward I heard something in the next room. "Shit, someone's coming," I said to myself as I knelt down behind the butcher-block table. Holstering my weapon, I pulled my German made Meridian knife out of its leather sheath. This elite knife had a blade that was made out of molybdenum vanadium. Amanda had sent it to me from Germany and its cutting edge was razor sharp.

Taking off my night vision goggles I set them gently down on the marble floor beside me. Poised, I waited. My heart raced with the combination of total fear, excitement, and adrenaline as I listened to the kitchen door open and heard the clicking sound of the light switch as whoever it was turned on the kitchen lights.

Listening, I heard the refrigerator door open. I peaked around the corner of the butcher-block table and saw that it was only one person. He was in his mid-forties, had pepper gray hair and stood about five-feet, six-inches tall. As he stuck his head inside the refrigerator I made my move.

In one quick move I stepped up behind him and reached around him with my left hand and grabbed him by the mouth. At the same time I quickly placed the razor sharp edge of my knifes blade against his throat.

"Shhh, one sound and you're dead. Do you understand?" I asked as I whispered into his left ear. Nodding his head yes, I continued. "How many people are in the house?" I asked as I turned him around to face the door of the kitchen and pushed the refrigerator door closed with my hip. Raising his hands he held up eight fingers.

"Bullshit!," I said angrily as I applied pressure to the knife. Grunting, he pointed at my hand wanting me to remove it from his mouth. "If you scream, you die. Understand?" I asked as my heart raced with excitement. Nodding his head yes, I slowly lowered my left hand and placed it on his shoulder.

"Only eight people are in house," he whispered in broken English.

"Is Walter Chang here?" I asked.

"Yes, upstairs asleep with his wife," the man replied.

"Where's the rest of the people?" I asked calmly.

"We leave tomorrow to go to Rome. Mr. Chang tell everyone to go and have vacation. No workers are here, only body guards," he explained with a trembling voice. "Please, you no kill me. Money is upstairs in safe," he added afraid I was going to kill him.

"Where are the other five people?" I asked calmly.

"Front room, they sleep now. We leave early to go to airport," he explained.

"Are they armed? Do they have guns?" I questioned.

"Yes," he replied in a whisper.

Lowering my knife, I pulled it away from his throat and brought it behind him. As I did I quickly clasped my left hand back over his mouth and drove the blade of my knife in between his fourth and fifth rib. The razor sharp blade sliced through the muscle in his side and entered his heart. His body tensed as he tried to grab my left hand, I twisted the blade of the knife, which turned his heart to mush.

Slowly, I lowered his lifeless body to the floor and pulled my knife out of his side. I placed my knife back into its leather holder, turned off the kitchen light, and put my night vision goggles back on. Pulling one of my silenced automatic pistols out of its holster, I cocked the hammer back and opened the kitchen door.

I was amazed at how long the expensive hand carved oriental table was as I walked through the master dinning room. There was crystal china everywhere. Leaving the master dinning room I walked down the hallway and looked into the front room. All of the furniture was oriental. There were statues, paintings, and vases everywhere. Most of which appeared to be from the Ming Dynasty. It was absolutely beautiful and priceless.

In the front room, I saw all the suitcases lined up to my left and five bodyguards as they slept soundly in front of me on the two large sofas and in the chairs next to them. One was snoring. Firing five quick shots I could smell the faint smell of gunpowder coming from my pistol barrel. All five of the guards lay still. The snoring had stopped.

I spent the next hour moving slowly through the entire estate. Checking to make sure no one else was here. I cleared the basement and lower section of the home first, then went upstairs and systematically began to check all the bedrooms and bathrooms.

Reaching the master bedroom, I realized that the man in the kitchen had told me the truth. There were only eight people here. The home was basically empty. Their bags were packed. They were leaving for Rome.

Very quietly, I slipped into the master bedroom and seeing the large master bed on the opposite side of the room I walked up to it. There laying in the bed in front of me was one of the Chinese Triads richest and most powerful men, Walter Chang and his wife. Raising my right hand I pointed my pistol barrel at Walter's face.

"The Sandman is here, Mr. Chang," I said out loud. My voice startled him and his wife. Opening their eyes they both looked around in the darkness of their bedroom. I could see them clearly with my night vision goggles. All they could see was the dark figure of a stranger pointing a gun at them.

"What? Who is it? Who is in my bedroom?" Chang asked.

"The President sends his regards, Mr. Chang," I said loudly as I pulled the trigger one time. My bullet caught Walter Chang mid-center in the face as his wife began to scream. My second bullet hit Mrs. Chang in the mouth. As it did the room fell into a dead silence.

I found the light switch, took off my night vision goggles, and turned on the light. Had I turned the light on while I was wearing the thermal night vision goggles, the bright light would have temporarily blinded me.

Looking over at the bed, Walter Chang and his wife lay motionless on their blood stained white silk sheets. Leaving the bedroom I went to the east wing of the house and signaled Ollie from the upstairs bedroom window. Using his flashlight he signaled me back. Turning on each light in the estate, one at a time, I began to search for Walter Chang's computer. Almost twelve minutes had passed before I heard Ollie yell.

"Sandman, where are you?" he shouted.

"Upstairs, turn the lights on as you come this way. The house is clear," I shouted back.

"Did you find the computer?" Ollie asked as he headed up the stairs toward me.

"Yeah, its up here. Wait till you see this," I answered.

"Where are you?" Ollie asked as he reached the top of the stairs.

"Down the hall. Third room from the end on the right side," I shouted back.

"Man, partner, this place is huge," Ollie said as he walked into the main computer room where I was waiting. "Holy shit," he added as he saw the system that Walter Chang had in place.

"Yeah, no kidding. What is all of this?" I asked, as I looked at all the computer equipment in the room.

"Amazing, would you look at this. He has six separate computers all hooked into the central mainframe system. This is state of the art technology," Ollie explained as he sat his nylon backpack down and holstered his pistol.

"You can crack this system, right?" I asked as Ollie sat down in the tall-backed, black leather chair located in front of the stainless steal enclosed system that had computer wires and telephone lines running directly into it.

"I certainly hope so. You might as well get comfortable this is going to take some time. You should have kept Chang alive so we could have gotten his access codes from him," Ollie commented as he began to type on the computer keyboard.

"No way. Walter Chang is old school triad. He would have never given us any information about anything. Did you see all the Ming Dynasty artifacts in this place?" I asked.

"Yes, I did. The inside of this home is worth at least a billion dollars. We should load some of it up and take it back with us. We could finance some of our operations with this stuff," Ollie said jokingly. "That's what Amanda did."

"What? What are you talking about?" I asked as Ollie continued to try his luck gaining access to the elaborate computer system.

"When we hit Klaus Gruber's estate. Amanda went back into the estate and loaded up on a bunch of the artwork. She shipped it all back to Carla. I don't know what Carla did with it, but I do know this, our Special Projects Black Operation account suddenly found an extra eight hundred million dollars in it," Ollie explained with a chuckle.

Picking up the telephone in Walter Chang's computer room, I called Carla, the telephone only rang once when I heard her voice pick up on the other end.

"Hello," she said coldly.

"This is the Sandman, we're in," I replied.

"Did you find his computer?" she asked.

"Yes," I answered as I watched something pop up on the computer screen.

"I'm in!" Ollie said excitedly. "Damn, I'm fucking good!"

"Yeah, no kidding, that was fast," I replied.

"Well, what's going on?" Carla asked. "Did you find any weapons at the estate?"

"Oh shit," Ollie said in a whisper as the three dimensional picture of the weapon appeared on the computer screen.

"That's one of ours," I said in a soft voice.

"What's one of ours? David, what's going on?" Carla questioned in a frustrated voice.

"Hang on, Carla," I whispered as I placed my left hand on Ollie's shoulder and began to read the information that was coming up on Walter Chang's computer screen.

"Where's the President?" Ollie asked as he pointed his fingers at the computer screen.

"Carla, secure the President and don't let Air Force One take flight anywhere. Call PEOC – Presidential Emergency Operation Center – and tell them six FIM-92-A American made stinger missiles are missing. If this information is correct, they're being sold to Walter Chang by Chantel Cafarelli for a cool six million each," I explained.

"What! What's that got to do with the President?" Carla asked in a paranoid tone of voice.

"Before one of the guards died, he told me they were all leaving this morning to fly to Rome. They must have been going there to oversee the shipping of these stinger missiles. Per Chang's computer data, one of the intended targets is the President and Air Force One. This estate now falls under the 1947 National Security Act. Get some people over here to secure it, but keep it very quiet and low key. Get a Delta Force or Navy Seal team in route to Milan, Italy. Ollie has this end covered. Have Neil track me by satellite, and get me to Milan as fast as you can. I have to get to Chantel and secure those stingers before she finds out that we hit Walter, and sells them to someone else. Is John Mitchell available?" I asked as I continued to watch all the data appear on the computer screen.

"He will be as soon as I pick up the other phone," Carla explained nervously. "Why?"

"Tell him I need back up and get him to Milan. Tell him I'll meet him at Via Hoepliz. Get our Elite Seal or Delta Force team to focus on La Scala but don't go in. Wait for me to find Chantel," I explained excitedly to my boss.

"You've got it. David, secure those stingers and kill that fucking bitch. Ben has our Lear there waiting for you and Ollie. You take the plane and get to Milan. I'll call Ben. Move! Move now!" Carla explained as she hung the telephone up in my ear.

I explained to Ollie everything that Carla had said and prepared to leave. Just out of curiosity I went back into Walter Chang's master bedroom before I left. There on the floor next to the closet door were six Samsonite black leather suitcases. Opening the first one I found it full of Mrs. Chang's clothing. Opening the second one I found it full of Walter's clothing, also. It was the other four that brought a huge smile to my face.

"Oh yeah," I said to myself as I found them filled with stacks of brand new one hundred dollars bills, each stack still wrapped tightly in their bank bands.

Taking all four of the suitcases with me, I put them in the new Ferrari. The keys were already in the ignition and I needed a ride. Little Jessy wanted a Ferrari like Magnum P.I. I guess now she had one.

* * * * * * *

Arriving at the international airport in Rome I was greeted by John Mitchell and our covert undercover agent who was stationed in Rome, Tomas Monti.

"David, this is Tomas. Tomas, this is Dave." John introduced as we moved quickly through the airport and climbed into Tomas' car. "There's a Delta Force team in route. Carla updated us on the situation," John explained calmly as Tomas pulled his silver Mercedes Benz out onto the main road and accelerated.

"Six stinger missiles that could kill a lot of people," Tomas explained with a rich Italian accent. Tomas was thirty-years old, stood five-feet, seven and one half-inches tall and weighed about 165-pounds. He had jet-black, wavy hair that he combed straight back and brown eyes. He dressed casual so he wouldn't stand out in a crowd.

"Yeah, somebody's ass is going to burn when the serial numbers of these stingers get traced back to where they're supposed to be stored. Dumb, real dumb," John explained as he shook his head from side to side slowly in disgust.

"Do you think that a stinger could take the President's plane out of the air?" Tomas asked as he glanced over at me.

"No, I doubt it. I do know this much. Its a heat seeking missile that boasts a top speed of mach one. It would do some damage to one of the engines but I seriously doubt it would take Air Force One out of the sky," I explained as I looked at my gold Tag Heuer divers watch. "It's almost 5:00 p.m., the information on Chang's computer said that this Chantel Cafarelli girl has them hidden in the basement of the La Scala. How hard do you think it will be to get down there, Tomas?" I questioned as I reached into my shirt pocket and pulled out the solid gold and diamond inlayed ring I had taken off of Walter Chang's right index finger just before I left his estate.

"Not hard at all. Is that real?" Tomas asked as I slid the ring onto the finger of my right hand.

"Oh yeah, it has an oriental diamond inlayed emblem on the face of it. I searched the computer on my way here and found out that this emblem is the sign of the Triad. I thought it might come in handy. So I took it. I figure that Chang didn't need it anymore," I explained jokingly as we all began to fall deeply into our own thoughts in mental preparation for our mission. Placing two drops of Methadrine under my tongue, I sat back and took in the sights of this beautiful country.

We were headed for Milan's famous opera house, which was called, La Scala. It was famous for its sweeping, curve design and for the role it played in the Italian history of opera. The Italian culture was well known for its opera singers. Throughout the entire world there are none better than the opera singers of Italy.

Tomas parked his car; we got out and began to stroll through Milan's Galleria Vittorio Emanuele. I was in awe at its 19th Century mosaic floor. The faces of the buildings were lined with round, white bulbed streetlights. The cement faces of the buildings were hand carved with the most beautifully detailed artwork I had ever seen. Looking up I saw large hand carved archways that connected the buildings on both sides of the street, from the rooftops.

"My God, Tomas, this is truly beautiful," I said as I looked all around trying to take in as much as possible.

"Thank you, we take a lot of pride in our country. Come my friends, we will eat here and wait for the Delta Force team to arrive and get in place," Tomas explained as we walked into the old Italian restaurant and sat down.

"Let me order for you. I guarantee you will love it. You have never tasted real Italian cooking until you come to Italy where Mama cooks in the kitchen herself," Tomas explained with a true pride for his country.

"And to think, not so long ago these beautiful streets were filled with the horrors of World War II," I said as I thought back and remembered my Uncle Tommy who had died fighting in that war.

"Yes, it is sad and a lesson we should never forget," Tomas explained as the cute Italian waitress walked up and took our order. We spent the next hour and fifty-one minutes eating, drinking Chianti wine, and listening to Tomas as he explained the design and layout of the famous Italian opera house, La Scala.

It was a few minutes past seven when I glanced over and saw the young, blonde hair American as he walked into the restaurant. He wore Levi blue jeans and a short sleeve pull over shirt. He stood six-feet tall and had a muscled body. It was his airborne jump boots and high and tight cut hair that told me this was the man we were waiting for.

"Is that our Delta Force boy?" John asked softly noticing that the young American looked over at our table. Nodding my head slightly, the young American walked through the crowded restaurant toward us.

"How do you know that he's a Navy Seal?" Tomas asked.

"Trust me, he's a seal," I replied as the young American walked up to our table with a forced smile on his face.

Before he could say a word I spoke, "I never saw a wild thing feel sorry for itself," I said as I looked up at him and took a sip of my wine.

"Hoo yah," he replied.

"Have a seat," I said. Waiting for the young man to sit down at the table with us I asked, "Hungry?"

"No time for that. Master Chief Bret Robinson Seal team two," he said as he extended his right hand out for me to shake.

Shaking his hand I introduced us, "I'm Dave, that's Tomas, and he's John."

"Nice to meet you, fellas," Bret replied as he shook hands with Tomas and John.

"I was told that Delta Force was coming. What happened?" Tomas asked with a curious look on his face.

"My team was closer," was all that Bret said.

"Ah," Tomas replied as he looked over at me and smiled.

"I've got a seven man team with me. Their keeping an eye on La Scala. My orders are to follow your instructions, Dave, so what's the game plan?" Bret asked.

"The woman selling the stingers is named Chantel Cafarelli. She's suppose to meet with Walter Chang of the Chinese Triad tonight at the opera. She has a private booth in the upper balcony. I have to meet with her first to make sure the stingers are here. If they are we take 'em down. If they're not its my job to find out where they are," I explained in a whispered voice.

"What if Chang shows up?" Bret questioned. It was a good question. Bret was trained well and covering all his bases. He wasn't taking anything for granted that could jeopardize his team and put them in harms way.

"Chang's dead," I replied calmly.

"His men?" Bret asked.

"All dead," I answered.

"Sounds like you've been busy," Bret commented with a grin.

"The opera starts at eight. The meeting is set for nine. Lets go take a look at La Scala and get ready," I suggested avoiding Bret's comment.

394

"Sounds good, lets get this done. The big brass at the Pentagon are wired tight right now because of this," Bret explained as we all got up and left the restaurant.

* * * * * * *

It was 8:45 p.m. when I walked into Milan's famous opera house, La Scala. Handing the girl at the entrance my ticket I asked the usher how I could find Ms. Cafarelli. Walking me up the stairs we stopped at one of the doors that opened to one of the privileged private balcony viewing areas.

La Scala was absolutely beautiful inside. It was old rustic and a theater that can only be described as surreal. It wasn't until I had talked to Tomas that I learned that an opera is a play in which people sing their individual part. In some cases the singer stands alone. His or her opera song is actually telling you a story. Now, what I once looked at as stupid had a whole new beauty to it. A beauty all its own, matched by none.

Opening the old wooden door, I stepped onto the open face balcony that sat high above the main body of people sitting in the theater seats below. There were four very old, but well kept, seats in this balcony. One of which had a beautiful Italian woman sitting in it. Her long black hair shined in the semi-darkness of the balcony. Her head was tilted slightly back and her eyes were closed, as she savored the moment of the beautiful song being sung from below. She appeared to be in her late forties, and wore a long, dark blue dress that had a touch of silver running through it. Her white, pearl necklace highlighted her olive skin

"What a waste," I thought to myself. "Such a beautiful woman. Why would she choose to cause senseless death to so many? But then again, who was I to judge her," I thought as I stood in the darkness and waited for the song to end. When it did, I stepped forward, and sat down in the seat next to her. Tomas had supplied me with a fine, handcrafted, black Italian made tuxedo. If nothing else, death was well dressed this night in Milan, Italy.

"I am sorry young man, but this balcony is reserved. You will have to find another," she said in a very polite manor. Taking off Walter Chang's gold ring, I handed it to her, and smiled.

"Ms. Cafarelli, Mr. Chang sent me, along with his deepest apologies for not being able to be here himself," I explained with a sincere look of regret on my face.

The next opera play had just began as she looked at the diamond inlay of the Triad symbol, then at the stage below. Handing me the ring she didn't speak for almost three full minutes as she watched the singers perform below.

"You are not Italian and certainly not Oriental. Who sent you to see me?" she questioned without looking at me.

"My employer is Walter Chang. He is here in Milan with a very bad case of Salmonella poisoning. Both he and his wife are not only throwing up all over everything, they are also fighting a major battle of diarrhea. Not that those details are any of your business. I have been trusted to deliver thirty-six million dollars to you and to you only. I will return the money to Mr. Chang and explain to him that by his sending his ring with me as proof of who I am and that I work for him, simply wasn't good enough for you. I assure you, ma'am that will be an insult not easily forgiven. You obviously do not know Mr. Chang very well. If you knew him you would have known that he never removes this ring from his hand without good cause. It was done out of respect for you. I am sorry to have bothered you," I explained as I stood up to leave and placed the gold ring of Walter Chang's back onto the finger of my right hand.

"And what would have happened had I not returned Walter's ring to you?" Chantel asked as she made eye contact with me once again. As she did the singing stopped. Everything in this authentic opera house fell silent as I bent down and whispered into Ms. Cafarelli's ear. Her hair had a smell of herb; her perfume was arousing to my senses. "I would have cut your throat," I whispered softly into her ear.

Turning to walk away, she said, "Wait." Stepping through the door I felt her grab my arm. "Please, you wouldn't deny a request from a lady would you?" she asked with a look of proper etiquette in her eyes. I didn't reply. I simply raised my eyebrows slightly. Pulling me back onto the balcony Chantel closed the door. "You wouldn't really kill a lady, would you?" she asked as she sat back down in her chair. Again I didn't respond. "Are you prepared to move Mr. Chang's merchandise?" she asked as the next song began.

The male singers voice was a deep, rich baritone as it floated softly through the air of the ancient opera house.

"Yes," I replied calmly.

"The money?" she asked as I stepped up behind her.

"Outside," I replied.

"All six crates are in the basement hidden behind the stage props. When the opera is over, I will go with you to get them. Does that suit you, young man?" she asked as she lifted her head upward to look at me.

"Yes," I replied as I reached into the right pocket of my tuxedo jacket. As I did I reached down and gently kissed the beautiful Italian woman on her forehead.

"A gentleman," she said with a smile as she lowered her head to watch the opera once again. Still standing behind her I bent down and whispered into her ear.

"Your right, I would never kill a lady," I whispered as I gently placed my left hand onto her left shoulder.

"I didn't think so," she replied softly as the singing continued.

"Who ever said you were a lady?" I asked as I pulled my right hand out of my jacket pocket. Just as I did, Chantel looked up at me once again.

Grabbing her under the chin with my left hand, I placed the tip of my ice pick at the base of her skull. Squeezing on her throat I watched as her big, beautiful, Italian eyes widened with fear. The touch of her flesh was soft as she reached up to grab my left hand. Pushing the ice pick into the soft tender flesh of the back of her neck, I whispered in her ear one last time. "The President of the United States send his regards," as I said it, I pushed down on the handle of the ice pick and then in one quick move, I thrust it upward into her brain. Severing her brainstem, killing her instantly.

Her body fell limply in my hands, as I pulled the ice pick out of the back of her head. Lowering her chin back down to its normal position, I gently let it go keeping her body in the upright sitting position. Stepping back and away from the dead body of Chantel Cafarelli I reached under the lapel of my tuxedo and spoke into the tiny microphone of my Seal team headset that Bret had taped there. "Balcony secure, team two, basement, hidden behind the stage props, six crates. Move now," I said calmly as I turned and walked out of the private balcony.

Leaving the mosaic opera house I stood out front as Seal team two breached the back service entrance of the theater and headed into the basement of La Scala. Seal team two found no resistance in the basement. Chantel was so confident in herself that she had no one guarding the deadly American made stinger missiles.

Bret and his team, along with the help of John and Tomas verified that the weapons were in fact still sealed in their wooden crates and quickly removed them from the belly of the famous opera house. Securing them in the truck they had waiting for them out back, Bret and Seal team two had disappeared into the darkness of the warm Italian night.

Seeing Tomas and John as they pulled up out front, I walked down the cement steps of the opera house and climbed into the backseat of Tomas' Mercedes Benz.

"Where to?" Tomas asked as he pulled away from the opera house.

Looking out through the back window of the Mercedes I took one last look at the legendary opera house known as La Scala.

"Let's go check out Chantel's home and see what we can find," I replied as I looked at my watch. "Man, its still early. We better call Carla," I suggested as John turned around in the front seat to look at me.

"I already called her. They were monitoring Seal team two from the Pentagon," John explained with a discontented look on his face.

"What's wrong, partner?" I asked curiously.

"This sucks, I didn't get to kill anybody," John replied as he turned to face forward once again in his seat.

"He is very upset about this, David," Tomas explained jokingly.

"John, if there's anyone at Chantel's house you can kill them. How's that?" I explained with a grin on my face.

"Oh yeah," John said calmly with a big smile on his face. I liked this guy; he needed the action just as much as I did. John Mitchell was in it for the action. That was the one thing that I understood very well.

Chantel Cafarelli owned a beautiful Italian villa on the outskirts of the city of Milan. Her chauffeur was just preparing to leave to pick Ms. Cafarelli up, just as we pulled up to the home. Between the chauffeur and three housekeepers inside the villa, my promise to John was kept.

We spent most of the evening searching the villa. We secured documents, computer files, and anything else that looked important. Just as we left the villa, we passed the Italian police cars that were heading to it. They had obviously found Chantel's body.

Securing everything in our Agency Learjet. John and I spent the next two days taking in the sights of ancient Rome, with our friend Tomas guiding the way.

Flying back to the Situation Room in the Pentagon I turned all the documents and computer disc's over to Carla along with Walter Chang's solid gold Triad ring.

Debriefing took several hours. After that our pilot, Ben, flew me back to Michigan. Thinking about my trip to Milan, I almost felt depressed inside. I knew if I ever wanted to eat an authentic Italian meal ever again, in my entire life, it wouldn't taste quite the same, unless I ate it in Milan.

Chapter Twenty-Four
A Special Love

Walking into my bedroom, I set down the last two suitcases I had taken from Walter Chang's bedroom. On the flight from Washington D.C. to the Pontiac Airport, I pulled two million dollars out of one of the suitcases. Just before I got off the plane, I gave it to my pilot, Ben. He wasn't sure what to do or how to take the gesture. Once I explained to him that it was for his children's college fund and his retirement courtesy of Walter Chang, Ben smiled and gladly took it. Agents for the CIA were under paid for the many hours of work they put in on the job.

Ben didn't think his job was really that important, but it was. He was responsible for the Learjet. It had to be ready to go at any given moment. The security of the plane fell on him. Lately, Ben had become my personal pilot. He loved the excitement, the adventure, and had become my friend. He was a good man who deserved the money. In our job we accepted the fact that we could die at any moment. Ben was married and had two small children. If that should happen, the money would go a long way to care for his loved ones. That thought alone would give Ben some inner peace.

Pushing the suitcases into the corner of my closet I heard a thump. Turning the overhead closet light on I pushed the rack of clothes to the side to see what it was.

"My duffle bag, damn, I forgot all about it," I said softly to myself as I reached in and pulled it out. Pulling it over to the side of my bed, I sat down on the floor, and opened it. I hadn't touched it since I shipped it home from Vietnam. So much had been going on in my life that I had completely forgotten about it until now.

The smell from inside the bag brought with it a sudden rush of memories. Our sniper's hooch, our missions, and most of all my friends: Nick, Butch, Chopper, Cookie, Johnny, Bell, and Mosier. Clothes, photographs, personal items. Everything was just as I had packed it. Digging down toward the bottom of the OD green duffle bag, I smiled.

"Hoo yah," I said as I pulled out the small medical cardboard box that held my supply of liquid Methadrine.

After I had been rescued from the POW camp in Cambodia, Chopper and Butch kept taking it away from me because the doctors at China Beach told me my heart was weak. I always found a way to steal it back from them. The thought of it brought a smile to my face as I opened the small box.

"What the hell is this?" I asked myself. The twelve tiny vials were still in the box, but on top of it was an envelope that someone had folded in half and placed inside the box. "I'll bet its a note from Chopper and Butch," I said out loud to myself as a smile spread across my face. I opened the envelope and pulled out the piece of paper that was inside. When I did, a heart filled emotion that I had never felt before, surged through me, and touched the depths of my soul.

"Kate," I whispered softly as the memories of Lieutenant Kate Donovan filled my heart.

A Marine medivac helicopter was flying Kate, a doctor, and a wounded Marine to the China Beach Army Hospital in Da Nang when it was shot down by enemy fire. We were just leaving a Marine firebase when we got the mayday call for help. We were only ten minutes away, but by the time we got to the crash site Kate, an Army nurse, had panicked and ran into the forest. The Marine co-pilot had been shot and killed when he had gone after her. The entire area was crawling with Viet Cong soldiers. I went after Kate while the rest of our team flew the wounded Marine, pilot, and now seriously wounded doctor out of the hostile area and to the medivac hospital. Kate had been shot in the leg. By the time I caught up to where she was, two Viet Cong soldiers were preparing to rape her. I killed both of them before they could sexually assault her, threw her naked body over my shoulder, and ran like hell.

We hid inside a cave that was behind and in the side of a waterfall. French Intelligence had discovered it long ago and turned it over to us. Our Black Op's team had supplied it with medical supplies, clothing, weapons, and equipment in case we would ever need to use it. It was inside the waterfall hideout where I treated the pretty, red headed Irish nurse.

We were in the cave for two days when I was forced to break radio silence. Kate was getting worse.

An all out assault was made on the area by joint combined forces of the Army and Marine's to include Navy and Air Force jet fighter's to rescue Kate in operation Fallen Angel. The rescue mission was a success and cost some of our soldiers their lives. Over a short period of time something had happened to Kate and I. We had never kissed, yet we both knew, as soon as our eyes had met, that we had fallen in love with each other in a war torn country. Fate had then separated us when Kate was wounded a second time, when she had come to the Bien Hoa Air Base to see me.

I was then called out on a classified mission and sent deep into Cambodia with Butch and Chopper to kill three North Vietnamese Generals. By the time we had returned from our mission, Katie had been sent home. She had given this letter to Cookie who had promised to give it to me upon my return, which he did. I had hidden it in this box and put it in my wall locker for safe keeping. I had forgotten about it, until now.

Reading the letter, once again broke my heart, and caused my eyes to fill with tears. "How could I have forgotten?" I asked myself. "How could I have forgotten the young woman who had stolen my heart?"

* * * * * * *

Calling Carla, I explained that I needed some time off. After telling her the story about Katie, Carla agreed. She thought it was a romantic idea and understood that it was something I was going to do with or without her permission.

Carla, being my friend, reminded me that Kate could very well have gotten married by now. If she was it would be fine with me as long as she was happy. I just knew deep in my heart that I needed to see Katie. Even if it was to look into her eyes just one last time.

Carla then cautioned me to stay armed and keep my sky pager with me at all times just in case she should need to contact me. Carla then told me that Walter Chang's red Ferrari was being shipped from the airport in Los Angeles to my home. It was being given to me as a gift for a job well done. Marge was transferring the title of the Ferrari over to me. It would be in my driveway when I got back. When I asked about the Rolls Royce Silver Cloud that was also at the Chang estate, Carla laughed and asked me if I had seen her new Rolls Royce yet.

Calling Agent Eckland, I explained that I was going to be gone for a while, Kathy was not very understanding about my wanting to see Kate again. I didn't really care what Kathy thought. I was going anyway.

Telling my grandparents and mother where I was going, I left my sky pager number with Andy just in case they should need to get a hold of me.

* * * * * * *

Ben had flown me to Billings, Montana. Once there I rented a new Ford Ltd and headed north to the address Katie had written in the letter. I was going to call first but decided against it. I wanted to surprise Kate. I could only hope she hadn't gotten married yet.

The long drive to Kate's mother's home was beautiful. I would find myself driving for miles without seeing a house anywhere. This was truly God's country.

Seeing the mail box with Kate's last name and address on it caused my palms to sweat as I pulled off the paved road and drove through the trees down the long driveway to Kate's mom and dad's home.

Seeing the horses as they grazed in the pasture off to my left and the barn and horse stables up ahead, I quickly realized that this was a very large horse ranch. This caught me by surprise. Kate had never mentioned that her parents were ranchers. I pulled up in front of the large log home, got out of my car, and stretched my muscles. The air out here was so fresh and clean I couldn't believe it.

"Can I help you, young man?" the older man asked. He stood six-feet tall, had sandy, blonde hair, and weighed about 185-pounds with a slender built. He wore a cowboy hat, chaps on his pants, and spurs on his boots, his face and hands were weathered.

"I'm looking for Kate Donovan, is she here, sir?" I asked politely.

"Wait here," was all that he said as he went up to the large main house and knocked on the door. Seeing a woman walk up to the open screen of the front door, the ranch hand said something to her, nodded, and then went back to his daily routine.

As she walked out onto the large front porch, I couldn't believe how much this woman looked like Kate. She was in her early forties, had long red hair, which was pulled back in a ponytail. She stood five-feet, six-inches tall, in a slender frame. Stepping off the porch she smiled in a kindly manner and walked toward me.

"My ranch foreman tells me that you're looking for my Katie. So tell me, young man, who might you be?" she asked in a rich Irish accent.

"Hello, ma'am, I'm sorry to have bothered you. I'm really not sure how to explain this. I met your daughter in Vietnam and..." I began to explain when she interrupted me in mid-sentence.

"Oh my, I know who you are. Your name is David, isn't it?" she asked as she finished drying her hands on the small dishtowel she had walked out of the house with.

"Yes, ma'am," I replied looking Kate's mother in the eyes.

"You saved my daughters life," she said as she held her hand out for me to shake. "I'm Sarah, Katie's mother," she explained as we shook hands.

"I'm very proud to meet you, ma'am. Forgive me for saying this but I now see where Kate gets her beauty. You're a very beautiful woman, ma'am, with all due respect that is," I complemented as I shook Sarah's hand.

"Ah, a charmer are ya," she said smiling.

"I really need to see Kate, is she here, ma'am?" I asked once again.

"Come inside with me, young man. We need to have us a little chat, you and I," Sarah explained as she placed her hand on my arm and led me into her home. The inside of the home was immaculate. It wasn't anything fancy like a rich man's estate but it was comfortable more in a way that I was use too.

Taking me into the kitchen, Sarah sat me down at the large oak wood table. She opened the refrigerator door, reached inside, and pulled out a glass bottle.

"My Katie put this in here just before she left. She said, 'Mama, don't let anyone touch this. David will come, I just know he will, and when he does I want you to give him this so he will feel at home," Sarah explained as she handed me the ice cold Pepsi and smiled. "I told my daughter, don't you think your David would much rather have some good Irish whiskey? 'Oh no, Mama,' my Katie tells me, 'David doesn't drink nor does he smoke, he drinks Pepsi,' my Katie tells me," Sarah explains as she hands me a bottle opener and a glass filled with ice.

"Where is she, ma'am?" I asked worried that Kate had gotten married and left.

"She left eighteen months ago, son. She went back to Ireland to spend some time with her grandparents. Oh, mind you now, the young men would come a courting, but Katie would have no part of it. I would tell my daughter, 'Katie go out and have some fun. Enjoy your life, darlin,' but she would do no such thing. 'I'm waiting for my knight in shinning armor. He'll come, mama, my David will come. I can feel it in my bones,' my Katie would tell me.

My daughter had trouble sleeping at night. Sometimes late at night she would wake up screaming. Covered with sweat, my Katie would be. Her entire body would be trembling. Her father and I would run into her bedroom. Oh my, I would hold her so tight in my arms my heart would just break at the thought of seeing her like that.

Scars, I would see on my Katie's back and legs. She would try to hide them from me, but I'd see. I'm not a stupid woman, I know something terrible happened to my daughter. A mother knows these things. Would you tell me what it was that happened to my Katie?" Sarah asked as she sat back in her kitchen chair and crossed her arms across her waist.

"I'm sorry, ma'am. That would be wrong for me to do. Your Katie will tell you when the time is right for her to do so. I will tell you this much, your daughter is a hero. A true hero in every sense of the word. I need to find Kate. Would you give me the address in Ireland that I can reach her at, please?" I asked.

"You mean the telephone number so you can call her, don't you?" Sarah asked with a slight grin.

"No, ma'am, with all due respect, I need the address. I need to see her, to look into her eyes." I explained.

"You're being serious, are you? You're willing to fly all the way to Ireland to see my Katie?" Sarah questioned as the thought of it caught her by surprise.

"Yes, ma'am, its what a knight would do. I would go anywhere in the world to find your daughter. Please, ma'am, will you give me the address?" I asked once again.

I spent the rest of the afternoon at the ranch. Sarah introduced me to each and every one of her ranch hands as the young man who saved Kate's life in Vietnam. After that, I wasn't the dark, complicated, stranger anymore; I was welcome.

I left the Donovan ranch around 4:00 p.m. just before supper. I wanted to get back to the airport. I had a long way to go and I wasn't going to let anything get in my way.

* * * * * * *

Calling Carla from our Agency Learjet, I let her know that Kate wasn't in Montana at her parents home. I then explained that I was going to Dublin, Ireland to find her.

Carla insisted that Ben fly me there and warned that I should stay armed at all times. Per Carla, General Boris Kalashnikov had been talking about me a lot lately. At this particular point and time I didn't really care about Boris or what he had to say about me. All that mattered was that I find Kate.

Our flight to Dublin was a smooth one. I told Ben stories about Vietnam and some of the crazy things Nick, Butch, Chopper, and I used to do. Several times Ben had laughed so hard that he actually had tears in his eyes. It was at those particular moments I was very grateful for the autopilot system, which was part of our plane.

Landing at the airport in Dublin my eyes showed me a whole new country of honest, proud, hard working people, for the first time.

I rented a car from the local car rental, I showed the address of Kate's grandparents to the older Irish man who rented me the car, and asked for directions. Rather than give me directions, Mr. O'Connor drew me a map and explained that without it I would most certainly get lost. He was born and raised here in Dublin and knew Kate's grandparents. The people of Dublin were a kind yet tight knit community. I could see right away they were very protective of each other.

The drive to the Donovan home was a peaceful one. It was a country of vast green meadows, rolling hills, and plush green forest. It was early summer; the sun was shinning and warm. I drove through the small town and took in the sights of the beautiful country.

It took two and a half hours for me to reach the small Irish built home of Kate's grandparents. Pulling off the hard packed gravel road I drove slowly down the winding driveway leading into the small valley that held within it the home of Kate's grandparents.

It was a small hand built Irish home with a red tiled roof. Parking next to the two toned silver and gray Chevy truck I turned off the car engine and got out to stretch my muscles.

It was both of Kate's grandparents that came out of the home to see who I was. Her grandfather stood six-feet tall, had dark, red hair, and wore a mustache. He weighed a good 220-pounds all of which was solid muscle. He looked to be in his mid-sixties. Kate's grandmother was a different story. She stood five-feet, ten-inches tall, and to my surprise had more of a light, reddish color to her hair. She was medium built with pretty blue eyes. You could tell by looking at her she was a pioneer. She was in her early sixties and wore no make-up. She didn't need any. She, as her daughter Sarah and granddaughter Kate, had a natural beauty all of there own.

"Are you lost, young man?" the older gentleman asked in a kind but no nonsense way.

"I hope not, sir. I've come a long way, from America. I'm looking for Kate. Is she here, sir?" I asked politely.

"And what business is it that you have with my wife, young man?" he asked with a curious look on his face as his wife took a step closer to take a better look at me.

"I apologize, sir. I didn't realize that your granddaughter was named after your wife," I explained as I extended my hand out to him. "My name is David, its very important to me that I find your granddaughter, Katie," I explained as he reached out to shake my hand.

"My name is Sean, its nice to meet you," Sean explained as he shook my hand. His handshake was strong and firm.

"Lands sake, Sean, this is him, the one that our Katie talks about. He's come all the way from America," the elder Kate said in a whisper.

"And what is your intentions when it comes to my granddaughter?" Sean asked with a very serious look.

"With all due respect to you and your wife, sir, my intentions are completely honorable. That is why I am asking you, sir, for your permission to see your granddaughter," I explained in a respectful old school fashion, to the man who was the elder of the home.

"Well put. I see that you have been raised with the proper up bringing of the old country ways. With that said you should understand this. If you should break my granddaughters heart or bring a tear to her eye, I will not hesitate to kill you," Sean explained calmly as he looked me straight in the eyes.

"As it should be, sir," I answered as I reached out to shake his hand once again.

"Good then," he replied, "I have work to do. My wife will take you to Katie," Sean explained as he walked away and headed for the barn just a short distance from his home.

"Well, young man, I think you and I should have a little talk before I take you to where my granddaughter spends her afternoons," Kate's grandmother explained as she and I both walked slowly together, past her home, and into the green, grassy meadow next to it.

"My granddaughter talks about you quite often. Then some days she doesn't speak a word. She'll just sit and pray to our God and gaze out across the meadows. It hurts me to see her like this; I love her very much. Did you know that Katie grew up out here?" the elder Kate asked as we strolled slowly across the meadow.

"No, ma'am, I didn't know that," I replied.

"Have you met my daughter Sarah yet?" the grandmother asked as she looked up at the white clouds above.

"Yes, ma'am. I met Kate's mother two days ago, when I went to their ranch in Montana looking for Kate," I explained.

"You went to Montana did you? Well, that has me a wondering. You went to Montana and two days later came all the way out here to see my granddaughter. Why is that? What is it you have on your mind?" grandma asked. Stopping to pause for a moment, I took a breath of air into my lungs and let it out slowly.

"I'm not sure how to explain it, ma'am," I sighed.

"Try saying it with your mouth. I'll figure it out," she replied as she slid her left arm through my right arm and began to walk with me once again.

"The first time I saw Kate she was hurt, so everything happened pretty fast," I began to explain.

"Ahhh, that would be when she was shot," grandma replied without looking at me.

"You know about that, ma'am?" I questioned surprised that Kate had said something to her grandmother.

"A girl will tell her Nana things she won't tell anyone else. I know all about the waterfall, the rescue mission to save my Katie, the explosion when she came to see you, which injured her a second time. I even know about my granddaughter's knight. You know that young man who stole her heart. You do know who that is don't you?" grandma asked as she glanced over at me and grinned.

"I thought it was the other way around, ma'am," I answered as I remembered the few moments that I had actually spent with Kate. "I don't know how to explain it, ma'am. We were in a cave that was lit by several torches. I had stitched Kate's leg up and with everything I had already been through I was scared to death. Not for me, ma'am, but for Kate. Hour after hour passed and all I could do was sit with her and hold her hand. When she finally woke up, she sat up and looked at me. That was the first time I actually got to look deep into her eyes," I explained.

"And what was it you saw in my granddaughters eyes?" grandma asked as we stopped and she turned slightly to the left to look at me.

"She took my breath away. She asked if I was her knight in shinning armor? Then she passed out and fell into my arms. It was then I knew that this was the girl I wanted to spend the rest of my life with," I explained as I dropped my head and looked down toward the ground.

"But your feeling guilty about something, are you not? What is it that troubles you, young man?" grandma asked in a motherly way.

"When I came home my life was kinda screwed up. One thing after another began to happen to me. I'm ashamed to say it, but I forgot all about Kate. How could I have done that?" I questioned as I looked up at Kate's grandmother and looked into her eyes.

"That doesn't matter, David. What matters the most is that when you did remember, you came searching for her. Maybe God didn't think the time was right. Maybe you both needed some time to pray and clear your minds," grandma explained as we began to walk once again.

"But Katie has been hurt and alone and I wasn't here for her," I replied feeling guilty for having forgotten.

"Oh, she has never been alone, we've all been here with her, and our blessed Lord never leaves her side. And now look at you. You're here in Ireland wanting to look into Kate's eyes one more time, needing to see if the magic that you once saw and felt is still there," grandma explained as we reached a high point of the meadow.

Looking ahead and slightly down I saw a small clear blue pond. Sitting next to it on a hand-sewn blanket was Kate.

"Kate," I said in a whisper as I looked down at the girl that once saved my life.

"I'm going to leave you here, David. In a few moments you and my granddaughter will both find the answers, you have been waiting for. Either way, the mystery is about to end and a new journey is about to begin, for both of you," grandma explained as she removed her arm from mine, turned, and walked away.

Walking toward Kate my heart and mind raced with a combination of both excitement and fear. She was sitting facing the pond with her back toward me. She was wearing a pink halter-top and white shorts. Her shoes and socks were sitting off to the far left side of the blanket, on the thick, plush grass. The closer I got, the more I could hear the old Irish tune she was softly singing into the warm afternoon breeze. I could feel my heart pounding in my chest as the memories of Kate and our short encounters together in Vietnam raced through my mind. Now, standing behind her and next to her blanket, she must have heard or sensed my presence. She stopped singing.

"Nana?" she said calmly as she tossed a small stone into the pond in front of her causing the calm clear water to ripple out in all directions.

"I'd prefer David, but you can call me Nana if it pleases you," I said calmly in my best Irish accent.

"Turning her head quickly to look back in my direction she jumped up.

"David!" she shouted as our bodies touched and she placed her hands on the sides of my face. "I knew you would come, I knew it, I could feel it deep down in my bones," she whispered as we looked deep into each other's eyes. Without another word being said our lips touched for the very first time.

Laying Katie down onto her blanket, a warm feeling flowed through me as I held her tightly in my arms. It was here in the green meadows of Dublin, Ireland that Katie and I made love to each other for the very first time. Along with this tender moment we found what we had both been searching for. A special love that brought along with it, peace.

* * * * * * *

Lying on the blanket next to Katie I rubbed my right hand gently up and down on the soft tender flesh of her back. Looking at the small scar's from the shrapnel wounds, and the longer scar from her surgery to remove the shrapnel from her spine, brought back with it the memories of the evening the rocket propelled grenade blew the army truck up from behind her, causing her injuries.

"Do they hurt?" I asked as I looked into Katie's pretty eyes.

"No, it was my heart that was hurting, but not anymore. If I should die this very day I'll die at peace now that I've seen you again," she explained as she lay next to me.

"We should get dressed before your grandfather comes looking for you," I suggested with a newfound look of concern on my face.

Seeing the worried look on my face brought a smile and laugh to Katie's face. "My Paw Paw is a good man. You'll like him once you get to know him," Kate explained as we both sat up and began to put our clothes back on.

"I already like him. I just don't want to see his Irish temper is all I'm saying." It was then that I remembered the satellite chip in my shoulder.

Looking up at the sky I couldn't help but wonder if Neil had been watching us from the War Room. Looking at my watch, it was almost 6:00 p.m.

After getting dressed I folded up the blanket, took Kate by the hand, and walked her back home.

"This is such a beautiful land, Kate," I said as I looked around in all directions.

"I know, that's why I came back here. I feel safe here. Dublin has a way of clearing the cobweb's out of my head," she explained peacefully.

"I'm sorry it took so long for me to get here, Kate. Will you forgive me?" I asked with a sincere heart.

"I fell in love with you long ago, David. You never have to say you're sorry to the woman that loves you," Kate explained as she reached up and kissed me on the cheek.

"It's because of how I feel for you deep in my heart, Kate, that I need to say I'm sorry. You should never hurt the one you love," I explained.

"Are you saying that you love me, David?" she asked as she stopped walking and turned to face me.

"Katie, I've loved you from the first time I looked into your pretty blue eyes. I just never realized how much I loved you, until this very day," I explained.

"Better be careful what you say to me. A good Irish woman will settle you down quicker than you can blink an eye," Katie explained with a smile and a twinkle in her eye.

"Don't make any promises you can't keep girl," I responded with a seductive look in my eye and a grin on my face. "I could get used to living out here."

"Ah, I might just have to keep you around then," Katie, replied as she tightened her grip on my hand and began walking once again.

I spent the rest of the early evening with Kate and her grandparents. Kate's grandmother fed me wild grain biscuits and Irish made rabbit stew. Both of which were delicious. Her grandfather on the other hand reminded me that real men drink 15-year old, pot still, Irish whiskey and not Pepsi.

After drinking two shots of Jameson Irish whiskey, I explained that only a fool would match shots of whiskey with an Irishman, just to impress the grandfather of the woman that he intended to marry. My statement seemed to please him as he nodded his head, grinned, and gave me back my bottle of Pepsi. We now seemed to understand each other a little better.

Even though they invited me to spend the night at their home, I declined. I then explained that even though I would be sleeping on the sofa, I felt it would be disrespectful to them because I wasn't married to their granddaughter. My statement made Kate grin and impressed the hell out of her grandparents.

Saying goodnight, I went out to my car, climbed into the backseat, and fell asleep with the scent of Kate's body on mine.

* * * * * * *

On day two I drove Kate to the city to meet Ben. Kate showed us the sights of Ireland. The look on her face as she pointed things out to us told me she wasn't ready to leave her beautiful homeland.

In Vietnam Kate had a touch of her Irish accent. But now that she was back home in the country she loved, I was getting to see a whole new side of her, a side that warmed my heart. Her accent was rich with the way of the proud Irish people, and I loved it.

It took us about ten-minutes to convince Ben to call his wife and have her fly out to meet him here in Dublin. Leaving their two young children with Ben's parents, Ben's wife Laura flew out to meet with her husband for a long overdue vacation.

We spent the next two weeks seeing the sights, relaxing, and having fun. During the second week we even took Kate's grandparents for a ride in our Agency plane. They had never been in a Learjet before and they loved it.

Leaving Ben and Laura, so they could spend some time alone, Kate and I went back to the little town she had grown up in as a small child, near her grandparent's home. It was a small town that sat far away from the big city. Everyone here knew each other on a first name basis. I had rented a small room at a place called Nell's. Nell was a widower who was in her late forties. Her husband, a local businessman, had died two years earlier from a massive heart attack.

At first, no one accepted me. I was the young, dark complicated kid that appeared out of nowhere, the outsider so to speak. Once they saw me with Kate and her grandparents, I was accepted. These were small time farmers living off of the fruits of their labor. Simple, proud, honest, hard working people, who I was finding out, were falling onto some hard times.

Nell, who owned the town's small but well stocked grocery store, had turned the upstairs of the building into a very nice apartment, which I was now renting. Nell was also the first cousin to Kate from her grandmother's side of the family.

Sitting in my upstairs apartment, Katie was explaining to me how their small town's local bank had been bought out by the big city's major banking chain. Along with the buy out, came a new set of rules, pay what you owe or lose your land. It was simple to see that the new, German banking firm, was trying to make a move on the people of Ireland by

410

taking away the land which had been owned by their families for over two hundred years.

Hearing the knock on my apartment door, I said, "Come in." Opening the old wooden door, Nell stepped into the room.

"I'm sorry for bothering the two of you, but I thought I best tell you. Katie, some of the men just took a gun away from your cousin Tom at the pub," Nell explained with a concerned look on her face.

"What? Tom's not a violent man. How could that be?" Kate asked as she stood up from the sofa and walked across the room towards Nell.

"I just got the call. They want you to come quick. You have a way of calming Tom down. One of the boys has gone to fetch your grandfather. I'm closing the store. Please, Katie, come with me. Something is wrong," Nell explained.

Locking the front door of her store we walked across the dirt street and headed down to the town's bar that was simply named, The Pub. The word had spread quickly that one of the locals was in trouble. Men and women alike were walking into the pub to find out what was going on. As Nell, Kate, and I walked in through the front door, we saw that Kate's grandparents had already arrived and the place was packed.

Tom was in his early thirties and stood five-feet, ten-inches tall, on a medium framed body. He had brown, ruffled hair, brown eyes, and was mad as hell.

"Calm down, Thomas, and tell me what's eating at you, that has you so riled up your carry'n your gun on you?" Sean asked calmly as we walked up and stood next to Kate's grandmother who had a worried look on her face.

"Its these new bankers Sean, they want their money or they say their taken me Daddy's farm. I'll kill the whole damn lot of 'em, I tell ya!" Tom replied angrily.

"How can they get away with it? They know your mother is in the hospital and recovering from her surgery. How can they want money at a time like this?" a man named John McTosch asked as he looked over at Sean.

"I borrowed the money from the bank to pay for my mothers surgery. What man among ya wouldn't have done the same, I tell ya. Now they tell me I have two weeks to pay up or I must get out. They won't even give me time to sell my back partial of meadow to help pay their damn money back. Their steal'n my Daddy's land is what those German bastards are doing," Tom explained as he tossed down a double shot of whiskey and shook his head sadly.

"It's not just you, Tom, they're after my land too and for a lot less than what I owe," another young Irishman named Danny McBaine explained.

"Why didn't you say something?" Sean asked quickly.

"For what, Sean? What could you do? The drought last year hurt all of us. Even your cousin Nell has most of us extended on our grocery bills, God bless her soul. It's going to be a good year for our crops this year, but the bank won't wait," Danny explained as he leaned back up against the bar.

"How much do you owe, Tom?" Sean asked.

"Forty-one thousand, just for the hospital loan," Tom explained as he looked at the elder Sean and shook his head sadly once again.

"How many others are in trouble and not speaking out about it?" Sean asked as hands began to rise throughout the bar. It was when I saw Nell's hand go up that I knew I had to do something.

"Nell?" Kate said in a whisper as she looked at her first cousin in surprise.

"They're good people, Katie, you know that. I've been carrying most of 'em all winter and spring. Why do you think I rented out the room to your young man? I'm almost broke along with the rest of 'em. We all came together, we'll damn sure go down together," Nell explained proudly.

When Nell said that I remembered our Black Op's Team. Brother and friend throughout life and into death, till the end. If one goes, we all go. If one stays, we all stay. Looking at these people who stood so strong, made me feel proud to know them.

As they continued to talk about their problems I thought about the thirty-two million dollars sitting in my closet. The money Walter Chang was going to use to buy the six stinger missiles.

"I can help," I said calmly as I looked at Kate and smiled slightly.

"How?" Kate asked in a whisper as she looked up at me.

"I have the money to help your friends," I whispered as I looked over at Sean.

"Paw Paw, my David has something he would like to say," Kate explained.

"What is it you feel the need to say, son?" Sean asked as everyone in the bar turned to look at me.

"With all due respect to all of you, I can help you with this trouble your facing," I explained calmly.

"And how would you do that? All together were talking at least a half a million dollars," John explained.

"I came here to buy my Kate some land of her own. Then I met all of you. A proud lot, you are. You're a lot like my people, the Armenian people. My people stand and fight together, just as you are doing right here, right now. I may not be Irish and maybe I'm young, but if it's your fight that you're facing, then it's my fight too. I have a half a million

American dollars on my plane," I explained as Kate ran her arm through mine showing her support for me.

"I've never taken a hand out from any man, I won't start now," Tom explained proudly.

"Hand out? What is it that you're saying to me, Tom? My skin isn't the same color as yours so I can't be a friend to you, is that it," I asked.

"I never said that," Tom replied as he downed another shot of whiskey and stared proudly back at me. "Don't put words into my mouth boy or I'll take you out to the street and teach you a thing or two," Tom added.

"Is that so?" I said as Kate's grandfather turned to look at me.

"Yes, it is. I'm not sure if your man enough to be courting my cousin, Katie," Tom said as he drank down another shot of Irish whiskey and slammed the shot glass down on the top of the bar.

"I'll tell you what Thomas, lets go out to the street and see if I can earn your respect. If you win, I'll leave and never return again. But if I win, you accept my hand in friendship and along with my hand you accept the loan of my money. You hear me, Tom? The loan of my money, not a damn hand out," I explained as I turned and walked out onto the street.

"Tom!" one of the women yelled trying to stop him from coming outside.

"David, you're not fighting my cousin!" Kate scolded.

"Back away, Katie, if I don't earn his respect now I'll never be able to look your people in the eyes again."

"Katie, get up here, girl, right now," Kate's grandmother shouted.

"Don't hurt him, David," Kate said as she slowly backed away from me. Kate knew I was a highly trained soldier and that worried her.

"I'll let him get a few good licks in first, but only a few," I explained with a grin as Kate stepped up onto the cement walkway and off the hard dirt street.

I knew that I was going to have to let Tom get a few good punches in on me. If I didn't Tom would feel shamed. He was a proud, young, Irishman, who had also been drinking, which fired up his Irish spirit along with his temper.

Stepping out onto the street to face me, Tom began to roll up the sleeves of his long sleeved shirt. Seeing Sean walk over to stand next to his wife and granddaughter, distracted me just enough. As I glanced over at them Tom threw three fast punches. All three hit me in the face causing me to stagger backwards about six feet.

"Thought I was drunk, didn't ya?" Tom asked with a wide smile as he began to roll up his other shirtsleeve.

"I never figured an Irishman got drunk on just a fifth of whiskey," I replied as I spit blood out of my mouth and onto the dirt below.

Tom had a punch that felt as though I was getting hit with a jackhammer. Just as I thought it, Tom unleashed all of his pent-up anger in a series of blows that rocked my world.

Just as he paused and smiled at me, I let him have it. My first punch was open handed and struck Tom in the sternum. I hit him just as he was exhaling his breath. When I did, it knocked the wind out of him. I stepped in quickly and followed it up with a left hook to the side of his nose and a right cross that landed on his temple. As the blood rushed out of Tom's nose he dropped to his knees. In a matter of seconds I had knocked the wind out of him and broken his nose. He was fighting hard to breathe. I felt bad, but had I not ended this fight quickly, Tom would have kicked my ass.

Stepping behind Tom I reached down and grabbed him by his elbows.

"Raise your arms, Tom, it will help to open your airway so you can breathe," I explained as I raised Tom's elbows upwards. When I did, he took a full, deep breath of air into his lungs and gasped. Sitting down on the dirt road, I tried to catch my breath and clear my head. I could feel a slight stinging in my left eye as I spit more blood out of my mouth and onto the ground.

"I'm going to have a black-eye," I whispered as I tried to rub my eye.

"You broke my nose. Where'd you learn to fight like that?" Tom asked as he sat down onto the road next to me.

"Vietnam, I was with a black operation team," I explained.

"Oh shit, you broke my nose," Tom said again as he tilted his head back. As he did Sean walked up and looked down at us. No one else said a word.

"I had to Tom, it was the only way to keep you from kicking my ass," I replied.

"Do you love my cousin?" Tom asked as he pinched his nose in an effort to try and stop the bleeding.

"Yes, I do," I replied as I looked up at Sean.

"Well then, that's good enough for me," Tom answered.

"Well, thank you, Tom, I'm glad to hear that," Kate's grandfather explained as he placed both of his hands on Tom's face and quickly snapped his nose back into place. When he did you could hear the bone crunch and Tom yell.

"Ahhh shit, damn ya, Sean, that hurt," Tom moaned.

"Alright, everyone back inside. This fight is over with," Sean explained as he helped us both to our feet.

Looking at Tom I extended my hand out to him, "I'd be proud to call you my friend, Tom," I said as I looked Tom in the eyes. The front of his shirt was covered with blood as he reached out and shook my hand.

"I, and I'd be proud to have you as one," he replied.

"Need a loan?" I asked with a grin and a sigh.

"I'd be grateful," Tom answered as he looked over at his elder, Sean. "He broke my nose, Sean," Tom said once again as he tilted his head back.

"Yes, well that's what you be getting when you put your nose in my future grandson's business," Sean answered as he patted us both on the back.

"Come on, I'll buy you boys both a drink," Sean said proudly as we went back into the pub.

"Let me see your eye," Kate said as she placed her soft hand gently onto the side of my face. "Oh my, your gonna have a shiner, ya are," Kate explained as we stepped up to the bar.

"What will you boys have?" the bartender asked as he looked at Tom, Sean, and myself.

"Whiskey," Tom replied, "and a lot of it."

"Give me a Pepsi," Kate's grandfather said as he looked at me and smiled.

"I'll have a whiskey," I answered, looking over at Sean.

"Cancel that Pepsi, Sam and bring me a whiskey. Better yet bring us the bottle," Sean explained proudly.

"Nana their gonna get drunk," Kate commented as she brushed the dirt off the seat of my pants.

"That's what our men do from time to time, its the Irish way," Nana answered as she stepped up next to grandpa and looked at Tom.

"Your wife is gonna skin your back when she sees that nose, Thomas," grandma cautioned with a smile.

"Yes, Kate, but you didn't have to remind me."

Pulling my money clip out of my pocket I pulled out the folded stack of hundred dollars bills and handed it to Sam the bartender as he poured us our drinks.

"I'm buying for the rest of the night, Sam. Make sure that everyone gets their fill," I said as I raised my shot glass up.

"To friends," I said out loud.

"To family," grandpa replied proudly as we tossed down the first round.

"Ohhh," I moaned out in pain as the Irish whiskey burned the inside of my mouth.

Handing me a bottle of cold Pepsi, Sean smiled as I took a big hearty drink. "Ahhh, now that feels much better," I said as I put my arm around Kate and gave her a squeeze. Smiling back at me, Katie took the bottle out of my hand and took a sip.

"So tell me, David, about that loan I'm in need of. I have to be honest with ya, I can't pay any of it back until my crop comes in," Tom explained as grandma plugged Tom's nose with gauge and placed a bandage across the bridge of it.

"I can have the money here by supper time tomorrow. Kate and I will have it at Nell's store. Come and get what you need. Take enough to pay off your bank loans and get your land deeds back free and clear from the bank. Make sure you take enough money to get you through until the fall. Don't worry about the money. Take what you need and pay it back a little at a time. It serves no purpose for you to try and pay it back right away. If you do that then you're left with nothing and you're no further ahead than you were before. I'll be leaving in a day or two to go back to the United States. Katie and I have talked it over and she doesn't want to leave Dublin. So then, Katie will stay here and look for some land to buy, land that we can build a home of our own on. I'll be sending some more money back here. Nell is a businesswoman. If she is willing, we'll open our own small bank and run it out of her store. What do you think, Nell, are you willing to do something like that?" I asked as everyone stopped drinking and looked over at Nell.

"I do it now, what would be the difference. Besides if it gets us away from these new German bankers, I'm more than willing," Nell explained proudly.

"Good then. For now, borrow what you need and tell your neighbors, family members, and friends. Get your bills paid off. There will be no interest on the loan," I explained.

"No interest, how are you going to make any money?" John questioned.

"I'm not trying to make any money. I'm trying to help my friends," I replied.

"Let the man finish what he's saying," Sean said as he raised his left hand. "Go ahead, son, what else."

"I'll have some friends of mine fly back here with more money. When it gets here I'll need a couple of you men to do me a favor," I explained.

"Name it, what's the favor you'll be in need of?" Tom asked.

"I'll have the money delivered to Kate and Nell, I'm going to need a couple of you men to drive into the city and buy a good size safe and bring it back here and put it where ever Nell tells you too. Make sure that it's a good size sturdy safe. Keep a close eye on Nell and my Katie for me and don't let any strangers or outsiders know we're running our own bank. I don't want anyone trying to rob Nell. God forbid that anyone of you should get hurt over something as stupid as money. So then, what do you say?" I asked as everyone looked at me in silence.

"You got my hand and my word on it. We'll get it done," Tom explained as he reached out and shook my hand.

"Good then, you've got you a new family owned bank," I said as I kissed Kate on the forehead.

* * * * * * *

I bought the back section of land from her grandfather, that Kate loved so much. When Sean told me Kate has always sat under the oak trees up on the hill over looking the small pond on his back section of land, I knew right then and there that would be where I would have our home built.

Ever since Katie was little she would go out to the pond and sing. She would make a wish and come back home. Kate called the small blue pond her wishing pond.

Sitting next to the pond, Kate and I talked about our plans for the future. She didn't want to leave Dublin and I wasn't ready to leave the United States quite yet.

My grandfather was ill and I wanted to be there with him until he passed away. Kate understood so we agreed that she would stay with her grandparents and help Nell with the small bank we were now putting in her store and at the same time Kate would hire Thomas and some of the other men from the town and over see the building of our new home.

I would go back to Michigan and continue to work for Carla and while doing so fly back and forth as often as I could to spend time with Kate.

Because I didn't want our relationship to be built on lies, I told Kate most of, but not quite everything that I had been involved in. Trusting each other was important to us. It also made it a lot easier to explain where and how I had gotten the twenty million dollars I was about to have sent to her.

"I see," Kate said with a serious look in her eye. "Take it from the bad and use it to help the good. I like that. I like that a lot," she told me just before I left Dublin.

My flight back home with Ben and his wife was a quite one. My lip was swollen, my left eye was black and blue from my fight with Tom, but it felt good. I was flying home a winner.

That was more than I could say for our President. Sitting back in our plane we watched as he waved goodbye and stuck both of his fingers up in a peace sign as he boarded the President's helicopter. Richard fought with the United States Supreme Court but after almost a year he lost and was forced to turn over all of his secret tapes. There were close to 3,700 hours of tape-recorded telephone calls and private conversations he had been forced to turn over. He gave them all up except for a ten-minute section of tape that had been secretly erased. Carla had covered her trail well, she was that good.

Rather than be impeached and most certainly convicted, Richard resigned. It was a smart move and a good deal. Richard resigned and the new President granted him a full pardon from any wrong doing.

The big boys at the top never go down. At least not when you're secretly trying to protect your country from a very serious communist threat against us. But then again, those are some of our best kept secrets.

Chapter Twenty-Five
Friendship

Walking into the Situation Room I was greeted by Carla and Ollie.

"So, tell me, how was Dublin?" Carla asked with a smile.

"Beautiful, simply beautiful," I replied as I sat down in Carla's office.

"I'd say he's in love. What do you say Ollie?" Carla asked as she looked at Oliver and raised her eyebrows.

"By the look on his face, I'd say your right," Ollie answered with a wide grin.

"How was Kate?" Carla asked.

"Beautiful, simply beautiful," I responded trying to keep a straight face.

"Are you leaving the team?" Carla questioned with a more serious look on her face.

"Eventually, but not right now. Kate is staying in Ireland and I'm staying here. I'll fly back and forth to see how things work out between us," I explained.

"The black eye tells me that she's quite a gal," Ollie said laughingly as he patted me on the back.

"Her cousin gave it to me, it's a long story," I replied smiling.

"You didn't kill him did you, David?" Carla asked with a worried tone in her voice.

"No, ma'am. I made friends with him," I answered. "So what's been happening around here, anything new?" I asked.

"Between Walter Chang's and Chantel's homes and everything you and John found and brought back, it's keeping us busy," Carla explained as she paused to take a sip of her coffee.

"Yeah and the stingers are causing a major problem for the Defense Intelligence Agency and the Department of Defense. We traced the serial numbers of the stingers and found out they came out of one of our military bases in Nevada. We arrested a Lieutenant Colonel and his Supply Sergeant three days ago. They swear they didn't know anything about how someone was able to steal from them, and they can't explain the bank receipts the FBI found in their homes," Ollie explained laughingly.

"Yeah, someone must have set 'em up by depositing a cool million in each of their overseas accounts," Carla added.

"Fort Leavenworth, Kansas has a prison full of idiots like them, so they should feel right at home when they get there," Ollie added. "Oh hey, before I forget, Neil said he needs to talk to you, ASAP."

"He lives in that room. What are you two up to?" Carla asked as I headed for the door.

"He's trying to trace a number for me. I'll let you know if it turns out to be anything worth while," I explained as I left the Situation Room and headed down the hall to see Neil in the War Room.

Neil was standing up watching intently as they monitored the movement of Seal team ten on the big satellite television screen. There was a new girl sitting at the computer terminal Carol was fired from. By the sound of things Neil had chosen well. This girl was dead on the money and serious about her job.

"Negative, team leader, break to your three o'clock and run for it. You're a half-mile from the water. Move damn it, move now!" she said anxiously but calmly into the mouthpiece of her headset.

"Moving to our three o'clock now," came the reply over the external speaker system.

Walking up to Neil I stood silently and watched.

"Shift position now, team leader, to your one o'clock. There's a rock formation dead ahead. Get in it and go silent. Bad guys coming up on your four o'clock. Stay silent, I've got my eye on them," she explained as she used her computer keyboard to zoom in on the area.

For the next ten minutes the whole room fell silent as we watched twenty-two enemy soldiers move in the direction of the Navy Seal team. Placing two drops of Methadrine under my tongue I felt my adrenaline begin to surge all through my entire body as the suspense began to build.

"Get 'em out of there," Neil whispered very softly as his eyes focused in on the enemy troops drawing nearer to our boys.

Placing my hand gently on Neil's elbow I shook my head, No, as my friend looked over at me. Another minute went by and all of a sudden the bad guys turned and headed southwest, away from the rock formation. Waiting to see that the Seal team was clear the girl at the control board gave the order.

"Team leader, your clear, move out now. Your people have just hit the beach to pick you up," she said calmly.

"Roger that, were moving," the team leader replied. A few more minutes passed and then he spoke again.

"Op's control we see 'em, thanks for your help, hoo yah, team leader out," he said as we watched the four man Seal team climb into the motorized rubber rafts and head out to sea.

Clapping our hands everyone in the room smiled as the girl that controlled the move took a bow.

"Damn, I thought they had bought the farm," Neil said in an excited but happy voice.

"Thanks for coming, Sandman. Come here a minute I want you to meet this lady," Neil explained as we walked across the room to meet his friend. "David, I'd like you to meet Sandy. Sandy, this is my friend David," Neil introduced.

Sandy stood five-feet, seven-inches tall, had shoulder length brown hair, brown eyes, and looked to weigh about 124-pounds. She looked to be in her mid-twenties. She wore blue jeans and a sweatshirt with a big picture of the face of Mickey Mouse on it.

"Its very nice to meet you, Sandy," I said as I shook Sandy's hand.

"Same here," Sandy replied with a smile.

"How did you know they wouldn't search those rocks?" Neil asked in amazement.

"They were looking for our boys to be on the run. At that point the most obvious thing to do was to lay 'em down," Sandy explained with confidence.

"Good call, Sandy," I said as a compliment.

"Of course you knew it, I just didn't expect Sandy to know it," Neil said to me.

"Yes you did. If you didn't, you wouldn't have hired her to join the team," I explained with a grin.

"Well thank you, David, at least you have some faith in me. Are you one of the Operation Control Specialists here?" Sandy asked.

"Sandy, this is the guy that Ms. Silverman and I was telling you about," Neil explained before I could respond to Sandy's question.

"You're the Sandman?" Sandy asked with a surprised look on her face.

"You never know," I answered.

"Oh my gosh, we used to talk about you and team one all the time. Especially late at night," Sandy said with a slight giggle.

"We?" I asked confused as to what she was talking about.

"Sandy just discharged from the Army. She's the first female ever to pass the course and become a member of the 82nd Airborne Special Forces," Neil said proudly.

"How far?" I said loudly looking Sandy in the eyes.

"All the fucking way," she shouted back proudly.

"Hoo yah. I'm damn proud to know you, Sandy. You can cover my six anytime," I explained as I shook her hand once again.

"Coming from you, sir, that's the biggest compliment I've ever gotten," Sandy explained.

"I'm nothing special, Sandy. I'm just part of the team," I explained humbly.

"Part of the team? Soldiers talk about you and Black Op's team one over campfires. Don't you know that? You're the Sandman, the best Black Operation's sniper ever. You shot a guy through the lense of his glasses at twelve hundred yards just as he was getting ready to cut the throat of an American POW. You're a legend," Sandy explained making more out of it than she should have. Looking at Neil I wasn't sure what to say.

"That's classified information how could she know that?" I asked.

"I don't know," Neil replied. "How do you know that?" Neil asked as he looked at Sandy.

"Some of the Marines that secured the POW, spread the word. Hell, your'e the guy that cut off Ho Chi Minh's head and shit in his neck. Whoa, what I'd have given to see that!" Sandy said excitedly.

"Don't believe everything the Marine's tell you," I said as I shook my head from side to side.

"If you ever get time I'd love to buy you dinner and talk to you about Vietnam," Sandy explained.

"I didn't cut off Uncle Ho's head," I said as Neil grabbed me by the arm.

"Yeah, right. Even I heard about that," he explained as he pulled me away and took me back to his desk, laughing.

"Thanks a lot, brother," I said as I sat down in the chair next to him.

"She'll call all of her friends tonight bragging that she met you," Neil explained as he sat back in his chair smiling.

"You wanted to see me?" I asked hoping to change the subject.

"Yes. Your buddy, Boris, is doing a lot of talking about you. He found out that Danny is the same Danny from your team and he thinks you're the one that helped to rescue him from Hanoi. General Kalashnikov is in direct communication with someone here in the States," Neil explained.

"Do you know who it is?" I asked excitedly.

"No, not yet. I swear to God, I'm working on it, but they never talk long enough for me to run the circuit on the call," Neil explained.

"The circuit? What circuit, what are you talking about?" I asked.

"It's the damndest thing. The call bounces from one state to another. I get a fix on the call in Texas and as I zoom in on the address it's coming from it bounces to New York, then to California, then to Maine. I thought we were the only ones with that kind of technology. That's how we set up the telephones for you and our other agents. It's state of the art and now it appears that the Russians have it to," Neil explained.

"Damn, keep trying to find out who it is would you?" I asked.

"Absolutely. How was your trip to Dublin?" Neil asked with a smile from ear to ear.

"I'm going to cut this satellite chip out of my shoulder," I threatened with a grin on my face.

"Hey, I'm not some pervert, brother. I switched over to different coordinates as soon as you kissed her at the pond," Neil explained with a sincere look on his face.

"Yeah, right," I responded coldly.

"You've got my word on it, partner. I would never betray your trust in me, not ever," Neil answered.

"Well, in that case, my vacation was fantastic. Come on, let's go get Carla and Ollie and I'll buy you guys dinner. What do you say?" I asked with a smile as I stood up.

"Sounds good to me, brother, let's eat, I'm starving."

* * * * * * *

I had been home for two weeks and the construction on my new in-ground swimming pool was almost complete.

I had sent Don to Dublin in one of my grandfather's Learjets. Along with him he took thirty million dollars. Twenty million was for Kate to start the new bank at Nell's store. The other ten million was to be deposited in a joint account that my grandfather had opened back in the early 1960's. I never knew about it until recently. But now that he had made the decision to tell me about it, I figured that now was a good time to add to it.

My grandfather had built the first hotel resort on the island of Aruba. He told me that one day Aruba would be the tropical island paradise everyone would want to go to. By 1985, he would prove he was absolutely correct. The Americana Hotel Resort Casino was packed!

"That's a big swimming pool," Andy pointed out as he took a sip of his ice-cold Budweiser beer.

"Yeah, the kids will enjoy it. I'll be going back and forth to Ireland for the next year or so. If you don't mind would you try to make sure that the girls get to use it whenever they want too, if I'm not here?" I asked.

"No problem," Andy replied as he took another sip of his beer.

"This girl you're seeing in Dublin, you really like her, huh?" Andy asked without looking at me.

"Yeah. I don't know how to explain it. As soon as I saw her again I felt at peace inside. I can't wait to take you with me to Ireland, brother. I promise you you're gonna love it there," I explained as I walked over to the refrigerator, reached inside, and grabbed an ice-cold bottle of Pepsi.

"I'll love to sample their whiskey," Andy said as he walked over to the bar and sat down.

"You'll meet your match there. Those Irishmen can drink!" I said shaking my head from side to side.

"So can we Indians. What are you going to do about Kathy?" Andy asked.

"I called Kathy right after I got back home. I kinda down played the whole thing for now. Neil said that she came to him a half a dozen times trying to find out exactly where I was," I explained surprised at what Neil had told me over dinner that night.

"Who's Neil?" Andy asked with a curious look on his face.

I had screwed up and made a mistake and Andy had caught it. No one except Kate knew that I was living a double life, balanced between the world of organized crime and the CIA. Thinking fast I answered. "He owns a bar that Kathy and I go to a lot in Virginia Beach. He's cool though. He covered for me. How long do you think it will take for those fella's to finish the pool?" I asked nodding my head in the direction of the men working on the pool. I was trying real hard to change the subject and it worked.

"It should be ready to swim in by next week," Andy explained. Just as he did the phone behind my bar rang. Picking it up I placed the receiver to my ear.

"Hello," I said.

"Hey, David. Boy am I glad your home. We just took your grandfather to St. Joseph's Mercy Hospital on Woodward Avenue. He wants to see you. He says it's important. Momo and Paul are on their way," Vito explained.

"Is he going to be okay, Vito?" I asked as my heart sank in my chest.

"I think so. I think he's getting ready to step down and retire. Get up here, will ya?" Vito asked sadly.

"I'm on my way," I replied as I hung up the telephone.

"What's wrong?" Andy asked as he sat his bottle of beer down on the top of my bar.

"Grandpa's in the hospital. Vito said he's asking for all of us to come up there. He thinks my grandfather is getting ready to step down and pass the ring on to his successor," I explained as I began to lock up the house.

"Andy, why do they call Sam Giancana, Momo?" I asked as my curiosity was getting the best of me.

"I don't know. Its one of those old school nicknames. That was long before I came around. Come on, brother, let's get going," Andy explained as we headed for his Ford Bronco to leave.

* * * * * * *

By 6:00 p.m. everyone had gathered at the hospital and stood at my grandfathers bedside. It was visiting hours and even though the rules for visitation said, only two visitors per patient, there were twenty-four of America's most powerful mob figures standing in my grandfathers private room. Giving each of the hospital security guards and nurses, that ran the floor, two brand new one hundred dollar bills, it was proof that back in those days everyone could be bought, if the price was right.

You could see that my grandfather was tired when he spoke to his room full of friends.

"The time has come for me to step down and pass the ring to the man who will replace me. I want to thank you, each and every one of you, for trusting me with your families and your lives. They say that when a man dies, if he can count his true friends on the fingers of his one hand, then he has lived an exceptional life. I look at all of you, who stand here with me now, and I know that I have been blessed. We have laughed and cried together, we have had good times and bad times together," my grandfather explained as the men in the room nodded their heads in agreement.

Looking around at these powerful men I could see that as my grandfather talked their memories of the old days were taking them back to another place and time.

"We have made millions of dollars and shared it equally among ourselves. Ah, where have the old days gone..." my grandfather said sadly.

"You have many more years ahead of you, Godfather," one of the men from the Gambino family said proudly.

"No my friend, I'm old and my health is not good. Today, some of you will be disappointed with me. Some of you may even feel angry with me," my grandfather explained calmly.

"No Godfather, never Godfather," the men in the room whispered softly.

"I ask you to trust me one last time. Have I ever lied to you? Mislead you or betrayed any of you?" my grandfather asked as he looked around the small hospital room at each of his long time friends.

"No, never, Godfather," they all responded with respect.

"Even though some of you will not understand now. I promise you that you will understand as time goes by," my grandfather explained as he slid his solid gold ring off of his finger.

His ring was solid gold with a flat black onyx gemstone in the middle of it. In the center of the gemstone was a rose that was hand cut from a flawless diamond. This ring was the symbol of the Brotherhood of the Rose. Some called it Mafia; some called it La Costa Notra. Those that were part of it called it, La Familya, which in Sicilian means, The Family.

Standing next to my grandfathers bed he reached out with his hand and gently raised my right hand. As he did, I stood in total surprise. I didn't want this. My heart was in Ireland. Sliding his ring on my finger, he spoke to me first in Sicilian and then again in Armenian.

"With this ring you also take my heart. Protect the men who stand in this room. Be fair and honest with each and every one of them. The family, and all who are part of it, is now in your hands. The Brotherhood of the Rose belongs to you, David. Protect it with your life," my grandfather explained as he leaned forward and kissed the diamond rose of my ring.

I wanted to say no, but to do so; I would have broken his heart.

It was Andy who raised my hand and bowed slightly. As he did he kissed my ring and spoke, "My loyalty is to you, Godfather," he said as Sam Giancana raised my hand and smiled.

"My loyalty is to you, Godfather," he said as he kissed my ring. Then came Paul Costalano and the rest of the men in the room. One by one they each kissed my ring and swore an oath of loyalty to me as their new Godfather.

Within an hour everyone except Andy, Sam, and Paul had left the hospital to return to their homes. As Andy closed the door to my grandfathers hospital room I was finally able to speak.

"Grandfather, why? This ring should go to Uncle Paul or Uncle Sam, not to me," I said as I reached down and held my grandfathers hand.

"David, I have already spoken with your uncles. This was also what they wished for me to do," my grandfather explained as he gently patted the top of my hand with his.

"David, with this new drug business we will have a whole new set of problems. We need you to run the family in secret just as your grandfather has. Your Uncle Sam and I will take all of the heat from the Fed's and law enforcement, just as the rest of the men that were in this room will also do. David, the FBI thinks I'm the Godfather. Before me, they thought it was Carlo Gambino. When the truth is that it's always been your grandfather," Uncle Paul explained as he looked over at Sam Giancana and smiled proudly.

"The reason we do this is so your grandfather would always have the freedom to move around without the FBI watching his every move. We stay in the newspapers and on TV and get all of the attention, all of the trouble and all of the press. They watch every move that we make but they can never bust us for anything. You want to know why? Because your grandfather was secretly and very quietly running the family business. Now it's your turn. Your smart like your grandfather and we trust you," Uncle Sam explained as he patted me on the back.

"I saw the faces on some of the men that were here. They smiled but they were not happy about this," I explained with a look of concern on my face.

"Don't worry about them. We know who they are and we have some of our people inside of their families, telling us everything they're doing.

We know what they're up to before they even have a chance to think about it," Paul explained with a cunning look on his face.

"Come on Godfather, we'll take you to the Red Fox and buy you a nice steak. Don't worry about it, everything is going to be just fine," Sam explained with a broad smile.

Saying goodnight to my grandfather we left the hospital and went out to dinner. For the first time since I've known them, they were wrong. After dinner, I still didn't feel any better about any of it.

* * * * * * *

It had been three days since my grandfather had passed his ring, and the power that came with it, over to me.

The work crew in my backyard was cleaning up. The pool and everything that came along with it was finished. All that was left now was to clean up some of the debris, rake out the lawn, and wait for the water truck to arrive so we could fill it up.

Looking at my watch it was almost 4:30 p.m. of what was turning out to be a beautiful Tuesday afternoon.

"Here, Godfather, eat this. Its my special barbecued horse ribs," Andy explained as he slid the large plate of beef spare ribs across the bar to me.

"Don't call me Godfather," I explained as I picked up one of the spare ribs and took a bite out of it.

"David, you're the youngest Don ever in the entire history of organized crime. Other men would kill for what you've just been given, and you don't want it. Why is that?" Andy asked, looking me straight in the eyes and waiting for an answer.

"It's not who I am, Andy. I don't need it, nor do I want the trouble that comes with it. Besides, you heard what I told Uncle Paul the other night over dinner. I'll do my best, but when my grandfather passes away, I'm going to pass the ring to him," I explained as I began to eat once again.

"Yeah, well I guess if that's what you really want to do then it's alright with me. I just can't picture myself working for some other family. I guess that maybe its time for me to retire," Andy said sadly.

"Yeah, me too," Don added as he looked over at me and took a sip of his beer.

"Not a chance. I said I was walking away from the mob. I never said I was walking away from you two or my family. Your friendship and loyalty to my grandfather alone has brought you both a lot more than either of you know. So don't worry about a thing. You're both staying right here with me until you decide to retire," I explained proudly as I looked at the two men who had dedicated their lives to my grandfather. "Hey, lets call Mrs. Carlson, Amy, and Dana, and invite the girls over for a pool party this Saturday. What do you think?" I asked knowing that the Girl Scout troop would love it.

"Hell yeah, I'll do the cooking," Andy replied.

"Sounds good to me, I'll be here," Don added as the telephone in my den began to ring. Getting up I went to my den to answer it.

"Hello," I said calmly.

"Are you available, sir?" the voice on the other end asked.

"Yes," I replied as I laughed out loud then hung up the phone.

Paul and Sam were right, no one knew who I was and that I was now running the Brotherhood of the Rose. They're sending their Godfather out on a hit. I loved it. I needed some action and this was right on time. Walking to the front door I opened it just as the doorbell rang.

"Your dry cleaning, sir. That will be five dollars please," the young delivery boy explained as I took the hanger off of his finger and handed him a fifty-dollar bill from my pocket. "Keep the change," I explained as I looked through the clear plastic bag that was covering the three-piece pin striped suit on the coat hanger, now on my left hand.

"Wow, thank you, sir. Thank you very much," the high school aged kid said happily as he turned and walked back to his delivery truck.

Closing my front door I headed back downstairs.

"Nice suite," Andy said as I stripped away the plastic bag and pulled the suit coat off the hanger.

"Yeah, it is," I answered as I pulled the manila envelope off of the copper wire of the coat hanger, from where it had been fastened.

"A hit? They're sending you on a hit?" Don asked with a surprised look on his face.

"Nobody knows who I am remember. Besides I need something to do," I explained as I tore open the top of the envelope and dumped its contents out onto the top of my bar.

Letting out a soft whistle Don asked, "Who in the hell do they want you to kill, the fucking President?"

"No shit, look at all of this money. There's gotta be close to fifty grand here," Andy explained as he began to count the stacks of money still wrapped in bank bands.

"Oh shit, I know this guy," I said as I began to read the information package inside.

"Who is he?" Don asked as he looked over at the 8x10 photograph I was holding in my hand.

"Yup, fifty thousand right on the money. Some body wants him dead real bad," Andy explained as he took a sip of his beer and looked across the bar at me. "Who is he?"

"Frank White, Gina's friend from New York. Get Gina on the telephone for me will ya, Andy. I need to talk to her," I asked as I tossed the photograph on the bar and took a sip from my bottle of Pepsi. "Shit, this will start a drug war in the Bronx," I whispered as I looked down at the picture of a young man who I happened to like.

* * * * * * *

The man who had put out the hit was Andre Shapiro, Frank White's business partner and long time friend.

Normally, that information would never be in the data information package. Whoever it was that sent this package, wanted the hit man to know that Frank White was being, what we called in the family, back doored. Frank had done nothing wrong. The hit was being put out on him for the soul purpose of greed, so Andre could take over what Frank had risked his life to build, a multi-million dollar drug business in the heart of the big apple itself, New York City.

I didn't tell Gina anything other than I needed to meet with Frank in private and that it was personal business.

Andy called Andre, he owned one of New York's major construction companies, and scheduled a meeting between us. I was to meet with Andre on Thursday at 1:00 p.m. in front of New York's Museum of Modern Art. There I would hire his construction company to build a four hundred million dollar casino I wanted built on the waterfront of the Detroit River in Michigan. Andre gladly accepted my request to meet with him.

At 6:00 p.m. that same Thursday night I was set to meet with Frank White at New York City's best new nightclub Show. Thursday would prove to be a very interesting day.

* * * * * * *

As we pulled our white stretch limousine up in front of the museum of Modern Art, I could see Andre Shapiro was anxiously waiting for us out front. Andy got out and opened the backdoor and invited Mr. Shapiro to step in to join me.

Andre was thirty-years old, had dark brown hair, brown eyes, and weighed about 200-pounds. He was six-feet tall and firmly built. He was also dressed in a twelve hundred dollar Armani suit and wearing a diamond face Rolex watch. The watch was a gift that Frank White had given to him for being such a loyal friend.

"Mr. Shapiro, thank you for meeting with me on such short notice. Please call me, David," I said with a smile as Andre stepped into the limo, took a seat across from me, and shook my hand.

"The pleasure is all mine, sir. I hope we can do business together," Andre said as Andy closed the car door, got back into the car, and began to drive once again.

"You come highly recommended," I explained as I reached toward the bar sitting to my right. I knew from the information package that I had on Andre that his drink of choice was, Chivas Regal Royal Salute twenty-one year old Scotch. He drank it straight up on ice.

"I'm told you're a Chivas man, would you like a drink?" I asked.

"Yes, sir, that would be fine. So you're building a casino on the Detroit River, huh? I've got some building plans I brought a long with me if you care to take a look," Andre explained anxiously.

"Yes, I certainly would," I replied as I opened the bottle of aged Scotch and poured Andre a drink. We spent the next twenty minutes driving through Manhattan. Seeing Andre shake his head brought a smile to my face.

"Whoa, I think I've had to much to drink," Andre explained with a yawn.

"No, it's not the Scotch. It's the Chloral Hydrate I put in it that's making you tired. Its called a Mickey Fin when you mix it with booze, it knocks you out," I explained calmly.

"What? Mickey Fin?" Andre said with a surprised look on his face.

"I'm the hit man that your contract on Frank White was given to. Frank's my friend. Thanks for the fifty grand," I said just as Andre fell over sideways spilling the rest of his drink and paperwork onto the floor of the limo.

It took us another ten minutes to reach the scrapyard where Uncle Paul had two of his men waiting for me. Pulling in we drove the limo up to where one of the men waved for us to park. Stopping the car, Andy got out and opened the backdoor. Reaching in he grabbed Andre just as I took the Rolex off of his wrist. Handing Andy the plain white envelope, he then pulled Andre out of the car, and closed the door.

Opening a bottle of Pepsi, I sat back and watched as Andy handed the envelope of cash to one of the men. There was ten thousand dollars inside the envelope. That's what I was paying them to do what they were about to do.

Picking up Andre's body, they carried it over and tossed it into the backseat of a wrecked Buick Limited and closed the door.

Walking back over to where our limousine was parked we sat back and watched as the big steel claw of the crane came down, picked up the wrecked Buick, and dropped it into the car crusher. The man standing with Andy then walked over to the large car crusher, reached up and pushed the big red button that activated the machine. It took about seven minutes for the car crushing machine to turn the old Buick into a small square solid mass of steel. Along with it was the last of Andre Shapiro. Andy then shook hands with the first man and waved to the second man that ran the crane. Getting back into the limo Andy started it up and drove us away.

"Crushing experience wouldn't you say?" Andy asked as he broke out laughing.

"He was wrong, Andy, Andre got what he deserved. Do you think anyone would ever believe it if you told them about how easy it is to kill someone and get away with it?" I asked.

"I seriously doubt it. Hell, I've been killing people for fifteen years now. No one would ever suspect me of being a Button Man. Do I look like a killer to you?" Andy asked as he looked back at me through the rear view mirror and smiled.

"Yeah, as a matter of fact you do. Its probably all of that dog meat you eat," I answered with a straight look on my face.

"Yes, Godfather," Andy replied as he raised his right hand and flipped his middle finger up at me.

"Don't call me Godfather," I said as I opened a cold bottle of beer and handed it to Andy. As I did I reached into my suit coat pocket and pulled out another white envelope. Reaching over the back of the front seat I handed it to Andy. "Thanks for your help, brother," I said as he took the envelope from my hand and slid it inside his suit coat pocket.

"Anytime, Godfather," he said once again to taunt me. Going to a strip club called Wiggles, Andy went in and picked up our original limousine driver. We dropped him off here, gave him five hundred dollars and told him to have fun until we got back. Even though he was one of Uncle Paul's men, I wasn't about to let him be a witness to our murder of Andre Shapiro.

With Gus back behind the wheel of his stretch limousine we headed to New York City's newest Nightclub Show, to meet with Frank White.

* * * * * * *

Walking into the Show Nightclub Andy and I were escorted to a private table Frank had reserved for our meeting.

"Hey, David, how's the motor city?" Frank asked with a big smile on his face as we shook hands and sat down at the table with him and his right hand man.

"You remember Deon, don't you?" Frank asked as he pointed at his friend.

"Absolutely, how's it going Deon," I said as I shook hands with Frank's enforcer. Deon didn't say anything. He just smiled and nodded his head.

"So tell me, your cousin Gina said you needed to see me right away. What's going on, you need some nose candy in Detroit?" Frank asked grinning as he looked around the table at all of us. Handing Frank the manila envelope I had brought in with me, I waited for his response.

"What's this?" Frank asked as he peeked inside the envelope in a playing manner. When he saw the 8x10 photograph of himself he dumped the contents of the envelope out onto the table, pointed his hands at it, and lost the smile that was on his face.

"What the hell is this," Frank asked again as he began to read the information about himself. When he got to the part about his long time friend, Andre, Frank's face turned a shade of pale and his mouth opened slightly. As he finished reading it he handed it to Deon and looked deep into my eyes,

"The contract came to Detroit. Your friend, Andre Shapiro was probably afraid you would be tipped off to a local hit coming out of your own town. The enforcer family in Detroit knows that you're my friend so they gave it to me," I explained calmly.

Frank White was a good guy, but he was well known for his very short temper and sudden outburst of rage. Knowing this I was being real careful with how I broke the news to him.

Setting the papers down on the table, Deon covered them up with the large manila envelope and whispered, "I'll take care of it," in Frank's ear. The look of betrayal on both of their faces told me they believed what they had just read to be true.

"I owe you one," Frank said as he pushed his chair back to leave. As he did I reached into my pocket, pulled out Andre's Rolex watch and tossed it on the table in front of where Frank was sitting. Seeing the watch, Frank picked it up turned it over, and read the inscription on the back.

"Where's Andre?" Frank asked with a look of pain in his eyes as he handed the watch to Deon.

"Gone," I answered calmly.

"You?" Frank asked with slightly raised eyebrows.

"Nobody threatens my friends, Frank. Lets just say that its been dealt with and leave it at that," I explained calmly.

Pausing for a moment Frank turned and looked at Deon. "Look at this. Detroit dealt with it. What do you think about that?" Frank asked his friend Deon. Nodding his head in agreement Deon raised his glass of champagne and still never said a word.

Drinking to our friendship to each other, Frank started to laugh.

"Son-of-a-bitch, that no good bastard. I loved him like a brother and he tried to have me killed," Frank said sadly with a laugh.

"The stronger you become, the more enemies you'll make. Its the life that we chose," I replied as I looked at Frank and smiled. We spent two hours at the nightclub Show. From there we went to the new Manhattan Gentlemen's Club 212-475-3200. Frank was pulling out all the stops. His mood was getting better. I think he realized just how short life really was. With that in mind, everything became one big party for him.

We ate at a place called Eating's Cheatin' at Sazerac House, 212-989-0313, where Frank and I watched in amazement as Andy and Deon, who were now very drunk, tried to out eat each other. Deon was no match for the Indian. Even Frank agreed that Andy had won, hands down!

From there we went to a bar called The Flat, 212-677-9477 and rounded out the night at a club called, Jake's Dilemma. By 4:00 a.m. I was burned out. New York was a fast paced party town. Even though I partied and was having fun my mind was on other things.

Saying goodbye to Frank and his enforcer, Deon, Andy and I spent the rest of the night at the Chelsea Hotel. We left New York City at 9:00 a.m. and headed back to Michigan in my grandfathers Learjet.

Looking at Andy, who was passed out and snoring in the seat across the isle from me, I couldn't help but smile. Placing two drops of Methadrine under my tongue I let out a sigh. "Would anyone ever believe any of this?" I thought to myself as my plane disappeared into the soft white clouds of the sky above.

* * * * * * *

Saturday's pool party was a day filled with laughter. Just off to the left of my new in-ground swimming pool, Andy had built a large outdoor fireplace, complete with a stainless steel barbecue grill. Tara and her Girl Scout troop arrived along with most of their mothers, at 9:00 a.m.

Being sprayed with the water hose for the eight hundredth time I let out a sigh. "What in the hell were you thinking, David?" I asked myself as thirty-plus young teenaged girls ran in and out of my house, dripping wet with water.

"I'll bet you weren't expecting all of the mothers to show up too, were you?" Tara's mother Amy asked as she gently pushed her sunglasses back up onto her nose and smiled.

"Are you kidding? All of you beautiful women in swim suits? You don't hear me complaining," I answered with a broad smile on my face.

"They're trashing your house," Amy pointed out as we watched a team of girls throw water balloons at each other. Some of which went straight into my basement through the open sliding glass doors.

"Its only a house," I answered calmly.

"You really don't care do you. Money means nothing to you does it?" Amy asked as Dana walked up to us with a worried look on her face.

"David, the girls are wrecking your house. Maybe we should leave?" Dana suggested.

"Don't worry about it. Its only water. Let 'em have fun while their still young enough to have it. Look at 'em, they're growing up way to fast. Before you know it they'll be graduating high school and going their own separate ways. But the two things that they'll take with them are these memories and knowing that they can always come to this home for help or if they need a safe place to stay," I explained as I reached down and picked up the water hose.

"Okay, remember that we warned you," Dana said with a half grin on her face as I raised the hose up and sprayed both her and Amy with water.

"Ahhhh!" they both screamed as they looked down at their water soaked swimsuit tops and then back up at me.

"Nice, real nice," I said smiling as I looked at both Amy and Dana's water soaked breasts.

"You like that, huh?" Dana asked playfully.

"Oh yeah," I said grinningly.

"Hey, Uncle David. You want a cold Pepsi?" Jessy shouted out from behind me.

"Yeah, please," I shouted back as I turned around to face Jessy.

Just as I did the water balloon full of ice-cold Pepsi hit me right in the face! Looking at Jessy standing thirty-feet away from me, wide-eyed and smiling, I couldn't believe I had gone for it.

Hearing Amy and Dana breaking out with laughter behind me, I raised the water hose above my head and began to spray the sticky soda out of my hair and off of my body. When I had finished rinsing myself off I looked at Jessy, who was now laughing at the sight of me as I stood in front of her dripping with water.

"You wasted a bottle of Pepsi?" I asked as I ran after her, chasing her into my house. Squealing with laughter she disappeared somewhere into the crowded maze of girls inside.

The girls and their mothers stayed until 7:00 p.m. and then slowly, one by one, left to go home. By 8:00 p.m. I found myself sitting at my bar looking at the mess they had made and left behind for me to clean up. Lowering my head I slowly rested it onto the top of my bar. "Oh, God," I moaned softly.

"Don't worry about it. We'll get it all cleaned up tomorrow. By the time we're finished you'll never even know they were here," Andy explained as he opened a bottle of Budweiser and took a sip of the cold beer.

"I know," I whispered softly. "I know."

* * * * * * *

It took us all day Sunday to clean up the mess the girls had left behind. I spent the entire day Monday with my grandfather who was now back at home. It was here at 151 South Telegraph Road in Pontiac, Michigan, that I sat in the backyard of my grandfathers red brick home and listened to him as he shared with me his best kept secrets.

"Within a week from the time of my death, one of the families will try to assassinate you. There will be no warning. So watch for it and be careful. The other families won't know what is being plotted against you, so do not blame them. Its this drug business. I never wanted this for you, David. I'm sorry," my grandfather explained sadly as he patted me gently on the back of my hand.

"Its okay, Grandpa. I'll take care of it, don't worry," I replied softly as I looked at the man who had raised me like his own son.

"Watch for Miami, that's where the hit will come from. Remember what I am telling you and don't forget," my grandfather warned again as an after thought.

Sitting back in the lawn chair, I looked up at the birds singing in the fruit trees of my grandfather's backyard. I was losing him; it was just a matter of time now. In the warmth of this beautiful summer afternoon, I sat with my grandfather in silence. Our minds took us on our own separate journeys of our younger days, when life was filled with laughter and happiness and was much more simple.

Chapter Twenty-Six
Looking Glass

After flying to Virginia Beach I found myself sitting in Kathy's kitchen drinking a Pepsi. Kathy had just gotten back home from an assignment Carla had sent her on in France and was now upstairs taking a hot shower. Walking into Kathy's den, I sat down at her computer system and picked up her secure phone line. I dialed Carla's number but noticed that Kathy's security phone had something added to it, a cord that ran into a separate gray colored box. A line then came from that box and attached itself to the main body of the telephone.

"Must be another one of Walter Shaw's inventions," I thought to myself, as someone answered on the other end of the line.

Using my voice recognition code, I waited for the CIA's mainframe computer to match my voice with the one they had on file in Langley. It took about ten seconds and then the phone made a high pitch screeching sound and hung-up on me.

"What the hell?" I said to myself as I hung up the receiver, picked it back up, and tried to call through once again. Within thirty-seconds the same thing happened all over again.

"Huh, that's strange," I whispered as I began to check the wires on the telephone and computer systems.

"Man, forget this," I said to myself seeing the maze of different sizes, colors, and shapes of wires spread out all over. Looking at the short wave radio I noticed it was set on radio frequency band 4287. It was then that I heard Kathy yell from the upstairs hallway.

"David, will you put on a pot of coffee, please? I'll be down in a few minutes," Kathy explained.

"Alright," I shouted back as I left the den and went back into the kitchen to make the pot of coffee. I really liked Kathy and was trying real hard not to screw up my friendship with her. She was fun to be with and fun to work with. She was also a cold-blooded killer when it came to completing a mission. Making the pot of coffee, I sat down at the kitchen table, and took a sip of my Pepsi.

"Sorry it took so long," Kathy said as she walked into the kitchen and gave me a quick kiss on the cheek. "I haven't had a chance to clean up for three days," she explained as she sat down at the table and began to brush out her hair.

"How was France?" I asked as I looked at Kathy and tried hard not to think sexual thoughts.

"I didn't have time to enjoy the sights. There's some nut case genius that invented some weird virus he thinks will help to control the world population," Kathy explained with a tone of frustration in her voice.

"What?" I replied totally confused at what she had said. "Did you find him?" I asked.

"No we missed him. We found his laboratory in the basement of his home and a lot of documentation. But he was gone and so was whatever it is he was working on," Kathy explained as I got up and poured her a cup of freshly brewed coffee. "I'm sure you'll hear about it. It's got everyone in Langley at full alert," Kathy continued as I handed her the cup of coffee and sat back down.

"The worlds turning to shit, kiddo," I commented as Kathy took a sip of her coffee.

"God, that tastes so good. Thank you, David," she said.

"You're welcome. You know, there are other things I make real well too," I mentioned with a grin on my face.

"Really? And what about Kate, is she one of them?" Kathy asked in a playful way.

"Ouch. Jealous, are we?" I asked as I batted my eyelashes at her.

"Maybe," Kathy replied smiling.

At that moment the telephone, in Kathy's den, began to ring, at the same time my pager began to beep. Reaching into my pocket I pulled out the pager and looked at the digital read out to see what the message was.

"It's Neil, says its urgent," I explained as Kathy smiled, got up, and headed to her den to answer her phone. Following Kathy into her den I cleared my pager and reset it.

"Hello," Kathy said politely. "Yes, ma'am... Do they know what it is?... Yes... Yes... Oh my God... Yes, ma'am... David? He's right here, ma'am... Yes, ma'am, we're on our way," Kathy said as she hung up the telephone and looked over at me.

"I'm to get you to the Pentagon as quickly as possible. I've got to change clothes, they want me there too," Kathy said excitedly as she ran out of her den and up the stairs to her bedroom. Reaching into my shirt pocket I pulled out my tiny glass vial of Methadrine and placed two drops of it under my tongue.

"Now what?" I asked myself as I tried to figure out what was going on.

* * * * * * *

Sitting down at the long glass-top table of the conference room, located in the basement of the Pentagon, I looked over at Ollie and nodded.

Looking back at me, Ollie raised his eyebrows and glanced at all of the people in the room with us.

This was the first time, since I had joined Carla Silverman's team, that I had ever seen this many people at one of these high security level meetings. Out of all of the people in the room there were only eight people I actually knew. Everyone looked worried and nervous. Something was very, very wrong. Watching Carla and Deputy Director Crock walk into the room I place two drops of Methadrine under my tongue and waited for her to speak.

"Ladies and gentlemen, thank you for coming on such short notice and so quickly. We have a situation we now believe to be of a critical nature, to not only the United States, but to the entire world population. You've each been given an envelope of which I would like to ask you to open now," Carla explained as I picked up the manila envelope sitting on the table in front of me and opened it up. Pulling out its contents I looked at the variety of 8x10 photographs first.

"With us in this room today are members of the Federal Bureau of Investigation, the Secret Service, the National Security Agency, the Central Intelligence Agency, Interpol, the United States Customs Service, and a few other people that for security reasons I will leave unmentioned.

The man you are looking at is thirty-nine years old American born François de Bourbeillon. He has a Ph.D in Psychotherapy and was once one of our Agencies's leading scientists in the field of Viral Chemistry. The man is a genius with an IQ well beyond three hundred and fifty.

He stands five-feet, ten-inches tall and weighs 181-pounds. He is single, has dark brown hair, brown eyes, and wears glasses. For reasons beyond our understanding Francois became obsessed with creating a virus that could be used as a weapon against our enemies. As you all know it's against international law to do so. When we tried to talk to him about it he became defiant and emotionally unstable.

It became evident that François was no longer thinking clearly so we discharged him from the agency. In short we fired him," Carla explained as she nodded her head at one of the men sitting next to Oliver. Standing up he addressed the people in the room.

"Hello, my name is Philippe Guillebon. I am an agent with the CIA stationed in Paris, France. After leaving America, François moved back to the home of his grandparents in Paris. Ms. Silverman issued the alert for me to place François under surveillance. As we continued to watch him we began to notice that he had begun to do research using monkeys and sheep. We then began to notice that he was withdrawing into his own little world. Last month while François was away shopping, I entered his home and stole some of the chemicals he had in his laboratory and shipped them back here to our people in Langley for analysis," Philippe explained as he motioned to the young woman who was sitting at the far end of the table.

"Hello, I am Lisa Morgenstern. I am the head physicist now leading the viral disease laboratory in Langley, Virginia. Upon receiving the chemical samples that Philippe recovered from the home of Francois de Bourbeillon, we immediately began to break down the chemical substance for analytical study. What we found was shocking!

François has created a virus from the fluid remains of dead monkeys and sheep. This virus destroys the white blood cells immune system of the human body. Once inside of the human body it multiplies rather quickly through the blood system.

The scary aspect of this is that it can be transferred from the infected carrier to anyone that he or she may have contact with in which bodily fluids are transferred. Such as with saliva, sperm, or the blood or bodily fluid of the carrier coming into contact with an open cut or sore of a otherwise healthy person.

Outside of the human body the virus dies immediately. Once you are infected however, it kills your immune system which leaves the human body defenseless against any bacteria or virus that it may come in contract with," Lisa explained.

"Excuse me, Doctor. Are you saying that if you're infected by this virus and you cut yourself on, lets say a rusty nail, an infection from that cut could kill you?" Oliver asked shocked by what he was being told.

"Yes, that is correct. A common cold that your body would normally fight off on its own, would now kill you in a matter of weeks if you are infected by this virus," Lisa explained as she calmly sat back down. Everyone in the room fell silent.

"Kathy," Carla said softly as she nodded at my field supervisor. Standing up Kathy addressed the room that now sat in shock at what they had just heard.

"Hello, I'm Special Agent Kathleen Eckland of the Central Intelligence Agency. I was sent to France with an International Warrant. I met with my fellow agent, Philippe Guillebon in Paris. We immediately went to the home of Francois de Bourbeillon, which is located on Bis Rue Laugier.

With the aid of French authorities we force entered the home. Unfortunately Mr. Bourbeillon had already fled. We have strong suspicion that Francois had been tipped off. He had left most of his equipment and much of his personal belongings behind," Kathy explained as she sat back down.

Taking my ink pen, I wrote one word on the back of a piece of paper in the manila envelope and showed it to Kathy. "Kathleen?" was what it said.

Feeling the heal of her left foot bury itself deep into the toe of my right shoe I winced silently as Kathleen turned, looked calmly at me, and smiled.

"Hello, I'm Frank Hooper of the FBI. Our Agency is tracking Mr. Bourbeillon through his credit cards and banking records. As of yesterday, Mr. Bourbeillon is believed to be in New Zealand. With a little luck, we hope to have him in custody within a few days," Special Agent Hooper explained proudly as he sat back down in his chair and looked at Ms. Silverman with a smile.

"Lets hope so Frank," Carla said calmly. "With the help of our friends at Interpol, the United States has issued a global alert asking all Law Enforcement Agency's, from around the world to be on the look out for Mr. Bourbeillon," Carla explained.

"Ms. Silverman, please excuse me but I need to ask one very simple question. Why? What would motivate this man to create such a deadly virus?" the older woman who was standing at the back of the room asked with a confused look on her face.

"Meredith, I believe your question can be better answered by Mr. Williams. Mr. Williams would you care to respond to this question, sir?" Carla asked calmly.

"Yes, I believe I would, ma'am," Williams answered as he stood up to address the room. "Hello, my name is Greg Williams. I am a Special Agent with the United States Secret Service. We believe that the motivation behind Mr. Bourbeillon's act of obvious insanity stems from the following. Our Agency has recently found out that François came from a very rich and wealthy family. His father however, divorced his mother a little over a year ago. He moved to Africa where he is now living with an African gentleman. To try to put it gently, they are living together as homosexual lovers. We believe the news of his fathers behavior was more than Mr. Bourbeillon could handle and that is what has pushed him over the edge causing him to create such a deadly virus," Greg explained as he sat back down.

"But how bad could this actually be? He infects a couple of people, probably his father and his father's lover. They die and that's it, right?" Meredith asked in a questioning tone.

"If only it were that simple," Lisa explained without standing up. "One infected person could carry the virus and never even know that they have it. For example, an infected prostitute will spread it to anyone that she has intercourse with. They go home and have sex with their wife and now the wife has it. If she becomes pregnant the unborn fetus now has it.

What if Mr. Bourbeillon infects himself with the virus and travels around the world having sex with both prostitutes and homosexuals? The consequences of such an act would cause a global epidemic, we have absolutely no cure for it at this stage of our research. Millions of people could be infected within one year's time. If we don't find this man and stop him before he infects just one person, in twenty years most of the worlds population, as we know it, could very well be gone," Lisa explained sadly.

"We believe at this early stage of our investigation that François intends to use his virus to infect the black and homosexual communities of the world. Even with the mind of a genius he doesn't seem to realize that a virus such as this won't stay contained within those minority groups. Just one infected person donating his or her blood to a hospital or blood bank will infect and kill thousands," Special Agent Hooper added.

"Is it possible that is his plan, mass murder?" someone asked nervously from the back of the room.

"It is a possibility," Hooper replied.

"Will we be releasing this information to the public as a public health and safety warning?" Meredith questioned.

"No not at this time," Deputy Director Brian Tully of the National Security Agency replied.

"Why not?" Meredith questioned. "Doesn't the world have a right to know?"

"First of all the majority of the world population wouldn't believe it. Second of all it could cause a panic if they did believe it, but most of all because we hope to catch Mr. Bourbeillon before he has a chance to infect anyone. If we can do that, then what the world never knew, won't hurt them, will it?" Mr. Tully responded.

"Let me remind all of you that what you have just been told is a matter of National Security and stays between us. You have all been called here because of the role you will each play a part in, as we attempt to stop Mr. Bourbeillon. Thank you for coming on such short notice. We all have a lot of work to do so lets get to it," Carla explained as calmly as she could. "Oh, by the way, Mr. Francois de Bourbeillon is now listed and wanted as an international terrorist," Carla added calmly as she glanced over at me and sat down for the first time since she had entered the room. Waiting for everyone to leave the conference room, Ms. Silverman locked the door.

Looking at Kathy, Oliver, Mr. Crock, Mr. Tully, and I, you could see by the look on her face that she was overworked, stressed out, and tired. Rubbing her hands over her face Carla spread her fingers and looked through them at the Deputy Director of the National Security Agency.

"Well, Brian, I guess this is what I get for not listening to you. Oh, God," Carla said sadly as she sat back in her chair and stared across the room. "We should have killed him as soon as he started acting strange."

"Hind sight is twenty-twenty," Mr. Tully responded with a straight look on his face.

"David, what we didn't tell everyone is that we believe that Francois may be headed to Norway. It's only a guess on our part, but with his money he could find safe haven there. You are hereby authorized to use any and all means available to you to track this bastard down. Find him, David. Find him, secure the vials of the virus he has with him, and then kill him. Mr. Bourbeillon will not be placed on public trial so that he can embarrass our government. Agent Eckland you are to go with David and assist him in any way needed," Carla explained.

"Yes, ma'am," Kathy replied with a professional look on her face.

"Coordinate your movements through Neil. He'll assist you with anything you need. Use our War Room's global satellite elimination mapping system if you need it. By the way, where is Neil? Why isn't he here?" Deputy Director Crock asked as he looked over at Carla.

"He's checking on a possible security breach with our system," Carla explained as she placed her left hand over her mouth and yawned.

"What? How bad of a breach?" Mr. Crock asked with a concerned look on his face.

"Its nothing to serious. He thinks it might just be a glitch in the computer. The computer did its job and scrambled it. Neil is just checking it out to be safe. That's why he's in charge of the war room. He is sincerely dedicated to his job," Carla explained.

"Well then lets get to it. Check in with Neil and get started on your hunt, David. Do what you do best and find this guy. As for you, Carla, go home and get some sleep. That's a direct order," Mr. Crock said sternly.

"Richard, do the words, fuck you, mean anything to you?" Carla replied with a grin on her face.

Getting up Kathy and I left the room and headed to see Neil. Kathy didn't have a high enough security clearance to get into the War Room so she waited in the hallway.

"You had to love Carla. She wasn't taking any shit from anyone," I thought to myself as I slid my new hard plastic Q-clearance identification card through the new security scanner attached to the door of the War Room. Hearing the security bolt slowly slide back, I entered the room.

"Hey David, boy am I glad you're here," Neil said as he turned around in his chair to look at me.

"Yeah, I know. I'm suppose to check in with you on this search for Bourbeillon," I explained as I walked up to where Neil was sitting.

"Yeah, I know, hey listen. Somebody tried to use your security voice recognition code to gain access to Langley. It's your code but it's not your voice. Did you call Langley in the past twenty-four hours?" Neil asked with a serious look on his face.

"Yes I did as a matter of fact, I tried twice. One call, right after the other, but the system scrambled on me both times. Then we got the call to report in, so here I am. Is that why you paged me?" I asked.

"Yeah. That and the fact that Carla said 'Get the Sandman here, now!'" Neil explained in his best Ms. Silverman voice. Scratching the back of his head Neil looked over at the mainframe computer system. "It must have been a power surge of some kind. Well, at least I know that it was you. That puts my mind at ease. So you're going after our mad scientist, huh?" Neil asked with a wide grin. "Yeah, me and the rest of the world. I'm taking Kathy with me," I explained.

"I see. And what about Kate?" Neil asked.

"This is business. Kate is personal. Wait until you meet her my friend. You're gonna love her. She's one of a kind," I said proudly.

"I'm looking forward to it. I've got relatives in Scotland," Neil explained.

"Your a Scotsman?" I asked, caught completely by surprise.

"Yup, and a fine one I am," he replied playfully. "So tell me. When are you leaving and what do you want to code name this mission?"

"We're leaving as soon as Ben gets here with our plane. As for what to name this mission? I have no clue, I'll leave that up to you. I'll catch ya later. We need to pack some things and get ready for a long run. I think this fella is a lot smarter than they're giving him credit for," I explained.

"What makes you say that?" Neil questioned with a curious look.

"You don't create a virus this deadly and do it over night in the basement of your home. I think he's been working on it for a long time. I also think he used our laboratory and technology to do it. This has nothing to do with his father turning gay and divorcing his mother. I may be wrong Neil, but my gut instincts and my sixth sense is telling me that someone in our agency put him up to this," I explained with a serious look on my face.

"The one thing I've learned to do is to respect your gut instincts and to start paying more attention to mine. You really think that someone close to us is playing Doctor Jekyll and Mr. Hyde?" Neil asked with a concerned look.

"Yeah, I really do," I replied. "Do me a favor and try to pull up all of Francois de Bourbeillon files. Not the new stuff, the FBI is looking at all of that. I'm talking about the records of what he ordered while he was working for the Agency. Go back three years from the time Carla fired him and lets see what you come up with. In this case, old buddy, the most obvious could be the least obvious. So keep it between us," I explained.

"I'll put Sandy on it right away. Be careful, Sandman, and good luck," Neil replied as I left the War Room.

* * * * * * *

Operation Code Name: Looking Glass
Target: Francois de Bourbeillon
Target Coordinates: Unknown
Mission Status: Red
Mission profile: Locate American born Scientist Francois de Bourbeillon and terminate target with extreme prejudice. Secure any and all of Bourbeillon's chemical and or biological instruments. Use military means to destroy the deadly virus known to be in his possession.
Time Frame: None.

The search for Francois de Bourbeillon was a peerless one. The FBI focused their efforts in New Zealand where his credit cards were being used to purchase small meaningless items.

Neil had begun to pull up information that led us to believe that Francois might be living with friends of his and his mother. For four months Kathy and I flew around the globe looking for Bourbeillon. We started in the beautiful country of Norway and from there we went to Germany, Holland, Belgium, Poland, Portugal, Spain, Latin America, South Korea, and the United Kingdom.

We found evidence that he had been in these countries to visit with his friends but what we did not find was Francois de Bourbeillon himself.

We were on our way to Sonkajarvi, Finland when I used the secure telephone and computer line on our Agency Learjet to call Neil.

"What in the hell are we doing wrong, David? Four months for Christ's sake. And we can't find this guy? He's always one step ahead of us. I don't understand it. We have all of this technology and all the manpower we need and we still can't find him. Mother fucker!" Neil said in a burned out and frustrated tone of voice.

"Lets go back and start at square one, Neil. The things my Seal team training taught me was to know when to withdraw and take a closer look at what was right under my nose all along. Okay then, the most obvious is the least obvious. Everything is subject to change at any given moment," I whispered softly into the telephone as my mind tried to refocus my thoughts.

"How's Kate, have you talked to her lately?" Neil asked.

"She's cool, I call her every other day," I explained as I looked over at Kathy who was sound asleep in her seat.

"You know that Carla sent Danny to the Farm, don't you?" Neil asked.

"I thought that Chopper had already been through the Farm?" I questioned confused to hear what Neil had just told me.

"No, after Carla recruited him, he went straight back to Vietnam. Carla wants to get him a Q-clearance. So she sent him to the Farm. Danny said that if you could do it, then so could he," Neil explained with a laugh.

"Good, I'd love to go out on some missions with my big brother again," I replied.

"By the way, before I forget, Chopper left a card here for you," Neil explained.

"A card? What's in it?" I asked.

"I don't know, Dave, it's sealed."

"Open it up for me would you?" I asked curious as to what Danny would have left for me.

"Well lets see," Neil said as he tore open the envelope. "Its a letter with a twenty dollar bill in it. It's probably personal. I'll keep it safe until you get back," Neil explained.

"Neil, your my friend and brother. Read me the letter will you? I trust you, bubba," I explained.

It took a few seconds for Neil to start reading the letter that my big brother Danny had left for me. I knew that for the most part Neil had never felt he was part of the real action. He was the only child of two honest and hard working parents. He thought of himself as being a computer geek. All of that changed when we went back to Vietnam to get Danny out of the POW camp in Hanoi, when I asked Carla to put Neil in charge of the War Room and our mission.

"Dear David, I knew with you that your friendship came from your heart. You've never judged me by the color of my skin. How rare that is when we live in a world of racism and hate. My mother and Ms. Silverman both told me that you were the one who brought my brothers from Team One back to Vietnam to rescue me. If I told you, finding that out, didn't make me cry, I'd be lying to you and lying is the one thing we don't do with each other. I knew deep down in my heart that if and when you found out I had been captured you would come looking for me. In that, I had no doubt. It gave me the strength I needed to fight back and stay alive long enough for you to find me. You were right about one thing, being a POW sucks! My mother thanked me for all the money I had sent her. She wondered why I had sent it to you first and not sent it directly to her. You're something else, David, something else indeed. Thank you for loving my mother as if she was your own. That's a lot of money, little brother. Some day when we go back to Cambodia and find that Buddhist temple again, I'll pay you back. For now, I am sending you that twenty dollars I owe you. Remember when you bet me twenty bucks that I couldn't climb up onto the top of our bunker and kick your butt? I never expected you to pull a shotgun on me. Never let it be said that I don't pay my bets. By the time you get this, I'll be at some place called the Farm. I told Ms. Silverman that I wanted to start working with you or else I would quit. She smiled and told me she was hoping I would say something like that. What the hell, how hard can it be after everything we've been through together. Now that I think about it, I still want to go back to Laos and kill that damn cat! What do you say, you up for it? Well its time for me to go. There's some guy that says he knows you, he's going to take me to the Farm. Says his name is Oliver, but once I finish my training at the Farm I can call him Ollie. I'm not sure what that means but then again I never was the smartest guy on our team, just the best looking and strongest. Thanks for coming back for me, Sandman. No greater love does a man show than to be willing to lay his own life down for his brother. I love you little brother and would die for you to prove it. Your brother and friend, throughout life and into death, till the very end... Danny.

Man, that's deep. Thanks for sharing that with me, David, it means a lot. I hope one day I can be thought of like that," Neil said softly as he thought about what Danny had written to me.

"You already are loved like that, Neil. You just haven't figured it out yet," I explained. "What did you pull up on Francois' phone records."

"Not much. Two years ago he ran a bunch of ads in some of America's biggest city's newspapers. The lab was paying people to test a new drug. There are a lot of collect phone calls that came in to the laboratory at Langley. Well, they were routed to his home through their telephone system anyway. Other than that there's nothing," Neil explained.

"Collect calls?" I asked.

"Yup, almost every one of 'em," Neil answered as I heard him shuffling through the stack of papers. "About eight-hundred people all total. It takes a lot for the FDA to approve a new drug," Neil explained.

"Were you able to get a copy of the newspaper ad's that he ran?" I asked as my mind began to focus in on a thought.

"Yeah, the newspapers keep all that stuff on file as a matter of public record, why?" Neil asked as his curiosity started to kick in.

"Did he pay all their expenses through the Agency's account?" I asked.

"Yes, the article says all expenses paid, round trip airfare, hotel, and meals for two days. Earn five hundred dollars per person," Neil explained as he read the article to me.

"Oh my God, Neil, Francois is a lot smarter than we thought. He's already hit the United States and he used our Agency to fund it, that's why we can't find him," I explained.

"You've lost me, brother, what are you talking about?" Neil asked.

"His acting weird was all a front. He wanted Carla to fire him so that it wouldn't draw any suspicion to his leaving. Damn, Neil we're not a pharmaceuticals company testing a new drug. If we were going to test something, we would use the military not the civilian population. Collect phone calls, which means people that are homeless, drunks, and prostitutes. He lured them in with the free round trip airfare, hotel, and food for two days. He paid them five hundred dollars each and injected them with his deadly virus. I'll bet they all went to his home or he met with them at a hotel close to the airport. I'll also bet that he gave some of the prostitutes, passports and credit cards and sent them to some of these other countries where his credit cards are being used in. They're spreading the virus around the world and leaving a credit card paper trail for us to follow to keep us looking for him in all the wrong places," I explained.

"Oh mother fucker, it was right under my nose all along and I didn't even see it. The most obvious was the least obvious," Neil answered.

"Call Carla and tell her what's going on. Then I need you to work your magic, brother. Punch up your computer and see if you can find out if there are any Red Cross or World Relief organizations in Africa doing any medical treatments for the African people, like flu shots or vaccine inoculations. Then call me back, Neil. I'll have Ben change course, tell Carla that we're headed to Africa. Then get her to call the center for Infectious Disease Control and have them start looking at the city morgues to see if the number of deaths has gone up and is it over things like a common cold or flu bug. I'm afraid we may be to late, Neil. Oh God, I hope that I'm wrong, but I don't think I am. Call me back and give me a vicinity to target in Africa that Francois might be doing relief work in," I explained as I hung up the telephone.

Telling Ben of what I suspected we immediately changed our course.

"Oh please let me be wrong, God," I prayed silently to myself as I sat back in my seat and closed my eyes.

* * * * * * *

Ben had altered our course and after receiving a call from Neil, we were now headed to Kenya, Africa.

Neil had found out that humanitarian relief workers were working in nearby remote villages, distributing food and medical supplies to those in need. With a little luck we might be able to get a fix on the location of Francois de Bourbeillon.

Carla had called the American Ambassador in Africa and asked him to make arrangements for us at the airport when our plane landed. The African people were good people but once we left the major city and ventured out into the remote jungle areas we would need someone with us that could speak the African language and also knew his way around the country. Without a guide to show you the way, if you should happen to wonder off in the wrong direction, you would soon find yourself to be nothing more than lunch for one or more of the wild animals who roamed the vast lands of this wild and beautiful country.

"Hey, Kathy, check this out," I said as I sat at the computer station at the back of our plane.

"What's up," Kathy asked as she walked up to where I was sitting and looked over my shoulder at the computer screen.

"It says here that its often difficult for a male rhino to gain entry into the females vagina and that it can take up to two hours," I explained with a serious look on my face.

"No kidding," Kathy replied as she continued to look over my shoulder at the computer screen.

"Yeah. Look at that," I said as I pointed to the picture of the male and female rhinos having sex. "To ensure conception, the male rhino can ejaculate once every sixty seconds for up to an hour!" I explained as Kathy read the material on the screen.

"Who in their right minds would sit back and watch two rhinos having sex and count how many times the male rhino ejaculates?" Kathy replied as I looked up at her and grinned.

"Talk about a stud, could you imagine what it would be like to have an orgasm every sixty seconds for a full hour? Hoo yah," I said smiling.

"Asshole," Kathy answered with a broad smile as she walked toward the front of the plane to keep Ben company. "Hey, Ben, David wants to have sex with a rhino," Kathy explained playfully.

"No kidding, he better be able to cum once very sixty seconds for up to an hour if he wants to raise a family with her," Ben said loudly as he put the plane on auto-pilot and headed toward the back of the plane to use the bathroom.

"Thanks a lot, Ben," Kathy said in a whisper as Ben walked pass her. I was laughing so hard that my stomach began to hurt. "Oh God, four months is two long to be flying around the world with each other. I need a break," I said to myself as I reached over and opened the small refrigerator next to our communications system.

I opened my bottle of Pepsi and took a sip as Ben stepped out of the bathroom and sat down next to me. Ben had become a very close friend to me. For the past four months he had been teaching Kathy and I how to fly the Agency Learjet. He was surprised at how quickly I was learning the art of his trade. I was not at the point that I could navigate the plane by map or visual land marking, I could take off and land the plane with ease. I explained to Ben that I had always been a quick study when it involved something I was interested in. It would also give Ben a chance to relax and take a nap or a break from his duties as our pilot. For me it was great fun, especially knowing I had two Learjet's sitting at home at the Pontiac Airport. The Agency would help me get my license and then I could fly myself to Dublin to see Kate whenever I wanted too.

"How bad do you really think this situation with the Frenchman is?" Ben asked.

"Bad, real bad. Neil checked with the laboratory in Langley and there's no record of any tests being held on any human subjects. Plus, out of almost eight hundred volunteers none of them ever came to Langley. A deeper check showed that the Holiday Inn hotel at the airport had a sudden influx of people housed and fed by the hotel as guests of Dr. Bourbeillon," I explained sadly.

"How can this happen and no one in the accounting office noticed that Francois was spending hundreds of thousands of dollars of the Agency's money? It doesn't make any sense," Ben replied in a frustrated tone of voice.

"His research was funded out of the Black Operation account. He had free access. The Agency thought he was working on an antitoxin for VX Nerve Gas and Botulin. Hell this is the same guy that came up with a vaccine for Anthrax. So when he's doing test studies on animals no body is thinking anything about it. Everyone thinks it's a project to protect us," I explained as I turned and typed on the computer keyboard.

"Look at this, Ben," I said as I showed Ben what just appeared on the computer screen, "I could only gain access to this information by using my Q-clearance. We just gave Saddam Hussein, the leader of Iraq, a ton of VX Nerve Gas, Anthrax, and Ricin Biotoxins. He's not even a duly elected president of the country. He's a damn dictator for crying out loud. And to make matters worse, he's a cold blooded killer," I explained as I watched the look of shock spread across Ben's face.

"Why in the hell would we do that?" Ben asked as he looked over at me for an answer.

"Keep this between us, Ben," I said with a serious look.

"I will, David, I give you my word on it," Ben replied.

"We're tracking two suitcase sized nuclear American made weapons, that came up missing at the end of World War II. We have friends in Iran that we've trained and give funding too. Their code name is The Blue Light Group. They're sending us information, they believe the leader of Iran, some guy called the Ayatollah Komaine, has the weapons or is about to receive them. Because of this, we're supporting this Saddam Hussein fella and giving him permission to use chemical weapons on the people of Iran," I explained.

"What are we, crazy? Why don't we just go in and get the damn weapons back?" Ben asked.

"As soon as the Iranian Blue Light Group gets a positive fix on exactly where they're at, we will. But for now Saddam is going to keep them occupied with a land dispute or holy war of some type. It's a real fucked up deal and we're going to sit back and act as if we have no idea why Iraq and Iran are fighting," I explained.

"Well at least we gave him only enough to use on Iran," Ben replied with a sigh of relief.

"Ben, now that we have given Saddam the real stuff, all that his chemists have to do is keep one vial of each. With that culture they'll be able to mass-produce the stuff. When they do, what will keep them from using it on us if they should get mad at us for some reason?" I asked calmly as I raised my eyebrows.

"And if he does, we'll simply deny any and all knowledge of it and say we have no idea how he got his hands on these deadly chemicals that just happen to be outlawed by the United Nations," Ben pointed out as he reached into the refrigerator for a cold drink.

"Bingo, and we sit back and act as though we're a peace loving country. It makes me sick to my stomach, Ben. I love my country and I love the American people, but I can't stand our government or the politicians that run it," I replied as I turned off the computer and took a sip of my Pepsi.

"Hoo yah to that. Can I ask you a favor, Dave?" Ben asked with a serious look in his eyes.

"Absolutely. What's up?" I answered as I looked over at my friend.

"Can I go with you when you and Kathy go in after François? I've always wanted to see Africa and real lions and I might never get a chance like this again. Plus after four months of being cramped up in this damn plane, I'm feeling a little cagey," Ben explained as he waited for an answer.

"Hell yeah!" I said with a broad smile on my face. "Just make sure you carry two handguns and load 'em with the Black Rhino ammunition. Welcome to the hunt."

* * * * * * *

Landing in Kenya we were immediately greeted by our guide. Our guide was an American, big game hunter, named Max Bowman. He wasn't a tour guide by any means. He was a very real, big game hunter, who agreed to help us out when he was asked to do so by the American ambassador to Africa.

Mr. Bowman was not only an expert shot with big bore weapons but he was also a seasoned hunter who had spent years hunting big game animals from all over the world. He also loved to brag about his young nephew, who according to Max, could shoot four-inch square blocks of wood out of the air, and do it with a fully automatic, high powered, machine gun. With Max's reputation, I believed him.

Max had hired an African friend of his named Contu, who was an experienced guide. They had six, four-wheel drive vehicles, tents, camping gear, and food. They also had five men to drive the vehicles and prepare camp.

After securing our plane we said our hellos and went into town to buy boots and proper clothing for our journey.

"My god its hot," Kathy sighed as she wiped the sweat from her forehead with the back of her hand.

"Your body will adjust to it in time," I explained as Contu and Max drove us out of the city and into the wilds of Africa.

"This is beautiful country," Ben commented as we looked in all directions taking in the sights.

"Yes, it is beautiful, but it is also very dangerous country, so do not wonder off by yourselves or you may get eaten by a lion," Contu explained in broken English.

The small remote villages of Africa are great distances apart from each other. On our drive to the first village we saw herds of elephants, zebras, wildebeests, giselles, and other animals I didn't even know the names of.

Africa was rich with diamond mines, which made billions of dollars a year. Yet the owners of those mines and the officials that ran the government did little, if anything at all, to help the African people.

Pulling our four-wheel drive Range Rovers into the first small village I couldn't help but feel sad. These people were malnourished and starving.

"Oh my, look at these people," Kathy whispered softly in a sad voice.

"Sure makes me glad to be an American," Ben added as we pulled up into the center of the village and stopped.

"Its another Vietnam, just a different jungle and a different color of people," Max added as one of the elder tribesman walked up to our vehicle and smiled.

The man looked to be in his fifties. His skin was a dark black, wrinkled, and leather looking. He wore homemade jewelry and was naked except for a cloth that he wore around his crotch. He was covered with dirt, his hair was matted, and he was missing some teeth. He spoke no English but when he spoke, he stood straight, and spoke with pride. He was the tribe's chief.

Talking to him in his native tongue Contu and Max showed the chief the picture we had bought along with us of François de Bourbeillon. Looking at the picture it only took the chief a second to answer. Nodding his head yes the chief pointed at the side of his left arm and then at everyone of the people in his tribe, men, women, and children alike.

"He says that the doctor was here three days ago and that he put a needle in their arms telling them that it would keep them from becoming sick. He says that the doctor is traveling to all of the villages in this area to help the people," Max explained as he turned in his seat to look back at us.

"Can he tell us how many people are with the doctor?" I asked. Saying something to the chief, Contu answered.

"The Chief says three people are with the doctor. They drive in two steel machines like ours, one is full of supplies."

Thanking the Chief for his help, we left the village. Looking at the village full of women and small children I felt a rage of anger that was slowly building up inside me.

It was getting late by the time we had left the village, so Contu decided to stop for the night and set up camp. I wanted to tell Max what was going on but couldn't. To do so would have been a breach of security. The workers had prepared for us a simple meal of Gazelle steak, wild rice, bread, fruit, and water. Simply put, cooked over an open campfire, it was delicious!

Sitting by the open fire, the sounds of the wild came to life as the sunset and night spread its blanket of darkness over us.

"We're never going to catch up with him. He has a three day head start on us," I explained as I tossed a small dry branch into the campfire.

"We don't even know which village he's going to next," Kathy added.

"I could fly us over the entire area but I doubt I could land our jet close to where ever Francois is without damaging the plane," Ben added.

"I've got a real nice twin engine back at the airport I can land anywhere in Africa," Max whispered as he poked the fire with a small stick, looked up at us and grinned.

"Now we're back in the game," Ben said with a smile as he looked over at me.

We spent the next several hours sitting by the campfire listening to Max and Contu as they told us some of their more interesting stories of hunting the wildebeests of Africa. Off in the distance we heard a lion roar.

"What was that?" Kathy asked as she slid a little closer to me.

"Lion, he's hungry tonight," Contu said softly as he stared into the blue and yellow flames of the large campfire, never looking up.

"They don't come into camp at night, do they?" Kathy asked.

"Only if they smell a woman," Contu replied as Max and I made eye contact with each other.

"What? What do you mean, Contu?" Kathy asked in a scared tone of voice.

"Women, they come if they smell women," Contu said calmly.

"Why, when they smell a woman? What's the difference?" Kathy asked as she looked all around in the darkness.

"Your meat is more tender than ours. It is sweeter, they like that," Contu answered as Max, Contu, Ben, and I all stood up at the same time and headed for our tents.

Leaving Kathy sitting by the campfire all by herself, she jumped up. "Oh hell no, there's nothing sweet about me. I'm one mean, sour tasting, bitch," she shouted out loud as she ran up to Ben and I.

"Yes, I can see that," Contu answered as we all broke out laughing at the joke he had just played on Kathy.

"You assholes," Kathy said softly realizing that Contu had been playing with her.

"I'm sleeping in here with you guys tonight," Kathy explained as she followed Ben and I into our tent.

"This should be interesting," I said jokingly.

Pulling her 15-shot Smith & Wesson automatic pistol out of her shoulder holster, Kathy cocked back the hammer and grinned.

"Don't even think about it. I'm more deadly than that fucking lion," she explained nervously.

"This is true," I explained as I reached into my shirt pocket and pulled out my tiny vial of liquid Methadrine. Placing two drops under my tongue I slipped the tiny vial back into my pocket.

"You guys get some sleep, I'll stay up and stand watch. I love it in the jungle," I explained as I stepped back out of the tent and into the darkness of the African night.

* * * * * * *

It took us most of the day to get back to the airport in Kenya. Max Bowman owned a beautiful twin engine Cessna. It took Max, Kathy, Ben, and I almost an hour to get our gear on board. By then it was getting to late to fly so we spent the night in Kenya.

* * * * * * *

It was six o'clock in the morning as our twin-engine plane lifted off. We were headed north on our search for Doctor Francois de Bourbeillon and the deadly virus he was injecting into the innocent people of Africa.

We flew across the vast plains of Kenya, Tanzania, and Ethiopia and saw herds of wild animals. The country was beautiful in its wildest state.

Landing at some of the small villages we talked to both Hutu and Tutsi tribesmen. Some were afraid to look at the photograph thinking that we had captured the doctor's soul and wouldn't release it. They had no idea what a camera or a photograph was. These simple people were still hundreds of years behind modern day technology. Some of them had already been inoculated with the deadly virus. Some of them were too afraid of the needle. They had never seen a syringe before.

Spending the night at a Hutu village we waited for the sun to come up praying that tomorrow would be the day we would find Francois and stop his insane madness.

* * * * * * *

We were north of the Sudan when Max spotted something.

"Down there, looks like two vehicles," he said as we flew low over the treetops of the small remote village.

Making a wide sweep we came back around for a second look.

"That's him," Ben said as he looked out through the side window of the plane.

Making another wide circle of the area we came back around and landed the plane.

Walking up toward the small village we could see both of Doctor Bourbeillon's vehicles. Lined up next to them were the people of the small tribe. The doctor was standing with his shirt sleeves rolled up injecting them one by one and then giving them a piece of hard candy for a treat.

Walking up to the doctor, Kathy began to speak.

"Doctor Francois de Bourbeillon, I'm Special Agent Kathleen Eckland. I have a warrant..." she was saying when I pushed her aside.

My first strike was open handed as I delivered a treacherous chop to the doctor's throat. The tribe's people jumped back. Some ran, some watched and pointed their fingers at us as the young children cried with fear.

Grabbing his throat the doctor staggered backwards with a look of shock and total paranoia on his face. As he did I kicked him just below and onto the side of his left knee. When I did his knee snapped like a twig and the doctor fell to the ground gasping for air.

The gunshot echoed in the air as I turned quickly to look behind me. One of Doctor Bourbeillon's aides hit the hard, dry, dirt ground. In his hand was an old .38 caliber revolver handgun. Standing off to his left, I saw Ben with his gun pointed at the man who was about to shoot me in the back.

"You two, get up against the fucking truck, now!" Ben ordered to the other man and woman who was working with Francois.

Without saying anything I turned back around and moved in toward the doctor. Reaching out with his right hand in an attempt to stop me, I quickly grabbed the doctor's hand by the center of his palm with my left hand, and twisted it back towards him in a goose necked position. When I did I struck the back of his hand hard with the open palm of my right hand. The sound of his right wrist snapping was crisp and sharp as it sent the doctor's body into an uncontrollable spasm of pain.

"David!" Kathy shouted out loudly in an attempt to help me to regain my focus and a clear way of thinking. Looking at Kathy she quickly nodded her head in the direction of the women and children who were afraid and crying at my outburst of pent up anger and rage.

Seeing them, I quickly calmed down. Walking up to the other man working with the doctor I asked, "What's your name?"

"Kyle," he answered.

"Do you know what's going on here?" I asked.

"Yes, you just killed my friend and seriously injured Doctor Bourbeillon," he replied.

"I didn't kill your friend, Kyle. My brother did," saying that I could see Ben smile at my calling him my brother.

"These vials are tainted. You didn't know that?" I asked calmly.

"What? What are you talking about? My friend Lori and I were vaccinated two weeks ago, we're not sick nor are we showing any signs of becoming sick," Kyle responded.

"You will be if I don't get you and Lori to a hospital right away. It poisons your liver, Kyle. Without your liver you die. It takes about a month for it to do enough damage to kill you. You're lucky we got to you and Lori in time. I'm sorry about your friend, but he pulled a gun on me," I explained.

"Oh my, all of these people. The doctor knew this?" Kyle asked.

"Yes he did. Listen, I need you and Lori to help me. We are going to drive these trucks out into the plains and burn this tainted virus. Then we'll come back here and fly you both to the hospital so you can be treated. How's that sound?" I asked.

"Yes, that sounds good," Kyle answered.

"Okay then, load up your equipment and let's get the doctor and your friends body into the back of the supply truck. Kyle would you ask some of the tribesmen to help out to get your friend and the doctor into the back of the truck?" I asked.

"I'll help," Max said as he turned to walk toward the doctor who had passed out from the shock of his injuries.

"No!" I shouted. "Don't touch them, Max. Don't get any of their blood on you. You can catch it that way. The tribesman, Lori, and Kyle are already infected so it can't hurt them," I explained quickly as I walked over to where Max was standing.

"You're not really with the American Red Cross are you?" Max asked.

"No," I answered.

"Mind if I ask who you people really are?" Max asked with a raised eyebrow and a curious look on his face.

"Ask me later," I replied.

Leaving Max and Ben to watch the airplane, Kathy and I rode with Lori and Kyle as we took both of the trucks, the doctor, the dead body of Kyle's friend, and the twenty cases of the deadly virus, out into the wilderness of Africa.

Unloading the twenty wooden cases of the deadly virus, I drove the thick rubber tires of the truck back and forth over the cases until I was sure that each vial was smashed. Remembering what our Agency scientist, Lisa Morgenstern, had said, "Once the body dies or the virus is exposed to the air it immediately dies."

"Kyle would you and Lori help the doctor out of the back of the truck and put him into the Land Rover, please. We'll all go back to the plane in one vehicle," I explained calmly.

"Yes, certainly," Kyle answered as he and Lori helped Francois out of the truck. The doctor was awake and in an excruciating amount of pain.

As they turned to help the doctor back to our Land Rover, I fired two quick shots. The first shot hit Lori in the face causing her body to flip backwards onto the ground. My second shot tore its way through Kyle's chest and exited out through his back taking with it his heart in a bloody spray of flesh and muscle.

The doctor fell, once again, to the ground.

"Please, why are you doing this?" he asked in an emotional tone of voice.

"Are you out of your fucking mind? Do you have any idea of what you've done?" Kathy shouted out angrily.

"What I've done? What I've done? Yes, I know what I've done! I'm saving mankind. The blacks, the prostitutes, the homosexuals, the drug users, their destroying the purity of humanity," Francois shouted out in anger and pain.

"Get out of the way, Kathy," I said as I fought hard to control my anger.

Starting up the truck I drove forward toward the doctor. Seeing the large rubber tire coming at him he tried to roll away but it was to late. His shattered knee and broken wrist kept him from moving quickly enough.

Rolling the left front tire of the truck over his left leg the doctor's screams echoed through the hot afternoon air. I took great pleasure in hearing him scream as I rolled the truck tire back and forth over both of his legs. Backing up the truck I pulled it around and slowly rolled the tire up next to his head.

His entire body was shaking with pain. He was going into shock. Moving the truck forward an inch at a time I heard his skull pop like a ripe melon. Backing the truck up I turned off the ignition and got out.

"You should have let the lions have him," Kathy explained as she pointed out across the open plains at the seven large cats watching us and slowly moving in our direction.

"Why, they didn't do anything to us. Why kill good lions?" I asked.

"What are you talking about? Kill the lions? They would have eaten that sorry bastard alive," Kathy explained.

"Yeah, and then they would catch the virus and spread it to each other. Doctor Morgenstern said once its exposed to the air it dies. Now they can eat all three of these bodies and not get sick," I explained as Kathy and I got back into the Land Rover and drove back to where Max and Ben were waiting for us with the plane.

Our flight back to the airport in Kenya was a quite one. To my surprise no one said a word.

Grabbing our gear, Ben and Kathy got into our Learjet and waited for me as I paid Max for his services.

"Thanks for your help, Max, what do I owe you?" I asked.

"A thousand should cover it," Max replied with a curious look on his face. Reaching into my pocket I pulled out a plain white envelope and handed it to Max. "There's ten thousand dollars in here, Max. You don't know us, you never saw us, and you don't know anything. We were never here, right, Max?" I asked calmly with a straight look on my face.

"I'd say thank you, but you were never here to thank," Max answered with a broad smile as he took the envelope from my hand and tucked it into his pants pocket.

"Your a smart man, Mr. Bowman. Thanks again," I said as I turned and walked to the steps of our plane.

"But if you would have been here, who would you people have been?" Max asked as I stepped up onto the first step of our plane. Turning to face Max I answered his question.

"We're America's best kept secret, Max. What do you say we just leave it at that."

Max never said another word, he simply grinned and waved goodbye.

* * * * * * *

Returning to the United States, I went back to my home in Michigan while Kathy and Ben debriefed at the Pentagon.

Two days later, with Ben at my side, I took my pilots test and passed it. A week later, I flew my grandfathers Learjet to Ireland and spent some time with Kate.

In time Dr. Lisa Morgenstern would discover that the deadly virus came from a monkey that was shipped to Dr. Bourbeillon from Central Africa. The virus was a combination of animal and human body fluids that led some to believe a human may have had sexual contact with the animal. Two years would pass before the world would be told about a deadly new virus called, HIV-AIDS.

It would be a young white child name Randy White, who would contract the deadly disease from a hospital. It was at the hospital that this young man would receive a blood transfusion, where someone had donated the diseased blood. In the end it would be that tainted batch of blood, which would end the young boys life. Finally, the HIV problem would receive national news media coverage.

Because of one person who created a disease with the hope of targeting homosexuals, drug users, people of poverty and color, over two hundred thousand people from around the world have already died. Over a million are now HIV positive.

Is there a cure? I believe that the answer to that question is, yes. Unfortunately, you'll never see it, because its one of our best kept secrets. Aids, cancer, diabetes, and a number of other diseases are all part of a multi-billion dollar a year business. Pharmaceutical companies alone, make billions of dollars a year by manufacturing medicines and pills that kill the pain and slows these diseases down.

Doctors, hospitals, pharmacies, therapists, clinics, and research laboratories make billions of dollars a year off the pain and suffering of those who have the deadly virus.

Why would they allow this to happen? The answer is simple: money, power, greed, and racial hatred. What better way to wipe out those you don't like, control the world population, and make billions of dollars in the process.

The AIDS virus alone affects mostly the homosexuals, prostitutes, drug addicts, and poverty stricken. The problem is that it didn't stay in these minority groups as some felt it would. It slipped out and still, those that hold the secrets don't care.

Gay men and women, in their lives grapple with sexuality and spirituality, politics, and religion, love, and death. AIDS alone depicts the horrors of this deadly disease and shows us the physical scars and suffering of its many victims and how ugly this disease really is.

The deadly virus is decimating the beautiful people of Africa and has reached its deadly touch out to the entire world.

To date, it has become a pandemic.

Gazelle shot in Africa by Author.
"Became known as supper."

459

Chapter Twenty-Seven
Code Name: Clean Sweep

Standing in my backyard, I looked through my telescope and out into space at a beautiful Nebula. My high-powered telescope had precision ground-glass lenses with anti-reflective coating and two separate Kellner eyepieces. It was mounted on an adjustable tripod and gave me optical clarity that was simply unbelievable.

Adjusting the telescope, I looked at the moon, where on July 20, 1969, Neil Armstrong and Edwin "Buzz" Aldrin Jr., made history by being the first men to walk on the moon.

"Yeah right," I said to myself as I walked away from my telescope and sat down in my lawn chair next to my swimming pool.

The large pool had lights in it making the clear blue water inside appear to sparkle in the darkness of the night. I had been home from Ireland now for almost two weeks and I was bored to death.

I couldn't help but wonder what had happened to me? Vietnam had changed the course of my life so dramatically that it sometimes confused me. When I was out on a mission or going out after someone to kill, I felt alive inside. I felt pumped, alert, and full of energy. But when I had no one to go after, I felt lifeless and drained of all of my energy. Something seemed to have snapped inside of me. Maybe it had happened while I was a POW in Cambodia. All I knew was, whatever it was that had happened to me, it had changed me, and I needed something to happen real soon or I was going to go nuts.

Hearing my telephone ring in my den, I got up and headed inside. While I was gone, Andy had installed a water proof external speaker box on the outside of the back of my house and put it just above my sliding glass doors. He had attached it to my telephone bank inside my den. Now if I was outside and the telephone or computer rang or beeped, I could hear it. Walking inside I looked up at the speaker box. "Crazy damn Indian," I said to myself as I headed quickly to my den. Once in the den, I sat down in my black leather chair and picked up the telephone.

"Hello," I said as I looked at my watch.

"Hello, kid, is your scrambler box on?" Carla asked.

"Always," I answered. "You sound down, are you alright?" I asked.

"Yeah, I guess so. It's this virus ordeal. I got a call from Lisa at the lab and she said that she has scientific proof that some sick bastard was either having sex with one of the monkeys that Francois had ordered from Central Africa, or he combined his body fluids or the body fluids of a dead cadaver with the monkey. Lisa said that without the 'Host Monkey' that

Francois used, finding a cure could take years, if we find one at all," Carla explained in a tired voice. "Hell, it could have been someone in Africa screwing the damned monkey for all we know."

"Millions of people are going to die a real horrible death if someone doesn't find a cure and find it fast," I explained.

"I know," Carla replied.

"If they found a cure, do you really think that the powers to be would let it be known?" I asked, curious to hear Carla's reply.

A long pause.... "I seriously doubt it, David. I received a memo just a few hours ago telling me that the research on this is being given to someone else. We are to resume normal black operation status. We're out of it," Carla explained.

"So the cover up has begun, huh?" I questioned.

"It sure sounds like it. To the power elite, this will only affect the Blacks, Homosexuals, Junkies, and Prostitutes. Why would the rich politicians care about them?" Carla explained in an angry voice.

"It's going to spread to everyone and to all age groups of people, Carla, you and I both know that. Now someone has pulled us out of the game to keep us from finding out who was secretly behind all of this? Boy oh boy, this really sucks, it's a man made virus for crying out loud. They created it for one purpose, Carla, to kill innocent people! Hell, at least we kill the right people to keep them from starting a nuclear war. This is something else. Now they're going to cover it up," I explained bitterly.

"I agree with you, David, but we need to keep our suspicions to ourselves for now. Who knows what they might try to do next. Remember, Presidents have the best protection in the world and they still get assassinated. We're out here on our own kiddo, so watch your back and be careful," Carla explained.

"Mind if I ask you a question?" I asked.

"Not at all, what's up?" Carla responded.

"I was looking at the McGruder film on the Kennedy hit. It was a triangulated crossfire. There were three sniper's that shot at him from three different angles, and the Secret Service agent driving the car, slowed the car down almost to a complete stop so they could take the shot. How is it that nobody else sees this?" I asked, suspecting that Carla may have been involved in the plot to kill President Kennedy.

"And what else have you noticed?" Carla asked with a soft voice.

"Oswald was never up stairs at the time Kennedy was shot. He had witnesses that all said he was downstairs in the cafeteria eating his lunch when Kennedy was killed. All the witnesses said he was just as surprised to hear that Kennedy had been killed as they were. What I find real interesting is that the FBI, Secret Service, local and Texas State Police were all searching for Lee Harvey Oswald before they had any idea as to what was really going on. The police announce that they found a .306 caliber rifle, but they then produce an Italian made Carcano rifle that's a total piece of junk. Don't you find that interesting, Carla?" I questioned.

"And?" Carla replied calmly.

"Jack Ruby was caught on tape gunning down Oswald and he's using a gun that has a hammer shroud on it. Plus, his finger is lying on the side of the gun pointing at Oswald. Ruby was a professional hit man who was dying of cancer. Would you like me to continue?" I asked slyly.

"No, you've said way to much already. Only a person with you're training would see what you were able to see. That's what we trained you for.

President Kennedy was a very sick man, David. He was on ten different kinds of painkillers and medications. He could barely walk because he was in so much pain. Most of the time the Secret Service had to use an electric lift just to get him on board Air Force One. He had a padded cushion on his rocking chair that he sat in while he was in the Oval Office at the White House. Had the world found out about how sick he really was, they would have forced him to resign. Let's just say that it was more of a mercy killing and leave it at that, shall we," Carla explained calmly.

"I see," I replied.

"Kennedy wasn't the saint that everyone thought he was. He ordered a mob hit on Marilyn Monroe to keep her from exposing the love affair he and his brother Bobby were having with her. She threatened to go to the press and expose them. They killed her, and young Bobby was there at the Monroe home when it happened.

When Senator Robert Kennedy attacked organized crime and went after Teamster President Jimmy Hoffa on national television; that pretty much sealed their fate. We have Jimmy Hoffa on tape talking to Bobby Kennedy. Hoffa called him from a payphone outside the White House. Hoffa warned him to 'back off before it was to late.' He even tells Bobby that the big mob boys are pissed off about him attacking the Teamsters. Jimmy tells him that the mob will kill his brother John, but Bobby wouldn't listen.

After the hit goes down on John Kennedy, Hoffa calls Bobby back at the White House, from the same phone booth, and tells him, 'Your brother's dead because of you. His blood is on your hands you little punk. I tried to warn you. Now back off or we're both gonna be next!' Then Jimmy hangs up the telephone. The FBI had it all on tape but J. Edger Hoover hated the Kennedy's so he kept it all quiet. Business as usual.

The next time you come to my office bring some Chinese take-out with you and I'll tell you all about our dirty little secrets," Carla explained, with a laugh and a sigh.

"That's a deal. Hey, whatever happened with that missing video tape Risa stole, did you ever find it?" I asked.

"The one of the alien autopsy?" Carla asked.

"Yeah, that one. Did it ever surface?" I questioned.

"No, but if it does, without Doctor Tansiri alive to verify that it's authentic, no one will believe it. We'll use our contacts in the news media to say that it's a Hollywood fake," Carla explained.

"Like you said, business as usual," I answered sarcastically.

"Yeah, pretty much. You better get used to it. Its how things are done at the top," Carla replied.

"Oh well, life goes on. So tell me, did you call me just to vent some of your pent up frustrations?" I asked playfully.

"Yeah, pretty much. This whole ordeal with Doctor Bourbeillon really has me upset. We've done a lot of dirty things before, but this one really pisses me off. It's nice to have someone that I can trust enough to talk to and share some of my inner feelings with. I haven't been able to do that in a very long time. Thanks for listening," Carla explained.

"Anytime, mom, anytime at all," I replied.

"Remember, keep this conversation and our suspicions between us and I'll talk to you later, okay? Have a goodnight, David," Carla explained as she hung up the telephone on her end.

Hanging up my phone, I sat back in my chair. For a while I had thought that Carla might have been the one behind Doctor Bourbeillon's secret experiment. But now I realized that I was wrong.

"It's a man made virus, from a monkey out of Central Africa and human body fluids. There was someone behind this killer virus other than Doctor Bourbeillon. Who in the world could it be?" I asked myself as I sat back in my chair and yawned...

* * * * * * *

It was a hot, clear, sunny Tuesday morning as I stood on the grass next to my driveway and watched as the middle aged man named Sonny pulled my new red Ferrari up and onto the car trailer. Watching as he climbed underneath the trailer he quickly secured the frame of the car to the steel car hauler.

Even though Marge had sent me a clear title for the car, I had only driven it one time since I had taken it from Walter Changs estate in California. So I was having it shipped to Ireland so Kate could have it.

Wiping the dust off of his hands with a clean rag, Sonny walked up to me and looked at the paperwork on his clipboard. "Alright then, we'll get this to Ms. Kate Donovan in Dublin, Ireland, all safe and sound for you. She must be a special lady to send her a car like this," Sonny said with a grin.

"Yes she is. She saved my life in Vietnam, I'd say that's pretty special wouldn't you?" I asked as I pulled out the certified check I had picked up from my bank, and handed it to Sonny. Looking at the amount that the check was made payable for, Sonny then looked back up at me and winked.

"That will do it, sir. You can let Ms. Donovan know that we'll have it delivered to her front door within 30-days. If you need anything else shipped overseas just let us know. Thank you for your business," Sonny said as we shook hands.

Watching him get into his truck and take the Ferrari away, I turned and looked at Tara and Jessy who were both watching me.

"That sucks," Jessy said with a look of disappointment on her face.

"Where did you learn to talk like that, young lady?" I asked.

"Andy and Don," Jessy said as she puckered her bottom lip with a pout.

"Listen, I know I promised you that I'd get you a new Ferrari, but you don't want that one. In a couple of years you'll both be old enough to drive. As soon as you get your driver's license I'll buy you a brand new one, okay?" I asked.

"Promise?" Jessy asked as she started to perk up a bit.

"I promise," I answered as Jessy walked up to me and gave me a hug.

"Thanks, Uncle Dave," she said.

"Your welcome," I replied as Jessy's mother pulled into my driveway to pick up the girls.

Watching the girls walk toward Dana's car I looked at Tara. "Hey butthead, aren't you going to give me a hug too?" I asked as Tara turned around and put both of her hands on the sides of her hips.

"Where did you learn to talk like that, David," she asked in a scolding manner with a serious look on her face.

"Andy and Don taught me," I said quickly.

Seeing Tara smile, she ran up to me and gave me a hug goodbye. "See ya later, Uncle Dave, and you can get me a Corvette when I turn sixteen," she said with a grin as she turned and ran back to the car.

"That's my girl," I said softly as Dana waved at me and backed out of the driveway.

The girls were growing up way to fast. They're young body's were starting to fill out and they were way to smart for their own good. I had already opened up separate trust funds for both Tara and Jessy. I had also put both of their mothers in my will and left Amy and Dana enough money to live very comfortably on, should something ever happen to me.

Walking back into my house, I heard the phone in my den ring. Walking into my den I sat down at my desk and picked it up. I left the black scrambler box on all of the time now, just to be safe.

"Hello," I said in a soft sexy voice.

"Damn, if I was a girl I'd have a wet spot in my underwear. Do you always answer the telephone like that?" Ollie asked jokingly.

"No not always, I usually say something smart like, 'Hello, Long Dongs Meat Shop'," I answered as we both began to laugh.

"I'm going to have to start calling you more often," Ollie replied.

"So, what have you been up to? Anything interesting?" I asked.

"No, not much. I'm selling a lot of weapons to the Contras. Don't ask me why but its what the big boys want, soooo," Ollie replied.

"Yeah, well after this ordeal with Bourbeillon, nothing that we do surprises me anymore. So what's up? You never call me," I asked, curious as to why Ollie would be calling me.

"To be honest with you, I really don't know. Carla asked me to get you on a secure line. She'll be here in a minute. She's in her office talking to Richard about something," Ollie explained.

"Interesting," I replied as I sat back in my chair.

"Just before she closed the door to her office I heard her tell Richard that she got a call at her home late last night. But then she closed the door to her office. It's probably from one of our Field Agents. Hang on, partner, here she is. I'll talk to you later," Ollie explained as he handed the telephone to Carla.

"Thank you Oliver, please close the door on your way out will you." Pause... "David?" Carla asked.

"Yes, ma'am, are you alright?" I asked. Carla never has someone else call for her so I knew that something was up.

"Yes, I'm fine. Listen, I was just talking to Deputy Director Crock. Well, let me start at the beginning.

I received a telephone call late last night from one of my most powerful informants. Remember the other day when we were talking about the Kennedy's and Jimmy Hoffa?" Carla asked.

"Yeah, why?" I asked.

"My guy inside the Mafia is telling me that the mob has a hit going down on Hoffa tomorrow. Hoffa tried to blow up Teamster President Fitzsimmons. The car bomb went off and almost killed Fitzsimmons' son Richard. Jimmy's stepson Chucky told Provenzano everything, it's a mess."

"Hang on, let me find my pen," I answered, even though I had my ink pen sitting on my desk right in front of me. Carla had just caught me off guard, and I didn't know if she was testing me or not. Could she have known who my grandfather was all along? Did she know about me? Opening my desk drawer, I closed it loud enough for Carla to hear it.

"Okay, I'm ready," I explained calmly, even though my heart and mind were racing out of control.

"It's going down at the Macus Red Fox Restaurant on Telegraph Road in Bloomfield Hills, Michigan, sometime around noon or shortly thereafter. My guy tells me that the family is bringing hit men in from New Jersey. They're not using their local talent. The order came down from Tony Provenzano out of the New Jersey crime family," Carla explained anxiously.

"Wait a minute, I want to make sure that I understand this. Your telling me that Hoffa tried to kill Fitzsimmons, and almost killed his son Richard instead. Now Tony Pro is going to hit Jimmy tomorrow in Michigan?" I asked. "Boss, I think you've got some bad information. Are you sure that you trust your so called man on the inside?" I asked, hoping that Carla would slip up and tell me who her informant was.

"First, they're not going to gun Hoffa down like they did with John and Bobby Kennedy. My guy tells me that they're going to make Hoffa disappear. And yes, I trust this man one hundred percent. He helped us with the Kennedy assassinations, the hit on Oswald and Jack Ruby. He was our man who had put together the plan for us to hit Fidel Castro. Sam's our snake in the grass, David," Carla explained.

"May I ask, just who are we talking about here? Sam who?" I asked calmly.

"He's the big man himself, David. The boss of the biggest crime family in Chicago. Sam Momo Giancana. He's been our best informant for over ten years now. If Sam tells me that Jimmy Hoffa is going to disappear tomorrow at noon, you can take that to the bank," Carla explained proudly.

Trying not to show any emotion I calmly asked, "Okay boss if you say so. What do you want me to do?" I asked.

"Do you know where this restaurant is in Bloomfield Hills, Michigan?" Carla asked.

"Oh yeah, everyone knows where the Red Fox is. It's a popular restaurant," I replied as I faked a yawn to appear as if I could care less.

"Go there tomorrow and find a place to sit in the parking lot where you'll be able to see everything. Watch and see what takes place in the parking lot with Hoffa. If anything should happen to go wrong, kill everybody including Hoffa. In exchange for the information, I promised

Sam that I'd have someone there to clean up the entire crew if anything should happen to go wrong," Carla explained.

"Alright, if you say so. I still think that this Sam fella is blowing smoke up your skirt, but I'll go there," I replied calmly.

"Thank you, David. Be careful, kiddo, these mob hit men are not to be taken lightly. They're very serious and they're deadly. Call me as soon as its over with, will you?" Carla asked.

"Okay, I'll talk to you tomorrow, sometime after one o'clock," I replied as we both hung-up our telephones.

Looking at my hands they were both shaking. I couldn't believe what I had just been told. The man that I had grown up calling Uncle Sam was a CIA informant. Everything that he had told me about trust, honor, and loyalty was a lie.

"Son-of-a-bitch, they're gonna hit Hoffa and not tell anyone about it, and Carla and the Agency wasn't going to do a damn thing about it. Sam has a lot of dirt on the Agency and they have an equal amount of dirt on him. No wonder they work so well together," I thought to myself as I tried to clear my thoughts and figure out what I should do next.

There was nothing that I could do about it. I already knew that the family had at least two FBI agents in their pocket who were ready to step in and take over the investigation once Hoffa was reported missing.

"Well, for now, I'm going to go for a swim in my pool and throw a steak on the grill for lunch. I'll worry about tomorrow when tomorrow gets here," I said to myself as I went up stairs to change into my swimsuit.

* * * * * * *

Black Operation Code Name: "Clean Sweep"
Status: Surveillance
Location: Macus Red Fox
Lock Coordinate: Telegraph Road, Bloomfield Hills Michigan
Target Ident: James Riddle Hoffa
Target Status: Active
Time Frame: Twelve o'clock
Mission Status: Surveillance at visual level only, parking lot of restaurant known as Macus Red Fox. Locate and observe meeting between New Jersey and Detroit organize crime members. Confirm assassination of Teamster President James Hoffa. At first observation of difficulty, terminate all parties present with extreme prejudice.

It was Wednesday, July 30, 1975, as I sat in my car and looked at my Gold Tag Heuer watch.

I had given one of the salesmen at our local Flannery Ford Dealership, five hundred dollars. For that he let me borrow one of their brand new Ford Thunderbirds equipped with a dealer license plate. If anything should happen to go wrong, I would pull off the license plate and burn the car. He would then report the new car as stolen and keep my new corvette that I had left at the dealership for himself.

The car was beautiful. It was such a dark blue that it almost looked black. It had black leather interior, was fully loaded, and still had the dealership shipping tag on the back left window.

It was a hot, sun shiny Michigan day. "It's eight minutes after one Jimmy, your late, that's not like you," I said to myself as I took a sip of my Pepsi and pulled my briefcase across the front seat, a little closer to me.

Looking out through the windshield of my car, I double-checked to make sure that I was parked in the best position possible. I had backed my car into the front left corner of the restaurant, closest to Telegraph Road. From this position I could see almost everything that was taking place in the parking lot, and still get away easily if anything should happen to go wrong.

"Hello Jimmy," I whispered to myself as I watched the brand new, dark green, four door, Pontiac Grandville pull into the restaurant parking lot and come to a stop next to the Macus Red Fox restaurant sign. Jimmy had pulled to the left of the sign with his car facing away from Telegraph Road.

Getting out of his car, I watched as he closed the car door and looked around the parking lot. He was wearing black slip on shoes, blue dress slacks, and a blue short sleeve pull over shirt, that had some kind of small design above the left shirt pocket.

"You certainly do look like a mob boy Jimmy," I said to myself as Jimmy put on his dark framed plastic sunglasses.

Jimmy had a small hunting lodge in the Northern Forest of Michigan, which I had flown up to several times. They would go up there to hunt but they never really did do any hunting. They would walk around drinking beer and discuss daily and teamster union business. There at his property up north, Jimmy would laugh and joke about how the FBI wouldn't be able to watch and listen to him while he was deep in the Michigan woods. As for me, I thought that if someone ever wanted to kill Jimmy, what a better place to do it than at his lodge deep in the woods.

Jimmy Hoffa was a no-nonsense man well known for his ability to fight to get what he wanted. He loved his wife and family, there was no doubt about that, but most of all he loved the men of the Teamsters Trucking Union. He was stubborn and bull headed. He was a hotheaded, cunning, smart, clever man who defended his truck drivers with a vengeance. He would do whatever was necessary to protect his men, his brother teamsters, and they all knew it. That's what made him so powerful. You had to admire and respect that, just as his men admired and respected him.

In short, James Riddle Hoffa was a legend. He did nothing wrong to deserve something like this. There would be a lot of rumors that would surface about him. But the truth is Jimmy was about to win his appeal which would allow him to run for Teamster president again. He felt Fitzsimmons had betrayed him so he tried to kill Frank but the hit failed. Now, Tony Pro, under orders from Bufalino, was goint to kill Jimmy and there was no stopping it.

Watching Jimmy, he seemed restless. He walked into the front entrance of the restaurant and came back out, and looked at his car. He said hello to two different men that had come out of the restaurant. Jimmy kept looking at his watch. He was nervous. His stepson Chucky was suppose to have had this meeting with Tony Jack from the Detroit enforcer family, all arranged, but nobody was here yet. At 2:15 p.m. Jimmy walked to the back of the restaurant and made a phone call.

You could drive around to the back of the restaurant and find a bakery. I don't know who Jimmy called but I couldn't help but wonder why Jimmy wasn't listening to his sixth sense. That little voice whispering in his ear, telling him that something was wrong. Jimmy was trying real hard to make peace with the New Jersey crime boss. He trusted Tony Jack from Detroit and knew that if anyone could help him settle this issue with Tony Pro, Tony Jack was the one.

Tony Jack was the younger of the two brothers who ran the enforcer family. There was Vito and Tony. Tony was given the nickname, "Tony Jack." When he and his brother Vito were kids they tried to jump onto an open boxcar of a passing train. Young Tony slipped, and when he did, the wheels of the boxcar cut off one of his legs at the knee. But don't kid yourself, it never slowed him down, it only made him stronger. Both he and his brother now owned a small orange juice delivery company that did very well.

Tony wasn't stupid by any means. He knew that Chucky told his stepdad, Jimmy Hoffa, that he, Tony Jack, was going to be meeting with him at the Macus Red Fox for lunch. While Jimmy was waiting patiently for Tony to arrive, Tony was at the Southfield Athletic Club to ensure himself a sound proof alibi. Tony would continue to ask well-known businessmen and spa attendants what time it was. He was so worried about making sure that his alibi was perfect, he forgot to take of his expensive watch.

Hearing the loud horn of a semi-truck tractor-trailer rig, I watched as the truck driver waved at Jimmy and Jimmy waved back at him. Everybody knew Jimmy Hoffa, even when they were driving southbound on Telegraph Road and Jimmy was standing next to his car in a restaurant parking lot.

Minute after minute passed. "I'll be damned, I'll bet that something happened and they're not going to show up," I thought to myself as I looked down at my watch.

As I looked back up, I saw a car pull into the parking lot and drive to the back of the building. Inside was a female driver who appeared to be in her thirties. A few seconds later I felt my heart speed up as I placed two drops of liquid Methadrine under my tongue, and opened the top of my briefcase. It was 2:30 p.m. as the black Lincoln, four-door, Town Car pulled into the parking lot of the Macus Red Fox restaurant and stopped.

Reaching into my briefcase, I pulled out my Mack-10, .9mm machine gun and then pulled out the two 60-round clips I had duct taped, back-to-back together. Without taking my eyes off of the black Lincoln Town Car, I quickly slid the first clip into the machine gun and chambered a live round into the firing position. There was no doubt about it, this was the car full of killers who had come for Jimmy. From my angle I could see the light colored New Jersey license plate on the back of the car. Lowering myself in my seat, I watched as four men got out of the black Lincoln and Jimmy began to walk towards them.

All four men were less than six feet tall. Three of them were medium build. Out of those three men, two of the brown haired men looked as if they were actually brothers. Their facial features were so much alike that it caught me by surprise. Maybe it was my training from the Farm that caused me to notice it, I don't know. The fourth man was more heavy set and had dark brown hair. He was the one that Jimmy loved as if he was his own son. He was the same person who I had seen at the restaurant-bar of the Pontiac Airport. He owed a huge gambling debt to Tony Pro, and to pay it off, he was now going to betray the one man who loved him the most, Jimmy Hoffa.

I couldn't hear what they were saying, but Jimmy's hand gestures told me he was upset because this wasn't what he had expected, Tony Jack wasn't with Chucky. Just as the four men shook hands with Jimmy, the young woman who had driven to the back of the restaurant, picked up her baked goods and was slowly passing by the Lincoln Town Car. As she did she looked at all five of the men and gave a half smile, as they looked back over at her.

As she pulled her car up to the entrance of the restaurant driveway, she looked up and down Telegraph Road. As she looked to the left, it appeared that she had seen me, smiled, and then pulled out onto Telegraph Road and headed south.

Watching as Jimmy talked to his stepson and the three Teamsters from New Jersey, I started my car and slowly pulled up behind them, made a quick left turn and checked the traffic on Telegraph Road. Pulling onto Telegraph Road I turned right and headed south. I already knew where they were going to take him. I felt safe knowing that they would never harm Jimmy while he was at the Red Fox restaurant, especially now that they all knew that there was a young woman who could identify all of them as the ones last seen with Jimmy once he was reported missing on Channel Seven Action News. Just down from the Macus Red Fox restaurant is a banquet hall called The Raleigh House. It sits back away from Telegraph Road and on the left hand side of the road, not quite a mile away from the Red Fox as you head south towards Detroit.

Passing the Raleigh House I could see a few cars parked in its parking lot up toward, and close to, its entrance at Telegraph Road. Car-pooling was becoming more popular, and a few people would meet at the Raleigh House, park one car, and take the other car on to work together. Knowing this, I wasn't surprised to see a few cars scattered around the front of the large parking lot.

What caught my eye was what I saw sitting at the back, far right, of the parking lot. There, as I drove by, I saw a large Sundowner R.V., two Cadillac's, one red the other white and a new looking burgundy Mercury. What surprised me was seeing Tony Pro from the New Jersey crime family, standing next to the motor home talking to Vito Jack from the Detroit enforcer family.

"Boy, do you have some fucking nuts," I said to myself as I drove by. "You come to Michigan, uninvited, just to watch Jimmy die." Sam Giancana wanted Carla to have someone witness the hit from the CIA. Was it because he knew that Tony Pro was going to be here, or was it because he wanted something else? "What a tangled web we weave," I said as I found a spot to turn my car around.

After turning my car around, I headed north once again. Seeing the large Raleigh House sign, I pulled onto the shoulder of Telegraph Road and off onto the gravel. I was still a good hundred yards away from the front entrance of the Raleigh House as I turned off the car and turned on the emergency blinkers. Wrapping a newspaper around my Mack-10, I tucked it under my arm and got out of the car. I then stepped to the front of the car, opened the hood and very quickly made my way into the woods, which surrounded the area of the Raleigh House.

Telegraph Road was a four-lane highway. Two lanes going north bound and two lanes going south bound. It was heavily traveled, and it wasn't uncommon to see several cars, broken down, sitting on the side of the road. You would see them with flat tires, engine trouble, or out of gas, and they would sit for an hour or two until a wrecker could come and pick it up for repairs. I knew that the car would be okay, what I was concerned about the most was whether or not Chucky or the hit men would recognize my car when they pulled into the Raleigh House, as being the same car that had just pulled out of the Macus Red Fox restaurant, just a few minutes earlier.

A good spy takes advantage of the fact that no one looks for small details such as that. I was counting on the fact that all of them would be thinking about killing Jimmy and would not be paying attention to their surroundings, other than to be watching for law enforcement.

Making my way quickly through the woods, I got to the edge of the tree line, nearest the south end of the parking lot, just as the black Lincoln Town Car pulled into the parking lot of the Raleigh Banquet House. Staying just inside the tree line and hidden from sight, I stood silently and watched, keeping my finger on the trigger of my small Mack-10, alert and ready in case anything went wrong. The black Lincoln pulled around and then backed in next to the burgundy Mercury. My mind and body raced with the full surge of adrenaline as I watched a moment that would become a part of America's history. Getting out of their car they all walked over to where Vito and Tony Pro were standing next to their motor home and smiling.

Shaking hands with each other, I could see that Jimmy felt uneasy. He was smiling, but he kept looking over at Chucky who would smile back at him and nod his head in a gesture that everything was all right.

Jimmy trusted Chucky and, in doing so, he stepped into the motor home with Vito, Tony Pro, and his stepson. Had it not been for his trust in his stepson, Jimmy would have never agreed to meet anyone without at least two of his armed body guards from his Teamsters headquarters with him.

"At least they're sitting down and talking it out," I thought to myself. I knew from the meetings I had attended, that the three men from the Teamsters union in New Jersey were the hit men. With this in mind, I knew that Jimmy still had a chance to change his mind, and if he did, this would all end peacefully.

Looking at my watch about fifteen minutes had passed when Jimmy came out of the motor home. He was far beyond upset, Jimmy Hoffa was in his truest form. He was pissed off, yelling, and he didn't give a damn who knew about it. One thing was for sure, from where I was standing, Jimmy Hoffa was not afraid of Tony Pro.

Chucky came out after Jimmy, trying to talk to him. Then came Vito, then Tony Pro. Jimmy turned around and laid into Chucky first. Then he walked back up to Tony Pro, stuck his finger in Tony's face and gave him holy hell. Jimmy's face was red with anger and the veins were bulging in his neck as he yelled at Tony. I could hear him, but I couldn't make out what he was saying.

"Give him hell Jimmy," I said to myself as Jimmy turned and walked away.

Chucky tried to say something to him once again, but Jimmy waved him off with his right hand in an, "I'm all done talking," gesture.

Walking over to the burgundy Mercury Marquis, Jimmy climed into the backseat and slammed the door shut. Thinking for a moment Jimmy then got out of the car.

Walking back toward the Town Car, I could see Jimmy telling the three Teamsters from New Jersey, he wanted them to return him to his car at the Red Fox restaurant. All three men opened the car doors, with the two men that looked like brothers opening the backset of doors. The younger looking of the two brothers, stepped back so Jimmy could climb into the backseat. As he did, he and his brother looked over at Tony Pro and Vito. Tony nodded his head yes. As Jimmy slid in towards the middle of the backseat, two of the men closed the car doors. As they did, the younger of the two brothers pulled his handgun, stuck the barrel of it inside of the car and pulled the trigger three times.

Jimmy saw it coming but it was too late. He was trapped in the backseat with nowhere to go. His body slumped over to the right, and then disappeared from my sight as the young gunmen slammed the backdoor shut.

All three of the gunmen walked up towards the front of the car and stood. Taking out their packs of cigarettes, they each lit their own cigarette and waited. It was then that Jimmy Hoffa showed them who was the boss. He sat back up and looked through the window.

I could see Jimmy's mouth moving as he sat all alone and yelled at them. "Holy shit," I thought to myself as I watched in awe.

Seeing this caught everyone by surprise as the older brother moved quickly to the opposite side of the car. Opening the front passengers side door, he reached in, pointed his gun over the front seat and fired all six rounds out of his revolver. All six bullets hit Jimmy in the chest. This time Jimmy went down and didn't get back up. It took nine bullets to end the life of James Riddle Hoffa. At the time of his death, just as it was all throughout his life, Teamster President Jimmy Hoffa once again proved that he was a man of steel. The look on Chucky's face told me that he regretted what he had done, but he was too afraid to do anything to stop it. Looking at my watch it was 3:10 p.m., on July 30, 1975, when Jimmy Hoffa had taken his last stand on a warm, sunny, Wednesday afternoon.

It was twenty minutes after three when the dark haired driver of the Lincoln Town Car flicked the butt of his cigarette out onto the black asphalt parking lot. Walking to the back of the Town Car he keyed open the trunk and pulled out a large piece of thick black plastic which had been folded into a square. From behind the trunk lid, he looked over at his boss, Tony Pro.

"Now what are they up to?" I asked myself as Tony ran the fingers of his left hand through his dark wavy hair and nodded, "Yes."

Leaving the trunk lid open, the three men got back into the Lincoln and wrapped the thick black plastic around the body of Jimmy. When they had the body secured and hidden from sight, all three carried it to the backdoor of the Raleigh House, opened the door, and went inside. When you go into the backdoor of the banquet house, just inside and to the left is a small hall type room. That is where the trash grinder is located. The out chute of the machine goes into and through the side of the cement wall, where its grindings fall into the large steel dumpster outside.

It's almost funny when you think about it. The mob has been running dead bodies through that grinder for years, yet nobody ever once questioned why you would even need it.

The large banquet hall could cater to four weddings' or parties at a time. I guess that would be a lot of trash, paper plates, plastic glasses and silverware, bottles, cans, paper table clothes, and streamers. "Yeah, I guess you would need a machine so strong that it could grind up metal cans and an occasional body, shoes, watch, bones, and all into two inch chunks," I thought to myself as I looked at my watch and waited.

Ten more minutes had passed when I thought to myself, "How hard can it be fella's, throw the body on the conveyor belt, push the button, and feed it into the machine for crying out loud."

Tony, Vito and Chucky had all gone back into the motor home to wait. They felt safe. You couldn't hear the gunshots. Just a muffled popping sound, because the shots were fired from inside the car. You seldom saw a cop in this area at this time of the day. They were more focused on the busier intersections of traffic.

Watching as all three of the New Jersey hit men came out through the backdoor of the banquet house, I couldn't help but think about what Tony Pro had said to Jimmy long ago when he warned him. "I'll make you a very powerful man Jimmy. But if you ever cross me, they won't find so much as your fingernail." The one thing about Tony Pro is that if he made you a promise, he kept it.

All three of the New Jersey men walked to the back of the black Lincoln Town Car and lit up a cigarette. While they stood there smoking, the two brothers pulled out their handguns and tossed them into the trunk of the Lincoln. These were the murder weapons used to kill Jimmy.

Walking over to the motor home Tony Pro, Vito and Chucky stepped back out and stood next to the large white Sundowner. Smiling, Tony Pro shook the drivers hand and patted him on the right side of his shoulder. It was then that the fourth man, Russell Bufalino, appeared from the back of the RV. I couldn't believe what I had just seen. It was betrayal at its finest moment. If Chucky tells Tony Pro and Vito that a girl drove by and saw them shaking hands with Jimmy at the Red Fox restaurant, these men would be dead within days. Tony Pro wasn't stupid, he would leave no witness behind that could put him at the scene of this crime, ordering these murders. The fourth man, who had stayed hidden, had now started up the RV.

Hearing a truck engine, I looked left from my hiding spot in the woods, and saw the garbage truck as it pulled in and pulled up next to the large steel trash dumpster.

Setting down an empty trash dumpster, the driver of the garbage truck picked up the old container and secured it to his rig. As he did, the passenger riding along with him, got out and walked over toward Vito. Vito walked toward him, met him halfway and pointed at the black Lincoln Town Car, as the Sundowner drove past them and left. Lowering myself down, I took one last look at the Dearborn Heights garbage truck as it drove away, carrying along with it the remains of Jimmy Hoffa. It was headed for the new million-dollar incinerator. Tony Pro and his men got into the red Cadillac and started it up. Vito got into the white Cadillac and Chucky got into the burgundy Mercury. The passenger from the garbage truck got into the black Lincoln and started it up. He was one of the men from the enforcer family out of Detroit. I doubted that he even knew what was hidden inside the trunk of his car.

Running quickly, I arrived at the edge of the woods next to where my Ford Thunderbird was parked just as the garbage truck drove past heading south on Telegraph Road. Behind the truck, I watched as the black Lincoln, both Cadillac's and the burgundy Mercury passed by, blending into the traffic as if nothing had ever happened.

Walking out of the woods, I closed the hood of my Ford Thunderbird, got inside and turned the car around. My curiosity was killing me. I wanted to know where that black Lincoln Town Car with the New Jersey license plates was going.

Within the hour I would watch from a distance as the large crane picked up the brand new Lincoln Town Car and set it into the car crusher of a nearby scrapyard, turning it into a small square block of steel. As was the plan, the remains of Jimmy Hoffa, along with the rest of the trash that was in the trash dumpster, were placed in the new incinerator and incinerated not just once, but twice to ensure that no trace of the Teamster President would ever be found. A few days later the brand new one point six million dollar incinerator would be dismantled and no one, not even the FBI, would ever ask why?

Within three hours from the time that Jimmy was suppose to meet with Tony Jack at the Macus Red Fox Restaurant, the hit and the clean-up was all over with and complete.

It wouldn't take long for Jimmy to be reported as missing. The Bloomfield Hills Police Department, along with the Michigan State Police, would act quickly in a sincere effort and attempt to solve the disappearance of the famous Teamster President. It wouldn't take long for the Detroit Bureau of the FBI to step in and take over the case. Phone calls would quickly begin to come in sending the FBI searching in all directions. All but the right one.

Most of the telephone call in tips, were made by mob members or their friends just to keep the FBI running. The FBI has a lot of good men and women in their ranks. It's too bad they didn't know that the two agents leading the investigation were dirty.

I believe that, in time, someone in the Bureau had begun to figure it out. Both field agents in charge of the Hoffa disappearance would be reassigned to two different areas of the Federal Bureau of Investigation. One of them would become a courier for the Bureau, flying documents around the United States. The other one would become a polygraph examiner for the Bureau. It was plain to see that because he was one of the lead agents in the original investigation, he would be the one called to give the polygraph test to any potential witnesses that might come forward to break the case.

I can guarantee you this. If he was the agent giving the test, no matter how truthful you were, he would make sure that you failed the test, and report who you were to the Detroit enforcer family. Interesting how that works out, isn't it...

* * * * * * *

After the hit, I went to see my grandfather at his home in Pontiac and told him everything that had happened. I then told him that one of my informants had told me Sam was an informer for the Agency and he tipped them off to the hit going down on Jimmy Hoffa.

"I know all about Sammy, I've known for years that he was working with the government. One day I promise you they will regret it. Momo will betray them. For now however, he uses them and they in return use him. It's business, David. It's how things are done, so don't take it personal," my grandfather explained as we sat in the backyard of his home at the picnic table.

"I just thought that you should know, Grandpa," I told him.

"Listen, as long as your grandmother is alive, don't ever tell anyone what you have seen happen today. Promise me that," he asked as he looked sadly into my eyes.

"I promise Grandpa," I replied.

"Times are changing, David, there's very little honor left among the families. With this new drug business all they see is money. If they thought that you were going to tell the police anything about this Hoffa business, they would kill your grandmother to silence you. Once we are both gone, if you should ever get into serious trouble, you can always use this to get yourself out of it. But if you should ever decide to reveal the truth, don't tell them the truth right áway. Give them enough to let the FBI know that you know something, but leave a way out for yourself in case you should need to take it. Remember, some of them work for the families. So tell me, how is this young lady that you go see in Ireland?" he asked as he began to smile and changed the subject.

"She's great," I replied with an even bigger smile.

"Do you love her?" he asked.

"Yes I do, Grandpa. I know that this will sound crazy, but the very first time I looked into her eyes I knew deep in my heart she was the one I wanted to spend the rest of my life with. With one look, she stole my heart," I explained, not sure if my grandfather would understand.

"That makes me feel better. That's how it was when I saw your grandmother for the first time. Oh mama, she was so beautiful, I told her right then and there, not to be seeing anyone else and that I planned to marry her. She has been my best friend ever since," my grandfather explained proudly.

"Kate is full-blooded Irish Grandpa, I'm not sure if Grandma will accept her," I explained with a look of concern on my face.

"The Irish are good people. They're a proud hard working people that helped to build this country we live in. If you love her, David, then so will your grandmother, don't worry," my grandfather explained as he patted me gently on the knee.

I spent the next three hours sitting with my grandfather in the backyard of his home. We watched the sun set together and, as we did, I felt an empty sad feeling inside of me. I knew that he didn't have much time left, he was dying…

Chapter Twenty-Eight
Code Name: Miami Heat

It had only been a week since the disappearance of Jimmy Hoffa. The FBI had now taken over the case and the cover-up had begun. The television news channels were giving the disappearance of the famous Teamster leader around the clock coverage.

Bored, with nothing to do, I flew to Langley, Virginia, to meet with Doctor Lisa Morgenstern to see if there were any new developments with the Bourbeillon Virus.

Using my Q-clearance identification, I was able to get into the CIA Biotechnology Facility, but I was told that I would have to wait for Doctor Morgenstern in her office.

Because Doctor Morgenstern was the Agency's leading virologist, Doctor Bourbeillons Mystery Virus was turned over to her and her team for study. This new virus was considered to be so dangerous that the virus and the testing of the virus had to be done in a level-4 Restricted Laboratory.

Seeing the beautiful young scientist walk into her office, I could see that she was in dire need of a break. Walking over to her large desk, she looked at me and paused for a second. Then she remembered me as she pointed her finger at me and spoke.

"You were at the meeting," she said in a curious way.

"Yes, Doctor, I was sitting at the table," I replied.

"Please, call me Lisa. Your name is?" she asked.

"Dave, I'm Carla Silverman's friend," I explained trying not to say too much about who I was or what I did.

"Ah yes.... did Ms. Silverman send you?" Lisa asked as she sat down in her plush leather chair behind her desk.

"No she didn't. No one sent me Lisa, I'm just troubled by all of this," I replied.

"You're the one that tracked down Doctor Bourbeillon, aren't you?" she asked.

"Yes I am. I guess maybe that is what's bothering me the most. I saw all of those innocent African men, women, and children he had injected with his virus. Is there any chance for them Lisa? Will you be able to find a cure, an antiviral we can give them to save them?" I asked sincerely.

"We have four levels of study and containment here at this research facility. Level-1 being the lowest with level-4 being the highest. I have classified this as a very serious and deadly level-4 virus," Lisa explained with a serious look on her face.

"Can you tell me anything about this virus?" I asked, hoping to learn more about it.

"Well, as in all level-4 viruses, this one is blood born and can be transmitted by other human bodily secretions. I've been doing a lot of work on what we now call the 'Lassa Virus.' The Lassa Virus infects the cells that line the blood vessels. They become leaky, so fluid in the vessels leak out. It makes people swell in the face and the neck, and they'll get fluid in their lungs and have respiratory failure. People can die from it anywhere from 7 to 14 days after infection. I have now created an antiviral for the Lassa Virus. If we treat the patient in the first week of the illness, the survival rate is 95 percent or more. But the Bourbeillon Virus is entirely different. It destroys the human body's immune system. Once your immunity system is gone, what was once a simple cold could now kill you.

The base core of the Bourbeillon Virus, which I have identified through its DNA signature as coming from a Spider Monkey from Central Africa, was genetically altered with an unknown synthetic substance. The problem with this new virus is that its base core has mutated; and in doing so it has changed its characteristics.

I've never seen anything like it before. Now that it has mutated, we have no way to identify the man made synthetic substance. Without knowing what that was, we're in trouble.

So you understand a little better, David, what makes a blood born virus deadly is that it will mutate and change its characteristics. They live on the brink of self-extinction because they have high rates of mutation. But that gives them an advantage because it allows them to avoid immune responses. With the right push, they can mutate themselves out of existence. That is the basis for some types of antiviral therapy. With high levels of mutation, they eventually self-destruct. But they're not going to do that without help.

In our present case, we cannot identify the second synthetic core element because the mutation process has altered it into something entirely different, something unknown," Lisa explained as her telephone began to ring.

Picking up her phone, she spoke for a few seconds and then told whoever she was talking to that she would be right there. Hanging up the telephone she looked at me and spoke.

"I'm sorry, David, there's a small problem that requires my attention. I'm afraid that I am going to have to go," she said as she stood up from behind her desk to leave.

"Lisa, thank you for taking the time to explain things to me. It's helped me to understand things a little better," I said as I shook Lisa's hand and walked out of her office with her.

"I'm sorry that I don't have better news for you, David. But tell Ms. Silverman that I won't give up on this, I'll keep searching," Lisa explained as she turned and headed down the long hallway of the research facility to return to her lab.

"Well, that is certainly not what I wanted to hear, " I said to myself as I left the high security research center and headed back to the airport.

"Adding the secondary synthetic substance, knowing that the core substance mutation of it would mask it, makes this a man made killer virus. If the word of this ever got out to the American public, it would be considered an act of genocide against mankind," I thought to myself as I drove toward the airport. "This is going to kill millions of people." Now I knew why they pulled Carla and our team out of the investigation. They needed to cover this up quickly. If the world found out that this virus was created in the CIA Laboratory by an American scientist, the American government would be held liable.

When this virus finally becomes known to the public, and is out in the open, we'll eventually blame it on a Spider Monkey that was shipped to the United States from Central Africa. We will put it right in front of the entire worlds eyes and they won't even see it because, if they did, they would realize that if we knew that it was a Spider Monkey, and we had the shipping records to show that it came from Central Africa, then we could also use those shipping records to locate the exact area in Central Africa that the monkey came from. With that we could start testing and find an antiviral to destroy it. But the world will never figure it out, because the most obvious is the least obvious.

* * * * * * *

After talking with Doctor Morgenstern I checked on my grandfather and then flew to Ireland to spend a few weeks with Kate. Our new, privately owned bank was doing well and had successfully bailed out the people of the little town that Katie had grown up in. With the help of Walter Changs millions, our very simple strategy had worked. All of Kate's family members and friends were now debt free and no longer owed this new German banking system anything. They are on their own, back on their feet and doing well.

To my surprise, even though I had told Kate and Nell not to charge any interest, the proud Irish people would have none of that. As they borrowed money to pay off the Central Bank, they demanded that Kate and Nell draw up legal bank loan agreements to include the same interest rate as that of any other bank. When I asked Kate, why, she explained that it was a matter of pride and doing what was right. With that in mind Kate and Nell were not going to argue with a bunch of their Irish whiskey drinking friends. I had to laugh, because she was right.

The wheat and barley fields were coming in nicely and gave a beautiful look of gold to the acres upon acres of farmland they were growing in. Kate's cousin Tom, and some of his friends, had gone into the big city and purchased a nice size bank safe. They had driven back to Nell's store and put it safely out of sight in the back storage room of the store. Tom, along with Kate's grandfather and some of their friends had already brought in building supplies and had begun to build Kate and I, what grandma called, Kate's dream home.

I had purchased a very large section of land from Kate's grandfather that surrounded her wishing pond. There was a small hill over looking the beautiful pond and meadow. The hill was covered by several large oak trees and surrounded by acorn trees, where a family of red squirrels made their home. It was up on the wooded hill where Kate had told the men to build our home.

I spent ten days with Kate, at which time, I learned the fine art of the Irish, on how to cut and lay stone. I now understood why Tom hit like a jackhammer and why the men were in such good shape. Picking up, cutting, and laying stone was no easy chore. Especially when each stone had to be set perfectly into its spot. If not, "a well built Irish home wouldn't be able to breathe properly," Sean explained proudly. I really didn't understand what he meant by that, but I wasn't going to question the man that I had grown to respect, while he stood there with his back straight, standing proud and looking at the newly set rock foundation of what was soon to be his granddaughter's new home.

Saying goodbye to Kate, I left Dublin and headed back to my home in Michigan where I needed to check on the family business.

* * * * * * *

Sitting in my kitchen I watched patiently as Andy made a pot of his famous dog meat chili.

"You're putting in too much chili powder, Andy," I explained calmly.

"No its not," he responded as he stirred the pot of boiling chili and added more chili powder.

"That's too much chili powder, brother," I said once again as I took a sip of my Pepsi, and watched.

"I know what I'm doing. You have to have enough chili to kill the strong taste of the dog meat. If not, you'll start raising your leg and peeing on your neighbor's tree," he explained.

"That's ground beef, Andy, not dog meat," I replied as I shook my head in disbelief as he added more chili powder. "I think that your suppose to add extra chili peppers, brother, not chili powder."

"I know what I'm doing, shut-up and wait until you taste this."

Seeing that I wasn't going to convince Andy he was messing up our lunch, I sat back and waited. It took about another ten minutes before the master chef felt that his famous chili was ready to eat. Grabbing two large bowls out of my kitchen cabinet, Andy filled them both up and set mine on the kitchen table in front of me.

"Try that and then tell me I don't know what I'm doing," he said proudly as he sat down at the table across from me.

"I think I'll wait for you to try yours first, big brother. A great chef as yourself deserves the honor," I explained trying hard not to laugh.

The chili looked great, but you could tell by the smell that my dear friend put in way to much chili powder. Sitting back in my chair, I crossed my arms across my mid-section and waited as Andy took a very large spoon full of the chili and shoveled it into his mouth. The look on his face was worth the wait.

"If I only had a camera," I thought to my self as I watched Andy's eyes get big and his lips press together. Spitting the mouth full of chili back into his bowl, he quickly took a large drink out of his bottle of beer. This was a big mistake. Beer and that much chili powder do not mix well together.

Spitting his beer out into his bowl of chili, he slowly raised his head and looked at me.

"That tastes like shit, I told you that was to much chili powder. Why don't you ever listen to your elders?" he scolded.

I was laughing so hard I couldn't even respond. Andy could be so funny at times.

Hearing my telephone ring, I got up and went into my den to answer it. Sitting down at my desk I picked up my secure line and placed the phone to my ear.

"Hello," I said as I tried to regain my composer and stop laughing.

"Well at least your in a good mood," Carla responded.

"A friend of mine just made a pot of his famous chili. It was a disaster," I explained as I wiped the tears of laughter from my eyes. "What's up?"

"Remember that fourth guy you told me about? The one that drove Provenzano out of the parking lot?" Carla asked.

"Yeah, what about him?" I asked, knowing he had just been killed.

"I just got a call form my man on the inside. The girl you said drove out from behind the restaurant went to the Bloomfield Police Detectives." Carla explained excitedly.

"And that surprises you?"

"To be honest with you, yes it does. Who in their right mind would stick their nose in a mob hit, that is the big question?" Carla asked.

"An honest law abiding citizen?" I taunted.

"I guess. Well anyway, now that the FBI has taken over jurisdiction, they questioned her and she picked all of their faces out of the FBI organized crime files. You were right; two of the shooters were the Briguglio brothers, Salvatore and Gabriel She also ID'd Thomas Andretta and Chucky O'Brien as being there," Carla explained.

"How do you know that Chucky didn't tell him?" I questioned.

"About the girl? No, she went to the FBI. I hope the family doesn't consider her a threat and kill her too," Carla replied.

"They won't mess with her. The only thing she saw was Jimmy shaking hands with four people and smiling. Without an eyewitness the feds have nothing. Hell Carla, they don't even have the legal authority to take over jurisdiction in the case do they?" I asked.

"Not really. But if push came to shove, they would find a reason," Carla answered.

"Well don't worry about the girl, nobody will mess with her," I explained once again trying to calm Carla's fears.

"I hope not, she's just a nurse in the wrong place at the wrong time. So how was Ireland?" Carla asked.

"It's beautiful at any time of year," I replied.

How's your grandfather? Is there anything we can do for him, David? If there is, all you'd have to do is ask," Carla explained in a kind tone.

"Thank you Carla, I appreciate your offer of help, but there's nothing that anyone can do. He spends a lot of his time lying down. We have an oxygen tank next to his bed now. He puts on the little plastic nasal apparatus every so often. It helps him to breath a little better. Its kinda sad Carla, he told me that he knows he's dying and all he wants is to die in his own bed," I explained sadly.

"Well, if there's anything that I can do, don't hesitate to ask. My other phone is ringing, I've gotta go. I'll talk to you later," Carla said, as she hung-up the telephone on her end of the line.

Hanging up my phone, I turned and watched as Andy walked into my den.

"I'm hungry, lets go and get something to eat. Because you screwed up the chili, you can buy. How's that sound?" he asked with a wide grin on his face.

"Yeah, that sounds good. I don't know what I was thinking about, putting all of that chili powder in the chili like that. That was a pretty stupid thing for me to do huh?" I asked with a serious look on my face as we both walked out of the den together.

"Don't worry about it, you're young, you'll learn as you get older. Have you ever tried any of my horse meat stew?" Andy asked as he put his arm around my waist and gave me a friendly hug.

"You don't put chili powder in it do you?" I asked with a grin.

"Hell no. You don't put chili powder in horse meat stew. You use a lot of Tabasco sauce. It helps to kill the taste of the horse meat. If not, you'll catch yourself pawing at the ground with your foot," Andy explained as we both began to laugh once again.

* * * * * * *

It was late August 1975 when I received a visit from my grandfather's attorney, Mr. Anthony Andolini.

Anthony was in his mid-fifties and was full-blooded Sicilian. Ever since he had graduated from Harvard Law School, he had worked for one man and one man only, my grandfather. He was what the family would call a wartime consigliore. His job was to protect the family by taking care of all the family's legal affairs. If a war should happen to break out between the families, Anthony would be my grandfather's closest friend and advisor.

Sitting in the basement of my home I watched as Anthony opened his briefcase and pulled out a handful of legal documents. Laying them out on the top of my bar, I poured Anthony a drink and listened to what he had come to tell me.

"David, now that you have taken over as the head of our family, your grandfather has asked me to stop by and fill you in on what's been going on. First, I work for you now, unless you would rather have someone else represent you on behalf of the family," Anthony explained as he looked up at me waiting for a response.

"Anthony, that would never happen. You are the family consigliore as it has always been and always will be. You are the power behind the family, so please stay with us and counsel me as you have my grandfather," I asked respectfully with a smile.

"Always Godfather, thank you for those kind words," Anthony replied.

"So tell me, what's been going on while I've been away, and what are all of these papers?" I asked.

"Well first, Frank White blew away one of the lieutenants in the Columbo Family last week," he explained looking up at me.

"What?" I responded.

"Frank sent one of his representatives to see Dominic about money that Dominic owed Frank. As you know all of Frank's men are black. So Dominic stands up and pisses all over the young man's pant leg and shoes."

"Where did this happen?" I asked curious as to why Dominic would do such a stupid thing as that.

"It all took place in the back room of Dominic's club. He was in the back playing poker with some of his men. So anyway, the young man stays calm and leaves to deliver the message that Dominic had given him to deliver to Frank. Frank walks right in and tries to talk to Dominic but Dominic talks stupid to Frank. So Frank pulls out his .45 and blows Dominic out of his seat.

We made all of the usual inquiries and Dominic's people all say that Frank was in the right. These are five of Dominic's closest men who sat right there at the table and witnessed the whole thing. We sent Don Meloche to represent you at Dominic's funeral. Your Uncle Paul met with Frank and talked to him, so everything is business as usual. Dominic disrespected Frank, so Frank blew him away.

Yesterday, Frank is on the headline news at a fundraiser. Frank's building a hospital in the Bronx and donated millions to get the project started. He had the Mayor, Senators, Congressmen, and Hollywood celebrities, there. Its big news for New York," Anthony explained as he took a sip of his drink.

"For a hospital?" I questioned.

"Its not just a hospital, David. It's a free clinic hospital for poor people, people who live in the projects. Without money or insurance they can't get medical treatment. With this new hospital, everybody gets help. It's a great idea. The only problem is that our sources inside the 5th Precinct are telling us the cops are all upset about it because they put Frank in prison and now he's out, rich, and living large. We sent word to him, so hopefully he'll watch his back. They're Irish cops and hot headed to boot," Anthony explained as I poured him another drink. "You know that you've got a yacht and a condo in Florida don't you?"

"No I didn't know that. My grandfather kept all of these things secret," I explained.

"Well, not really, these papers need your signature. Just sign next to the 'X' and I'll take care of the rest. Every five years your grandfather trades in his old yacht and picks up a brand new one. The new one just came in. It's docked at the marina in Florida. I had to fly down to sign for it. He ordered it special for you, David. It's a gift. His way of thanking you for taking over and protecting the family. Your gonna love it, its huge," Anthony explained with a broad smile.

"God, I'm gonna miss him when he's gone," I said sadly.

"Yeah I know, we all are. The one thing about your grandpa is that he always planned ahead for the future. I need you to sign next to the 'X' right there," Anthony explained as he pointed to the spot that he wanted me to sign on the bank papers.

"Your grandfather has two overseas accounts that are in both of your names. The first account has well over two billion dollars in it. You also have close to a billion in Barer Bonds that we have locked away in his safe at his resort in Aruba," Anthony explained as I signed the papers and handed them back to him.

"He made all of this money without selling drugs?" I asked.

"Your grandfather would never touch drugs, not ever, and you shouldn't either. What he does do is take a small percentage from the profits of each family. We're talking booze, gambling, prostitution, and that includes the casinos in Vegas. He has been doing it since the late thirties. He invested wisely and let the money build on its own interest. Your grandfather is one of the smartest men that I've ever had the privilege of knowing; he's a genius when it comes to making money. He makes it for himself and for everyone else all at the same time. He always gives them the biggest percentage. That's why they love him so much," Anthony explained proudly.

"How did you meet my grandfather, Anthony?" I asked.

Laughing out loud, Anthony paused for a moment as his memory took him back in time.

"My parents migrated into the United States from Sicily. They came through Ellis Island, but were both killed in a car accident shortly after they were given their American citizenship. I was just a kid, all alone and living on the streets of New York. I was starving to death, boy oh boy. It was hard back in those days.

Anyway, I walked up to your grandfather, put my hand in my coat pocket, you know with my finger pointing at him from the inside like I had a gun in my pocket, and told him to give me a dollar or I was going to kill him," Anthony explained shaking his head from side to side with a big smile on his face.

"Yeah, what happened?" I asked anxious to hear the story.

"Well, your grandfather was a big man, but I looked him right in the eyes and didn't back down. I was hungry, David; I hadn't eaten anything in three whole days.

Your grandfather looks at me and puts his hands in the air and then as calm as could be he says, 'where's your mother and father?' I told him that they died in a car crash, and he was going to die from my bullets if he didn't give me my dollar! 'You don't have any family to take care of you?' he asked me as he lowered his right hand and reached into his pants pocket. I tell him don't you try anything funny or I'll shoot.

Your grandfather pulls a brand new silver dollar out of his pocket, looks me in the eyes and says, 'you know that your finger is sticking out through the hole in your pocket don't you?' All of my clothes had holes in them and were worn pretty thin. I was so desperate I wasn't paying any attention to the fact that my finger had poked out through the hole in my coat pocket. I looked down and saw my finger and thought, 'awe shit,' turned and tried to run, but he grabbed me before I could move an inch. I figured, what the hell, at least if he kills me, I won't be hungry anymore," Anthony explains as his memories took him back.

"So what did my grandfather do?" I asked.

"He looks me in the eyes and says, 'you can run away like a coward or you can start acting like a young man you're age should and come with me,' then he let me go and walked away. I didn't know what else to do and I had nowhere to go or anyone that cared about me, so I followed him.

He took me to a little Italian restaurant and fed me. The best part was that he talked to me, not at me. He respected me and talked to me like a father would talk to his son, it was great.

After that he brought me back home to Michigan and raised me like I was his own son.

I went to law school and became the best attorney that I could be. I wanted to make him proud of me. I've had offers from big law firms, but I won't leave the old man. He never left me and I damn sure won't leave him. So, that's my story," Anthony explained as he raised his glass in a toasting manner.

"Well, I do know this, my grandfather brags about you to everyone. He loves you like a son, he always has," I explained.

Anthony and I spent the rest of the day talking about the family business and our plans for the future. He then became very serious and told me about the dark side of the family business and how treacherous it could really be if you didn't watch yourself.

I had grown up knowing Anthony all of my life. He was a man who I had always respected and who would now play a big part in my life.

* * * * * * *

Sitting at my desk I had just reached over to turn on my computer when my phone began to ring. Caught by surprise, it startled me. I hadn't been able to get any sleep. My nightmares were now back in full force and haunting me every chance they could. Picking up the receiver of my telephone I placed it to my ear and spoke.

"Hello," I said coldly as I began to yawn from my lack of sleep.

"Boy do you sound like shit," Kathy commented.

"Yeah well I feel like it too. I think that I've had maybe six hours of sleep in the past three days. So what's up, pretty lady?" I asked trying to change the subject.

"We got a call on our undercover line. Remember Danny Patron, the big Cuban, suspected of being a terrorist out of Florida?"

"Yeah, what about him?" I asked as I yawned once again.

"Well, Matt and Adam have confirmed that he is involved with a terrorist group out of the Middle East."

"What does that have to do with you getting a call on our undercover phone line?" I asked impatiently.

"I'm getting to that. Danny Patron called the number that you gave him when we were in Florida with him. He's invited you to a party that he's having at his estate and from what Matt and Adam are telling us, Danny has some big time bad guys that he's also invited. Carla wants us to go. She believes that Danny wants you there to set up an overseas deal. So what do you say?" Kathy asked.

"When is it?"

"This Saturday, I'll meet you at the airport in Miami. Ben has already been notified. He'll meet you at the Pontiac Airport. He'll call you to set up the time. This is a rich mans playboy type party, so dress accordingly," Kathy explained excitedly.

"Gee that means that you'll have to dress in two band aides and a G-string huh?" I teased.

"Maybe, see ya in Miami," Kathy teased in a sexy tone of voice as she hung the phone-up in my ear.

Hanging up the telephone on my end I couldn't help but wonder. "Why would Danny Patron invite me to one of his parties? What is he up to? I guess I'll find out soon enough." I headed to my bedroom; I needed to get some sleep no matter how bad the nightmares get.

* * * * * * *

Stepping off the Agency's plane in Miami, I placed two drops of Methadrine under my tongue and smiled as I watched Kathy walk up to me. She was wearing a pair of Daisy Duke cutoff jean shorts, a pink halter-top, and sandals. It was a beautiful 95-degree sun shiny afternoon. Seeing Kathy dressed like this made it even hotter.

"So what do you think?" Kathy asked as she struck a pose for me.

"Oh yeah, most definitely hot," I commented as I looked at her firm little breasts. "Where are Matt and Adam?"

"They're with Patron. Sometimes I wonder about those two," Kathy explained as we walked through the Miami airport and headed to her new all silver Porsche convertible.

"Why?" I asked as we climbed into the precision made German sports car.

"They've been bang'n Patron's girls left and right. I really think that they're starting to like Danny a lot more than they should," Kathy explained as she started the engine and drove us out and away from the airport.

"Its all part of deep undercover work, you know that. They'll probably end up with the clap," I said laughingly.

"Good, that'll teach 'em, did you ever get any sleep?" Pulling my tiny vial of Methadrine speed out of my shirt pocket I held it up and smiled.

Reaching into her purse, Kathy pulled out a small plastic medicine bottle and handed it to me.

"What's this?"

"They're sleeping pills called Seconal, better known as 'Reds.' Take one or two just before you lay down to go to sleep and see if they help you," Kathy explained as she ran a red light without paying any attention to what she had just done.

"I don't do drugs," I explained as I held up the see-through plastic bottle and looked carefully at the red capsules that were inside.

"Are you out of your rabbit ass mind? What exactly do you think that vial of Methadrine speed is?" Kathy asked sarcastically.

Slipping the bottle of pills into my pants pocket, I turned my head and looked up at the sky. I knew that I was addicted to the liquid speed, but deep down inside I knew that I needed it to help me to fight the ghosts of my past. Kathy's comment had struck a nerve. Real partners would have never said that.

"I'm sorry, partner, I didn't mean that the way it came out."

"Sure you did, and your right Kathy, but don't judge me until you've walked in my shoes," I explained calmly as we headed to our undercover estate in West Palm Beach.

* * * * * * *

Setting down my suitcase I walked into the large den and smiled. Matt and Adam were both on telephones in our Palm Beach estate.

The estate was huge in terms of a normal Palm Beach home. It was completely furnished with an Olympic size swimming pool in the back

40-acres. Close to the swimming pool was a large tennis court. The den was complete with a full-size, well-stocked bar.

Hanging up the telephone Matt looked at me and smiled. "Hey, brother, long time no see. How have you been?" Matt asked as we shook hands and Adam hung up the other telephone that he was on.

"What's up, Dave?" Adam added as I shook his hand too.

"I see that you guys have been living large and enjoying life," I said smiling.

"No shit, Patron is an animal. These Cuban women are unbelievable," Matt explained as he walked behind the bar and pulled a cold Pepsi from the refrigerator.

Sitting down at the long mahogany topped bar, Matt handed me the bottle of Pepsi and poured himself and Adam each another drink.

"So what's so important that has Danny wanting to see me?" I asked as I took a sip of my cold soda.

"They're wanting to do a major arms deal overseas. We told them that you still have some big time military connections in Vietnam and now that the new President is pulling all our troops out of South East Asia, they can be purchased real cheap," Matt explained with a grin.

"Not only that, Danny has some major league bad guys coming to this party to meet with him and hopefully put together some business deals with you. He even has some boys coming out of the Middle East, from Afghanistan, Iran, Syria. Some representatives from Iraq are coming on behalf of Saddam Hussein from his Mukhabarat Intelligence group," Adam added.

"The Agency is already selling Hussein a ton of weapons," I replied, confused as to why he would want to purchase more from an unknown source.

"Saddam will buy weapons from anyone who has mass amounts to sell, the man is a psycho. The best part is we're being told by Patron that Luis Enrique Villalobos is suppose to be attending this party," Matt explained anxiously.

"I've heard that name before, who is he?" I questioned.

"Ollie suspects that Luis is the main man who is running large amounts of assault weapons to the Contras. We just called Carla about Luis. Ollie is in route to Miami to attend the party, and he's bringing a new set of orders along with him," Adam replied smiling as he took a sip from his drink.

"Yeah, our mission profile might be changing when Ollie gets here. Tomorrow may prove to be a very interesting and productive day," Matt added as he raised his drink in a toasting manner.

490

"It sure sounds like it. I'm going to need to use your secure line fella's. I need to talk to Carla and I mean right now," I explained as Matt slid the telephone across the bar top to me.

* * * * * * *

Elite Wet Work Operation
Code Name: Miami Heat
Target: Luis Enrique Villalobos
Location: Miami Florida
Coordinates: Unknown
Mission Profile: Termination

Oliver arrived late Friday night around 9:00 p.m. and came straight to our home in West Palm Beach. We spent the rest of the evening talking about our new mission orders and all of the possibilities of what could go wrong during tomorrow night's party at Danny Patron's estate. I was bothered deep inside by the one question now eating away at me. Turning to Ollie, I figured that if anyone would know the answer, he might.

"What I don't understand, Ollie, is how are all of these people, most of whom are directly connected to terrorist groups, coming to the United States for a meeting and none of our people in the Middle East know about it?" I asked worried as to what the answer might be. Taking a deep breath of air into his lungs, Ollie let it out slowly and looked up at me. The look on his face told me that something was wrong.

"Nixon is gone, and the new President is catching a lot of heat from the Congress about us. They're complaining that the CIA is spying on Americans trying to find Communist sympathizers rather than spying on our enemies overseas. The bureaucrats are pulling on the purse strings. They're starting to cut back on our funding, and from what Carla told me just before I left her office, they're trying to pull the CIA out of the Middle East altogether," Ollie explained with a worried look on his face.

"What, are they nuts? Syria and Afghanistan are the terrorist training capitals of the world for Christ's sake. No wonder these people are walking into the states undetected," I said angrily.

"Carla says that if Congress gets its way, by 1979 we'll be down to less than 200-agents in the Central Intelligence Agency. They're more worried about their image than they are about protecting the country. Nixon loved the spy game, I mean, he really got into it, but now that he's gone were going to feel the effects of it," Ollie explained sadly.

* * * * * * *

Pulling up to the large metal cast iron gates of the Patron estate I looked down at my Gold Tag Heuer watch and smiled. Our gold inlayed invitation said to be here by 5:00 p.m. It was now 7:00 p.m., and the sun was just beginning to set over the horizon.

Remembering what old "Blue Eyes" had told me in Las Vegas about the real big players and power money people never showing up for the fight until a few minutes just before the main even starts, I held true to form and came two hours late.

I was wearing a black silk shirt with black dress slacks by Armani and a pair of low cut slip on Gucci dress shoes. Kathy was wearing a pink silk see-through shirt with a white and very tight, mini skirt and a pair of black suede heels. She accessorized with a pair of crystal earrings and a crushed diamond face Rolex watch. Oliver, Matt and Adam were dressed similar to me. Without a doubt we looked rich and like well cared for Mafia wiseguys.

Pulling our stretch limo in through the gates, Matt handed the heavily armed security guard, who was standing at the gate, our invitation. Waving us through, we parked our car next to two Rolls Royce's and got out.

The estate was packed with people and the party was powered up. Walking toward the back of the estate we stopped and looked around for our host Danny Patron. The booze was flowing like water, half naked girls were laughing and jumping into the Olympic sized swimming pool in Danny's backyard, and the music was booming, all Cuban sounds of course.

"Boy this guy sure does know how to throw a party doesn't he?" Ollie asked with a serious look on his face.

"Ease up brother and relax. It's a party so have fun and smile. If you look to serious, they'll think that something is wrong," I explained as I saw Danny walking towards us, smiling.

"Hey, my brother, where have you been? You were suppose to be here at five o'clock," Danny explained, smiling as he looked through Kathy's blouse at her firm breasts.

"Karen, say hello to Danny," I said as I introduced Kathy to Danny using her undercover name.

"Hello, Mr. Patron, this is a very nice party," Kathy replied smiling.

"Please, call me Danny, and thank you, we Cubans love to have a good time," Danny explained as he looked over at Ollie.

"Danny, I hope that you don't mind, I would like you to meet my main man from Bangkok. He handles all of my overseas shipments. Oliver, this is my business partner and friend, Danny," I introduced, using Ollie's real name just to play it safe. If we should happen to run into someone that Ollie knew from overseas, I didn't want them to call Ollie by his real name, and give Danny any reason to think that I had deliberately lied to him.

"Oliver it's good to meet you. If you're David's partner then your always welcome at my home. Come; let's get something to drink. Are you hungry? I've got home cooked food that is so good it will make you cry with sadness if you can't eat it all," Danny explained as we walked over toward his outside bar to get a cold drink.

We spent the next two hours eating, drinking, dancing, and mingling with Danny's guests. They are rich and powerful businessmen; a couple of United States Senators were even here having fun. But what we didn't see were the people from overseas. The ones who were connected to the international terrorists of the Middle East.

There was plenty of booze, plenty of women, and plenty of cocaine, but where were the bad guys?

"Matt, what's going on?" I asked as I took a sip of my Pepsi from a crystal wine glass.

"Stay loose, Sandman, Danny is real slick, you've got to watch him. Don't misjudge or under estimate him, David. He is not a man to be taken lightly. If Danny says the heavy weights are coming, then you can take that to the bank. They're here, the question is where?" Matt explained as we continued to act as though we were having a good time.

Looking to our left we watched as one of Danny's men approached us.

"Excuse me, sir, but Mr. Patron would like to speak with you and your friends. Would you come with me please?" he asked politely.

"Absolutely," I replied as we followed the bodyguard across the back of Danny's estate, heading toward the beach. Walking across the thick plush green grass and through the palm trees, I saw Danny and several of his men standing next to a small waist-high pole with a metal box attached to it. Seeing us coming, one of Danny's men flicked the switch on the metal box and the entire area lit up with bright lights.

"Hey, David, I have some very important guests I would like you to meet. Unfortunately we will have to take a little ride to go see them. Do you mind?" Danny asked calmly. He was trying to read my face for a reaction but I was already way ahead of him.

"I don't mind at all. If you say there alright with you, let's do it," I responded as I reached into my pants pocket and pulled out my tiny vial of Methadrine. Looking up I could hear the small helicopter coming as I placed two drops of the liquid speed under my tongue and returned the tiny vial back to my pocket.

"This is going to take two trips. David, why don't you and Oliver come with me and Matt and Adam can bring Karen with them on the second

493

trip," Danny said loudly as the small Bell helicopter landed just off to our left.

Ducking down we ran over to the helicopter and climbed in. Within a matter of two minutes we were lifting off and vanished into the darkness of the hot Miami night, heading out across the ocean.

Turning in his seat to look back at Ollie and I, Danny spoke.

"I have a small boat about sixteen miles off shore in international waters. I have some friends on board I would like to introduce you to. Because of who they are and where they come from, I have a need to protect them, so we are having a small party out here also.

As soon as we get off, my pilot will return to my home and pick up the rest of your friends," Danny explained.

"What is this about, Danny?" I questioned curiously.

"Matt told me that the war is over in South East Asia and America is pulling out all its troops and you have shit loads of weapons for sale that your people are stealing out of Vietnam. If you want to sell them, these are the people who will buy everything you have. Matt was being truthful with me wasn't he?" Danny questioned.

"Not completely, Danny. I'm not a thief; I don't steal. We're just rerouting large shipments of weapons, ammunition, and explosives to a secure spot we have control over. The military is in such a hurry to pull out and come home they're not paying any attention to where it's going. To be honest with you, they really don't give a damn about any of it. I've got an awful lot of stuff Danny. Are you sure your friends can handle it?" I questioned, already knowing they could.

"Oh yeah, these people are oil rich," Danny answered as he turned back around in his seat.

Off in the distance I could see the lights of Danny Patron's yacht. It was lit up like a small city and almost just as big as one.

"Holy shit, that's got to be at least 250-feet long," I said in awe as we approached the yacht and landed on the helicopter pad at the back of the ship.

"Two hundred and sixty-eight feet to be exact. Do you like it?" Danny yelled as we jumped off the helicopter and moved quickly down the steps to the top deck of the ship.

The yacht was completely lit up with bright lights and a big band was playing music from somewhere inside of the main structure of the ship. It had banners and flags flying from bowsprits and railings. Its elegant design alone told me that this boat cost Danny a small fortune.

There was food and drinks everywhere and a 10-piece orchestra playing soft smooth mellow music to the big time guests of Danny Patron.

The yacht had a staff of 30 people onboard tending to the guests, not to include fifty of the most beautiful women in the world onboard tending to any other needs the rich Arab guests might have.

Walking inside the main cabin area of the yacht the mahogany-topped bar glistened under the lighting from above. The bar was lined with exotic brands of liquor, champagne, and Dom Perignon. I had no doubt the ladies on board were all high-class call girls and being paid a fortune to be here.

"You own this yacht, Danny?" I asked as the bartender poured me a glass of Dom Perigonon.

"No my friend, I lease it from time to time from a place in Miami called Celebrity Yacht Cruises. It costs me about thirty grand a night. That's with food, booze, staff, the whole nine yards. I could buy it, but its easier to lease it and it costs me a lot less in cash and headaches," Danny explained as one of his guests walked up to me smiling.

"Danny, I always knew you were a class act, now I see I was right. Hello Detroit Mafia," Frank White said as we shook hands.

"Frank, why doesn't seeing you here surprise me? How have you been, I hear you blew away one of Paul's lieutenants," I said with a grin.

"You two know each other? This is so good. We sell our drugs to one and buy our guns from the other. I love America," Danny said laughingly. "Come on, fella's, I want to introduce you both to the men who run the Middle East."

"Weapons huh? You must have a bunch," Frank said with raised eyebrows.

"Frank, I'd like you to meet my overseas partner. This is Ollie, Ollie meet my friend, 'The King of New York,' Frank White," I said as I introduced Ollie to New York's biggest drug dealer.

"Frank, good to meet you."

"Same here," Frank answered as he and Ollie shook hands.

We spent the next hour being introduced to some of the most dangerous men of the Middle East, while Carla and Neil monitored my movements by satellite through the computer chip in my shoulder.

Just as we were getting ready to sit down to discuss the mass sale of weapons that the Agency had authorized Ollie and I to sell, Luis Enrique Villalobos came on board. It was the girl with him that caught my attention. She was olive skinned, young, and beautiful, and in her hand she was carrying a Russian built suitcase size nuclear weapon. Walking toward us Danny walked up to greet Luis with open arms.

"You see that?" Ollie whispered calmly as he took a sip of his drink.

"Uh huh," I replied as Danny walked over and introduced us.

"David, Oliver, Frank, these are two of my close friends, Luis and Sonya," Danny explained as we all said hello to each other and walked into the room Danny had prepared for our business discussion.

We were in the meeting for about five minutes when Kathy, Matt, and Adam entered. They each had a drink in their hand and sat down next to Ollie and I.

"How are things going?" Kathy asked as she whispered in my ear.

Saying nothing, I used my eyes to draw Kathy's attention to the Samsonite gorilla that was now sitting next to Sonya's feet across the room from us.

Looking up at me I knew that Kathy saw the weapon of mass destruction and realized that we now had a problem. Our mission profile had just changed.

My mind raced as Ollie explained what we had for sale and showed the Middle East buyers a variety of photographs of our merchandise. I needed to get my hands on that A-pack weapon before Sonya was able to tell anyone what she was carrying with her. I knew who she was. I remembered seeing her pictures in the CIA computer files. She was Sonya Sarasyn, a well-known assassin with the Albanian Guerrillas.

What I noticed was that she was uncomfortable. She kept shifting and moving her lower body in her seat. My training from the CIA Farm was about to pay off in a very big way.

"Excuse me, gentlemen, but I am going to need to step out for a moment. A little to much Dom Perignon I believe. My business partners speak for me. So whatever you decide and agree upon has my blessings," I explained as I politely excused myself to go to the bathroom.

I knew by the way that Sonya was acting that her body movements were telling me that she needed to pee and that she would be heading to the restroom any minute now. The problem was, we had brought no weapons with us. To do so would have been a big insult to our trust in our relationship with Danny.

Walking up to the bartender I asked where the restrooms were located and found out that they were, downstairs and toward the bow of the large ship.

Moving quickly, I stopped and picked up two mixed drinks that were made in eight ounce glasses, from one of the young ladies that was serving drinks, and then headed down the steps and toward the bow of the large yacht.

Finding the restroom I went in and poured both glasses of liquor into the toilet, fruit and all, and then flushed it.

To my surprise, this whole area of the yacht had very few people in it. Stepping back into the hallway I found the supply closet. Just as I opened the door to the closet, I saw Sonya as she walked down the stairs and headed toward the bathroom. Waiting to hear the bathroom door close, I then checked to make sure that she was inside and then looked at what was in the supply-cleaning closet. I knew what I needed and could only hope that the two chemicals were here. Seeing both plastic one-gallon bottles brought a smile to my face.

Opening the bottle of bleach I poured it into the first glass and then screwed the plastic cap back onto the plastic bottle. Picking up the second bottle of ammonia, I poured it into the second glass and then screwed the plastic cap back onto the plastic bottle. Picking up both of the glasses, I pushed the closet door closed with my foot, walked over to the bathroom door and waited.

Hearing the toilet flush, I set both of the glasses down next to the door and prayed that no one else would come down here to use the toilet or bedrooms.

As Sonya unlocked the bathroom door and opened it, I caught her by surprise as I kicked her in the sternum. The kick was so vicious and unexpected, that it drove Sonya backwards, causing her to drop the suitcase that she was carrying with her as she fell to the floor.

Grabbing both of the glasses, I tossed them into the bathroom, one on top of the other, in front of Sonya, and quickly pulled the door shut.

As the ammonia and bleach chemicals mixed together, they caused a chemical reaction to occur. A white vapor appeared that held within it a deadly toxic gas.

Hearing Sonya coughing, she fought hard to pull the door open, but it was to late. Within a matter of seconds I could hear her body drop to the bathroom floor. Holding my breath I opened the door, reached inside and flicked the switch next to the light switch into the 'On' position, and then closed the door once again.

It was the switch for the ceiling exhaust fan. It was now 'On,' and venting the deadly fumes out of the confined area of the bathroom.

By their selves, ammonia and bleach are strong smelling, but if you combine the two chemicals in equal amounts, they become deadly.

Seeing one of the men from Syria walk down the steps with a pretty little blonde, I watched as they both laughed and walked into one of the many bedrooms that were located down on this level.

Stepping next to the door by the supply closet, I opened it and took a look inside. It was a small bedroom and it to was empty.

Moving quickly, I opened the bathroom door and saw that all of the fumes were gone. Holding my breath I went in picked up Sonya and carried her body into the bedroom. Placing her on the bed, I stepped out of the bedroom and closed the door behind me, locking it.

Walking back to the bathroom, I tossed a towel into the sink, soaked it in cold water, and then after picking up both of the glasses, I spread the soaking wet cold towel over the tile floor and pushed it around with my foot to let it clean up any remaining chemical that might still be lingering. Leaving the wet towel on the floor, I picked up the suitcase and left the bathroom.

Walking back upstairs, I stepped outside and walked over to the rail at the side of the yacht and tossed both of the glasses over board and into the water.

My heart was racing with the combination of adrenaline and fear. That was to close and had to be done way to fast for me.

Taking several deep breaths of air into my lungs I let them out quickly as I tried to calm myself down.

"David, are you alright?" Kathy asked as she and Adam walked outside looking for me.

"We don't have time so listen closely. Take this and get it back to the house in Palm Springs," I said as I handed Adam the A-pack nuclear weapon. "Kathy, call Carla right away. Tell her what we found here. Then tell her to wake up John Mitchell and have him come and pick this up immediately. Tell Carla that Sonya Sarasyn is on board this ship and that her body is down stairs in the bedroom, next to the supply closet across from the bathroom. Tell her that we need a cleaner to get that body out of here as soon as the ship docks. We can't let Danny or Luis find out that Sonya is dead. Go now, the helicopter pilot is taking people back and forth," I explained quickly.

"John Mitchell, Sonya Sarasyn and a cleaner, I got it. Lets go, Adam," Kathy said as she and Adam took the suitcase with them and boarded the helicopter. Watching it start its engine and lift off, I began to calm down and felt a lot better, as I watched Kathy and Adam disappear into the darkness of the night.

About eight minutes had passed when I heard Danny talking to some of his guests as he walked out onto the deck.

"Hey, David, where have you been?" he asked smiling.

"I've been out here trying not to throw-up."

"Oh man, brother, are you getting sea sick?" Danny asked with a concerned look on his face.

"I'm not sure, it might be the booze, Danny. I have an allergic reaction to booze, that's why I drink Pepsi. One of your staff gave me a couple of white pills. She said that it was for motion sickness. Its starting to kick in now. I'm feeling a lot better. Sorry my friend I don't want to ruin your party," I explained sincerely.

"Hey fuck this party, I'm worried about you."

"I'm feeling better now. How's Ollie doing with the big boys?" I questioned trying to change the subject.

"He's real good, he ain't giving 'em an inch. He smells money and your partner is selling everything you've got. The men from Mukhabarat Intelligence, Saddam Hussein's boys, they're out bidding Syria and Iran. Ollie's gonna make you rich tonight," Danny said smiling as he patted me on the back.

"No, brother, he's making us rich. You're my partner on this, Danny. Whatever I make, twenty five percent of it goes to you for putting this meeting together. I appreciate your help, partner," I explained as I placed my hand on Danny's shoulder and looked him in the eyes.

"Anytime my friend, any time," Danny replied smiling.

It was 3:00 a.m. when Ollie, Matt, and I said goodbye to Danny, Frank, and the rest of the men that we had met on board Danny's yacht, and lifted off in the helicopter.

John Mitchell flew in and picked up the Russian made suitcase sized nuclear weapon and flew it to Nevada to be stored away in an underground area of the Mercury Test Site Facility.

"Well we lost Luis," Kathy said sadly as Matt poured everyone a drink at our bar.

"Luis is nothing compared to Sonya and recovering that Russian made weapon. If any of those buyers would have known what that was, they would have killed everyone on that yacht to get their hands on it. What I'm curious about is how fast you were able to kill Sonya and recover the weapon," Ollie explained as he turned to look at me.

"Yeah, Dave, how did you do it? We didn't even have any weapons on board with us," Matt asked as he handed me a glass of cold Pepsi.

"Normally I wouldn't tell you," I said as I thought about it for a minute. "One of the things that my Seal team instructors used to always tell me was everything is subject to change at any given moment. Last night was a perfect example of that. I knew that she had to go to the bathroom just by observing her body movements. That's something that they taught us at the Farm. With that knowledge, I figured that the best place to get her would be when she was alone in the bathroom. I also knew that there was no way that she was going to leave that A-pack weapon behind in a room full of third world Arabs," I explained.

"How did you know that? You knew that she would take it with her to the bathroom?" Kathy asked.

"Because I wouldn't have left it behind. Would you have?" I asked curious as to what her answer would be.

"No, I guess not. We moved it real fast once we got our hands on it," Kathy explained looking back over at me.

"I grabbed two drinks from one of the waitresses and took them downstairs with me. Once I found the bathroom, I dumped them out and looked to see if there was an air exhaust system inside. Its a small area, located close to all of the bedrooms, so I figured that there would be, and there was.

Wherever there's a bathroom, there's going to be cleaning supplies, so I found the closet that all of the cleaning supplies were in. I then filled one of the glasses up with bleach and the other with ammonia," I explained calmly as I took a sip of my Pepsi.

"Bleach and ammonia?" Adam asked with a strange look on his face.

"Yeah, their both caustic, but if you mix them in equal amounts, they have a chemical reaction to each other that causes them to become toxic and very deadly. Your local food store or drug store is full of chemicals that are deadly if you mix 'em together. You just need to know which chemicals that your looking for," I explained.

"So what did you do, throw them in her face when she came back out?" Matt asked.

"Oh no, that wouldn't work. It would burn and make her gag and choke, but the mixture would be all wrong to make it turn toxic. What I did was I set the glasses down next to the bathroom door and waited. Think about it, nobody pays any attention to their surroundings when they step out of the bathroom. As soon as she opened the door I kicked her in the sternum," I explained as I took another sip of my drink.

"Why there? Why not in the face? You know, in the nose or throat?" Kathy asked.

"No that wouldn't work for what I was trying to accomplish. I needed to hit her somewhere hard enough so that it would knock the wind out of her. I wanted her to fight to catch her breath, that way she would suck in a lot of the vapor right away. I know what its like not to be able to breathe. It scares the hell out of you and causes you to panic.

I kicked her so hard that it not only knocked the air out of her lungs, it drove her body backwards so fast that she hit her back on the edge of the sink and fell straight to the floor.

I knew that I had her because I was watching as she opened the door; she was exhaling as I kicked her. So anyway, I grabbed both of my classes and tossed 'em right in front of where she was bent over. Then I pulled the door shut and held it. There's an exhaust fan right next to the light switch, but she never noticed it. It really wouldn't have mattered anyway. She was fighting hard to catch her breath and inhaled a lot of the fumes. She was dead within 60-seconds from the time that I kicked her, and the rest is history. I just hope that Carla gets that body out of there before any of the work crew notices it," I explained.

"Don't worry about that, the cleaners would have taken care of that as soon as the ship docked," Adam explained.

"The Sandman strikes again. Only you could have pulled something like that off so fast. Good job, partner," Ollie said as he patted me on the back smiling.

"I don't know about all of that, but at least we got that weapon before one of those terrorist groups got their hands on it," I said as I stood up and walked outside.

Walking over to the pool I sat down in one of the chairs. Raising both of my hands up about chest level, I extended my fingers and took a close look. They were both shaking. I needed some sleep, I had been awake far to long, powered up on Methadrine. Reaching into my pants pocket I pulled out the plastic bottle of sleeping pills that Kathy had given me, and looked at the red capsules that were inside.

Sitting back in my chair, I took a deep breath of air into my lungs and let it out slowly. It was a beautiful, hot, sun shiny day. The warm rays of the sun felt good as they reached their slender fingers down from above and touched my skin, almost as if they were trying to revitalize me.

"Come on, David, calm down. Don't let it win, calm your heart down and relax. Your going to be alright," I said to myself as I closed my eyes and tried to focus my thoughts and stop my body from trembling.

"David," Matt shouted out from the sliding glass doors that led from the back of the estate to the pool area.

"Yeah," I responded curious as to what he wanted.

"We just got a call from Neil. They got Sonya's body out of the yacht undetected. We're good to go," Matt explained.

Giving Matt a thumbs up, I closed my eyes once again. As I did I felt a sharp pain shoot across my chest heading toward my left arm. It was only for a second, but in that second of time it hurt like hell.

I thought about Kate and my grandparents and then I thought about my life and all of the people that I had killed.

My mind seemed to float softly as my memories took me back to the first two Viet Cong soldiers that I had killed on my first outing as a sniper. I had killed them both with one-shot from my .300 magnum snipers rifle. That one bullet had blown the one young soldiers head completely off of his body, leaving nothing but a bloody stump where his head had once sat above his shoulders.

"Damn, how many people have I killed?" I asked myself as I tried to remember.

Taking a deep breath of air into my lungs I let it out slowly. As I did a gray haze filled my mind and darkness set in once again....

Chapter Twenty-Nine
Scorpion Sting

Tormented by my nightmares and the ghosts of my past, I said goodbye to Kathy, Ollie, Matt and Adam. Kathy and Ollie were headed to the Pentagon for a full debriefing on, "who, what, when, where, and why," everything happened the way it did while we were with Danny Patron. The retrieval of yet another Russian suitcase-size nuclear weapon, which was found in the United States, had the power players in Washington D.C. up in arms. As for me, I knew that I needed to get away for a while and get some much-needed rest.

Thinking about what Anthony had told me about my grandfather buying me a yacht and owning a condominium in Florida, I called Kate and asked her to fly in and meet me at Jacksonville International Airport in Amelia Island, Florida. She anxiously agreed.

Meeting Kate at the airport, we rented a car and headed north. The drive was 27-miles. Just having Kate with me seemed to calm me down. She had a way of making me feel at peace deep within my tormented soul. Kate was without a doubt my guiding angel.

I couldn't figure out why my grandfather chose Amelia Island for his hide-away until I had actually gotten there.

The marina was located on Front Street on downtown Fernandian Beach.

Parking our car, I took Kate by the hand and walked out onto the thick boardwalk of the marina. Seeing my grandfather's yacht not only shocked me, but also brought a smile to my face.

She was 163-feet of sleek power and elegant design. It had American, Armenian, and Italian banners and flags flying from the bowsprits and railings. Fully staffed, it took twenty people to run and operate this yacht. In short, it was breathtaking and huge! She had crystal glassware and a beautiful full-length mahogany-topped bar.

To my surprise, the captain of the ship was a woman. She was from Uruguay and was half Japanese. She stood five-feet, seven-inches tall, had shoulder length dark brown hair, and brown eyes. She was 28-years old and lived on board the yacht. Her name was Barbara, and she was indeed, one beautiful woman. Kate and I hit it off right away with Barbara, and explained that we were not the rich and famous type snobs who felt they were better than everyone else in the world. She then laughed and told me that I was just like my grandfather, kind and easy going; to me that was a very big compliment.

We spent the night on board our yacht, where I cooked dinner for the ladies.

The next day Kate and I set out to see the sights. Barbara had explained to us that Amelia Island had a very deep history. Europeans had first settled here in the 1500's and by the 1800's it had become what president James Monroe called a "Festering Fleshpot," filled with pirates, smugglers, and illegal slave traders. A more licit golden age in the 1870's, when it first became a tourist destination, left the islands main town of Fernandina Beach, filled with Victorian homes with gabled roofs, elaborate verandas and window's walks. All of which is located on 13-miles of white sandy beach.

We took the ghost tour at St. Peters Episcopal Church Cemetery. We ate at Brett's Waterway Cafe, which is next to the marina, and the Beach Street Grill at the corner of Beach Street and Eighth Street. We spent a few nights at the Fairbanks House, and a couple of nights at the Florida House Inn. Most of all, we spent hours upon hours walking barefoot on the white sandy beach picking up seashells, talking and watching the sunrise and sunsets. Nights turned into days and days turned into nights as Kate and I made plans for our future together.

We spent two weeks together on the island and then said our goodbyes once again. Kate needed to get back to Dublin and I needed to go and check on my grandfather's condition. I wanted to spend some time alone with him. I needed to thank him for loving me as if I was his own son. Most of all, I needed to make sure he knew just how much I really did love him. Most people never tell their loved ones just how much they truly do care about them. Before you know it, they're gone and it's to late to express your true feelings toward them. I wasn't going to let that happen to me. Not when it came to my grandparents.

Flying back to Michigan, I spent a few days with my grandparents. We shared a lot in those two days. Most of all we expressed our feelings toward each other and in doing so we were able to find a very special feeling of inner peace.

* * * * * * *

I was sitting at my desk, looking at my computer screen, drinking a Pepsi, when my phone rang.

Picking up the telephone receiver I place it to my ear. "Hello," I said calmly.

"Hey, partner, good job in Florida. No one was expecting that," Neil explained.

"No kidding, I almost shit when I saw Sonya walk in. But then when I looked down and saw the A-pack nuke, I almost fell out of my chair," I replied.

"I'll bet. The brass is really upset about it, but there isn't a damn thing they can do about it. The Russians insist that all of their weapons are accounted for.

Hey listen; Kathy got a big promotion out of the whole ordeal. She now has clearance to get into the war room," Neil explained.

"She has a Q-clearance?" I questioned.

"Oh hell no, she's just been upgraded on her security access level, that's all. I'll bet she didn't even do anything to earn it did she?" Neil asked in a joking tone of voice.

"She looked hot as hell," I commented.

"I'll bet she did. She asked me exactly where it is you go when you go to see Kate. I really think that Agent Eckland has a bit of jealousy building up inside of her she's not letting you see. So, my friend, be careful," Neil advised.

"Thanks for the advice. You didn't tell her where Kate lives did you?"

"Hell no, I reminded her that I run the war room and I can jerk anyone's clearance if I feel they may be a threat to any of our missions or operatives. She wasn't sure how to handle that, so she reminded me that she was your direct supervisor and that she had a right to know. So, I told her to go ask Carla," Neil explained laughingly.

"Have you had any luck on tracing those numbers for me?" I asked.

"I'm getting close, but I don't have a fix on who it is here in the States that Kalashnikov is talking to. Not yet anyway, but I'm closing in on him. They talk about you a lot lately, so we monitor those numbers around the clock," Neil explained.

"I do appreciate it, brother, thanks."

"No problem, partner. Do you mind if I ask you a question?" Neil asked.

"Not at all, what's up?"

"Your the only one that ever got away from General Kalashnikov, Colonel Ky or Major Dinh. Everything our intelligence listening post in Russia is picking up, tells us that Boris is taking this very personal, and wants to kill you himself. How did you do it? I mean, damn, they tortured you for 89-days. How did you get through all of that without breaking mentally?" Neil asked in a sensitive way.

"I went to 'Sere,' it gave me the edge," I replied.

"Sere? What's that?" Neil questioned.

"Survival, evasion, resistance, and escape school. They were brutal, but then again, so was Colonel Ky and Major Dinh. I got real lucky, Neil. Another 24-hours in that camp and I would have been dead. Just another body dropped off at the edge of the camp to feed the animals with. Even after I had killed Major Dinh and escaped, I had gone as far as I could. Had it not been for that long range, Australian Reconnaissance Team finding me, I would have died out in the jungle. I had gone as far as my body, mind, and spirit was gonna go. God bless those Aussie's," I explained.

"Man, all of that specialized training came through for you in the end didn't it?" Neil asked.

"Yeah, that and an awesome God who never gave up on me. But now it all comes back to haunt me, Neil, the memories. I can't even close my eyes without seeing the faces of the dead. I seldom get any sleep. Not like you do anyway. I fall asleep, don't get me wrong, but I always wake up trembling and scared to death from the nightmares I have. That's why I use so much Methadrine. Its the price I pay, brother, for the life I chose to live," I explained.

"Yeah, I guess, but you sure do live out every man's fantasy. I envy you."

"Yeah well don't envy me, Neil. It's not all you think it is."

"What, are you nuts? You're a Navy Seal who went Black Operations with the Army and CIA. Shit, man, you heard what Sandy said about you. People talk about the Sandman over campfires at night. That's you, brother. The one who rides the pale horse of death. Your a frigin' legend for Christ's sake," Neil explained with a touch of excitement in his voice.

"I was not a Navy Seal. That's a misconception, Neil. I spent six weeks training with them. I had to pass hell week just to qualify, but after that I spent the rest of my training, one on one, with an E-9 Master Chief, who taught me the special tricks of their trade. They gave me an honorary Trident Pin. They wanted me to stay and try to finish out the six-month course, but I couldn't. I was there for one reason and one reason only," I explained.

"What was it? What was that one reason? If you don't mind me asking," Neil questioned.

"To learn the elite, covert tricks of their trade. They taught me how to do Black Op's work, not how to do Navy Seal work. There is a big difference, brother. Hell, the 'Farm' was a lot harder and taught me a lot more. Stuff the Seals don't even know. That's what I got off on.

Anyway, like I said, its no big deal. But I will share this bit of information with you. Its a consistent fight with me. I really enjoy what I do. It wouldn't take much to push me completely over the edge and turn me into a full fledge killing machine. The good part of me fights with the evil part of me everyday. Sometimes I really feel that the good part of me is starting to lose the battle. If that happens, I don't know what I might turn into. It's scary, Neil, it really is," I explained sadly.

"Yeah well, I still envy you. You're the Sandman, brother, and everyone is afraid of you. You'd piss in Satan's pocket and not think twice about it."

"Fuck Satan, he's a bitch," I replied calmly as my other telephone began to ring.

"Listen, Neil, I gotta go, I'll talk to you later. Stay on that trace for me, will ya?" I asked.

"You got it," he replied as I hung up my telephone and picked up the other secure phone.

"Hello?" I whispered softly into the telephone receiver.

"If your done chit-chatting on our Agency telephone, do you think you could spare a moment of you time to speak with me. You do remember me, don't you? The one that you do such great work for," Carla said half jokingly.

"Hummm, let me think a minute. The one that I work for? Oh yeah, the foxy lady with the great set of legs. How ya doing, boss?" I replied playfully.

"Turn on your computer, I'm sending you some intel," Carla explained as I turned on my computer and watched the screen, as a picture of a Russian appeared on it.

"Who's this?" I asked.

"His name is Ivan Lacinov. He's a diplomatic attaché. Guess who he works for?

"Russia?" I replied dumbly.

"Duh, no shit, damn you catch on quick don't you? He works for your old buddy Boris and he's coming to America," Carla explained.

"So? They have an Embassy here, remember?" I added.

"Our Delta Force listening station monitoring all of the airwaves, to include Boris' telephone lines, just came up with some great tactical intel. Ivan is not coming to the Russian Embassy my dear friend. He is meeting with a diplomat from China, at Mercer Island in Washington."

"Your kidding me. I wonder what they're up to?" I replied.

"That's what we need you to find out. Our intel says they're meeting at someplace called 'Lid Park,' on West Mercer Way, in three days. There's some festival going on out there this weekend called the 'Seafair Festival.' The people of Mercer Island even have the Blue Angels fly overhead. I'm sending you all of the details Delta Force gathered. I need you to get there ahead of time, survey the area and retrieve the black ballistic nylon briefcase the Russian is going to be carrying. Our intel says whatever they're up to, it's all in that attaché briefcase Ivan is passing over to the Chinese to take a look at. We think it has something to do with oil, and they may be planning to invade one of the Arab countries. Do whatever you have to do, David. Kill Ivan if you have to, but get us that briefcase," Carla explained in a very no-nonsense tone of voice.

"Send me everything you've got and tell Ben to meet me at the airport. You want Kathy in on this now that she has war room clearance?" I asked.

"That wasn't my idea, kiddo, Mr. Crock promoted her before I could object to it. Sure take her... on second thought, don't tell her anything. I have something else I need her to do for me. I'll call Ben and have him call you. Get that attaché and bring me the security briefcase," Carla explained once again as she hung up the telephone.

Hanging up the telephone on my end, I called Marge at the CIA's Technical Services Division. I was going to need a few things only Marge could get for me. If Ivan was one of Kalashnikov's most trusted friends and personal attaché, I was going to enjoy killing him just to spite Boris. That would hurt him, and that's exactly what I wanted to do.

Picking up the telephone I called Marge at her office. Ben could bring what I need along with him when he came to pick me up. I had three days to apply the 7-P's. "Proper, previous, planning, prevents, piss, poor, performance." Seal team training the master chief's way...

* * * * * * *

Ben and I arrived at Mercer Island within thirty-hours from the time we had gotten the call from Carla. Marge had moved quickly to prepare the items I had requested. I wasn't sure if I would need them, but it was better to carry a few extra things with me now, rather than to wish I would have later if I needed them and didn't have them.

We had rented a car and drove in on Interstate Highway-90.

Mercer Island was located on the other side of Lake Washington. Because I already knew Ben wanted to be more active, along with the fact he had saved my life in Africa, I took him along with me. Worried that I might get lost, Ben became my personal driver and back-up man on this operation.

I really didn't need him along to complete this task, but when I explained it to him that way he looked at me and said "Yeah right," and then thanked me for letting him tag along.

The first place we went was "Lid Park." From here there was a great view across the lake to Seattle. It was wooded, and to my surprise, had quite a few people walking around enjoying the park.

"There's an awful lot of people here, Dave. How are you going to kill Ivan without someone noticing you?"

"I'm not sure. Lets rent a room and find Tully's Coffee Shop and have a cup of coffee. I'm going to need to think this out. We have two days to plan it out before he actually arrives, if our intel is correct anyway. So lets have lunch, and see what everything looks like," I explained calmly as I placed two drops of Methadrine under my tongue and headed back toward our car.

We found Tully's Coffee House at 7810 South East 27th Street. It was a small coffee house and in all honesty, served a great cup of fresh brewed coffee. The people were friendly; the place was clean and quiet. Sitting down at the table we drank our coffee and talked.

"What do you think Boris is up to?" Ben asked.

"With him you never really know, but the one thing I do know is the general doesn't do anything small time. Whatever it is, if he's teaming the KGB up with the Chinese, its gonna be big."

"Do you have any idea as to how you're going to kill Ivan. Is that something you plan out ahead of time? If you don't mind me asking, that is," Ben asked in a low whisper.

"Well, I live by a certain set of rules. Rule number one, 'always expect the unexpected.' Rule number two, 'everything is subject to change at any given moment.' I very seldom kill people the same way, unless I have no other choice. What really turns me on is thinking of different ways to kill people. It's all part of the hunt, man I really love it. All of our intel on Ivan tells me he's a very cunning and dangerous man. With that in mind, I brought along some extra goodies in my 'bag of death'," I explained.

"Your bag of death?" Ben questioned with a curious look.

"Yeah, I carry a black leather doctors bag or an attaché case along with me most of the time. I keep all kinds of neat stuff in there. On this operation I brought it along because I'm not sure how this is going to play out," I explained.

"Well I'm grateful your letting me hang out with you, partner. I really get off on watching you do your thing."

"No problem, Ben. By the way, I never thanked you for saving my life in Africa. Thank you, brother, I appreciate it. I'm so used to working with Chopper, Butch, and Nick that I always knew my back was covered. I'm glad you were there, cuz, Kathy sure wasn't paying any attention."

"Are you kidding, I actually got to blow away a real live bad guy. I loved it. I'm glad I was there to back you up," Ben explained as he took a sip of his coffee.

"Did Carla rent us a room somewhere close by?" I asked.

"No, I took care of that while I was waiting for Marge to put together your bag of death, as you put it. We've got a room at the Holiday Inn."

"Damn," I said softly.

"What? Damn what?" Ben asked.

"I'll be right back, I need to make a call," I explained as I got up and walked over to the pay phone.

Calling information, I got the number for the Holiday Inn. Calling the hotel I waited for the front desk to pick up and answer.

"Hello, Holiday Inn, may I help you?" the young female voice asked politely.

"Yes, ma'am, could you please tell me if Mr. Ivan Lacinov has arrived yet?" I asked. It was what I called in Vietnam a WAG, 'Wild Ass Guess.' Today was Thursday afternoon. If we came two days early what would keep Ivan from doing the same thing.

"Sir, Mr. Lacinov has arrived but unfortunately he has stepped out for lunch. Would you like to leave a message?"

"No, I'll just stop by to see him later tonight. Could you tell me what room Ivan is staying in please?" I asked politely.

"Yes, sir, Mr. Lacinov is staying in Room 204," she explained.

"Okay, thank you, ma'am, and you have a nice day," I responded.

"Your welcome, sir," she answered as she hung up the telephone.

Hanging up the pay phone on my end I walked back over to the table and sat down grinning.

"You look like the cat that just ate the canary. What's going on?" Ben asked excitedly.

"Remember I told you to always expect the unexpected? Well, partner, Ivan Lacinov is already here."

"What? Where?" Ben asked in a whisper as he leaned forward to hear what I was about to say.

"Holiday Inn Room 204," I explained as I took a sip of my coffee.

"Shit, he's not suppose to meet with the Chinese diplomat until Saturday at 1:00 p.m.," Ben commented with a confused look on his face.

"He meets with them on Saturday, that doesn't mean he's coming here on Saturday. He came early so he'd be familiar with the area, with his surroundings, in case something happens and he needs to get out fast. I think we should pay old Ivan a little visit tonight, what do you think?" I asked calmly.

"We? You want me to come along with you? Oh hell yeah! Tonight sounds good to me," Ben answered with a big smile on his face, as he took a sip of his coffee.

"I'm going to make a 'wet work' agent out of you yet. You love this just as much as I do," I explained as my mind began to think about all of the scenario's that could take place tonight. Now what I needed to figure out was exactly how the Sandman was going to put Ivan to sleep....

* * * * * * *

The Holiday Inn was a two-story structure with roughly 160-rooms to it. Its main office lobby was separate from the rooms themselves. Inside was a real nice bar-restaurant. It was at that restaurant Ben and I decided to eat our evening meal and wait to see if Ivan would also show up to eat here.

I already knew from our intelligence reports that Ivan Lacinov was a seasoned KGB agent. He stood six feet, eight inches tall, had dark brown short hair, brown eyes and weighed in at close to three hundred-pounds, all of which was muscle. In short, Ivan Lacinov was a highly trained killing machine, and was not to be taken lightly. His skill at killing people was why General Kalashnikov had sent him on this assignment.

It was 7:00 p.m.; we were almost finished with our meal when Ivan stepped into the dining area.

"Holy shit, look at the size of that guy," Ben said softly as we continued to eat.

"Uh huh," was all I said in reply.

"The Farm teaches you how to fight with guys that big?" Ben asked. "Ivan is going to be treacherous, David," Ben added as Ivan sat down at one of the tables.

"They don't teach you to fight with anyone, Ben. They teach you to out think them and kill them. If for some reason you do have to fight someone, you focus on one particular body part. Fight that part and not the whole body. See how big he is?" I asked.

"Yeah," Ben replied.

"If you have to fight a man as big as he is, you take out his knee. He'll drop like a ton of bricks," I explained as I took a very careful and detailed look at the big Russian.

Remembering what my instructor had taught me while I was at the Farm, I let the training take over. It only took a few seconds and then I saw exactly what I needed to see, and smiled.

"Don't tell me that you already have a plan?" Ben asked as I took a sip of my Pepsi.

"He's wearing body armor under his clothes. Do you see it?" I asked.

"No, you see body armor?"

"Oh yeah, that's why he's carrying the briefcase with him. His personal data information sheet says that he showers every night before he goes to bed. That's because the body armor makes him sweat. Its thick and heavy," I explained as I pulled out my money clip to pay for the meal.

"Your going to use his body armor to kill him?" Ben asked, with a totally confused look on his face.

"No, my friend, I'm not," I answered.

"Oh, you're going to kill him while he's in the shower. Now I get it," Ben replied with a look on his face as if he had figured out the last piece of the puzzle.

"Nope, see his feet?" I asked as we stood up to leave.

"Those aren't feet, they're fucking battle ships," Ben answered jokingly.

"Stepping up to the cash register I paid for our meal with a brand new one hundred dollar bill and told our waitress to keep the change. When we were outside, I continued our conversation.

"Okay, his feet. Your going to hit him in the head with one of his own boots and kill him. So tell me just exactly how are you going to pick up the boot? They're huge and have got to weigh a ton," Ben explained with a chuckle.

"He's a diplomat, Ben. He's wearing a suit, and by the looks of it a rather expensive one at that. But Ivan is a soldier and a trained KGB agent. He's not wearing dress shoes; he's wearing nicely polished, all black leather, jump boots. I'm going to use his boots and let Ivan kill himself," I said smiling as we headed to our room to prepare.

"Now I am lost. How?" Ben asked.

"I've had an idea for quite awhile now and I swear to God it will work, but I've never been able to try it out on someone. Well, tonight we're gonna try it out on Ivan. If it works, I'll send it to the Farm and they can teach the new recruits how to do it," I explained as we stepped up to our room and keyed open the door.

"And if it doesn't work, then what?" Ben asked.

"I'll shoot Ivan in the chest ten times with some Black Rhino rounds and we'll grab the briefcase and run like hell," I said as I began to laugh and stepped into our hotel room.

* * * * * * *

It took less than five minutes for me to open my black leather doctor's bag and fill a syringe with 30cc of Heroin. Carefully placing the red plastic cap over the needle, I placed the syringe into my top left shirt pocket. I then checked my handgun to make sure it was fully loaded with a clip of Rhino rounds.

Placing my lock pick gun into my pocket, I handed Ben the black Russian made ballistic nylon briefcase I had asked Marge to send me. Pausing for just a second, I pulled out my small glass vial of Coo-da-day poison.

"That's from the Colombian poison arrow frog, isn't it?" Ben asked as he watched me apply a few drops of the deadly poison onto the tip of the needle of my syringe and carefully place the cap back over the tip of the needle once again.

"Yes it is. The pure Heroin will kill Ivan but I'm not taking any chances. He's a big man and I want to make sure that he dies fast. These Rhino rounds will cut through him like a hot knife cuts through butter. The problem is I've seen what these bullets are capable of doing. They'll go through Ivan and the wall behind him. If there is anyone in the room next to him, I might end up killing innocent people. That my friend is against my personal set of rules. So now with just one poke of this needle Ivan will be dead within 30-seconds. It will take him that long to figure out that he's just been assassinated. By then it'll be to late. Remember, Ben, your there to observe and nothing else. Keep your weapon in your hand, but don't use it unless you absolutely have to understood?" I asked as I placed two drops of liquid Methadrine under my tongue and put the tiny vial of speed back into my pocket.

"Understood, man this is scary, David," Ben replied.

"Stay here if you want to, but I've got work to do," I explained as I walked out of our hotel room with Ben right behind me.

It was already dark by the time we reached Ivan's room. Knocking on the door, I waited.

"What are you doing? You already know he's not in his room," Ben explained as I knocked once again and looked to my right and left to make sure no one was watching us or coming down the walkway.

"You don't listen very well do you? Always expect the unexpected. How do you know he didn't bring a friend along with him like I brought you along with me?" I asked as I slid the tip of the lock pick gun into the lock and pulled back on the lever three times.

"What if he has the door wired to explode?" Ben asked.

"He has the attaché case with him. If he didn't, I'd be concerned about that, but he does, so I'm not," I explained as I clicked open the door lock. Placing the lock pick gun back into my jacket pocket, I opened the door.

"Hello, hotel security. Is anyone here?" I asked as a precautionary measure just to play it safe.

I didn't trust Russians or the Chinese. So I was playing this operation very safely. I really didn't care about me, but I had Ben along so I had to be extra careful to assure his safety.

Stepping inside we closed the door behind us and turned on the light.

The room had two double beds in it. Across from the beds was a large dresser with a full size mirror on it. Next to it was a 21-inch TV set sitting on a television stand. The bathroom was on the far left with a small walk in closet across from it on the far right side of the room.

Ivan had brought three suitcases along with him. His suits and dress slacks were spread neatly out across the one large double bed nearest the front door. His underwear, socks and T-shirts were stored neatly away in the dresser drawers. His extra side arm was holstered and laying on the bed close to his pillow.

"Turn off the light, Ben, we'll hide in the closet and wait for him to take his shower," I explained as Ben turned off the light and locked the door to the room once again.

Looking at my watch it was almost 9:00 p.m. when Ben and I heard the front door of the hotel room open. Hearing it close and the lock bolt click shut caused my heart to race with excitement and fear. My adrenaline was at an all time high as I tightened the grip of my left hand onto the butt of my 15-shot Beretta. Looking over at Ben I could see that he was nervous as Ivan began to sing a Russian song in his native tongue.

He set the attaché case down on top of the dresser, went into the bathroom, turned on the water in the bathtub, and then got undressed.

So far everything was going well until he sat down to use the toilet. Hearing him fart, which was followed by the thumping and splashing sound of human waste hitting water, was quickly followed with a stench that was nothing less than toxic. I knew that most Russians eat a lot of garlic, but when you combine it with vodka and God only knows what else he had eaten, it caused a smell that made my eye's burn and made me want to vomit!

Watching Ben slowly reach up and pull his T-shirt collar over his nose and mouth upset me. It was an unnecessary movement that could have alerted Ivan to our presence in the room. I should have known better. I was forgetting the basic set of rules. This would not happen again, I promised myself that.

Hearing the toilet flush, Ivan pushed the bathroom door closed. Waiting, I listened as the big Russian stepped into the bathtub of water; I then made my move.

Slowly opening the closet door, we both stepped out, and carefully and quietly closed the closet door behind us.

Stepping over by the bed I reached into my shirt pocket and pulled out the syringe full of pure Heroin and deadly poison mixture.

Even though I was wearing my leather gloves I was very careful as I pulled the plastic cover off the needle. Putting the cover back into my pocket I slipped the syringe into Ivan's right boot with the plunger facing the toe of the boot. Holding the boot on an angle I watched as the syringe slid quietly up and into the boot. It was now out of visual sight with the needle pointing towards the heal of the boot. Setting the boot back down onto the floor in the exact same position I had found it in, I then took the attaché case Marge had sent me and switched it with the briefcase Ivan had placed on the top of the dresser.

Reaching into Ivan's pants pocket I pulled out his diplomatic credentials and replaced them with the new set of credentials Marge had sent me. The new set had Ivan's name and photograph on it but only identified him as a Russian citizen, not a diplomat. Putting the fake credentials back into his pants pocket I motioned for Ben to open the front door of the hotel room. As he did we quickly stepped out of Ivan's room, pulling the door closed behind us in a very slow and quite manner.

Walking at a normal pace, we went back to our room and gathered up our belongings.

Within fifteen minutes from the time we had gotten back to our room, we were packed, in our car, and driving out of the parking lot of the Holiday Inn.

"We're not going to wait and see what happens?" Ben asked curiously.

"No we're not. We got what we came for. We need to get this back to Langley as quickly as possible," I explained as I tried to calm myself down from the full surge of the adrenaline rushing through me.

"Man, I wanted to watch that big mother fucker die. Do you think that your syringe trick will work?" Ben asked as we drove the 12.5-mile an hour speed limit.

"Oh yeah, I got him, I guarantee it. But he's been drinking, so the odds are that after he takes his bath, he'll lay down and go to sleep. He won't put his boots back on until tomorrow morning unless we speed things up and spook him tonight," I explained calmly as I began to mentally slow my heart rate down a bit.

"I never thought about that," Ben said softly.

"You never thought about accidentally hitting one of those coat hangers in the closet either when you pulled the collar of your T-shirt over your nose. That little stunt could have gotten us into a shoot out with Ivan," I explained as I looked over at Ben.

"You're right, Dave, I wasn't thinking. The smell was so foul I couldn't handle it. I'm sorry, partner."

"You don't handle it, Ben. You accept it, over come it, and move forward," I explained.

"How do you do that when it smells that bad?" Ben asked.

"You do it the same way you over come any other problem on a mission. You triumph over it by sheer will, pure tenacity and absolute determination. You do it the way your Seal team instructor teaches you to do it. You don't think about it, you just fucking do it. No matter what it is, you overcome it and defeat it. Nothing is impossible on a mission or in your daily life," I explained in a strong serious tone of voice as my anger began to over power me.

"That's how you survived the POW camp isn't it?" Ben asked sensing that I was upset.

"Damn right it is. I take a lot of pride in the fact that I was able to spend six weeks with the United States Navy Seals. Those instructors crammed six months of training into my head, in six weeks. I owe them my life Ben. The one E-9 Master Chief was a die hard, loyal, no-nonsense son-of-a-bitch who taught me well. I triumphed over that POW camp and everything they did to me for 89-days. I beat those rotten bastards by using sheer will, pure tenacity and absolute pure one hundred percent determination.

I just killed one of General Kalashnikov's personal friends, and that dumb bastard doesn't even know that he's dead yet. This won't end until Boris Kalashnikov and I meet face to face, and when we do, the Sandman is gonna put that commie red Soviet bastard to sleep," I said angrily.

Something had just snapped in me. I had just unloaded a lot of pent-up anger and bitterness onto Ben. The memories of Vietnam, the people I had killed, the Americans I had watched die, and the 89-days of being tortured by Major Dinh and Colonel Ky were starting to eat away at the fibers of my soul. I needed to push all of the hate, bitterness and anger back inside my inner closet and put a bigger pad lock on the door of my dark side. The ghosts were starting to sneak out. I couldn't allow that to happen if I wanted to remain sane.

Sensing that I was over the edge, Ben didn't say anything else to me for the rest of our trip. He flew me back to the Pontiac Airport and dropped me off. Ben then took the Russian attaché case back to Langley and dropped it off so it's contents could be analyzed.

As I had expected, Ivan Lacinov had taken his bath and went to bed. The next morning however, when Ivan woke up and got dressed, he put on his boots. When he did, as he slid his right foot into his boot, he pushed his toes into the deadly needle. As he did, the forward thrust pushed the syringe backward into the toe of his boot. As that happened, the toe of his boot pushed the plunger of the syringe forward injecting Ivan with 30cc's of the pure Heroin, and two drops of deadly CIA poison known as Coo-da-day. As Ivan screamed out in pain and pulled his foot back out of his boot, the needle and syringe were still stuck deep in between his toes.

Grabbing the syringe, Ivan pulled the needle out of his foot. When he did, he put his fingerprints all over the plastic syringe.

It was twelve o'clock Friday morning when the cleaning lady keyed open the door to Room 204 of the Holiday Inn and found the dead body of Ivan Lacinov laying on his bed with a syringe in his hand. The Mercer Island Police Detectives would investigate and find the black nylon attaché briefcase. Opening it up they would find an ounce of Heroin and three magazines, a Playboy, a Penthouse, and a Hustler. The medical examiner would state on the death certificate that Ivan Lacinov died of an accidental overdose of Heroin, an illegal narcotic. The investigation into Ivan's death would be closed within 72-hours. His body would be shipped back to Russia at the expense of General Boris Kalashnikov. Boris would file formal complaints to the United Nations alleging that a Russian diplomat had been assassinated by the Chinese government. The Peoples Republic of China would vigorously deny the acquisition.

All in all it turned out to be a pretty interesting week. The question now was what was in the attaché diplomatic briefcase?

I wasn't sure why I had gotten that angry. It wasn't in my nature to vent my frustrations like that, especially using that much foul language. The battle between me and the Sandman, lurking within, had begun once again.

I flew to Dublin and stopped in Kerry County at a place called 'Paddy Cullen's Pub.' Instead of ordering a Pepsi, I had a pint of Paddy's best Irish brew. From there I found myself in Bray at the outskirts of Dublin. I was in a place called 'Ard More Pub.' I was on my third pint when Kate and her grandfather walked in to get me. Someone at the pub had called them to let them know that I was there and drinking, which was something that I seldom ever did. I remember saying hello to Kate and asking her grandfather to join me in a drink. But what I don't remember is throwing up all over the bar and passing out.

I woke up in front of the round stone fireplace of our new home, to the crackling sound of a fire within it. Kate was holding me in her arms and patting my forehead with a cold damp cloth. Looking down at me she smiled.

"You don't drink very well," she explained calmly.

"No I don't, that's one of the reasons I prefer not to," I moaned as my head began to throb.

"Wanna talk to your woman about it?" Kate asked, as she looked deep into my eyes.

"Yes I do. That's why I came home to you," I replied.

"What's wrong, David, what has you so tormented that you'd get drunk?" Katie asked as she ran her hand gently across the left side of my face.

"Why won't our home stop spinning around?" I asked as darkness over powered me and I passed out once again....

Chapter Thirty
Straight Pin

I had spent two weeks with Kate talking about my inner battle and how I had taken it out on Ben. She was quick to remind me that that was what real friends were for, and Ben would forgive me.

Calling Ben at home, I apologized for venting on him the way I did. He was quick to remind me that real friends never have to say they are sorry to each other. He was also quick to tell me he was glad to see I hadn't lost my focus or my edge, and if I needed someone to vent on, he was there for me 24-hours a day, 7-days a week. I now felt better knowing I hadn't lost my friendship with a man who had become one of my true friends.

It was the telephone call from Andy, which brought me back home to Michigan.

Frank White and his men had just shot it out with the Chinese – Hong Kong – Triad in New York. It was over Heroin and control over the drug called 'China White.'

Over thirty Chinese Triad members were killed in the gun battle, which started inside a Triad controlled building, to the streets outside.

When it was over the Chinese Triad members who had just received a major supply of the expensive white powder were dead. Frank and his men walked away with over a ton of 100% pure Heroin, all of it stored neatly in 50-gallon barrels. Calling Anthony, Andy, Don, and some of my most trusted family members to my home; we met to discuss how Frank's actions might affect the five New York crime families.

We learned from our people inside the local police precincts that Frank's biggest problem now was a rouge group of Irish cops had had enough of Frank White and his men. Another war was about to begin and I didn't want any part of it. Both Frank and his men, and the Irish cops who were about to go after Frank, were proud and serious. The major flow of illegal narcotics into New York was about to spark a very bloody and deadly fight between Frank White and the men who called themselves New York's finest. The question now was, how far was each side willing to go for what they each believed to be right.

* * * * * * *

"Don't let them get me. Please, brother, remember your promise. Oh God, I can't feel my legs. Please don't let 'em get me. Remember the pit?" Nick said as I held him in my arms.

The Viet Cong sniper's bullet had hit him in the lower back, severing his spine and blowing a large hole out through his intestinal track as it exited through his stomach. My best friend was dying and there was nothing I could do to save him.

"Don't worry, big brother, I'm here. I'm not going to leave you, I promise," I said as tears filled my eyes.

"Drop your weapons, do it now," the voice explained over the mega phone in broken English.

"Oh, God, please, shoot me, Sandman, please don't let them get me," Nick pleaded.

"They're not going to touch you, don't worry," I explained as I raised my pistol up and held it in my right hand.

"Drop your weapon, we won't hurt you. We want to help you. You cannot escape, you are surrounded," the Vietnamese Officer said once again.

Looking down the path to my left I could see the scope of choppers sniper's rifle pointed at me as sweat ran down from my face and into my eyes and mouth.

"Don't give up your position, I love you, brother," I mouthed without saying a word.

"Drop your weapon, do it now," the Vietnamese Officer ordered more sternly.

"Please, David, please don't let them get me," Nick said again with a panicked look in his eyes.

"I've got you, big brother, don't worry," I said once again.

"Tell my mom and dad that I did my best. Tell them that I love them with all my heart," Nick said as he began to cough up more blood.

"I'll tell them, big brother, I promise," I said as I cocked the hammer of my pistol back into the firing position.

"I love you, Nick, I'll see you on the other side, I said as I placed my left hand over Nick's eyes and turned his head slightly to his left.

"Thanks, David. I love you, little brother," Nick said again in a soft voice as I placed the barrel of my pistol up against the right side of his head at the temple.

"No, do not shoot him, we will help you, drop your weapon now!" the voice ordered as it echoed through the forest.

"Fuck you, asshole," I shouted with tears in my eyes as I pulled the trigger.

'Boom....'

Sitting up quickly I fought hard to catch my breath.

My body was completely covered with sweat and trembling.

"Nick," I whispered softly in the stillness of my bedroom, as I looked around in the dark. "Oh, God, why couldn't it have been me who was killed instead of my brother Nick? Why, God, why?" I asked as I laid back down letting my emotions overwhelm me.

* * * * * * *

I had laid in my bed for almost four hours staring at the sealing. God must have been busy because he never answered my question as to why?

Looking at my watch it was almost five o'clock in the morning as I got out of bed and went to take a shower.

After my shower, I got dressed and went downstairs to check my computer and grab a cold bottle of Pepsi.

While I was in Ireland my grandmother had been taken to the hospital for surgery. The doctors had operated on her and removed a tumor from the inside of her stomach. When I had gone to see her I found out that the tumor was the size of a baby's head. The good news was that she was resting comfortably and she was going to be alright.

It was 9:00 a.m. when I called Carla at the Situation Room to check in with her.

"Hello," Carla said in a rather cold tone of voice.

"Hello, boss, how's everything going?" I asked.

"Well, if you tell me you're alright, everything will be going fine. How are you, are you alright?" Carla asked.

"Yeah I'm okay. I was just having a little anger management problem and battling with my personal ghosts. I've got them under control. For the most part I'm feeling better now. I guess I just needed to vent a little bit," I explained calmly, hoping we could change the subject.

"Did you find anything worth while in Ivan's briefcase?" I asked.

"Yes as a matter of fact we did. It seems we were right. The Russians are wanting to invade one of the Arab countries and we think they are wanting the Chinese to join them. We're still trying to decrypt the computer discs we found inside of the attaché case.

We also sent your little needle in the boot trick to our people at the Farm," she explained with a chuckle in her voice.

"Oh yeah? That's cool, what did they think about it?" I asked.

"They loved it. It's original and has proven to be very effective. They're going to incorporate it into their nasty book of deadly tricks. They wanted to know what you call it?" Carla asked.

"I'm going to call it 'The Scorpion's Sting.' I'm going to name it after you," I explained proudly.

"The Scorpion's Sting, huh? I like that. It is a very deadly bite and a great way to kill someone and make it look like something they did to themselves. It certainly was a great idea. I'm almost afraid to ask you how you came up with the idea," Carla explained.

"The most obvious is the least obvious. I've got a few more ideas I'm going to experiment with. I'll let you know how they turn out," I responded.

"How's Kate?" Carla asked.

"Calming, loving, understanding. Shall I continue?" I asked playfully.

"No, I think I get the idea. Listen, kiddo, I'm glad your feeling better. I've gotta go, I have a lunch date with Neil. He's going to update me on our latest intelligence information on your friend General Kalashnikov. Of course he can't just tell me here in my office. It has to be over lunch, and I'm buying. If not, Neil swears I'll regret the day I introduced you both to each other. I think you're corrupting him. Neil is starting to act cocky just like you," Carla explained.

"That could be a good thing, mom. At least he's not timid anymore. He has more confidence in himself. It says a lot about him, and it builds character in him. Neil's a good man, you should be glad you've got him on your team," I explained.

"I am glad that I've got him on my team. And yes he is quite a character just like you. I'll see you later, David," Carla said as she hung up the telephone.

Hanging up the telephone on my end I began to laugh. I was starting to feel better; maybe it would turn out to be a good day after all.

* * * * * * *

It was almost 5:00 p.m. when I heard a knock at my front door. Opening the refrigerator in my kitchen I pulled out a cold bottle of Pepsi, opened it, and walked over to my front door to see who it was. Opening the door I smiled when I saw my Uncle Paul.

"Uncle Paul, this is a surprise, please come in," I said as I invited Paul Castellano into my home.

"David, its good to see you," Paul said as he walked over and sat down on my sofa.

"Are you hungry? Would you like something to drink?" I asked.

"No, I'm fine. I was just visiting with your grandfather. Why didn't anyone call and tell me that your grandmother is in the hospital?" he asked in an almost scolding way.

"I thought Don called you? I'm sorry, Uncle Pauly, I thought you knew," I replied as I sat down next to Paul on the sofa.

"Well at least she is going to be alright. That woman is such a saint," he said as he paused to think for a moment. "They said they took a tumor out of Helen's stomach the size of a baby's head for Christ's sake. How was she able to eat anything?" Paul asked.

"Yeah I know. She's stubborn and didn't tell anyone she wasn't feeling well. I guess the pain finally got so bad Uncle Jack noticed something was wrong and rushed her to the hospital. We're lucky, it could have killed her," I explained.

"Yes I know. Oh mama, the times we used to have back in the old days," Paul said as he thought back to their younger days and smiled.

"Is everything alright? You look troubled," I asked, knowing Paul didn't come to my home for a friendly visit.

Opening his briefcase he pulled out a manila envelope and handed it to me.

"I have a serious problem," Paul said as I opened the envelope and looked at the pictures inside.

"No such thing as a problem, Uncle Paul. Who is this guy and how does it concern you?" I asked.

"His name is Saul Rosenberg, Doctor Saul Rosenberg to be exact. Saul owns a pharmaceuticals manufacturing company in Beverly Hills. He is also a very rich and powerful man. Saul is the best neurosurgeon in the United States. He has strong political contacts, and like most of the rich and famous men of the world, Saul has a number of politicians in his pocket. One of these politicians has decided to run for President of the United States," Paul explained as he took a deep breath and let it out slowly. Sitting back on the sofa Paul looked at me with a very worried look on his face.

"What's going on Uncle Paul?" I asked as I sat back, turned sideways, and looked at the man I had grown up knowing as my uncle.

"We have been making an illegal drug called PCP out of Saul's pharmaceutical company in Beverly Hills."

"Angel Dust? Your making Angel Dust? Holy shit Uncle Paul, the cops are going crazy about that crap. One criminal gets pumped up on angel dust and it makes him super human. It takes eight to ten cops to subdue him and put him in handcuffs. There's some cases where guys get so strong because of the effect of the PCP they actually break the damned handcuffs," I explained, even though I knew Paul already knew all of this.

"We've made millions on the PCP alone. We split the profit three ways. But now that our friend is running in the up and coming presidential elections, Saul is demanding certain promises and guarantees be made to him once our friend wins the election."

"And if not?" I asked with raised eyebrows.

"Saul reminded us that most of our profits from the sales of the PCP went into our friend's campaign fund to help support his run for the presidency," Paul explained with a sigh.

"And he can connect you to this money laundering campaign ordeal?" I asked.

"Oh yeah. If Saul makes a deal with the FBI, God forbid, he has enough on my friend and I to put us both in prison," Paul explained sadly.

"So, why don't you send one of your boy's over and blow Saul away?" I asked. "Problem solved right?"

"Can't do it like that. A murder investigation might lead right to us. Saul has to many rich and politically connected friends. They would demand a very thoroughly conducted investigation. We need Saul dead but there can't be any mistakes with this one. It has to look natural. The forensic medical examiner won't leave any stone unturned. They'll go over his body with a fine-toothed comb. Which, is why I came to you. Who do you think I should put on this?" Paul asked.

"Leave this package with me, Uncle Paul, I'll take care of it. There's something I have been wanting to try out. Saul might very well be the perfect person to try it out on. Besides, I need to pick something up for Kate and I want to buy it at Tiffany's in Beverly Hills," I explained with a grin.

"David, don't do this on your own. We can't risk anything happening to you of all people," Paul explained as he patted me on my left knee with his right hand.

"Does Momo know about this?" I asked.

"Sam? No, I came to talk to your grandfather about it first. John said to talk to you right away about it, so here I am," Paul explained.

"Like I said, Uncle Paul, don't worry about it and don't talk about this to Sam or anyone else. Give me a week to study the personal data information sheet on Saul and I'll put Saul Rosenberg to sleep for you," I explained.

I spent the next two hours talking to Paul about the problems with Frank White and the New York Police Department. We then talked about other family business and my plans to turn the ring over to him when the time comes.

I wanted to tell Paul what I knew about Sam and his connection to the CIA. But deep down inside I felt he already knew about it. You don't become a powerful man like Paul Castellano without knowing something like that.

* * * * * * *

I flew to California and rented an all silver Lamborghini. Anything less would have made me stand out in the crowd once I got to Beverly Hills.

Driving past the 8-story Italian Renaissance-style City Hall building, I couldn't help but feel impressed by its structure and design.

California is full of beautiful women who where now trending out with the new G-string style bikinis. I found it hard to drive and stare at the women at the same time, but I somehow managed not to wreck the expensive Italian made sports car while taking in the sights. Once I got to downtown Beverly Hills, my first stop was Tiffany's. Even though everyone in Beverly Hills seemed nice, I couldn't help but feel a bit uncomfortable. Most rich people feel and act as if they are better than everyone else. This part of California seemed to keep that belief very much alive.

Tiffany's was a very rich and high-class store. If you had to ask how much something was, then you had no business being there in the first place.

The young lady behind the counter was pleasant, cheerful and very helpful as she showed me a variety of wedding rings. I settled on a six-carat, flawless, golden jubilee diamond set in a platinum setting. As soon as I saw it I knew it was the ring I wanted to give to Kate on our wedding day. I then picked up a set of matching diamond earrings to make the set perfectly complete.

Setting my briefcase on the countertop, I opened it and told the sales lady to simply take whatever she needed to complete the sale.

Even though I had roughly a half of a million dollars in brand new one hundred dollar bills in the briefcase, she took out what she needed as if it was an everyday thing and rang up the sale.

Taking the black velvet holders the ring and earrings were in, I placed them in my briefcase and gave the young lady two thousand dollars as a tip for her help and service. Lucky for me the ring was already the exact size of Kate's ring finger. Someone else had ordered the ring but cancelled the order the day before I had arrived. So it all worked out well for both of us.

Tossing my briefcase in the passenger's seat of the car, I headed to the 90210 district of Beverly Hills' elite multi-million-heir, rich and famous group. Finding the home of Saul Rosenberg was simple. It was the biggest one in the neighborhood. It sat back off the road and on plush, green, manicured grass. It was white and your typical rich mans home with the Rolls Royce parked out front. The homes in this neighborhood were spread out a bit and were not located right next to each other like the small middle class neighborhood I had grown up in.

As I drove by, I took a look at Saul's home and the area surrounding it. In doing so, I made a mental map in my mind to compare against the blue prints, which were given to me by Paul in the personal information package.

I already knew that Saul was married and had two children. Both children were grown and in college. The son was in Princeton and the daughter in Yale University. Saul now lived with his wife, Ann, who he had been married to for almost twenty-five years. They had a housemaid named Gilda, who came five days a week – Monday through Friday – to clean, cook and do the normal 'kiss the rich man's ass work'. Gilda was married to a man named Hans, who was from Sweden. Hans did all of the lawn and gardening work, which included caring for Saul and Ann's cars.

Saul and Ann were very meticulous about their eating habits. Breakfast was at 6:30 a.m. sharp. When they were home, lunch was to be served at noon. Their evening meal however, was served at 6:00 p.m. Because of the new high tech security alarm system Saul recently had installed, I would use the evening meal to enter their home and bypass the new electronic system.

I looked at my Gold Tag Heuer watch and realized it was slightly past noon. I would find a place to have lunch, rent a room, and wait for the afternoon to pass. I had some diagrams of Saul's home to study, now that I had seen it, this would give me the time needed to do it.

* * * * * * *

Renting a room at the Beverly Hills Hilton, I spent the majority of the afternoon drinking Pepsi and studying the information on Saul Rosenberg.

I was fascinated with a man named Walter Shaw who had invented the black 'scrambler box,' call forwarding, and conference calling. I had spent a lot of time reading about him in the personal index area of the CIA computer system. The two big reasons that Walter Shaw Sr. was in the agency's computer system was that he was the man who created the 'Red Phone' – untappable phone line – that connected the President of the United States in the Oval Office, to the President of Russia at the Kremlin. The other reason was because the American government had ripped Walter Shaw Sr. off and in doing so stole his patents from him. This could make a man with Walter's genius a serious threat if he should ever decide that he wanted a little Sicilian revenge.

Walter had a son named after him, Walter Shaw Jr. Walter Shaw Jr. was angry at the fact that the American government had ripped off his father. So Walter Shaw Jr. was quickly becoming the best jewel thief the world had ever seen. Walter Jr. had been trained by another master thief who was also a member of organized crime. This mans name was Pete Salerno, a charming, deep voiced Italian, who during World War II, had been trained by the Secret Service in the art of breaking into the homes and safes of high ranking German Officers to steal their documents.

Walter Shaw Jr. had broken away from Pete Salerno and was now on his own. At this particular time Walter Jr. had put together a young group of cat burglars who were quickly becoming known by Florida law enforcement officers as The Dinner Set Gang. The cops didn't know who they were yet, but the Dinner Set Gang was ravaging the homes of Florida's elite rich and walking away with millions in diamonds, jewels, and gemstones.

Walter Shaw Jr. didn't waste time trying to by pass high tech security systems. Instead, he and his gang waited until the family of the home they wanted to break into was eating dinner. Walter Jr. would then walk right into the home through the unlocked front door, go up to the owners bedroom, while the family was eating dinner in the other room. Brilliant, simply brilliant. The most obvious was the least obvious.

I had been studying Walter's technique from the Agency's computer system and now planned to use it along with my own special technique of assassination to kill Doctor Saul Rosenberg this evening.

*   *   *   *   *   *   *

Using a Hollywood make-up kit and some of the tricks that Carlos the Jackal had taught me, I disguised my self to look as though I was fifty years old with graying hair. I didn't plan for anyone to see me, but I also remembered my training. 'Everything is subject to change at any given moment' and 'always expect the unexpected.' Simple rules, which had kept me alive thus far.

It was 4:30 when I called Saul Rosenberg's home from my hotel room. It was their maid Gilda who answered on the other end of the line.

"Hello, Rosenberg residence, may I help you?" she asked politely.

"Yes, ma'am, may I speak to Mr. Rosenberg please?" I asked. I wanted to double check to make sure that Saul was going to be home for dinner tonight. A man with his political status could very well have a dinner engagement to attend to. The last thing I wanted was to walk into the house and run right into Hans or Gilda.

"I'm sorry, sir, but Mr. Rosenberg will not be home until 5:30," she answered.

"Oh I see. Could you tell me when would be a proper time for me to call Mr. Rosenberg back. I wouldn't want to interrupt his dinner," I explained calmly as I looked in the mirror and touched up some of my face make-up.

"The Rosenberg's will be sitting down to eat at approximately 6:00 p.m., they're usually finished with their evening meal by 6:45. A good time to call would be anytime after 7:00, but please do not call after 9:00 p.m. the Rosenberg's settle into bed shortly there after, sir," she advised kindly.

"By nine o'clock my wife and I are usually in bed ourselves. I'll call Saul after seven. Thank you for your kindness, young lady, and have a good afternoon," I explained as we said our goodbyes.

So far so good, my plan was moving forward and I now knew that Saul would be in his dining room shortly after six o'clock with his wife. Looking at my watch I placed a couple of drops of liquid Methadrine under my tongue and sat back in my chair. It wouldn't be long now and I would soon test two theories of Walter Shaw Jr. How to walk into a home at dinnertime, and my new thought on how to kill a man and make it look natural without using Coo-da-day poison.

* * * * * * *

There was a mild breeze blowing through the evening air as I parked my car. The gray rain clouds were starting to roll in overhead. A tropical storm was brewing off the coast of California. Getting out of my car I locked the doors, adjusted my sunglasses on my face and smiled. "I love it. Come on rain," I said as I looked up at the darkening clouds beginning to swirl slightly above my head.

Walking down the street I headed to the home of Saul Rosenberg, carrying my black doctors bag in my hand.

The storm was about to break loose which had people heading home to button down for the night. The good thing about a rainstorm is they always seem to make people tired and sleepy. It would all work to my advantage. Death was in the air tonight. The Sandman was coming, and as usual, my next victim had no idea that he had just sat down to eat his last meal.

Seeing Saul's home I walked up the long driveway, past the shrubs, and then up to the large polished oak wood doors at the front of his home.

Looking at my watch it was 6:12 p.m.. By now according to the Dinner Set Gang rules, Saul and his wife, Ann, would be sitting down at their dinning room table to enjoy a lush green salad or soup. Their maid Gilda would be busy in the kitchen preparing to bring out the main course of the meal.

Reaching up for the brass-polished doorknob, my heart raced with excitement as I turned the knob and pushed the door open quietly.

The rain had just begun to fall behind me as I stepped inside, looked quickly around and gently closed the door behind me.

Moving across the large front room I headed directly to the large spiral stairway leading to the second story of the home.

Moving quickly up the stairs I could hear Saul and Ann as they talked about their affairs of the day while eating their evening meal. My mind raced with excitement as I made my way up to the second floor of the house.

"No wonder Walter Shaw Jr. loves his work. This is a pure adrenaline rush," I thought to myself as I moved down the hallway and found the master bedroom. Looking inside the bedroom to confirm nothing had changed, and that this still was the master bedroom, I stepped into the bedroom across the hall. Taking a quick look around, I walked over to the large walk-in closet, opened the door, stepped inside and pulled the door closed behind me. Sitting down on the floor of the closet I placed my doctors bag on my lap and tried to calm myself down.

For some strange reason, walking right into someone's home like this, while the owner's were inside and unaware of my presence, had me so excited I was almost having trouble breathing.

Looking at my watch, I knew I had approximately five hours before I would pay my visit to Mr. Rosenberg.

* * * * * * *

Saul and his wife, Ann, had gone into their bedroom at 9:18 p.m. and by 10:00 p.m. their bedroom light had been turned off.

Shining my pen flashlight at my watch I checked to see what time it was. It was 11:35 p.m. as I very carefully and quietly stepped out of the bedroom closet.

The storm outside had gotten worse. The wind was blowing, the lightning was flashing and lighting up the inside of the bedroom.

Walking up to the bedroom window I pulled back the curtain and watched as bolts of lightning boomed out their angry cry in the darkness of the night and raced across the black sky above.

"This is way to easy. If people ever knew how easy this kind of work really was, they would never believe it," I thought to myself as I watched the rainstorm blow on the palm trees, causing them to sway gently in the wind.

Setting my black leather bag on the bed I unzipped it and pulled out the small aerosol canister of sleeping gas Marge had given me from the CIA's Technical Services Division. Screwing the small thin rubber tube onto the end of the nozzle I took a deep breath of air into my lungs and let it out slowly.

"Sandman's coming, Saul," I said to myself as I picked up my bag and walked over to the bedroom door. Opening the door I stepped out into the hallway and carefully set my leather bag down on the floor keeping it close to, and snuggled up against the hallway wall.

Lowering myself down onto the thick carpet floor I stretched my body out along the wall lengthwise. Holding the aerosol canister in my left hand I gently slid the thin rubber hose under the door keeping it close to the edge of the door closest to the wall. With the hose now in place, I slowly reached up with my right hand and place it on the metal valve to release the gas from the canister. Just as I did the bedroom door opened in the darkness! Without moving a muscle I watched as Ann walked out of the bedroom, her silk nightgown brushing gently across the top of my head. Holding my breath I didn't move as panic and pure adrenaline raced through my entire body.

Pausing for only a second, Ann yawned and walked past me down the hallway to the stairs. Quietly I pulled the hose back out from under the door, grabbed my leather bag and made my way back into the bedroom across the hall. Closing the door, I kept it open just enough so that I would be able to see when Ann returned to her bedroom.

"My face was only a few inches from her left foot. Thank you, Lord, for the training I received at the Farm and with the Seals," I thought to myself as I tried to calm myself down.

A steady flow of Adrenalin and pure excitement was surging through every pour of my body as I stood in the darkness of the bedroom.

The flashes of lightening filled the bedroom momentarily. The whole situation and my entire surroundings made me feel like I was in one of those old Bella Lugosi horror movies.

I didn't know where Ann had gone and I wasn't about to go and look. She was gone for almost fifteen minutes. Then she finally came back down the hall and returned to her bedroom, closing the door behind her once again.

I knew she hadn't gone to the bathroom because she had gone downstairs. That, plus the fact that she had a bathroom in her huge master bedroom. I could only assume that she had either forgotten to do something or she had gone downstairs to make sure the house was secure for the night. Either way, I would now have to wait for Ann to fall back asleep before I released the gas into her bedroom.

* * * * * * *

It was 1:30 a.m. as I laid back down next to Saul's bedroom door. Sliding the thick rubber hose back under the bedroom door, I gently turned the valve on the aerosol canister of sleeping gas. Because the carpet was thick and fit snugly against the bottom of the bedroom door, I didn't need to block the bottom of the door with a towel. The fumes of gas would all stay inside the room. It was a fast acting gas. Just a few breaths of it into your nose, mouth, and in your lungs would knock you out cold for an hour.

Waiting for the aerosol canister to empty, I pulled the hose back out from under the door and placed the hose and empty canister back into my black leather bag. Pulling out the small surgical breathing mask, I placed it over my nose and mouth, picked up my bag and opened the door to Saul's bedroom. Stepping inside I turned on the bedroom light, leaving the bedroom door wide open behind me. Walking up to the side of the bed, I set the bag down on the nightstand next to the bed.

Reaching over I grabbed Saul by the shoulders and shook him vigorously.

"Wake up, Saul," I shouted out loudly. I knew that both he and Ann were in a deep surgical state of sleep, but it never hurts to double check and play it safe.

Opening my bag, I pulled out an empty syringe, a three-inch long flat end straight pin, a small jewelers hammer, and a tube of Krazy Glue. With my left hand I used my fingers to separate the thick hair on the top of Saul's head, slightly off center and to the left.

I then took the three-inch straight pin and carefully pushed the tip of it directly into one of the hair follicles. Using the tiny jewelers hammer, I then gently tapped the flat end of the pin, pushing it through the skull and into Saul's brain about two inches. As the metal needle entered Saul's brain, his body jerked slightly. His breathing became labored as his brain hemorrhaged inside of his skull, giving Saul a major stroke.

My next move was going to be to remove the straight pin and insert the thin needle of the syringe in through the hole and into Saul's brain. I was then going to inject a syringe full of air into Saul's brain, causing it to explode from within. But to my complete surprise, I didn't need to. Saul Rosenberg had stopped breathing.

Checking for a pulse I found none. "I'll be damned, see ya Saul," I said with a chuckle as I opened the tube of Krazy Glue.

Pulling the needle out, I quickly placed a tiny drop of glue at the base of the hair follicle, sealing the tiny puncture hole. Taking a close look at the scalp, I could see no sign of blood or glue, due to the fact that the glue dries clear and only a small touch of it was actually needed on the skin.

Putting the syringe, hammer, glue, and straight pin back into my black leather doctors bag, I zipped it shut. Pulling out my pocket comb, I carefully combed Saul's hair back into its normal pattern and returned the comb to my pocket. I then walked to the other side of the bed and checked Ann's heart rate to make sure it wasn't irregular. Seeing that her heartbeat and breathing were normal, I walked back over to Saul's side of the bed and picked up my bag. I took one last look at Saul and noticed that the muscles on the opposite side of his face were all drooping as if they had no firmness or texture to them at all. It was the tell tale sign of a major stroke. After one last look at Ann, I turned off the light and walked out of the bedroom. Taking off my surgical mask I tucked it into my leather bag and headed downstairs to the front door.

Pushing the delay circuit button on the security alarm box attached to the wall next to the front door, I opened the door, pushed the lock button back into the lock position on the doorknob, and pulled the door closed behind me. Turning the doorknob to make sure that it had locked shut once again I smiled.

Walking out from under the shelter of the overhead entryway, I immediately became soaked from head to toe from the heavy tropical rainstorm.

*   *   *   *   *   *   *

I spent the next week sightseeing in California. I went to see the Lego Land Theme Park in Southern California, and to Huntington Beach, which was famous for being known in the summer as Surf City, U.S.A.. I ate at the Long Board Restaurant and Pub and watched the girls of the West Coast as they walked around in their skimpy bikinis.

The best part of all was the four days I spent at Disneyland Adventure Theme Park. Even at my age, I had a great time hanging out with Mickey Mouse and his friends.

After seeing everything I wanted to see, I flew back to Michigan. It was then that I received the call from Andy, and was told that I better hurry.

My grandfather was dying....

Chapter Thirty-One
The Hit

Pulling into the driveway of my grandfather's home, I knew right away that his condition was bad. There were to many cars here, which told me that the end was near. Parking my car behind my mothers red Pontiac, I ran inside hoping that I wasn't too late to say goodbye. It was Andy who met me at the door.

"How bad is it?" I asked already knowing the answer by the look in his eyes.

"We're losing him, hurry, David," Andy explained as he placed his hand gently on my shoulder.

Walking through the kitchen and into the dinning room I saw my mother, Uncle Jack, Aunt Mary, and several other family members. The looks on their faces caused my heart to sink deep into my chest. Walking into my grandfather's bedroom I saw his private nurse standing next to his bed.

Looking at my grandfather brought tears to my eyes as I sat down next to him on his bed. Reaching down, I gently picked up his hand. His eyes were glazed over with a foggy look to them, and he was having a hard time breathing.

"He can't see you, David, but he can hear you if you talk to him," the nurse explained.

"Isn't there anything that you can do?" I asked in a soft tone of voice.

"He's old, David, I don't know how he is able to hold on like he is. I think he is fighting until he knows that your grandmother is going to be all right. He won't leave until he knows that his wife is going to be okay. He loves her that much," she said as she stepped out of the room to give me some time alone with the man who I grew up to love as a father.

Putting my face close to his ear, I ran the fingers of my left hand through his hair as I held his right hand in mine.

"I'm here grandpa, its me, David. I'm here with you, your not alone, don't be afraid," I said gently into his ear. "I just saw grandma. She's okay, grandpa, don't worry. The doctor said she can come home tomorrow," I explained as he continued to struggle for each breath of air.

"I'll take care of Mamo, don't worry, Babo, everything will be okay. Don't fight, rest now. It's okay, Babo," I explained using the Armenian words for grandmother and grandfather.

"Please, Holy Father, don't let my grandfather suffer like this anymore. If your going to take him, then please, I beg you, take him to heaven with you now," I prayed out loud as tears filled my eyes and ran down both of my cheeks. "I love you, Babo, rest now, don't fight it, don't be afraid, I'm here with you," I explained as I gently squeezed his hand in mine.

As I said it, he took in a deep breath of air and let it out quickly. Then he took in another deep breath of air and let it out slowly. With that last breath of air, my grandfather left this life; he was gone.

* * * * * * *

Even though I knew for quite some time that my grandfather was dying, his death overwhelmed me. As promised, we brought my grandmother home from the hospital the day after my grandfather had died.

His funeral was massive, to the point that our local police officers had to block a number of intersections to allow the funeral precession to pass by going from the funeral home to the cemetery.

There were hundreds of cars lined up one after another, with license plates from all over the United States.

Family, friends, relatives all attended, coming to say goodbye to a kind and gentle man they had all grown to love.

To my surprise, the heads of most of the organized crime families, to include hit men, Judges, Politicians, Senators, Congressmen, and many more, all came to say their last goodbyes.

What touched me the most was when Carla, Kathy, Butch, Joe, Cookie, Bell, Mosier, Tom and my dearest friend Danny, all walked in together to pay their respects to a man they never knew. It was their friendship to me that brought them here on the saddest day of my life.

After the funeral services were over, everyone began to leave the cemetery to head to the Stien House Restaurant. We had booked the entire restaurant for all of our family and friends to gather for a traditional farewell meal. It was here at the cemetery that I found myself sitting all alone next to the freshly dug grave of my grandfather.

I felt so numb and empty inside that I didn't hear the two men who had walked up to me, until they both sat down on the lawn next to me.

With my eyes filled with sadness I looked to my left, and then to my right, and saw Butch and Danny sitting at my sides. No words were said; none were needed. My two brothers were at my sides again. That alone said it all.

Almost an hour had passed on this beautiful October afternoon, when I finally came to terms with the grief I felt over the loss of my grandfather. Andy and Don had now returned to the cemetery. Walking up to us, they sat down and introduced themselves to Butch and Chopper.

"Out of all of the people I've killed and watched die, I've never felt this kind of sadness before," I explained as I looked over at my closest friends.

"I heard what the nurse told you about your grandfather not wanting to leave until he knew that your grandmother was alright. But I really think that he was fighting to hold on until you got there," Don explained as he took a sip out of his bottle of beer.

"I don't know why," I replied sadly.

"You're the one who gave him the peace of mind to let go and move on to the next plain of existence. As soon as you said that prayer, he relaxed and left. He wasn't afraid of the unknown anymore. You shouldn't feel sad, David, you should feel good that you were the one who was there with him at the very end," Andy explained with a sad comforting smile.

"I guess so," I said as I looked over at Danny and smiled half-heartedly.

"You okay, little brother?" Danny asked as he put his arm around my shoulders and gave me a brotherly hug.

"Yeah, I'm gonna be alright. Its good to see you again, big brother," I replied.

"We came as soon as we heard. Carla called all of us to let us know," Butch explained.

I figured you guys would all be at the Stien House eating and getting drunk," I said as I started to feel a little better inside.

"One goes, we all go. Brothers and friends throughout life and into death, till the very end, remember?" Danny asked with a serious pride filled look.

"Yeah, if you're not there, neither are we," Butch added as he gave me a brotherly pat on the back.

"Boy, I miss you guys. I think I could eat something. I haven't eaten for three days," I explained.

"Well then we better get going, I hear the food is fantastic. Carla and the rest of the gang are stuffing their faces," Danny explained as we all stood up and headed to our cars.

"I've got a big house, fellas. What do you say we grab the rest of the guys and you all camp out at my place for a few days," I suggested hoping that they would say yes.

"Sounds good to me," Butch answered quickly.

"Hell yeah, I'm in. We've got a lot to catch up on," Danny added.

"You guys ever had any of my dog meat chili?" Andy asked jokingly with a straight face.

"Dog meat chili? Hell no," Danny answered. "Hell, chili ain't chili unless you use one hundred percent rat meat, with a lot of chili beans."

"Rat meat, what are you nuts?" Don asked with a disgusted look on his face.

"So, it's been said," Danny replied as he looked over at me and winked.

"Oh boy, this is gonna be an interesting week," I thought to myself as we got into our car's and headed to the Stien House to meet up with our friends.

After leaving the Stien House, Carla and Kathy headed back to the Pentagon to attend to some Agency business. Cookie, Danny, Butch, Joe, Tom, Bell, and Mosier all agreed to come back to my place to spend a few days. This would give us time to talk about our plans for the future, and what we were now all doing with Carla at the Agency.

Pulling into my driveway, I was met with a pleasant surprise. Ben had flown to Dublin and brought Kate back to Michigan.

Seeing Kate made everything seem alright again. Now our black operations 'Team One' was complete. The original team with our special adopted nurse was back together once again.

We spent the next five days together, eating, drinking, laughing, and telling Danny about the details of our rescue mission into Hanoi to save his life.

Danny asked me if I would show him the stungun I had used to shock him with, not once but twice. I, being smart enough not to let him get his hands on it while I was in the same room with him, told him that I didn't know where I had put it, nor was I going to give him the combination of my safe so he could get it.

It was here in my home, in the company of my brothers, that I officially proposed to Kate and asked her if she would marry me. Even though I had already asked her once by her wishing pond, I felt that it was only proper to do it once again now that we were all together as a family.

Handing Kate her diamond ring, she cried as I put the engagement ring on her finger and then said "yes."

It was Thursday afternoon when Kate and I flew all of the fella's back home in my Learjet.

Our last stop took us to New Orleans. Danny wanted his mother to be able to meet Kate. Even though I had given Danny's mother the money, she kept her home just as it was.

"The memories," she explained, "are something that I don't want to let go of. This is my home where I raised my two sons. This is where I will one day slip away to meet the Lord."

We spent several hours with Danny and his mother; and then Kate and I flew back to my home in Michigan so Kate could meet my grandmother and family.

We spent all day Friday with my grandmother. As my grandfather had told me, my grandmother loved Kate. They got along with each other as if they had known each other all their lives.

It was almost six o'clock in the evening when I got the call from our family attorney Anthony Andolini.

"Hello," I said as I answered the telephone at my grandmother's home.

"David?"

"Yes, Anthony, is that you?" I asked as I looked across our dinning room and into our Sun porch. My grandmother was showing Kate all of our family album pictures. They were both smiling and having a nice time together.

"Yeah, its me. Listen I didn't want to say anything earlier with your grandfather passing away and the funeral and all," Anthony began to explain.

"What's wrong, Anthony?" I questioned.

"Frank White is dead."

"What?" I responded with a shocked tone of voice. Stepping down the hallway so my grandmother and Kate couldn't hear my conversation I asked, "What happened?"

"Remember I told you that the cop's from that one New York Irish precinct had it out for him?"

"Yeah, I remember," I responded.

"Well last week the cop's gunned down Deon, Frank's number one man and best friend. Deon took out a couple of the cops before they were actually able to kill him. Well, during the funeral for one of the cops, Frank and his driver pull up and, right in front of two hundred fucking cops, Frank blows away that red headed son-of-a-bitch cop that started the hole thing between them."

"What? Frank blew away a cop during a cop's funeral? When the place is crawling with law enforcement officers?" I questioned with a surprised tone of voice.

"Called him up to the back window of his limo and emptied both barrels of a twelve gauge shotgun into his face at point blank range. Then Frank rolled up the window and they drove away.

"They got away?" I asked.

"Oh yeah, the other cops were in such shock at what had just happened, that Frank and his driver drove away without a scratch or a shot being fired at them.

Well, this afternoon Frank ran into 'em and they shot it out in the street at noon right in front of God and everyone else.

Frank was able to jump into the back of a taxicab, but the cab driver got scared and jumped out of the car. Frank died a few minutes later in the back of the cab. He had been shot and bled to death. I thought you should know. Your Uncle Paul called to fill me in. Frank died but he took a bunch of them with him," Anthony explained sadly.

"Damn, I liked Frank. This isn't going to cause any problems for Paul and the five New York families is it?" I asked knowing how some cops can be.

"No not at all. One of your Uncle Paul's long time friends died almost two weeks ago. I don't know if you knew him or not. He was a big time doctor out of Beverly Hills California. The guys name was Saul Rosenberg, I met him a few times. He seemed like a pretty good fella for a rich snob type," Anthony said jokingly.

"No, I never heard of him. Was it foul play or a natural death?" I asked anxiously.

"The guy had a massive brain hemorrhage while he was asleep and in bed with his wife. The medical examiner's autopsy report listed the cause of death as a stroke. Hell from what Paul was telling me, his friend Saul wasn't that old, early fifties. It's to bad, but it happens. At least he died in his sleep. Paul asked me to let you know about Saul's death. I figured you knew him," Anthony explained as both Andy and Don walked up to me to see if everything was all right.

"No, my grandfather probably knew him though. That's probably why Paul wanted me to know," I explained.

"How are you doing? Are you alright?" Anthony asked with concern for my well-being.

"Yeah I'm okay. It hit me harder than I thought it would. Some of my friends from Vietnam came to the funeral and then spent a few days with me at my place. That helped me out a lot. I'm alright though, thank you for asking," I explained.

"Hey, I watched you grow up. Remember, I'm here if you should need me. Even if you just need someone to talk to. Don't hesitate to call," Anthony explained.

"Thank you, I'll call if I need you. How are you, Anthony, do you need anything?"

"Me? No, David, I'm fine. Your grandfather took very good care of me in his Will. I'm set for the rest of my life. Hey, before I forget, did you get a chance to go and see your new yacht?"

"Yeah, I took Katie with me. Christ, it's huge. It's a beautiful boat. I met Barbara. I wasn't expecting to find a female captain on board," I explained with a little humor in my tone of voice.

"Don't be fooled by her age or her looks. She made her 'bones' with the family by blowing away a Miami businessman. She's a 'made woman.' If anything should ever happen, you can trust her one hundred percent, David. Don't ever forget that," Anthony explained.

"I didn't know that, thanks for telling me," I replied surprised at what I had just been told.

"Listen, tell your grandmother I called and that I'll stop by in a few days to see her. I gotta go, David, I'll see you later. Remember, call me if you need anything."

"I will, Anthony. Thanks for calling."

"Alright, I'll see you later," Anthony said as we both hung up our telephones.

"Frank's dead," I explained as I looked over at Andy with a sad expression on my face.

"Cops?" Andy asked.

"Yup, he took a bunch of them with him though," I explained as we walked into the kitchen to get something to drink.

I spent the next hour talking to Don and Andy about family business.

Don was going to head back to his home, which was only one block away from my grandfathers home. Andy was going to spend the weekend with his mother at her home. They loved to sit up and watch late night movies together. Andy's mother's name was Elsie. She was a no-nonsense sweet heart of a lady who loved her son with all of her heart and soul.

It was almost 8:30 p.m. when Kate and I said goodbye to my grandmother and headed back to my place for some much needed sleep.

I had been awake to long as usual, and to make matters worse, the jet lag from flying to Washington D.C. then to New Orleans and back to Michigan, was really starting to catch up with me.

It was almost midnight by the time Kate and I finally climbed into bed to get some sleep. We were both totally exhausted. Tonight, being together with each other, we would hopefully be able to get some much needed sleep.

* * * * * * *

Hearing the telephone ring startled me awake. Groggy and still half asleep, I looked at the clock on my nightstand as I picked up the telephone and place it to my ear.

"What?" I said in an angry tone of voice. It was 2:00 a.m. and I had finally fallen asleep just to be startled awake again by my telephone.

"David, Andy's been shot," the female voice said frantically in a fast and emotional tone of voice.

"What?" I shouted back as I jumped up out of bed and began to pull my pants on.

"Andy's been shot. He's hurt real bad! Oh my God, David. He's in his car. It's off in the ditch. The first road after you pass over the I-75 freeway of M-15. Please, David, hurry, I'm calling an ambulance, hurry," she pleaded as she hung up the telephone.

Pulling on my boots, I grabbed the keys to our Lincoln Continental Mark Five.

"David, what's wrong?" Kate asked as all of my comotion woke her up.

Grabbing my briefcase out of my closet, I yelled back to Kate as I ran out of the bedroom and down the hallway of my home. "Andy's been shot, call Don now! Tell him M-15 across I-75, the first gravel road to the left. Bring help now!"

"What? David, no!" she shouted back as I ran out of my home and climbed into my bulletproof silver Mark Five. Starting it up I floored it as a wave of total fear rushed through me.

Andy was a very close friend to me. He was my brother, and the thought of him being hurt enraged me deep inside.

Lucky for me I had grown up in this area and wasn't far away from the area where the girl told me Andy was laying injured.

I was now on Dixie Highway heading into Clarkston Township, where I had grown up as a child. Speeding past the Palace Restaurant, I saw three Oakland County Sheriff's patrol cars parked in the parking lot. They were eating their supper. Within another minute I had sped past Maybe Road and was turning onto M-15 where it forks off of Dixie Highway where my friend Mike Roy owns the Roy Brother's Gas Station. Flooring it, the big 428-horse power engine pressed my upper body back into the drivers seat as I sped forward heading toward the town of Clarkston. We had taken both of our new bulletproof Lincoln Continental out of the airplane hanger where we kept them stored. We used them for my grandfather's funeral.

Andy was going to meet Kate and I at the Pontiac Airport on Monday. He was going to fly along with us when I took Kate back home to Dublin.

"Oh please don't be dead. Hang on, Andy I'm coming, help's on the way, brother," I said out loud to myself as I reached over next to me and flicked open the latches on my briefcase.

Pulling out my Mack-10 machine gun, I quickly slapped a fully loaded 60-round clip into the feed position of the deadly weapon. Looking down at my speedometer, I was moving at an even one hundred miles an hour as I shot through the small town of Clarkston heading toward the spot where M-15 crosses over the top of the I-75 Freeway. Crossing over I-75 I saw the gravel road ahead on my left. I knew this area well. It was heavily wooded and some of the above middle class families had started to build beautiful homes out here. The homes were not close to each other, which allowed for a lot of beauty and privacy at the same time.

Turning the steering wheel fast and hard to the left I slammed on the power brakes at the same time. This caused the large heavy Lincoln to power slide to the left. My timing was perfect. I was in a straight line with the gravel road as I pushed the gas peddle to the floor once again. Tires squealed on the asphalt and then hit the loose gravel road. As the Lincoln gained speed, all that I could hear was the four barrel carburetor sucking air into its system and the rattling of loose gravel as my car tires spun it upward off of the road and bounced it around into the metal fender wells of my vehicle.

"Oh, man," I said as I could see the red taillights of Andy's car off in the distance ahead of me. My heart raced as I tried to clear my thoughts and focus my thinking.

I was on a full adrenaline surge of rage, anger, and excitement as it all hit me at the same time.

Drawing closer in the darkness, I had forest on both sides of me as I passed quickly by several of the beautiful homes that sat back and away from the gravel street.

Andy's car was facing nose first into the ditch that ran along the side of the road.

It was then, in the darkness of this wooded area of Clarkston, Michigan, that reality set in as I slowly began to wake completely up.

"Andy? Andy is at his mothers house," I said to myself, as everything seemed to go into slow motion.

"David, no!" Kate had yelled. I thought that she had yelled 'no' out of worry for Andy, but it wasn't. She was yelling 'no' to stop me from running out of the house knowing that I was still half asleep.

"Oh shit, I've been set up," I said as I looked at my speedometer and then out through the front windshield of my car.

I was traveling at close to seventy-miles an hour, on loose gravel, as I switched my headlights to high beams.

It was too late; there were two of them, one on each side of the small gravel road. Everything seemed to be running in slow motion as they both stepped out from behind the trees. Raising their 12-gauge, High Standard riot shotguns, they pointed them right at me and opened fire! It was a combination of deer slugs and double 00-buckshot that hit the thick bulletproof windshield right in front of my face.

Flames jumped out of the end of their shotgun barrels almost three feet in the darkness of the night. Then, the bulletproof window broke loose from the window frame of the car and fell inward onto the steering wheel and dashboard of my car.

"Shit!" I yelled out as I spun the steering wheel hard to the right, held on to it, and laid down on the leather front seat to my right. The slugs and 00-buckshot sounded like angry hornets as they entered the open hole where my windshield used to be. The big Lincoln Continental slid sideways across the loose gravel road and then slammed its left driver's side of the car into the tail end of the car that was nosed into the ditch. As it did, I reacted quickly. Turning off the ignition to the car, the engine went dead as I turned off the headlights at the same time.

"Oh shit, mother fucker," I whispered as I slid my body down off of the front seat and onto the floorboard. Pressing my body lengthwise up under the dashboard I flipped the safety switch off on my Mack-10.

"If they throw a grenade into the car through the open hole of the front window, I'm dead. Awe shit! What's wrong with you, David? Grandpa warned you that within a week from the time of his funeral, they would try to kill you. He told you not to forget, and you did," I said to myself as my mind raced trying to figure out what to do next.

Everything was still. It was so quiet that it was almost spooky. Then I heard footsteps as the leather soles of their shoes crunched on the loose gravel beneath their feet. They were walking toward my car.

"Come on, Frank, let's get the hell out of here, he's dead," the first voice said as I tightened the grip on my machine gun.

"The old man said to make sure that we put two in his head," the second voice replied.

Far off in the distance, I could hear police sirens.

"I hit him twice in the head with slugs for Gods sake, I'm telling you, he's fucking dead! Come on, lets get out of here."

"Old man Tortelli said that this guy is dangerous and that we better not fuck up or he'll kill us. I gotta put two in his head I'm telling ya."

"Your gonna shoot a dead man in the head after I blew his head off with a shotgun? I'm telling you he's dead. Somebody's coming Frank, lets go now!" the first man said as I heard him run down the gravel road away from my car.

I could hear more cars coming now.

"Ah shit, he's dead," Frank said, as he took off running in the same direction as his friend did.

I could hear the car doors open, then close. Then the engine started and they sped away in the opposite direction, spraying gravel all over as they did.

"Old man Tortelli, huh? Son of a bitch, my grandfather was right. He had told me to watch Florida. That's where the majority of the drugs were coming in through. Your hit men blew it, Gino. Now I know that you ordered the hit," I said to myself in a whisper as I heard a number of cars come to a stop on the gravel road behind my car.

I wasn't about to look up until I knew for sure who was out there. 'Always expect the unexpected.' I had forgotten the golden rule and it almost got me killed.

Hearing the car doors open I heard people run up behind my car.

"Wait! Freeze, don't go up there," it sounded like Andy's voice, but I wasn't sure because of the thick body of the car and my position in it.

"David's in there! Oh, man, no," the next voice said.

"David, don't shoot, little brother. If you do you'll never be able to eat any of my dog meat chili again," Andy shouted out loud letting me know it was him.

"Andy?" I shouted back.

"Come on, boy, the cops are right behind us, lets go!" Andy shouted back.

Climbing out from under the dash, I opened the passenger's side door of my car, grabbed my briefcase, and climbed out.

There were six cars with Andy and Don. Each car had four of my grandfathers most trusted men in it. All of whom were heavily armed.

Handing Don my briefcase I looked over at Andy who had just walked up to me.

"You okay?" he asked with a concerned look on his face.

"Yeah, I'm fine."

"You sure you're alright?" he asked again.

"Yeah, I'm alright," I replied.

Just as I did, Andy punched me as hard as he could in the left side of my jaw! I flew backwards about six feet and bounced off the trunk of my car. Shaking my head from side to side, I tried to refocus my thoughts.

"Shit, you fucking asshole!" I stuttered as Andy and Don grabbed me by my arms.

"That's so you remember not to be so stupid the next time," Andy explained as we ran to our cars and drove off. The sheriff's deputies had just pulled off of M-15 and onto the gravel road. The neighbor must have reported hearing gunshots. Because they were at the Palace Restaurant eating, it gave us the extra few seconds we needed to get away.

"Where to?" Andy asked with an angry look on his face.

"Pontiac Airport, we're going to the mattresses. Let's get everybody to the yacht. I need sometime to figure out how I want to deal with this."

Going to the mattresses was an old Mafia term used when a war was about to break out between the families. What it meant is that you go to your safe houses. Someplace that no one other than your closest men, your inner circle, knows about. From there you send out your soldiers, your hit men to systematically kill off your enemies.

I had forgotten about Kate. She was home all alone.

"Shit, Kate's by herself, get me back to my house now!" I said as concern for her safety raced through my mind.

"Kate called us, that's how we knew where to find you. I've got six of our men there with her now. Don't worry about Kate, David; everyone knows that she is an innocent non-family member. They won't touch her, if they did the families, and I mean all of the families, would turn against whoever was behind the attack on her life.

The boys are taking Kate to the Detroit Metropolitan Airport. Don't worry; she'll get home safely. Do you have any idea who's behind this attempt on your life?" Andy asked knowing that all hell was about to break loose.

"Yes I do, its old man Tortelli out of Miami. I heard one of the shooters telling his partner that old man Tortelli said to make sure that they put two in my head," I explained as we made our way to the Pontiac Airport hangers where our planes were kept.

"It's a good thing you were driving the bulletproof Lincoln. If you would have been in one of your other cars, we would be burying you next to your grandfather," Don said as he looked over at me from behind the steering wheel of the car.

"Bulletproof my ass, the fucking windshield came out of the damn window frame of the car. As soon as this is all said and done, I'm going to deal with those assholes in California who ship us our cars. Mother fuckers," I said angrily as I placed two drops of Methadrine under my tongue.

"Call Anthony as soon as we get to the airport. Tell him to report the car stolen. Then I need him to meet us at the yacht as quickly as he can. Let him know what happened," I explained as the liquid speed kicked in and I started to calm myself down.

"The God damned windshield blew out? That car cost your grandfather ten thousand dollars, and then another twenty five thousand to have that company in California make it bulletproof," Andy explained as he shook his head from side to side in disgust.

"We'll deal with them later, right now I have bigger problems," I explained.

"I'll call Paul and Sam as soon as we get to the hanger. They'll want to know about this so they can retaliate against Tortelli," Don said as we turned off of M-59 and onto Airport Road in Pontiac.

"No, don't call anyone. I want Anthony to use our contacts in the newspapers to run an obituary notice on me. I want it to say that I was killed tonight in a car accident. Just call Barbara and tell her what happened. Tell her to get her crew together. I want to be out at sea as quickly as possible. We'll need to let my grandmother know that I'm alright. I don't want her to worry. She's been through enough already. I'm not going to fight back the traditional way. I'm going to make sure that all of the families fear me. I've got an idea, but I'm going to need you guys to help me pull it off. I'm not taking this personal; it is business, nothing more. I'm going to show Tortelli what a good businessman I am," I explained as we pulled into the Pontiac Airport.

* * * * * * *

We reached Amelia Island and boarded our yacht by 9:00 a.m. Sunday morning. There were twelve of my best triggermen with me to include Anthony, Andy, Don, and our Captain Barbara and her crew. Barbara had cut her work crew down to herself and eight other staff workers. My 163-foot yacht had a total of twenty-five people on board, which left us plenty of room to move around the huge ship freely.

By ten o'clock we had left port and were past the 12-mile international waters zone. It was time to put our heads together. Time to plan out a death hit on the head of the Miami crime family, one Gino Tortelli.

Gino was the elder of the family. He was a sixty-two year old full-blooded Italian with three sons. Bela was the oldest, followed by Vincent, and then their younger brother Joseph, all of whom were made men in the world of organized crime.

Bela Tortelli was 38-years old, Vincent was 36, and Joseph, the youngest of his sons, was 30. This caused a problem, which was one that concerned Anthony deeply.

"We hit the old man and all three of his son's will seek revenge against you, David. They won't give a damn what the Commission or the other heads of the families have to say about it. It won't be business to them. They'll take it personal," Anthony explained as we sat around my beautiful mahogany-topped bar pouring ourselves a cold drink.

"Bullshit! I say that we kill the whole fucking family; Gino, his son's, his wife, his dog, cat, and gold fish," Andy snapped back.

"You know better than that, Andy," I said as I began to laugh at how angry he still was.

"Fuck that, David, they tried to kill you for God's sake," Andy answered angrily.

"It was business, Andy, it wasn't personal, so don't take it personal," I explained calmly as I opened a bottle of cold Pepsi and looked at my wartime consigliore.

"You're the head of our family now, David. We take it very personal when someone tries to whack you," one of my hit men explained as he stepped up to the bar and looked me straight in the eye.

"I appreciate that, Ron, but don't lose your focus on this whole ordeal," I answered as I winked at him in an effort to ease the tension building in the room.

"Your taking this awfully calm, David," Don added as he took a sip of his beer.

"Anger clouds your thinking my friend and right now we all need to think clearly. Besides that, it was a great plan on Gino's part," I explained as I took a sip of my drink.

"How's that boss?" Kyle asked with a curious look on his face.

"He thought it out. He must of had some type of a personal data package on me. His hit men, the one that answered to the name Frank, told his partner that Gino said I was extremely dangerous. How would he know that? He also told them that if they fucked up the hit, I'd kill them," I said pausing for a moment to think back to what Frank had said. "Or maybe he meant that he would kill 'em if they botched the hit on me. We might be able to use that to our advantage. Anyway, he had a girl call and used Andy as the bait to lour me out fast before I had a chance to wake up and think it out with a clear mind. They got me to drive myself out into a dark wooded area without any bodyguards. It was a great plan, I gotta give him that. Had I not been in the Lincoln I'd be dead right now. By the time it dawned on me I had been set up, it was too late. His boys had already hit the windshield of my car, right in my face with three shots each. I gotta hand it to him, he had me. I'm alive because I had grabbed the wrong set of keys to the right car," I said as I raised my bottle of Pepsi in a toasting gesture. "Thank you, dear Lord, you saved my life," I added as I took another drink of my soda.

"Okay, we all agree that we got lucky last night. The question now is, how do we respond to this?" Anthony explained as several of our galley crew began to bring in our lunch.

* * * * * * *

We bypassed Freeport and went to the Island of Nassau. We docked there and began to make calls to our people back in the States.

From the information our family members were giving us, our plan was working. Anthony made all the appropriate calls as soon as we had left for Florida. The families had all been notified that I had been killed in a car accident late Saturday night. It came as no surprise to hear that Gino

Tortelli had asked the Commission to put together a meeting of the heads of all the families to discuss who would take over the seat as 'Godfather.'

Everyone agreed, however, the meeting would not take place right away. Uncle Paul recommended that they wait and meet in three weeks. This would give everyone time to prepare for what was sure to be a heated meeting as everyone jockeyed for position in the ranks of organized crime.

* * * * * * *

A week had passed when we received information that all three of the Tortelli brothers had flown to the Bahama Island of Freeport for a vacation.

This was the first time all three of the sons had been together at one time. Our plan was working, we had put them to sleep, so to speak. They had no reason to be worried about anything. They were celebrating and enjoying life to its fullest.

What they didn't know was that death was watching them. The Sandman was mounting his pale horse and preparing to gather their souls.

* * * * * * *

"What did you find out, Andy?" I asked anxiously.

"All three of Gino's boys are in Freeport. They're spending a lot of time at a small casino there called, 'The Joker's Wild.' Their pilot is scheduled to fly them back to Miami in five days. Their flight schedule has them landing in Miami at noon Saturday," Andy explained as he and Kyle walked up to the bar to grab a cold drink.

I had sent Andy and Kyle to Freeport to confirm that our information was correct about the Tortelli brothers being on the island. They had flown to the island in the small Bell helicopter that sat on the helipad of my yacht.

"Alright, I want to hit all three of the sons as they get off of their father's Learjet in Miami. I want to coordinate this hit so that I have Gino on the telephone just as his boys are getting gunned down. Can we make this work?" I asked as I looked around at my grandfather's most trusted people.

"Why don't we just hit 'em here in Freeport?" Ron asked as he looked over at Kyle and Andy, who had spent the day watching the Tortelli brothers.

"Bad idea, they don't stay together. When they all do get together in one spot, they have broads with 'em," Kyle explained.

"Yeah, we wouldn't want to hit an innocent person by mistake. That could cause a lot of trouble for the families," Don added.

"It would be a lot easier at Miami International. I've got a cousin who is the head supervisor over baggage handling. He's in charge of loading and unloading all of the passenger's baggage on the planes," Niki said with a smile. Niki was one of the two female hit women who were with us on this family outing. She was a 24-year old hit woman who joined our family at the age of fifteen after her mother died of cancer and she had no where else to go. She stood five-foot, one-inch, had long waist length brown hair, and big brown eyes. She made her bones with the family at the age of sixteen after Andy had taught her all the tricks of the trade.

My grandfather had put her through high school and taken care of her. She was free to leave at anytime, but loved what she did; and loved being with our family so much, she decided to stay with us rather than go on to college. Her young looks helped her to get close to most men, making them think they were about to score a young high school cheerleader. Instead, they found themselves dying at the hands of a very beautiful and very deadly young hit woman.

"Are you sure that your cousin will turn his back and let us use his uniforms and equipment, Niki?" Anthony asked.

"Absolutely, I can get us in and out of the airport," Niki responded.

"Alright then, we have four days to get in place," Anthony explained.

"What about Gino?" Don asked as he took a drink of his cold beer.

"We don't touch Gino. We kill all three of his sons. Then we let him live with the guilt, knowing that they died because of him. That kind of guilt will eat him alive like a cancer, plus he has a bad heart. Once he finds out that I'm alive, he'll kill both of his shooters, Frank and whoever that other guy was. I want them dead, and I'm going to use Gino to kill them," I explained as I took a bite out of some cold shrimp.

"I got an idea boss, you want to hear it?" Niki asked with raised eyebrows and a smile on her face.

"Absolutely, I've got one too. Let's see if we're thinking a like," I answered as I pushed my plate of fresh cold shrimp aside and reached into my pocket for my tiny vial of liquid Methadrine.

* * * * * * *

By Friday we were back in Florida and in place. Just as Niki had said, her cousin had given her two of the Miami International Airport baggage handlers blue coveralls. He had also made sure that a luggage train – a motorized vehicle that pulls the flat luggage carts loaded with passenger's luggage to and from the large commercial aircraft – was also available for our use.

We were now set. All we had to do was wait until noon tomorrow, and hope that everything went according to our plans.

It was a beautiful sun shiny Florida day as I looked at my watch and placed two drops of Methadrine under my tongue.

Andy was on one of our telephones talking to Ron who was at the international airport.

Ron was on a pay phone located next to a large set of windows, which looked out onto the docking area for some of the commercial and private flights. Niki's cousin had let her look at the private sector flight computer, which told us the spot Ron was looking at was the exact spot the Tortelli's Learjet would pull up to once it landed. It would be at that spot where the Tortelli brothers would get off of their plane and enter the airport terminal.

It was also at that same spot where two of my best shooters would drive by in a fully loaded luggage train and gun down all three of the brothers. We were going to use two silenced Mack-10 machine guns. The .9mm ammunition would tear them to shreds and the sounds of the large commercial airline jet engines would help drown out any sounds of gunshots should the Tortelli brothers happen to get lucky enough to get a shot off with one of their own handguns.

The odds of them actually carrying any weapons with them on vacation were slim. However, I had to remember one of the golden rules. 'Always expect the unexpected.' It was better to play it safe now, rather than be sorry that we didn't later.

I had six other shooters in the large airport. They were all standing in strategic spots. If airport security, or any plain clothed law enforcement officer should happen to see what was going on and pursue my two shooters, my other hit men would take them out. Everyone comes home except the Tortelli's on this one. I live by a set of codes. My people are never expendable. We are all family. Each member of my family is always protected, no matter what the cost. Money meant nothing to me; it was only a tool we used to acquire the things we want in our life times. Our people, however, are priceless to me. I can replace money. I can't replace my family if I should happen to lose one of them.

They all know my feelings on this issue and it makes for a strong bond of loyalty within our inner circle and throughout our entire family.

My attorney, Anthony Andolini was sitting next to our other telephone. He had called the Tortelli home on Wednesday and made arrangements to talk to Gino at twelve noon today. He had left a message telling the elder Tortelli he wanted the Florida family to take my family in and make it all part of the Miami crime family, now that my grandfather and I were both gone.

Gino Tortelli, a man of greed, knew that such a merger of the two powerful crime families would make him a very powerful man among the inner structure of the world of organized crime. He would be anxiously waiting for Anthony's call at noon today. They weren't expecting any problems. They had their guards down. This would turn out to be their fatal mistake.

"The plane just landed," Andy explained as he talked to Ron who was our eyes at the airport.

"Picking up the other telephone, Anthony dialed the number to Gino Tortelli's private home.

"Yes, is Mr. Gino Tortelli there please?" Anthony asked calmly.

"Ron said that the Tortelli Learjet is pulling into its 'off loading' spot," Andy explained as I listened intently to both of the conversations at the same time.

"Mr. Tortelli, how are you, sir, this is Anthony Andolini from Michigan."

"Their plane is at a full stop, engines are off," Andy whispered.

"Yes, sir, it is tragic losing both John and David. We were not expecting it," Anthony explained as he took a sip of his drink and winked at me.

"The side door is opening," Andy whispered with a devilish grin on his face.

"Yes, Gino, yes I understand," Anthony said into the phone.

"Steps are down," Andy said softly.

"Yes, sir, well that is why I called you. You never really know who to trust anymore. It's a dangerous business we are in," Anthony explained to Gino.

"Their stepping off the plane. Our shooters are in motion," Andy explained as he pointed at me.

"Hang on, Gino, I have someone who wishes to speak with you," Anthony explained as he handed me the telephone.

"Gino, how are you?" I said as my adrenaline began to surge through my entire body.

"I am fine, who is this?" Gino asked in a curious tone of voice.

"It's me, David, your Godfather. Tell your hit man Frank that he's a piss poor shot. Did you really think you could kill me, Gino?" I asked as I watched Andy.

"All three of the Tortelli boys are down. Our people are moving out of the area," Andy explained with a smile.

"David, is it really you? Oh this is such good news," Gino said in a panicked tone of voice.

"You tried to kill me, Gino, it's business. So, now I complete the family business you started. I have just killed all three of your son's, Joseph, Vincent, and Bela. This is the price you pay for your betrayal. They're dead because of you, Gino. 'Bah-fong-gue'," I explained, telling him to go fuck himself in Italian.

"No!!!!!" he screamed into the earpiece of the phone as I hung it up in its receiver.

"Talk to me, Andy," I said as my heart raced with excitement.

"Alright, Ron, get everyone back here as quickly as you can," Andy explained as he hung up the phone on our end.

"We're good, they're moving out through the airport. How did Gino take the news?" Andy asked with a broad smile as we shook hands.

Standing up, I hugged both Andy and Anthony. "He screamed 'no,' so loudly that I can't hear out of my left ear," I said smiling.

"As soon as everyone gets back here to the yacht, pay each of them twenty-five thousand, that includes Barbara. Then give Barbara three thousand for each of her work crew on board," I explained as I thought about Niki and Tracy, our two female shooters.

I had used both of the women on this hit to do the shooting. My logic was that if anything should happen to go wrong, once they took off the blue coveralls, no one would pay any attention to two young women. They would be searching for two men, while our girls walk right past them.

"Give Niki and Tracy both fifty thousand each. They earned it today.

Anthony, would you call Sam and Paul? Let them know I'm alive and tell them what happened and how we responded to it," I explained.

"You got it, I'll call them both right now. They can notify the rest of the families," Anthony explained as he poured himself another drink.

"What about Gino?" Andy asked with a look of concern on his face.

"Give him a week to bury his son's. Then have Uncle Paul set up a meeting between Gino and I out here on the boat. Tell Paul to guarantee Gino's safety. By then Gino will have killed both Frank and whoever was with him on the night they tried to kill me. We'll settle this business with him then," I explained as I stepped behind the bar of my yacht and opened up the refrigerator. Pulling out an ice cold Pepsi, I opened it up and took a sip.

"Now, what do I do with Gino?" I thought to myself as I sat back down in my leather chair and called my grandmother and Kate to let them both know I was alright.

* * * * * * *

It had been eight days since the hit went down on the Tortelli brothers.

We spent a few days partying on my yacht, then I sent everyone back home after paying them for a job well done. The only ones left on the yacht were Barbara, Don, Andy, and Mike, our helicopter pilot.

Arrangements had been made by Paul for Gino Tortelli to fly out to my yacht and meet with me to make the peace between us. Paul said that Gino was uneasy about meeting with me all alone. Then Uncle Paul asked him if he really thought it was a smart idea to insult me a second time? Standing behind my bar, I could hear our small Bell helicopter as it landed on the helipad at the back of our yacht. Andy and Don both went out to greet Gino and bring him in to meet me and make the peace between us. I could see right away by the way he looked as he walked in through the door, that the loss of his three son's had already taken a toll on him.

"Gino, thank you for coming," I said as I gave him a gesture with my left hand to have a seat in one of my soft leather chairs.

"Thank you for inviting me, Godfather. What do I say to you?" he asked as I stepped out from behind my bar, walked over, and sat down in the chair next to him. "There's nothing to say Gino. What's done is done. It's time to move forward and settle these issues between us," I explained as Andy handed both Gino and I a drink.

"All that I want to know, Gino, is why? Why would you want to kill me instead of talking things out like men?" I asked.

"All of the narcotics come through Miami. I know that you and your grandfather, 'rest his soul,' are against the drug business," he said as he nervously finished off his drink.

"Andy, get Gino another drink. Yes, it's true I hate the drug business. But my grandfather gave you his blessings. I would never go against that," I explained as Andy took Gino's empty glass from him and handed him another scotch on ice.

"Oh, mama, my boys are gone, what have I done?" he said remorsefully as he took another large drink from his glass. Without responding, I watched as the Chloral Hydrate mixed with the scotch began to take effect.

Looking at his half empty glass, Gino then looked up at me. Leaning forward, I took the glass from Gino's right hand before he dropped it on my carpet.

"But," he mumbled as his eyes rolled up into their sockets and he passed out from what's known as a 'Mickey Fin.'

Several hours passed before Gino woke up. We had taken off all of his clothes and placed his naked body into a metal wire cage known as a lobster trap.

At the right side of the metal cage we secured two scuba air tanks and ran the air hose in through one of the open square wire holes in the cage. We then placed the breathing apparatus into Gino's mouth and put the underwater goggles on over his eyes so that he would be able to see and breath while submerged under water.

I could see the look of total fear and panic on his face as he realized what was about to happen to him. The wire lobster trap cage fit snuggly around his body and gave him no way to fight or move once we had placed him inside it, and fastened it shut.

"Calm down, Gino, you have enough air in those tanks for one hour. I want you to stay down there, on the ocean floor and think about what you tried to do to me. In forty-five minutes we're going to pull you back up," I explained as Don and Andy grabbed the ends of the cage and set it into the water with Gino facing upwards toward the surface.

"Let him go," I said as Andy and Don let go of the wire cage.

Looking over the side of the boat I watched as Gino and his cage slowly disappeared from sight and vanished into the depths of the clear blue ocean of the Florida Keys.

"Andy, did you tie a line onto Gino's cage?" I asked calmly.

"Nope, I thought Don did," Andy replied as we continued to look over the side rail of my boat.

"Me? I thought you did?" Don explained calmly.

"Oops, see ya, Gino..." I said softly with a grin on my face.

Chapter Thirty-Two
Pay Back

I had just gotten back home from the hit on the Tortelli family. Walking up to the front door of my home, I saw the note someone had attached to the brass doorknocker. Opening it up I read it.

Dear Uncle David,

Where have you been? Are you okay? I miss you.

Love Tara

Tara was growing up and with all of the things that had taken place in my life lately, I had forgotten to call her.

"Oh boy," I sighed to myself as I unlocked the front door of my home and walked inside. Locking the door behind me I went upstairs to use the bathroom. Looking into my bathroom mirror I smiled. I hadn't noticed at the time, but I had gotten quite a suntan while I was in Florida.

"Cool," I said to myself as the telephone in my den began to ring.

"I really need to put extension phones upstairs," I thought to myself as I ran down the stairs and unlocked the security doors to my den. Sitting down at my desk I picked up the secure phone and checked to make sure that my black scrambler box was still on.

"Hello," I said calmly.

"Where in the hell have you been?" Kathy asked sternly.

"Florida, why?" I asked knowing that I couldn't lie to her about my location. Now that she had access clearance to the CIA War Room at the Pentagon. She could find out exactly where I was at by asking Sandy to locate me by satellite through the satellite chip in my shoulder.

"Why haven't you answered our page? What did you do, leave your pager at home?" she asked sarcastically.

"No, my pager is in my pocket," I answered as I reached into my left pants pocket and pulled out my satellite sky pager. Taking a look at the digital face of the pager I saw that it was blank. The battery had gone dead and I had forgotten to check on it.

"Oops, my battery went dead, sorry. I'll put a new one in it as soon as we're finished talking," I explained.

"Explain that to Carla, she has been trying to contact you".

"Yeah? What's up?" I asked.

"I don't know. She's been trying to contact you for several days. She's been at the hospital with someone. She seems real upset about something, but she won't tell us anything about whatever it is. All that she said was, find David; I need the Sandman.

Do me a favor and drop whatever it is that your doing and get to her office. I'll call her at the hospital and tell her we found you and you're on your way. Ben is already waiting for you at the Pontiac Airport," Kathy explained.

"Alright meet me there, I'm on my way," I replied as I hung up my telephone.

"What could possibly be so bad that Carla, with her heart of ice, could be upset?" I wondered as I got up and began to lock everything back up again.

* * * * * * *

It was almost midnight by the time I walked in through the front doors of the Pentagon. Showing my Q-clearance identification to the security guards, I quickly made my way to the elevators.

The Pentagon never sleeps. The men and women who work here are always on duty, protecting the American citizens and the country we love so very much. They do a tiresome job which no one ever thanks them for.

Walking into the Situation Room I went right into Carla's office and sat down. I could see right away that she was tired and that she had been doing a lot of crying.

"I'm sorry, mom, my pager went dead. I forgot to check the battery. What's wrong kiddo, talk to me. Whatever it is, we'll fix it," I explained as I sat, genuinely concerned for the woman who had become my very close and dear friend.

"How do you fix a ten year old little innocent girl who has been raped?" she asked as she threw her hands up in the air and began to cry once again.

I could feel the anger building up inside me as I reached into my shirt pocket and pulled out my tiny vial of liquid Methadrine. Placing two drops of the powerful speed under my tongue, I returned the tiny glass vial back to my shirt pocket and waited for her to regain control of herself.

"Her name is Neve. She is the daughter of one of our Joint Chiefs of Staff. Oh Jesus, why?"

Long pause... "It took a hundred and fourteen stitches to sew her vagina back together." Long paused as Carla blew her nose on a handkerchief.

"She's comatose, David. She's in complete shock. The doctors don't know if she will ever come out of the coma." Another long pause.... "Neve has severe head trauma from the beating she took from that vicious bastard." There was another long pause from Carla as she tried to regain her composer.

It took everything I had to control the rage building up inside me as I sat and waited for Carla to continue.

"David, Neve is my goddaughter. I'm her godmother, and I don't know how to help her? I feel so fucking helpless," Carla sobbed.

"Do you know who did it?" I asked coldly.

"Yes," Carla answered as she opened her top desk drawer and pulled out a manila envelope.

"He left fingerprints all over the place. His name is Istvan Bastick," Carla explained as I opened the envelope and pulled out his photographs.

"He's from Turkey? A fucking Turk, that figures," I said in a whisper of a voice. I was going to enjoy this; I hated Turks.

"His family is rich and powerful in his native country of Turkey. He owns a small restaurant in downtown San Jose. That's where he lives now. I don't want him dead, David. Death is to good for him. I want him to suffer. I want him to be in constant pain for the rest of his worthless fucking life. I don't want you to go, David," Carla explained as hate filled her eyes.

"What? This piece of shit rapes an innocent child and your telling me that I can't go after the cocksucker?" I snapped back angrily.

"No, you can't go. I need someone more sinister, more medieval in his way of thinking, someone that would scare the shit out of Satan himself. I need the Sandman to go...."

* * * * * * *

Taking Kathy and Ben with me, I filled them in on what the 26-year old Istvan Bastick, of Turkey, had done to little Neve.

Within the hour we had refueled the Agency's Learjet and were in flight to San Jose. Once there we rented a car and drove to the 'Grand Hotel Costa Rica' in downtown San Jose. Renting a room, using one of my fake identifications, Kathy and I spent the night at the hotel. It was almost 1:00 a.m. and there was little we could do until the sun came up in the morning. I asked Ben to stay with the plane to make sure no one tried to steal the tires off of it. That's right, you heard what I said. We were in San Jose, and in this part of the country everything is fair game, if you're a good enough thief.

* * * * * * *

It was 5:00 a.m. when I reached over and turned off our alarm clock. Kathy was still asleep and I didn't want the portable alarm to go off at 6:00

a.m. and wake her up. I already knew what I wanted to do to Istvan, so there was no reason to wake Kathy up this early in the morning.

She had been up along time and needed her sleep. I had a job for her to do, but it wouldn't be until after lunch.

Leaving our hotel room, I went downstairs to the lobby cafe of the hotel and ordered my breakfast. It was odd, because I actually felt hungry this morning. Usually I had no appetite when I was using the powerful liquid speed. But this morning I felt like eating steak and eggs with a lot of A-1 Steak Sauce and an ice cold Pepsi, which was exactly what I ordered.

I already knew that Istvan lived here at the Grand Hotel Costa Rica, but I didn't want to touch him here at the hotel. I was going to make this child molester scream so loud that his great, great, great, grandparents would wake up from their graves and beg me for mercy.

Istvan owned a small restaurant just down the street from the hotel. It was called, 'Turkish Delight' and served a combination of Turkish and American meals. The tourists who came here on vacation love it. I, on the other hand, was going to use his restaurant to cause him a lifetime of torment, suffering, agony, and pain.

I never left anyone alive, not ever. This was going to be a new experience for me. I just wasn't sure if I could do it without killing him. For those of you reading this book, I promise you that I'll try. It's just going to be really hard for me. It's not the Sandman's way of delivering death. But, it's going to be real, real close.

* * * * * * *

I was sitting in the hotel lobby waiting for Istvan to come down from his room.

Looking at my watch it was nine o'clock sharp as Kathy stepped off of the elevator, saw me, and walked over to where I was sitting.

"Asshole," she said rather loudly as she sat down next to me.

"Chill out, pretty lady, there's nothing going on right now anyway. Besides that, you needed some sleep," I explained as I watched the crowded lobby full of people moving about.

"Has the pervert come out yet?" Kathy asked as she slipped on her sunglasses.

"No, but he should be out any minute now. He opens his restaurant at 10:00 a.m. sharp. It's after nine now so he should be stepping off of that elevator any second now," I explained as I placed two drops of Methadrine under my tongue."

"Let me try some of that stuff, I need to wake up," Kathy asked as she reached her hand out wanting me to give her my vial of liquid Methadrine.

"Hell no! You'll get addicted to this shit and end up strung out on it just like me," I answered as I slipped the tiny glass vial back into my pants pocket.

"One drop isn't going to kill me," she responded.

"Forget it, grab a cup of coffee out of the cafe," I countered.

"There he is," she whispered softly.

Istvan had just stepped off of the elevator and was walking toward us. Walking past us he headed toward the front doors of the hotel, stepped outside, put on his sunglasses and turned to the left. He was on his way to his restaurant to open up for the day.

Istvan stood five-feet, ten-inches tall and had a muscular build. He had jet-black hair that he combed straight back, brown eyes and was clean-shaven.

"I wonder how many other kids he has raped?" Kathy asked bitterly.

"I don't know. Don't get me started, Kathy. It's taking everything I have inside of me to not walk into his restaurant and put six rounds in his fucking chest. Come on, lets go take a look around the area," I explained as we both stood up and walked outside.

* * * * * * *

We had spent most of the morning checking out the surrounding area, just in case anything should happen to go wrong and we needed to make a fast exit.

The Turkish Delight Restaurant opened its doors to its customers at 10:00 a.m. sharp, but didn't actually start serving food until 11:00 a.m. It was between 10:00 a.m. to 1:00 p.m. when the lunch crowd came in to eat. From 10:00 a.m. to 11:00 a.m. was coffee hour. It was at this time you could order a number of different blends of exotic Turkish coffees. Turkish coffee was served in small cups equivalent to an American shot class which we would serve our whiskey in at a bar. The very tiny Turkish coffee cups are made out of ceramic and are hand painted. The coffee itself is very thick and is extremely rich in flavor.

Between 1:00 p.m. and 4:00 p.m. you can still order food, but the second big rush of customers starts between 4:00 p.m. and ends around 7:00 p.m. The restaurant closes at 9:00 p.m. for the night.

Kathy and I had called Carla to confirm that we had located our target. The one thing for sure was that we were not going to waste any time on this assignment. Istvan had seriously hurt a child, and in doing so, he had hurt someone very close to me, Carla. This was going down tonight no matter what the consequences might be.

It was 6:30 p.m. when Kathy and I walked into the restaurant known as the Turkish Delight and sat down to order our evening meal.

Kathy ordered a meal that was made out of goat meat, cabbage, and rice. I ordered a hamburger with a double order of french fries.

Istvan walked around to each table and personally talked to each of his customers to make sure their meal was all right and they were enjoying themselves.

It was a smart way to do business. My grandparents and my Uncle Jack and Aunt Mary did the same thing at their restaurants. It made your customers feel welcome and like they were part of your family. It also made them enjoy themselves so much that they always came back again.

Smiling, Istvan walked over to our table to greet us.

"Hello, welcome to my restaurant. How is your food?" he asked politely.

"This is delicious, I have never had anything that tasted quite like this before," Kathy explained, fascinated by what she was eating.

"Oh, I am so happy that you like it. And how is your meal sir? Is everything alright with it?" he asked with a broad smile on his face.

"It's not bad, it would be kind of hard to screw up a hamburger and french fry meal, don't you think?" I asked with a grin.

"Anyone can cook a hamburger. You throw it on the grill, flip it over and its done. French fries are a completely different story. How are yours?" he asked.

"Crisp and hot, they're good," I answered.

"Would you like to know why they are crisp and still hot and not soggy and cold?" he asked.

"Yes, I would. Why is that?" I questioned as I dipped one of my fries into some A-1 Steak Sauce and took a bite out of it.

"I keep my deep fryers set at a much hotter temperature than any other restaurant does. As soon as the french fry touches the hot grease, it is immediately shocked on the outside. This keeps the grease from soaking into the potatoes as it cooks," Istvan explained proudly.

"Smart thinking. Is this the only restaurant you own?" I questioned.

"Yes for now it is. I would like to open one just like it in the United States somewhere in New York. There it would be Turkish and Mexican food. What do you think? Would people enjoy a restaurant like that?" he asked with a curious look.

"Are you kidding, they would love it. My wife and I just closed a deal on a restaurant in downtown Manhattan. We're traveling around the country now trying to decide what kind of food to serve. In New York people want food that is exotic and different. A restaurant like this would make millions in its first year. You wouldn't be interested in becoming partners with us would you?" I asked with a serious look on my face.

"Are you serious?" he asked.

"Absolutely. We have the building in a prime location. If we could use the Turkish Delight name and you taught our chef how to cook Turkish-Mexican food, we would be in business. How's a fifty-fifty split sound?" I asked smiling as I reached out to shake his hand.

"I am Istvan Bastick and yes I am interested. I think that we should talk," he answered with a smile as he shook my hand.

"How about after you close up tonight. This is a cozy restaurant, we could talk right here?" I asked as I looked over at Kathy who was nodding her head 'yes' in agreement, and then back over at Istvan.

"Tonight would be perfect, I have nothing to do. I close at nine. Is that to late for you?" he asked.

"Not at all, we'll stick around and wait for you to close up, then I'm going to talk you into becoming my business partner," I explained with a smile on my face.

The hook was set. The thought of a restaurant in downtown Manhattan and a fifty-fifty split of the profits had his mouth watering. Greed, it gets them every time.

* * * * * * *

I had sent Kathy back to our hotel room at 8:15 p.m. to pick up my stungun and my roll of heat duct tape. She took it out of my suitcase, put it into her purse, and was back at the restaurant by 8:35.

Saying goodnight to the last of his work crew, Istvan locked the front door to his restaurant and turned off the lights to his sign outside. Looking at my watch it was almost 10:00 p.m. when the young Turk turned and looked at Kathy and I.

"Another busy night," he said smiling. "I am sorry to have kept you both waiting for so long."

"It was worth it, the food here is excellent. I'm anxious to see how you have your kitchen set up to accommodate for two different types of cooking. The kitchen in our new restaurant is huge. It also has two large walk in coolers and two walk in freezers," Kathy explained.

"Really? This could work out well. We could use one cooler and one freezer for the Turkish food, and the other two for the Mexican food. Come, let me show you how I have my kitchen set up to handle two different styles of cooking," Istvan explained as Kathy and I got up to follow him into his kitchen.

I was real proud of Kathy; she had given us a reason to go into the back section of the restaurant. The restaurant faced the main street of downtown San Jose. It also had an all window front that allowed you to see out through the windows as the people outside walked by. Someone walking down the sidewalk would be able to see into the main section of the dining area, even this late at night. We were now heading into an area of the building where no one would be able to see or hear us.

Stepping through the wooden doors separating the main dinning area from the kitchen I wasted no time. As soon as we stepped through the doors and into the well-lit area of the kitchen I jammed the end of my stungun into the back of Istvan's neck and pulled the trigger. Counting to five I released the trigger as Istvan's body dropped to the hard tile floor beneath him.

"Well, that was quick," Kathy said with a surprised look on her face.

"Fuck this piece of shit. Just looking at him makes me sick to my stomach. Give me the duct tape," I said as I tucked the hand held stungun into my back pocket. Pulling off all of Istvan's clothes, I quickly taped his legs together at both the ankles and the knees. I then pulled his arms up over his head and taped his arms together at the elbows and wrists.

Walking through the kitchen I looked for the deep fryer. Finding it next to the large stove, I turned its switch back on.

Grabbing Istvan's body, I picked him up and laid him length wise out on to the stainless steel table next to the deep fryers.

It didn't take long for the grease that was already hot to begin to boil once again in the four large grease wells of the deep fryer system.

Istvan had just started to come to as I grabbed his arms at the elbows and stuck both of his hands into the hot boiling cooking oil.

"This is for the little girl you raped," I explained.

His screams were deafening but short, as he quickly passed out from the pain and shock that had now traumatized his body.

Pulling his arms upward I looked at what was once a perfectly good set of hands.

"Those are done," I said laughingly.

The smell of cooked flesh filled my nose as the boiling oil dripped off his charred hands. The skin had cooked, blistered, and melted all at the same time, within a matter of seconds.

His body quivered as I turned him around on the long stainless steel table.

Grabbing him by the knees I then dipped both of his legs, halfway up to his calf muscles, into the deep fryer. Holding them in the hot boiling oil for about three seconds was all it took. Istvan's body began to jerk wildly as the hot oil scorched, blistered, and cooked his feet and calf muscles in a violent outburst of cooking madness.

"Grab him," I yelled as I quickly pulled his feet out of the bubbling oil.

Grabbing Istvan by the waist and chest Kathy pressed down on his body in an effort to contain his convulsions.

"What's going on, why is his body doing this? He's out cold from the shock of being cooked alive," Kathy asked.

"It's a muscle reaction. It's his body's way of saying that it can't take anymore," I explained as I set Istvan's legs back down on the stainless steel table.

The smell of burnt human flesh was sickening. His body was calming back down now. Picking up a small saucepan I dipped it into the hot boiling oil, and turned off the deep fryer. Holding it above his crotch I poured a small amount of the boiling oil out of the saucepan and onto Istvan's penis, testicals, and lower stomach. As I did, his flesh began to pop and sizzle as the hot oil burned its way quickly through the skin and into the muscle below.

"Oh yeah, he'll never use that again," Kathy said as she began to laugh out loud.

Tossing the saucepan back into the hot oil of the deep fryer, I walked over to the cooks counter and picked up a small pearing knife. Lifting Istvan's eyelids, one at a time, I pressed the tip of the sharp knife into each of his eyeballs. When I did, his eyes hemorrhaged, causing a white liquid substance to ooze out as each eye turned a foggy white in color.

"Oh shit, the Sandman's here, isn't he?" Kathy asked as she looked up at my face and backed away from Istvan's body.

"No, he's not. You don't ever want to see the Sandman, Kathy, I told you that before," I explained as I tossed the small knife into the deep fryer.

"Call an ambulance, tell them that there's been a terrible accident here and that Istvan has been badly burned. Tell them that we need emergency assistance now. The telephone number is up there next to the telephone on the wall," I explained as I pointed at the list of emergency numbers next to the telephone.

Calling the emergency numbers for both the hospital and police, we wiped off the telephone to make sure that there was no fingerprints on it, and then quietly left the restaurant. Walking across the street, we waited and watched to see what would happen next.

It took about five minutes for the emergency medical team and police to arrive. They were inside the restaurant for quite awhile, working hard to stabilize Istvan's traumatized body.

When they brought him out on the stretcher he had IV tubes attached to his body. It was a good indication he was going to live, which surprised me. That kind of trauma should have stopped his heart from the shock and killed him. If he did survive, he would be in burn treatment therapy for years. He would never be able to see, or use his hands or feet again. As far as being able to pee, he would have to do that through a plastic tube.

The one thing for certain was Istvan Bastick would never rape or cause harm to anyone ever again.

* * * * * * *

We left San Jose the next day and flew back to check on Carla. A week later Carla called the hospital to check on Istvan's condition. He was listed as critical but the doctors believed that he would make it. At least what was left of him would anyway.

Sadly enough, little Neve remained in a coma.

Chapter Thirty-Three
Code Name: Perdition

It had been several weeks since Kathy and I had returned from San Jose and our mission to go after Istvan Bastick. I couldn't figure out how Istvan's body was able to take so much of the sever burning I had put it through. He should have gone into shock and died right away. To my surprise, I found out from Neil, that Istvan was an opium addict. He had been smoking it twice a day for the past five years. The very powerful opium narcotic is the only thing that numbed the pain of being deep fried enough to keep his body from going into a deep enough shock to stop his heart, and kill him.

We had moved on Istvan so fast no one had the time to prepare a data information package on him. But then again, I guess it didn't matter. In the end he paid the ultimate price for his sick perverted deeds.

It was Halloween and Tara, Jessy and the entire Girl Scout troop had gathered together and decided that I needed to have a Halloween haunted house party at my home. They spent the entire week redecorating my home for the event. Between Mrs. Carlson, Tara's mother Amy, Jessy's mother Dana, and my visa gold card, the house looked like something you would see in an old Bela Lugosi movie.

The girls dressed me up to look like count Dracula, Andy as a blood thirsty Indian, and Don as Frankenstein.

The party started at twelve o'clock noon only because they all wanted to eat at my place.

It was a beautiful early fall day, the sun was shinning, the music was playing and the barbecue grills were fully loaded with hot dogs, hamburgers, and hot spicy Italian sausages my Uncle Sam Giancana handmade just for the occasion. Of course I now had to go to Sam's home to learn the fine art of Italian sausage making and to help him re-supply the case of sausage he had just sent to us. For some reason, Sam wanted me to come to his home, and this was his way of getting me there. So I promised him I would come and let him teach me how to make Escarole after the party was over.

"You know your crazy for letting them trash your house like this," Amy said laughingly.

"My house loves it and you look absolutely gorgeous," I explained as I looked at Amy's black vampire outfit. The girls had broken with local vampire legend of long black flowing female gowns. They dressed Amy in a black silk blouse; tight black leather pants and black leather low cut heal shoes. To keep it in simple terms, Amy looked good enough to eat!

"Well thank you my dear," she said in a long drawn out sentence as she ran her long fingernails through my hair.

"Maybe we should go to my den and make some little vampires," I responded with a hiss as I bared my fake set of vampire fangs and bit Amy gently on the neck with them.

"Oh God, promise?" she replied with a giggle.

"Alright you two knock it off," Dana said as she handed me her glass for a refill of Hawaiian Punch. Standing behind my bar, I refilled Dana's glass as she sat down on one of my bar stools.

"This is so cool, David, thanks for letting the girls do this," Dana said smiling in her nurse outfit.

"You haven't seen anything yet, ladies, wait until it gets dark and I throw the dry ice into action. The whole floor of the house will look like its foggy from the floor to your knees," I explained smiling.

"Do the girls know about this?" Dana asked curiously.

"Nope, I've got a couple of fella's coming over around ten tonight with chainsaws. They took the chains out of them, but they'll be noisy and scary as hell. They're going to be dressed up like leather face from the Chainsaw Massacre movie," I explained with a grin.

"That's the movie you took all the girls to see at the Cinema Showcase Theater two days ago isn't it?" Dana asked surprised at the stunt I was about to pull on the girls.

"That's why I agreed to take them to see the movie. When my guys show up with their chainsaws running, we're going to have some fun. I've got a special added bonus surprise I'm going to add to it. I promise your gonna love the way this Halloween party ends," I explained as I raised my glass of Pepsi in a toasting manner.

"These girls are crazy, they just threw Don into the swimming pool. Give me a beer would you, brother?" Andy asked as I popped open the top of an ice cold long necked bottle of Budweiser and handed it to him.

"I thought you guys drained all the water out of the swimming pool for the winter?" Dana asked curiously.

"We did, there's no water in the pool," I replied as I took a sip of my drink and looked over at Andy.

"Oh my God, Jessy!" Dana shouted as she and Amy ran outside to check on Don's condition.

"Is Don okay?" I asked.

"He's a professional hit man. Don jumped up and climbed out of the pool and started chasing 'em. He loves this shit," Andy said laughingly.

* * * * * * *

Looking at my watch it was almost ten o'clock at night. I turned off all of the lights in the house and had candles burning. The girls all gathered in the basement to tell scary Halloween stories to each other about headless people with hooks instead of hands.

Sneaking into the back storage room in my basement, I pulled a bag of dry ice out of my deep freezer and poured the entire bag into the metal air conditioning duct system.

My heat and air conditioning vents were located at the carpet level of each room. This would allow the cold foggy sensation from the dry ice to filter it's way through the floor duct system and enter the rooms without anyone noticing it.

Pouring a pan of hot water on the dry ice it immediately began to hiss as I closed the lid to the duct system and turned on the small fan that would push it down the lines and into the rooms.

Leaving the storage room, I stepped back behind the bar and nodded at Andy.

Within a matter of a few minutes the fog began to roll in through the floor vents and cover the entire floor about six inches in depth.

Looking at my watch, it was thirty seconds to ten.

"You know it gets foggy just before you die don't you?" I said in my best Count Dracula voice.

"What?" Tara asked as they looked over at me. They were so engrossed in their horror stories they hadn't noticed they were sitting in a low level fog.

"The Sandman, he comes to collect your souls in the fog," I repeated.

"Oh my God, look at the floor!" Jessy shouted out.

Just as she did Ron and Jerry, two of the family's hit men, started up their chainsaws and burst in through the sliding glass doors like masked wild men. Every girl in the room began to scream, cry and run in all different directions of the house. Waiting for about forty seconds, I reached under the bar, pulled out my Colt .45 automatic pistol, which was loaded with blanks, and opened fire at the two crazed killers who had just broken into my home. Slapping their selves in the chest, the small bags filled with chicken blood burst open, leaving big red bloody blotches on their dirty white T-shirts as they both fell to the floor.

Within a minute of starting it had ended. The house was filled with scared, screaming, emotionally frantic young girls. Ron and Jerry had switched off the chainsaws as they fell to the floor. The smell of gunpowder and exhaust fumes from the chainsaws lingered in the air.

"Good shot, David, you got both of them," Andy yelled as he walked over and knelt down next to Ron to see if he was dead.

The fog from the dry ice had almost completely covered both Ron and Jerry's bodies. Mrs. Carlson, Amy, and Dana had almost gotten the girls calmed down when Ron sat up and stabbed Andy in the chest with a fake Hollywood stunt knife. Grabbing the knife, Andy groaned, called out my name, and fell to the floor. The girls were now completely in shock, filled with panic and screaming as tears of horror ran down their cheeks. Raising my gun I fired two more, very loud sounding gunshots at Ron. Slowly, Ron fell backwards into the foggy mist.

"Tara, go check and see if Andy's dead would you?" I asked loudly over the top of their screaming. Buried in her mother's arms, my adopted niece was now screaming out of control.

"David," Amy shouted as I turned all of the lights back on from the main control panel located on the wall next to my display of liquor by the bar.

"Happy Halloween," Andy, Don, Ron, and Jerry shouted out loudly as they all stood up out of the foggy mist.

As soon as they stood up out of the foggy mist, the noise level from the screams went up to 6.1 on the Rictor Scale. I was laughing so hard I had stomach cramps and tears in my eyes. It took almost fifteen minutes to actually calm all of the girls down and get them to believe it really was a Halloween prank.

* * * * * * *

It was noon of November 1, 1975, as Andy flipped our Porter House steaks over on the grill for our lunch. My home was completely trashed as I looked at it and sighed.

"That's what you get for pissing off a bunch of thirteen, fourteen, and fifteen year old girls," Don explained with a laugh.

Thinking about it for a few seconds, I began to laugh. "I think a couple of them pissed in their pants," I explained.

"Want me to call a maid in to clean the place up?" Don asked.

"Nah, I'm going to leave it like this for awhile. I kinda like the way it looks," I explained as I lifted up some of the angle hair the girls used to make it look like cobwebs.

Hearing my satellite pager beep, I checked to see who it was. Looking at the digital read out I saw it was Carla. The code read triple zero, a private code Carla used when it was an extremely urgent matter.

Walking into my den I sat down at my computer desk, picked up my secure phone, and called Carla right away.

"David?" she asked as she picked up the phone on her end of the line.

"It's me, what's going on?"

"Are you scrambled on your end?" she asked.

Looking over at Walter Shaw's black 'scrambler box' I saw that it was on. "I'm secure on this end."

"We're in serious trouble, kiddo, I really need you more than ever," Carla said in a worried tone of voice.

"Have I ever let you down yet?"

"No," she answered. "That's why I'm calling you."

"What's wrong?" I asked curious as to why Carla was so upset.

"I just got a call from one of my most trusted United States Senators. Sam Giancana is schedule to testify in front of a Senate Committee. He's going to tell them about the connection between organized crime and the CIA, from Castro to the hit on Kennedy. If he makes it to that Senate Hearing, Congress will not only indite some of us, they'll shut down the CIA all together, David."

"What? Why would he do that? The mob would kill him," I explained, shocked at what I was being told.

"My guy doesn't know what the FBI has on him. But whatever it is, he's agreed to cooperate and tell it all. He's even going to go into details about the Mafia families, the casinos in Vegas, and tell them who the inner structure of the family members really are. My Senator told me that Sam has promised to reveal who the best kept secret of the Mafia is. There's a new Godfather and Sam won't tell the FBI who it is yet. He's promised to tell it all to the Senate Commission at this special Senate Hearing on organized crime. I can't believe it. I trusted him, he was one of our best allies," Carla explained sadly.

"That's why he wanted you to have someone there to witness the Hoffa hit. He's going to say that the CIA was overseeing the whole thing and were the brains behind it, son-of-a-bitch!

We've got less than a week before he's scheduled to testify. Once he walks into that Senate Hearing, they'll put him into protective custody. Then, we'll never be able to get to him. How do we kill the head of the Chicago crime family and get past all of his men to do it? Tell me, David, can it be done?" Carla asked with an almost frantic tone of voice.

"I'll take care of it," I said calmly as a sad feeling of betrayal began to fill me.

"Are you sure you can get to him?" she questioned.

"Does anyone else know about this?" I asked.

"Just you, me, and the man that called me," she replied.

"Keep it that way. Not a word, Carla. Don't mention a word of this to anyone. I'll take care of it," I said again as I hung up the telephone.

Carla had used keywords like, 'the families best kept secret,' and 'who the real Godfather is.' So, I knew without a doubt the Senator's information was correct. Sam had waited for my grandfather to pass on and now, for some reason; he was going to destroy everyone.

His testimony would hurt our country by destroying the CIA. It would hurt the families, and the innocent women and children the men of our families were husbands and fathers too. That was something I could not let happen.

"Come on, brother, the steaks are done," Andy, shouted from the basement of my home.

"I'm coming," I yelled back. "I'm coming for you to, Sam. The Sandman's coming and you invited him into your home to teach death how to make Italian Escarole."

* * * * * * *

I spent the next day talking to Kate on the telephone. I told Kate earlier I was involved in organized crime and then I explained to her, who my grandfather was. I also told her I had no desire to be the Godfather. I was only going to stay until my grandfather had passed away. After that I was going to leave the family and move to Dublin to live my life out in peace with her.

Unfortunately I would have to stay 'in' just a little while longer now to clean up the Sam Giancana problem, but I couldn't tell her about Sam.

I had stayed on the phone with Kate for most of the day. The telephone bill was going to be huge, but I didn't care. I was still spending Walter Chang's millions.

Before talking to Kate, I called Marge at Langley's Technical Services Division. I needed a silenced .22-long pistol that couldn't be traced if I should need to throw it away. I didn't want to use the .22 magnum I already had in my possession. A good forensic expert might take an extra long look into the death of Sam, especially if he was about to testify at a Congressional Senate Hearing.

The one thing about mob hits is that if the hit man is a real professional, he will identify the hit as a mob killing. This can be done in several different ways, and for a very good reason.

It's called a 'Signature Hit.' What that means is that your telling a trained police detective it's a mob hit and your telling him why it happened. If you shoot a person twice in the back of the head or twice in the side of the head, and you use a small caliber weapon, such as a .22-long pistol, your letting the police know its a mob hit. If you place a penny in the victim's mouth that is telling the police the person was killed because he was either a snitch or was about to cooperate with law enforcement against the family.

Every good homicide detective will always look in the victim's mouth. They even do it on television now, but normal everyday citizens never understand why they are doing it or what they are looking for. In either case, the police investigation will be closed in 72-hours and the homicide file will be placed in what is known as a 'Dead File.' Law enforcement officers know they will not be able to solve that particular homicide because the shooter, or hit man, was serious enough to tell them to back off and leave it alone.

The CIA will sometimes use a signature hit of its own. They will use a .22-long or .22 magnum pistol and shoot their victim once in the back of the head. They will then press the barrel of the pistol up into the fleshy part of the victim's neck, under the chin and close to the neck muscle. They will then fire six shots on an angle, up and into the brain of the victim. If it's done correctly, according to the instructors at the CIA Farm, it severs the brain stem of the victim. Either way, death is instantaneous. This hit tells international law enforcement officers the American CIA is responsible for the assassination and that it's to be left alone. Again the homicide investigation will immediately be placed in a 'Dead File' and closed.

Calling Ben, I told him to pick up Kathy and meet me at the Pontiac Airport. We were flying to Chicago. I felt that Sam might be on edge. He wanted me to come and see him so I now figured he might possibly be trying to set me up. Maybe not, but it was a gut feeling I was not going to ignore.

My thinking was that if I had Kathy along with me, the presence of a pretty, young female might help to calm Sam down a little bit or as I use the term, 'Put him to sleep' and get him to relax.

When I called Marge back, she told me that an undercover operative would meet me in Chicago at a place called the Matchbox Bar on North Milwaukee Avenue. The gun I had requested would be delivered to me there.

I also wanted Kathy along for another reason. If Sam was getting ready to testify at a Senate Hearing in Washington D.C., both he and his home might very well be under FBI surveillance. I would need to check out Sam's neighborhood for at least one full day and one full night before going to his home to see him. I wasn't about to walk up to his front door and have the FBI sitting in the home across the street from his, taking pictures of me.

* * * * * * *

Wet Work Operation
Code Name: Perdition
Target: Sam Momo Giancana
Location: Chicago

I locked up my home and headed to the Pontiac Airport to meet with Ben and Kathy. To my surprise, I found them both sitting in the airport restaurant eating prime rib steak. Sitting down at the table I told them to take their time and ordered a cold Pepsi for myself.

Placing two drops of Methadrine under my tongue, I thought back to the meetings, which took place here. This is were Tony Provenzano had flown in to meet with Tony Jack and his people to talk about the future killing of Jimmy Hoffa. If people only knew what took place right under their noses everyday, they would understand what a dangerous world we really do live in. But then again, maybe its better they don't know, huh?

After Ben and Kathy had finished eating, we flew straight to Chicago O'Hare Airport and rented a new triple silver Ford Thunderbird from Avis Ford. Driving away in our new rental car we searched for the Matchbox Bar and found it at 770 North Milwaukee Avenue. Parking our car down the road, Kathy and I walked over to the bar.

The Matchbox is a red brick faced building with the front door facing the corner of the street. Once inside, I understood why they named it the Matchbox. It was so small the bartender only had thirteen-inches extra to move around in behind the bar. Don't misunderstand me, it had a very long bar, but there was only thirteen-inches of space between the bartender's back and the cash register and liquor display behind him.

"Now I understand why they named it the Matchbox," Kathy said jokingly as we sat down at the far end of the bar.

Kathy ordered a glass of Vodka straight up and I ordered a Pepsi while we waited for our contact person to show up.

"I notice you drink a lot of Vodka," I commented with a grin on my face.

"Yeah, I grew up drinking Vodka as a kid. It doesn't phase me at all. I think I'm immune to it. I could drink it all day and still be sober. So tell me, David, who are we going after?" Kathy asked quickly changing the subject.

"A big mob boy, but the Fed's might have his house under surveillance. So we're going to need to sweep the neighborhood and check every house to make sure its safe before we go and pay him a visit," I explained as our contact person walked into the bar and took a look around.

"That's our boy," Kathy said softly as we watched him walk over to us.

"Sorry it took me so long to get here. Believe it or not I had a flat tire," he explained as he sat down next to Kathy.

"Don't worry about it. Tim this is Dave. Dave this is Tim. Tim works for Marge," Kathy explained as she introduced us to each other.

"Hey, Dave," Tim said with a nod.

"Tim," I replied as the bartender came over to take Tim's order.

"What can I get, ya?" the bartender asked with a smile.

"Give me a cold Bud, would you?" Tim asked.

"One cold Budweiser coming right up," the bartender replied as he went to get Tim his beer.

Keeping his hands below the bar countertop, Tim reached in under his jacket and looked around to make sure that nobody was watching him. At the same time Kathy opened up her purse. In one smooth and quick move Tim pulled the silenced .22 magnum pistol out from under his jacket and placed it into Kathy's purse. Kathy closed her purse just as the bartender walked back over to us and handed Tim his drink. Paying for his beer Tim took one long drink from his beer bottle. Setting the bottle back down on the bar he looked over at us.

"I'll catch you guys later. I have another package to deliver. I've got to have it in Dallas, Texas by noon tomorrow. Stay safe, guys," he explained as he patted Kathy on the back of her left shoulder and left the bar.

"Marge sure does keep him busy. Tim is always on the move," Kathy explained as she finished her drink.

"Come on, let's get out of here," I said as I pulled a ten-dollar bill out of my pocket and set it under my glass for the bartender.

"Where we going?" Kathy asked as we left the bar and stepped out onto the sidewalk out front.

"Let's rent a room at the Sheraton Hotel. I need to call Neil," I explained as we made our way back to our car.

* * * * * * *

Renting a room at the Sheraton, we ordered a large pizza. I then called Neil at the War Room. I had called Neil before I left my house and asked him to call all of the local, state, and federal law enforcement agency's in and around the area of Sam's home. I told him to see if there were any active undercover operations or surveillances taking place in this particular county of Illinois. It's a common practice for law enforcement. It helps to keep one agency from accidentally blowing the undercover operation of another agency by accidentally walking into their operation as its taking place.

"Hello," Neil said as he answered his end of the line.

"Hey, buddy, what's up? Were you able to find out anything?" I questioned.

"I called everyone in the tri-county area around Sam's home, there's nothing going on with any of the Sheriff's Departments, State Police, FBI, DEA, ATF, or the United States Marshals. It sounds like you have a clear path, Dave," Neil explained.

"Always expect the unexpected, I'll still take a quick look around just to play it safe. What's our time frame on this?" I asked.

"Try to hit Sam by tomorrow, he's scheduled to testify in four days from today. Can you get him, Dave?"

"I'll get him, don't worry about that," I replied calmly as the pizza delivery boy dropped off our pizza.

"I've never seen Carla this worried before. I saw her in her office rolling her glass cyanide capsule around between her fingers," Neil explained.

"Really?" I replied caught by surprise at what he had just told me.

"There was some goodie-two-shoes bureaucrat who wants to shut down the Agency. Sam's testimony is all they'll need to do it. Carla knows that. She also knows she could take down a lot of people, including a few Presidents," Neil replied.

"She'd never do that, she'd kill herself first just to shut down the Senate investigation and protect everyone in the process," I explained.

"Damn right she would, she's die hard loyal. You cut her and she bleeds red, white, and blue. She asked me earlier if I thought you'd be able to get past all of Sam's security and kill him. She knows you will, but she needed a little reassurance," Neil explained.

"What did you tell her?" I asked as Kathy handed me a piece of pizza and a bottle of Pepsi.

"I reminded her that there was a damn good reason she brought you into the Agency and gave you all that special training. Hell, brother, you met Carlos the Jackal and swapped secrets with him and lived to tell about it," Neil said with a slight chuckle in his voice.

"I don't know anyone named Carlos, Neil. I have no idea what you're talking about. Who in the hell told you something like that?" I asked. No one knew about Carla's connection to Carlos or her sending me to be personally trained by him. "Why would Neil say what he had just said?" I asked myself.

"Man, I just assumed that's where you learned how to disguise yourself so well. Remember how you disguised everyone to look like Russians when you went into Hanoi to get Danny out of that prison camp? That was pure genius," Neil explained.

"Yes it was. It was also three months of training in Hollywood, California with a special effects crew that taught me how to use their

Hollywood make-up kits," I replied hoping to convince Neil that that was where I had learned how to use the art of disguise.

"No shit, I never knew that," he answered surprised to hear that I had gone to California to train in Hollywood.

"You're so funny, Neil, Carlos the Jackal, huh? That's original. Listen, tell mom to calm down. By tomorrow night the Sandman will have collected Sam's soul. I'll talk to you later. Page me if anything changes," I explained.

"You got it, stay safe," Neil said as we both hung up our telephones.

"Who's Sam?" Kathy asked as I took a bite out of my pizza.

"Chicago's legendary gangster, mob boss Sam Giancana," I answered with a wink of my eye.

"Holy shit! We're going to kill the head of the Chicago crime family? How do you think the other families are going to respond to a hit on one of their big boys?" Kathy asked with a touch of concern in her voice.

"Don't worry about it, I know the Godfather. He's a real good friend of mine. If they object, I'll kill them to. Did you order any A-1 Steak Sauce for the pizza?" I asked smiling.

"You know the Godfather, David, this isn't a joking matter. How are we going to get into his home and past all of his security?" Kathy asked with a look of concern on her face.

"Have I ever let you down, Kathy?" I asked calmly looking Kathy straight in the eyes.

"No you haven't," she answered.

"Then trust me will you?" I replied as I took another bite of my pizza. "We need A-1 Steak sauce for this pizza," I mumbled as I continued to chew.

* * * * * * *

It didn't surprise me at all to find Sam's home in the middle class suburbs of Oak Park, Illinois. My grandfather once told me, "Never show off what you have. Stay in the middle. When you let people see that you have a house, car, boat, anything better than theirs, they get jealous. When that happens, they call the police and say, 'Hey where did he get the money to buy so many nice things?' Then the police watch you and put their noses in your private business. Never let the police stick their nose in your life. Once they do, you will never be able to get their nose out of your business ever again."

These were the words of a very wise man, and Sam was living by them.

He lived in a middle class neighborhood. What I liked most were the awnings over his windows. My grandfather had red and white aluminum awnings over the windows of his red brick home too.

Kathy and I parked our rental car a block away from Sam's home and walked into his neighborhood. Holding hands we slowly walked down the sidewalk and past Sam's home. Every so often we would stop and hug each other or give each other a gentle kiss on the lips. If any of Sam's neighbors should happen to be watching us, it would make them think we were a young couple in love simply taking an evening walk.

What we were really doing was looking in the windows of their homes to see if any undercover police surveillance teams were watching Sam's home. The good thing was that I had been trained very well at the CIA's Farm. As I had explained to Kathy before we left the hotel, "Look beyond the curtains, sometimes a highly trained surveillance agent will put the back of a chair or some other item of furniture close to the window. It's there to distract you. A good cop trained in the art of undercover surveillance will sit far back in the room and as far away from the window as possible. This type of cop or Federal agent is very dangerous because he knows what he is doing and he is doing it very well," I explained to her.

Walking to the end of the block, we crossed the street and walked back down the side of the road Sam's house was on.

"See anything that appears to be out of place?" I asked.

"Nothing, it looks clear. How are we going to get into his house, David? Do you think he will have any of his men inside with him?" Kathy asked as we walked up the sidewalk in front of Sam's home.

"No, he's all alone, this is his car," I explained as we walked up the driveway and past Sam's car. "He's not expecting any trouble, so his guard is down. Don't act surprised when I introduce you to him. Just smile and be yourself," I explained as we walked around the side of his home and stepped up to the backdoor.

Knocking on the screen door, I placed two drops of Methadrine under my tongue and waited.

"Oh boy, you've sure got some nerves of steal," Kathy whispered as I knocked on the screen door for a second time.

Hearing the wooden door inside open, I smiled when I saw Sam's face.

"David," Sam said with a surprised look and excited voice.

"Hello, Uncle Sam, I hope that you don't mine, I brought my girlfriend along with me. She said that she wants to know my Uncle Sam's secret recipe for making Italian sausages and Escarole," I explained as Sam smiled and opened the outer screen door.

"Kathy, I would like you to meet my Uncle Sam. Uncle Sam this is my girlfriend Kathy," I introduced.

"Mr. Giancana it's a pleasure to finally get to meet you. David has told me so much about you that I feel as though I already know you," Kathy explained calmly with a broad smile on her face.

Kathy was shocked to find out that Sam was my uncle, but she was also very well trained and never showed it. She was blending right into my lead and playing her hand out as we went along.

"It's very nice to meet you, please come in. Why didn't you call?" Sam asked as we stepped inside his home.

"Call? I thought that you said to be here on the 5th to make Escarole and sausages? That's what Tony told me when he brought me the case of sausage you sent over for the girl's Halloween party. You want us to come back another day?" I asked with a slightly confused look on my face.

"No, no, today is the right day. Come on, let's go downstairs to my kitchen," he replied as we walked down the stairs and into the basement of his home.

"I only meant, why didn't you call? Everybody calls me but you. You are just like your grandfather 'God rest his soul.' Oh how I miss him," Sam explained as we walked over to the small kitchen Sam had set up in his basement.

"You have two kitchens in your home, Mr. Giancana?" Kathy questioned.

"Don't you call me Mr. Giancana, Kathy, you call me Uncle Sam. If your with my nephew, then that makes you part of my family, okay?"

"Okay, Uncle Sam," Kathy answered shyly.

"And the answer to your question is yes. I have two kitchens. I like to make my sausages down here. It's quiet and peaceful. I also like to cook my main foods down here. You know, the sausage, the turkey for Thanksgiving, things like that. It keeps the greasy food smell out of the upstairs part of my home. Even David does most of his cooking in his basement, don't you, David?" Sam asked as he poured us a glass of vintage red wine.

"Absolutely, I learned that from my grandmother," I answered as I looked over toward the counter by the sink.

"How is your grandmother, is she alright?" Sam asked as he opened his refrigerator and began to pull out some packages of meat.

"She has cancer in her stomach, Uncle Sam," I explained sadly.

"What? What cancer, I thought that the doctors took the tumor out of her stomach?" Sam replied with a troubled and concerned look on his face.

"They did," I answered.

"Oh, mama, what next? Why Helen? Did your grandfather know?" Sam asked as he opened the first package of meat.

"No, none of us knew, Uncle Sam. We just found out. She'll have to go into the hospital for radiation treatments," I explained sadly.

"Is there anything I can do?" Sam asked.

"No, Uncle Sam, all that we can do now is to pray for her."

"That I can do. All right now I want you to watch what I am doing. The trick to making a good Italian sausage is that you grind up 80% beef and then you grind up 20% pork and mix it all together. Now then, you see this fat on the pork?" Sam asked looking over at Kathy and I.

"Yes, Uncle Sam, you cut that off and throw it away right?" Kathy asked curiously.

"Oh no, young lady, you grind that up with it," Sam explained.

"Won't that make it greasy tasting?" Kathy asked.

"No, there's not that much fat. Listen, if you buy hamburger at the food store it already has fat ground up in it. Do you know why?" he asked.

"No, I don't," Kathy answered as she turned to look at me. "Do you know why they do that?" she asked me.

"Yes, I do, it's so that the meat won't burn. If you cut a piece of raw steak and throw it in a frying pan it will burn up real fast. That's why the butcher always leaves a small strip of fat around the outer edge of steaks, pork chops, ribs, or they grind a little bit of it up in the hamburger. It greases up the pan and the meat so that it won't burn," I explained.

"Is that right, Uncle Sam?" Kathy asked.

"That's exactly right," Sam answered as he began to put the chunks of beef into the meat grinder and turn the handle to grind it up.

"What about prime rib?" I've never had prime rib with fat on it," Kathy questioned.

"That's because you trim it off as it's cooking, but you leave it in the baking pan. Do you know why prime rib is so tender?" I asked Kathy.

"You marinade it over night?" she asked in a questioning way.

"No, that's not why. Tell her why, David," Sam said as he put some more raw beef into the meat grinder to grind it up.

"When you own a restaurant like we do, we go to the slaughter house and pick out ten cows. We then tell the man that works there to spike seven of them and cut the throats on the other three."

"What?" Kathy responded with a surprised look on her face.

"What they do is they wrap a chain around the back hoofs or ankles of the cow. Then they put a hook in the chain and use an electric wench to pull the cow up into the air so its head is facing down toward the ground. Then he takes a razor sharp knife and he cuts the cow's throat. The cow then relaxes and bleeds to death. While that's happening most of the blood drains out of the meat because the cow's muscles are all relaxed. That's why the meat is so tender. The other seven cows are going to have a spike driven into their forehead and right into their brain. When that happens all of their muscles tense up and they die. That's why the meat is a little tougher so you use those cows for your regular steaks, roasts, and hamburger," I explained with a smile.

"I'll be damn, I never knew that," Kathy said in a soft whisper.

"Those are our family secrets, so don't tell anyone else. We never tell our secrets to anyone outside of our family," Sam explained as he looked down at the meat that he was pushing into the meat grinder.

"That's right, we never tell our family secrets to anyone, especially a Senate Hearing," I whispered softly.

As I did Sam stopped cooking and looked up. The first shot struck him in the back of his head, slightly below mid-center. He shook his head one time and staggered backwards about a foot. His body collapsed and fell to the floor.

To my surprise, Sam was still breathing. He was staring up at the ceiling and blinking his eyes, as the cold barrel of the silenced .22 magnum was pressed under his chin, just above his Adams apple. Placing the gun on a slight angle, six more shots were fired upward and into Sam's brain.

Looking at my watch it was 8:00 p.m. November 5, 1975. Chicago's legendary crime boss lay dead on his basement floor, shot to death while making his favorite meal of Escarole and Sausages in his basement kitchen.

Looking at Kathy she was breathing heavily, her eyes were wide and filled with excitement.

"Let's go before Judith shows up and catches us down here," I explained as I picked up both of our wine glasses. Drinking the wine out of both of the glasses, I wiped them clean with a dishtowel and then placed them back up on the shelf next to the rest of the glasses.

Heading back up the stairs we left the same way we had come in, wiping everything down with the dish towel on our way out to make sure we weren't leaving any fingerprints behind.

It was a cool, clear November night as Kathy and I walked hand in hand back to our rental car and drove away.

We didn't go back to our hotel room. Instead we drove straight to the airport where Ben was waiting for us. Turning in our rental car, we climbed on board and flew away.

For some strange reason, I didn't feel bad at all. I thought that I would, but I didn't. Sam had made himself expendable and put himself in the position he had ended up in.

To me it was business, protecting both of my families, the Mafia and the elite covert black operations group of the CIA.

After all, Carla had become a very special friend to me. In many ways she was almost like a mother to me, and we all know that every red blooded American boy would kill to protect his mother. It's the American way of doing things and keeping your best kept secrets secret...

Note: Sam Momo Giancana was mad at Dezi Arnaz for producing the television series: The Untouchables and wanted to kill him. He was also responsible for the murder of actress Marilyn Monroe, which was called a suicide in 1962. Sam was one of the men responsible for the deaths of John F. Kennedy and Robert Kennedy. He was upset with them because they betrayed him and relentlessly prosecuted organized crime in the 60's.

For you the reader, Sam was actually killed eleven days before Teamster President James Riddle Hoffa. But for the story line of this book I placed this hit in the November 1975 time slot.

Sam Momo Giancana died in the basement kitchen of his Oak Park home while cooking his favorite meal of Escarole and Sausages, on the night of July 19, 1975 at the age of 67.

His girlfriend Judith Campbell Exiver was not at his home that night.

Chapter Thirty-Four
Phosphorous

After the Giancana hit I flew back to my home in Michigan and called Neil at the Pentagon.

"Talk to me, brother, how did it go?" Neil asked.

"It's a done deal, forget about it," I replied as I took a sip of my Pepsi.

"Is it true that you took Kathy with you on this hit?"

"Yeah, I'll tell ya, buddy, killing someone makes that girl horny. She's kinda strange sometimes," I replied.

"Next time your in town I'm taking you out to dinner. I wanna hear all about this hit. Did he know why he was dying? I hope you don't mind me asking, this kind of stuff intrigues me. How did you get past all that security and whack a mob boss as big and dangerous as he was? Man oh man, you are the universal assassin," Neil explained with a chuckle.

"How's Carla?" I asked avoiding his questions.

"Over the edge. First the ordeal with her goddaughter and then this Giancana shit. He could have destroyed us. Mom needs a vacation, she's burning out," Neil explained with an almost sad tone to his voice.

"Is she in?"

"Yeah, you wanna talk to her?"

"Yeah, transfer me over to her office will you? I've got an idea," I explained.

"You got it, brother, thanks, Sandman, you saved our asses on this one," Neil explained as he transferred my call over to Carla's office.

"Hello," Carla said in a tired voice.

"Hello sexy, feel better?" I asked.

"I don't know how you did it, David, and that little bitch Kathy won't tell me anything either. She said that you threatened to cut her tongue out if she even thought about telling anyone how you got into Sam's house. Is that true, or did the little bitch blow smoke up my ass?" Carla asked hoping that I would give her enough reason to fire Agent Eckland. For some strange reason, Carla did not like Kathy.

"It's true, it's no one's business. How you feeling?" I asked.

"Like shit. They found Sam's body already. I'm wondering how bad the fall out will be now?" Carla explained.

"Listen to me, the local cop's won't give a damn. The FBI won't investigate it because they'll be afraid that the word might leak out to the press that Sam was going to testify in front of a Senate Hearing about the connection between the CIA and the mob. We should leak that tidy bit of information to the press ourselves."

"Are you crazy?" Carla asked surprised at what I had just told her.

"Crazy? Oh yeah, crazy like a fox, pretty lady. Everyone will think the mob hit Sam to silence him. Let them take the blame. Then whoever was behind all of this will lay low and run for cover. They won't really know if the CIA hit Sam or if the Mafia did him in. Either way whoever is behind all of this Senate Hearing crap will be to scared to say a word about it or release any information in regard to what they had on Sam. They'll know that if they do, their dead," I explained calmly.

"Good point, it would bring the whole ordeal to a final end. I'll have to think about it," Carla replied with a yawn. "So why are you calling me? Do you miss me or did Neil tell you that I'm falling apart?" Carla asked with a fake laugh in her voice.

"Neil never said a word about you. Thanks for letting me know that you're falling apart," I explained.

"Shit, that was a dumb thing for me to say, huh?"

"Yeah, but you and I have an agreement between us. Remember? No secrets."

"I remember," Carla answered in a soft voice.

"Good, you owe me three favors now. One for the Morimoto Soba bet that you lost, one for the Istvan Bastick ordeal, and now one for this hit on Sam. Am I right? You owe me, no matter what I ask you for, you promised that you would do it, no questions asked. Did you mean it or were you lying to me?" I asked, hoping that Carla would commit herself to our agreement.

Without saying another word I waited silently for her reply. I could hear her take a deep breath of air into her lungs and let it out slowly.

"Yes, I remember, what do you want?" she asked.

"No matter what it is, I have your word on that right?" I asked once again trying to give her no way out of what I was about to do to her.

"I owe you three, I promise that no matter what it is, I'll do it," Carla replied knowing that I was setting her up.

"Good, you have a ton of vacation time coming. Tell whoever it is you report to that your taking the next thirty days off. Then pack your bags. I'll pick you up tomorrow. I'm taking you on an all expense paid vacation," I explained with a broad smile on my face.

"David..." she began to say.

"Listen to me, Carla, I don't have very many friends, so the ones I do have, I happen to care about very much. I happen to care about you a lot more then you know. Pack your bags or I swear to God, I'll quit. I'll cut the satellite chip out of my shoulder, leave the keys to this house on the kitchen table and I'll walk away. I don't lie to my friends, so if they lie to me I walk away. It's up to you, Carla, you coming with me or am I leaving?"

"You're really serious aren't you?" Carla asked.

"You bet I am, I'm also burning out. I need to get away for a while. What do you say, feel like running off with a younger man?" I asked.

"Pick me up at my home, here's the address..."

* * * * * * *

As soon as I had hung up the telephone from talking to Carla, my family attorney, Anthony Andolini called to tell me that Sam Giancana had been killed. Anthony and I talked for almost two hours. I then told him that I was leaving for a while and put him in charge of our family until I returned.

I then called Kate to tell her that I was taking Carla on vacation, and then explained why I was doing it. Kate understood and told me that after I helped Carla, she needed me to come back home to Dublin. When I asked if she missed me she laughed and said, "I always miss you. I have a surprise for you so when your done please come home."

Assuring me that everything was all right, I knew that her grandfather, cousin and friends had finished building our house that over looked Kate's wishing pond. "Women were so predictable," I thought to myself as we continued to talk.

Before I knew it we had talked for almost four hours. Saying goodbye, I packed my suitcases and laid down to take a short nap. Carla might turn out to be more of a handful than I might have expected. So I thought that I better at least try to get some rest.

* * * * * * *

The murder of Sam Giancana was the top story of the day for the news media, but was also short lived. Conspiracy theories were running rampant that the mob silenced one of their own. Hearing that made me smile. "Carla must have fed the information to someone in the news media," I thought to my self as Carla's limousine pulled up next to my Learjet.

Watching Carla step out of the limo broke my heart. Neil was right; she was completely burned out and over worked. Carla had dark rings around her eyes, which was a tell tale sign of being over stressed and in desperate need of sleep. Looking over at me she frowned and gave out a sigh.

"You look like shit," I said with a forced smile. I was really concerned for her well being now. She was really looking bad.

"Well thank you my dear, I don't think anyone has ever complimented me quite like that before," she replied with a grin.

"That's because people tell you what you want to hear rather than tell you the truth. You look like shit, that's the truth. But the Sandman is going to resurrect you. After spending thirty days with me, you'll be back on top and good as new," I explained as Carla's limo driver walked up to me carrying her luggage.

"Where would you like me to put these, sir?" he asked.

"Just toss 'em on board would you please," I replied.

"You got it," he said as he put Carla's luggage on board my plane.

"Thank you, Gene, take the next month off with full pay and benefits, I'll call when I need you to come and pick me up," Carla explained as her limo driver stepped off of my plane and nodded his head in acknowledgement.

"Okay, hot shot, here I am as promised," Carla said with a look in her eyes that I had never seen before.

"This won't hurt, I promise," I replied as I helped her on board.

Leaving Washington D.C. we flew south. It was just Carla and me now. Our first stop was the Yucatan Peninsula, as we descended on the ever so beautiful Cancun, Mexico. Landing in Cancun I was directed to a small hanger that I had called ahead and reserved for my plane. After tucking the plane away safely we hired a driver and headed for the luxurious digs of the Oasis Cancun Resort.

The Oasis was seven stories tall and, of course, I had called ahead and reserved two luxury suites, next to each other, on the seventh floor. After putting our luggage away we both took a shower and headed downstairs to have supper.

The Oasis Cancun Resort has a great restaurant which serves the best Mexican food I have ever eaten. It was almost 7:30 p.m. by the time we finished our drinks and desert. Jet lag was setting in from our long flight so we decided to call it a night and head back upstairs to our rooms to talk, have a few drinks and get some much needed rest.

Sitting on the balcony of Carla's suite, I poured her a glass of Dom Perignon and sat down next to her.

"God, I'm stuffed, I haven't eaten like that in a very long time. This is beautiful, David, thank you," Carla explained as she leaned over and kissed me on the cheek.

"You're welcome and no, I'm not that easy. I never sleep with a woman on the first date. Especially if I think she is ready to fall asleep on me," I said jokingly.

"Sleep, I haven't had a full eight hours of sleep in the past three months. If the American people only knew how much we sacrifice to keep them safe," she said as her mind started to drift and her thoughts began to take her back to all the things she had done in her career in the name of God and country.

"Oh no you don't, you're on vacation, pretty lady. Leave the job in the Situation Room. The world won't fall apart without you. This next four weeks is all about relaxing, sleeping, eating great food, and taking long walks on the beach with me. So please stop thinking about work, will ya? Let's just relax and have a great time," I explained with a look of concern on my face.

"You really do care about me, don't you?" she asked with a long yawn.

"More than you know," I replied as I quickly reached over and took the glass from her hand.

I had put five hundred milligrams of Chloral Hydrate in Carla's drink. She was so overly exhausted she was wired tight. The 'knockout' drug, known as a 'Mickey Fin,' would help her get the much-needed rest she deserved. In fact, Carla was out like a light and was actually snoring.

Picking her up I carried her over to her queen size bed and gently tucked her in.

"Get some rest, mom, I'll stay right her to keep an eye on you, I promise," I whispered as I kissed her tenderly on her forehead.

* * * * * * *

Carla had been asleep for almost eighteen hours. Sitting on her balcony, I had the sliding glass doors open and was eating my lunch when I heard her get up and out of bed.

Turning my head to see if she was alright, I watched as she walked across the room and went into her bathroom. Ten minutes later she came back out and walked over to her bed. Taking off her blouse, pants, bra, and socks, she laid back down and quickly fell asleep once again.

Walking into the room I looked at her and took a sip from my glass of Pepsi.

Carla didn't have an ounce of fat on her entire body. I already knew she had a great set of legs. She had shown me those when we had flown to Pavel Malenkov's estate in the mountains of Switzerland after Morimoto Soba. But seeing her now surprised me. This girl was built and in short, was one very beautiful woman.

Walking back out on the balcony I sat down and finished eating my lunch.

It was a hot, beautiful sun shiny day. A cool breeze was blowing in my face and entering the room causing the window curtains to dance to its tune.

Closing my eyes my mind took me back to Vietnam. It was almost as if I was there again, sitting on top of the bunker next to our sniper's hooch. After a long mission we would be so tired and so wired up because of it, that once we fell asleep, we would actually be out cold for two to three days straight.

I understood very well what Carla was going through, the Chloral Hydrate had worn off now. If it still had been in her system, she would never had been able to open her eyes, let alone get up to use the bathroom.

She was over the worst part of being totally exhausted. She was sleeping now because she was tired. Her muscles and neurological system were regenerating themselves. She would be out for at least another day or two. I knew that from experience.

Picking up the telephone which was sitting on the table next to me, I called Anthony Andolini to see how things were going at home. Anthony told me that things were going as expected. Most of the families were preparing to go to Sam's funeral. The FBI was still searching for Jimmy Hoffa's body and coming up empty handed. Other than that, everything was running smoothly.

My second call was to Neil at the Pentagon.

"Hello," he said.

"What's up, little brother?" I said as I took a bite out of one of my jalapeno pepper.

"Hey, Sandman, how's Cancun?"

"Nice but I'm cutting this satellite chip out of my shoulder as soon as I hang up the telephone," I replied calmly.

"No you won't, it might just save your life one day. How's Carla?"

"She's been asleep for almost nineteen hours. You were right, she was on total burn out mode," I explained.

"I'm shocked she actually agreed to take a vacation. For what it's worth, thanks, she really needed this break."

"So did I, so it all works out. How are things going with you?" I asked.

"We are installing a brand new state of the art computer telephone tracing system. The guys are working on it right now," Neil explained proudly.

"What's it do?" I asked.

"Well, with our old system, to trace a call we had to have the person we were trying to get a location on, stay on the phone for at least one full minute. In some cases it would take even longer than that. With this new system the computer will give us the exact location and address within one to three seconds. I'm hoping we will now be able to find out who this mystery caller is that's been calling Boris Kalashnikov from here in the

States. I'm also hoping it will help us to trace all of those numbers you brought back when you down loaded the Gruber and Malenkov computers. This could be a real big break through for us. It's got me excited," Neil explained.

"Man, that sounds good. It'd like to know who's giving Kalashnikov information about me," I replied.

"Whoever he is, it might help us to speed up the 'Skip Trace' system that he's using. I'd still like to know how the Russians got that technology. It's really strange, Dave, the only time we have ever caught them using it is when they call Boris from here in the United States and talk about you. They're trying real hard to make sure we don't catch them using it. Thank God, we did catch 'em, huh?"

"No kidding. You do great work Neil; we all appreciate how hard you work, brother. You put in a lot of hours, buddy, don't burn out on us," I explained concerned that he might end up like Carla had.

"Hey, I'm doing what I love to do, but I'm also smart enough to take a break if I need one. Now that I'm training Sandy as my second in command, I can relax a bit more. Sandy is a real sharp cookie. She's not like that airhead Carol was."

"That's good, that's real good. Speaking about Cookie, how's my old team doing?" I questioned.

"They're like you, Sandman, they're unstoppable. Once they start on a project or an assignment, they don't stop until it's done. Which reminds me, Chopper called me. He's in Germany with Amanda tracking down a very serious lead on two A-pack nuclear suitcases. He wanted to know how you were doing," Neil explained.

"That's my big brother. Man, I love that guy. Tell him I'm okay now. He's worried because of how hard I had taken it when my grandfather passed away. They always kept an eye on me. Brothers and friends to the very end. That's the code we live by. Tell him that I'll call him as soon as I get back," I explained.

"I'll tell him, but you'll have to do it from here. I can't give you his code numbers, you understand don't you?"

"Absolutely, I would never have expected you to, unless it was an emergency situation. Listen my friend, I'm going to let you go for now, I'll call you later, alright?"

"Okay, buddy, don't stay out on that balcony to much longer, your liable to get a sun burn," Neil said with a chuckle.

"You've been watching me all of this time?" I asked with a shake of my head.

"You're right here on the big screen, brother, live at five and soon to be in full color. They're also installing a new color screen in the War Room, no more black and white. God, I love modern technology," Neil added.

"Tell me something, who is Carla's favorite singer? You know, like a music artist that does concerts. Does she listen to music?" I asked

"Believe it or not she's very versatile in what she listens to. Right now she's been talking about going to a David Bowie concert if she ever gets the time. Why?" Neil asked.

"She has the time now. See if you can get us tickets to one of his concerts, but not for at least three weeks. Can you do that?" I asked hoping that Neil would say yes so I could surprise Carla with it.

"If Bowie is in concert in three weeks, you'll both be there. Are you into his kind of music?"

"No not at all, I'm into classical and country. But I'll put up with David Bowie if it makes Carla smile," I explained with a sigh.

"I hear ya, I can't stand Bowie. Call me next week and I'll let you know where he's playing," Neil explained.

"Alright, brother, page us if you need us, I'll call you later," I said as I hung up the phone and waved my hand up toward the sky.

My third call was to Kate. After seeing Carla looking as hot as she did, I needed to remind myself that I had someone a thousand times more beautiful waiting for me in Dublin. I just hoped that a telephone call and a cold shower would be enough to do the trick.

When your twenty-five years old and as horny as I always am, it was going to be difficult. For you it's easy, your sitting at home reading this book. I'm the guy sitting out here on the balcony of the Oasis Resort in Cancun, Mexico eating jalapeno peppers and drinking ice cold Pepsi. "Gee, I wonder what James Bond would do?" I asked myself. "But then again, Carla did say I was better than Bond, didn't she...."

* * * * * * *

It had been 58-hours since Carla had fallen asleep in her room. She was now tossing and turning every few minutes on her bed. Her body was rested; she was ready to wake up.

Picking up the telephone I called downstairs and ordered Carla a nice meal. I knew from past experience that after a long over due sleep, especially two and a half days worth, when you wake up, you're both hungry and very thirsty.

I then called the flower shop, which is also located in the main lobby of the resort and ordered Carla three-dozen red roses. I was betting it had been along time since anyone had bought her flowers.

Writing a short note to Carla, I set it on the dresser, walked out of her room, and locked the door behind me.

* * * * * * *

It had been four hours since I left Carla's room. Sitting at the outside in-ground swimming pool, I took a sip of my Pepsi and smiled as Carla walked toward me with a drink in her hand. She was wearing a yellow halter-top, white shorts, and a pair of sandals. Her hair was pulled back and tied in a bun with a red rose tucked neatly into her hair on the left side of her head. Seeing her dark Ray Ban Aviator sunglasses is what made me smile.

These gold wire-framed glasses were made especially for Secret Service and deep cover agents. The lenses were almost black. The person wearing them can see out through them with crystal clear clarity, but if you're looking at the person who is wearing them, you can't see their eyes. The lenses are to dark to see in through. This allows the person wearing them to act as if he or she is looking in one direction when they are actually looking off to the left or right.

"You are so sweet," Carla said as she bent down and kissed me on the lips. "Do you know how long it's been since anyone has bought me flowers?"

"No, how long?" I asked.

"I was seventeen and he was the young man taking me to my high school prom."

"You mean it's been four years since anyone has bought you flowers?" I responded with a straight face.

Laughing out loud Carla pulled a lawn chair up next to mine and sat down next to me. "I wish I was twenty-one years old again. God, I feel so much better. How long was I asleep?"

"About two and a half days, fifty eight hours to be exact. You do look as though you're feeling better. How was your lunch?" I asked.

"Steak, eggs, toast, freshly sliced fruit, coffee and of course the Sandman's signature drink of choice, ice cold Pepsi? What's not to love about a meal like that?" Carla asked smiling.

"Wanna take a walk?" I asked.

"I'd love to," Carla answered as we got up and headed toward the beach.

We spent the next four hours walking bare foot on the beautiful beach of Cancun, with the water swirling around our feet and ankles.

It was the first time Carla and I had ever really had a heart to heart talk with each other. We talked about things I won't discuss, but they were very deep feelings about ourselves. Things you keep hidden for fear that if you did talk to someone about them, they wouldn't understand. It was the beginning of a very special relationship. One I would value all the days of my life.

That night, while we were eating dinner, I slipped four small orange tablets in Carla's wine glass without her noticing it. We call them brown bombers; they are very small, but an extremely powerful laxative. A hospital would give you four of these pills the day before you were scheduled for surgery. Within about six hours these very tiny pills would give you a major case of diarrhea and would flush out the entire contents of your stomach and intestinal track. It does such a good job, it also flushes out all of the toxic build-up in your digestive system.

What most people don't realize is that when your sick, or you have a flu bug, or food poisoning, or you just feel bad for no reason at all, the best thing for you to do is to take a powerful laxative. In Vietnam, if we started to get sick we would drink a half or full bottle of Milk of Magnesia and within two hours we would feel our stomach start to gurgle. When that happens we would then start drinking large amounts of warm water. A few minutes later all hell breaks loose, and you get a massive case of the runs. It will smell so bad it will almost make you want to throw-up. What your actually doing is flushing all of the bacteria, and build-up of toxins out of your body. When you do that, your natural immune system isn't on over load anymore trying to fight these things off and you'll immediately start to feel better. Didn't know that did you? Well, I knew Carla wouldn't take them on her own if I asked her to. I also knew that if I was truly going to help her, I needed to flush the toxins out of her system.

By ten o'clock Carla excused herself for the night because she was getting stomach cramps. I then told her what I had done and why I did it. I also explained to her that she needed to start drinking a lot of warm water.

"When nothing but water is coming out you'll be clean and feeling great. Then all you have to do is eat something and the 'runs' will stop, I promise," I explained.

* * * * * * *

It was 6:00 a.m. when I heard the knock on my door. Opening the door I saw Carla smiling at me.

"Buy you breakfast?" she asked as I stepped out into the hallway and closed the door to my room behind me.

"No, you are on vacation, I'm paying for everything. How you feeling?" I asked as we stepped into the elevator. We were the only two people in the elevator so we continued to talk.

"Well, Doctor Dave, I feel like a million dollars. I don't want to sound gross, but my God, David, I had chunks of stuff coming out of me that was horrorable smelling," Carla explained.

"Red meat, they say when you die you have at least six pounds of decaying meat stuck to the lining of your digestive system. That's why we feel bad and get sick most of the time. It's also what causes cancer. It's toxic, that's why it smells so bad.

"Your rested and your flushed out, now the vacation begins," I explained with a smile on my face.

We spent another five days in Cancun walking on the beach, swimming, water skiing, eating, and listening to Mexican music.

From Cancun Mexico, we then flew to the tropical Island of Aruba and stayed in the penthouse suites of the Americana Resort Hotel.

The Island of Aruba was a tropical paradise very few people knew about in 1975. My grandfather had told me that the Island of Aruba would one day be the hot spot everyone would want to go to. By the early 1980s he would prove to be right.

We spent a week in Aruba scuba diving, playing golf and sailing on the crystal blue waters surrounding the island.

Calling Neil, I was pleased to hear that Sandy had gotten us two front row tickets to a David Bowie concert in Paris.

Our next stop was Paris, France. Once there, we went to the Pavillon de Paris. Which was located at Pav. Paris Olympia 3 FNAC.

On stage we watched a young David Bowie work his magic and put on one hell of a concert. Sitting in the front row I looked over at Carla.

"You really like this kind of music?" I asked in a loud voice so she could hear me over the concert music.

"Hell no, I enjoy the same kind of music that you do, Bach, Beethoven, and country," Carla replied with a smile on her face.

"But Neil said you had mentioned you wanted to go to a David Bowie concert," I explained with a confused look on my face.

"I was joking around with him when I said that," Carla explained as she began to laugh out loud. "Is that why you brought me here, because you thought I wanted to see David Bowie perform live in concert?"

"Yup," I replied with a nod of my head and a stupid look on my face.

"God, I love you for caring so much about me," she replied as she kissed me on the right side of my cheek.

Looking at Carla I felt good inside. She had a twinkle in her eye again. She was well rested and had a beautiful dark suntan. She was back to being the healthy, feisty, woman who took charge of situations that American Presidents were to afraid to touch.

After the concert we went to dinner and were enjoying a nice French meal when both of our pagers went off at the same time. Looking at the digital read out we both looked up at each other and said at the exact same time, "Neil."

"I'll call," I said in a low voice as I motioned for the waiter.

"No, David, I'll call. If Neil paged us both at the same time something's wrong and I need to know about it," Carla explained.

"May I help you, sir?" The waiter asked politely.

"We need to make a phone call. Do you have a telephone we can use, please?" I asked.

"Why yes we do, sir, I will bring it to your table for you," he replied as he turned to go and get the phone.

"I've never been at a restaurant before where they bring the telephone to your table," Carla explained.

Sliding the small assortment of flowers sitting in the middle of our table over to the right I smiled.

"Phone jack," I explained as I nodded my head in the direction of the plug-in that was also part of our table.

"How did you know that was there?" Carla asked with a surprised look on her face.

"That's why you sent me to the Farm," I replied with a serious look as the waiter came back and plugged the telephone into the jack.

"There you go, sir."

"Thank you, my friend, I appreciate your help," I explained as I slid the telephone over to Carla.

Dialing the phone, we waited for Neil to pick up on the other end.

"Anybody ever tell you how pretty you are?" I asked as I looked across the table at my friend.

Tilting her head slightly to the right, she smiled. My question caught her off guard. It was then that the overseas connection went through and Neil answered.

"I'm not secure on this end, talk to me son, what's going on?" Carla asked as I listened to the one sided conversation.

"What? Where did they spot him?.... Who called?.... Tell him to meet us at the airport in London. We'll be in the air within the hour, I'll call you back as soon as we are airborne," Carla explained as I motioned for the waiter to bring us our check. Hanging up the telephone I saw the look of the scorpion in Carla's eyes.

"A member of 14-Intelligence Company was with one of our operatives at a London nightclub called Fabric. They spotted Takeo Kutaragi just as he was leaving the club. They lost him in the crowd but they know Takeo is somewhere in the immediate area. 14-Intelligence Company is putting a net around the entire area. We need to get to London, David," Carla explained with a serious look on her face.

Handing the waiter two, one hundred dollar bills, I told him to keep the change, so he would leave.

"You're still on vacation," I replied.

"David, you saved me from almost having a complete nervous break down. I've never had this much fun before. No one has ever cared about me like this before," she said softly as she gently bit her bottom lip and paused to control her heart felt emotions.

"Who's Takeo Kutaragi?" I asked.

"He's an assassin who works for the Japanese Yakuza. Last year he tortured an American DEA agent in Columbia. The Cali Drug Cartel had caught the agent and then called in Takeo because he's so good at torturing people.

The Columbian's filmed it all. It took three days and then he poured a gallon of gasoline on the American agent and set him on fire. They then sent the tape to the President of the United States.

Three months ago Takeo did the same thing to one of our deep undercover agents in Russia. He sent that tape to us at the Pentagon. He burned one of my boys to death...." Carla explained as her eyes filled with tears and she lowered her head to compose herself. Taking her handkerchief out of her purse she wiped the tears from her eyes and looked back up at me with a forced fake smile.

"Let's go," I said in a soft voice as we both stood up and walked out of the French restaurant.

* * * * * * *

Wet Work Operation
Code Name: Phosphorous
Target: Takeo Kutaragi
Location: London, England
Coordinate: Unknown

Takeo Kutaragi was a 24-year old Japanese assassin and a blood member of the feared Yakuza. His specialty was the unique way he could torture a person. He knew exactly what to do and how to bring his victim to the edge of death without actually killing him. His longest documented torturing of another human being was in Brazil, which lasted six full days and nights.

The FBI serial killer psychological profiling program had listed Takeo Kutaragi as an unpredictable, homicidal maniac who had mastered the art of ancient medieval ritual torture. The FBI believed that killing someone in this long, tormenting, vicious way was a sexually stimulating experience which excited Takeo so much that torturing just one of his victims would give him multiple orgasms.

What made matters even worse was the fact that Takeo had trained in the Japanese theater of arts at an early age, and in doing so, had become a master of disguise. This was one of the reasons he had twenty-three international warrants out for his arrest, from twenty-three different counties around the world. Interpol had been searching for him for over ten years.

For British and American intelligence agents to spot Takeo walking out of a nightclub was a very rare thing indeed. In fact, the person they saw might very well be someone who looks like Takeo, but in all reality, really isn't him at all.

"From this point forward, we better make every move count and be very careful," I warned as I lifted the wheels of my Learjet off of the dark cool asphalt of the French International Airport and took flight heading to London, England.

* * * * * * *

It seemed like our flight had taken forever. Carla called Neil and had him reserve rooms for us at the well known Metropolitan Hotel, in downtown London. It would be there that we would meet our undercover operative Eric LoGiudice.

Landing at London's Heathrow Airport, we were met by a man named Sterling Townsend. He was the director of the Elite British 14-Intelligence Group. He was also one of Carla's closest friends.

Securing our plane we climbed into Sterling's limousine and headed to one of 14-Intelligences secret offices located on Grosvenor Street. Nothing was really said until we got inside and locked the door behind us.

The office building was located next to a popular magazine publisher, which made it easy for British Intelligence Agents to blend in late at night with the steady flow of people who were coming and going in the building next door.

The office we just entered looked like a normal office. However, once we walked through the main front section of the office and into the back room, a whole new world opened up to us.

There were computers, telephones, short wave radios, and undercover surveillance equipment throughout the entire room. Six British 14-

Intelligence Agents were inside gathering information on our target, Mr. Takeo Kutaragi.

"Sterling, are you sure it's him?" Carla asked as she set her purse down and took a seat next to the long wooden conference table located in the center of the large room.

Sterling Townsend was, in my opinion, the older image of England's James Bond fiction character. He was in his early fifty's, had graying hair that was neatly trimmed and combed straight back. He stood six feet tall and weighed 185-pounds, all of which was muscled. He had deep blue eyes and a thin mustache which was also graying. He was well dressed, clean cut and well mannered. Most of all, he had a deep British accent and was plainly a man who not only deserved respect, but was also completely in control.

"Quite certain," he replied as he pointed to a large wall map of the entire downtown area of London. We have agents watching a five-mile area around the nightclub where Mr. Kutaragi was last seen leaving. I must say he is a slippery fella. Both of our agents had gotten a very good look at him. And in a blink of an eye he had vanished. Slippery, very slippery. We believe he is staying in one of our local hotels. We have them all covered so if Takeo does pop his head up once again, we'll spot him," Sterling explained with confidence.

"Why would a man like Takeo be here in London? That has me puzzled," Carla explained as she looked from Sterling over to me.

Placing two drops of Methadrine under my tongue, I kept my thoughts to myself and looked over at Mr. Townsend.

"That also has a number of our agents worried. You have just asked the million dollar question," Sterling commented as he lit his pipe and sat down next to Carla. As he did our London based agent, Eric LoGiudice, and his British 14-Intelligence friend walked into the room to join us.

"Anything?" Sterling asked as he looked over at his operative.

"Nothing, sir, we lost him, but I am telling you, it was him, it was Takeo Kutaragi," he answered as he looked over at Carla. "Ms. Silverman, it's good to see you again, ma'am, you're looking well."

"Thank you Mark, it's good to see you too. I'd like you to meet David. David, this is Mark, he is one of the best agents I have ever met," Carla explained as she introduced us to each other.

"Mark, it's my pleasure," I said with a smile and a nod of my head as we shook hands.

"Same here, David, it's nice to meet you," Mark replied.

"I see that you're hanging out with the Italian Judge," I commented as I looked over at Eric and smiled.

"Hey, buddy, how you doing?" Eric greeted as we shook each other's hands.

"Good, Judge, how about yourself?" I asked as everyone sat down at the table and started pouring cups of tea to drink.

"I feel a lot better now that your here," Eric answered with a smile.

"Judge?" Mark asked with a confused look on his face.

"LoGiudice, in Italian means 'the Judge'," I explained.

"Interesting," Mark replied.

"I see you bought your secret weapon, ma'am," Eric said as he looked over at Carla who was also his boss.

"Secret weapon?" Sterling asked with one raised eyebrow as he looked over at Carla and then over at me.

Giving Eric her 'what are you doing look' she answered Sterling, "I'll explain later. But I want to make something very clear right now. If we catch Takeo and take him alive, David will deal with him. Is that clear, gentlemen?" Carla explained as she looked at each of the men in the room one at a time.

"Let's catch him first and worry about what we're going to do with him after we have him in our custody," Sterling explained calmly as he puffed on his pipe.

"Here, here," Mark responded in agreement.

We spent the next three hours making plans and listening to Sterling's agents as they called in with up to date information on their search for Takeo.

It was almost 2:00 a.m. when Carla, Eric, and I left the secret office of Great Britain's most feared intelligence group.

Eric drove us to the Metropolitan Hotel. Once in our room we had a meeting of our own. Takeo Kutaragi, if caught, wasn't going to be leaving England alive.

* * * * * * *

We had been in London now for four days and there was absolutely no sign of Takeo Kutaragi. In all reality that didn't really surprise anyone. Everyone already knew that the Japanese assassin was good enough to evade the worlds best law enforcement agents for ten years and at the same time continue to catch his victims, take days to torture them, and still get away, after he would finally kill them. There was no doubt in anyones mind, Takeo was the master of this particular manhunt.

"I think we may have lost him, sir," Mark explained as he talked to his boss.

"What do you think, Carla? Do you think that he spotted us and quietly slipped away in the darkness of the night?" Sterling asked.

"It's possible, he is very good at what he does. Damn I wanted to catch that bastard," Carla explained in a frustrated voice. "What do you think, David, is he gone?" Carla asked as an after thought.

"His safe haven is in Japan. He knows that no one can touch him there. He's here in London for a very good reason, ma'am. I'd say that he is still here and he's after someone. The question is who is he after and where will he strike? But then again that's just my opinion, ma'am," I explained calmly as I took a sip of my Pepsi.

"Good observation, young man. I tend to agree with your way of thinking. Who is he after? That is the burning question," Sterling added as he finished his meal.

We were eating lunch at one of London's more popular restaurants. At the same time, we were also staking it out to see if Takeo might just happen to show up for lunch.

It was a quiet December day. It was Wednesday and the temperature was dropping outside. In a week it would be Christmas and I wanted so very much to spend it in Dublin with Kate at our new home.

"Why, Mr. Townsend, how are you?" the elderly lady said to Sterling as she walked by our table to leave.

"Oh my, how are you, Fran? It's been such a long time," Sterling replied at the sight of his old friend.

"It's been far to long, my dear friend. Will you be attending the Prince's Trust Benefit this Saturday evening? I would like so very much to see you there," Fran explained.

"My oh my, I have been so busy with other matters that I had completely forgotten. I will try to be there, I promise," Sterling replied as he raised his teacup up in the air in a toasting manner and smiled.

"Oh that would be lovely, I hope to see you there. Ta, Ta," she said with a polite smile as she gave the rest of us a light wave goodbye with her hand.

"Charming lady," Carla commented with a smile.

"Yes quite, and a dear friend. A grand lady," Sterling replied.

Looking over at Carla I raised both of my eyebrows with an intense look of surprise on my face.

"What? What did I miss?" Carla asked unsure as to what I was trying to tell her.

"Mr. Townsend, where do they hold the Prince's Trust Benefit?" I questioned calmly.

"The Royal Albert Hall, it's a grand benefit. All of London's elite will be there," Sterling said proudly.

"And so will Takeo Kutaragi," I explained as I stood up quickly to leave.

The most obvious was once again the least obvious. If my gut feeling was correct, and it always is, Takeo was going to assassinate some one at the Prince's Trust Benefit this Saturday night.

Hearing Carla say, "Oh shit," and Sterling mumble "Oh no, not the Prince," confirmed my gut feeling. The question now was, who was Takeo after.

* * * * * * *

It was Saturday night as Carla and I walked into the Royal Albert Hall. Looking around I could see that this was going to be one of London's biggest partygoers events of the year. Everyone who was anyone was here.

Some of London's top music performers were here to sing and also enjoy the party. In all actuality the event was called, 'The Fashion Rocks for the Prince's Trust Benefit.'

With her arm draped through mine, Carla put her mouth close to my ear and whispered, "How are we ever going to find him in a crowd this size?"

"He won't be himself, we already know that. Look at each person beyond your normal way of looking at people. You're looking for something out of the norm. Sterling has the place crawling with MI-6 and 14-Intelligence Agents. Eric is keeping his position within a few feet of ours. I told him to stay close and be ready for anything. But that doesn't mean anything. Takeo is one of the best. He also knows that this event will be crawling with undercover agents. All we can do is enjoy the party and hope that we get lucky," I explained with a fake smile.

"I'm so glad you're here with me, David. Please use all of your skills tonight. I want to look this bastard in the eyes before he dies," Carla explained as she tightened her grip on my arm.

This was one of the biggest charity events of the year. Everyone was attending the grand event. Between songs different people would get up on the stage and talk to the large crowd of people. Drinks were flowing, people were laughing, and everyone was having a grand old time.

The Queen arrived with her son Prince Charles. To my surprise the Queen didn't stay very long. She smiled, waved, and talked to people as she mingled with the large crowd. Within the hour she had left. When she did, the Prime Minister showed up with some of the Royals. The Prime Minister stayed and was clearly having a very good time.

"I'm going to take a walk through the crowd, I'll be right back," I explained as I nodded at Eric to follow me.

"What do you think, buddy?" Eric asked as we slowly made our way through the crowded hall.

"He's here, I can smell him," I replied.

"Your kidding, you can smell him? What's he smell like?" Eric asked with a puzzle look on his face.

"Death," I replied, as I carefully looked each person in the room over from head to toe.

We had arrived at 7:00 p.m., it was now almost 10:00 p.m. and there was still no sign of Takeo.

The Prime Minister was on the stage talking into the microphone to the crowd as the next band set up to perform. He was telling jokes, and the crowd was laughing and clapping their hands. It was then that I saw something out of 'the norm,' as my instructor at the CIA Farm would describe it.

"There he is," I said quickly as I tapped Eric on the arm, never taking my eyes off of my target.

"Where?" Eric asked excitedly.

"Up by the stage," I replied.

"I'll get Carla," Eric responded.

"No, there's no time, he's moving closer to the end of the stage where the Prime Minister will have to walk down the steps to exit. Follow me Eric, keep your eyes on the nun," I explained as we slowly made our way through the crowded room of people.

"You sure that's him?" Eric asked, worried that this might really be a real nun.

Reaching into my suit jacket pocket, I put my right hand on the stungun I had hidden inside.

Without taking my eyes off of the nun I whispered to Eric, "If she tries to run shoot her," I explained as I moved up even closer, like a wild cat stalking its prey.

"You got it," Eric replied nervously.

I was within six feet of the nun as the Prime Minister finished his joke telling session. Smiling at the crowd he waved his right hand at everyone and headed toward the end of the large stage where the steps were located.

Watching the nun clap her hands once again, I had no doubt I was now within arms reach of Takeo Kutaragi.

As the Prime Minister stepped down off the stage and onto the first step, my heart raced with excitement when I saw the nun lower her right hand and twist her wrist. When she did I saw the syringe drop downward from under her sleeve and into her hand.

A full surge of pure adrenaline rushed through my entire body as I pulled my right hand out of my pocket.

The Prime Minister was now on the last step and about to step out onto the main floor of the hall. As he did the nun made a quick turn toward him as I pressed the stungun into her lower back and pressed on the trigger. As I did the next British rock group began to play. The music was loud enough to cover the sound of my stungun. The surge of electricity flowing through the nun's body caused her to jerk as every muscle in her body tensed up. It was at this same time the Prime Minister walked past us completely unaware that he was about to be injected with God only knows what.

Releasing the trigger on the stungun I quickly wrapped my left arm around the waist of the nun to hold her up and keep her from falling to the floor. Placing the stungun back into my pocket, I turned the nun's body around toward me and picked her up in my arms.

"Eric, the exit, move now, clear a path," I said as Eric quickly picked up the syringe from the floor where the nun had dropped it.

"Oh my God, is she alright?" One of the young women asked as I walked passed her carrying the nun.

"She'll be fine, she just needs a little air, that's all," Eric replied as we made our way to the exit door. Stepping through it and out into the cool night air I bent down and dropped the nuns body down onto the cement sidewalk.

"You got any handcuffs?" I asked as I pulled my silenced .22 magnum out from under my suit coat and pressed the barrel of the gun against the nuns forehead.

"Cuff's?" Eric asked with a surprised look as Carla, Sterling and a dozen of Sterling's agents rushed outside and gathered around us.

"That's a nun," one of the agents said quickly.

"Anybody have any cuff's?" I asked as I began to get frustrated.

"Here you go," one of the female agents said as she handed me a pair of handcuffs.

Rolling the body of the nun over onto her stomach I cuffed both of her hands behind her back.

Kneeling down next to me, Carla looked at the nun and then back over at me.

I knew what she was thinking. She wasn't sure if this was Takeo or not but she wasn't going to second-guess or question me. To do so would tell Sterling and his agents that she didn't trust me.

Grabbing the nun's fingers I showed them to Carla.

"Ever see a nun with a manicure before?" I asked.

"No can't say that I have," Carla responded calmly.

"How about a nun wearing a Japanese made watch?" I asked with a grin as I lifted up the long black sleeve of the nun's habit uniform.

Carla was now smiling as the nun began to come out of her stunned state of condition.

Rolling her over I pulled her long black habit up around her waist.

"Well, well, look at that. A nun with a set of men's nuts. Hello Takeo," I said with a smile as Takeo regained consciousness.

"Superb work young man, we've got him," Sterling explained in a sharp British accent, as he looked around at his agents with a smile on his face.

"Grand job, David. Sherlock Holmes would be proud of you. Now I know what you meant, Eric, about David being Ms. Silverman's secret weapon," Mark said proudly.

"Tech seven to all agents, we have Takeo in custody. I repeat, we have our target secured," one of the other agents said into his radio lip mike.

"He was getting ready to inject the Prime Minister with this, sir," Eric explained as he reached into his pocket and carefully pulled out the syringe Takeo had dropped to the floor. Handing the syringe to Mr. Townsend, an angry look appeared on his face for the first time since I had met him.

Holding the syringe up toward the outside lights, Sterling took a long careful look at the liquid inside it.

"Gordon, get this to the lab would you old chap. Let's see if we can find out what this is," Sterling explained as he handed the syringe to his agents.

Takeo was now fully alert. His head and eyes were moving in all directions at once as he tried to analyze his next move.

"Hello, Mr. Kutaragi, you murdered one of my agents and sent the film of his death to me at my office," Carla said coldly as she stared Takeo in the eyes.

Reaching into my pocket I pulled out my stungun once again.

He was too calm and had a smile on his face. He was getting ready to do something. When I saw his tongue move under his lower lip I pressed the prongs of my stungun quickly into Takeo's leg and gave him another ten-second jolt of electricity. Putting my stungun back into my pocket I then holstered my handgun.

"Eric, look inside of his mouth would you. Look between the lower lip and his gum," I explained calmly.

Holstering his weapon, Eric knelt down next to Takeo and opened his mouth. Looking inside, he reached in with his fingers and felt around. It only took Eric a second to find what he was looking for. Pulling out the small glass capsule of Cyanide Poison, Eric held it up for me to see and smiled.

"I think he wanted to take the easy way out, huh?" Eric asked as he handed the capsule to Mr. Townsend.

"You have trained him well, Carla," Sterling commented.

"Yes, I have. I have always said that David is better than your James Bond. Now even you know that to be true," Carla explained with a nod of her head as she looked over at me proudly.

"Well, I don't know if I would go so far as to say that. Our Bond would think of a unique way of disposing of Mr. Kutaragi. Let's see if your David can impress us with something that I have never seen before. Believe me, Carla, I have seen it all," Sterling explained as he pulled his pipe out from the inside pocket of his suit coat and calmly lit it.

Looking at me Carla tilted her head slightly to the right and raised her eyebrows.

Placing two drops of Methadrine under my tongue I put the tiny glass vial back into my pocket.

Looking up at Sterling I asked, "May we borrow a car, sir?"

A crowd of people had started to gather around curious to see what had happened to cause all the security from inside, to run outside so quickly. As the London police moved the crowd farther back from our perimeter, three Chrysler Town Cars and two Chevy Blazers pulled right up next to where we had Takeo laying on the ground. All five of the full sized vehicles helped to block the view from the crowd of people who were still coming outside from the Royal Albert Hall to take a look. Takeo was wide eyed and fully alert when Eric and I helped him up and quickly pushed him into the backseat of one of the Chryslers with dark tinted windows.

"Where to?" the young female agent from British 14-Intelligence asked as Eric and I climbed into the backseat and sat at each side of Takeo. Carla and Sterling climbed in and sat down in the front seat next to the female driver.

"South, about four miles there's a cemetery on the left side of the road. I saw it as we drove past on our way here. I think the sign read, White Chapel Cemetery," I explained as we quickly drove away and left the Royal Albert Hall for the last time.

Much to my surprise, Takeo Kutaragi still hadn't spoken a word.

My first thought was to take Takeo to the Bronson and Ive's Funeral Home. Once there I thought about strapping Takeo down to the stainless steel embalming table and replacing his blood with a Formaldehyde Cocktail. This could be done in the same way as a mortician would do when he embalms a dead body to prepare it for the funeral display.

The only difference would be, I was going to do it to the Japanese assassin while he was still alive. The Formaldehyde would make his blood boil and burn him from the inside out. The problem was that once the Formaldehyde hit his heart or brain, it would kill him instantly. At least that's the way I figured it would work anyway.

Takeo left a signature on almost all of his hits. Once he tortured his victims, he would then soak them down with gasoline and set them on fire, burning them alive until they finally died. This method of death gave me an idea on how the Sandman would introduce Takeo Kutaragi to his final end.

It was almost midnight as we pulled into the White Chapel Cemetery in London, England.

"Pull up to that small white building next to the chapel would you?" I asked as I reached over the shoulder of the blonde haired female driver and pointed at the building.

"Oooookay," she said in a long drawn out way.

As we pulled into the cemetery, one of the black Chevy Blazer, four-wheel drive vehicles parked itself sideways across the front entrance to keep anyone else from coming into the cemetery. At this late hour it was doubtful that anyone would come in. However, we also didn't know if Takeo had any friends around to back him up and help him if something should happen to go wrong, as it did.

The secret British Intelligence group wasn't taking any chances either way. That's what makes them the elite black operations group that they are still to this day.

Parking our cars in front of the small white building next to the cemetery chapel, the drivers of all four of the vehicles turned out their headlights and shut off their engines all at the same time.

"I'll be right back," I said softly as I climbed out of the vehicle.

The first thing I noticed was how still and quiet everything was. I wasn't one to get spooked easily, but I have to admit I felt a chill run up my spine as I walked up to the side door of the small white building next to the chapel.

Turning the doorknob, it was locked.

"Shit, who locks a door in a damn cemetery?" I said in a low tone of voice as I reached into the inside pocket of my suit jacket and pulled out the small lock pick set I had borrowed from Eric the day after Carla and I arrived in London. Opening the small leather holder, I pulled out the rake and tumbler picks and quickly went to work on the door lock.

To my dismay it took me almost three full minutes to pick the lock before it finally clicked open. Yeah, I know, I'm supposed to be good at this stuff. But you try picking the lock on the door of the crematorium building, at midnight, in a cemetery, with only the light of a full moon to assist you.

Uh-huh, that's what I thought. Just keep reading. I promise your gonna love what I do to this sick bastard.

Opening the solid wood door I ran my hand along the inside wall to my left, found the light switch and turned on the light.

The small room wasn't that big, it was about 24-feet by 24-feet on the inside. There was a desk in the far left corner with a filing cabinet sitting next to it. The top of the desk was cluttered with papers, and had a cold cup of coffee and a half eaten Big Mac hamburger still sitting on top of it. Across the room was the square metal door of the propane-fueled oven used to cremate dead bodies.

Walking over to the oven, I pushed down on the lever used to open the oven door and then pulled the thick steal door open. The door itself had a small yet very thick heatproof window in it. Seeing that brought a smile to my face.

Reaching inside the oven I pulled out the metal table that moved easily on metal rollers. I then took a look at the temperature gauge and the fuel ignition button. "This was going to be very simple," I thought to myself as I turned and walked back out to our car where Takeo was waiting. Opening the backdoor I reached in and grabbed the Japanese assassin by the arm.

"Step out here a minute, Mr. Kutaragi. I would like to talk to you for a moment," I explained as Eric, Carla, Sterling, our driver and all of the agents in the other three vehicles all opened their car doors and stepped out into the cool breeze of the December night.

"I am going to ask you a question, Mr. Kutaragi. Who sent you here to kill the Prime Minister of England?" I asked with a calm voice as I reached into my jacket pocket with my right hand and grabbed my stungun.

I already knew Takeo wasn't going to say anything. He was a highly trained Yakuza Warrior. To even show fear of any kind now that he was in the hands of his enemies, would be insulting to not only him, but also to the Master in Japan who trained him from the time he was a young child.

"What's the matter, Takeo, afraid to talk now that you've been caught?" Carla asked as her eyes filled with hate and anger just at the sight of him.

"He's not afraid, ma'am," I said as Takeo and I stared deep into each other's eyes.

"Mr. Kutaragi is a very proud and highly trained Yakuza Warrior. To speak to us would bring dishonor to him and disgrace his Master," I explained. When I did I noticed that Takeo tilted his head ever so slightly to the right. It surprised him that I not only understood but also at the same time gave him his respect as a fellow assassin.

"Search him, Eric," Carla said coldly.

Searching Takeo's entire body all that Eric could find was one lone room key. Handing it to Carla, Eric looked back over at me and waited to see what my next move was going to be.

"Is there anything you would like to say to him, Sterling?" Carla asked coldly as she continued to look at Takeo through hate filled eyes.

"No not at all. In fact, I agree with David. Mr. Kutaragi will go to his death, no matter how horrible it may be, in total silence," Sterling explained as he pulled out his pipe and lit it. "I've seen his kind do it before," Sterling added.

"Just so you know, Takeo, it was your hip's that gave you away," I explained as I dropped my head slightly and gave him an oriental bow.

The look in his eyes told me that he understood as he returned the bow as a show of respect. In doing so he acknowledged to me that I had caught him fair and square, because he had slipped up and made a mistake that would now cost him his life.

Grabbing him by the arm I led him into the crematorium and walked him up to the oven. I thought he would try a martial arts kick as one last attempt to strike back before he was put to death. But he didn't. Instead, much to my surprise, he sat down on the metal table, looked at me, and nodded his head once again and then turned his body length wise and laid down on the table.

"My God, you're going to cremate him alive?" Mark asked in a whisper as I slid Takeo's body into the oven and sealed the door closed behind him.

Looking in through the small window of the oven door I could see that Takeo's face was now covered with tiny beads of sweat. His mouth was moving, he was praying.

"You're not really going to do this are you?" the driver of our car asked nervously.

Looking over at the young female I noticed that the other agents were still standing outside securing the small room we were in, only a few were looking inside.

Showing no emotion, I reached up and pushed the fuel start button. When I did a line of small flames appeared all around the entire top and bottom of the oven. These were the small pilot lights that would burst into flames as soon as I pressed the fuel ignition button, which I had not done yet.

Takeo's body was jerking wildly as the heat inside of the oven slowly began to burn and blister his skin. Reaching up, I quickly turned off the oven and opened the door. As I did I could feel a rush of heat hit me in the face as the cool December nights air rushed in to replace it.

The rancid smell of burnt flesh quickly filled the small room we were standing in. Looking into the oven, Takeo tilted his head slightly back and looked at me. His entire body was now trembling; his eyes were wide with a look of fear in them.

"Shall I call an ambulance, sir?" the young female agent asked excitedly as she looked over at her boss.

"Step outside Hanna and wait out there with the others please," Sterling asked as he puffed on his pipe. Mr. Sterling Townsend was standing straight and proud in true British fashion, showing no emotion.

Lowering her head Hanna walked out of the small room and joined the other agents.

"Did you have an orgasm yet?" I asked as Takeo and I looked each other in the eyes.

"Sandman's here, asshole, say goodnight," I said as I slowly closed the oven door and locked it shut once again.

Pressing the fuel start button, I heard the hiss of propane gas as the pilot lights all relit themselves again.

Looking in the tiny window I saw Takeo's body kicking and jerking wildly.

Pushing the ignition button, the inside of the oven burst into flames. When it did we all stood in silence and listened to Takeo scream.

"So much for being a true Yakuza Warrior," Eric said jokingly as the screaming stopped.

Adjusting the temperature of the oven to 1,900 degrees, I looked over at Carla and then at Mr. Townsend.

"In three hours there will be nothing left but a pile of ash. Are there any good restaurants open this late at night around here? I'm hungry," I explained as I looked over at Eric.

"How about Takeo? He'll be done in, oh I'd say, another five minutes," Eric explained as he looked at his watch and broke out laughing.

"I believe you were right my dear. This was original and a first. Amazing, simply amazing," Sterling explained as he calmly tapped the burnt tobacco out of his pipe and let it fall to the floor near his feet.

"I told you he was better than your Mr. Bond," Carla bragged as we all walked outside and stood in the cool night air.

"Well, I don't know? James would have probably...." Sterling began to say as Carla cut him short in mid sentence.

"Don't even try it, Sterling," Carla explained as we all walked back over to our cars and drove away.

Takeo Kutaragi died in the early morning hours of December 20, 1975. In his death he took with him the secret of who had sent him to kill the

Prime Minister of England. In my opinion, he died with honor as a true warrior.

Carla and I spent the night at the Metropolitan Hotel in London. We received a call at 7:00 a.m. December 21st. It was from Neil. Carla's goddaughter Neve had come out of her coma. She couldn't remember anything about the assault or being raped, which to us was a blessing. Little Neve was going to be just fine, which was going to make this a very special Christmas indeed.

Flying Carla home so that she could spend Christmas with Neve, I had only one thing left to do before I flew to Dublin to spend Christmas with Kate.

* * * * * * *

Flying back to San Jose I went straight to the trauma care burn unit of the local hospital to see Istvan. Everyday the medical staff would scrape off layer after layer of dead puss oozing skin from Istvan's badly burnt body, which was a long and painful process for him.

His pain was so horrible that the doctors caring for Istvan had ordered that he be placed on a continuous Morphine IV that was fed directly into his blood stream.

Even with all of the Morphine flowing through his body, Istvan laid completely still, moaning, groaning, and wincing in pain and agony.

"Are you a friend of his?" the intensive care unit nurse asked in a whisper of a voice.

"No, ma'am, his family called and asked me if I would stop by and check on his condition," I answered calmly.

"Who would do such a horrible thing to another human being?" the nurse asked as she checked the IV drip that fed the Morphine into Istvan's system.

"Death, no one escapes death when the Sandman comes to collect your soul," I explained as I stared at Istvan.

"Mr. Bastick did, he's still alive," the nurse replied with a grin as she turned and left the room.

Reaching into my shirt pocket I pulled out a small syringe and removed the plastic red colored cover from the needle. Slipping the thin needle into Istvan's IV bag, I quickly injected 30cc's of deadly Potassium Chloride into the bag. Placing the cap back over the thin needle I put the syringe back into my pocket, turned and looked at Istvan.

Leaning forward I placed my mouth close to his ear.

"Behold, I saw a pale green horse and upon it sat death, which was followed by the grave. The Sandman's here, Istvan. I'm here to collect your soul. It's time to go, Istvan. This is the price you pay for what you did to little Neve. Say goodnight," I whispered in a cold and deadly manner.

He seemed to become paranoid at the words I had spoken to him. The Potassium Chloride entered his blood stream quickly. Within seconds Istvan Bastick's heart stopped as he let out his last breath of air.

Turning, I walked out of the hospital and flew to Dublin to spend Christmas with Kate.

I tried, I really did. But once the Sandman brings death to your door, he must collect your soul. Now with Istvan dead, I felt much better.

* * * * * * *

Sitting in front of our fireplace I held Kate in my arms as we watched the yellow blue tipped flames dance on the logs in front of us.

It was almost midnight of December 24, 1975. Our brand new home was finished, and in short, it was beautiful. Kate had decorated the entire inside of the home with candles, Christmas lights, and a large Christmas tree. Under the tree we had all of our Christmas presents neatly wrapped with colored paper, ribbons, and bows. Our home was about three thousand square feet in size. It was hand crafted by Kate's grandfather and relatives. They had built it out of large rocks and solid oak timber. It even had hand made red ceramic shingles for a roof.

When Kate picked me up at the airport she blindfolded me just before we got home to ensure that I would be completely surprised when I saw our home for the very first time. Surprised isn't the right word to describe how I felt. Awed and amazed would be a more accurate description as to how I actually felt.

"Thank you Kate, this is the greatest surprise I have ever had in my entire life. Our home is perfect, I really do love it," I whispered into her ear as I gently kissed her on the side of her neck.

"It pleases me to hear you say that, David, but the house isn't the surprise I've been wanting to tell you about," Kate explained as she turned in my arms to face me.

"It's not?" I asked with a surprised look on my face.

"No, love, I wanted to give you this surprise on our Lords birthday, which is right now," she explained as our large solid oak wood grandfather clock struck twelve midnight. It was early Christmas morning.

"Close your eye's," Kate said with a large smile and a twinkle in her eyes.

Closing my eyes my heart raced with excitement as I smiled and grinned.

"Ready?" she asked playfully.

"Yes, dear, I'm ready," I answered in a soft voice.

Placing her mouth close to my ear, I could feel her breath on the side of my neck, which smelled like fresh mint.

"You're going to be a daddy, I'm pregnant with twin boys. Merry Christmas my love," she whispered as she kissed me tenderly on the lips...

Chapter Thirty-Five
Broken Arrow

Sitting in the pilot's seat of my silver Learjet, I looked out through the side window. Seeing Kate blow a kiss and send it to me gave me a warm feeling inside.

When Kate had gotten up one morning and quickly ran to the bathroom to throw-up, Kate's grandmother took her to see their family doctor. It didn't take a genius to figure out that Kate was pregnant. What shocked everyone was when the doctor gave Kate an ultrasound examination and confirmed that she was not only pregnant but was pregnant with twin boys.

Her grandfather and cousin Tom immediately went to the pub to celebrate and commence in the fine Irish tradition of buying drinks for everybody and getting drunk.

I didn't want to leave Kate but I needed to fly home and check on my grandmother and turn the family over to Uncle Paul in New York.

Waving goodbye, I took flight and flew back to Michigan. It was January 15, 1976.

When I got home I went straight to my grandmothers house to check on her condition and tell her about Kate.

The news about Kate being pregnant with twin boy's not only excited my grandmother, but it seemed to give her a new found source of hope. Her cancer was slowly spreading, but now she was more determined than ever to beat it, so she could see her great-grandsons.

Uncle Paul was in the hospital having some minor surgery so instead of flying to New York to see him, I sent flowers and a message to let him know that I wished him well and that I would fly out to see him when he was feeling better. Going back to my home I found myself sitting at my desk drinking a bottle of Pepsi with a large grin on my face. I was going to be a daddy.

Thinking back to Vietnam and how I had first met Kate brought back fond memories. Picking up the telephone I called my closest brother and friend, Chopper. To my disappointment, he was still in Germany with Amanda, tracking down the information we all hoped would lead us to the nuclear weapons we were all trying very hard to recover.

My second call went to Neil.

"Talk to me," Neil said after he picked up his telephone.

"Hey, partner, Happy New Year," I responded cheerfully.

"David, same to you, partner. Hey, man, Carla looks great. When she got back from her vacation and your trip to London, she actually walked in and kissed me on the cheek. Talk about a woman revitalized," Neil explained with a chuckle.

"She's a great gal, we had a really good time," I explained as I took a sip of my Pepsi.

"How's it feel, being the guy who caught Takeo?" Neil asked.

"That was a combined effort, brother, I didn't catch him, we all caught him," I replied.

"Bullshit, Carla said you told Takeo it was his hips that gave him away. Everyone, and I do mean everyone in our division is trying to figure out what in the hell you were talking about. Mind explaining what that meant to a young rookie computer geek like me?" Neil asked hoping that I would tell him what few people knew about hips.

"Takeo was good, Neil, he was real good, but he was dressed in a nun's habit. If it wouldn't have been for the fact that the habit he was wearing was just a tad bit snug, I would have missed it," I explained.

"Geez, Dave, you would have missed what?" Neil asked impatiently.

"Women, their hips are higher up on their bodies frame than men's are," I explained calmly.

"What? Are you serious? I've never heard that before. Are you being serious with me or are you playing with me?" Neil asked.

"I'm being serious. I wouldn't lie to you. Women have higher hips than men. It's because they give birth to babies. At least that's the way it was explained to me at the Farm. Women are built different than we are, especially in the area of their hips. It's got something to do with the birthing process and the birth canal," I explained.

"No shit! You caught Japans most dangerous terrorist because of his hips? Call me Mary and kiss my ass, that's amazing. Leave it to the Sandman. You're versatile, brother, damn your good," Neil explained proudly.

"Just lucky, I got off on the training I learned at the Farm. After hours I'd go to where my instructors lived and asked them to teach me their special secrets, the stuff they don't teach just anybody. That impressed the hell out of them. So they would spend hours teaching me things they never taught anyone else. You guys should send them a message and tell them it was private training about the difference between men and women's hips, which helped us, catch Takeo. It would mean a lot to them," I explained seriously.

"Yeah, I'll bet it would mean a lot to them to know that their training brought Takeo's killing spree to an end. I'll make sure they get the message," Neil explained.

"So, how's little Neve doing? Is she alright?" I asked.

"That little lady is doing great. The way I understand it is Istvan snuck up behind her and hit her in the back of the head with God only knows what. The doctors believe it was the first blow to the head, which knocked her out cold. That was the only good thing about the whole ordeal.

When she went into the coma, I guess it was the combination of the blow to the head followed by the vicious beating he gave her which caused her to get brain clots.

It took almost two months to dissolve the clots with medicine. Once the doctors dissolved the clots, Neve woke up. By then all of the surgery had completely healed. So it was like she went to sleep and woke up two months later, and to her, nothing happened. Talk about a miracle," Neil explained.

"No kidding, that's great. God, I hate those sick bastards who hurt little kids," I said bitterly.

"Don't we all, thank God we were able to find out who it was. I hear you deep fried him," Neil commented with a slight laugh in his voice.

"Let's just say you can stick a fork in him, he's done," I answered jokingly. "Anything new on who it is, here in the States, that's talking to Kalashnikov about me?"

"The new system we had installed is working great, but there have been only two calls to Boris about you since we had it installed. They've got a skip jump system that's a lot like ours. I'm slowly eliminating states trying to get me closer to the main source or exact location the main call is coming from. I'm narrowing it down Sandman, it's only a matter of time now and we'll have him. I'd sure like to know who in the hell this is and be able to get a close-up look at his system," Neil explained.

"Good, I'm going to pay that Russian spy a very personal visit as soon as you tell me who it is. Just promise me, brother, you won't tell anyone who he is when you find out. I want this guy to meet the Sandman one on one," I explained in a serious tone of voice.

"This will be between me and you only. I won't even tell Carla until you tell me its okay to do so. I promise you that," Neil replied.

"Thanks, brother, I appreciate it. Is Carla in her office? I need to talk to her," I asked.

"No, as a matter of fact she flew to Switzerland for some super secret meeting. The rumor is, she might be leaving the Agency for a bigger and better top secret position somewhere else," Neil explained sadly.

"What?" I responded surprised at what I had just heard.

"Please keep that between us, David. It's just a rumor. I know the Congress is killing us right now. If what we're hearing has any truth to it, they're cutting our budget this year and talking about pulling all of our spies and agents out of the Middle East within the next three years. Where's Nixon when you need him the most?" Neil explained sadly.

"I don't think she is going to leave. She would have said something to me while we were on vacation and away from everyone. At least I would have thought that she would have anyway."

"Maybe, maybe not, time will tell. She's suppose to be back in her office Thursday. Stop by or give us a call then, unless of course we call you first," Neil explained with a chuckle in his voice.

"Alright, buddy, I'll talk to you later," I replied as I hung up the telephone on my end.

Things were changing and the politicians in Washington D.C. were about to make a major mistake. If they did, America would be in danger like it's never been in before.

* * * * * * *

"There you go, brother, that should do it. You now have telephones in your bedroom and down here behind the bar. I'll send you my bill," Andy explained with a grin as he set his tool kit down on my bar and opened the refrigerator to grab a cold beer.

Picking up the telephone I placed it against my ear. It was dead! Looking over at Andy I handed the receiver to him. "It's for you," I explained with a straight look on my face.

""Yeah right," Andy replied as he opened his long necked bottle of Budweiser and took a drink.

"Really, it's for you," I explained once again as Andy took the telephone receiver from my hand and placed it against his ear.

"Shit!" he mumbled as he left the basement and headed back upstairs to my den.

"The line's dead," I whispered to Don who was sitting across from me at the bar with a curious look on his face.

"The only thing he's really good at is killing people. Did you ever try eating any of his dog meat chili?" Don asked with a serious look on his face.

"Oh yeah, but only once," I replied as the telephone began to ring. Picking up the telephone I placed it against my ear. "Hello," I said cautiously into the receiver.

"It was a loose wire, it's working now," Andy explained.

"How in the hell did you get the telephone to ring like that?" I questioned.

"Ancient Indian secret," Andy replied.

"Like the recipe to your dog meat chili?" I asked knowing full well it would piss him off.

"Fuck you, that was your fault not mine," Andy responded. As he did my front doorbell rang.

"Answer the door on your way back, would ya?"

"Oops, I forgot to tell you," Andy replied.

"You forgot to tell me what Andy?"

"Tara called earlier when you were taking your shower. She's bringing a few of her friends over. They're going to cook us supper tonight," Andy explained as the doorbell rang once again.

"As long as its not dog meat chili," I replied as I hung up the receiver to my telephone.

It took Tara, Jessy, Karen, and Judy almost three hours to make Andy, Don, and I supper. I kinda felt that Tara wanted to ask me something, but wasn't sure how to do it. It doesn't take three hours to make Kraft Macaroni and Cheese and boil hot dogs. After we ate I took Tara to my den for a moment and closed the door.

"Have a seat," I explained as I sat down on my black leather playpen sofa.

"What's up, Uncle Dave?" Tara asked.

"I've watched you grow up for the last five years of your life. I know when something is bothering you. Would you like to talk about it?" I asked in a fatherly way.

Looking down at her feet there was a long pause. Raising her head Tara looked into my eyes.

"Your going to move away aren't you?" she asked with a sad look on her face.

I hadn't really taken the time to think about how my moving to Dublin was going to effect the young girl who I loved like a daughter.

"Come over here and sit next to me would you please?" I asked as Tara stood up and tears began to fill her eyes. "Awe, Uncle Dave," she whispered as she sat down next to me and put her hands over her face.

Putting my arm around her I pulled her close to my chest.

"I'm going to tell you some of my best kept secrets. I want you to listen carefully to what I am going to say to you, okay?" I asked as I raised her chin with my finger so we could look each other in the eyes.

Nodding her head 'yes', I wiped the tears from her cheeks.

"I promised you along time ago I would never lie to you. So, I'm going to tell you some stuff I need you to try and understand. First, I love you so very much. You're the daughter I never had. Nothing will ever change that. I'll always be a part of your life. I told you about my girlfriend Kate, remember?" I asked.

"Yes, the red headed nurse from Vietnam. Your angel, right?"

"Yeah, she's a special angel God sent into my life. A lot like you are. The only difference is that Kate's pregnant," I explained.

"What? Really? You're going to be a daddy. That means I'm going to be an Aunt, huh?" Tara asked with a surprised and now happy look on her face.

"Well, a little more than that," I explained. "Kate's going to have twins," I said with a broad smile on my face.

"What!" Tara yelled out in excitement.

"Two little boys to be exact," I said proudly.

"Oh shit, two little boys, this is so cool," she replied.

"That's the first time I have ever heard you swear. You're growing up to fast," I sighed.

"Sorry about that, I swear sometimes."

"It's cool, just remember, you're a young lady and try not to swear around other people."

"Okay, I'll be careful," Tara responded.

"Listen, I'm going to move to Dublin, Ireland. But I'm going to keep this house. Kate and I will be living in Ireland and flying back here to live too. All of my family is here. You and your mom, Jessy and her mom, my mom, dad, sisters, aunts, uncles, and my grandma. I'm leaving but not the way you think I am. Kate's family lives in Montana. They have a huge horse range out there that's beautiful."

"Really? Do you think that one day you could take me there to see the horses?" Tara asked with raised eyebrows.

"Absolutely," I replied.

"Now I understand why you're gone so much," Tara explained nodding her head.

"Well, the other super big secret is that sometimes I do some very special work for our government," I began to explain.

"Really? Your what? Like a secret agent or a spy or something really neat like that?" she asked as she looked over at my desk with the computer and three different telephones on it. "Oh man, that's why you said we can never come into this room," she whispered slowly as she began to analyze things out in her own mind.

"I can't tell you what I do. It's not that I don't trust you Tara, so don't you think that, because I do trust you. So don't tell anyone else."

"No one? Not even my mom?"

"No one sweetie, especially your mom. Not Jessy, or even Don or Andy," I explained with a serious look in my eyes.

"Don and Andy don't know either?" she asked with a surprised look on her face.

"No one knows, just you and Kate. I shouldn't have told you anything at all. I can't tell you any more than that. But what I can say is that what I do helps to keep America safe. There are a lot of bad people out there who would like to hurt us and destroy our country. What's important to me is that you understand there's a bunch of Americans who are willing to risk their lives, even die if need be, to stop the bad guys from hurting us," I explained.

"And your one of those good guys, huh?" she asked me as she pressed her lips together and looked into my eyes.

"I sure hope so. Do you understand I'm not leaving you, but things will be a little different?"

"Can I come to Ireland to see you and Kate?" Tara asked.

"Absolutely, I hope you come to our wedding," I explained as I leaned forward and kissed Tara on her forehead.

"This is so fucking cool..." she began to say as she caught herself swearing again. "Oops."

"Don't smoke cigarettes, don't do drugs and don't break the law, promise me that, Tara," I asked sternly.

"I don't do any of that stuff. Can I call you Dad instead of, Uncle David?" she asked shyly.

"Yes you can, as long as you never, ever forget who your real father was. It's important that you never forget him. He's a real special father who loved you and your mom so much that he was willing to go and fight in a war on the other side of the world, just to keep you safe here in America. He died to protect us all. He's a real hero Tara, always be proud of that, understand?" I asked.

"I've always been proud of my Daddy, one day I'll tell my children about him," Tara said smiling.

"That a girl, are we cool now?" I asked.

"Yeah, I understand now. Now I'm not afraid of losing you anymore. But now that you're my second Dad, can I have some money to go shopping with?" she asked with wide eyes and a big smile on her face. Just as she did my telephone began to ring.

"I knew you were setting me up, you little shit," I said as I stood up and walked over to my desk to pick up my phone.

Reaching into my pocket I pulled out my gold money clip and tossed it over to her.

"Take what you need," I explained with a grin as I picked up the telephone and turned on the scrambler box.

"Hello," I said calmly as I watched Tara pull two one hundred dollar bills out of my money clip and look up at me for approval.

Smiling, I said "Just take it all."

"David?" Neil said in an exited tone of voice.

"Yeah, what's up?" I asked.

"Broken Arrow, Ben is on his way to pick you up. Carla's in route back to her office. Move now, brother, this is a Code Red Broken Arrow," Neil explained as he quickly hung up the telephone.

"Shit!" I said loudly as I hung up the telephone. Neil had just given me a top-secret government code word for a missing nuclear weapon. Code Red meant it was a direct threat against our country, which gave it top military and national security priority.

"Tara, I gotta go. I love you sweetie, but you have to leave this room," I explained as we both ran out of the den.

"Tell Andy to keep an eye on the house," I said as I ran upstairs to grab my coat and the keys to my car.

* * * * * * *

It only took about twelve minutes for me to get to the Pontiac Airport. In that short period of time Ben had already landed, turned the plane around and was ready to take off again. The side door was open and the jet engines were still running as I ran over to the plane, climbed in and pulled the door closed behind me. Securing the side door I quickly climbed into the co-pilots seat and fastened my seat belt.

Ben had the plane moving before I could even close the door which told me that whatever was going on was going to be real hot and without a doubt very dangerous.

I waited for Ben to take off and get us airborne once again before I said anything. I didn't want to break his concentration. Once in flight, I spoke.

"How bad is it?" I asked as I pulled out my tiny vial of Methadrine and placed two drops under my tongue. My heart was racing with excitement and a full surge of adrenaline anticipating his response to my question.

"Whatever it is, partner, it's hot! They've called me four times already to see if I've picked you up yet. They've never acted like this before. They have four other Learjet's in the air bringing people in. Hang on, Dave; I'm getting a call.

Roger that operation control, he is on board, we are in route to your twenty. Estimated time of arrival one hour fifteen minutes, do you copy? Roger that, Pale Horse out.

"Sorry about that, Neil is driving me hard on this one," Ben explained.

"Pale Horse? That's your code name? I've never heard you use that code name before. I thought you were Op's One?" I questioned.

"I use to be, but once they assigned me to you and you only status, Neil renamed my call sign to Pale Horse. You know, from the book of revelations. Death rides the Pale Horse. Your mounted and riding now, partner," Ben explained smiling as he looked over at me and switched the plane over to autopilot.

"Just don't paint this plane pale green. I swear to God I'll shoot you if you do," I responded. Nothing really surprised me anymore when it came to call signs or code names. Our elite group worked real hard at what they did in the name of God and country. So when they came up with unique names to match a particular situation, it made them feel good. It was a small price to pay for the great job they always did for us.

As soon as we landed military police rushed me to the Pentagon. Running up to the front door I showed the security personnel my Q-clearance and ran straight to the elevator. Once downstairs, I ran straight to the Situation Room.

There were two people inside, both of whom were very busy taking on the telephones. After seeing me come in, Ollie walked out of Carla's office with a serious look on his face.

"Hello, partner, follow me, everyone is meeting in the Conference Room down the hall," Ollie explained as we quickly left Carla's office.

"Why down there?" I asked.

"We're assembling a special team. People are still coming in," Ollie explained with a worried look on his face.

Grabbing Ollie by the arm, I stopped him in the hall.

"What's wrong, partner?" I asked as I looked deep into my friend's eyes.

"It's a suicide mission, David, if you guys get caught our government will deny knowing you. The odd's are really against you on this one. Please think it over before you agree to do this," Ollie explained in a whisper as several people walked past us and down the hallway.

I had never seen Ollie act this way before. He was truly concerned for my safety. Something was wrong. Showing our identifications to the two military police officers standing in the hall, guarding the door to the conference room, they checked our names against the list of names on a piece of paper on their clip board, and then opened the door to let us in.

Stepping into the large room a wide smile spread out across my face when I saw who was already waiting inside.

"Hello, youngster," Cookie said with a smile as he walked up to me and gave me a hug.

"Hey, pop, how ya doing?" I asked.

"Hello, Sandman," Tom Burke and Joe Knight both said at the same time. As they did we all started laughing as we shook each other's hands.

"David, thanks for getting here so quickly," Deputy Director Crock said as he walked over to shake my hand.

"No problem, sir. Boy all we need now is Bell, Mosier, Butch, and Chopper, and we'll be ready to rock and roll," I explained jokingly.

"Agents Bell, Mosier, and Hartford are already here, son, they're in the War Room with Neil looking at the target information. We're just waiting for Carla and Danny to arrive now," Richard explained calmly.

"How bad is it, sir?" I questioned.

"It's going to be a challenge that's for sure. Let's wait for everyone to get here and we'll all talk it over and do a little brainstorming," Richard explained as he reached over and picked up his cup of coffee and took a sip.

Looking at my gold Tag Heuer Diver's watch it was a little past ten. Sitting down at the table I looked over at Cookie, Tom, and Joe, and without saying a word we were already tuning into each other's energy. All we could do now was sit it out and wait.

* * * * * * *

Code Name: Broken Arrow
Target: Ayatollah Khomeini
Location: Tehran Iran

It was 1:30 a.m. when everyone finally arrived, including my big brother Danny. It was Carla who took charge and controlled the meeting.

"Alright gentleman, yesterday afternoon we confirmed through our CIA listening post, which is located in the mountains north of the town of Astara, and also through a whiskey-number intercepted by the National Security Agency, who had been targeting the personal telephone number of a man known in Iran as the Ayatollah Khomeini, that the Ayatollah is in direct possession of two of our missing A-pack suitcase size nuclear weapons.

As you all know, a whiskey-number is the code word designator for the National Security Agency's highest-priority intercepts. Whiskey-numbers go directly to the Presidents' desk, eyes only, by way of the DCI.

Please take a very close look at this man's picture," Carla explained as she walked around the conference room table and handed each of us an 8x10 color photograph of the Iranian known as the Ayatollah Khomeini.

"This photograph was given to us by the Defense Intelligence Agency. The Ayatollah is the leader of an Iranian militant group known in Iran as Sepa-E Pasadran – the Iranian Revolutionary Guard Corps. These are some very dangerous fundamentalist bad guys who call themselves, The First of Allah.

Danny has been working very closely with a group of Iranians who we have trained here in the United States. They are the Iranian Paramilitary Guerrillas known to us as The Blue Light Group. The Blue Light Group are our eyes and ears in Iran," Carla explained.

"Do we know where the weapons of mass destruction are, ma'am?" Joe asked.

"Yes, they are hidden in a secure room at the Ayatollah's Palace in Tehran," Carla explained.

"Shouldn't we be sending in a Navy Seal team or Delta Force to retrieve these weapons, ma'am?" Cookie asked with a look of concern on his face.

"Yes, we should, but unfortunately we can't. If we send in any type of military force, no matter how small they may be, and they get caught or end up shooting it out with the Iranian Military, the country of Iran would declare a holy war against the United States. That act alone could unite all of the Middle East countries against us, even our allies. The Ayatollah is a radical Shiite Islamic Extremist. He hates the United States of America. Our intercepts have confirmed that in eight days from today, the Ayatollah is going to turn both of these nuclear weapons over to a terrorist group from Syria. The Syrian Terrorist Red Cell group is going to bring them both to the United States to detonate them in two of our major cities, Washington D.C. and New York," Carla explained with a troubled look on her face.

"You've confirmed this information, ma'am?" Tom asked.

"Absolutely, we've confirmed it through both Israeli Mossad and Kuwaiti Intelligence. They have the Syrians talking about it on tape."

Everyone in the room fell silent, including me. Some of us looked at the desk, others looked around at each other. It was our old commanding officer who broke the silence, Captain Mosier, now CIA Special Agent Mosier.

"The President is looking for someone to volunteer and go into Iran to breach the palace and retrieve the weapons. That's why Black Operations Team One has been asked to attend this meeting," Mosier explained as he looked around the room at all of us.

"Let's cut to the chase. Here's the simple facts, Butch, Chopper, Sandman, Cookie, and Joe are all halo jump qualified," Bell began to say.

"So am I, sir," Ollie quickly pointed out as he looked over at me and winked.

"Oliver, we're going to need your expertise here. You would be more effective helping Neil and Agents Mosier, Eckland, and Bell control this operation from the War Room," Deputy Director Crock explained.

All of a sudden I understood, Ollie was right, they didn't expect who ever went in to get out alive. Ollie was being groomed for some higher position. They didn't want to lose him. It was what we call, a Tell and Crock, just told by telling Ollie he couldn't go.

Our whole team caught it, and to be honest with you, it gave me a sick feeling inside knowing that I may never see my family, Kate, or my son's ever again.

Looking over at me, my big brother Danny smiled.

"What do you say, Sandman, me and you just like old times? Let's put on some James Brown and rock and roll."

Again the room fell silent as every eye in the room focused their attention on me. Looking up at Carla I saw it in her eyes. Then she slowly shook her head no, telling me not to volunteer.

"You can't go, Danny, neither can Butch, Cookie, Joe, or Tom," I explained as I sat back in my chair and rubbed my hands over my face.

"Bullshit, you go I go, that's our code. We all go or none of us go," Danny shouted back.

Looking over at both Bell and Mosier, I could see that my big brother was starting to get upset. "What in the hell is going on here, sir?" he asked angrily.

"Sandman's right, Danny, he's the only one who's qualified to go," Mosier explained with a concerned look on his face.

"Fuck that!" Danny shouted back as he slammed his hand on top of the large wooden table.

"Danny, listen to me," Bell said calmly. "As big as you are and being a black man on top of it, you would stand out like a sore thumb. The rest of the team are all white men. David is Armenian, he is olive complected which means he will blend in perfectly with the Iranian Blue Light Group. He's also the only one in this room who has been trained on how to detonate a suitcase size A-pack nuclear weapon and handle the plutonium or uranium core if he needs to remove it safely and hide it.

It's your call, Sandman. Nobody will blame you if you say no," Bell explained, as we looked each other in the eyes.

"Do me a favor, Danny, if anything happens to me, go to Dublin and take care of Kate. Promise me that, big brother," I asked as I looked over at my best friend.

"Bullshit, David, you're not going into that towel-head ass country without me," Chopper snapped back as he looked into my eyes.

"Promise me, big brother. You'll understand when you see Kate again," I said in a whisper of a voice. We both knew there was no sense in arguing. Someone had to go and the clock was ticking. Time was running out. If just one of those weapons made it into the United States, millions of Americans would be killed.

"I promise, I give you my word as your brother and your friend," Danny said sadly.

"I'm not jumping out of any fucking air plane!" I said loudly as I looked over at Ollie.

"Yes you will. I told you in China you would and you will. Its who you are, David," Ollie explained as he shook his head in disappointment because I volunteered to go in alone.

* * * * * * *

We spent the next 24-hours putting a mission plan of action together. I was going to halo jump into the mountains near the town of Astara, close to where our CIA Listening Post was located. The Blue Light Group would pick me up there and help me get to the Ayatollah's Palace in Tehran.

Once I retrieved both nuclear weapons, I would make my way across the border into Iraq and go to a small village just outside of Bagouba, called Aswan. My team would pick me up in the garden area of the small village.

A halo jump approach can be hazardous to your health in many different ways. You cannot shoot effectively and steer a parachute at the same time, which means a single man on the ground with a submachine gun can kill you quickly. The winds in this area were unpredictable. They shift quickly, which could blow me off course and put me somewhere on the next mountain ridge. Plus, jumping out of a perfectly good aircraft into minus-sixty degree Fahrenheit air at seven miles above the ground is dangerous all by itself. Dangerous and stupid I might add.

The tricky part of this would be trying to work out the halo harp, or high altitude release point for my jump by using the Magellan GPS and overlaying the route on our defense mapping agency pilotage chart.

We were doing all of this totally blind. We had no idea, for example, about the wind conditions on this particular mountain. Under normal conditions, winds flow upslope on warm days in mountainous terrain. But there is also what's known as unpredictable valley breezes, which create wind shears, violent updrafts, and unpredictable turbulence. Between the physical conditions and the fact that I was gong to be jumping blind, I was going to have to overcome a high DVF to reach my target on time and do it all in one piece.

Now, there's a mathematical formula for determining the harp during a jump like this. The formula is known as the modified D=KAV, where D equals the gliding distance in nautical miles, K equals the canopy drift constant, A equals the altitude and V equals the wind velocity in knots. But D=KAV doesn't do any good if you don't know the wind velocity, the gliding distance is variable, the altitude is give or take a couple of thousand feet, and the landing zone conditions are unknown. So what was going to happen at the time of my jump was that my jumpmaster, a Seal Master Chief, was going to have to read the air currents and wind as I come in.

I was going to have to jump in at an altitude of 37,500-feet, or seven miles, and pop my chute at a low enough opening to avoid being picked up by radar from the Iranian radar site at Parsabad.

After a carefully planned brainstorming session, the final plan broke down like this. Bell, Mosier, Neil, and Ollie were gong to control the operation from the War Room by Satellite Visual Communication. Butch, Chopper, and Tom would be waiting for me in the Garden Village of Aswan just outside of Bagouba in Iraq. Cookie and Joe would be standing by with a Black Operations helicopter to pick us all up once I reached the Garden Village. We had one last meeting before Air Force pilots flew us to our starting points to begin the mission. It was our most trusted friends, Bell and Mosier who did the talking.

"This is going to be the ultimate challenge for our team. We have been given a vast new arsenal of high tech weapons and a visual strategy that will prove to be merciless. You will all be wearing live communicator headsets linking you to each other and to us here at the War Room in the Pentagon.

This is a hazardous mission. Sandman, you are to penetrate deep into enemy territory undetected. Expect close-quarters combat. Strike with surgical precision, breach and clear the estate by any means necessary. There will be no negotiations, David. Retrieve both nuclear weapons and eliminate the threat against our country. Stealth intelligence and teamwork are going to be your ultimate weapons. This is unconventional warfare at its best. If you get caught, David, Washington will deny knowing you. We on the other hand will track your every move by satellite and find a way to get you out. You've got my word on that, son," Bell explained with a sincere look on his face.

"Listen, let's not kid ourselves here. If anything goes wrong I'm going to detonate both of those weapons in the heart of Iran. I don't make a very good POW. Been there, done that, remember?" I said as they all fell silent and nodded their heads, remembering back to our time together in Vietnam as Black Op's Team One. "Besides that, they won't keep me alive long enough for you to find me and get me out. So, I'll take them all on a happy carpet ride to see their Allah," I explained with a grin. I was trying to stay up beat and positive but deep down inside I had a real bad feeling.

"Brothers and friends, throughout life and into death, till the very end," Mosier said proudly.

"Hoo yah" we all shouted as we stood up to leave.

"Let me talk to you a minute, David," Neil said as he pulled me aside and away from the others.

"Burn this name and address into your mind," Neil explained as he handed me a piece of paper to look at. It was the name of a person who lived in the high Iranian plateau town of Nara in Northern Iran.

"If anything goes wrong, get to this person, she'll hide you and get you out of the country through a backdoor. Take this with you. It's a thin layer of lead, covered with a surgical tape. If you need to disappear, tape it over your satellite chip and you'll go dark on my computer screen, but we'll still be able to hear you through your radio transmitter."

"What's wrong, partner? Your worried about something aren't you?" I asked.

"You're my friend and I don't want to lose you. Something isn't right about all of this. Like you said, always expect the unexpected, right?" Neil asked with a forced smile.

"That's right," I replied as I took the round thin lead disc from Neil and placed it in my pocket.

"If I whisper into your ear piece and tell you to check your water supply, that will mean that something's very wrong and you need to go dark and abort all your plans. Get to Riyadh and find a way home. Break all communication and run like hell," Neil explained with a serious look in his eyes.

"I trust you, Neil, if you give me the word, I'll go dark and disappear. Thanks, partner," I said as we shook each other's hands.

Leaving the War Room I was starting to feel a little better. Neil was covering all of the bases just in case things went FUBAR, fucked up beyond all repair. He was learning well and remembering the little things I had taught him over the past few years.

Carla walked me to the front door. I knew that she was upset with me for accepting the mission. But deep down in her heart she knew there was no other choice.

"Your upset with me, aren't you?" I asked.

"No not really, just concerned about your safety. You're like a son to me, so keep David here will you? Let the Sandman go from this point forward.

Khomeini and his people are dangerous, don't hesitate to use your weapons. Remember they are terrorist and you're in their backyard. Remember your training and come home safely," Carla explained as she gave me a gentle kiss on the cheek.

"Anything else I should know? You know, like, why us? We've all been doing this long enough to know that this is a Delta Force operation and not something we should be doing. If I'm going to die you could at least tell me why I'm dying," I explained as I looked deep into Carla's eyes.

"I volunteered the team, you're all being tested, David. I can't tell you anymore than that, at least not now," Carla explained in a very careful way.

"But you shook your head no, you were telling me not to go. Why would you do that if this is a test?" I asked.

"To see if our country meant more to you than your own life. I know you, David, no matter how dangerous it is your going to go, especially if it's a direct threat against your country. But don't kid yourself, David, this is as real as it gets. Those weapons are there and the Syrian's are going to bring them here to detonate them. Danny and Amanda have worked hard tracking them down. The question is now, can you get to them and get them out.

This is something completely different from what you're used to doing. You've got the best team of people working with you. You have state of the art technology with satellite surveillance covering your every move and everything around you for miles. You have new weapons we are going to start to issuing to all our Seal and Delta Force teams. Personally, I truly believe that if one man can do this and get in and out of a hostile country like Iran, you're the one. You have the best-trained men at Operation Control: Mosier, Eckland, Bell, Neil, and Ollie. You have a deadly team ready to come to your aid at Aswan: Butch, Tom, and Danny. And you have two of the best helicopter pilots in the world standing by to fly in and pull you all out with Cookie and Joe.

I have told some very powerful people that my boys can do anything, and I meant every word of what I said. Climb onto the Pale Horse and ride. Get those weapons out of there, Sandman, or die trying," Carla explained.

I don't know where she had been or who she had been talking to. What I did notice was that Carla had a different tone in her voice. She was acting more like a boss than a friend.

Turning around, I didn't say a thing, I simply walked over to the black van with the dark tinted windows waiting for me and climbed inside. I knew now, without any doubt in my mind, if I survived this mission, it would be my last. She was risking my life to prove a point and to me that was unacceptable. When this was over, I was going to quit.

* * * * * * *

The four men in the van were CIA, they took me to a location, which I will not name for security reasons. It was there I picked out my weapons and tactical gear for this mission. From there I was taken to the Air Force Base where I waited for the rest of my team.

It didn't take long before Butch, Danny, Tom, Joe, and Cookie all came walking into the pilots briefing room, where I was waiting for them.

"This is bullshit, Sandman, and you know it," my big brother Danny said in an angry tone of voice. Danny, Tom, and Butch were all carrying .50-caliber sniper's rifles. With these weapons they could make a two thousand five hundred meter shot with no problem at all. They were dressed in desert tiger stripe camouflaged battle dress uniforms.

"Yeah I know it is. Carla said that we're being tested for something. Personally I don't like risking my life or any of yours just to prove a point to people who obviously don't give a damn about us. When this is over, I'm done," I explained calmly as I looked over at the five men who were my most trusted friends.

"When this is over you'll be bored and ready for the next mission, " Butch said jokingly.

"No, big brother, I'm done. The only way I would come back is if one of you guys needed me for something. Kate needs me and I need her. This is it for me," I explained as the room fell silent.

Our thoughts all took us in different directions. The memories of our past, the good times, the bad. But most of all it was the reality that we may never see each other again which brought along with it a deep sadness.

We were flown to a military base in Saudi Arabia where we said our goodbyes. Like Danny said, "It was time to put on some James Brown and rock and roll."

* * * * * * *

To you the reader, if you have read my first book A Sniper's Sin, and now are reading this one, you know that as a sniper in Vietnam or an assassin for the Mafia and CIA, I travel light. Today would be a completely different tactical operation. Because of this, I will be dressed in a completely different way.

To my surprise it was a Delta Force team flying me into Iran, and not a Seal team.

To make this entry work to my advantage I was going to halo jump in from an altitude of 37,500-feet and I was gong to do it just as the sun began to set in the west. If our timing was right, I would have just enough light to see where I was going. This would allow me to land in a relatively safe area, if I could find one free of trees, rocks and God only knows what else that might be waiting for me down there at ground zero. As I land, if I haven't killed myself on the way down, the sun should set within minutes of my touch down, and darkness would blanket me with her night.

We were flying in an all black C-130. I was wearing what is called BDU's Basic Black Battle Dress uniform with a seal CQC, close quarters combat vest. Cinched around my waist was a tactical pistol belt. Descending from it and attached to my right thigh, was a ballistic nylon holster which held my new suppressed Heckler & Kock USP-9 pistol and five spare fifteen-round magazines. My left thigh supported six thirty-round submachine gun magazines loaded with .115-grain Winchester silvertip bullets. Strapped to my back, next to my parachute was a scabbard holding H&K's ubiquitous MP-5 submachine gun in .9mm, with a knight-wt-technology suppressor screwed onto the barrel, and a seventh full mag of silvertips within easy reach. I also had eight Mark 3A2 concussion grenades and two Deftec No. 25 flashbang grenades in modular pouches velcro'd to my CQC vest. Each concussion grenade contained a half-pound of TNT. They worked wonders in enclosed spaces such as small rooms or the interior's of tanks.

Along with all of this, I carried a spare radio, lip mike, ear piece, twenty feet of shaped linear ribbon charged explosive on a wooden spool, primers, wire and an electric detonator, a pair of eighteen-inch bolt cutters, an electrician's screwdriver, lineman's pliers, a short steel pry bar, and a first aid kit. I also carried a pair of two-liter bottles of drinking water. My fanny pack contained a handful of nylon restraints and a small roll of waterproof duct tape. Strapped to my right calf I wore a Mad Dog Taiho combat knife with a nonmagnetic blade. Wound around my waist was twenty feet of caving ladder with modular titanium rungs and stainless steel cable-rail. With all of this extra weight I still had my parachute and breathing mask attached to a small oxygen tank, which I needed to survive the halo jump at such a high altitude.

From the point of my insertion to my target area was going to be difficult in the best of conditions, but I really had no choice, if there was the slightest possibility that I would need to use something, I either carried it along with me or did without it when the time came. I chose to play it safe and expect the unexpected. I was already powered up on Methadrine and the sun was beginning to set as the rear cargo door of the big C-130 plane began to open up.

"Ready?" the Jumpmaster Delta Force officer asked with a dead serious look in his eyes.

"I'm not jumping out of this fucking plane!" I shouted back as my fear of heights began to overwhelm me, and I took a step backwards.

Listening into his earpiece, he quickly pointed at the open backdoor when the pilot radioed to him that we were over my jump zone.

"Go!" he shouted.

Running toward the open rear door I yelled once again, "I'm not jumping out of this plane," It was at that moment I fell into the soft white clouds and vanished from sight.

At this altitude it should take about four minutes to reach the ground. Falling through the evening sky the panoramic view was nothing less than spectacular. To see what it was that I was now seeing would leave no doubt in anyone's mind that our God was alive and performing the miracles of life as we know it.

To the east I could see a wave of darkness sweeping across the vast desert and heading in my direction. To the west I could see multi-colored lights glistening over the edge of the horizon as the sun moved further from sight.

I was a few minutes behind schedule, night was quickly setting in. I was going to have to go for broke and pull my chute at the lowest point of opening possible. Watching my altitude gauge I pulled my ripcord and popped my chute at 800-feet. At the high rate of speed I was descending, it deployed quickly and jerked me backwards at 500-feet. Catching a slight updraft I glided myself into a small clearing halfway up the side of the mountain.

Feeling my feet touch the ground, I took off running and quickly began to pull in my parachute. Pulling off my oxygen mask I watched in awe as the last remaining remnants of light disappeared and a wave of darkness swept over me.

Dropping to my knee's I fought to calm myself down and then said a silent prayer, thanking God for getting me back down to earth safely. It took about ten minutes before I was ready to stand back up. It took that long for me to stop shaking.

Pulling off my oxygen tank and nylon chute harness, I rolled the tank and mask inside the cute and hid them under some wooded debris. Pulling my headset and tiny mouthpiece out from around my neck I quickly put them on and spoke into the mouthpiece to see if I was live on our secure satellite feed.

"I'm down, talk to me," I whispered into the mouthpiece.

"We hear you, Blue is closing in on your position to pick you up. They saw you and will be at your twenty in five," Neil explained, telling me that the Blue Light Group saw me come in and were coming to get me.

"Chopper?" I whispered checking to see if Danny, Cookie, Butch, Tom, and Joe could hear me from their position in Aswan.

"Twenty-twenty," was all that Danny said.

Keying the mike with my finger I sent back a tsk...tsk... sound. When I did both Danny and Neil returned the same tsk... tsk... back to me.

The one thing we were taught in Seal team training was keep it simple and never trust anyone who tells you a radio frequency is secure. From this point forward very little will actually be said over the airwave.

Keying the mike, we can say a lot just by sending the static tsk... tsk... sound back and forth to each other.

To you the reader, you have to understand that this is not a Hollywood movie. If we can unscramble a secure radio frequency, then we must operate under the frame of mind that the bad guys are listening to every word we say too. Which brings me to a second point; I want to share with you while I am waiting for our Blue Light friends to arrive. This is considered an unconventional combat warfare operation. The bad guys, or in this case, the Iranians, will be referred to in Seal team terms as Tango's. So when you hear us talk about Tango's remember those are the bad guys on this mission.

Hearing some movement just off to my right I quickly knelt down and pulled my MP-5 H&K submachine gun out of its scabbard.

"Black Knight?" someone whispered from within the trees. This was the code name the Blue Light Group had been given to identify me. I knew now not to shoot, this was my counterparts and escort, the Iranian Blue Light Group.

"Sand Castle?" I responded. As I did four young men my age came walking out of the cover of the trees.

"Come, my friend, we must move quickly. I want to get you to Tehran and to my home before the sun rises once again."

Shaking each of their hands, I said nothing. We were on the move and operation Desert Heat had just begun.

* * * * * * *

Special Warfare Operation
Code Name: Desert Heat
Target: Home of the Ayatollah Khomeini
Location: Tehran, Iran

Mission Profile: Breach and clear the estate palace of the man known as the Ayatollah Khomeini. Find, secure, and remove two American A-pack suitcase size nuclear weapons. Close quarter's combat expected. Eliminate the threat and withdraw to Aswan, Iraq.

Making our way on foot we walked through a series of precarious ravines which s-curved inland. From there, we got into a car and drove toward the town of Nara. Changing cars at Nara we began our drive to Tehran. Looking at my watch, it was almost 4:00 a.m. when we finally reached the home that would be my safe haven for the night.

For security reasons to protect the identity of our secret allies in the Blue Light Group I will call the leader of the group, Mazur.

Mazur's home was located on the outer edge of the city of Tehran. Once inside, we all began to feel a little more at ease. Sitting down at his dining room table Mazur's wife, Anonna, made us all something to eat. At 5:00 a.m. everything stopped so Mazur and his friends could say their morning prayers.

Placing two drops of Methadrine under my tongue, I placed the tiny glass vial back into my pocket and closed my eyes. It was time for me to pray also. I was in an unknown country with four young men which I had never met before. I was going to need all of the help I could get and the one person I could always count on was God.

After we ate our breakfast, Mazur handed me photographs of not only the outside but also the inside of the Ayatollah's palace.

"How did you get pictures of the inside of his home?" I asked in total surprise of what I was looking at.

"I have many friends, all of who do not like this Shiite. He is sick in the mind," Mazur explained with a smile.

"How so?" I asked as I studied the photographs.

"Many of us believe that one day he will try to over throw the Shaw. If that happens, those of us who are Sunni Muslims will live in constant fear of his dictatorship. Time will tell if this will happen. For now we must get these bombs out of his hands," Mazur explained.

"I have two questions for you, my friend. Is this palace heavily guarded? And do you know which room the suitcases are in, by any chance?" I questioned.

"Some days the Ayatollah is guarded but most of the time no. My friend who works inside the palace, during the day time, tells me that the security room is this one," Mazur explained as he tapped his finger on the photograph to show me which room I should be looking for.

"What time does your friend leave the palace to go back to his home?" I questioned. I knew that once I got inside the palace I was going to kill everyone in sight. I didn't want to kill Mazur's friend.

"She cleans for him, and leaves at four o'clock in the afternoon," Mazur explained with a grin.

"She, huh? That is good Mazur. Do you have any other friends inside the palace after 4:00 p.m.?"

"No, after 4:00 p.m. it is the enemy that lives within," Mazur answered as we both began to study the pictures.

"Why don't you and your friends get some sleep. At six o'clock tonight we will drive by and take a look at the palace. Then we will decide what day to strike," I explained calmly.

"Okay, we will sleep now. Come, let me show you where you can wash and the room where you can rest in," Mazur explained as he patted me on the back.

After washing up, I went into the bedroom Mazur had for me to sleep in. Closing the door, I walked over to the corner of the room and sat down on the floor. From here I could see both the window of the room and the door. Pulling my new Heckler & Kock pistol out of its holster, I sat and waited. Even though I was told that Mazur could be trusted I wasn't going to take any chances. I was in the badlands. There would be no sleeping until this was over.

* * * * * * *

It was almost 3:00 p.m. when I heard Mazur moving around. Within minutes everyone was up and moving about once again. Mazur's young wife Anonna began to prepare a meal of lamb kebob and pilaf rice for us to eat. By six o'clock that evening we were in Mazur's new Mercedes Benz and driving through the streets of Tehran.

Mazur was a young businessman whose father. Well, lets just say that he and his friends were all oil rich and leave it at that shall we.

Tehran was a busy city. A lot of its people were closing up their shops and businesses and heading home to their families. What surprised me most was the fact that women in this part of the land were considered second-class citizens and basically had no rights at all.

By 6:35 p.m. we were driving by the Ayatollah's palace. It was big, but not as big as I had expected it to be. You have to remember, this was early 1976 and he was considered a religious leader, but had not as of yet, over thrown the Shaw who was the current ruler of Iran. That would happen in 1978.

"Look there he is," one of Mazur's men whispered as we drove by the front wrought-iron, black colored metal gates of the Ayatollah's home.

The Ayatollah was standing out in front of his home talking to a dozen men who I assumed to be his bodyguards. They were dressed in their traditional robes and wearing their Turbans. They were standing next to a dark gray Rolls Royce and four silver Mercedes Benz four-door sedans.

Driving down the road, we pulled into a parking area and watched to see what he was up to. The sun was beginning to set in the west. It would be dark in a few minutes, and unknown to Mazur and his friends, I was ready to make my move. Placing two drops of Methadrine under my tongue I listened as Mazur and his men talked.

"What do you think he is up to?" the driver asked calmly.

"I am not yet sure. I don't know if he is coming or going?" Mazur replied as we sat at a distance and watched the Ayatollah and his men laugh and talk with each other.

Pulling off my head dressing Mazur had given me to disguise myself; I reached around my neck and put my Seal ear and mouthpiece on. Keying the transmitter I sent a message to both Neil at the War Room in Washington, and to Danny who was standing by with Butch and Tom in Aswan.

"Tsk... Tsk...," I signaled quietly as Mazur and his men continued to watch the palace some three hundred yards away.

"Tsk... Tsk..." came the first reply.

"Tsk... Tsk... Tsk...." came the second which brought a smile to my face.

The palace had steel gates at the entrance and a black wrought-iron fence surrounding the entire estate. The home itself was big, but not huge. It was beautiful, and without a doubt, the home of a multi-millionaire. But the property it was sitting on was small. Getting past the fence and to the palace itself would only take a matter of 90-seconds at best.

Looking out the window and then at my watch, the sun was gone. It was 7:00 p.m. and the darkness of the night had set her veil upon me once again.

"They're getting in the cars," the driver said softly.

"We should just kill them all now, while they are all together and unarmed," the passenger sitting in the front seat added coldly.

"No it would draw to much attention. Our friend must get those weapons out of the house. That is our priority," Mazur explained.

"They're leaving," the driver added.

Looking out through the front window of Mazur's car we sat quietly and watched as the Rolls Royce and four Mercedes pulled out through the front gates. As they did the last car stopped. One of the men got out of the car, closed the metal gates, got back into his car and pulled out to join the other four vehicles that had stopped to wait for them. Watching them drive down the street Mazur looked over at me. When he did his eyes widened.

"What are you doing?" he asked wondering why I had quietly pulled off my headgear and robe. Underneath I had on my BDU's and was fully armed and ready to go.

"Pull around to the back of his home and let me out. Then come back here and wait for me, I'm going in," I explained coldly as I began to mentally prepare my mind for the surprises that might be waiting for me inside.

"But?" Mazur began to say. Catching himself in mid-thought he pressed his lips together and nodded in agreement.

"Move, now!" he told his driver sharply.

Starting the engine of the Mercedes the driver pulled out slowly, so as not to draw any unnecessary attention to us. Pulling around to the back of the palace, I quickly jumped out of the car and ran toward the wrought-iron fence, as I did Mazur and his men drove away. I hit the fence at a dead run and was over the top of it and running toward the back of the palace within seconds. Placing my back up against the wall next to the backdoor I reached over my shoulder and pulled my MP-5, H&K submachine gun out of its scabbard. Taking several deep breaths I tried to calm myself down. The combination of adrenaline, speed, and fear had me so powered up that I almost felt dizzy.

Reaching over to the doorknob, I checked it to see if the door was locked. Turning it I smiled, it was unlocked. Leaving the door closed I stepped back and looked at the windows. There was one light on down stairs and three lights on upstairs. Looking in through the window next to the backdoor, there was enough light coming in from the hallway that I could see the room I was about to enter was empty. Opening the door I moved in quickly and locked the door behind me.

Waiting a few seconds to let my eyes adjust, I could hear someone talking in the room in front of me. I could also hear music playing softly, which seemed to be coming from somewhere upstairs. Moving slowly I made my way through the large kitchen and carefully peeked into the next room.

The room was large, and was full of wall decorations and ancient art. Sitting on the sofa was a young man armed with an AK-47 assault rifle. He was talking to someone on the telephone.

"Shit," I whispered to my self. To kill him while he was talking on the phone would alert whoever it was he was talking to that there was trouble here at the Ayatollah's home. All I could do now was wait and pray this Tango didn't stay on the telephone to long.

I didn't like this kind of stop-and-go ops. My training had taught me that an operation like this should flow, much like a single knock out punch. One single, powerful, decisive, kinetic motion from start to finish. But here I had no choice other than to wait it out.

Luckily for me this Tango was only on the telephone for a few minutes. Watching him hang-up the phone I moved in behind him fast and fired one shot from my silenced MP-5. The .9mm bullet entered the back of his head and blew most of his face off in a spray of red crimson blood, bone and brain, all over the plush white carpet in front of him. His body fell forward in a dead heap as I moved over and turned off the lights in the room. This would work to my advantage in case the Ayatollah and his men came back home while I was upstairs.

Moving up the stairway to the second floor of the home, I slowly and warily checked the hallway inch by inch as I eased around. It was empty.

"Oh fuck; one, two, three, four, five, six, seven, eight doors lined the hallway, four on each side." Here are the rules for hallway clearing; you do not go passed a closed door unless you can make sure it can't be opened. Remember the door to the basement in Klaus Grubers estate in Germany. That mistake almost cost me my life. Lucky for me the first six doors to these rooms were open, the last two were closed.

Inching my way down the hallway I checked each open room just to play it safe, and stopped to listen when I reached the last two doors remaining before I got to door number nine which was my target suite and door ten which was the Ayatollah's personal bedroom.

Listening, I could hear at least four people in each of the closed doored rooms. If I used my Deftec flashbang grenades, I would stun everyone in both rooms, but I would then have to get into each room and kill everyone inside. This would be hard to do because of the smoke that would fill each room from the explosions.

Fuck it, I was about to give the term dynamic entry a whole new meaning. Because the doors to these rooms opened inward I was going to have to make one fluid-cat like move. Setting my MP-5 down on the floor I opened two of the modular pouches on my CQC vest and pulled out two of my mark 3A2 concussion grenades. Placing one under my chin I held it there by tilting my head forward. Pulling the pin out of the first grenade I slid my submachine gun forward with the toe of my boot so it was up close to my target suite. My heart was racing as beads of sweat ran down across my face and dripped to the floor.

Reaching up I set my hand on the first doorknob and took a deep breath of air in through my nose. Letting it out slowly I quickly opened the door, rolled the grenade into the room and closed the door. Lifting my chin, the second mark 3A2 fell neatly into my hand as I pulled the pin, opened the next door and rolled it into the room. Slamming the door shut I heard men screaming as I leaped to the floor and tried to get out of the way. I was almost on the floor when the first concussion grenade exploded followed by the second one. Each Mark 3A2 grenade contains a half-pound of TNT.

I was lucky, the walls to the palace were made of thick cement, which helped to protect me. The laws of physics also prevailed, proving that TNT can be hazardous to human flesh.

Reaching over for my submachine gun, I was caught by surprise as I began to stand up. Just as I did the bedroom door to the Ayatollah's suite opened up. She stood five-feet, seven-inches tall, weighed about 120-pounds, had olive skin, long beautiful black hair, and big brown eyes. She must have been asleep because she looked confused and was screaming.

In one cat-like move I reached down to my right calf and pulled my new Taiho combat knife out of its sheath. As I did I lunged forward sending the razor sharp stainless steel blade of the knife deep into the young woman's stomach. Twisting the knife in my hand I pulled upward slicing open her soft tender flesh, pulled out the knife, and pushed her body backwards.

Her eyes were wide and filled with tears as the effects of being gutted alive set deeply into her mind. She then fell backwards onto the carpeted floor of the Ayatollah's bedroom and began to flop around like a fish out of water.

Securing my knife back into its sheath, I reached into another one of my modular pouches and pulled out a Deftec No. 25 flashbang grenade. Checking the door to the security room I found it locked. Pulling out my shaped linear ribbon charged explosive I ran it all the way around the inside of the door frame, inserted a detonator, and took cover. Dropping the hammer I blew the big, heavy, carved wooden suite door off its hinges, pulled the pin on my flashbang grenade, and rolled it into the smoke filled room. Letting it detonate I picked up my MP-5 and cleared the doorway of the security room. Keeping my back against the wall I moved to my port side scanning the room with my machine gun.

The Deftec had blown out a couple of the windows because the smoke was venting out pretty fast. It didn't surprise me to see two heavily armed men as they tried to stand up still stunned from the flashbang grenades. Firing five shots into each of the Tangos chests I watched as they both flew backwards into a dead heap onto the floor.

Moving quickly through the room I checked to make sure it was clear.

I know, your wondering why I rolled the grenades into the rooms instead of tossing them in, right? Well, the answer is simple, if you toss a grenade into a room a Tango could catch it and throw it back out at you, or it could bounce off a piece of furniture and roll back out the door to you. Therefore, you roll it in on the floor so he can't catch it and if it does hit something, it might spin but will stay in the room. See you're learning something important. Don't believe what you see in a Hollywood movie, it's bullshit!

Moving across the room I found another thick, heavy, wooden door. This was the door our A-pack weapons were behind, according to Mazurs female friend. Trying the door, it was locked. Now I was really screwed, I had used all of my ribbon charged explosive to blow open the first door.

Pulling another Mark 3A2 grenade out of my CQC vest I duct taped it to the doorknob. Pulling a bed sheet off the bed I quickly tore it into thin strips, tied the ends together, fastened one end of it to the grenade pin and moved back out into the hallway with the other end of the long strip of sheet.

Laying down on the hallway floor and as far away from the open suite door as I could possibly get, I pulled on the strip of bed sheet. The explosion was deafening. Jumping up to my feet I ran back into the room and looked into the room I had just blown the door off of. To the far left of the small room I saw both of our suitcase size nuclear weapons. To the right of the room were a stack of solid gold bricks and a four-foot wide, three-foot deep, five-foot tall stack of brand new one hundred dollar bills in American money.

Grabbing handfuls of the American currency I began to stuff it into my fanny pack. Picking up both of the A-pack suitcases I carried them out into the open room. Tearing two wider strips of bed sheet off of the original sheet, I tied the ends of the sheets to the handles of the suitcases so that both suitcases were now tied together with a three-foot section of sheet in between them. Sliding my MP-5 submachine gun back into its scabbard on my back, I placed the three-foot section of sheet around my neck and stood up.

"Perfect," I said out loud to myself. I now had both of the nuclear suitcases hanging at both sides of my body. I needed to be able to carry them and have my hands free to shoot with.

I had to get out of this palace. I had been in here way to long and the explosions were bound to have been heard by someone on the outside. Stepping back into the hallway I looked down the long hall toward the stairs.

"Oh shit," the light had just come on down in the main living room where I had shot the Tango in the head.

"Don't panic, David, stay calm and think it through," I said to myself as I heard the distinctive sound of Iranian voices as they came up the stairwell at the end of the long hallway.

Pulling two more Mark 3A2 concussion grenades out of their pouches, I pulled the pin's on both grenades and rolled them both like bowling balls down the hallway. I rolled them hard enough that they both reached the end of the hallway and disappeared into the stairwell just as the first Tango reached the top of the stairs. The double explosion was earth moving. Moving to the window, I unwrapped the caving ladder from around my waist, hooked the titanium rungs to the doorframe of the wall I had blown the second door off of, and tossed the cable-rail out the window.

Climbing out through the broken window I climbed down the ladder, hit the ground and pulled my USP-9 pistol out of its holster. I could hear gunfire at the front of the palace; I ran across the back of the palace estate and climbed back over the wrought-iron fence. Mazur and his men had attacked from the front of the palace, which help to distract the Ayatollah's bodyguards long enough for me to escape from the rear.

I could hear police sirens coming in the distance. I was on the run in Iran, dressed in an all black battle dress uniform, heavily armed, with two suitcase sized nuclear weapons dangling at my sides. To make matters worse, Mazur and his men where not only shooting it out with the Tangos, but weren't here to pick me up, and the police were closing in on this area fast. Taking off on foot, I found myself alone in a hostile, foreign country. I was in the Caspian Region of Northern Iran. If I could find a place to hide until Mazur and his men could find me and pick me up, I might make it out of this alive. Keying my radio transmitter I had no choice but to break radio silence.

"I've got both of the children, I'm on the run with no babysitter," I whispered into my radio mike as I moved as far away from the palace as I could.

"Where's Sand Castle?" Neil asked.

"Heavily engaged, they just left my twenty," I replied.

"Go to your secondary until they can come back to pick you up," Neil explained.

"I wish that I had one," I answered as I reached a small housing complex. Looking at my watch it was almost 9:00 p.m. My heart was racing, I was covered with my own sweat and my fear factor was starting to become a very big reality in my life.

"Hold, I'm trying to re-establish with Sand Castle," Neil explained as he tried to reach Mazur by radio.

Seeing the cars in the parking lot of the housing complex I made my way closer to the entrance of the parking lot. I knew I couldn't risk being seen walking through the lot full of cars looking for one to steal. I also knew this whole area was going to be crawling with Iranian police and military soldiers as soon as they found all of the bodies in the Ayatollah's home.

Watching a middle-aged man walk out of the apartment building I waited to see what he was going to do. Climbing into an old Chevy pick-up truck, he started the engine and turned on his headlights. I could hear more police sirens coming into the area behind me close to the Ayatollah's palace. Watching as the old pick-up truck made its way slowly through the parking lot, I moved across the street and squatted down next to the pile of garbage bags next to the entrance.

As soon as he pulled up to the street I moved in quickly, opened the drivers door to his truck, and shot him one time under the left armpit. The look of surprise and shock at seeing me almost matched the look of pain and fear as my .9mm bullet ripped its way through his chest and tore a hole through his heart.

Pushing his lifeless body over into the passenger's side of the seat, I tossed both my suitcases into the cab of the truck and on top of his body, climbed in, and drove away. Holstering my pistol I wiped the sweat from my eyes and tried to focus my thoughts. Driving down one of the small side streets I heard Neil as he spoke to me through my earpiece.

"Knight, Castle is out of the area with one pawn down. Try to find a safe place until the smoke clears," Neil explained.

"Roger and out," I answered as I watched the long line of Iranian military jeeps, trucks, and heavily armed troops pass by in front of me as I pulled up to the main highway. As they passed me going to my left, I turned to the right. I was going to get as far away from this area as I possibly could.

Mazur was heading in the opposite direction with one of his men either wounded or dead. I couldn't count on his coming back to get me now. Within a matter of minutes the Iranian military's revolutionary guard would have this entire area sealed off. I needed to get out of the capital city of Tehran and to the mountains to the north.

If Mazur was doing what I thought he was, he was trying to draw the police and military in the opposite direction, and lead them as far away from me as he possibly could at the same time. He was buying me some time by drawing all of the attention to himself.

Driving slowly, I made my way out of the city and out onto the desert highway to the north. Outside the city was nothing but barren wasteland stretching for hundreds of miles; spanning a vast area far more permeable than anything I had ever seen before. There were a few natural barriers which were nothing more than acres of squat scrub brush.

It was almost midnight when I stopped the truck on the deserted highway and drug the dead body of the old man out into the desert.

Covering him with sand, I returned to the truck and drove off once again. I was almost out of gas, and out in the desert miles from nowhere. I was in big trouble, and I knew it.

Turning the old Chevy truck around so that it was facing the direction I had just came from, I punched a hole in the side of the front left tire and left the truck parked on the side of the road. It was a common thing to see cars and trucks stranded or broken down along the sides of these desert roads. Leaving it like this would give me time to get far away from it before anyone realized the old man was missing.

Moving north, I stayed on the paved section of road with my senses at full alert. I had read enough in the CIA computer data bank about the Middle East to know that it was dangerous being out here alone like this, especially this late at night. There were thieves and desert-roaming bandits all throughout this entire area who enjoyed nothing better than an unfair fight.

I walked for about a mile and then headed west into the desert leaving the asphalt road behind me. Contrary to what you might think, it gets damn cold out in the desert at night. About four hundred yards into the desert sand and away from the public road, I dug in for the night. Like I said, it was to dangerous for me to go any farther in the dark. Especially while I was carrying two suitcase sized nuclear weapons along with me.

Pulling off all of my gear, I took off my BDU's. Staying true to rule number one, always expect the unexpected and rule number two, everything is subject to change at any given moment, I remembered rule number three, don't forget rules one and two!

Folded between my back and chest were a pair of desert colored, camouflaged, tiger striped, fatigues. I had them hidden between my Kevlar vest and my BDU's. Shaking the sand off of my black BDU's I put them back on and then put my tiger striped fatigues on over top of them.

Why tiger stripes and not regular camouflaged jungle fatigues you ask? No trained Seal would ever wear anything other than a black battle dress uniform or tiger stripes. Didn't know that either did you? Well now you do. Some more of the Sandman's best kept secrets.

Putting my gear back on, I spent the rest of the night fighting with the sand fleas. The extra fatigues helped to keep me a little warmer. Now all I could do was wait. I took some comfort in knowing that Neil was tracking my every move by satellite. He might not be able to see me in the darkness of the night, but that little white dot on the large wall screen in the War Room let him know exactly where I was at all times.

* * * * * * *

Looking at my watch it was ten-minutes past five in the early morning hours. Placing two drops of Methadrine under my tongue I watched as the sky over the horizon to the east began to turn a brilliant yellow-orange and gold color as the sun began to rise.

Tsk... Tsk... Tsk... echoed in my ear as I tucked the tiny glass vial of liquid speed back into my pocket. Three Tsk sounds told me that it was Neil in the War Room at the Pentagon. Two Tsk sounds would tell me it was Danny standing by with his team in Aswan, Iraq.

There was a slight breeze in the air coming in from the north. I could smell water, which told me I was getting close to the Caspian Sea. From there I should be able to get a Seal team to pick me up. Things were starting to look up. I was actually starting to feel better about all of this. Then, just as things were looking good, two things happened. Looking up toward the northeast I saw four Mi-17 Soviet built Russian helicopters appear on the horizon just as Neil broke radio silence.

"Black Knight, don't say anything. Just listen. Whiskey intercept has verified that a call was made from the U.S. to the Kremlin. Call went to General Kalashnikov identifying you as the one who breached the Ayatollah's estate. Our listening post has confirmed they're coming in through Turkmenistan to begin a wide sweep. Abort Caspian! It's heavily mined and monitored with ground motion censors. They know its you. They also know what you're carrying, go west to Turkey, move now. Black Knight you've been betrayed from an unknown source. Check your water supply now!" Neil whispered in my earpiece.

All of a sudden my heart stopped as I watched the four Russian helicopters turn from four to seven. They were moving northwest heading to the Caspian Sea to cut me off. Waiting for them to disappear from my sight, I pulled out the small lead disc Neil had given me before I had left the Pentagon. Pulling the shinny paper part of the adhesive tape off, I reached in under my two shirt tops and pressed the sticky part of the tape to my skin. The lead disc was now in place and covering the satellite locater chip in my shoulder. Grabbing both of the nuclear suitcases I broke out into a dead run and headed east to the mountains roughly two miles away.

"Black Knight we've lost you on our screen, Tsk me so I'll know you're alright." The War Room couldn't track my movements now. The thin lead disc was blocking the satellite signal. The problem was they couldn't still see me, so they would be trying to find me at my last known coordinates, which I was a good mile away from by now.

"Black Knight, Op's control," Neil said again to let me know I was in total black out or what we would call Dark Mode.

"Where is he, dammit?" Bell asked.

"Double check the satellite feed, Sandy," Neil asked. Neil was holding his transmitter button down so I could hear them talking at the War Room. It was his way of letting me know I was off of their screen.

"I want to know who in the hell that call came from and I mean right fucking now!" Deputy Director Crock shouted in the background.

"The NSA is tracing it, Sir," Neil explained.

"Come on, Sandman, send us a signal so we'll know you're alright," I heard Ollie say in the background.

"Where is he, Neil?" Carla asked.

"I don't know, ma'am, it could be rain clouds or a weather problem blocking our satellite feed. It happens from time to time. Let's give it a few minutes and see if it clears up," Neil explained.

"That or he doesn't know who to trust now. If he went rogue on us, he'll head straight to his support team," Mosier explained.

"We just received a message from our listening post in Northern Iran, ma'am. The Iranian military is in direct contact with the Russians. They're closing in from the rear but they're moving in the blind. They're not sure if the information sent to the Kremlin is true or our way of tricking everyone into going in the wrong direction to help Black Knight escape into Iraq or Turkey," Ollie explained. Just as he did, Neil cut off the communication signal between us.

I was leaving a trail in the sand that a blind man could follow but I had no choice. Out in the open like this I was dead meat, the only chance I had to possibly make it out of this mess alive, was to get into the mountains which were a good mile away. The temperature was beginning to rise, the sun was coming up fast, and I was running out of time.

Did I make it to the mountains? Yes I did. I was young, healthy, pumped up on fear, Methadrine, and adrenaline. I was also tired, out of breath, and scared. That's right, scared. Let me tell you something about fear and being scared. It gives you that extra edge that you need when your body is telling you that you can't go any farther. Let me tell you something else, pain, fear, and being scared are good things. Why, you ask? Because it lets you know your still alive.

Here at the base of the mountain I found a ten-acre dense patch of thorny overgrowth. Taking a few minutes to catch my breath I could feel my heart pounding in my chest. I was covered with sweat, my muscles ached, and it was getting hotter by the second. Standing up I began to climb into thick scrub at the base of the mountain. I was in the hills the Iranians called the Kuhe Asbinasi. From here I would set up my own little observation post and watch the bad guys. I needed to know what I was up against. So, from here I would try to get a fairly good count on how many

Russians were coming into the area, check their weaponry, and learn their behavior patterns.

From this spot, I was about eighteen kliks or just under eleven-miles from our CIA listening post. All of which was up hill, through some of the roughest landscape that God (and/or Allah) had ever created. The secret listening post sat at an altitude of eighteen hundred feet, in a two hundred by two hundred yard earthen pocket. I also knew the listening post was shielded to the west by a ridge climbing as high as three thousand feet in some places and to the north lay a series of jagged, three hundred-foot cliffs making an approach from that direction much too time consuming.

Why am I telling you all of this, you're asking yourself? Because I also knew that the main road, from the CIA's secret listening post, ran due south, up, through a series of precarious ravines that S-curved inland, heading toward the high Iranian plateau town of Nara, and from there, on to Ardabil, where the CIA's old single-runway airfield (altitude: 4,317 feet above sea level) could be used to aid in my escape.

If I could get to Nara and reach Neil's contact person there, I might just make it out of this mess alive.

Why not go straight to the listening post for help? It was too risky, plus I didn't want to bring any undue attention to that location. Now your wondering how I knew about the CIA listening post, aren't you? Because you spent money on my book I'll tell you. Well, that and because I need to catch my breath.

While at the Air Force Base I used Colonel Hugh Jamieson's computer system to access the agency's computer at the Situation Room. I did my homework on this entire area just in case rule two came into play. Remember rule two? Everything is subject to change at any given moment, well it had.

So then, my friends, if you don't have any more questions, I'm out of here! Now then, after explaining all of this, getting out of this mess should be as easy and sweet as a piece of Armenian baklava, right? Sure it was, at least so I thought.

* * * * * * *

I had been on the move all day and night. It was now getting close to daybreak. I had decided against my first thought in which I was going to set up my own observation post to monitor the Russian's movements.

I was trying to get to the ravines on the other side of our listening post so I could reach the high plateau town of Nara. I was just under two miles from where I wanted to be. The distance I was traveling, under normal circumstances, could be covered in a relatively short period of time. But covering this distance on foot through these mountains had become a long, grueling, arduous hike. I was in the middle of hostile territory, operating in the blind, and trying not to make any noise that would alert the various Iranian military, Revolutionary Guard, Russian's, and or the Fundamentalist Tango units who might just happen to be out prowling around this area looking for me.

And so, I proceeded meter by meter, moving cautiously through the dry streambeds, climbing the rough rock outcroppings, picking my way so as not to leave the sort of tracks the security units look for. Did I know for sure they were looking for me or that hostiles were operating in this area? No, I did not. But as my Seal team instructors would continually remind me, "Never assume that the enemy is not looking for you. Assumptions like that can get you killed or captured."

It was getting late in the evening and the sky was quickly metamorphosing from black to blue, which meant it was time for me to dig in for the day. Now then, when it comes to concealment in this sort of terrain, as Master Chief Jeff Mareno would also say, "It's fucking hard to do." In heavily wooded areas, you can use the natural, thick vegetation to help you conceal your position. The same goes for jungle venues. Thick forest is a great help because it allows you to augment your ability to camouflage yourself by using the natural lighting, and shadows to your advantage, just as you saw me do in my first book, A Sniper's Sin.

But here in Iran, the light during daylight hours was direct and strong, and the lack of vegetation would make camouflage difficult. But then again, I was trained by the Navy Seals, so I knew as a sniper, what to look for.

After about five more minutes of crawling, climbing, and clambering around, I found a small cave with an opening partially covered by a short outcropping of rock and large irregularly shaped boulders, adding to its concealment possibilities. Dropping behind its natural cover I set down both A-pack weapons. I was tired and it was time to take a break.

From what I could see the cave was about twenty feet deep with a ceiling about seven-feet high. Small, cozy, and, all, in all perfect for what I needed. I had pushed my luck about as far as I possibly could thus far. Moving around in the day light was a big no, no. But given no other choice I fell back on my training and did what I was trained to do. "Don't think about it, just do it and get the job done."

Sitting down, I pulled off my gear and took a drink of water. It was then I noticed that something smelled real foul in this cave. Looking around I quickly realized it was me. Closing my eyes, I tried to think of who could have betrayed me and called my bitter enemy in Russia, General Boris Kalashnikov? Who knew I was here? Carla, Neil, Kathy, Sandy,

Ollie, Bell, Mosier, Crock, Tom, Joe, Cookie, Butch, and Chopper. There was no way any of these people would ever betray me. Or would they? Mazur and his Blue Light Team. Maybe they had gotten captured? That must have been it. I was simply to damn tired to think about it right now. I needed to rest and prepare for my next move...

* * * * * * *

It was the sound of helicopters which woke me up. I must have been completely burned out and exhausted, because I had actually fallen asleep and didn't have any nightmares. I don't even remember dreaming about anything.

Pulling my H&K USP-9 pistol out of its holster I looked at my watch. It was almost 3:00 p.m. The shade in the cave gave me some relief from the blistering heat waiting for me outside.

Peeking out through the opening of my cave I watched as two Soviet helicopters passed by slowly. They were about a hundred yards off to the south of my position, but the face of the black haired KGB Russian caught me totally by surprise. I remembered seeing his face and reading about him in the Defense Intelligence Agency's files in the Classified Data Bank of the CIA computer. I was sure it was him. The DIA had hundreds of surveillance photos of him.

His name was Oleg Lapinov, and here he was, riding in that helicopter; it looked like he was wearing Civvies. He had thick, black eyebrows, a thick, black mustache, and from everything I had read about him, he was real bad news and one of General Kalashnikov's personal friends. Was Oleg related to Ivan Lacinov the big Russian I had killed with the scorpion sting? Yup, they were cousins. Did I care? Oh yeah, this guy was all muscle and Mr. Nasty. Just looking at him told anyone with a trained eye that Oleg was a stone cold killer.

He had started out as a young KGB hood and had actually worked for Uncle Joe Stalin, making political dissidents disappear in East Germany just after World War II. Later, he had played a big part in the KGB's advance group which infiltrated Prague just before the Soviet invasion of Czechoslovakia in 1956. Recently, he had been running training camps for transnational terrorists right here in the Caucasus.

What made things even worse was that I also recognized the man sitting behind Oleg. He was also in the DIA surveillance package. His name was Ali Sherafi. Ali is one of the original members of the Ayatollah Khomeini's militant Sepa-E Pasadran, the Iranian Revolutionary Guard Corps. He was alleged to be in favor of Khomeini and was supporting an overthrow of the current Iranian government. They wanted the Shaw out and Khomeini to take over.

Why am I telling you about all of this? You'll find out. The big thing is that these Russian's were working hand in hand with the Ayatollah and his revolutionary guardsmen. I needed to get word to Danny in Aswan, so he could relay this intel to Crock and Carla at the War Room. All of a sudden a bigger picture began to make itself known. In their search for me, they just told on themselves. The Russian's were working with Sherafi, which meant that they were supporting Khomeini's thoughts about an overthrow of the current Iranian government. A government I might add which worked with ours.

It was almost 5:30 p.m. when I left the cover of my small cave. Placing two drops of Methadrine under my tongue, I stretched out my muscles, and headed toward the town of Nara.

* * * * * * *

It was almost midnight when I reached the high plateau town of Nara and found the home of Mrs. Mara Rishi. There was a small light on in the front room of the tiny, brick home. To describe this town to you would be hard. It was ancient, yet simple.

Looking around to make sure no one was watching, I pulled out my pistol, cocked the hammer back, and knocked on the old, wooden front door of the home. When I did it only took a few seconds for the door to open.

The woman I was looking at stood five-feet, six-inches tall, was slender built, had long, black hair, big, brown eyes, and olive skin. She looked to be in her mid-thirties and was beautiful.

"Mara?" I asked cautiously.

"Yes," she replied in a whisper.

"I am the Black Knight, I need help," I said softly as I took another quick look around to make sure I was still unseen.

"Come quickly," she answered as she opened the door wider and I stepped inside. Closing the door behind me she locked it and stepped around to the other side of the small front room to get a better look at me.

"I'm sorry that I look and smell so badly, it's been a long trip," I explained.

"You are Oliver's friend, yes?" she questioned cautiously. Now I began to feel a little better. Ollie must have given the information about Mara working for us, to Neil, so Neil would pass it along to me.

"Yes, ma'am, I need to get out of this country. Can you help me?" I asked as I set down the two suitcases and holstered my weapon. I looked really bad. The thorn bushes and jagged sharp edged rocks I had been climbing through for the past two days had torn my clothing to shreds.

Let me tell you something. The one thing the satellite or topographic maps don't show you are things like thorns that shred your BDU's, heat, attack trained sand fleas, vicious brown gnats, malevolent horseflies, and blood thirsty vampire mosquitoes. All of which, I might add, I had been fighting with over the past forty-eight plus hours. My body was covered with bite marks, scrapes, cuts, and bruises. Simply put, I was fucked up! But the one thing my Seal team instructors had taught me was, no matter how bad it gets, the Seal way is to overcome all obstacles and tough it out, which so far is exactly what I had managed to do.

"Come with me," Mara explained with a grin as she pinched her nose. Looking down at the two suitcase A-pack weapons Mara sensed my concern. They will be okay, I live alone. Please come with me now," she said once again.

Taking me outside and into her backyard she pointed to a large tub of water used to water her livestock.

"The soap is next to the tub, you can bath while I find something clean for you to wear," she explained as she turned and went back inside.

It took ten minutes for me to take a quick bath. The soap burned, but all in all it helped to disinfect my cuts, bites, and scrapes.

Giving me a clean, white, man's Arab robe and sandals I put them on and quickly washed my BDU's, fatigues, and under clothes.

The homes here were not very close together but I still needed to hurry and get out of sight. Going back into the house, I closed the door and locked it.

"Please come and sit down," Mara explained as she motioned toward her kitchen table.

"How long has it been since you have eaten?"

"Three, maybe four days, I don't remember," I explained as I looked around nervously.

"Please relax, you are safe here," she explained as she handed me a large bowl of lamb, rice, and bread.

"Do you have a telephone?" I asked.

"No, but my cousin does," Mara explained.

"I need to get a message to Oliver, can you do that for me?" I asked as I began to eat.

"Of course, that is why I am here," Mara explained with a grin.

"Mara is a very pretty name," I commented as I continued to eat.

"Thank you, my mother named me Mara because I was born right here in this very house, in Nara."

"Mara, from Nara, that is really neat. Your mother is a wise woman," I explained.

"Yes, my family lives in your new New York City now. Thanks to Oliver, I know that they are safe," she explained with a smile. "What is your nationality?" she asked as she took a long hard look at me.

"Armenian, my great grandparents, Vector and Sophia Negoshian, came to America after the Turks invaded our country in 1915."

"Oh," Mara said excitedly as she clapped her hands and smiled at me. I have some Armenian friends in Turmenistan. They are, how you say in America, Mafia, yes?" she asked to make sure her choice of words were correct.

"Really?" I asked.

"Oh yes, they will get you back to America safely. Oliver was smart in sending you," Mara explained with a smile. I spent the next week at Mara's home waiting for her friends to come and pick me up.

On day eight I met two young Armenian men, Ben Hagopian and Leo Gopigian, both of whom were full blooded Armenian. These two young men would take me out of Iran and to a safe place.

Taking twenty thousand dollars out of my fanny pack, from the money I had stolen from the Ayatollah's safe room, I gave it to Mara as a way to thank her for helping and keeping me safe.

Leaving the town of Nara, Iran, we began our journey to Naryndzlar, which is an ancient Armenian fortress town, high in the Caucasus Mountains, at the very northern tip of Autonomous, Karabakh.

They took me to a mountain almost eight thousand feet high. Higher than Denver. Higher than Geneva. It was here at the top of this mountain I was taken to an old hotel made from a fourteenth century monastery. It was isolated and impossible to get in and out of without people knowing.

Here I had the protection of the heavily armed Armenian Mafia. Even though there were twenty-five thousand Russian troops scattered through Armenia and Autonomous, Karabakh, I was hiding right under their noses, in a country controlled by Russia and protected by both the Russian and Caucasian mafias.

"Geezus, these are my people," I thought to myself as I sat down on the bed in my hotel suite. "Wait until they find out who I am."

Naryndzlar was accessible by a single, two-lane gravel road that wound up through the narrow mountain passes. The village itself contained no more than three, maybe four-dozen homes, a tavern, and a small guesthouse. From the end of the main street an old-fashioned funicular railway climbed one kilometer up the steep mountainside to the hotel above.

For you, the reader, here's some background. During the heyday of the Soviet Union, which I am now in, Naryndzlar had been a retreat for top Soviet officials and heroes. Yuri Garain, the Russian Cosmonaut, had been given a two-week vacation at Naryndzlar as a reward for his record-breaking trip into space.

Khrushchev, Brezhnev, Andropov, have all stayed here too. At this particular point in time, 1976, this place had become a vacation retreat for Russia's top Vory, the organized crime bosses, and the financial oligarchs who were the real leaders of the Russian Federation. It is run by the Chornye, which is shorthand for Chornye Smorodiny, or Caucasian Mafia. Here you could get the best of everything that money can buy. And believe me, they had the money to buy the best of everything and everybody.

Within an hour I was introduced to a man named Steve Sarcasian who was the head of the resort and crime family. He introduced me to the managers, the assistants, the people in the dining room and the bar. Even the women. He told me what clan they came from; what crime family they belonged to; who their Vory are; how they think; what they do; how they do it. I knew it all, he told me everything.

The hotel itself had fifty or so rooms and eight suites, all of which were spread over two floors. The corridors fanned out along the natural ridge of a small plateau in a gentle crescent from the old monastery building, which served as the reception area and lobby, and housed the main dining room and bar. On the inner side of the crescent, the rooms looked down into the valley below. On the other side, the view was spectacular. I could see northeast, across a series of Craggy Mountain Peaks that towered as high as three thousand meters. From the lobby area, an old circular stone staircase wound down to the monastery basement, which had been converted into another bar.

There were three other major structures on the plateau, which were perhaps fifteen, maybe, twenty acres in all. The first was a large, three-story dormitory like affair built at the very edge of the plateau on the southeast side, so as to not disturb the view, which housed the staff and security people.

A second two-story structure contained the communications equipment and had more dorm space for a reinforced security force when Kremlin leaders were in residence. Finally, there was a good-sized aircraft hanger built to house the helicopters which ferried the VIP's from the big airports at the Armenian capital, Yerevan, 175 klicks to the west, the Republic of Georgia's Capital City, Tbilisi, 240 klicks northwest, or the small, single-runway airfields at Stepanakert or Agdam.

Please note that I am giving you the up-to-date information on this area so you can look it up on a 2004 map. At this particular point and time this is all the motherland of Soviet Russia – the big red threat to America.

I had been at the resort for almost three days now. I had given Mara my spare VHF secure radio and told her to wait 48-hours from the time I left to call Chopper and deliver an abort message to my back up team. She would also read a detailed message I had given to her, to Chopper, and explain to him that Oleg and Ali were both in Iran and working with the Ayatollah's Revolutionary Guard. Whether she was able to get through to Chopper or not I didn't know.

Telling Steve I needed to use his communications equipment, I was taken to the two-story structure and left alone to make the call I needed to make. I wanted to make sure Chopper had gotten the message from Mara. I wasn't sure how much juice was left in the battery of the transmitter.

Setting the large short wave radio to our secure frequency number I keyed the mike.

"Bishop One, Black Knight," I said in a whisper of a voice. "Bishop One, Black Knight," I repeated again.

"Knight this is Bishop One," Chopper responded.

"Did you get my message?" I asked.

"No, caller ran out of power to transmit," came the reply.

"Do they know who back doored me?" I asked, wanting to know who leaked the information of our operation to the Russian's.

"Negative. Taliban, Al Qaeda, Syria, Mukhabarat, and Palestinian's are all searching for you," Chopper explained.

"Shit," I replied. I hadn't realized that many people from that many terrorist groups were searching for me.

"Something happened to your chip, we can't locate you for recovery," Chopper explained.

"Abort, go home, I'm too hot. I'll find a way out on my own," I explained.

"Bullshit, tell me your twenty, we'll come and get you," came the response.

"Tell Op's Control that Oleg Lapinov and Ali Sherafi are in bed together. The Russian's are supporting Khomeini. Abort your position and get back to Operation Control. I'm going under until the weather clears," I explained.

"Black Knight, don't do this," Chopper advised.

"To much chatter, gotta go. Remember your promise. Till the end, big brother," I explained as I switched off the power to the short-wave radio and turned the frequency dial to a different sitting. I didn't want to stay on the radio for too long just to be safe. I was way to hot. Every terrorist nation was looking for me now. They wanted these nuclear weapons to use as an international bargaining chip or to detonate in the United States.

There was only one thing left for me to do. Find a safe place to hide them and return to the United States.

On day four a very large helicopter arrived at the mountain top fortress. Going out to meet the middle aged man who had just arrived, Steve immediately brought him over to see me.

"Mr. Knight, I would like you to me Mr. Japridze," Steve introduced as we shook hands and sat down at a table to order our lunch.

It turns out that Mr. Japridze was a Georgian Autortiet. Which is like a Godfather, or a Vory, but in the economic area, not so much the criminal area. Mr. Japridze controls the major banks and business. He also sat on the board of the World Banking Federation, which made him a Russian diplomat with diplomatic immunity.

"Steven tells me you need safe passage to Switzerland. Well, young man, I believe that I can get you there safely. For a matter of fact, I will be leaving for Switzerland this Sunday. I have a business meeting there that I need to attend to first thing Monday morning. Would you like a ride?" Mr. Japridze asked with a smile.

"I would be grateful, sir, thank you," I explained as we ordered our dinner.

Today was Wednesday, it wouldn't be long now and I would be on my way home.

Business in Russia was the same as it was anywhere else. It didn't matter what you knew. All that really mattered was who you knew, and Steve Sarcasian, being a powerful mob boss with the Armenian Mafia, knew all the right people.

* * * * * * *

It was Sunday morning. I had spent the last three days talking to Steven about family business in the United States. We made arrangements for the New York family to ship supplies of weapons, alcohol, and pharmaceutical drugs to Steven. Not illegal drugs like Heroin, but hospital drugs like Penicillin, pain killers, antibiotics, all of which the people of Russia were in dire need of. Not to mention that real American made pharmaceutical drugs were worth ten times more in Russia than illegal drugs were.

Saying goodbye to Steven, I left the fortress resort hotel at the top of the Caucasus Mountains in Naryndzlar. Using his diplomatic credentials Mr. Japridze got me safely to Switzerland.

Just before I left Naryndzlar, Steven gave me a change of clothing and a beautiful all leather carry-on shoulder bag. I put my five remaining Mark 3A2 concussion grenades, my last Deftec No. 25 flashbang grenade, my ballistic nylon belt, holster, H&K USP-9 automatic pistol, and five extra fifteen round magazines all into the leather travel bag.

I left my H&K MP-5 submachine gun and the extra thirty-round magazines that were loaded with .115-grain Winchester Silvertip bullets with Steven. I also gave him fifty thousand in American one hundred dollar bills for his help and for arranging to get me safely to Zurich, Switzerland. All of my other little goodies I kept with me and carried in my new travel bag.

Landing at the Zurich International Airport in Switzerland made me feel a whole lot better about what was happening to me. I still had a little over three hundred thousand dollars with me. This was the money I had stolen from the Ayatollah's safe room. The one of many valuable lessons I had learned while I was being trained at the CIA Farm, if cash is available, grab it, you never know, it may come in handy down the road. The money, even though I had grabbed it at the spur of the moment, was now giving me aid in my escape.

I was in Switzerland with no passport, identification, or credentials. I was carrying two suitcase size A-pack nuclear weapons and a travel bag containing enough explosive power to cause some serious damage. What I needed to do now was find a hotel room with a telephone and call for help. It was all down hill now – a piece of cake.

Stepping off of Mr. Japridze's private jet, he walked me pass the Swiss security and customs agents with a simple showing of his diplomatic immunity credentials. It came as no surprise that everyone knew him by name.

Walking through the airport terminal, we were heading toward the front doors where the diplomat's limousine was waiting for him. It was then that I heard the female voice ring out calling my name.

"David?" Is it really you?" she shouted.

Turning my head to see who it was, a smile appeared on my face.

"Sasha?" I said in a surprised tone of voice.

"Yes, it is I. Have you come to see me?" Sasha asked as she walked up to me excitedly, placed both of her hands on the sides of my face and kissed me tenderly on the lips. The question and kiss both caught me by surprise. So I avoided the question and enjoyed the kiss.

"How have you been?" I asked.

"Why you have not called me, huh?" she asked in a seductive way.

"I have called, no one is ever home. But I am here now and I would like you to meet a friend of mine. Sasha, this is Mr. Japridze. Mr. Japridze this is Ms. Sasha Malenkov."

"Yes I know, I do business with her father Pavel. How are you, Sasha? Is your father here with you?" Mr. Japridze asked.

"No, he is in town on business, but he will be home later tonight. Would you come to our house for dinner? I know he would love to see you before tomorrow's big meeting?" she explained.

"And I would like to speak with him also. I would be honored to have dinner with you and your father. So tell me, young lady, who is this good looking young man you are with?"

"Oh, I forgot," Sasha said with a giggle. "This is my cousin Otto Sakorzenki. He has come to visit and to go skiing," Sasha explained as she introduced us to her cousin Otto.

Otto was in his late twenties, medium built with black hair, brown eyes, and a neatly trimmed mustache. He stood about five-foot, ten-inches tall and weighed close to 175-pounds. Shaking hands, we said hello.

"And you, David, you will come and stay at my home too, yes?" Sasha asked with wide eyes.

"Sasha, I need to make some phone calls, and...." I began to say as she cut me off in mid-sentence.

"I will not hear no for your answer. My father would be so upset to hear that you are here and have not come to our home to stay and say hello. We have many telephones. You can make your phone calls from my home. Is that not right, Mr. Japridze?" Sasha asked.

"How does one say no to such a beautiful young woman, huh?" Japridze asked with a grin as he looked over at me. "Come my young friend, we will spend the evening at the Malenkov mansion," Japridze said as Sasha ran her arm through mine and we left the terminal.

Whispering something to his limo driver, Mr. Japridze, Otto, Sasha, and I were taken to the far side of the airport where the large Malenkov helicopter was waiting for us. Climbing on board, we were flown to the Malenkov Estate.

Climbing off the helicopter I couldn't help but smile. The estate was huge and nothing had changed since the last time I was here.

It hadn't been that long ago when Carla and I had come here so I could kill Morimoto Soba.

It was Sunday afternoon, and most of the staff and employees were gone. Walking inside, Sasha took Mr. Japridze and I to the second floor of the four-story estate and showed us to our rooms. I set both of my suitcases and my travel bag down next to the closet in my bedroom, when I turned I found Sasha standing in the doorway watching me.

"I am so happy you are here once again," she said softly.

"So am I, but I need some time to go shopping. I have nothing to wear for dinner tonight," I explained sadly.

"This is not a problem. I have closets full of men's clothing. Please take what you want," Sasha explained as she walked into the room and opened the doors to the closet. Inside it was full of brand new suits, dress shirts, jackets, and shoes and boots, in all different colors, designs, and sizes.

"We have many different guests come to visit with us. Sometimes they need things, so my father keeps everything extra, just in case. I am so glad that you are here," Sasha explained as she gave me a tender hug.

"So am I. I really do need to make a telephone call. I need to check on my grandmother, she has a cancer," I explained with a sad expression on my face.

"I am sorry to hear that. The best time to call is after six or seven o'clock at night. The overseas lines are not so busy then. For now you can shower and change into something comfortable. My father will be home soon and we will have supper then, okay?" she explained politely.

"Okay," I answered softly as I gave the Russian beauty a kiss on the forehead.

"Oh, I know what you want. Yes I do, maybe later I say yes to you again," she said playfully as she turned and walked out of the room closing the door behind her.

"Oh yeah," I whispered to myself as I walked over to the bedroom door and locked it. Taking off my clothes I went into the bathroom and took a hot shower. I let the hot water run over my body for the longest time. I also kept the door to the bathroom open so I could keep an eye on both of the A-pack suitcases.

After my shower, I shaved and found a real nice Italian made Armani three-piece suit. To my surprise, it fit perfectly.

Placing two drops of Methadrine under my tongue, I opened my carry-on leather bag, pulled out my .9mm automatic pistol, and tucked it in between my belt and the small of my back. Yes, I checked to make sure it was loaded and ready to fire.

I set both of the nuclear weapons in the closet. I then slid my leather bag under the bed next to the nightstand. Finally, laying down on the soft mattress of the bed I couldn't help but wonder what the night might bring now that I was back in Switzerland with Sasha.

* * * * * * *

For the first time since this whole mission had begun, I could feel all of my muscles relax. Laying on the soft bed I looked at my watch, it was almost 6:00 p.m.

Hearing the elevator doors open down the hall, I grinned. "Supper, then a call to Carla. In twenty-four hours I'll be on a plane and heading back to the good old U.S. of A.," I thought to myself as I heard a light knock on the bedroom door.

"David, are you awake? It is time to eat. My father is anxious to see you," Sasha whispered in three slow sentences. "I have a surprise for you," she added playfully.

Standing up I walked over to the bedroom door, unlocked it and then opened it. The smile on my face quickly vanished when I saw the barrel of the silenced Russian-made .9mm automatic pistol pointed straight at my heart. The impact of the three quick shots hitting me at point blank range in the chest sent me staggering backwards. The smell of gunpowder filled my nose as I felt my entire body go limp. Falling backwards I knew right away that Otto was a professional. Each time he had pulled the trigger of his gun, he stepped forward keeping the barrel of the gun within inches of my heart with each shot. He didn't look angry at all, it was just business for the young Russian hit man.

Feeling the corner of the bed catch me behind my left knee, I fell backwards as my body and the back of my head bounced hard on the floor below. The pain in my chest was indescribable. It shot straight through my body like a red-hot dagger. The impact of the bullets hit me at 850-foot pounds of pressure per square inch, and knocked the air out of my lungs. Laying still I fought hard not to panic. I stared up at the ceiling keeping my eyes open as if I were dead.

"Is he dead?" Sasha asked as she walked into the room followed by her father and Mr. Japridze.

"Three bullets in the heart, he is dead," Otto explained as he holstered his weapon.

"Where are the weapons?" Japridze asked anxiously.

"There, in the closet," Sasha responded quickly.

"I will get them," Otto explained as he turned and walked to the opposite side of the bedroom toward the closet.

"No!" Pavel shouted in a panicked voice. "Do not touch them. They may be booby-trapped. Come, I will call someone who knows how to disarm such things," Pavel explained as he turned to walk out of the room.

"Remember our deal, Pavel, you get the American, I get the weapons," Japridze explained as he and Otto followed Pavel out of the room. My eyes were burning and my lungs were on fire from not being able to blink or breathe.

"Remember your training, David, no pain, tough it out, stay calm," I reminded myself as Sasha walked up to take one last look at me.

"You thought that you would get my pussy. Instead you got dead. Stupid American," she said in a cold low voice as she spit in my face.

"Sasha, come it is time for dinner," Pavel shouted from the end of the long hallway.

"Yes, Papa, I am coming," she shouted back to her father as she turned and walked out of the room to join them at the elevator.

Blinking my eyes, I took in one fast long breath of air. I wanted to scream the pain was so bad. Reaching behind me I groaned out in torment as I pulled my automatic pistol from the small of my back and cocked the hammer.

As your reading this it is important that you remember two things. Do as I say and not as I do, because if you do as I do, you will find yourself laying on the bedroom floor of an estate in the Swiss Alps with three 9mm bullets buried deeply into your Kevlar bulletproof vest.

Was I stupid? Yes. Did I forget rules one, two, and three? Yes I did. Why wasn't I expecting the unexpected and forgetting that everything was subject to change at any given moment? The answer is simple, I was thinking with the head of my dick and not the head that was on my shoulders as God had intended for me to think with.

Was I in serious pain? Yes. Was I upset or angry? No. I was far beyond upset and angry, I was straight, down right, one hundred percent, fucking pissed! Am I swearing a lot in this chapter? Yes, and for that, I apologize. But if you had been going through what I had been going through lately, you would be swearing too.

Sitting up I slowly lowered myself back down to the floor. I felt dizzy and my eyes were sending me a blurred message. I could feel a small knot beginning to form on the back of my head where it had slammed against the floor.

"There's no time for this, David, get up now," I told myself as I sat up and toughed it out as my Seal team instructors had taught me to do.

I pulled my leather bag out from under the bed, unzipped it, and pulled out two extra fifteen round magazines for my pistol. Slipping them into my back pants pocket, I then reached back into my bag and pulled out my Deftec No. 25 flashbang grenade.

Have I ever told you what a Deftec does? No? The body of the Deftec No. 25 is made of thick steel and weights almost two-pounds. It has small vent holes located at both its top and bottom. It has a sound level of 185 decibels at five-feet, with a flash factor of 1.8 million candela lumens and a duration of nine milliseconds. It also has a one-point-five second fuse. To put it in non-technical terms for you , they are fucking loud and fucking bright. Which is as it should be, because they have been disorient to disorient bad guys in life-and-death situations.

There is a downside, however. It is this; if you, the good guy, are to close to the fucking thing when it goes off, you end up almost as disoriented as the bad guy your trying to throw off balance and gain the advantage over. This is why we train as follows:

Step One. Gently toss the flashbang into the center, or toward the far side, of the space you want to occupy. Do not simply drop it in the doorway.

Step two. After it explodes, make entry.

In short, it temporarily blinds and deafens you.

Making my way to the bedroom door, I peaked around the corner of the doorframe and looked down the hall. It was all clear, so, I made my way down the hallway, avoiding the elevator, because they would hear it, and quickly made my way down the stairs located next to the elevator.

Because it was Sunday, I knew there would only be one or two staff working to cook and serve the evening meal. Now on the main floor of the estate, I kept my back against the wall and slowly made my way toward the dining room. The closer I got to the door, the more I could hear as they sat at the long dining room table and ate.

"You will be rewarded well when you return to the Motherland, Otto. Many men have tried to catch this American," Pavel explained proudly.

"Yes, Father, Uncle Boris will be very pleased when you call him with this good news," Sasha added as they continued to talk and eat.

I couldn't believe what I was hearing. Uncle Boris? Pavel Malenkov was either directly related to or extremely close friends with my most hated enemy, General Boris Kalashnikov.

"So what is it that you will do with these American nuclear bombs?" Pavel asked.

"They will be going to the PLO in Palestine. From there my friend, Yasser Arafat, will have his people sneak them into Israel where they will detonate them. It will be American weapons that destroy the Israeli scum on the Earth. We will finally be rid of them once and for all," Japridze explained coldly.

"And what is it that you get from all of this? You destroy Israel for what reason?" Otto asked curiously.

"For their money, what else. Most of their wealth is in our World Bank. Who is it to say what they had when they are all dead?" Japridze commented with a snicker in his voice.

"You steal all of their money, Palestine takes their land and has their own country, and America takes the blame from the United Nations. This is good and how it should be. But what about the Armenian who called you asking for your help to save his friend?" Pavel questioned with a touch of concern in his voice.

"Sarcasian the Mafia boss? What will he know? I will tell him that I delivered his fellow countrymen safely to Zurich. He will not question me, we have done too much business together, he trusts me," Japridze explained.

At least I knew now that Steven Sarcasian wasn't involved in this. He had simply called the wrong man for help.

Hearing the maid come out with more plates of food I pulled the pin out of my flashbang grenade and rolled it into the room. I turned away from the door and the flash explosion but it still made my ears ring.

Moving into the room, the rancid smell of explosive and smoke filled my nose. Locating the young Russian I fired two shots hitting Otto in the chest and knocking him out of his chair and onto the floor. Moving in fast I shot Japridze in the face. My .9mm bullet struck him in the left eye and blew the back of his head off as his body fell backwards, chair and all, to the floor.

Walking past Sasha who was still stunned and blinded from the noise and the flash of the Deftec, I walked up to where Otto was laying on the floor. Even though I could plainly see that the front of his white shirt was completely covered with his own blood, I shot him two more times in the head.

The maid had dropped her tray of food and had stepped backwards with both of her hands clenched tightly over her face. Firing one shot my bullet struck her in the chest, blowing a melon size hole out through her back. Her body hit the wall behind her and slid slowly down towards the floor, leaving a wide smear of red crimson blood on the white wall behind her.

Walking over to Pavel I quickly placed the barrel of my gun against the side of his head at the temple. "Say goodnight asshole," I said loudly as I pulled the trigger. The bullet went straight through his head but to my surprise he didn't fall out of his chair. Instead his upper body fell straight forward causing his face to slam down into his plate of food. Blood was squirting out through the hole in his head with each beat of his heart. As his heart stopped, so did the flow of blood.

Hitting Sasha in the side of her head with the butt end of my gun, I knocked her out of her chair and ran quickly into the large kitchen. Standing in the far corner of the kitchen was a middle-aged woman with pepper gray hair. Her whole body was trembling from head to toe with fear. Looking into each others eyes, I raised my gun.

"Say goodnight, bitch," I said coldly as I fired one shot into her face, turned and walked back into the dining room.

Sasha was just starting to stand back up as I walked over to her. There was a trickle of blood running down the side of her face from where I had hit her with the butt of my gun. The effects of the flashbang grenade were wearing off quickly now.

"You thought that you would get my pussy. Instead you got dead, stupid American, huh?" I mimicked as I grabbed her by the hair with my left hand.

I had a horrible pain in my upper chest that was shooting into my left shoulder, but I was too pissed off to care. I was so pumped up on adrenaline and fear that I could feel my heart pumping in my chest.

Turning her head so that she could see her dead father I whispered into Sasha's ear. "Say hello to Daddy."

Seeing her father laying face down in a plate full of food and blood, her eyes widened as she began to cry and scream.

"I don't need your pussy you Russian bitch, I've already had it," I said in a loud and angry tone of voice.

Pushing her head forward I forced her to bend over as I slammed her head down onto the table next to her fathers. Her face was now laying in the pool of blood that belonged to her father. I wanted to torture this bitch. I wanted to make her scream for hours but I didn't have the time to waste.

Pushing the barrel of my gun into the back of her head she began to beg for her life. For a moment I thought about letting her live. I could use her later on if I needed to. She would also inherit her fathers billions.

Looking down at her long black hair I thought about the hours I had spent alone with her in her bedroom. The scent of her body, the tenderness of her soft warm flesh. It hadn't been that long ago that I had made love to this Russian beauty. The memory brought a smile to my face as I pulled the trigger of my gun one more time.

The bullet shot straight through her head and into the thick hand carved wooden tabletop. When it did her legs kicked out from underneath her. Letting her long black hair go, her body slid off of the table, and fell to the floor.

"Once the Sandman comes for you, Sasha, he doesn't leave until he collects your soul," I said softly as I looked down at her dead body.

Ejecting the clip from my gun I tucked it into my pocket and pulled a fresh clip out of my back pocket and reloaded my weapon. I had fired nine of my fifteen bullets. That's right, if your trained properly you always try to count your spent rounds. It doesn't matter if it's a pistol, rifle or submachine gun, you always try to keep track of your ammunition. A trained Navy Seal carries 300-rounds of ammunition into combat or on any Black Operation's mission. That's not a lot of ammo, so you best make every shot count.

I had five full fifteen-round clips left and six bullets remaining in the clip I had just taken out of my gun. That gave me 81-rounds remaining.

Before this was over, I had a feeling I would need each and every one of them.

Sitting down in Sasha's chair I picked up the bottle of red wine chilling in the sterling silver ice bucket, popped the cork, and took a long drink. I set my pistol down on the table and reached up and rubbed my face. When I did I winced when my hand ran across the power burn on my chin and neck. When Otto shot me, the muzzle flash of his weapon had burned the flesh on my face.

Walking through the estate I locked the front doors, the back doors, the kitchen doors, and the doors to the service entrance. Why did I do that your asking yourself? Because I was hurt, I needed a shower and a fresh change of clothes. I had blood on me from shooting Pavel and Sasha at point blank range in the head; the blood pressure from the heart causes the blood to squirt out through the hole in the skull. Anywhere else on or in the body, no; but a headshot is messy. Its not like you see on television or a Hollywood motion picture. That's fiction, this is real life you're experiencing now, and it's messy.

Going back up stairs I went to my bedroom, stripped down, screamed from the pain in my rib cage, and took a hot shower. My chest was already turning black and blue from the bullets impacting my bulletproof vest. Finishing my shower I put on a fresh change of clothes and climbed into the elevator. Taking the elevator to the fourth floor of the estate I went to the end of the hall where Pavel's communications room was.

Opening the unlocked door I grinned. "He only locks this door when he has his private parties. So much for trusting your friends," I said out loud to myself as I sat down at the large desk and picked up the telephone. Dialing for an overseas line I called straight through to the War Room. Reaching under my shirt I pulled the adhesive tape off of my shoulder, which had the thin lead disc still attached to it.

"Hello," Neil said anxiously.

"Hey, partner," I answered.

"Where are you?" Neil asked cautiously.

"Check your satellite screen. I need a passport, identification, and a ride home," I explained as I rubbed the pain in my chest with my right hand.

"Holy shit," Neil whispered.

"I'm on the move, tell Bishop that I need a ride."

"How in the hell did you get to Pavel's estate? Better yet why would you go there of all places? Are you nuts?" Neil asked.

"I'm going to give you a direct feed into his computer system. Download everything and then virus his system. I gotta go," I explained calmly.

"Where are you going?" Neil questioned.

"Lines not secure you've got the high tech system, I'm sure you'll find me. I'm on the move, partner, don't trust anyone except Bishop and his team. Are they available to come and get me?"

"Yes, I'll have them in route in a matter of minutes."

"I gotta get out of here."

"Did you..." Neil began to ask and then caught himself.

"Connecting your line to the computer. Tell Ollie it's all his and to have fun."

"He's standing right here beside me. Stay on the move, partner. Your being hunted, we'll find you," Neil explained.

"I know, it's deeper than you think. I just had a run in with some of them. This place is a mess. It needs a good cleaning," I explained. I had just told Neil that everyone here at the Malenkov Estate was dead.

Setting the receiver of the telephone into the computer phone cradle, I turned on the system and then left the communications room.

Going back to my room I picked up both of the A-pack suitcases and my leather travel bag. Going back downstairs I headed to the front door. Just as I reached up to unlock it, the doorbell chimed.

"Oh shit, this must be the guy Pavel said he was going to call to check for booby traps," I thought to myself as I slid both suitcases over to the opposite side of the door.

Looking at my watch it was almost 8:30 p.m. I pulled my gun out from where I had tucked it into the small of my back. I quickly checked to make sure a live round was in the chamber and that it was ready to fire. Clicking off the safety I opened the door being careful to keep my gun hand behind it, and out of sight.

"Otto?" the tall young Swiss man asked. He stood six-feet, three-inches tall, had sandy blonde hair, a mustache, blue eyes, and was neatly dressed. He looked to weigh about 240-pounds and was carrying a medium sized metal suitcase.

"Yes, and you are?" I questioned as I looked around to see if he was alone.

"Ian, Pavel called me," he answered with a half smile as he raised his metal case slightly.

"Ah yes, I am sorry, please come in," I asked.

"The American, he is dead?" Ian asked as he stepped inside.

Closing the door behind him I quickly raised my weapon.

"No," I said in a low voice as he slowly turned his head to look back at me.

"But you are," I said, as Ian's eyes got wide, I fired two shots. The first shot hit him in the right shoulder. The second shot caught him in the neck and caused him to stagger backwards about six feet. Reaching up to grab his throat Ian fell forward and dropped first to his knees, then to the floor.

Walking up to his body I fired one more shot hitting him at the base of the skull where it meets the neck. The bullet severed Ian's brainstem, went through his neck, and buried itself into the hardwood floor.

I found his car keys in his pocket. "I need to borrow your car, Ian," I explained as I tucked my pistol back in between my belt and the small of my back. Picking up my suitcases and bag I stepped outside and locked the door behind me.

Walking over to Ian's silver Chevy, four-wheel drive, two door, Blazer, I put my suitcases and bag on the backseat, climbed in, and started it up. Lucky for me it was an automatic transmission. My chest was killing me so shifting a manual four speed transmission would have caused me a great deal more pain I really didn't need right now. I put the Blazer in drive, took one last look at the Malenkov Mansion, and then drove away.

* * * * * * *

It took me almost three hours to drive from the Malenkov Estate, that was hidden deep in the Swiss Alp's, to a small out of the way hotel called the Suisse. I didn't want to stay at any of the major hotels in the big tourist areas. If the bad guys were still looking for me, I figured they would have all the major hotels under surveillance. I also knew that someone on the inside of our elite group was leaking information to Boris at the Kremlin. Because of this I wasn't going to stay in one spot for more than 24-hours at a time.

I found the Suisse on Piazza Mazzini 23. It was a modest hotel with wood floors and hand carved furnishings set in a Fifteenth Century Palazzo over looking the lake. It was clean, beautiful, and the service was excellent. 011-39/031-950-335 well that's what the phone number would have been if any of this was true, which of course its not.

Asking the young lady at the front desk if they had a doctor on call, she said yes. Explaining that I had been in a skiing accident and had hurt my chest, she called him at his home. It was almost midnight when the middle aged doctor arrived at my hotel room. With one look, he had no doubt in his mind that I had broken a number of ribs. I needed X-rays but we settled for a chest wrap. As he tightly wrapped the cloth material around my badly bruised chest, I moaned, groaned, winced, and gave some serious thought to shooting this nice doctor. The pain level was rising quickly. Paying the doctor for his services, he handed me a large bottle of painkillers and grinned.

"You're going to need these," he explained as he patted me on the shoulder and advised me to take skiing lessons.

After thanking the doctor for the house call, he left. When he did I placed two drops of Methadrine under my tongue and popped two of the 800-milligram capsules into my mouth and laid down.

* * * * * * *

It was 1:00 in the afternoon, as I boarded a train for Como. Even though I had only been at the Suisse Hotel for less than twelve hours, I heard that little voice in my head, my sixth sense, telling me to move and do it right now.

The train ride to Como took three and half-hours. The sight seeing view was beautiful. Between the chest wrap, painkillers, and Methadrine, the pain and agony in my chest had eased up to almost nothing. But I wasn't kidding myself. I couldn't take another hit like that in the chest and walk away.

Once in Como I took the express ferry for a one-hour cruise to Bellagio where I ate supper and spent the night at a small boarding house.

At 7:00 the next morning I was boarding the train once again. This time I was heading to Venice. After a four-hour train ride I hopped onto the No. 82 ferry and got off at the Accademia Bridge. I spent the day at the Hotel Galleria on Campo della Carita 878A, 011-38/041-523-2489. A Seventeenth Century Pallazzo at the foot of the bridge on the Grand Canal. I went to see the Accademia Gallery and the Doge's Palace, window shopped at Calle Larga XXII Marzo, and then sat around the Piazza San Marco.

The next morning I took the train from Venice to Innsbruck, which was a five-hour ride. Once there I went to the old cobble stoned town of Altstadt and rented a room at the Weisses Rossl Hotel. The Weisses Rossl dates back to 1410 and was only a ten-minute walk from the train station. It was located on Kiebachgasse 8 at 011-43/512-583057.

The next morning I took a taxicab to the Pension Paula, a hillside chalet just outside of town on Weiherburgasse 15 at 011-43/512-29262. I had just finished eating my lunch when I looked up and saw Danny, Butch, and Tom walk into the small chalet restaurant. Standing watch at the doorway was John Mitchell, the nuclear explosives expert. Scanning the restaurant they saw me and walked over to the table I was sitting at.

"Damn, boy, your a hard one to catch up with. When you go dark you go pitch black don't you," Tom said with a serious look on his face.

"Where's the suitcases?" Butch asked with a tense tone to his voice.

Reaching into my pants pocket, I pulled out my room key and handed it to my brother.

"Both of my suitcases are in my room. I've got a leather carry-on bag up there to. Grab it for me would you?" I asked as I took a sip of my Pepsi.

Reaching under the lapel of his coat Danny whispered into the lip mike of his satellite radio set.

"We've got him, he's okay," was all he said.

Danny, Butch, Tom, and John were all dressed in regular plain clothes, so that they wouldn't stand out in the crowd of people. But if anyone was paying any attention at all, they would have noticed the small earpiece in their left ear and the thin wire which ran from it, around their ear, and disappeared under the collar of their shirts.

"You alright, little brother?" Danny asked as I stood up and set a twenty-dollar bill on the table to pay for my meal.

"I am now. It's been a long, hard, bloody run. boy, am I glad to see you guys," I whispered.

"If you ever tell me to abort again, I'm going to beat your ass, boy," Danny said as he punched me playfully in my left shoulder.

When he did, a razor sharp pain shot through my chest, like a hot dagger, and then down my left arm. Wincing out in pain, I bent my upper body forward and placed my right hand on the top of the table to steady myself. That playful little tap actually made my head spin.

"Awe shit your hurt aren't you?" Danny asked with a concerned look on his face.

"I'll be okay, big brother, just get me out of here, will ya?" I responded.

Leaving the restaurant we climbed into the two taxis waiting for us out front. Driving to the outskirts of town Cookie and Joe were both waiting for us there in an all black unmarked helicopter. Climbing on board we lifted off and headed to a secure location the Agency had in Venice.

For reasons of security, I won't tell you where the CIA's safe house is located in Venice. I will say that it is a nice size private estate and heavily armed on the inside.

Once inside, we all went into the large front room and sat down.

"Take off your coat and shirt, youngster, and let me take a look at your chest," Cookie told me as John set both of the suitcases down on the floor across the room from me.

"Sandman, you got the keys for these?" John asked with a curious look on his face.

Taking the small brand new key out of my shirt pocket, I tossed it across the room to Agent Mitchell.

"I'm all taped up Cookie, Doc said it's some broken ribs. I'll be okay, I've been through this before," I explained as John unlocked both of the suitcases and opened them up to make sure they were secure and stable.

"What the fuck is this?" John asked with a surprised look on his face. Reaching into the suitcase he pulled out one of the many thick hard covered books inside and held it up in the air for everyone to see.

"That's Mark Twain, it's a pretty good book," I explained with a straight look on my face as everyone in the room turned to look at me with a "What the fuck is this?" look on their face.

"Youngster, you did get both of the nukes out of the Ayatollah's place, didn't you?" Cookie asked with a concerned look on his face.

Looking over at my friend and mentor, I raised both of my eyebrows and gave him that "No shit asshole" look.

"Okay, wrong question. We know you got 'em, the question is, what did you do with 'em?" Cookie asked realizing that his first question was dumb.

"I wrapped 'em both up in thick logging chains and dumped 'em. There somewhere in the Caspian Sea off the coast of Pakistan at about 2,000-feet below sea level." I explained with a straight face.

"You're kidding right?" John asked.

Reaching up, I unbuttoned my shirt and pulled it open. Pointing at the three bullets still lodged in my Kevlar bulletproof vest, over my heart, I answered John's question.

"Does this look like a joke to you? They were coming at me from all angles, so I deep sixed 'em rather than let them fall back into terrorist hands."

I then went on to explain what Mr. Japridze had said to Pavel, Otto, and Sasha about his plan to turn the A-pack weapons over to Yasser Arafat, so his people could detonate them both in Israel. Everyone then agreed it was better to dump them in the ocean than risk loosing them if I would have been caught and killed.

I never mentioned Mara or Steven Sarcasian and his fortress resort high up in the Caucasus Mountains. Instead, I told everyone that I made my way south across Iran and snuck into Saudi Arabia. I told them that I met with a young woman who lived in a housing complex in the town of Riyadh and paid her to help me.

Now you, the reader, have been on the run with me, so you know that it's not true. Did I hide both nuclear suitcase size A-pack weapons somewhere between the Ayatollah's Palace in Tehran and the hillside chalet in Pension Paula in the old town of Altstadt in Venice? Yes I did. Am I going to give them back to the CIA? No, I'm not. Now you're wondering why right? Well because those two nuclear weapons could be part of a whole new story, plus you never know when they might just come in handy one day.

We spent the night at our safe house and flew back to the United States the very next morning.

Carla, Deputy Director Crock, ranking members of the National Security Agency, and the Defense Intelligence Agency debriefed me. Debriefing took almost three hours. Carla, by the way, was smiling from ear to ear.

I then went to the hospital for X-rays. I had six broken ribs Even though some people would say that I don't have a heart, I actually do have one. It was time for a rest, while the search for the person on the inside who betrayed me, was intensifying.

* * * * * * *

In 1979, Russian KGB General Oleg Lapinov was placed in charge of the Spetsnaz Alpha Team that assassinated the president of Afghanistan just prior to the Soviet invasion of that country. In the 1980's he'd directed a ruthless policy of extermination against Afghan Mujahideen leaders. By 2000, he would show up once again as the Kremlin's Chief Advisor on oil policy in the former Republic's. Simply put, he was Moscow's liaison with the Lovrushniki – which is KGB slang for the Georgian, Azeri, and Armenian Mafia's. He would tell them how far they could go in collecting dan, or protection money. He would also set the limits on how big a Tusovka, or piece of the action they could slice for themselves.

Ali Sherafi, was one of the original members of the Ayatollah Khomeini's Militant Sepa-E Pasadran – the Iranian Revolutionary Guard Corps who called themselves, The Fist of Allah. In 1979 he played a very big part in the take over of the American Embassy in Tehran. In 1999, top secret intelligence reports would show that he tried to mount a coup against the current Iranian government because he thought it's policy of rapprochement with the west was evil and anti-revolutionary.

But he still had a few Rabbi's left amongst the Mullah's and they had, according to the stories Iranian sources were floating, saved him from prison, and sent him into a kind of exile, as an Agricultural Expert, to consult with the governments of the Caspian Region about improving grain exports to Iran.

And if you believe that cover story, I have a real nice piece of oceanfront property to sell you. It's just outside of Clarkston, Michigan....

Chapter Thirty-Six
Kate's Angel

I spent the next three days in the hospital under the watchful eyes of military doctors, heart specialists, and Special Agent Eckland, who were all worried about my condition

Even though Kathy was my field supervisor, she had also become a good friend to me. She was pretty, had a great body, and was fun to be with on 'wet work' operations. She was also a very rare type of woman. She was as cold blooded and heartless as could be when it came to killing people, which for me, worked to my advantage.

For three days she tried to pick my brain and get me to confess to where I had stashed the two nuclear suitcases. She wasn't buying the story that I deep-sixed 'em in the ocean.

Staying true to my way of doing things, I smiled, laughed, joked, and held my ground sticking to my story and doing it with style.

After signing myself out of the hospital, Kathy and Ben flew me back home to Michigan.

Once there, I found myself being cared for by Kathy, Tara, and Jessy. Trust me when I tell you that you don't ever want to be stuck in a house with three young women who all believe they know exactly what is best for you.

I had been badly injured in Switzerland. From the start of my mission to its finish, I had pushed and abused my body well beyond its limits. It was the Seal way of doing things. I didn't have to like it; I just had to do it. There was no room for failure, because a trained Navy Seal never fails, not ever.

Even though I am the first to admit that I am not a Navy Seal, I was trained by them to become a Black Operation Sniper. They also blessed me when they gave me my Trident Pin, and in doing so, made me an honorary Seal. It was their way of accepting me as one of their own. Along with that Trident Pin, came the responsibility to up hold their code. In doing so I could not fail, no matter how badly I had been injured. Not as a POW in Vietnam, nor as a 'wet work' Operative for the Agency. I only wish now that I had gone back and finished the training with them. That would have been the greatest honor of all.

Hearing someone walking down the hallway toward my room, I smiled when I saw Tara walk in holding a bottle of Pepsi in one hand and bag of Lay's potato chips in the other.

"What's that?" Tara asked when she saw the gold Trident Pin I was holding in my right hand.

"It's called a Trident Pin," I explained as I set it down on the nightstand next to my bed and looked back over at my adopted daughter.

"Is it special?" she asked with a curious look on her face as she handed me the bottle of Pepsi and bag of chips.

"Yup, real special, just like you are," I explained.

"Really, do you really think I'm special?" Tara asked as she sat down on the side of my bed next to me.

"Yes I do. Your father would have been so proud of you. You look a lot like him ya know," I explained with a wink of my eye.

"Yeah, my mom tells me that a lot. Can I ask you something?" Tara asked with a serious look on her face.

"It doesn't matter, even if I say no your still gonna ask," I answered as I took a sip of my Pepsi.

"Kathy said you got in a car accident and that's how you hurt your chest so badly. Is that true?" Tara asked, as she looked deep into my eyes waiting for an answer.

"No it's not, it felt more like a semi-truck hit me, not a car," I explained. I didn't want to lie to Tara so I answered with a different form of the truth.

"Hurts pretty bad, huh?"

"Only when I talk to much. Do me a favor and call your Uncle Andy. Tell him to come over and save me from a house full of women," I said jokingly in an attempt to change the subject.

"When I get married will you walk me down the aisle?" Tara asked.

"You bet I will, just do me a favor and enjoy your life while you're young. Don't get married right away. Travel and see the world first. Once you get married, everything changes. It has a way of slowing you down and keeping you from doing all those little things you wish you would have done if you wouldn't have gotten married," I explained.

"You sound just like my mom," Tara said as the doorbell rang. "Andy," we both said at the same time. "I'll go see," Tara said quickly as she ran out of the room and disappeared from sight. Tara was growing up way to fast, and to be honest with you; I wasn't ready to see that happen.

From up here in my bedroom it sounded as though the girls were all excited about something, but I couldn't tell what it was. It took a few minutes before Tara stuck her head back in through the open doorway of my bedroom with a huge smile on her face.

"Guess who's here?" she asked gleefully.

"Donald Duck?" I said with a grin.

"You're such a butthead Dad, no it's not Donald Duck," Tara explained as she stepped off to the side.

Seeing Ben and Carla walk into my bedroom caught me by surprise. Seeing Kate peak in through the door behind them filled my heart with joy.

"I let you go off to play with your friends and look what happens," Kate said jokingly as she walked up next to my bed and kissed me tenderly on the lips.

"I felt that Kate needed to be here, so I sent Ben to Ireland to pick her up."

Kate wasn't showing that she was pregnant yet but her face was sure glowing.

"Thanks, boss," I said with a smile as I looked at Carla.

"Oh don't thank me, I brought my suitcase along to," Carla explained.

"Yes dear, when Ms. Silverman called me to tell me that you had been hurt, I insisted that she spend a few days with us," Kate explained smiling.

Looking around the room at Kate, Carla, Kathy, Tara, and Jessy I couldn't help but let out a sigh.

"Ben, don't you leave me alone with these women," I explained with a serious look on my face.

"Hey, I love you like a brother, but, dude, you're on your own. See ya, later," Ben said with a smile on his face and a wave of his hand as he walked out of my bedroom laughing.

"I called Amy and Dana too. Their both coming over to join the party," Kathy explained with a big grin on her face.

"You guys have a good time. I'm going to go and see my grandmother," I explained as I started to get out of bed.

"Oh no you're not, there is no need for that. Andy is bringing her over. She should be here any minute," Kathy added with a wide smile.

"Some friend you turned out to be," I responded as I gave Kathy a dirty look.

"Your grandmother is going to teach us all how to cook your favorite Armenian dishes. That's why Carla agreed to come over and spend a few days with us," Kate explained anxiously.

"You talked to my grandmother?" I asked surprised that Kate had called her.

"Of course, we call each other everyday. Your grandmother and my Nana have become quite good friends. My Nana has asked her to come to Dublin for a visit. Isn't life just grand," Kate said proudly in her Irish accent.

"Oh this is gonna be fun," I said in a low soft voice as I sat back against my pillow and groaned.

* * * * * * *

Well, as you can imagine, the girls went wild. The smell of Armenian food filled the house. Baked pastries, stuffed grape leafs, lamb, pilaf rice, you name it and believe me they were cooking it. Oh, by the way, did I forget to mention that I was the one paying for everything? How careless of me to have forgotten to mention that little, but expensive, tid bit of information.

In all honesty, I really didn't care. The memories of this four-day escapade or female bonding session, which would be more accurate, I hold close to my heart. There were four generations of women in my home. Tara and Jessy were fifteen. Kathy, Kate, Dana, and Amy, were all in their very early thirties. Carla was in her very early forties and my grandmother, who I loved with all of my heart and soul, would always tell us on her birthdays that she was just turning twenty-one. And no one argues with the wisdom of their grandmother, right? Of course not.

I also noticed that Kate was paying a lot of extra attention to Tara and Jessy. Much to my surprise Kate asked Tara if she would be her made of honor at our wedding. Of course when Kate asked her, they both cried. It's a girl thing.

Even though I had no say, what so ever, in the matter, this group of wise women set a date for our wedding. Kate wanted to be married next to her wishing pond. So they chose May 15th, as our wedding day. It would be a warm spring day, the flowers in the field, wild flowers that is, would be in bloom. All in all it would be a perfect setting for a very special day.

May 15th was also Kate's grandmother's birthday. So with that in mind, our wedding reception would also turn out to be one big birthday party for Grandma Katie.

Watching the girls say goodbye to each other, which of course took almost two full hours, brought a warm smile to my face.

Carla walked over to me to say goodbye. "I can't believe that you stayed for four days," I explained with a broad smile on my face.

"Are you kidding, I wouldn't have missed this for the world. I've never felt this happy before," Carla explained.

"Thanks for staying. You know that you're always welcome here at my home," I explained.

"I know, I'm also highly upset with you, kiddo," Carla said sternly.

"Me? Why?" I asked.

"Why didn't you tell me that Kate was pregnant? I never would have let you go into Iran, had I known," Carla explained with a sincere look.

"Yes you would have," I replied in a low voice as I knelt forward and gave Carla a kiss on the cheek.

"Did you really deep-six those two nukes?" Carla asked very quickly trying to catch me off guard.

"They're deeper than the Titanic."

"Well, get some rest and heal up. Your gonna need all of your strength raising those two son's of yours," Carla explained with a wide grin.

"Yeah, I know. Did Kate tell you what we're going to name them?" I asked as we began to walk over to the front door.

"Yes, she did, it will mean a lot to them. How very special, David, special indeed. Call me in a few days, will ya? I need to get back to the Pentagon to see if it is still standing," she said jokingly as she walked over to Kate to say goodbye once again. As she did, my secure phone began to ring.

Walking into my den I picked up the receiver and placed it to my ear.

"Hello," I said softly.

"Are you available, sir?" the voice on the other end asked.

"No," was all that I said. When I did the phone on the other end hung-up. I was in no shape to go out on a mob hit. This was the first time that I had ever said no. I couldn't help but wonder how he felt about that.

Kate spent the next two weeks with me at our home in Michigan. Because of my injury, the FAA wouldn't let me fly, so Ben volunteered to take Kate back to Dublin for me, when she was ready to leave and return home.

There were a lot of things that needed to be done to prepare for our wedding. And according to Kate, I would only get in the way, as all men do. I found that statement to be interesting. Especially coming from a young woman who, for the past three weeks, ate bananas and sardines, and asparagus with strawberry ice cream and dill pickles. Okay, her body is going through some changes. I can deal with that. But when she started craving Cap'n Crunch cereal and horseradish, mixed 'em both together with chocolate milk and ate it, that was a bit much. But when Andy saw Kate eating it and then went in to the kitchen and mixed a bowl for himself, I couldn't help but wonder how crazy this Indian really was? He actually sat down next to Kate, on my front room floor, and ate his bowl with dill pickles. So of course Kate had to have pickles with hers too.

I couldn't help but wonder how anyone could eat all those ingredients mixed together and still live. I called my mom and grandmother for help and got none. I called Kate's grandmother for help, she laughed at me and handed the telephone to her husband, Sean.

When I explained it to him he laughed, told me "It had only just begun," and then went on to explain that, "It's the women in our lives that make good men go to drink'n."

"No shit, Grandpa. They're crazy," I explained as I said goodbye and hung up the telephone.

Going into the kitchen I made one of my famous bologna, A-1 steak sauce, and whip cream sandwiches, opened a bottle of Pepsi, and ate by myself.

* * * * * * *

Over the next three months I spent a lot of time with Neil at the War Room. We were trying desperately to find out who it was that had leaked the information about me being in Iran to Boris in the Kremlin.

Ollie was working his end, Neil and I were working our end, Kathy was working her end, and Danny with the Team One guys were working their end of the intelligence network.

Now your wondering, Kathy? A girl? And I have to be the first to admit, even though she is as cold hearted of a killer you could ever meet, as a woman she could do a lot.

I'll bet that you're all out there thinking that I'm going politically correct on you, right? Next thing you know I'll be saying that there should be women Navy Seals, Rangers, and Green Berets. No, absolutely not! But let me tell you, women can do a lot in the military. Not as Seals, lets leave that to bad Hollywood movies. But they can work the holy crap out of intelligence assignments. They can serve as military attaches. They can do almost anything except fight as part of an elite combat unit.

The problem is that today's military sees itself as a social, not a fighting, organization. So we end up with situations like the Navy has, in which 18 percent of all females serving at sea get pregnant, and cannot perform their duties. That is no way to make war. And believe me, if we had to go to war with all of those pregnant silhouettes aboard, we'd be in serious trouble.

One way to begin to solve the problem would be to follow the Marine Corps example of keeping men and women separate. If that practice were followed in the Army, Navy, and Air Force, there would be far less problems in our military today.

But that is unlikely to happen with the current Pentagon mind set, which is the product of leaders who have never had to shoulder the responsibility of leading other men into battle. Indeed, the majority of our leaders, both in the administration and in the congress, have never served in the military, and therefore, see it as an alien culture, something to be mistrusted.

Okay, enough with the sermons. My point is that Kathy can be ruthless at the intelligence level. Look at Carla for instance. When General Boris Kalashnikov was having his surgery, Carla paid off the right doctors in Russia and had a satellite chip implanted into his left shoulder. She knows that Boris is a threat to America, and a very powerful military leader and politician in Russia. Now, if he becomes a major problem, we can find him at any given moment and kill him no matter where he is on the planet. And who did it to him? A woman.

So, anyway, everyone was working their end of the network, but without the mysterious caller calling Boris, we were once again stagnated.

I was healing up pretty good now and the FAA gave me the thumbs up to fly again. Flying to Dublin, I took my guest list to Kate so that she could send out our wedding invitations. Between her lot and mine, all I can say is thank God we're getting married in a very large meadow.

Kate had all of her relatives, family, and friends coming in from Montana, Ireland, and Scotland. I had all of my relatives and friends coming, but I also had to invite all of the family members of my organized crime family. To leave them out would have been an insult, which is something I would never do.

It was going to be big, festive, and above all a hell of a lot of fun. The estimated cost for the alcohol and beer alone was going to be twenty thousand dollars. That's not to include the food, ice, plates, cups, napkins, silverware, etc. If I ever get to see the Ayatollah Khomeini again, please remind me to thank him, because it's the money I stole from his safe room that's going to pay for all of this. After I thank him, remind me to kill the bastard.

* * * * * * *

May 14, 1976

The weather forecast called for sunshine and warm weather for the next five days.

Kate's parent's, Scott and Sara Donovan, had arrived on the 7th of May, and were staying with their parents, Sean and Katie, at their home.

My parents and grandmother had also arrived a week early to help out if needed and were staying with Kate and I at our new home on the hill over looking the beautiful meadow where Kate's wishing pond was.

Uncle Paul from New York, and some of the other heads of our families, had sent refrigerated, semi-tractor trailer trucks to us. They were loaded with Budweiser beer, American and Irish liquor, and more steaks and chickens than I had ever seen before in my life.

Danny, Butch, Cookie, Tom, Bell, Mosier, Tara, Amy, Jessy, Dana, Ollie, Kathy, Ben and his wife, had all arrived yesterday and were staying at Nell's boarding house and the small local motel on the outskirts of town.

We had reserved a fleet of rental cars and limousines, which were waiting, at the airport for our guests to arrive from the United States. We also had helicopters standing by for our VIP guests, like Uncle Paul and his bodyguards.

We had leased rooms in all of the local hotels and motels throughout the entire area. We were expecting around eight hundred plus people to be here tomorrow. In reality, by the time the reception would begin, with all the local towns people who we had also invited, the number would be closer to twelve hundred.

A lot of the local town people had volunteered to man the barbecue grills, serve drinks, and help out in anyway needed. It was their way, as Kate told me, of saying thank you for our opening the bank at Nell's, and helping them out, plus Kate was one of their own.

Stages had been built, speaker systems had been put up; everything was set and ready to go for our wedding tomorrow.

Taking Kate by the hand, we walked down to the wishing pond and sat down to be alone.

"I saw an angel here today," Kate explained as she gently rubbed her tummy.

"An angel?" I asked delicately.

"Yes, an angel. She was right over there, smiling at me," Kate explained as she raised her right hand and pointed toward the front edge of the wishing pond.

"Okay," I said in a slow fashion.

"Don't okay me, David, I'm not daft. I know an angel when I see one. She was so beautiful. When I walked over toward her she smiled at me and told me not to be afraid, that everything was going to be alright," Kate explained as she gazed in the direction from where she said she had seen her angel.

"Well, that's good news," I said softly as I looked at the side of Kate's face.

The sun was beginning to set and I swear to God I could see a radiant white and gold glow all around Kate's body. Blinking my eyes twice to clear my vision, I thought I had been seeing things, but the white and gold glow was still there.

"You're glowing," I whispered in amazement as I reached out to touch the beautiful aura all around her.

"What?" Kate asked with an angelic look on her face.

"Your glowing, I swear to God, Kate, I can see it. Its all around you, its beautiful," I explained in a mesmerized way.

"All pregnant women glow, its God's way of keeping us safe," Kate explained as she looked deep into my eyes.

"I never thought I could feel this way, Kate. Sitting here with you and the boys. I don't feel empty or alone anymore," I explained softly as I looked at the woman who had stolen my heart, so long ago.

"What do you mean, empty and alone?" she asked.

"I don't know how to explain it. Ever since Vietnam, I've felt dead inside. It was like a Vortex, a black hole that continued to suck the life out of me. A cold, dead, empty feeling. I kept trying to fight it, and now, all of a sudden, it's gone.

I look at you and I feel a kind, gentle peaceful feeling inside of me again. Like I used to feel before I went to Vietnam. You are my angel, Kate, my saving grace," I explained in a soft whisper as I leaned forward and gently kissed the mother of my children on her lips.

"See, I told you my wishing pond is a special place. Even the angels come here to comfort us and take away our pain. Oh, how our God does love us, David. Don't ever forgot that," Kate explained as she leaned over and gently laid her head on my chest.

Placing my arms around her, I held her close to my heart where I knew she would always be. It was here, sitting with Kate and my two boys, next to her wishing pond, that I had finally found peace.

* * * * * * *

It was exactly twelve o'clock as I stood looking at Kate. The minister had begun the wedding ceremony. Kate's father, Scott Donovan, had walked her across our butterfly filled golden meadow to the sound of Scottish bagpipes, and gave her hand to me, along with his blessings.

Scott and his father, Sean, were full-blooded Irish. Kate's grandmother was Scottish and had moved from Scotland to Ireland after marrying Scott's father, Sean. Grandma Kate's last name was Connery. By no means were we going to leave the Scottish tradition out of our wedding. Grandma Katie had told us that it had always been her dream to see her granddaughter married to the sound of Scottish bagpipes. And by God, that is one wish Kate and I were making come true. Standing next to me were my best men, Danny and Butch. Standing next to Kate were her maids of honor, Tara and Jessy.

Kate was wearing her grandmothers wedding dress. The beautiful hand made white dress had been worn by her grandmother, her mother, and keeping with their family's tradition, it was now being worn by Kate. Of course Grandmother Katie had to let it out a tad bit to make room for her grandson's, which as Grandma Katie explained, "Was no problem at all."

The sun was shinning, the meadow was filled with little butterflies, and purple, red, white, and blue wild flowers. A gentle breeze blew across the meadow as Kate and I took our wedding vows.

Ever since Kate was little she had sung a song standing out here by her wishing pond. Today, as she said, "I do," she looked into my eyes, smiled, and recited a line from her childhood song, to me. " My Irish eyes are smiling, their smiling just for you. For every time I see your face, you make my heart feel new."

Looking at my bride I held her hand, looked into her eyes, and said, "My love for you is forever and a day. When I put my arms around you, it is there that they will stay. Smile with me, laugh with me, cry and be sad with me. And when the world stops turning, spinning slowly to a stop. Take my hand, don't be afraid, and together with our children, fly away with me into the night."

Raising her white veil, I kissed my bride. "Well, I don't know about the rest of you, but I could sure go for a sip of fine Irish whiskey," the minister explained to the crowd of our friends and relatives.

And with that our wedding reception and Grandma Katie's birthday party had begun.

I had always thought that the Armenian's and the Italians knew how to party, but I'll tell you what, we didn't even come close to the Irish and Scottish men and women when it came to having a good time. Oh how I do wish that my grandfather could have been here to see this.

The men were lining up to kiss and dance with Kate. They were filling her bridal purse with handfuls of hundred dollar bills. The women were all lining up to kiss and dance with me.

The smell of grilled steaks and barbecued chicken was floating through the afternoon spring air. Everyone was laughing, the music was playing, and for the first time in a very long time I felt good about myself.

It was about two o'clock in the afternoon when Kate picked up a microphone to speak to all of our friends.

"Your old lady is getting ready to say something, little brother," Danny explained as he put his big arm around me and gave me a hug.

"Man, she is beautiful, Sandman," Butch added as he took a long drink from his bottle of Budweiser.

"Hello, everyone," Kate said out loud to get the crowds attention. As she did everyone turned to look at her. "Everyone of you are asking me what David and I are going to name our twin boys. So I have decided to tell you, but first, there's a wee bit of story that I need to tell you first,"

Kate explained with a big smile and a giggle as she looked over at me for approval.

Smiling, I nodded my head, 'yes', and took a sip of my Pepsi.

"I met my husband in Vietnam. David, was part of a very special black operations team who would go out and try to rescue American POW's. His three teammates were and always will be his, and now our, best friends and brothers. Now then, if you look over there," Kate explained as she pointed toward, Danny, Butch, and I. "David, is standing with his brothers. That big fella is Danny, who we lovingly call Chopper. The other young fella is Butch, who I might add are both still as handsome as ever," Kate explained smiling.

"David's third brother was killed in the war while they were trying to desperately rescue a captured Marine pilot. His name was Nick, and even though we may not be able to see him, I just know that Nick is here with us today," Kate said lovingly as she looked over at me, giving me a tender look.

"Now then, our first born son will be named, Daniel Jonathon. After you, Danny, and David's grandfather John, who has gone to be with our Lord," Kate explained proudly as she looked over at Danny.

"Awe, little brother," Danny said as he looked from Kate over to me, totally surprised by what he had just heard.

"But I'll tell you what, little Danny better not come out as big as you are or you'll both be in some serious trouble," Kate said jokingly as everyone began to laugh and clap their hands in agreement. Looking up at my best friend, I saw that his eyes had filled with tears.

"I love you, big brother," I whispered to my friend.

"Damn, David, awe man," Danny tried to respond but he couldn't. Seeing his mother Mrs. McBride walk over to him smiling, brought a warm feeling to my heart.

"They're name'n their baby after me, mama," Danny said to his mom as his voice broke with emotion.

"There's no greater love than that, than for a man to name his child after his brother," Mrs. McBride explained as she gave her son a tender hug.

"Our second son will be named, Nicolas Sean, after our dear friend and brother Nick and my grandfather Sean Donovan. Nick's parents have honored us by being here with us today," Kate explained as she pointed over at Nick's mom and dad who were sitting with Cookie, Joe, Tom, Bell, and Mosier.

"Your son will always live on, not only in our hearts, but also through our son, Nicolas," Kate explained as everyone clapped their hands.

"Now, Butch, we haven't forgotten you, dear brother. It's just that there was only room for two on this first trip. But I promise you our third born will be named after you. Let's just hope its another boy," Kate joked as she looked up at the sky smiling. "Thank you, Lord, for blessing us with such dear and wonderful friends," she whispered. After she did the band started back up and the party continued.

"Brothers and friends, throughout life and into death, till the very end," Butch and Danny said proudly as they raised their drinks.

"Hoo yah," I replied as I raised mine.

The Scottish group began to play a song called, Auld Lang Syne, which was according to Kate's grandmother, written in the Eighteenth Century by a Scottish poet named, Robert Burns. The phrase means, a nostalgic look at the past. The song says, 'Let's celebrate over some drinks,' which was exactly what was happening at this particular point in time.

At 2:30 we brought out the birthday cake for Kate's grandmother. Seeing the twenty-one candles that garnished the top of it brought a big smile to Grandma Katie's face.

It was a few minutes past three when Kate and I walked over and stood next to her wishing pond. Looking over at the crowd of people we couldn't help but smile and laugh.

"You don't mind that I told everyone what our boy's names are going to be, do ya?" Kate asked smiling.

"Not at all, honey, it was a special moment."

"I thought I saw Danny cry," Kate said as she looked over at Danny who was preparing to enter a drinking contest with Andy and Kate's cousin Tom.

"It brought tears to his eyes," I explained as Danny, Tom, Butch, and Andy got up from their table and began to walk across the meadow lawn toward us.

"We are so blessed, David," Kate whispered softly.

"Yes we are," I replied as I kissed Kate on the forehead.

"You do have some big friends, David," Kate commented with a grin. Looking over at Danny I saw him raise his glass of whiskey at me and smile.

"He is a big man, that's for sure," I remarked.

"Not Danny, those two," Kate explained as she pointed at the other two men walking toward us, along the edge of the pond.

They both stood about six-feet, five-inches tall and weighed a good 240-pounds each, all of which looked to be solid muscle. One of the men had brown hair, the other had black. They were both carrying a nicely wrapped wedding gift and were smiling.

Looking over at them I tried to place their faces in my mind, but couldn't remember either of them. The black haired fella nodded his head at me in a friendly gesture. Smiling, I nodded back at him.

"I don't know those guys," I commented as I looked over at Danny, Tom, Butch, and Andy who were walking toward us on our right side.

It was then that everything seemed to go into slow motion. Both Danny and Andy saw it coming first. I saw their smiles disappear as they let go of their drinks and quickly reached under their suit jackets to grab their guns. Their eyes were fixed on the two men walking directly toward Kate and I.

As I saw Danny's mouth move and the panicked look in his eyes, I looked back over at the two men who Danny was yelling at. I remember hearing Kate scream, "No." When she did she turned quickly to face me, wrapped her arms tightly around my waist and began to push me backwards with all of her might. Her quick reaction caught me off guard and caused me to stagger backwards. It was then that I saw what Kate, Andy, and Danny had seen. Both men had dropped their wedding gifts. I watched the packages tumbled end over end, falling to the ground as they pulled their weapons out from under their jackets.

"No, Kate!" I screamed as I tried desperately to turn my upper body and move Kate out of the way. I really tried, I swear to God I tried, but Kate's pushing me backwards and refusing to let go of me, caused me to lose my footing. I heard the gunshots as we both fell backwards. I could feel the impact of the bullets as they hit my wife in the back. I could hear people screaming and children crying as the air filled with gunfire. Feeling my back hit the ground, I wrapped my arms around my wife and began to roll her over and onto her back.

"No, David," she cried out. "Please my love, let me lay here on top of you for just a moment," she whispered. Her face was next to mine, I could feel her breath on the side of my face. My hands and forearms felt warm from the wetness of her blood.

The gunfire, as quickly as it had started, had now stopped. Danny and Andy were the first to run over to us. Kneeling down next to us I saw it in their eyes. Rolling my wife gently to the side I sat up and held her tightly in my arms.

"Why, Kate, why?" I asked as my heart tore out of my chest and I began to cry.

"Because I love you so very much," she whispered.

"Please don't leave me, Kate. Please don't leave me," I begged.

"I can't feel the boy's, David," my wife said softly as she pulled her left hand around and touched her stomach.

"Katie, oh God, no!!!" Kate's mother and grandmother began to scream as their husbands Scott and Sean held them both back.

"Oh my God, no!" Carla whispered as she pushed her way through the crowd to get to us.

"Let me through," the town's doctor yelled. As soon as he saw Kate, he knew and simply lowered his head with sadness.

"I'm here, Kate, don't be afraid, I won't leave you," I whispered as tears ran down my face.

"I'm afraid that I'll have to take our boys with me, David. Their going to need to stay with their mother," my wife explained as she raised her head off of my chest to look at me.

"I understand, Kate. They'll be safe with you," I cried.

"We'll be waiting for you in heaven, my love," Kate whispered.

"No, Katie. Please, honey, oh please, Lord, take me, not my wife and children," I screamed as I began to lose control of myself.

"Look, David, its my angel, she's here," Kate said softly as she looked over to our right and up toward the sky. Looking at my wife I saw a beautiful white glow radiate all around her body as she raised her hand up toward the sky.

"Oh my, it's the Lord, David, he's here to take us to heaven," Kate explained as a smile appeared on her face. Bending forward, I kissed my wife gently on her lips.

"Yes, Lord, the boys and I are ready. Come boys, we must go with Jesus now," my wife said in a soft heavenly voice as she continued to look up at the clear sky above.

As she did her hand slowly lowered as I pulled her body gently against my heart once again. "I love you, Katie, I love you so very much," I whispered into Kate's ear as I once again began to cry.

Chapter Thirty-Seven
The Pale Horse

I buried my wife and two sons under the large oak tree which sat next to our home at the top of the hill. From there they could look out across the meadow at the beautiful wishing pond she loved so very much.

I didn't disturb Kate's body. Instead, I left her as she was at the time she had died in my arms; wearing her grandmothers wedding dress with the white, lace veil draped gently over her face. Because she still carried both of our unborn children inside of her, there was no embalming. The children stayed inside of their mother, where I knew my wife would keep them safe.

I don't remember very much about the funeral. I remember there were a lot of people who came to pay their respects and say goodbye to the young, brave woman who was one of their own. With no doubt in my mind, I knew my wife Kate, was an angel sent from heaven to experience life here on God's green earth.

The news of the shooting spread quickly throughout both Ireland and Scotland, as well as, throughout the organized crime families in America.

Most of the guests who had come to our wedding had stayed for Kate's funeral. After the funeral they slowly began to fade away returning to the world of their own individual lives. Our new home was filled with unopened wedding presents and had our uncut wedding cake still sitting silently on our kitchen table.

My brothers, Danny, Butch, and Andy had refused to leave my side. Danny had taken away my pistol and refused to give it back. He knew I didn't want to be here anymore, and was afraid I would take my own life.

You know what? He was right; I didn't want to be here anymore. The one person I truly loved had been viciously taken away from me. All of my hopes, all of my dreams, were gone now. There was no more laughter in my life, no more smiles.

Our friends from the town had bought a beautiful white marble headstone and place it at the head of my wife's grave. On it, these words were engraved:

Kate, Daniel, Nicolas

Angels sent from heaven to bless our lives. Taken home by our Lord himself.

To young – To soon. May 15, 1976.

I came here to find peace and happiness with Kate. Instead, I brought with me death to the ones I loved the most, my wife and children. I tried so very hard to understand why Kate would do such a thing, knowing that our unborn children were inside of her.

"When you love someone as much as the two of you loved each other, you sometimes react to a situation without thinking. That is what our Kate did when she saw you were in danger. Don't be angry with her or with God, David. She did the same thing you would have done for her," Grandmother Katie explained as she laid white roses at the head of my wife's grave.

"You'll always be part of our family now, son. This is your home now, don't ever forget that," Grandfather Sean explained. Taking his wife by the hand they turned and walked back across the golden meadow to their home.

I wanted to cry but there were no tears left. My heart was gone now, and along with it went my soul. All I could see was the darkness that had now consumed me. The blood in my veins ran cold with the darkness of time guiding its way through the black hole where my heart used to be.

It had been three days since I had buried my wife, and in that time period I had never left her side. Kneeling down next to her, I stared at the loosely packed earth that covered my wife and children. Unable to contain the darkness that had consumed me, I looked up at heaven and screamed with an angry, bitter, hate filled vengeance.

"Give me the power of your mighty sword, Father. Give me revenge!"

* * * * * * *

Sitting next to Kate's grave I looked out across the meadow and watched as some of the fish would break the calm surface of the wishing pond's water, and swallow up some of the small bugs floating on top.

Hearing some movement off to my right I watched as Danny, Butch, and Andy stepped out of my home and walked toward me. Danny sat down next to me and handed me a bottle of cold Pepsi. When he did the expression on his face told me that someone had called him.

"You need to eat something, little brother. You haven't eaten anything since…" watching Danny I understood that he had stopped in mid-sentence because he didn't want to say, since the wedding.

I knew and understood that these men were also in pain because of what had happened. But I didn't care about their feelings. That emotion was gone in me now. It was sucked out of me. Swallowed up by the vortex, the black hole that took away the last ray of white light energy in my life. I only had one emotion left, and that emotion was hate.

"Since my wedding, Danny. See?" I said as I raised my right hand and showed Danny my wedding ring. Kate had bought me what is known as a king's ring. It was made out of white gold. The sides were brushed. It had six flawless large diamonds forming a circle at the top of it, and one diamond in the middle, a total of seven diamonds. Inside she had the jeweler engrave the words; 'United As One', which is exactly what we were, for the rest of eternity.

"You need to eat something is all I meant," Danny explained with a sad look on his face.

"I will, God is sending me something," I said with a blank expression on my face.

"Manna?" Butch asked with a curious look.

"No not Manna," I replied calmly.

"What then?" Butch asked.

"He's sending me revenge. Its best eaten cold," I explained as I took a sip of my Pepsi.

"Carla called, she ran the fingerprints and photographs of the two shooters through our computer bank. She got a positive identification of 'em right away. Their KGB, Sandman, their Kalashnikov's men," Danny explained as he watched the expression on my face for a reaction.

Taking another sip of my Pepsi I looked out across the meadow. What had just been said to me came as no surprise. I had already figured as much. The size of the two men, the boldness of the hit. To do it at a wedding in broad daylight, knowing that some of the guests would be armed. It was a suicide hit; I knew that. What I was waiting for was Neil. Through him God would feed me.

"Yeah, and ten minutes later Neil called," Butch explained.

I was just getting ready to take another sip of my Pepsi. The lip of the bottle was almost at my mouth. Without moving a muscle I waited, frozen in the position.

"He said that he needs to see you immediately. He said you'd understand what that meant. He sounded really upset, and then he hung the telephone up on me," Butch explained with a pissed off look. Placing the bottle to my lips, I took a sip, and then turned to look at my wife's grave.

"I'm going to have to leave for awhile, honey. I'll be back, I promise," I whispered as I stood up and walked over to my home to take a shower. God had answered my prayer; it was time to eat.

* * * * * * *

I flew straight to Washington D.C. and went right to the Pentagon. Walking into the War Room I watched as Neil turned around in his chair.

When he saw me he turned a pale shade of white and his hands began to tremble.

"Sandy, do me a favor will you, and take a break? I need to talk to David privately," Neil explained.

Watching Sandy walk past me, I could tell by the look on her face that she wanted to say something, but she didn't know what to say. So she simply patted me on my shoulder and walked out of the room, closing the security door behind her. Walking over, Neil locked the door and turned to face me.

"It's my fault, Sandman," Neil explained as his eyes filled with tears.

"How so?" I asked calmly as I placed two drops of Methadrine under my tongue and looked into Neil eyes.

"The most obvious was the least obvious. The reason I could never get past their system is because it was our system they were using," Neil explained.

"Explain that to me, would you please?" I asked calmly.

"The skip jump calling system the caller was using is this one," Neil explained again as he pointed at the War Room's computer system.

"The person calling Kalashnikov was calling from their home and running it through my computer system. I didn't catch it until they called Kalashnikov from Ireland and call forwarded it through their home here in the United States.

We're the only Agency with Walter Shaw's call forwarding system. The call came through on the 13th of May, but this time I couldn't hear what the caller was saying. They were using one of our secure satellite phones. That's how I caught it. I just didn't catch it in time. I didn't figure it out until the day before yesterday. Once I did, I got a positive lock on it. I know who's been calling General Kalashnikov and giving him the information about you and how to get to you at your wedding," Neil explained sadly. Taking a deep breath of air into my lungs, I let it out slowly.

"Who killed my wife and children," I asked in a soft cold whisper.

Stepping closer to me, Neil whispered into my ear, and then began to cry. "I'm sorry David," he sobbed.

Putting my arms around him, I gave him a hug. "It wasn't your fault, it was mine. Don't blame yourself," I explained as I stepped back, wiped the tears from his cheeks, and patted him on his shoulders. "You caught 'em, that's what counts now. I'm going to need your help," I explained calmly with a forced smile on my face.

"I'm here, partner, just name it," Neil replied as he regained his composer.

"Check and see if you can tell me where I can find these people," I asked as I walked over to Neil's computer station and wrote the names down on a pad of paper. "Don't tell anyone anything until after I'm finished," I explained, as I looked Neil in the eyes.

"Not a word, I promise you," Neil answered.

"Good, I'll be in touch," I said as I turned and walked out of the War Room.

All the signs had been right there in front of me. They were right under my nose; I was looking right at 'em. They we're so obvious that I never paid any attention to them. The most obvious was indeed, the least obvious.

To me, betraying a friend ranks right down on the bottom of the scumbag list with child molesters, rapists, and people who beat up on children, women, and animals. You don't send them to a psychiatrist for therapy so they can whine about how daddy abused them as a child. You don't arrest them and try them in courts of law because that's a waste of time and money. There's a very simple, quick, and effective way to cure sick demented pieces of shit like that. You give them the Sandman double tap'.

What's the Sandman 'double tap' you're asking? It's very simple; you shoot 'em twice in the head! See, problem solved.

Walking into the Situation Room I walked straight into Carla's office, closed the door behind me, sat down in the chair across from her desk and looked her dead in the eyes. I could see it by the look on her face that she was trying to think of something to say.

"I'm so very sorry, David," she said in a soft tone of voice with a motherly look on her face. "I was going to stay and try to help you after the funeral but I knew that Danny, Butch and your friend, Andy, were there with you. So, I came back here to try and find out who the two men were that killed you and your family," there was a long pause as Carla looked down at her hands and then back up at me with a forced smile on her face.

"Do I look dead to you?" I asked coldly.

"Yes you do, David. I can see it in your eyes. The David I have come to love is gone. I look into your eyes and all I see now is the Sandman, I see death," she explained.

"You owe me two favors with no questions asked. I need those favors now," I explained.

"You're the son I never had! After everything we've been through together, don't you understand that? When they killed your wife and babies, they murdered my daughter-in-law and grandchildren. Don't you ever insult me and ask me for favors!" she shouted out as tears ran down her cheeks. "Just tell me what you need dammit and its yours, just don't shut us out, David. We're all family here; we need to be part of this. We all need to be involved for our own individual reasons. Don't you shut us out, David. Don't you dare shut us out."

My mind was racing now; I wasn't expecting this. Deep down inside of me I felt the old me trying to find his way back out of the darkness that had consumed him.

Carla had stood up and walked around her desk. Her face was red with anger; her eye make-up was streaked on her face from her tears. Standing up, she wrapped her arms tightly around me, and broke down crying again.

It took a few minutes for Carla to calm down, and then her telephone rang. Answering the phone she wiped mascara from her eyes.

"Where are you? Give us a few minutes and we'll be right there, I need to wash my face... I'm okay, we'll be there in a minute," Carla explained into the telephone and then hung it up. Walking into the small bathroom that's attached to her office she washed her face, dried it, and then turned to face me.

"Please come with me," was all she said. Leaving her office we walked down the hallway to the high security, sound proof, conference room. Opening the door we stepped inside. Closing the door behind us I heard the security locking system bolt the door close.

Looking around the room I saw Butch, Danny, Joe, Tom, Cookie, Moseir, Bell, and Neil all sitting around the large wooden conference table. To my surprise it was Danny who stood up to speak.

"I want to say something to you," Danny said with a very serious look on his face as he pointed his finger at me.

"I joined the Army because I wanted to fight. I joined the Black Operation's Intelligence Unit because I wanted to be trained to be the best killing machine I could be. So the Navy Seals trained me to be the best commando sniper in the world. I was a first round draft pick for the NFL, David. The Dallas Cowboys offered me millions. I didn't want to sack some punk ass quarter back or break bones. I wanted to be the best, so I joined Black Op's Team One, and that's exactly what I became, one of the best killers in the world.

We took an oath, one goes we all go; one stays we all stay! Don't think you're walking out of this room without us, because that ain't happen'n, not this time it ain't. Take a look around this room, Sandman. Remember us? We were, we are, and we always will be Team One. Brothers and friends throughout life and into death, until the very end, remember? The only exception is Neil and Carla, but we adopted them just like we adopted Kate.

They killed our sister, they killed little Danny and little Nick. Our namesakes, our babies. No body does that and lives, nobody!

Neil knows something, but he won't tell us. Because he made a promise to you. I respect that, but I'm going to kill this cocksucker if he doesn't tell me who betrayed you and Kate. I swear to God I'll snap his fucking neck like a dry twig.

Look around this room, Sandman. Do we look like saints to you? If they took every GI Joe wanna-be in this Pentagon and totaled up the number of people that they've killed, they couldn't come anywhere close to the body count that Team One has.

I know your hurt. Shit, hurt hell, look at you. You're dead, the Sandman has consumed you. But let me tell you something else I know. My little brother David is still in you somewhere and he'll find a way back out and get you under control.

Remember what you told me right after you became part of Team One?" Danny asked.

In all the years that I've know Danny, he's never talked this much nor has he ever been this angry with me. Tilting my head slightly, I tried to remember what it was that I had said to him. Shit, we talked about so much, how was I suppose to remember?

"Your grandfather always told you to never do anything in the heat of your anger. Because when you do, your not thinking correctly and you make careless, stupid mistakes that will either get you caught or killed. You told me your grandfather said that when you're mad or upset you need to simply walk away and calm yourself down.

Then, when you're ready, at the time you choose, at the place you pick, after you've planned it all out, then you make your move and strike back. I never forgot that, but I think you have. That's all I got to say," Danny said as he sat back down.

Everyone in the room was watching me in complete silence, waiting to see what I was going to say. As soon as Danny had sat down, it happened. I don't exactly know how to describe it. It was a warm flow of pure energy that moved right through me. It was so intense that it made my whole body quiver.

"Kate," I said in a whisper of a voice, caught by total surprise. Raising my hands I cupped them over my nose and mouth. "Its Kate, she's here, I felt her, she walked right through me," I explained.

"What?" Carla said as she stepped up next to me and placed her hand on my left shoulder.

"I can smell her," I explained as I placed my hands over Carla's nose.

"Oh my God, I can smell her, its her scent," Carla said softly with a surprised look on her face.

Big Danny was the first to jump up and run over to me. Grabbing my hands he smelled them and smiled.

"It is her," he said as he leaned closer toward me and sniffed. "I can smell our angel, she's all over you, little brother," he whispered with a big smile on his face.

It was at that exact moment, when I felt my wife walk through me, that the David she loved so very much began to fight back against the dark side.

My wife was trying to tell me something; she was trying to help me, and reaching out from heaven to do it. No, not to kill someone, Kate would never do that. But I really do think that she was trying to pull me out of the vortex and help me to clear my head, and that's exactly what she did. She didn't want me working for the dark side.

Now don't get me wrong, I hadn't changed my mind. No, no, no, I was still seeking revenge and that's exactly what I was going to get. I just wasn't walking around like a zombie anymore. Kate knew she was the only one who could pull me out of the trance I had fallen into. And Kate, being Kate, did it the only way she knew how, by making her presence known to me. The memories of my wife came flooding back through me. "God, I miss her so much," I said as I looked at my big brother, Danny.

"I know, little brother, I know, so do we," Danny said as he wrapped his big arms around me and gave me a big brother type hug. As Danny held me close to his chest, Carla wrapped her arms around Danny and I. Then came Butch, Cookie, Joe, Tom, Mosier, and Bell.

"You forget who's family you belong to now?" I heard Bell ask Neil.

"I thought..." Neil began to say from where he was seated.

"One of ours is hurting inside, so we all hurt just like you do. That's what makes us a team, a family. Get up here, boy," Bell explained.

When he did, Neil stood up, walked over to us and wrapped his arms around us. In doing so, even though he had never danced with death as we had done together as a team, Neil had officially become part of our family now.

Some people might think that what had just happened, a family hug, would be corny or weak. But they'd never been through what we had been through together. We didn't know it at the time, but it was this bond of loyalty that would soon take us on a whole new adventure, and would change our lives forever.

"Your not going to like what I'm about to do," I explained as we ended our bond of friendship hug.

"Just make it nasty and we'll enjoy every bit of it," Butch said as he looked over at me.

"Turn on some James Brown motherfuckers, its time to rock and roll," Danny shouted out with a big smile on his face.

I didn't tell them who had betrayed Kate and I. That was something I needed to do on my own. So for now that bit of information stayed between Neil and I.

I did however, lay out the plan I had put together for KGB General Boris Kalashnikov. And to be honest with you, now with this multi-talented team at my side, there would be no way to stop us.

While they started doing the research, I put together a brand new doctors bag of death. The Sandman, was about to make a house call and seek revenge.

*   *   *   *   *   *   *

The person I was going to see lived two miles from the Pentagon, in a very expensive condominium complex. It only took a few minutes on the CIA data information bank computer to gather all of the information on this person I needed.

Using my new lock pick gun I entered in through the front door of the apartment and locked it closed behind me. Walking into the bedroom I stood silently and waited for the person to come home.

I had taken a piece of thin 100-pound, fishing line and cut it into a three-foot length, tied a knot every two inches across the whole length of the line, and then tied a metal key ring onto each end of the line. You know, an O-ring like you put your car keys on.

Normally, I would use a piece of piano wire, but the fishing line would work just as well. I now had what is known as a garret.

I wrapped one side over the other, pulled it through the center, and slid my first finger of each hand into the metal O-rings.

Now it looked like a big looped snare. Here's what's going to happen. I'm going to toss the loop quickly over the head of my victim and then jerk it shut around their neck. Because it's so thin, it will bury itself deep into the flesh and muscle of my victim's neck and choke off, not only their air supply, but also the arteries at the side of their neck that supplies blood to the brain.

Oh yes, my victim will panic and claw at their throat trying to pull it loose. But they won't be able to. You want to know why? Because the small knots that I tied in the line will inner lock with each other. The only way to remove it will be to cut it out and that's not going to happen, I promise you that.

It was six o'clock in the evening when my victim came home.

Walking into the bedroom, I watched as this person took off their coat, shoulder holster and weapon, and hung them both in the bedroom closet.

Then this person stripped down naked and went into the bathroom to take a long, hot shower.

Where was I you're wondering? Under the bed watching. Who is it your asking yourself? Be patient my dear friend. I am. Hell, I'm letting this NSA agent take a shower before I kill them. Now you're really confused aren't you?

Did you hear that? The shower just turned off. You're about to find out who this person is.

Sliding out from under the bed, I walked across the bedroom and stood behind the bedroom door. I could hear her as she walked out of the bathroom on the thick shag carpeted floor and back into her bedroom. As soon as she passed the door I struck. Slipping out from behind the door I stepped up behind her and tossed the deadly garret over her head. When I did, I jerked as hard as I could on the O-rings that I held in my hands.

The thin deadly line sunk deep into the soft smooth flesh of her neck, and locked itself in. When it did, I released the O-rings, stepped back and kicked the bitch in the center of the back. She was already in a full panic when I kicked her. Her naked body bounced face first onto her bed and then turned quickly to face me.

"Hello Carol, remember me? The Sandman's here you fucking cunt," I said coldly as I watched Carol dig her long fingernails deep into the tender flesh of her neck.

Her eyes were bulging and her face was already turning blue. I walked up and took a closer look at her. Her mouth was wide open as she twisted her body wildly in all directions. She was kicking her legs out without even thinking about it. Jumping on top of her I held her down on the bed and watched. She was struggling and trying to fight for air, but she wasn't getting any.

Fear and panic are a terrible enemy in a case like this.

She kept jerking her head up and down as she tried to fight for air. I took great pleasure in watching her suffer.

"You're lucky, Carol, you're dying a lot faster than your friend is going to die," I whispered out to her. She was weakening quickly now; her body was relaxing. Her face was puffy and blue; her eyes were wide and filled with the horror of what was happening to her. Then she relaxed, her dead eyes staring up into mine.

You remember Carol, don't you? She used to work in the War Room with Neil. Remember, Carla turned the controls over to me when she sent the Seal team to the high ground. I sent them around and through the valley and from there to the ocean while the Navy blew away all the bad guys on the top of the cliff with their attack fighter jets. See now you remember.

Carla fired Carol and sent her back to her supervisor where she had worked with the NSA.

Carol blamed me for getting her fired from the War Room. Because of that, it made it real easy when another person approached Carol and offered to buy the top-secret security codes that controlled the master computer system in the War Room. With those codes they also gained access to my satellite chip code. General Kalashnikov must have paid a lot of money for that information because an NSA agent, earning field grade pay, could never afford a two hundred thousand dollar condominium like this one.

Picking up the telephone on the nightstand next to Carol's bed, I dialed a secure number and called for the CIA cleaners. The cleaners would come and dispose of Carol's body and all evidence that would suggest a crime had been committed here. What's really special about the CIA cleaners is that we have cleaning crews stationed all around the world ready to clean up any mess we make at any given time. Just like they did in Florida when I killed Danny Patron's buddies Mr. Cruz, his bodyguard, and ATF agent Julio Garcia.

I'll bet that the ATF is still scratching their heads and wondering about whatever happened to their undercover agent. But then again, they're the same Agency that murdered all of those women and children at the Branch Dividian Complex in Waco, Texas, trying to get David Kuresh. Did you know that President John F. Kennedy was getting ready to dismantle the ATF? Remind me later and I'll tell you about that.

Hanging up the telephone I left Carol's apartment and headed to the airport.

Once I got there, I climbed on board my Learjet and sat down in the pilots seat. As I did my sky pager began to beep. Pulling it out of my pocket I looked at the digital readout on the face of it, it was Kathy.

Looking at the read out, I cleared the pager and put it back in my pocket.

Carla had told Brandi to install a secure phone and computer system in both of my planes just in case I was ever in one of them and she should happen to need me. That system was located at the back of my plane with an extension phone next to the pilots seat here in the cockpit. Picking up the phone I called my Field Supervisor, Special Agent Kathren Eckland.

"Hello," she said on the other end of the line.

"Hello, boss," I replied with an empty tone in my voice.

"David, hi. I called Carla to see if she had heard from you and she told me that you were back in the States. I know it's a stupid question, but are you alright?" Kathy asked in a kind and concerned voice.

"No I'm not, I feel empty inside as a matter of fact…." I said as I paused, took in a deep breath of air and let is out slowly. "I'm in my plane now. I was just getting ready to fly to Langley and turn in my Q-clearance."

"David, don't do that, please don't do that," Kathy asked in a gentle tone of voice.

"I'm done, Kathy, I don't want this anymore."

"David, listen to me. I'm not just your field supervisor; I'm your friend. Everyone knows your hurting, please give it some time before you make a decisions like that," Kathy asked gently.

Pausing for a moment, I looked out through the windshield of my plane at a United Airliner that was just coming in to land.

"I don't know, Kathy. I feel so lost right now," I answered.

"When is the last time you had any sleep or something to eat?" she asked.

I didn't answer.

"That's what I thought. I'll bet you haven't eaten or slept since it happened, have you?"

Again, I didn't say anything.

"I'll make you a deal, I've got a six bedroom home here. Five bedrooms of which are empty. Come over here, David, and stay with me for a few days. Get some sleep and then make your decision. I'll even cook you one of my prime rib dinners. How's that sound?" Kathy asked.

"You can cook?" I asked knowing that would piss her off.

"Only when I'm worried about a friend of mine. Please, David, give me a chance to change your mind. At least let me help you, please, David. Two days, that's all I'm asking. What do you say, partner. Is that to much for a friend to ask for?"

Yawning, I paused for a moment. "I guess not. Two days and then I quit," I replied.

"You want me to pick you up at the airport?" Kathy asked in a more upbeat tone of voice.

"No, its getting late, I'm going to sit here in my plane for awhile. I'll fly out tomorrow, how's that? I'll be at your place sometime after lunch, okay?" I asked.

"That sounds great, David. I'll be looking forward to it."

"You really can cook, huh?" I asked as I yawned once again.

"Time will tell, won't it? I'll see you tomorrow," she replied.

"Okay, I'll call you from the airport after I land."

"Sounds good, fly safe, David and please be careful," she asked.

"I will, sleep tight, kiddo, and I'll see you tomorrow," I explained as I hung up the phone.

Yawning for a third time I sat back in my seat and watched as the runway lights turned on. It was getting dark and I needed some rest. Sitting back in my seat I let my mind take me back to Ireland and happier times when I was with Kate.

"Oh Katie, I miss you so very much," I whispered out into the darkness of the night.

* * * * * * *

It was one o'clock in the afternoon by the time I got to Kathy's home in Virginia. The clouds in the sky were turning dark gray and were moving in from the east. A severe thunderstorm was heading in this direction, which was fine with me. I loved thunderstorms and the more severe they were, the better I like them.

We were sitting in the kitchen of Kathy's home. I was drinking a Pepsi, and Kathy was sitting across the table from me sipping on a glass of vodka with orange juice and slicing some fresh mushrooms for our prime rib dinner tonight.

"I know you don't want to talk about what happened, but I just wanted to tell you that I am so very sorry. I feel guilty that I wasn't closer. Maybe if I had been I could have done something to have stopped them. I was over by the grills talking to some of the people from town when it all happened," Kathy explained as she took another sip from her drink.

"So, what's been happening in the world of espionage while I've been gone?" I asked trying to change the subject.

"Right now the big priority with us is what happened in Ireland with you and Kate. Neil said that he's stonewalled on trying to figure out how it could have all happened. He thinks it has something to do with what you did in Iran. Everyone is working on it, that's for sure. I'm working on the Russia angle with the DIA boys. We'll find out who's behind it, David, we'll get 'em," Kathy explained with a positive look on her face.

"I think I'm going to go and lay down for awhile," I commented as I looked at my bottle of soda.

"Good idea, see, your starting to relax a bit and that's a good thing. It's going to start raining soon. The weather report says that it's going to be a real bad storm," Kathy explained as she glanced across the kitchen and looked out through the window.

"Good, rain makes nice sleeping weather," I said as I got up and headed toward the bedroom.

"I'll wake you up around six, supper will be ready by then," Kathy shouted out enthusiastically.

Walking into the guest room, I closed the door behind me and laid down on the queen size bed. Closing my eyes I knew I wasn't going to be able to sleep but at least I could relax my body and let it get some rest.

* * * * * * *

It was now a little after seven in the evening. The thunderstorm was in full bloom outside. The dark thunderclouds completely engulfed the entire area of Virginia. The rain was pounding on the roof above our heads. The bolts of lightning were lighting up the interior of the house. Each loud thunderbolt the storm threw down at us had its own unique booming sound.

Kathy had set the dining room table with a candelabra which held six candles each. All of which were lit. The lights had been dimmed and the yellowish-blue flames of each candle danced its reflection on the sides of the leaded crystal glassware garnishing the table.

She served prime rib, baked potatoes, corn on the cob, sour cream with chives, hard crust French bread, and a tray of sautéed mushrooms, onions, and green peppers. Sitting in the hand-blown leaded crystal ice bucket, was a very old bottle of vintage aged Chianti red wine dating back to 1871. Kathy had set the mood perfectly with the classical music composition of Bach's Fifth Conchairto in c-minor playing softly in the background.

Sitting next to Kathy at the table I looked over at her with a half smile on my face.

"With the storm outside and all of the lightning, I almost feel like we're in one of those old Bela Lugosi horror movies," Kathy commented with one of those scared little girl looks on her face.

"Its perfect," I replied with a smile.

"Just give it a few days, David. I just know you'll start feeling better again real soon. I have faith in you," Kathy explained with a look of confidence.

"Yeah, I'm starting to feel a bit more relaxed already. I asked God for something and he's giving it to me," I explained as I raised my glass of Pepsi and took a sip out of it.

"After everything that's happened to you in Vietnam, the POW camp in Cambodia, and now this with the death of your wife and children, you still believe in God? My gosh, David, he killed your wife and children for crying out loud," Kathy said as she began to eat.

"All my life I've had a feeling, deep inside me, that I was sent here, in this life time for a purpose, but I never understood what it was. I'm constantly battling the dark side that's always trying to consume me. After Kate and my unborn children were murdered, the dark side almost won. I was so overwhelmed with hate that it actually had me for awhile, but not now," I explained as I poked at my prime rib with my fork.

"Really? Then what happened, you saw God smiling down on you? You're the Sandman, David. You kill people for a living, and the last I heard, that's against your God's commandments isn't it?" Kathy asked calmly as she continued to eat.

"Kate saw her guardian angel, and then she saw Jesus. He actually came to take Kate and my boys home with him to heaven."

"David..." Kathy began to say until I raised my hand to cut her short.

"Just hear me out Kathy, because I really need you to understand what it is I'm trying to tell you."

"Okay, I'm listening. I don't agree with you, but I'm listening," Kathy said as she set down her fork and gave me her full attention.

"I know that God is real, but when I lost my family, I became so bitter that I had surrendered to the darkness that had consumed me from the inside of my soul. I cried out to God and begged him to give me revenge, and to grant me the power of death. And you know what? It was at that moment that I saw and felt his presence. I've never told anyone about this Kathy, but I saw an angel, I really did. She stood by Kate's wishing pond and floated through the air and came right up to me while I sat next to Kate's grave," I explained in awe.

"Oh really, and what did the angle say?" Kathy asked sarcastically.

"She explained that God had not forsaken me, and that it was Kate's time to go to heaven. Her name was written in the book of life. Then the angel told me the greatest lie Satan has ever told is to convince people that he doesn't exist. The Arc Angel Michael, God's warrior angel, battled Satan in heaven and cast him down here to earth. Then the angel reminded me of the time that I had prayed in Vietnam. I was in a chapel and I asked God to give me a sign so I would know that I was doing the right thing. I had killed people and at that time I was battling with the evil part of me. (Note: Read my first book, A Sniper's Sin.)

God gave me the sign that I had asked for. When he did, I told God I would be his warrior angel here on earth. I had forgotten all about that prayer until last week when God sent one of his angels to remind me and comfort me. I'm here to kill evil people, Kathy, she told me that."

"An angle told you that you were sent here by God to kill evil people?" Kathy asked with a more serious look in her eyes.

"Uh, huh," I answered as I took another sip of my Pepsi.

"Well, I'd say that you've been doing one hell of a good job so far," Kathy responded totally absorbed now, in my story.

"It gets better, Kathy. When the angel told me that, she slowly waved her hand out across the meadow towards the wishing pond. When she did I looked, and there standing next to the wishing pond was a large pale green horse."

"What?" Kathy said as she rubbed the goose bumps on her arms and looked around the darkly lit room.

"I saw it Kathy, I really did. It wasn't a real, live, flesh and blood animal. It was in spirit form. It wined out to me and then pawed its right hoof down toward the ground. It had an all black leather saddle and harness with big silver conchoes attached to the leather.

Then the angel told me, 'God has granted you your prayer. You, David, have been given the power over death. You are the rider of the pale horse.' When she said it, she flew right through me and then disappeared into the darkness of the night.

I got up and walked over to the horse and climbed up onto its saddle. As soon as I did, an ice-cold chill ran through my veins. I've been cold ever since. Feel my hands," I explained as I reached my hand out to Kathy.

Just as she touched my hand a bolt of lightning let out a large boom and lit up the inside of the house with its flash of light. It scared Kathy so bad that she let out a scream.

"Shit!" she shouted out as I began to smile. "David, you bastard, you scared the shit out of me with that story," she said as she began to rub the goose bumps on her arms once again.

"You don't believe me?" I asked with a grin.

"You should tell that story to the girls the next time they have a sleep over at your house," Kathy said in a scared tone of voice.

"I have been given the power to grant you your wish, Kathy," I explained with a straight look on my face.

"Yeah right," she replied still a bit shaken.

Standing up, I walked over, and stood behind my field supervisor. Reaching forward, I began to gently rub her shoulders.

"David, sit down and eat would you? Your food's gonna get cold," Kathy explained as she began to calm down.

"Don't you want me to grant you your wish first? Once I do that, then I'll eat. How's that?" I suggested.

"Okay, grant me my wish," Kathy said playfully.

"Close your eyes," I said softly.

"Okay, my eyes are closed," she replied with a giggle.

Leaning forward I whispered into her right ear. "I know who you are, Kathy," I said softly into her ear as I pressed the prongs of my stungun into the side of her neck and pulled the trigger.

* * * * * * *

While Kathy was stunned I had taken off all her clothes and then set her back down in her hard backed wooden chair. I then duck-taped her wrists to the arms of the chair, and her ankles to each of the front legs of the chair.

She was now coming out of the stun. Cutting a piece of the tender prime rib, I placed it in my mouth, and began to chew. The thunderstorm outside had intensified; it was getting bad outside, but not as bad as it was about to get in here.

"What are you, crazy? Untie me right fucking now!" Kathy demanded.

Placing another piece of steak into my mouth, I turned to look at Kathy and began to chew once again.

"Listen to me, David you're emotionally over the edge. I'm you friend, David, try to focus and untie me," she said once again in a calmer voice.

"You kept telling me that you wanted to see the Sandman. You should be careful what you wish for, because now that's exactly who you're going to see," I said calmly as I set my fork down next to my plate and turned my chair sideways to face her.

"Someone has lied to you, David. Please let me go before this gets out of hand," she asked as a bolt of lightning struck the ground somewhere nearby and lit the inside of the dimly lit home, once again.

"You betrayed me, it was you, Kathy," I explained with a calm voice as I looked into her big blue eyes.

"David, I love you, you're my friend, my mentor. I would never do anything to hurt you, I swear to God I wouldn't," she said with a worried look on her face.

"Let me tell you what I know for a fact. When the CIA recruited me in 1971 it was a mans voice I talked to on the telephone at my moms home in Clarkston, Michigan. I had fifteen minutes to get to the Pine Knob Ski Lodge to meet with that person. But when I got there it was you who approached me. When I asked about the person I had talked to on the telephone, you assured me that you were alone and there was no one else with you.

I agreed to join the Agency after you told me it's only a matter of time before the KGB sends someone to Michigan to kill me. You also told me that you threatened to quit the Agency if they didn't let you be the one to recruit me. It was that important to you to meet me. To meet the legendary Black Operation's Team One Sniper, the Sandman. You didn't care about recruiting Danny or Butch. Your whole focus was on me," I explained calmly as I took a sip of my Pepsi.

"David, listen to me," she began to say.

694

"Shhh," I replied in a soft voice as I placed the first finger of my left hand against my lips. "Let me finish. I come to your home and find all of this," I explained as I waved my hand around the room, "I make the comment that the Agency is taking real good care of you. But you tell me that the Agency hasn't paid for any of this. You said your family is rich. Okay, I'll buy that. After all, I have a lot of rich friends who live in beautiful homes just like this one.

God, I was so stupid. I was looking at everything. It was all right under my nose, right in front of my face, out in the open, and I didn't see it because I trusted you. The most obvious is the least obvious, always expect the unexpected and never, ever, forget these rules. Yet with you, I did."

"David...." She began to say.

"If you interrupt me again, I'll cut out your tongue," I said coldly as I looked deep into her eyes. I could see little beads of sweat as they began to form on her forehead and cheeks. She was getting scared.

"I even saw the small satellite dish you have hidden on your roof. You have three computers connected to three separate telephone lines. If Neil or Carla tried to down load your computer all they would be able to access is the computer that Brandi installed for the Agency. Neil called Brandi she said she only installed one computer and one telephone on a secure line in your home. Your short wave radio was set to frequency 4287. When I asked who's frequency that was, you told me it was dead air and that you were just scanning the airwaves to see how far out you could reach with your set. You said it was just a hobby of yours, that you liked to talk to people you didn't know from far away countries.

I never thought anymore of it until Sasha Malenkov took me into her father Pavel's secret communications room to use the telephone. He had the same radio frequency 4287 on his short wave set, and so did Klaus Gruber at his home in Germany. When I tried to remember where it was I had seen that frequency before, Sasha and Ollie both distracted me, and then I forgot about it. Look at these paintings here in your home. They're worth millions. And this," I said as I picked up my glass of Pepsi. "It's leaded glass crystal, your home is full of it. There's only one country in the world that makes leaded glass crystal and that is Russia.

A few months ago I was in your den while you were upstairs taking a shower. You had a box attached to the receiver of your telephone. It wasn't Walter Shaw's black scrambler box, I saw that. This was something entirely different. When I used your telephone to call Neil and gave them my voice recognition code the mainframe computer analyzer scrambled the line and cut me off. Neil thought that it was a power surge of some kind, a computer glitch, but it wasn't was it, Kathy. That box on your telephone receiver changes a woman's voice into a man's. If you flick the switch on the side of the box it changes a man's voice to a woman's. That's why the computer scrambled my call. It was a different voice coming through on the other end of the line, not mine.

You love to drink vodka; you said you grew up drinking it as a child at home. That's normal for a Russian family isn't it, Kathy?" I asked.

She was starting to sweat real bad now; fear was starting to set in on her now. "You love to kill people. It turns you on sexually just like it did to Takeo Kutaragi," I explained.

"When Carla fired Carol you went to her and convinced her that it was all my fault. Then, you bought her a brand new condominium in exchange for the top-secret computer satellite codes Neil uses in the War Room.

You were always trying to get Neil to tell you where I was. You knew that you couldn't let the KGB kill me at my home or here at your home. If I was to kill one of them, before they were able to kill me, the news media would go crazy. 'KGB agents kill decorated Vietnam veteran at his home in Michigan!' Congress would demand full retaliation. It would turn into an international incident, and you couldn't let that happen could you?

Even Carla never trusted you. She knew there was something not quite right about you, but she just couldn't figure it out. You almost got away with it but you made three very big mistakes.

On May 13th you called the Kremlin and personally talked to General Boris Kalashnikov. You called from Ireland and ran the call through the Walter Shaw's call forwarding system at your home. When the call went through to Boris it was scrambled on your end so Neil couldn't hear what was being said. You used your secure satellite phone to make the call. That was your first mistake. That's how Boris knew I would be in the meadow on May 15th.

When the hit went bad and my wife sacrificed her life to save me, you made a second call to Boris to tell him that his men missed me and that they had both been killed. Once again you used your secure satellite phone. That was your second mistake.

But your biggest mistake was that you under estimated Neil. Because of the first call on the 13th of May, Neil refused to come to my wedding. Instead he stayed loyal to a promise he had made to me. Neil sat in the War Room and watched that computer system like a hawk watches its prey. As soon as you made that second call on the 15th, when the hit went bad, Neil used one of the Agency's Keyhole-13 top secret satellites to lock onto the call. And when he did, it identified your secure satellite phone as being the caller. When that happened he called your home number and locked on to it. That's when all hell broke loose and he found out that you had been using his system to cover your tracks all along," I explained calmly as I reached over and picked up the vintage bottle of Russian wine.

Using the cork screw I popped out the cork, tossed it, and the cork screw onto the table, and took a drink of the wine straight out of the bottle.

"Russian made in 1871. Let me tell you what else I know. My bitter enemy, General Boris Kalashnikov of the Soviet Republics KGB, has a wife named Nadia. He also has three children, Katrina is the oldest daughter, Eva is the second daughter, and Ivan is his youngest child and only son," I explained as I reached down and picked up my black leather doctors bag. I had gone to my bedroom to get it after I had stunned Kathy and knocked her out.

Setting the bag on top of the dining room table I opened it up and pulled out a pint size glass bottle and a brand new syringe.

"Katrina, it's a pretty name. In America it's pronounced Kathy. Radio frequency 4287 belongs to Boris Kalashnikov in Russia," I explained as I unscrewed the lid of my glass jar. "You're the daughter of Boris Kalishnikov. Because of you, Katrina, my wife and children are dead," I explained as I dipped the needle into the clear liquid and filled the syringe.

"Revenge is what I cried out and asked God for, and that's exactly what he's giving me. Revenge, its best eaten cold, and I'm as cold as it gets right now. This is Sulfuric Acid. It eats through steel. If it touches human flesh it burns its way right through it. It turns flesh, muscle, bone, and even human teeth into a liquid state. Take a real good look, Katrina, your wish has come true, its been granted. Look into my eyes," I said in a soft whisper of a voice as the storm raged on outside. "The Sandman is here and he's going to make you scream for hours," I explained looking into her eye.

"You thought if they killed me in Ireland one of the Irish Revolutionary Army or Protestant Paramilitary groups would be blamed for it," I said as I slowly lowered Kathy's chair backwards and down to the floor. "Nobody would have cared," I explained as I tried to control my anger.

Kathy was strapped to the wooden chair and was now laying on her back with her feet in the air.

"David, please don't do this! Wait, let me talk please!" she screamed. "I can help you kill my father. David, please don't do this. They threatened to kill me if I didn't help them," she cried out as she begged for her life.

"The bottom of your feet are filled with hundreds of nerve ending. You also have one of your smaller charkas in each foot."

Grabbing Kathy by the foot she screamed out once again.

"I'm pregnant! Please, David, I'm pregnant with your baby." Her whole body was trembling with fear as she continued to beg me not to hurt her.

"My baby?" I asked with a surprised look on my face.

"Yes, I didn't want to tell you because you were getting married to Kate. Please, David, I love you. I'm going to have your baby," she pleaded.

"That's to bad," I said coldly as I shoved the thin razor sharp needle into the ball of her right foot.

I injected both of her feet in several different spots with the powerful acid. In the ball above the heal and between the toes. Her screams were deafening. Her feet were popping and hissing as the acid turned her flesh and muscles into a bloody liquid state. Sitting back down in my seat, I ate my meal while Kathy screamed in tormented agony and the storm outside raged on. To me, it was music to my ears. Looking over at her, she was screaming at the top of her lungs as she twisted her body in a wild frantic attempt to break free from her restraints.

Filling the syringe once again, I grabbed Kathy by her hand and smiled. Inserting the needle into the palms of her hands and then under each of her fingernails, I injected her once again with the powerful acid. All of my anger, rage, and hatred had come to the surface. The effect was immediate as her flesh began to boil away and drip from her body and down to the carpet beneath her.

Reaching into my black leather bag I pulled out a syringe full of Morphine and injected it into her hip. She was going into shock, which is what I didn't want to happen. That would kill her to quickly, so the Morphine should help to slow down her death. What I was doing to her was nothing short of medieval, but that was the mood I was in and it felt good.

Sitting back down in my chair I sat and watched as Kathy's hands and feet disenigrated right before my very eyes. It took about two minutes from the time I had injected Kathy the second time, when the Sulfuric Acid finally reached the femoral arteries in her feet. When it did, the large arteries hemorrhaged and began to squirt blood out from around her ankles. With every beat of her heart, a massive amount of blood would shoot out of the large open vein spraying in all directions of the room. Seeing this, I knew right away that Kathy would bleed to death within a matter of minutes.

"Damn, I should have injected you in the spine instead," I said sadly knowing that she was about to die from the massive loss of blood. "Oh well," I said out loud as I pulled my knife out of my bag and walked back over to Kathy.

Pulling her chair back up to its upright position, I placed the razor sharp knife under Kathy's chin and cut her throat. Finishing what I had come here to do, I picked up the telephone and called for a cleaner.

Leaving Kathy's home, I walked out into the thunderstorm carrying my suitcase in my left hand and my black leather doctor's bag in my right.

The rain beat down hard on my body. It almost felt therapeutic in an odd sort of way. It was almost as if God was trying to cleanse my soul.

Looking up into the darkness of the night I let the rain dance on my face. As it did, I knew that the rain was a lot like me. We were both dancing in the face of death.

* * * * * * *

Leaving Kathy's home I flew straight to the Pentagon where my team was waiting for me. I walked into the Situation Room and I found everyone waiting for me. After I killed Kathy and returned to my plane, I called Neil to let him know I was on my way back to his location. I also asked him to assemble our team and explain to them what he had discovered in regard to Carol and Special Agent Kathy Eckland.

Sitting down at the conference table Neil was the first to speak. "Everyone has been briefed on what took place and the role that both Kathy Eckland and Carol Vance played in it. All of our computer codes and satellite codes are being changed as I speak. We have no idea the extent of damage these agents have caused to our National Security," Neil explained as he rubbed his left hand over his face with a sigh.

Neil had been working around the clock, non-stop on this project and it was beginning to show by the look on his face.

"Is it that bad, Neil?" Tom Burke asked.

"I have learned a lot of things from David. As you all know, he's taken me under his wing and has been teaching me things whenever time allowed. The one thing David has taught me that applies here is to never assume everything is alright. With that in mind, we have notified the President and a clean sweep of our countries security system is underway with our Agency, the Pentagon, NSA, DIA, and DOD. All security codes are being changed across the board, and from this point forward all of our top secret codes will be scrambled and changed every fourteen days," Neil explained as he looked over at Carla.

"Everything else is ready. We've just been waiting for you to get back to make the next move," Carla explained with an angry look on her face.

"This is going to have to flow smoothly, bam, bam, bam. We'll start in Canada and make our sweep from there. Once we get to Russia, things could go bad if Boris detects foul play," I explained as I looked at Cookie, Joe, and Tom.

"Don't worry about Boris, thanks to the satellite chip Carla had surgically implanted in his shoulder, we know exactly where he's at every second of the day," Tom explained with a broad smile on his face.

"Yes, and for the next 72-hours he'll be at Causeway Bay, in Hong Kong," Cookie added with a grin as he looked across the table at Carla and winked.

"Perfect, put on some James Brown then, because its time to rock and roll," I said in a cold voice as we all got up and left the Situation Room.

Everyone knew where they needed to be and what their role would be. I had the best assassination team at my side, with state of the art technology at our fingertips. It was now time for us to make our sweep.

* * * * * * *

This was going to go in three stages. The first stage took us to Canada where we were going after Boris' second born child, Eva Kalashnikov.

Eva had gone there to study at the National Ballet School of Canada. It had been her childhood dream to be the first young Russian to dance for Canada's national company. At the age of twenty-four she was already an accomplished ballerina and had studied dance theater in her own home town of Moscow.

Eva was young, slender, and had shoulder length, jet-black hair. To make it simple, she was beautiful. Parked out front of the National Ballet School we sat in our all black limousine and watched as the students slowly came out of the building to head home for the day. Looking at my Tag Hauer watch, it was three o'clock in the afternoon.

"There she is," Butch said as he sat watching from behind the steering wheel of the car.

"I'll get her," Carla explained as Butch got out and opened the back door for her.

Getting out of the car, Carla walked up to Eva and showed the young Russian beauty her State Department credentials, with a sad look on her face.

My heart raced with excitement as I sat and watched from behind the dark tinted windows as Carla explained to Eva that her mother had been killed in a car accident in Moscow. Carla then explained that we had been sent by her father, and would take her to the airport where he had a private diplomatic jet waiting to fly her back to her motherland.

Eva burst into tears as she held her hands over her face and cried. We could have told her a number of different things that would have gotten her into the car, but that wasn't the way we had been trained to handle a situation like this.

We need to pull Eva off her square so she wouldn't have time to think and possibly figure out that something was wrong. To accomplish this you want to trigger the persons deepest emotion, and there's no better way to do that than to tell the person that their mother has passed away.

Had Eva been thinking, she would have realized that had a tragedy really taken place, it would have been someone from the Russian embassy or Canada's diplomatic services who would have come to get her, not an American. But Carla insisted on being in on this hit, and her State Department credentials, even though they were fake, were the perfect hook.

Helping Eva into the limousine, Carla climbed in behind her. Closing the door Butch got back into the car, started it up, and began to drive away.

Handing Eva some Kleenex tissue, she blew her nose and continued to cry as Carla reached around Eva's shoulder to comfort her.

Stopping for a red light, Butch lowered the tinted glass window behind him, which separates the driver from the passengers in the back. Turning to look back at us, Butch raised the car phone in his right hand.

"Eva I have good news, your mother isn't dead," Butch explained with a smile.

"What, my mother is alive? Please let me speak with her," she said with excitement in her voice as she moved forward to take the telephone from Butch's hand.

As Eva moved forward I grabbed her from behind. Placing my left hand on her forehead I pulled her back toward me, reached around with my right hand and placed my knife against her throat.

"Your mothers not dead, but you are," Butch said in a cold, deadly tone of voice as my razor sharp blade sliced its way through the soft tender flesh of Eva's throat, cutting her esophagus in half. Watching Butch turn back around, the divider window behind his head raised back up as our car began to move forward once again.

As we expected, Eva panicked and swung her arms and kicked her feet out wildly in all directions. Pulling her soft, tender back, up against my chest, I kept my hand firmly on her forehead and wrapped my right arm, with the knife still held in my hand, around her slender waist. Feeling her body jerk wildly against mine, I placed my mouth next to her right ear.

"Your father killed my wife and two sons. Now I've killed you," I explained as the gurgling sound in her throat began to lessen and her body slowly relaxed in my arms.

I had been careful not to cut through the carotid arteries that ran along the side of Eva's neck. Had I cut through one of those arteries, there would have been blood squirting out of her neck and all over us. Instead I kept the blade of the knife straight and cut through her esophagus, which caused her to suffocate and drown in her own blood. It was a fairly clean kill. There was blood all over the front of her shirt, but all in all it wasn't too awfully bad.

"Give her to me, I'll do the rest," Carla explained as she reached over and grabbed Eva's dead body by the arm.

Driving to the airport, a CIA cleaning crew was waiting for us in a white Ford van parked next to our plane. They would clean the limousine and dispose of Eva's body. Climbing on board I carried only one suitcase along with me as Ben pulled the side door of our Learjet closed and smiled.

* * * * * * *

Sitting in our silver stretch limousine, Cookie, Joe and I watched patiently as Ivan Kalashnikov tried to learn how to surf. That's right, you heard me correctly, surf. Ivan had come to the United States to spend a few weeks with a young female friend of his, Annika Hediger.

Annika was German born, but living in California. She wanted to be an actress and was attending the School of Arts and Theater in Los Angeles. She was twenty-two years old, had long, sandy, blonde hair and blue eyes. She also had a hard body look that could easily make her a model. She was a looker, there's no doubt about that.

We had our limo parked off the main road on the sand in Huntington Beach. It was almost twelve noon. Joe and Cookie were both eating their lunch, which consisted of two Big Mac hamburgers, large fries, an apple pie desert, and a Coke.

Placing a couple of drops of Methadrine under my tongue, I sat and watched as Annika was trying to teach Ivan something that had to do with the art of surfing.

"What in the world is she trying to teach him?" I asked as Ivan fell off of his surfboard and back into the blue Pacific Ocean.

"She's trying to teach him how to switchfoot," Cookie explained as he took a bite out of his burger and began to chew.

"Switchfoot?" I questioned with a dumb look on my face.

"Yeah, switchfoot. What, you don't know how to switchfoot?" Cookie asked as he turned his head to look at me.

Raising my right hand I extended my first finger, placed it on my wire rim, dark tinted, gold Ray Ban Aviator sunglasses and slowly pulled them down to the end of my nose. All that it took was one look.

"Oh yeah, that's right, I forgot, your from Michigan," Cookie explained without changing the expression on his face.

"And?" I asked.

"Switchfoot is a surfing move where you change the direction your feet are facing while your riding the board. If your left foot is forward, you switch your feet so that your right foot is forward. First, you need to catch the right wave. When you find the wave you're looking for, you paddle hard, put your hands on the board, and stand up with your knees bent a little. You keep your legs shoulder width apart with most of your weight on your back foot. Once your steady, jump, and switch feet. Its an art for any surfer who's long boarding," Cookie explained calmly.

"And you know how to surf and do a switchfoot?" I asked.

"Yo dude, like, I had a life before Nam," Cookie said jokingly.

"That's a scary thought," I countered with a grin as I looked back out through the car window and watched as Ivan deep sixed himself once again.

"He'll never get it right. His posture is all wrong, plus he's a Russian," Cookie explained as he took a sip of his drink.

"Meaning what?" I asked totally confused by his statement.

"Russian's don't surf," Cookie explained as both he and Joe began to laugh out loud.

"There's way to many people around here, fella's. We're gonna have to wait for them to leave and follow 'em," I explained as I looked at all the people walking all around us.

"No problem, we go to Plan B right, partner?" Joe asked as he looked over at Cookie and smiled.

"That's right," Cookie replied.

"Why do I feel all alone right now?" I asked in a confused voice.

Laughing for a few seconds Joe then explained. "Ivan is staying with Annika at her place. Annika owns a one story house on Lemoyne Street in the city's Echo Park neighborhood," Joe explained as he reached over and started the car.

"Tonight at seven o'clock, Annika is taking Ivan to the Henry Fonda Theater in Los Angeles. From there they're going to the Viper Room to party, and then they're going to the Largo Music Club in West Hollywood to listen to some mellow music," Cookie explained with a confident look.

"How did you find all this out in such a short period of time?" I asked with an impressed look on my face.

"We do the intelligence work and you do the 'wet work', remember?" Joe asked as he pulled our car back out onto the road and drove us away.

"Yeah, intel work is hard shit to do," Cookie added as he looked back over at Joe and they both began to laugh.

"Okay," was all I said as I picked up my bottle of Pepsi and took a sip.

"Right now we'll go and check out Annika's house. Its over where Sunset Boulevard curves into the Silver Lake neighborhood of Los Angeles, I think," Cookie explained as he looked at a map of L.A..

"I'm impressed, you guys are something else. This is great intelligence work," I explained, proud at how hard my two teammates had worked to gather all of this intelligence information in such a short period of time.

"Today is Ivan's 23rd birthday," Joe explained as he looked into the rearview mirror at me. "Wanna know how we got all of this highly classified Russian intel on a KGB's General's kid?" Joe asked with a serious look on his face.

"Yeah, I really would," I answered.

"I called his mom and told her I was a friend of his. I speak Russian, remember? The most obvious was the least obvious, youngster. His mother told me everything," Cookie said with a broad smile as he moved his eyebrows up and down like Groucho Marx.

* * * * * * *

Contrary to Cookie's way of thinking, and map reading, Lemoyne Street was not in the Silver Lake neighborhood of Los Angeles. Even though I had tried to point out that the Silver Lake neighborhood and the city's Echo Park neighborhood sounded like two completely different neighborhoods to me, Cookie and Joe weren't buying it.

According to my dear friend and mentor, Cookie, "This is California, youngster, nothing here is how it seems to be."

They were the intelligence part, and I was the lowly 'wet work' guy. "Okay," I thought to myself as I sat back and watched my two dear friends play Ricky Ricardo and Lucy.

After driving around lost in L.A. for almost a full hour, I asked them if they wanted me to show them the art of map reading.

Frustrated, Cookie handed me the road map. "Okay, smart guy, show me your special top secret art of map reading," he explained.

"Do me a favor, Joe, pull into that Shell gas station up ahead would you? I gotta pee," I explained as I took a careful look at the road map. Pulling into the gas station, Joe parked the car and turned off the engine.

Opening the backdoor of the limousine I called the gas station attendant over to our car.

"Excuse me, but could you tell us how to get to Lemoyne Street in Echo Park?" I asked politely with a smile.

"Lemoyne? Sure no problem. You go down this way for three blocks and turn left at the light. Then go down four blocks and turn right next to

Matt's Party Store. You'll find Lemoyne Street about a half mile down on the left," the young attendant explained.

"Thanks, pal. I appreciate it," I said as I looked over at both Joe and Cookie and smiled. "See I found it for you," I said as I patted Cookie on the shoulder and handed him back the map. "That's how they trained me to find a road or street if I'm ever in an unfamiliar area, while I studied at the school of common sense," I explained jokingly as I got out of the car to go and use the restroom.

Much to our dismay, when we found Lemoyne Street and Annika's house, we also found six other people there. They appeared to be getting the place ready for a surprise birthday party, obviously for Ivan.

"We don't have time for this," Cookie explained in a low voice as we watched from a distance.

"Let's get out of here. This limo stands out like a sore thumb in this neighborhood. Let's go find the Henry Fonda Theater, Viper Room, and Largo Music Club, and check 'em out," I explained in a frustrated voice.

Cookie was right, we didn't have time to sit around and wait like this. To make my plan work, we needed to get to Russia before Boris got back from Hong Kong and we were running out of time.

* * * * * * *

Well, we were right. Annika and her friends had a surprise birthday party for Ivan at Annika's house. After the small birthday dinner party, they all tagged along and went with Annika and Ivan to the Henry Fonda Theater and then to the Viper Room.

We went inside to check on them at the Viper Room. The music was loud and the booze was flowing. The problem was it was also packed with people. I could have killed Ivan easily and got away with it, but to do it in such a manner wouldn't fit into my master plan for his father, Boris. So, once again we waited as I picked up our secure satellite phone and called Neil to let him know we were going to be late for the third stage of our sweep.

It was 11:00 p.m. when Annika and Ivan left the Viper Room. When they did the rest of their friends stayed behind and continued to party at L.A.'s hot spot.

"Finally," Joe commented when we pulled out of the parking lot and followed Annika as she drove Ivan to the Largo Music club.

Watching Annika and Ivan walk into Largo's, Joe, Cookie, and I began to go over the different scenarios of how to make this work to our advantage. I know, your reading this and thinking just go in and tell him that his mom or dad was killed like we did with his sister, Eva, right? Well, that won't work here, because Annika is with him. If Ivan should happen to leave with us and not return, she might call Ivan's mother to see if he's aright. She might call her own mother and father, who could possibly be good personal friends with Nadia and Boris Kalashnikov, and they might call Russia and talk to Nadia. As my Seal team instructors always told me, 'Never assume that everything is going to be alright. Assume the worst possible scenario is going to take place, and work it from there.'

"Fuck, its almost a quarter after twelve. Go in and bring 'em both out to the car will you?" I asked as I pulled my silenced .22 magnum pistol out of my black doctor's bag and checked to make sure it was loaded.

"What about the girl?" Joe asked with a curious look.

"We're out of time, brother. She's collateral damage as far as I'm concerned," I explained calmly.

"That's cool with me, Sandman. But she is innocent, she's not part of this," Joe explained to make sure I was thinking correctly.

"So were my wife and kids," I said coldly as I looked up at Joe and then over to Cookie.

"Hoo yah, I'll go and get them," Cookie explained with a sinister look in his eyes as he got out of the car.

"Hoo yah, let's rock and roll," Joe said as he pulled his silenced pistol out of its shoulder holster and cocked the hammer.

Ivan was the son of a KGB General. Even though he had just turned twenty-three years old today, I had to assume that his father had been training him to follow in his footsteps one day. With that in mind, I had to also assume that Ivan was a very dangerous young man.

Walking up to their table, Cookie introduced himself as a KGB agent. Talking in a low Russian voice he then slid his KGB credentials across the small round table for Ivan to see.

On the stage, a young dark haired girl played her guitar and sang in a low sultry murmur of a voice. Handing Cookie back his credentials, Cookie explained to Ivan that his father, Boris, had a surprise for him for his birthday and that he had sent a private limousine to take both him and Annika to a private dinner club in Beverly Hills.

As we had assumed, even though this special birthday gift had him smiling and excited, Ivan still asked Cookie a few questions about Russia, the KGB, and then topped it off with, "If my father called you today, did he call you from our home?"

"Your father is in Hong Kong," Cookie countered.

"Where in Hong Kong?" Ivan asked politely.

"Causeway Bay, he is staying on Tung Lo Wan Road," Cookie answered. "You can come to your party or stay here. It matters not to me," Cookie said in an angry tone of voice as he stood up and left the Largo Club.

This was in true character for a Russian KGB officer. They're arrogant and short tempered, and do not tolerate being questioned by anyone, especially someone as young as Ivan, general's son or not.

Cookie did his job well, young Ivan and his girlfriend Annika took the bait and followed him out of the club and to where we were waiting for him in our car. Opening the door to the limousine Annika climbed in smiling, while Ivan walked to the rear of the car to look at the license plate. Seeing the Russian diplomatic license plate, Ivan smiled and apologized to Cookie.

"Being the son of a great general, I must be careful. You understand, yes?" Ivan explained with a smile as he climbed into the car and sat across the seat from me.

Climbing into the car behind Ivan, Cookie closed the door as Joe pulled out of the parking lot and onto the main street.

"And you are who?" Ivan asked as he looked over at me with a broad smile on his face.

Reaching behind me I pulled my gun out from between my lower back and the seat. Pointing it at Ivan's chest, I answered him, "Death," I explained as I fired two shots into his heart as Annika began to scream.

Much to my surprise, before I could shoot Annika, Cookie had reached over, grabbed her by the head, and in one fast, cat like move, he snapped her neck like a dry twig. Putting my gun back into my leather bag, I pulled out my knife and looked over at Cookie.

"It never hurts to keep in practice, right?" he asked with a grin as he reached his hand out toward me for the knife.

Handing Cookie the razor sharp knife, I picked up the secure phone and called Neil.

"Send a cleaning crew to the airport, we have a car that needs to be cleaned. Tell our team we're on our way," I explained as I hung up the telephone and looked through the side window and out into the night.

* * * * * * *

Our flight to Moscow seemed to take forever. Rather than try and sneak into Russia, Carla called the United States Special Operation Command, based at McDill Air Force Base in Tampa, Florida and told them to prepare our diplomatic jet for a special covert operation.

Flying to McDill Air Force Base, Joe, Cookie, and I met Tom, Carla, Butch, and Danny and boarded the diplomatic jet from South Africa. Yes, you heard me, South Africa. We were flying to Russia as an African research team going to speak to Russia's Lower House of Parliament. The Russian's thought we were coming to their country to discuss new viral infections spreading throughout Africa, Ebola, Lassa, and the New Bourbeillon virus, which had not yet been named, HIV.

This would work in two ways for us. First, the Africans really were coming to the Duma to speak to the Lower House of Parliament, on Wednesday. Second, it helped us to get Danny into the country without drawing a lot of unwanted KGB attention to us. After all Danny is a very big African American, and you don't see to many black people in Russia. At least not in 1976 you didn't.

We were cutting it close. Our plane would be landing in Russia on Monday. Boris was scheduled to be back home early Tuesday and the South African delegation was also scheduled to arrive Tuesday at noon.

To the reader, there are six phases of any Spec War or Elite Covert Operation like this, which are: permission, insertion, infiltration, actions as objectives, exfiltrations, and post mission. That's the standard for all Seal Team Spec War Missions.

As Black Operations, we try to follow these standards if at all possible. Permission is the hard one when you halo jump into Iran, like I did to avoid being detected. So the permission aspect of it is that we've invited ourselves. See how simple that was? Permission granted.

Landing at Russia's International Airport we were greeted by several of Russia's top viral research scientist. Using our South African credentials and diplomatic immunity identification, we were taken to the National Hotel. Marg had put our South African credentials together for us at the CIA's technical services division and as it always is with Marge, they worked perfectly.

Let me tell you exactly where we are in Russia at this point. The National Hotel sits on a corner diagonally across from a large gate that leads into Moscow's Red Square and the Kremlin. The Duma, which is the Lower House of Parliament in Russia's Kremlin, is nearby across from one of Russia's most elegant shopping streets. The Okhotny subway station is just around the corner and the Kiev Railway train station sits within walking distance nearby. This would give us several avenues to escape by if anything should happen to go wrong.

Bell and Mosier had already called ahead and told our CIA undercover agents in Moscow we were coming. They also explained to them what it was we were going to need to make this mission successful. With this knowledge, our Moscow agents would have everything ready for us.

During our flight from Florida to Russia we continued to go over every detail of our operation. Step by step, inch-by-inch, we covered everything. Why? Because we knew that once we stepped off our plane we would no longer be able to say a word to each other about our attack plan.

The one thing we knew for certain was that the KGB had every hotel room, restaurant, park bench, and home, bugged so that they could listen in and monitor every word being spoken, not only by outside foreign visitors, but also by their own people. Hence the phrase, "Big brother is watching and listening," just like the American government is now doing to us in 2004. Kinda makes you wonder who our real enemies are doesn't it?

Moscow is every bit the way you see it shown on television and in the movies, or better yet, as you would see pictures of it in National Geographic Magazine. It's old, rustic, and beautiful to say the least. The National Hotel was the same way.

We had three Hotel Rooms reserved by the South African delegation, waiting for us upon arrival. All three rooms were right beside each other, each room with two single size beds and their own bathroom.

Carla and I stayed in one room together, Cookie and Danny stayed in the second room, while Tom and Butch stayed in the third. Remember, Tom, Cookie, and Carla all speak perfect Russian. Danny, Butch and I don't, so this pairing has us covered in case someone should happen to say something to us.

Because of our training, it only took us a few seconds to find all of the bugging devices carefully hidden throughout each room. I had actually found one device which had been meticulously hidden underneath the polished hard wooden floor at the base of a tiny wood crack. I had to hand it to them, they were good at the spy game, but so were we.

Your wondering why we don't turn the radio on full blast and run the water in the shower and sink of the bathroom to cover the sound of our voices aren't you? They only do that in bad Hollywood movies. Listen, if I was monitoring a listening devise and someone came into the room and cranked the radio up full blast and then turned the water on in the shower and sink, I would know right away that they did it to disguise the sound of their voices. Its what I call, a tell. They would be telling on themselves and I'd catch it and know right away something was wrong. With that in mind, I would put them on around the clock surveillance, twenty-four hours a day, seven days a week.

I hate Russians, just as much as I hate Turks, but I also am smart enough to respect the Russian Intelligence Services, also known as the KGB, and with that in mind I will assume they are smart enough to catch me if I tried doing it to them. What we don't need right now is to fall under the watchful eyes of the KGB at this point. Why? Because we're getting ready to make our move, that's why.

Looking at my watch it was almost four o'clock p.m. so we all headed down stairs to the hotel restaurant to have our supper and wait for our contact agent to show up. Looking at the menu I then looked up at Carla,

Tom and Cookie, all of whom I might add were watching Danny, Butch, and I smiling.

"I'll order for you guys," Cookie said in a low voice. Yes, the menu was written in Russian and I don't read Russian either.

"Thanks," I answered as I pulled my tiny vial of Methadrine out of my shirt pocket and placed two drops of it under my tongue.

"Forget it, our ride is here," Carla explained calmly as a middle aged, black haired woman approached our table.

That's right, a woman. I told you woman can work the holy shit out of the intelligence network. They also make great spies because in 1976 no one would have ever thought that we American's would use women as spies.

Walking up to our table smiling, she spoke in Russian and acted as if we were long lost friends. Standing up, I went back to my room to pick up my silver metal suitcase with the large orange and black biohazards material emblems on the front, back, and each end. Leaving the hotel room I joined the rest of my team downstairs in the lobby and left the hotel.

Parked out in front of the National Hotel were two black Lincoln Continental Town cars, with diplomatic license plates on them from South Africa.

The woman, who had come into the restaurant to get us, drove the first one and a second, younger woman with dark brown hair drove the other. Climbing into both of the town cars we drove away.

"Do you have everything ready?" Carla asked calmly.

"Yes, ma'am," was all our driver said as her eyes carefully scanned every direction. She never moved her head to look around. A KGB surveillance team would notice that and wonder why she was acting so nervously.

Instead, she used the rear view and side driver's door mirrors to check and make sure we weren't being followed.

She took us to a small business supply warehouse about five miles from the National Hotel. As soon as we pulled into the parking lot and up to the front of the large warehouse garage doors, Carla jumped out of the car and pulled open the door. Driving our cars inside and out of sight, Carla stepped into the warehouse and pulled the door closed behind us. It was quite obvious that Carla was no rookie at this Cloak and Dagger game.

"Everything is in the back of the delivery truck," our driver explained as we all walked over to the dark blue Ford van and opened the side door.

Grabbing what we needed, we left the warehouse in two teams and headed for the Kalashnikov estate.

We found the home of General Boris Kalashnikov in a heavily wooded area of Russia approximately ten miles out of town. The large mansion sat back and away from the main road. It had a long winding driveway surrounded by large beautiful trees and thick green grass. It was a large two-story estate that, I would guess, had been built sometime in the 1920's.

The sun was just beginning to set as we pulled up to the front of the estate and heard two tsk... tsk... sounds. Danny had just signaled they were ready. Carla and I were going to make entry through the front door of the estate. Cookie, Tom, Danny, and Butch had already come in from the back, through the woods, and would make entry through the backdoor and side servant's entrances.

Stepping out of the black Lincoln, our driver opened the trunk and stood watch as I pulled out the small two-wheel hand dolly and stood it upright on the asphalt driveway. I then reached back into the trunk and pulled out the wooden shipping crate with, 'Fragile, Ivory Statue, China,' stenciled on it, and placed it on the dolly.

Wheeling the crate to the front door Carla pressed the doorbell while our driver stood next to the trunk of our car, keeping within easy reach of her .9mm submachine gun. If anyone came up the driveway, she would handle it.

There were five expensive cars parked near the front entrance, which told us that Nadia had company. Ringing the doorbell a second time we stood patiently and waited for Nadia. The entire team knew it was very important to me that I was the one that would kill the General's wife. Everyone else in the house was fair game. Nadia, just as it was with his three children, would be killed by me. Watching as the large hand carved wooden doors opened, I smiled when I saw the very beautiful face of the woman known as Nadia Kalashnikov.

Speaking in Russian, Carla showed Nadia her credentials and introduced herself as a female KGB agent. She then apologized and explained that the package had arrived late and that the General had instructed her to deliver it to his wife before he arrived home from China.

Telling Nadia that the package was a gift for her, you could see Nadia's eyes light up with excitement. Inviting us into her home I followed Nadia, being very careful to keep my body positioned between Nadia and Carla. As I did Carla reached into her purse and pulled out her silenced .9mm H&K pistol, while our driver reached into the car and keyed the transmit button on her hand held radio, twice. This sent a double tsk... tsk... sound back to Danny telling him that we had just entered the Kalashnikov home. Danny and the rest of our team would now enter in through both the back door and servant's entrance and begin their sweep.

Stepping inside, Carla closed the door behind us as Nadia called out in an excited voice to one of her servants, asking them to come and help with the large shipping crate. As Nadia called out to her servant I slowly moved my right hand behind me and pulled out my Taiho combat knife.

I could hear a faint thump and then a second one off in the distance of the house in another room as bodies began to fall to the floor. Team One was moving forward. Nadia called out once again and this time a well dressed man, who looked to be in his early sixties, walked out of the room closest to us and off to our right. He was smoking a large Cuban cigar and smiling.

Stepping up next to Nadia I could hear the classical composition of Beethoven in concert playing softly in the air. The inside of the home was beautifully made with hand-polished wood and large wooden oak beams across the ceiling.

As the older man walked toward us talking to Nadia, Danny and Tom made their way into the hallway from the back. Seeing them, Nadia yelled out to her friend just as Carla raised her pistol and fired two quick shots into the big Russian's chest.

Stepping forward, about a foot, I reached up and grabbed Nadia by the throat with my left hand and at the same time buried the razor sharp stainless steel blade of my knife into her chest sideways between the third and fourth rib. Using the force of both my hands, I slammed her body backwards and up against the wall she was standing next to.

I could see her eyes were wide, which was caused by the combination of fear, pain, and confusion. She had reached up with both of her hands and grabbed my right hand, which still held the knife now buried deep into her chest.

Carla had already ran up to the man she had shot, and shot him two more times in the head to make sure he stayed where he was. She then moved quickly into the room the man had come out of to begin her sweep from our end.

Searching my eyes with hers, Nadia tried to figure out why this was happening to her as she gasped for short quick breaths of air.

"Your husband killed my wife and children. Now I've done the same to him," I whispered as I leaned forward and kissed her gently on the lips. "The kiss of death," I whispered softly as I looked deep into her eyes.

Feeling her heart pulse with every beat through the blade of my knife, I quickly pushed the handle to the right, then to the left, and then to the right again. Causing the blade inside of her to cut her tender Russian heart in half. When I did her body jerked out in pain three times with each thrust of my blade. Her mouth opened slightly as a gurgling sound creaped slowly out through her throat. It was then I felt her body go limp in my hands as it slowly slid down the wall to the floor beneath her.

It was also then that I heard Danny shout out, "Clear." Then Carla yelled out the same. From the time of entry the sweep took four minutes to complete. The Kalashnikov estate was now clear and everyone in it, with the exception of our team, was dead. Along with Nadia, one cook, two female servants, and eight dinner guests lay dead in the Kalashnikov home.

Checking their identifications for intelligence data gathering purposes it brought a great deal of pleasure to our entire team to learn that we had also just killed the mothers and fathers of both Nadia and her husband, Boris.

Using our secure satellite phone, Carla called Neil at the Pentagon's War Room, where Neil, Bell, and Mosier were carefully monitoring Boris Kalashnikov's every move. Hanging up the telephone Carla placed it back into her purse and then looked at all of us.

"Move quickly, gentlemen, Boris' plane left China two hours ago. He's on his way home and we're running out of time," Carla explained as she reached down and grabbed the ankles of Boris Kalashnikov's dead father, and began to drag it down the hallway toward the kitchen.

Picking up Nadia's body I carried it out to the car and tossed it into the trunk. Pulling out my knife I reached into the trunk and finished what it was I had come here to do.

Carrying the rest of the bodies downstairs we tossed them into the wine cellar, one on top of the other. Looking at them I couldn't help but grin. They looked like a bunch of rag dolls piled up like that.

We spent the next hour cleaning up the blood spill the best we could while Danny and Cookie prepared a few little surprises for Boris.

Taking one last look at the message I was personally leaving for Boris, I closed the refrigerator door and looked up at my team quietly standing by watching me.

"You sure you don't want to wait here until Boris gets home?" Cookie asked.

"No, there's no time. The real South African research team will be here in a few hours. We better be in the air before they land," I explained as we headed for the front door and back to our cars.

We didn't go back to the warehouse or to the National Hotel. Instead, we called Joe, who was waiting with the plane, and told him we were on our way. Joe had stayed with the plane to make sure the KGB wouldn't be able to board it and snoop around, possibly planting listening devices.

It took us an hour to get back to the airport. Using our diplomatic credentials we were allowed to pass through the airport terminal and enter the boarding section where our private Learjet was waiting for us. As we were walking out, I felt a fury of anger flair up within me as I watched my bitter enemy, General Boris Kalashnikov and four of his heavily armed KGB body guards, walk into the terminal no more than forty yards away at the off boarding area. Turning, they came our way. Walking past us, Boris looked over at me and then looked away. Within a few seconds he slowed his pace down and turned to look back over at me as I passed through the doorway and disappeared from his sight.

"He saw you, Sandman," Cookie said in a low voice as we walked out of the terminal and toward our plane.

"Uh huh," I replied as we reached the plane and climbed on board.

"Get us out of here, Joe, Boris saw David," Carla said quickly in an anxious voice.

"He saw me, but he couldn't place my face. The last time I saw him my face was bloody, bruised, and swollen. I was pale looking, dirty, and I had my big handlebar mustache. As soon as he gets home he'll remember where he saw me before. Do we have his home telephone number?" I asked as Joe and Cookie taxied our plane out onto the long runway to prepare for take off.

"What are you gonna do call him up?" Butch asked with a surprised look.

My memories took me back to the POW camp in Cambodia and then to the death hooch where I had been tortured by Colonel Ky and Major Dinh. I thought of Sergeant Tom McBride, Jerry, Larry, and all of the other young Americans who had been so brutally tortured and murdered because I refused to cooperate. Then I thought of my wife Kate and our two unborn children. I could still feel her breath on my face and see the look in her eyes when she told me that she couldn't feel her babies anymore, just before she died in my arms.

"Damn, right I'm going to call him. I got something that I want to say to him," I said bitterly as the force of our jet taking off pushed me back in my seat.

We were in the air for almost thirty minutes and well out over international water when Carla dialed the telephone and placed it to her ear. Within a few seconds she said something in Russian, smiled and handed me the telephone. "I called him at his home, he must have just walked in, its him, your old buddy Boris," Carla explained as I placed the receiver to my ear.

"General, how are you?" I asked in English.

"Who is this?" he asked bluntly in broken English.

"You sent two of your men to Ireland to kill me. Instead, they killed my wife and two unborn children," I said coldly as I tried to control my rage.

"Ah, it is you, David, the sniper from Army Intelligence, yes?" he asked arrogantly.

"I was just there at your home. Don't hang up the telephone or it will explode. Don't open your doors or windows, Boris, if you do your home will explode. Your friends, Colonel Ky and Major Dinh, taught me a special little trick. So I have used it to let you know that it was me, Boris, the Sandman, who has taken your family from you."

As I said it I could hear the sound of his breathing change, "Nadia? Nadia?" he yelled out, calling for his wife.

"I took great pleasure in killing her and your three children. I kept their bodies and left the rest for you," I explained. I could hear him moving through his home quickly now. He was turning on light switches and yelling something out in Russian.

Listen very closely, Boris. Stop moving and listen," I told him. I could hear he had stopped moving. He was breathing heavier now into the mouthpiece of his telephone, he was worried.

"Do you hear it, Boris?" I asked in a whisper of a voice.

"What I am suppose to hear. You lie like all Americans," he responded in a weak effort to convince himself that I had never been in his home.

"It's quite, so very quiet. It's the sound of the grave, the sound of death, Boris. Bury your dead and then know this. I'm coming for you, Boris. You'll never know when, you'll never know where. But as sure as I am a child of the God of Abraham, and his chosen Angel of Death, I swear to my God I am going to look you in the eyes as I cut your worthless fucking heart out," I said angrily.

"Otsosi pedik!" he shouted back, which is Russian for blow me.

"Nyet," I said bitterly, which is Russian for no.

"I left something for you in your refrigerator and downstairs in your wine cellar. I'm coming for you next, mother fucker, and when I'm finished with you, I'm going to zamochit baklan," I explained, telling him in Russian that I was going to piss on his grave, as I hung up the telephone and handed it back to Carla.

"I thought you didn't know how to speak Russian?" Carla asked with a surprised look on her face.

"Remember what George Bernard Shaw said, 'the best kept secret is the secret that keeps itself,'" I explained as I sat back in my seat and looked at my teammates and friends.

"Boy we'll never be able to top this hit. We walked right into the general's house and shit in his stew," Tom said proudly.

"It could get a lot worse and a lot more dangerous than this, gentlemen. Oh yeah, a lot worse," Carla explained as she dialed her satellite phone to let Neil, Bell, and Mosier know we were on our way home.

Looking over at Danny he patted his big hand over his heart and then pointed his finger at me and smiled. It was his way of telling me that he loved me. Nodding my head back at him I felt so grateful that God had blessed me with friends as true as these.

* * * * * * *

Because this was an unauthorized hit, there was no debriefing when we returned to the Pentagon. To be honest with you, when we got back to the War Room to see Neil, Bell, and Mosier it was a solemn moment. We shook hands, gave each other a brotherly hug and then went our own separate ways for a long over due rest.

They say that when the great KGB General, Boris Kalashnikov, opened his refrigerator and found the heads of his wife, son, and two daughters staring back at him, he screamed so loud his friends in China heard him. When he found his mother and father dead in his wine cellar, it pushed him into the vortex of the darkness of his soul. For now Boris will live with the guilt and pain of his past sins, just as I do.

I could have stayed at his home and killed him, but that would have been too easy. I wanted the death of his loved ones to consume his soul. He couldn't call anyone for help until he found all of the Semtex Czechoslavakian C-4 plastique explosives we had set throughout his entire home. Semtex I might add, is five times more powerful than our American C-4 plastique explosives. Did he find them all? Maybe, maybe not, time will tell won't it? After all the most obvious is the least obvious place to hide something, right?

Now your wondering if Boris and I will meet again aren't you? The answer to your question is yes, we will. And when we do, it will be the bloodiest and most costly battle of all.

But for now, I'm going back to my home in Dublin to see Kate and my boys. All of a sudden I feel cold, alone, and so very, very tired.

Chapter Thirty-Eight
The Best Kept Secret

Flying back home to Michigan, I spent a week with my grandmother at her home in Pontiac. Her cancer was slowly spreading throughout her body. Even though she was terminally ill, she still had that old country grandmotherly way of touching my heart and making me feel just a little bit better inside.

I then flew to New York to talk to Uncle Paul about the future of organized crime. I also told him about our family counterpart in Naryndzlar, Steven Sarcasian, and made arrangements to ship the medical supplies I had promised him. I gave Paul the telephone numbers and short wave radio frequency codes Steven had given to me. Now Paul would be able to contact Steven and open up a whole new line of business, and my promise to Steven will have been kept.

Then I spent a few days with Andy and Tara to make sure they were all right, and to see if they kept an eye on my house. I tried my best to smile and act as though everything was all right with me so they wouldn't worry. But to be honest with you, I felt empty and cold inside.

* * * * * * *

I had been back home in Dublin for almost three months. Sitting next to my wife's wishing pond, I felt a cool gentle breeze blowing in my face.

I took another piece of cheese-flavored popcorn out of the large bag and tossed it into the wishing pond. The puffed corn only sat on the calm surface of the water for a second. Then, with a quick splash of water, one of the fish came to the surface and gulped it down. I noticed that Kate's fish liked the cheese-flavored popcorn a lot better than the plain old regular popcorn. This made me wonder if fish have taste buds? I was going to soak some worms in Irish whiskey and toss 'em in to the fish to see if they'd get drunk, but then changed my mind when Kate's grandmother asked me, "Are you daft boy?" I guess that meant it wasn't a very good idea after all. So instead, I soaked them in Pepsi, and believe me when I tell you, the fish loved it.

I liked sitting out here, especially at dusk, just as the sun would begin to set in the west. If I listened carefully, I swear to God I could actually hear my wife singing her favorite song. I didn't take any of Kate's things out of our home; I left it just as it was. Her clothes, personal belongings, everything was still exactly as she had left them. I liked it that way. It kept my wife close to me at all times, which was just as it should be.

As peaceful as it was here, I could still feel the darkness within me as it tried to resurface and steal my soul.

* * * * * * *

It had been four months since I returned from Russia. My nightmares were a constant reminder of Kate's death. Every time I closed my eyes I would see her face as she looked into my eyes and told me that she could no longer feel our babies inside of her.

Sitting next to the big oak tree, I looked over at my wife's grave and wondered what our two boys would have looked like had they been born. Me, with black hair and olive skin, and Kate with her fair complexion and beautiful red hair. I should have never come here. Had I just stayed away, Kate would still be alive today.

The pain in my heart was giving me a bitter chill deep down in the depths of my soul.

Taking a sip of my Pepsi, I set the bottle down and picked up my silenced .357 magnum pistol. I hadn't heard from Carla, Neil, Andy, or anyone else for four months.

"I don't want to be here anymore, God. If you don't have anything else for me to do here on earth, then I'd like to come home now and be with my family," I said softly in prayer.

It was almost 1:00 p.m.; there was a strange kind of quietness flowing through the meadow valley today. How many people had I killed? Why didn't it bother me to kill people?

"Is this what I was born for, God? Is this why you brought me here to Earth, to ride the pale horse, deliver death, and collect souls? If it is, then please give me a sign, because if its not, then I'm coming home," I prayed calmly as I looked up at the white clouds above.

I waited another minute for God to answer me, but there was none.

"I'm coming home, Kate. I'm coming home to you and the boys," I whispered softly as I raised my gun and placed the cold blue steel barrel of it against the side of my temple. Reaching up with my thumb I cocked back the hammer. "I love you, Kate," I said softly as I placed my left hand on her grave.

Just as I started to apply pressure on the trigger I felt something thump me on the top of my head. Hesitating for a moment, I felt it again, except this time the dark brown acorn bounced off of my head and landed in my lap.

"What the heck?" I said as I lowered my gun and looked up at the large oak branch above my head.

Thump… sounded the third acorn as it bounced off of my forehead. Setting my gun down, I stood up and stared at the large female red squirrel.

"Don't play with me squirrel. The only reason I haven't shot you and put your fat butt in the cooking pot is because you were Kate's pet," I explained as she dropped another acorn down on my head.

"You little shit, prepare to die," I said as I picked up my gun, raised it, and pointed it at Kate's pet.

It was then I felt something warm on my hand as it slowly pushed my hand down so the gun was pointed at the ground. I could smell the fresh scent of mint as it blew gently across my face. It was the smell of Kate's breath.

"Katie," I whispered as I closed my eyes. "I don't want to be here anymore, there's nothing left for me to do." I could feel the touch of my wife's hand on the side of my face. Then I heard the sound of the helicopter as it came over the hillside and swept down into our valley.

I could see right away it was one of our new Pavelow Special Operations Helicopters, but what was it doing here in Ireland?

Looking up at the red squirrel I then touched the side of my face with my hand.

"Were you and your squirrel trying to stop me, Kate? Does God still have something left for me to do here on earth?" I asked as I turned back to watch as the helicopter swept across our meadow and landed down by our pond.

Hearing the engine turn off I watched and waited as the long rotor blades of the helicopter slowly stopped spinning.

Within a few seconds a smile spread across my face as I watched Neil step out of the helicopter and walk toward me carrying three boxes of flowers in his arms. He didn't speak to me. Instead, he knelt down next to Kate's grave and opened the long thin boxes. Pulling out three-dozen red, white, and yellow roses he placed them at the head of my wife's grave, lowered his head, and prayed.

I was so blessed to have friends like this, I really was.

Finishing his prayer, he made the sign of the cross in front of his face and chest, and then stood up to face me.

"Hey, partner," he said as we gave each other a quick hug. "Sorry it took so long for me to finally get here to see you, Kate, and the boys. A lot has been happening."

I can't tell you how good it made me feel when Neil said, me, Kate, and the boys. How many people would have said that? Not many I assure you.

"It's good to see you, brother. How's everyone?" I asked.

"Well that's one of the reasons I came to see you," Neil explained as he reached down into one of the flower boxes and pulled out a small cassette tape recorder sealed in a see through security wrap. Handing the recorder to me he then explained, "Carla asked me to give you this. It's sealed because whatever is in it is for your ears only. I'm suppose to wait here for your answer. Do you mind if I use your bathroom? It's been a long flight," Neil explained.

"No, not at all, go ahead. Tell your pilot to come up to the house. There's food and stuff in the refrigerator. You guys help yourself and make something to eat," I replied as Neil waved for his pilot to come up and join him as they walked over to my home and went inside.

Sitting down next to the oak tree I pulled out my small Bear pocketknife and cut open the air sealed plastic wrap. Its razor sharp blade cut through it easily. I couldn't help but wonder what could be so important that Carla would seal it this way. Pulling out the small Sony cassette player, I pressed the play button.

"Hello, David. I hope you're starting to feel better now that you've been away for a while and with your family. Oh how our little trip to Russia made me feel so alive again. After what had happened to you and your family, I really needed to kill someone. There's something I need to talk to you about and I think now is the time to do it, just in case something should happen to me.

After we came home from Russia, I resigned and left the Central Intelligence Agency and my position as Director of the Situation Room. The powers to be are pulling all of our agents out of the Middle East, and by 1979 will have cut our Agency down to less than two hundred agents. In doing so they're putting our country in grave danger of a terrorist attack. This doesn't come as a big surprise to me. For the past fifteen years I have been involved in a very covert secret project that I have now been asked to run. The world isn't run by presidents or world leaders. Those people are figureheads placed in positions of leadership so that the mass populations of people have someone to look at.

In truth, David, the world is really run by a handful of very powerful men who you never see or hear about. These are the men who control the World Bank. If you control the bank, you own the world, and therefore are responsible for what happens to the world and all that live within it. If the World Bank should fail, or be destroyed by terrorists or evil-minded people, the world, as we know it, would collapse, and that is something we cannot let happen.

Now then….(there was a long pause here in the tape). How do I say this to you? My father passed away almost a year ago. He was one of the nicest, kindest, most gentle people that you would ever meet. He was also one of the most dangerous, much like you are. My father was one of the men who controlled the World Bank. (Another long pause) He was your grandfather, David.

Before your grandfather married Helen, he had an affair with my mother. I am a product of that love affair. John wanted to marry my mother. But my mother knew he was the head of the organized crime families. So, she asked him to stay in the background because she was afraid someone might try to kidnap or harm me if they new I was his daughter. Reluctantly, he agreed and later met your grandmother whom he fell in love with and married.

I spent a lot of quality time with him. He used to take me places and we would shop and talk, and as I got older it was quite obvious that I was very much like my father. So, with his help, that is how I became the woman I am today.

I know who you really are, David. It's also how I knew to send you after Sam Giancana. Please, don't be angry because of what I am telling you, but instead listen with an open mind. In the Army you signed up to be a crew chief on a helicopter. But I knew if you followed that path, I might never get to meet, you. So a military Army doctor was paid to say you were a little color blind on real light and real dark colors. Because of that, you would not be allowed to be a crew chief due to the different colors of wires in a helicopter. Determined to stay in the Army and go to Vietnam, you asked your Sergeant Major for help, remember? And he asked you if you had ever thought about becoming a sniper? Didn't you find it the least bit interesting that on your first morning in Vietnam, someone was standing right there inviting you to join him for breakfast? Then, he introduces you to Johnny, who takes you under his wing and begins the process of testing your skills to see if you have what it takes to become a Black Operation's Sniper? The Agency had been following your every step long before you knew it.

Remember when you went to California to train with the Seals and when you got back to Vietnam, Bell and Mosier told you they had been receiving daily reports on your progress? Reports that were quite detailed. I was the one sending them those reports.

When you came home you blew up a house and killed three Florida drug dealers to protect your grandparents. That's when some of the mystery began to reveal itself to you, and your grandfather told you one of his best-kept secrets, remember?

We recruited you and sent you to the Farm for elite covert spy training. After that you were given the governments highest top-secret security Q-clearance. No one gets a Q-clearance that easily, David, no one. You did so that it would put you in direct contact with me. The rest is history.

Dad always told me to keep my family and secrets close to my heart, and that's exactly what I have been doing, until now. No one else knows about you or any thing else I have just told you and they never will. I promise you that.

I now sit in my fathers seat at the World Bank, but its very dangerous for me now. There are four of us who run and own the bank. Out of the four, I am the only woman. The other three men know me, so everything is fine right now. Even though I respect them, I have to keep in mind that they are getting old and will one day be gone. When that happens, who knows what might happen.

For now however, we are about to open a brand new operation that will span the world globe. Because of this, I cannot say anymore about it, not even to you.

What I want you to know is that I love the way you took such special care of me when I was in need. Not the laxative part, (laughs) but the sincere part that came from your heart. I am so very proud to have gotten to know you in such a special way, David. The blood that runs through our veins is the same and is what makes us so special, and so strong.

If by some chance your getting tired of sitting around, I could sure use your help with this new project. I have asked Neil to wait for your answer. If you decide to decline this invitation, I will certainly understand, and will do my best to stop by from time to time to see you, Kate, and the boys. However, if you decide to join me, there will be no turning back once you arrive here. Either way, always know that I love you and will keep you close to my heart. Until the very end of time..."

It was here that the tape ended. I couldn't believe what I had just heard. Carla was my aunt?

"Now, it's all starting to make sense," I said to myself as I turned off the tape recorder.

I couldn't help but smile when I took a moment to think about it. Oh how my grandfather had kept his secrets so very well hidden.

I could remember watching him walk around the backyard in his coveralls, pulling weeds out of the vegetable garden, and those times when he would simply leave for a few days to go see his special friend. I now understood who that special friend was, it was his daughter, Carla. That's why she kept asking me if there was anything she could do to help him. I wondered why she had cried so much at his funeral and had given him a gentle kiss goodbye as he lay in his casket. I thought it was because she was my friend. Now I knew it was because she was his daughter.

"I'll be damn, the best kept secrets are the secrets that keep themselves," I thought as I looked over at Kate's grave.

722

"This is why you kept me from killing myself isn't it, honey? Do you want me to go and see what this is all about, or should I stay here with you and the boys? Oh how I wish I could talk to you," I said.

I felt the thump of another acorn hit me on the top of my head and then bounce into my lap. Holding the dark brown acorn in my hand a smile spread slowly across my face as I looked down at it.

"I guess that's your way of telling me I should go, huh? Okay, honey, I'll go and help Carla out for a while. I know now your spirit is always with me. God, I never thought I could ever feel this way about anyone. I'll be back, honey, I promise. I love you, Kate," I said to my wife as I ran my hands across the thick green grass above her.

Standing up, I looked across our meadow and knew it was time to go. Walking across the meadow, I went to Kate's grandparent's home to tell them I would be leaving for a while and asked them to keep an eye on Kate, the boys, and our home.

I then went back to my home to pick up a few things and tell Neil I would be leaving with him. Smiling, he told me, "Turn on some James Brown cuz it's time to rock and roll."

I didn't know then how deadly it was going to become. But then again, it was the game of death, I played the best.

* * * * * * *

We flew back to the United States and then climbed aboard another all black Pavelow Special Operations Helicopter. From there Neil and I flew to, well lets just say a very secret place somewhere in Montana.

Our pilot never spoke a word. He was wearing black BDU's and was heavily armed. Once we got to a certain area, an EC-130 gunship helicopter appeared out of nowhere and escorted us the rest of the way in.

Looking at Neil, I saw him smiling at me.

"You been here before?" I asked with a curious look.

"I resigned when Carla did. I wanna tell you, David, but I can't," Neil explained.

"I thought we were friends," I questioned.

"That's why I can't tell you. You're the one who taught me the rules of the Cloak & Dagger business, remember?" Neil countered.

"Yeah, it looks like I taught you to well, huh?" I replied with a half smile.

Our pilot flew us to a small horse ranch and landed our helicopter in the same pasture where a half dozen mustang horses were grazing. When the helicopter landing this close to them didn't spook them, I knew there was more to this ranch, then met the eye.

Climbing out of the helicopter, Neil walked me inside the small ranch house and took me down into the basement. Walking across the basement, we stepped into a small wooden fruit cellar and closed the door behind us. It was only ten feet by ten-feet in size but the small video camera secured to the top right corner of the metal ceiling told me we were about to go for a ride, and that's exactly what happened.

Within a few seconds the inner section of the small fruit cellar began to lower itself downward. It was an elevator. I knew from the feel of the descent and from my experience at the Pentagon we had gone down at least five-stories deep.

When the back wall of the cellar open we stepped out and entered a whole new realm of reality.

There standing twenty feet away from me, I smiled when I saw my brothers, Danny, Cookie, Tom, Joe, Butch, and Johnny of all people.

"Oh yeah, now we're a team again," Tom said smiling as we all shook hands and said hello to each other.

"Where you been, Johnny?" I asked excited to see my friend once again.

"Right here, working on this project," he explained as I took a look around at this new high tech underground communications center.

Everything in it was state of the art advanced technology; polished stainless steel walls, see-through bulletproof windows, satellite communications with an operations command center far more advanced than anything I had ever seen before, doors that opened by themselves when you walked up to them, and fiber optic technology was everywhere.

You the reader have to remember, that this is 1976. We never had any of this kind of stuff back then.

To the back, far right of this very large room I saw a long office with an all glass window front, which allowed the occupants inside to observe everything taking place inside this room.

Next to the command center was another large room, which was the Global Satellite Observation Room. From there, agents could monitor the movements of anyone or anything in ten different countries around the world at any given time, and do it all at the same time.

Looking up at the glass office about fifty feet above the floor, I watched as Carla talked to both of our old commanders, Bell and Moser.

Looking out through the office window she saw me. When she did and our eyes met, she placed her hand over her mouth, surprised to see me. Saying something to Mosier and Bell, who now looked out through the window at us, they all three stepped into the office elevator and came down to talk to us.

"She looks surprised to see me," I commented as I looked up at my teammates.

"None of us expected you to come, youngster, you surprised us all," Cookie explained with a proud look on his face.

"I knew you'd come, little brother. The Sandman I know would never miss out on a fight like this," Danny explained with a serious look on his face.

"A fight like what?" I asked as Carla began to speak.

"I can't begin to tell you how pleased I am to see all of you again. Especially here as a team. You were all invited to join this new operation without knowing that any of the rest of you had been invited. The reason for this approach was because we wanted you to join us because you wanted to do something to protect mankind as a whole, and not out of your loyalty for each other.

Our mission is a very simple one. We are here to protect the world from those who would seek to terrorize and destroy it. You are the first team to be assembled in this multi-country task force. As you can see, we are far more advanced, with technology ten years ahead of the rest of the world.

As we stand here and talk, terrorist groups and red cell splinter groups are growing stronger around the world. It will be our job to find them and identify their leadership structure, along with the masterminds that control, order, support and finance them, and when we do, we will assassinate them.

We have full authority around the globe, we answer to no one, not even to the United Nations. If during any of our missions, law enforcement, or military forces of any kind should happen to get in our way, you are authorized to eliminate them. With our advanced technology, that should not happen.

We have unlimited funding available to us around the world. You will also have state of the art weaponry available to you; planes, ships, helicopters, all of which are available and strategically located around the world. We also have nine other Sections of operation just like this one, all of which are located in different areas around the world.

We have direct communication with other intelligence agencies around the world. British MI-6, Israeli Mossad, Kuwaiti Intelligence, and German's Top Secret Counter Intelligence Division Bundersamt fur Verfassungsschutz, just to name a few.

We will be assassinating presidents, and the world leaders of any country who pose a direct threat to world peace. Gentlemen, this will, by no doubt, be the ultimate challenge for you. You will be armed with a vast arsenal of weapons to include, laser and pulse weapons, poisons, and ..

gases. You will also have a visual satellite targeting system and a support team here at Section to use that system to provide you with up to the minute stealth intelligence that will be merciless.

Your job, if you choose to stay, will be to penetrate deep into enemy territory, and to do it undetected. You will breach and clear their estates and strike with a deadly, surgical precision, eliminating the threat with no negotiations, no matter what the cost may be to your team. This isn't going to be easy. We fully expect to lose some, if not all of you, at one point or another.

Please take a moment to think about this. You can step back into the elevator and leave now. I assure you, no one will fault you if you decide to leave," Carla explained.

It was at this point we all took our own moment to think about what we had just been told. Our thoughts took us back to Vietnam and what we did there together, as a team. Then with what we had been through together with the Central Intelligence Agency.

"Do we get workman's' comp and health insurance coverage with this job? Because I ain't doing it without full dental and optical coverage," Butch explained jokingly as he looked over at the rest of us and grinned.

Looking over at Danny, I saw him smile at me. "I think we should turn on some James Brown. What do you say, Sandman, you feel like dancing in the face of death?" he asked.

"Johnny?" I asked.

"I'm in," Johnny answered.

"Neil?" I asked.

"I stay with the team," he replied.

"Joe?" I asked.

"Somebody has to fly you in and out. I'm in," he replied as he looked over at his best friend Cookie.

"Cookie?" I asked looking at my mentor.

"We swore an oath to each other. One goes; we all go. One stays, we all stay. I stay with the team," he answered as he looked deep into my eyes.

"What about you, youngster?" Cookie asked.

Reaching into my shirt pocket, I pulled out my tiny vial of Methadrine and placed two drops of the liquid speed under my tongue. Placing the tiny vial back into my shirt pocket I pulled out the dark brown acorn I had put in there, and looked at it.

"I don't want to live forever, I say we do this," I said in a low, cold voice.

"They're in Carla, team one is yours," Bell explained as he nodded his head at us in agreement.

Walking over to the wall just off to our right, Carla reached up and pulled down the white sheet hanging on it.

There, hidden behind the sheet was the new gold crest emblem of the new top-secret counter-terrorism, counter-espionage, world protection services.

"Gentlemen, welcome to the World Security Bureau," Carla greeted as she looked over at me and smiled...

Note to reader

In the world of covert intelligence operations, a Q-agent knows that he must do bad things, to bad people, for the good of his country.

To believe in a supernatural source of evil, is not necessary. Men, alone, are a source evil enough onto themselves.

Forgiveness, is not an option. Forgiveness is between those that we go after and God. Our job is easy, "Arrange the meeting."

To do this, we become the warrior, in whom the old ways, have joined the new.

Comments and Questions can be sent to the Author via E-mail to: thesandman1944@yahoo.com

Allow time for replies.

Epilogue

Little did I realize, as I stood here next to my brothers, that my prayer had been answered and that I had indeed been chosen, by my creator, to ride the pale horse into the bloodiest battle of all.

Our journey of international assassinations will quickly shift directions when a lost ancient scroll written in Palaeo Hebrew is discovered. The writings of the scroll will not only reveal the hidden location of the lost Ark of the Covenant, but it will also reveal the true name of the creator of all things. When the scroll falls into the hands of Boris Kalashnikov, we will meet once again as bitter enemies for one final battle between good and evil. Our hatred of each other will consume us and claim the lives of our closest friends.

It will be then that Danny and I will enter the hidden chamber under the great Sphinx and find the Golden Ark. When we do, what is revealed to us will change our lives forever.

Covered in blood I will arm both of my suitcase size nuclear weapons to deliver one final strike against evil, and destroy the scroll and the Ark, to keep it from falling into the hands of darkness.

Where is the Ark of the Covenant? What did the sacred writings say? What is the true name of our Father, the creator of heaven and Earth? Will I tell you?

If I do, the lives of those who read the third book of the Sandman Diaries will never be the same. The words of truth will reveal the lies of evil, and in doing so; it will change your life forever.

But then again, that's a whole new story isn't it....

Made in the USA
Columbia, SC
30 October 2023